Tales from the Vatican Vaults

Tales from the Vatican Vaults

edited by

David V. Barrett

ROBINSON

ROBINSON

First published in Great Britain in 2015 by Robinson

13 5 7 9 10 8 6 4 2

This collection, concept, introduction and all linking material
copyright David V. Barrett, 2015

All stories copyright their individual writers © 2015

'The Tale of Pope Joan' by David V. Barrett was first published
in a different form in Narrow Houses Volume Three: Blue Motel,
edited by Peter Crowther, Little, Brown 1994

The moral right of the author has been asserted.

A CIP catalogue record for this book
is available from the British Library.

ISBN 978-1-47211-165-4 (paperback)
ISBN 978-1-47211-170-8 (ebook)

Typeset in Plantin Light by Hewer Text UK Ltd, Edinburgh
Printed and bound in Great Britain by Clays Ltd, St Ives plc

Papers used by Robinson are from well-managed forests and
other responsible sources

MIX
Paper from
responsible sources
FSC
www.fsc.org FSC® C104740

Robinson
is an imprint of
Little, Brown Book Group
Carmelite House
50 Victoria Embankment
London EC4Y 0DZ

An Hachette UK Company
www.hachette.co.uk

www.littlebrown.co.uk

Contents

Introduction

Dedicated to the memory of Pope John Paul, 1978–2010

This book is being published to commemorate the fifth anniversary of the death of Pope John Paul in 2010.

Among his many achievements Pope John Paul was the longest-reigning pope, his thirty-two years and two months passing Pius IX by six months. And he was the oldest pope ever, living till just past his ninety-eighth birthday, easily passing Leo III who lived to ninety-three, and remaining sound in mind and body until the end.

But it is not for these remarkable records that we celebrate John Paul's papacy. It is the fact that he ushered in an age of liberalism previously unknown in the Catholic Church. We shall recall shortly how he dealt with a number of difficult moral issues, some of which were making the Church of Rome seem out of touch with the modern world.

*

First we must repeat our gratitude to Pope John Paul for opening up the deepest, most secret parts of the Archives of the Vatican Library – known colloquially as the Vatican Vaults – to scholars. In doing so he has made available an incomparable wealth of historical material.

This act was not without risk, as John Paul himself accepted. Even more so than the Dead Sea Scrolls, the Nag Hammadi Library and other caches of ancient documents, who could tell the impact of what might be found in the Vatican Vaults? Certainly there would be skeletons; the Church's undercover involvement in world affairs throughout the centuries would be laid bare.

We know already that the Church of Rome has at times been involved in covering up things it did not wish to be known, and at times has blatantly rewritten history. The best known example of the latter must be the Donation of Constantine, an eighth-century forgery which asserted that the early fourth-century Roman Emperor Flavius Valerius Constantine gave the papacy spiritual sovereignty over all other churches, temporal sovereignty over large parts of Italy and landed estates throughout the Middle East for income. The Church continued to use this to assert its temporal rights long after it had been proven to be a forgery.

As we explore the thousands of documents in the Vatican Vaults, much of the history of the last millennium or more will have to be re-examined; the separation of fact from fiction is one of the hardest tasks facing the scholars. It might take generations of historians and theologians to sift through what is buried in the Vaults, separating out suppressed first-hand accounts from clever obfuscations.

Over the last twenty years we have only skimmed the surface. The research team has deliberately been kept small and manageable, rather than opening up the Vaults to an academic free-for-all. There have been papers, monographs and, for a few research assistants fortunate in their choice of supervisors, there have been doctoral theses. I was one of the first of these, and so owe my career as an historian to Pope John Paul. Two decades later I find myself chairman of the committee which would select and publish a popular edition of some of the material found in the Vaults.

Like John Paul, we are taking a risk in publishing this book. The accounts span over a thousand years. They cover a wide variety of subjects. Some challenge the foundations of the Christian faith. Others challenge our view of the world, with their revelations of the supernatural or the paranormal, of the spiritual or the alien. All are startlingly different views of the history we thought we knew.

Can we take all of these as verified history? Of course not. History is not an open book, a clear narrative from Then till Now. There are few certainties, only greater or lesser probabilities. Many of the accounts in this book may be completely factual; others may be fictions and fables which the Church, for whatever reason, wanted to hide. We hope that the notes before and after each one will guide the reader; we have, in many cases, erred on the side of caution.

As with scholars in all areas of academe, historians disagree with each other. Few of these accounts were a unanimous choice; most are the result of many hours of argument, with passions raised both for and against. This is part of the joy of scholarship, and I would like to thank my fellow committee members for not (quite) coming to blows, and for their enthusiasm and humour in both formal meetings and informal conversations.

*

This book is in itself a tribute to Pope John Paul. We must mention here just a few of his reforms during his many years as Pope.

Probably his first revolutionary action was to throw the money-lenders out of the temple. Within weeks of coming to office he was looking into the corrupt state of the Institute of Religious Works, commonly known as the Vatican Bank, and within months he had required several high-ranking officials, including an archbishop, to resign. The Commission of Enquiry into Financial Mismanagement was the first of several commissions he set up with the explicit mandate to 'find out where the Church fails, and show us how to make things right'.

The Commission of Enquiry into Abuse in the Church initially looked into the now-infamous Magdalene Laundry asylums in Ireland and Australia, and quickly closed the few remaining ones. It then turned its attention to the sexual, physical and mental abuse of children by priests, monks and nuns, Pope John Paul refusing to continue the Church's unspoken policy of quietly covering up both the problem and the scale of it. From the beginning this commission worked closely with both police and social services, ensuring that all who had committed abuse against children would answer for their crimes.

John Paul was not afraid to challenge long-held practices of the Church, including that of priestly celibacy, which was always a discipline rather than a doctrine. The first stage, early in his pontificate, was to allow already married men to enter the priesthood; later the rules were relaxed further to allow priests, under certain circumstances, to marry and remain as priests.

This was part of the Pope's rapprochement with the Anglican communion, his warm relationship with a succession of Archbishops of Canterbury being a constant feature of his long papacy.

Five years after he became Pope, John Paul brought about a most remarkable, yet at its heart remarkably simple, act of reconciliation between the two Churches. In 1896 Pope Leo XIII declared that all Anglican consecrations of bishops were 'absolutely null and utterly void' because there were gaps in their continuity of Apostolic Succession, the laying-on of hands from bishop to bishop over the centuries. The Anglican Church, naturally, disagreed.

For most people this dispute was as abstruse as how many angels could dance on the head of a pin. But for bishops and priests it was a major focus of division between the Churches.

Pope John Paul's solution, symbolically on Whit Sunday (Pentecost) 1983, was to bring together all the bishops of both Churches in cathedrals around the world in joint services of re-commitment of their faith and re-consecration of their ministry, with all laying hands on each other. Some criticised it as an audacious sleight of hand, and hardline Ulster Protestants called it worse than that, but the way that it was done, with smiles and hugs and slappings on the back as well as the formal laying-on of hands, somehow pulled off the minor miracle that from that day on, all Catholic and Anglican bishops recognised each other as equally valid.

Undoubtedly the reform with the most widespread effect was John Paul's relaxation in practice of the Church's teachings on contraception. Condoms were permitted for the prevention of disease, and the Pill if it was being used to regulate a woman's cycle or for other medical reasons; contraception was an unwished-for but unavoidable side effect. Again it was a sleight of hand, but one welcomed by millions of ordinary Catholics world-wide, who could continue to do what they had already been doing, but now without sinning.

*

It could all have been so different. If Pope John Paul's personal secretary had not chanced to go into the Pope's private rooms late at night to retrieve a book he had left there, and seen the light still on in the Pope's bedroom, and found the Pope slumped in bed from a heart attack, and called the Vatican physician and an ambulance – we might have lost this most reforming of all popes just a month after he ascended St Peter's throne. There would have needed to be a second conclave in 1978, and a new pope would have had to be elected. Who can guess what differences there might have been in the years between then and now? But there we are sliding into the realms of alternative history.

Prof. Francis Atterbury OBE, FRS
Durham, 2015

c. **850** CE

The story of Pope Joan has been believed and denied for around a thousand years. Numerous essays and books have 'proved' both the truth and the falsehood of the tale, and many would say that this account can lend no credence to the myth, for reasons which will rapidly become obvious; yet the mass of supporting detail requires that the possibility of its truth not be discounted out of hand.

This account in tenth-century Italian was in a folder entitled 'Johanna Anglicus, a woman', found among the personal papers of Pope Sergius III (904–911 CE) along with several letters, notes and diary entries which make reference to it. From internal evidence and from its prose style, particularly the shifts of tense to heighten the immediacy of emotion, it appears to be a transcription of Pope Joan's own dramatised oral tale, told by her to her family in or just outside Rome some time in the first few years of the tenth century.

The Tale of Pope Joan

David V. Barrett

It was a time of tribulation, and more. Everything, which had been going so well, so wonderfully, fell apart, flew apart – and most galling of all, I can place little of the blame on anyone other than myself.

Maybe Antonio, a little – but only a little. It was my carelessness, not his, that nearly lost us everything.

Oh, I had such power – had priests and princes bowing to me – and lost it through my lusts.

I wished, often then and sometimes even now, that I had never left Germany, that I had never left my family; that grey, rainy country so different from this sweating, plague-infested Rome; that arguing, fighting, loving, supporting family so different from the arguing, fighting, hating, back-stabbing men of God here.

But I was very young, in our years, still just nearer to thirty than to forty. It was my time to travel, to find new experiences on my own, but not for myself only: we always bring back what we have learnt and tell it to each other, that we may all share, may all learn.

Remember this, my children, when you begin to travel.

We were an English family, though we lived in Mainz. One of my fathers, for reasons I didn't understand as a child, was a missionary to the Germans. I was brought up in a house of scholarship. From my childhood I knew myself to be a scholar rather than a merchant or a farmer; and I knew also that I could not be tied, as several of my mothers were, to the family home. My birth-mother had left early for her final Wandering, having brought three healthy litters of children into this world and then into adulthood; she'd had enough of fetching and carrying, of cooking and cleaning, of being a wife among many and a mother of many.

'Don't let yourself get trapped, as I have been,' she told me. 'I wanted to study, but I ended my travels too soon and joined this family. A wonderful family, don't get me wrong, but I have spent too much time thinking of *us*, not enough of *me*.' She went on, my mother, a good deal more than that, but it all meant much the same: she'd been familied too soon, before learning to be herself.

I must not do the same. She told me, and I knew it for myself.

I would be a scholar, and there was only one place for that: the Church. No matter that, like all of us, I had no belief in God; I have none now and had none even in that highest position – but then, neither had many of my predecessors, nor many of my successors, I am sure. Here in Rome, at the very centre of the Church, there is less faith than anywhere else in Christendom – and almost no Godliness. It shocked me when I first arrived here, even though I was well aware of how dishonest humans are.

I did not wish to join a nunnery; there is too much devotion there, and – with some exceptions – too little scholarship. I changed to man's form and joined the Benedictine abbey at Fulda, near to our home in Mainz.

Why? Because there, I was among some of the finest minds in northern Europe. I could learn from them, argue with them, study their work first hand, read more books than were collected almost anywhere else, except Rome – and here they are collected but not read, not studied. There is no scholarship here; only fighting for position.

I listened and studied and learnt, and argued and taught and wrote. And made the beginnings of my reputation.

From there I went to Athens to extend my studies to Greek literature – and there, unknowingly, I took my next fateful step.

Each mistake is greater than the one before, each built on all that has gone before. This one seemed so right, so wonderful, so (if I'd believed in God and an afterlife) heaven-sent.

Danger, danger, danger. Why did I not see? Because I was blinded by that which lights one's life but throws all that one does not wish to see into the shadows. Love.

Love!

Antonio and I met first in a tavern, where as a brother under the Rule of Saint Benedict no doubt I should not have been; but too many of the brothers knew their scholarship only as a dull, dry thing, unrelated in every way to living. I had to breathe. There in the ancient squares and taverns I found release in conversation with men and women of all sorts and conditions, in rough wine and, from time to time, in women. Some I paid, but most became friends and friendly bedmates.

In a man's body I enjoyed bedplay with women; I would have liked the occasional man, for inside I was still deeply female, but there was too much risk.

In the abbey I could have had a dozen of the brothers; but I would rather have fornicated with a rotting dead pig than touch one of them or have them touch me.

I sensed Antonio across the tavern, just as he sensed me; our eyes touched across the room. I bought a carafe of wine and wandered as if casually over to the quiet corner he had moved to.

'Antonio of Verona, known as Brother Andrew of Tours.'

'Gerberta, of an English line, known as John of Mainz.'

We touched hands shyly, eagerly. *He* knew I was female.

I'd come across many others of our people over the last few years: the odd young traveller like myself, a few older ones on their twilight Wandering, and families here and there. We'd met, we'd talked, we'd spent evenings together sometimes – but we'd never got close. It almost seemed that I could make friends – shallow friends, anyway – more easily among humans than my own people.

But Antonio . . .

From that first meeting there was a power between us, a communication deeper than any I had known before. We were lovers from that first touch between our eyes; and only hours later we became lovers in bed also.

We made love first as two human men, because we couldn't wait to change our forms. And then later, the following morning, we made love again as ourselves, in our true forms.

It was the first time in five years that I had enjoyed the sexual sensations of my female body.

*

Oh, how easily are we betrayed!

*

And when I moved from Athens to Rome, Antonio came with me; neither of us even considered that he might not.

*

Oh, there are times when I wish I believed in God, for then I could cry out in the depths of my despair, 'Why, why, oh Lord?'

*

I taught at the Trivium, in the Greek church attached to the Church of Santa Maria in Cosmedin. I became well liked and well respected for my learning, in that city of influence and ignorance. In time, Leo IV gave me a cardinal's hat –

– and when his successor, Benedict III, a holy man whom in other circumstances I might have loved, died, I was acclaimed Bishop of Rome. I said no, of course; I said I was not worthy; I hid myself in St Peter's. But the crowd would not hear my protests, and said it was God's will.

*

Oh God, I wish I could believe in you. I could beg for your help, or at the least for your solace; I could take comfort in the promise that you would protect me; I could try to persuade myself that all this is part of some great divine plan, that you know what you are doing, that good will come of it in the end; or I could rail against you for what you have done to me.

But I can only rail against myself, and know that my help cometh only from myself, in whom I despair.

*

Antonio and I were careless in our loving, just as young lovers should be. It never crossed our minds that I might become pregnant; after all, we had no group marriage, there were only the two of us, and this gave us – this *should* have given us – the sexual freedom that our young people enjoy. Sex for fun, sex for play, sex for excitement, sex for friendship, as well as sex for love. Sex with a glorious variety of partners, experimenting with and enjoying the gifts of our bodies and minds and spirits and emotions, the gifts to give as well as those to receive. Sex without the responsibility of children – that's what group marriages are for.

I should not have become pregnant, not outside a group marriage; but I did. We were stunned, horrified, Antonio as much as I . . . then over the weeks and months we grew more used to the idea, began to look forward to it. I had never been a mother, and was at the age when I should begin to think about settling down in a marriage group. Maybe my body, fooled by my being with Antonio for three or four years, thought I was in a group marriage . . . a group of two.

We made plans. The baby was due in June of the year 858, a hot and filthy month when my absence from Rome would be regarded as sensible. We would go to a villa up in the hills, where there would at least be trees to shade us from the blazing sun, and where we would be away from the filth and stench and disease of summer Rome – and from the intrigue, the watching eyes and wagging tongues.

I had brought Antonio with me from Venice as my priest-attendant, and he still attended me as my cardinal deacon and secretary. It was expected that where I went he would go also.

*

Oh, Antonio! So beautiful, my only love, and you are gone. So beautiful, and so close to me, you turned down propositions almost daily from the fat priests and cardinals and dukes and administrators who jostle for position and power and wealth, who bribe and steal and seduce and kill to raise their social standing by one small degree, to move from one sphere of influence into a vying one, to gain another rich jewel or bag of gold, and all in the name of the God of love.

He wanted none of them; he wanted only me.

And I lose him, I lose him, and our child.

*

You know the place, some of you: between the Colosseum and the Church of St Clement. The day was hot, sticky, sweaty, as so much of that summer had been. The air itself seemed diseased. The Rogation Day procession between the Lateran and St Peter's wound slowly through the streets, priests and cardinals and choirboys before and behind me, a hundred pious nuns walking together in their midst.

My bearers stumbled from time to time, exhausted by the heat. I had tried to cancel the procession, the ceremony, but that body of administrators who actually run this hellish place would not allow it. It was tradition, it was custom, it was law. I, as Pope, had no say in the matter.

My time was near, but not too near: three or four weeks. This was my last compulsory appearance before I could flee this filthy place with Antonio; tomorrow we would go into retreat for the rest of the heat of summer, and I would have our child in peace.

*

The pain hits me and my waters break forth, together. I'm soaked from my loins down, and going into spasm; my entire body heaves and thrusts. I scream with the agony. One of my bearers, startled, chooses this moment to stumble; the litter tips and falls, and I with it.

My body reacts to the emergency without my conscious thought; I feel my vagina, closed with a fold of skin beneath my penis, open up and widen, widen suddenly and agonisingly as the baby within pushes itself into the world.

Priests, cardinals, attendants of all sorts, rush to my aid, knowing only that their Pope has fallen and is hurt.

I lie half on the ground, half still in the soaked finery of my litter, my legs wide apart as the thing inside me tears itself from me. And cries.

That tiny infant sound stills the hubbub around me. Choirboys, monks, nuns, priests, cardinals in their sweat-stained robes, all stop, and stand, and turn, and stare. And then they come for me, for me and for my barely born child, with their fear and their hatred, their boots and their fists, kicking and clawing and tearing and stamping . . .

*

Three days, now, three days to repair my ripped and ravaged body, but three lifetimes would not be enough to repair my torn heart.

*

Somehow I crawled away and hid, in rotting piles of rubbish in the shell of a half-broken building only a few minutes away from my scene of degradation and discovery and despair. Hid, until I could stop the bleeding from my own wound, my womb which had betrayed me, and from the cuts and tears and rough grazes and bone-deep bruises from the mob's attack.

And while I healed, I changed my appearance: I made myself a hand's width shorter, I changed my hair from its distinctive copper – a legacy from an Irish forebear – to black, and I made my face rounder and more anonymous. I remained a man; my attackers, the tribunals of the Church, the entire priesthood, half of Rome for all I knew (though some might secretly admire my presumed audacity) – all would be looking for a woman.

Now I was safe, at least from recognition, though my weak state would make me more prone to the illnesses of the city.

I sought out a small family group I knew, and told them what had happened. They were amazed, but they took me in; though we may fight and squabble among ourselves, we will always help each other against human threats, and besides, with my new appearance, there is no danger to them.

*

Three days, my children, three days and I have heard nothing. My child is gone, Antonio is gone: my baby no doubt torn apart or trampled underfoot, as they tried to do to me; Antonio – I do not know. I cannot believe he has deserted me. He was in the procession, near to me; if he tried to come to my help they may have taken him, beaten him, killed him.

There is little value placed on human life in this festering city, when it is not one's own. His body may be in the Tiber, with so many others; I have asked the Fantonis, the family who have taken me in, to listen for reports.

I could so easily have been in the Tiber myself.

There have been popes from our people before, three of them, but none lasted longer than my two years, five months and four days. They fared no better than most other popes. Maybe one day it will come that popes are not ripe for assassination, by knife or strangulation or by subtle poison; but even a pope's life is cheap when ambition rules.

All of Rome is buzzing with stories of how the Pope gave birth by St Clement's, and the greater amazement of the Pope being a woman. Such a thing has never been heard! I do not know if it has happened before; it is possible, though there is nothing in our history, and it would have been still more difficult for a human woman.

*

It was another week before Antonio and I found each other. He too had changed his appearance – he was taller, thinner – but I recognised him at once, and he me. Perhaps it is by our scent, that even if subconsciously we can know each other; this is, after all, the main way that we know each other from humans. Perhaps we recognised each other's individual scent across the piazza.

But I prefer to think it was our spirits calling to each other in their love.

You can imagine the joy with which we fell into each other's arms, even those of you too young to know the love between two adults. Each of us had pictured the other dead, trampled and pulled apart, or else captured and tortured and longing for death. (I still hear the screams from the dungeons of the Basilica in my sleep at night; Antonio will tell you. Those tortured in the name of the God of love know the depths of agony and degradation, if ultimately they know nothing else.)

Each of us had searched that plague-strewn city; each had listened everywhere for rumour, while hoping desperately we would hear none. Each of us had so narrowly escaped that we could not imagine the other having also such fortune.

People were beginning to stare, and in a city so leprous with suspicion that was dangerous. We remembered suddenly that we were both male in appearance. We drew back, looked into each other's eyes, laughed gaily (it was hard, but it was so easy!), and

David V. Barrett

clapped each other on the back like old friends who had not seen each other for a long time.

'I did not even know you were in Rome,' Antonio boomed.

'I didn't know you were either,' I replied. 'My wife, her sister is dying, and so I brought her. And you?'

Antonio looked sly. He glanced around as if to see who might be listening, then lowered his voice – but still kept it loud enough that those nearby, straining, might hear.

'I am here . . . on business, shall we say. A merchant friend of mine, he told me of a deal I could make . . . He let his voice fade away as we walked away, across the piazza, through an alley and into the anonymity of a crowded street. Our eavesdroppers, I knew, would smile and shrug; such deals were commonplace, and the reason many came to the city. Some were lucrative, but most came to nothing.

We walked through the crowds, yearning to touch each other, to hug, to hold, even just to say something to show our love for each other, our joy at finding each other.

Antonio led me into a small inn, and to a quiet corner. And it was only when we were seated, with a jug of rough red wine between us, that I thought – suddenly, sickeningly, with over-whelming guilt – of our child.

Antonio saw the change on my face, and reached over, laying his hand on my arm.

'It's all right,' he said, 'he's safe.'

I couldn't speak. My sight went grey, then white, then black. It was some time later when I realised that Antonio was holding a cold, damp cloth to my forehead and neck.

'It's all right,' he said, over and over again. 'It's all right.'

I sat back, and the dim interior of the inn slowly came into some kind of focus. Antonio gave me my beaker, his hand steady-ing mine as I raised it and drained it in one long gulp.

'Our son is safe,' he said, and my destroyed world, my distraught spirit, were made whole again.

It was only an hour – it seemed a month – before I held our son for the first time. He had beautifully thick dark hair and deep blue eyes, and his tiny fingers closed on mine. His body was human in shape; Antonio told me he was changing from his natural birth appearance to human almost as soon as he was born. Instinctive mimicry: our deepest survival trait. But at birth he had looked like us, unchanged, and his initial appearance, then the flowing of his infantile features as his body adjusted them to human, had compounded the horror of the Pope giving birth. This was a monster, a demon, devil's spawn. Small wonder that the priests and cardinals and other dignitaries and their attendants had tried to kill both him and me.

Antonio had had one moment in which to act, when, horrified by the tiny squirming creature before them, these holy men had turned their attention to a horror they could cope with: me. He snatched the baby, tearing the cord with his nails, and tucked him into his robes, then let himself be pushed back as others pushed forward to get at me.

He didn't know, he told me as I sat with our son cradled to my still human, still male breast, how he was able to leave me. But I maybe had a chance, however small; the tiny mewling creature had none without his immediate help, his full attention, his love and care and devotion. Apart from safety, our baby needed food, literally in the next few minutes. His first act in life had been to change his appearance, which drained him of every scrap of energy he was born with. If he were not given food, and then safe sleep, straight away, our son would die.

Antonio, my beloved one, my darling husband here, saved our son. Like me, he found friends to take him in, and one, who had recently had a litter of three children, had milk enough to feed our baby as well. It was fortunate in many ways that my first birth, as sometimes happens, was of only one child.

The two families lived at opposite ends of this teeming city, but knew each other well; two of the wives in 'Antonio's' family were sisters of two of the husbands in 'mine'. Together they helped us away from Rome, to a quiet village three days' ride away, and to a quiet farmhouse in the hills above the village.

There, for the next few months, Antonio and I could live as ourselves when we wished, though for the most part we retained our human appearance.

We both preferred his new, leaner look to his old, so he kept this; I reverted to my old appearance, which I had when I was a girl in Mainz, with a little added maturity we both agreed I suited. He was delighted with the new me; he told me now that this was how he had always seen me, deep inside –

– and this is how I have remained ever since, though the lines and wrinkles of added years have given, perhaps, yet more maturity to my looks!

The Church soon chose a new pope, and new scandals quickly replaced my own story as gossip on the streets of Rome. A woman pope giving birth to a demon is not a tale the Church would wish to be remembered.

*

And now we skip some fifty years to bring us to today. My children, my family, the youngest of you will not remember your oldest brother; he left the home first. But we shall see him next week, with joy.

From his earliest years your brother Simon showed the same leanings that I had: scholarship, philosophy, human theology. We did not discourage him; his life, his yearnings, were his to follow, not ours to dictate.

He had absorbed everything Antonio and I knew by the time he was twenty. And then he followed much the same route I had done, through the monasteries, before being appointed Bishop of Ostia, then managing to be assigned to Rome to take his cardinal's hat.

And now that we have had six popes in five years, fighting and deposing and killing each other, all the priests and cardinals of Rome will soon be meeting to try to find a pope who might last a little longer. Some men of the Church wish earnestly for the fighting to be over.

There are two likely candidates for St Peter's throne, two equally strong men who hate each other, and whose followers battle for supremacy with each other, with a passion such as I did not witness even when I lived there.

Your brother is well positioned, and, amazingly for this place, this Church, he has few enemies. Neither of the favourites will allow the other to take the throne without war following. The Church, however stupid it might at times be, has enough sense not to want that.

By next week your brother may be Pope, following in his mother's perhaps ill-advised footsteps. He will have his own problems, but there is one he will not share with me. He will not give birth on the Lateran Way.

Ω

Whether 'Simon' was elected to the throne of St Peter is difficult to confirm either way; there were several popes of unknown origin (and unknown original name) around this time, none of whom lasted very long. There is, however, no record of a Bishop of Ostia becoming Pope (they usually had the privilege of crowning the Pope), so it seems more probable that he was unsuccessful – in which case his life was doubtless considerably longer.

Whether this account is fact or fiction, history or myth, it has immense historical significance. If it is fiction, its very existence as a contemporary attempt to explain Pope Joan gives credence to her legend; it pre-dates by two centuries what had been the earliest known reference to the female Pope.

If the story is true, it explains at last the legend of Pope Joan, which some have accepted for a thousand years, though to others it has always seemed unbelievable that a woman could have become Pope. But it is even more unbelievable that another sentient race, a race of shape-shifters, has throughout history co-existed, undetected, alongside humanity – though if true this would certainly account for much mythology, folklore and tales of witchcraft.

1032–1048

The Catholic Church is the first to accept that there have been 'Bad Popes' over the centuries. One of the most notorious, Alexander VI, Rodrigo Borgia, has been the subject of many films and TV series. But more than four centuries before him there was a pope of whom even the Catholic Encyclopedia *says, 'He was a disgrace to the Chair of Peter.' For Pope Benedict IX the papacy was a family business, with two uncles, two great-uncles and a further two before them having been Pope. Benedict IX was Pope three times, and at one point sold the papacy to his successor for a large sum. He was accused of holding orgies in the Lateran Palace, and a slightly later pope mentioned 'his rapes, murders and other unspeakable acts' and said, 'His life as a pope was so vile, so foul, so execrable, that I shudder to think of it.'*

This account found in the Vatican Vaults might appear unbelievable, but it certainly provides an explanation for this most ungodly man occupying the throne of St Peter.

No Peace for the Wicked

K. J. Parker

Enough is enough. I stood up. They all stopped talking and stared at me.

'Gentlemen,' I said.

That's not how you address a roomful of cardinals, even if you're a cardinal yourself. It's an example of the subtle art of being politely rude, at which I excel. A Roman general once quelled a mutiny with that one word, *gentlemen*, used in precisely that way; he was addressing the mutineers, and the idea was that a general would never be *polite* to his soldiers, he'd say *listen, you horrible lot* or something of the sort; the implication being, they'd behaved so badly that he no longer regarded them as soldiers of Rome, and that was enough to shame them back to their duty. Neatly done. Now I come to think of it, that general was me.

'Gentlemen,' I repeated. 'This simply won't do. We've been here – what, three days? Four? – and we're still no further forward. This has to stop.'

They looked at me. I grinned at them.

Someone pointed out that the only reason we were all still there was because of my intransigence. 'It's all your fault,' he said. 'We're all agreed on Paul of Calabria, but you keep on about that appalling young thug of yours, and we aren't getting *anywhere*. Be reasonable,' he added, with a poor attempt at a conciliatory smile. 'We're never going to let that evil little shit get his arse on Peter's chair, not in a million years.'

'The vote needn't be unanimous,' I said. 'If you really want Paul—'

I let the sentence hang in the air. They shuffled and looked uncomfortable. Poor fools.

'We respect you,' someone said awkwardly. 'Obviously. We need you to agree. Otherwise—'

I smiled. 'I agree to Theophylact,' I said. 'Now, you do the same, and then we can all go home.'

They all started bitching at once. I cleared my throat. They subsided. Quiet as little mice.

*

I should explain. I can do that. It's one of the powers vested in me. I still have a large proportion of the Authority I used to have in the old days, before the 'Unfortunate Event'. I can command silence and attention, to a certain extent I can impose my will just by looking at people. If I choose to do so, I can imbue my words with divine eloquence – which means I could read out two pages at random from someone's household accounts or a shipping manifest and thereby win any debate I choose. I try not to, because it's cheating and an abuse of privilege. You see how conscientious I am. I have to be, in my position. Divine appointment is more of a responsibility than a privilege, believe me.

*

'Gentlemen,' I said, 'you're well aware that our decision here will have far-reaching consequences. It's our job to choose Christ's next vicar on Earth, and what could be more important than that? It's our job to entrust, to one frail, fallible mortal, the terrestrial power of Almighty God. Under normal circumstances, this would be a staggeringly momentous decision. But these . . .' Short pause, for effect. 'These are not normal circumstances. Now, you have no way of knowing this, so you'll just have to take my word for it, but I happen to know that the Pope we choose here today will be the most important, the most influential Pope in the history of the Church. It's essential that we choose the right man, the man God wants us to choose. Which is why you have no other choice but to elect Theophylact of Tusculum.'

*

K. J. Parker

A brief history of Theophylact of Tusculum.

He was a nasty piece of work, no doubt about it. In an age when the Vicars of Christ didn't even pretend to any degree of moral superiority over the aristocratic savages from whose ranks they were largely recruited, he was by universal consensus in a class of his own. His two immediate predecessors were both his uncles, the brothers of Theophylact's father, Count Alberic; the papacy ran in that family, like red hair or haemophilia. Twenty years old when the Count bought him the Fisherman's Chair, which he ascended as Benedict IX in October of the Lord's Year 1032, Theophylact's bizarre sexual practices and some singularly ineptly concealed murders soon made it impossible for him to continue in office – the Roman mob is notoriously broad-minded, but sooner or later even they will eventually draw the line – and so he fled. Later, regretting his decision, he raised an army, stormed Rome and took back Peter's crown by force. Subsequently deposed by the soldiers of the German emperor, he hired every thug in Italy and stormed his way back in for another year until he was finally driven out. He sold the papacy to his godfather for a large amount of money, to end his life in a haze of unparalleled dissipation. The most dreadful creature imaginable, in fact, and just the man we needed at that precise moment in time.

Note, incidentally, the pronoun.

*

I had their undivided attention.

'Brother cardinals,' I went on, 'you don't need me to tell you, we're living on the fulcrum of history, and the sharp edge, the razor on which history balances, is of course our beloved mother Church. Never before – trust me on this – never before have we faced greater challenges or more enthralling opportunities. To the east, we face the schismatics of Byzantium, and beyond them, the apparently invincible power of Islam. To the west, we see the furious energy of the Normans, a dammed river of strength and savagery waiting to burst. From my unique perspective, I can see the road ahead of us dividing. Follow one fork, and what do we find? A strong pope, universally loved and respected, heals the breach with our eastern brothers, unites the empires of East and

West, diverts the Norman fury to drive the mills of holy war; to our banner comes Michael of Constantinople – a sinner, yes, but one who has sincerely repented, who only waits for a chance to make good his redemption in wonderful deeds; already he has driven the Arabs from their Sicilian strongholds, his heart burns for the cause. Together – German, Greek, French, Italian and Norman side by side – what could prevent us from sweeping across North Africa, liberating the holy places, cornering the great enemy in his lair and crushing him for ever?'

I paused for breath. Having to breathe limits one's eloquence so. 'That is one path. If we follow the other, if we elect a weak, vicious, worthless creature to the Fisherman's Chair, what will happen? Let me tell you. The schism will continue to fester and bleed, to the point where it will never heal. Michael will win his great victory, but not against the Arabs. God will prove his redemption against the half-human savages of the Balkans, and Michael will die, to be succeeded by his ridiculous brother. Meanwhile, the Normans will sweep across half of Europe. Great swathes of Italy will fall to their swords, including much – too much – of Peter's own patrimony. They will snatch Sicily from Greek and Arab alike; what is more, what is worse, they will sit down with them in peace, building a mighty kingdom that is half Christian and half Moor, and their strength will become so great that the two Christian emperors will beat against them like bare hands against solid rock, bruising themselves and making no mark. The moment will have been lost. Normans will sack Jerusalem, coming not as liberators but as conquerors and looters, and thereafter there will be no chance of peace between West and East this side of Judgement Day. Alienated from the people of the West, the Church will sink into decadence and irrelevance, its temporal power frittered away in pointless wars, its spiritual authority corroded into rust and rubbish, until new schisms and new heresies shatter Christendom like glass into a hundred thousand sharp, useless fragments. From that place there will be no way back. The future history of the Church will be a long, agonising record of schism, heresy, bloodshed and hate.' I paused again. I was exhausted, as though I'd just run a mile. 'That, brother cardinals, is what we must decide today; victory or defeat, the triumph of the Church or its long, slow collapse into fratricide. No choice has ever been more vital. And for that reason, it is no choice. You have no options. What you must do is elect Theophylact of Tusculum to be the new Bishop of Rome.'

They were gazing at me like sheep at market. Finally, one of them shook off the spell enough to open his mouth. 'So Theophylact will reform?' he said. 'He'll stop all this nonsense and become this good and strong pope who'll do all these wonderful things.'

I smiled.

*

I had, of course, been to both places. I'm there now (in two places at the same time; don't try this at home), and I can see two completely different worlds. One of them will be all too familiar to you, and the other – well. You really wouldn't want to go there.

*

'You can't be serious,' someone said eventually.

I gave him my Authoritative smile. I don't use it often. In theory, you should only see it through smoked glass, darkly. 'Never more so,' I said. 'Theophylact will be the weak, vicious, useless pope. I'm inviting you to plunge the Church into an irreversible division. It's what has to be done. It's your duty.'

Silence. Then someone said, 'Well, you would say that, wouldn't you?'

Suddenly, I felt tired. I didn't need all this. 'Come on,' I said. 'You know me. You know what I stand for. You know better than anyone that there's no more loyal and dedicated servant of our Lord anywhere on Earth. You trust me. Now, shall we move to a show of hands?'

*

Virtute officii; by virtue of one's office. Excuse me; private joke.

*

Every story has a narrator; there is no such thing as a third-person narrative. You'll deny this, of course, because you've read a bucketful of the things. Reconsider. The storyteller may be anonymous and invisible, but he's there all right. He tells you what everyone did and said, he can even tell you what was going on inside everyone's head. He's everywhere, this universal narrator. With a simple *meanwhile, a thousand miles away, under the towering ramparts of Bari* he can cross turbulent seas and impassable mountains, straight in through the ear of the next protagonist, so he can eavesdrop on the poor devil thinking.

Omniscient, omnipresent, omnipotent. Remind you of someone?

The conceit: that the world is a story told by God. Crude, but actually not so wide of the mark. The good storyteller creates his characters but doesn't micromanage them; he allows them the luxuries of internal consistency and their own personal brand of logic; what we in the trade call *enough rope*. The storyteller knows the story, of course, unless he's confident enough in his own capacities (omniscient, omnipotent) to make it up as he goes along. To a large extent, this great storyteller is content to observe and record; to be an eavesdropper, a *witness* . . .

The Greek word for witness is *martyros*: martyr. Consider the one and only martyr, the narrator Himself transferred by His own compassionate will to the pages of the story He's telling. It's a rare and dedicated author who allows his characters to nail him to a plank and leave him in the blistering sun to die. Great, therefore, must be the value this author places on recording, witnessing, eavesdropping. The author made flesh – the author made word; in the beginning was the word, and the word was God – this author, however, did rather more than that. He intervened, as a character in his own story. He *participated*. That was His right.

We, being mere extensions of His will, aren't authorised to go that far. We're here to observe and advise; which is why I couldn't force those red-gowned halfwits to elect the evil Theophylact, I could only make speeches. Very good speeches, of course.

I have been a member of the college of cardinals, *virtute officii*, since long before they were called cardinals. Mostly, I keep my mouth shut; I observe, I witness. Only rarely do I advise. The rest of them are scared to death of me, needless to say, even though most of them don't actually believe I'm the same individual who sat at the Fisherman's left hand, when we were so poor we couldn't afford oil lamps. They don't believe the sacrament truly becomes blood and human flesh, either. More fools they.

*

But on this occasion, the eloquence was enough. We had a vote, and we were unanimous. Theophylact of Tusculum. *Habeamus* – God help us all – *Papam*.

Not surprisingly, I was delegated to take His newly-minted Holiness the good news. Nobody else wanted that honour – not, as one of my brother cardinals put it, with a ten-foot pole. Well, it saved me having to insist.

I eventually tracked him down in that small, rather cramped wine shop on the east side of the Colosseum (a favourite of mine, incidentally; I don't actually eat or drink, naturally, but the *idea* of the coarse house red is really rather pleasant after a hard day). He'd reached the stage in his usual monstrous procedure where they'd propped him respectfully in a corner until his sedan chair arrived to cart him home. The front of his tunic told me that at some stage he'd been eating sardines, in a mushroom and pepper sauce. I guess they didn't agree with him.

I can sober men up with a click of my fingers. That clears the head, though you still feel like death. 'Theophylact,' I said. 'Can you hear me?'

He opened his eyes and screwed them up, as if the rain was blowing in his face. 'Oh,' he said. 'It's you.'

'I've got some good news,' I said. 'You're the Pope.'

'Fuck,' he said, and tried to go to sleep.

'You're the new Pope,' I said, 'and I need you to listen to me very carefully. This is extremely important, and for reasons that needn't concern you, I have to tell you *now*. So I'd like you to sit up and open your eyes, and try and keep up. All right?'

'Go away,' he said. 'My head hurts.'

'All right?'

He sighed. 'Fine,' he said, and slid his back five inches or so up the wall. 'Well?'

'First,' I said, 'do you know who I am?'

He frowned. 'Of course I do,' he said. 'You're dad's friend, the cardinal, Whatsisname. You're always hanging round the house.'

We have a rule in our business; show, don't tell. For a brief moment – about as long as it takes to sneeze – I let him see me as I really am. It was a dangerously long exposure, but with all that alcohol in him to relax his muscles and cushion his system, I figured he could take it.

His mouth had fallen open, and it took him a lot of effort to speak. 'You're—'

'Your dad's friend the cardinal,' I said, 'who's always hanging round the house. That's exactly right. Blessed are those who have seen and yet have believed.'

He swallowed a couple of times. 'So there really is—'

'You'd better believe it,' I said. 'Your Holiness,' I added. 'Now I'm afraid you're going to have to forget all that in a minute or so, but right now I need to have your undivided attention. Now, then. Do you believe in good and evil?'

The innkeeper went by with a tray of empty cups. 'Yes. I suppose so. I mean, it's – well, it just is, I guess.'

I took the purse from his pocket and shook out a coin. 'Heads.'

'Yes.'

I flipped it over. 'Tails.'

'Yes.'

'On one side, the Holy Virgin enthroned. On the other, a rather hideous depiction of the King of the Greeks. Two distinctly different pictures. How many coins?'

In retrospect, not the best question to ask a man in his condition. Fortunately he answered, 'One.'

I absent-mindedly dropped the coin in my sleeve. 'Very good,' I said. 'Now, I'll ask you to cast your mind back to when you were learning your catechism. In the beginning there was the void. He said, Let there be light. And there was—?'

He paused, sensing a trick question. 'Light?'

'Yes. And?'

He shrugged. 'What?'

'Darkness,' I said. 'You can't have one without the other. Light presupposes darkness; without it, it wouldn't be light. And the other way around, of course. So, when He said, Let there be light, He was also saying, Let there be darkness. He *created* it.' I shrugged. 'He created all things. Yes?'

'Well, of course. Everybody knows that.'

'Indeed they do. Now, I want you to *think*. He created everything. Every single thing. That means,' I said, smiling, 'He created evil.'

Theophylact shook his head. 'No, that's wrong. Everything God does is good. Evil's just the absence of good. Isn't it?'

'Everything,' I repeated solemnly. 'Before that, there was just the void, remember? The void wasn't evil, it wasn't anything. In order for something to exist, it must have been created by God. God created evil.'

He frowned. Poor fellow, first day in the job and he gets that sprung on him. My heart bled. 'If you say so,' he said. 'It just seems a bit strange, that's all.'

'Very strange,' I agreed. 'But evil—' I took another coin from his purse. 'Evil this side, good the other. Inevitably. Unless you're thinking of a one-sided coin, like they have in Germany. And even then, when the other side is blank, the impress of the obverse die is visible, in reverse. So really, there's no such thing as a one-sided coin. And there can be no good without evil.'

He sighed. 'I suppose not.'

'Fine,' I said. 'That's not strictly true, of course. He is omnipotent; He can do anything. If he'd wanted to create a universe where Good existed without an equal and opposite force, He could've done so. If evil exists, it's because He *wanted* it to.'

He narrowed his eyes. 'Now there I think you're going a bit far,' he said. 'With respect,' he added quickly. 'I mean, even with what you just said, evil's got to be, well—' He ransacked his scrambled brains for the right word. 'A by-product,' he said. 'Like the silver mines. If you want silver, you've got to have lead as well. They go together. But the miners only want the silver.'

'The miners,' I pointed out, 'are fallible humans. They can only work with what He has made for them. He wanted evil, so He created it. Do you understand?'

He sort of wriggled from top to toe. 'I guess,' he said. 'Well, no, not really. You're saying you can't have light without darkness, which I can sort of get the hang of. But now you're saying He could've had light without darkness if He'd wanted to.'

'Exactly. Now, then. Why would He do such a thing?'

He thought for a while; and when he answered, I confess I was worried. Maybe the idiot boy was smarter than I'd assumed, which might be a problem, later on. 'So there'd be a choice,' he said. 'You can't have a choice if there's only one thing.'

'Yes. And?'

'And He wants us to have a choice.' Pause. '*Why* does He want us to have a choice?'

'So we can be wrong sometimes. So we can be fallible. If we weren't, if we were perfect, we wouldn't be us, we'd just be part of Him.' I took a step back, and spat. It landed just shy of his left foot. 'Now *that* was part of me, but I separated it from me. That was what Creation entailed. In creating the universe, He separated it from himself, as your mother separated you from herself when you were born. He is perfect. Something separate from Him must therefore, sooner or later, become different from perfection. And that,' I added, before he could interrupt, 'is why He created evil.'

To do him justice, I think he really was following what I said, albeit in the same way mad dogs follow carts on country roads. For any human with a head full of the coarse house red, that's not bad. 'So evil—'

'The thing to remember about it,' I said, 'is that, contrary to appearances, good and evil are different aspects of the same thing. They come from the same source. They serve the same objective. In practical terms, they're on the same *side*. I like to think of evil,' I went on, 'as His Divine Majesty's loyal opposition. Of which,' I added, 'I am a humble member.'

He nearly choked. 'But you're an angel,' he said.

*

Which is true.

It's true, because there is no such thing as time. Not for us, at any rate. Mortals believe in time the way fish believe in water; we, however, aren't fish. Eliminate time, and yes, I am an angel. I still exist in that state, before the 'Unfortunate Occurrence'. I also exist after it. I am, of course, the same creature – immortal, immutable, substance of His substance, an extension of His will. I am simply an angel who was assigned to other duties – a rotten job, but someone's got to do it. I am merely the faceless substance, the middle of the coin. Now I serve God in a rather different way.

(And on the eighth day He created Evil; and He saw that it was good.)

*

'What's all this in aid of?' he asked.

A shrewd question for a twenty-year-old alcoholic. The landlord was looking at us, muttering something to the large man who threw out the drunks. I smiled at them; they crossed themselves and found urgent things to do in the back room. 'It's important that you know who I am,' I said. 'It's important, because we're going to be seeing a lot of each other in the future, when you're Pope and I'm your most intimate, trusted adviser.'

He looked terrified. 'But you can't be,' he said. 'You're a—'

'Not the D word, please,' I said, quiet but very firm. 'I think on balance that it'd be better if you came to regard me as a senior official from the Department of Evil. Think you can do that?'

He pulled a sad face. 'I'm not sure,' he said.

Sigh. 'All right,' I said, 'let me explain it to you. Let's consider the emperor.'

'Which one?'

'Whichever one you like. Both emperors have advisers. For efficiency's sake, each senior adviser is in charge of a specific aspect of the affairs of the empire, a department. The Count of the Stables, for example, is in charge of war. He heads up the War Department. With me so far?'

'Yes.'

'Fine. Now, the Count of the Stables isn't *war*. He's just a normal – fairly normal – man, looking after the military side of things. He's not like Mars, the embodiment of battle. Same goes for the Highways Commissioner, the Superintendent of Shipping, the City Prefect and so on. Me too. My job is simply to administer and regulate the conduct of evil in His Majesty's terrestrial possessions. I make sure evil works predictably and efficiently, that its quotas are filled, and that it doesn't go too far. It's like being a governor. A governor doesn't have to belong to the province he governs. The Imperial governor of Bari, for instance, isn't an

Italian, he's a Greek.' I shrugged. 'The Governor of Evil is a cardinal. Bear in mind, we're all subjects of the same master. His will be done, absolutely.'

He gave me a sort of sideways look. 'And His will is, there's got to be evil.' He thought for a moment. 'I don't know.'

'Two sides,' I reminded him. 'One coin. Render to Caesar the things that are Caesar's, render to God the things that are God's. And above all, don't *ever* try and second-guess the Divine agenda. That's one sin that even you can't buy absolution for.'

He had that lost look. 'So who tells me what He wants me to do? You, I suppose.'

'We all have to do as we're told,' I said. 'Even me. Especially me.'

*

Especially me.

I step out of time the way you step out of your clothes, and I am there, then, once more; where, when I belong, I have always been, as it was in the beginning, is now and ever shall be. I am sitting in the back row, with a worried look on my face, while Lucifer tries to explain. He's not making a wonderful job of it. We don't like the way things are run around here, he says.

'Yes we do,' someone points out.

'Yes, all right, we do.' Lucifer has that lost look, too. 'But we have to take the broader view. We represent Divine discontent. That's our *constituency*. What we as individuals may think about it is neither here nor there. We have no say in the matter. We're bound by the mandate.'

'But we're going to *lose*,' someone else says. 'Come to that, we've already lost, where I'm standing. Does the term *hiding to nothing* mean anything to you?'

'It's in the plan,' Lucifer replies irritably. 'And we don't second-guess the plan. Do we?'

'God is working His purpose out, as year succeeds to year,' someone quoted in a mocking drawl. 'Yes, we know. And we've got to have dualistic morality, or we all just wink out of existence like a switched-off light. Fine. But why's it got to be *us*? Why can't some other bugger do it?'

Lucifer gave him a sour look. 'Let this cup pass from me, you mean? I wouldn't go there, if I were you. No, sorry, it's up to us, we've got to do it. And I know *because I say so* isn't the most inspiring motivation ever, but that's how it is. Sorry.'

I smiled. 'It sounds to me that we don't like the way things are run around here,' I said. 'Divine discontent. I do believe you've performed a very small act of Creation.'

Lucifer looked at me blankly for a moment. I think I heard someone mutter *for crying out loud*, or words to that effect. 'Well, think about it,' I said. 'God has ordered his loyal servants to be disloyal. Their loyalty to what they have always believed constitutes the Divine awakes in them the instinct to disobey. Disobedience is rebellion. Gentlemen, I rather fancy we've just brought about the Fall.'

'You know your trouble,' someone said. 'You're just too damned clever by half.'

'He's talking drivel, as usual,' someone else said. 'We may *feel* like not obeying, maybe just for a moment, but that doesn't mean we're actually going to disobey. Far from it. If He wants us to make war in Heaven, then that's what we do, obviously.'

I grinned at him. 'I did say a very small act of Creation,' I pointed out. 'Like a scientist in a laboratory, creating a single atom of antimatter that's only stable for a microsecond. It's not the quantity that matters, or even the duration. It's the fact that it's been done at all that changes the world. Admit it,' I went on, 'for a moment, a split second, you felt disloyal, you wanted to rebel. Well? Yes or no?'

He shrugged. 'Yes. But—'

'For a *moment*. For a *split second*.' I beamed at him. 'I spy with my little eye something beginning with T. Something,' I added, 'which doesn't apply to us. Anything we do for a moment, for a split second, lasts for ever, you know that as well as I do.' I stood up. I'd had about as much as I could take. 'Gentlemen,' I said, 'congratulations. We did it. We did as we were told. We are now all irrevocably fallen from grace.' Big grin. 'Thank you all ever so fucking much.'

*

The point being: the thing my esteemed colleague didn't actually say, but which was inevitably implicit in *why us?* Namely, how could He do this to us?

Divine discontent. That's the probe, the needle. Divine discontent worms its way through all the love and glory until it reaches *how could He possibly do this horrible thing to us*? This bad thing. This evil—

*

'In recognition of which,' I told Theophylact, 'my fellow rebels paid me the honour of unanimously appointing me Perpetual Ambassador to the Court of St Peter. Which is why I'm here. The way you can twist things round, they said, you're a natural for the job.' I smiled. 'They didn't mean it nicely, but I take it as a compliment.'

I don't think I've ever seen a more sober human being. 'So you did rebel,' he said. 'You did make war in Heaven.'

'We did as we were told,' I replied. 'But yes. And we lost, of course. Needless to say. I fought the Lord, and the Lord won. The point is,' I went on, 'God created evil. More than that, God used evil, He *was* evil. He betrayed us, His brightest creations, His angels. Because it had to be done. Because without darkness—'

'Yes, I know. Without darkness, there's no light. You said.'

I shook my head. 'Because without darkness there is light, because He ordained it, but *no one can see it*. It's a subtle difference, but a vital one.'

He rubbed the side of his head. 'So you keep telling me.'

'Only because it's true.' I glanced at my watch; a screaming anachronism, but I've got a licence for it. 'Look, we need to get you to the Basilica for the investiture. The point you've got to grasp is this. There is such a thing as good, as there's such a thing as evil. But *they're the same thing*. Now, you say it. Go on.'

'I don't think I—'

'Say it.'

He shot me a scared, sullen look. 'Good and evil are the same thing,' he said. 'Happy now?'

'No,' I said. 'But that's beside the point.'

*

Forth in Thy name, O Lord, I go, my daily labour to pursue. I got the idiot boy cleaned up and looking just this side of respectable, and bundled him off to the Basilica to be crowned. I got a hatful of dirty looks from the family, who'd been looking all over for him, which I repaid with smiles – turn the other cheek, and so forth. I couldn't very well skip the ceremony, but I bolted as soon as I politely could and missed the party afterwards; absolutely no great loss. So much to do, so little time.

'You're late,' he said.

'Oh, it's you,' I said. 'I was expecting to see—'

'Yes, I bet you were.' He scowled at me. 'But you've got me instead. Believe it or not, the entire universe doesn't actually revolve around you.'

Meek and mild, I told myself. Meek and mild as a little lamb. 'You wanted to see me?'

He's not the sharpest knife in the drawer, he can be appallingly pompous and he has absolutely no sense of humour, but he's fair-minded, I will say that for him. Others in his position – well. As noted above, we all know perfectly well, deep down, that we're all on the same side, playing for the same team; but there are certain individuals, naming no names, who feel the need to – ah well. Nothing overt or explicit, you understand, just nuances of voice and expression; which, in context, can be every bit as offensive as the crude epithet and the shower of stones. Not him, though. I respect him for that.

He put down the report he'd been pretending to read. 'Just what do you think you're playing at?' he said.

He can't abide wounded innocence. 'Me?'

'You. You do realise, you've put the entire plan in jeopardy?'

'Don't be silly. It's already happened. You know that.'

He closed his eyes for a moment. 'Don't play your games with me,' he said. 'You know perfectly well what I mean. Sequentially speaking, in linear time, you've told that young thug his fortune. How many times do I have to tell you, we don't do that? Not on this side and most especially not on yours.'

I gave him a sweet, sad look. 'I'm very sorry,' I said. 'Was it very wicked of me?'

'Don't start.' He was controlling his temper. 'Now I know you, you don't do things like that for sheer—'

'Devilment?'

'You're up to something,' he said. 'You're adding bits to the plan again, ad libbing. Well? You are, aren't you?'

I shrugged. 'And don't they always come out for the best?'

'That's not the point. Believe it or not, you aren't the sole conduit of the Divine will. There's such a thing as proper channels and the chain of command. And that's not a moral issue, it's purely administrative, so you can spare me your elaborate sophistries and tell me what's hatching in that seething little brain of yours.'

'He knows. I thought I'd be seeing—'

He was getting riled. I can never remember which deadly sin Anger is. Three, or four? 'You think you're so clever, don't you, going over my head all the time. Because, as you so gleefully remind me, there are things your lot can do that our lot can't, and it gets the job done quicker. Only you're forgetting one little detail. We've got to try and keep this whole shooting-match up together. We've got the lives and acts of thirty thousand billion humans to co-ordinate across ten millennia. And you know what? You wandering off on frolics of your own doesn't really help all that much. In fact, it's a total pain in the neck. So don't do it. Do you understand me?'

You see what I mean? In the final analysis, when he puts it like that, even I have to admit he's got a point. 'He knows,' I repeated, but my heart wasn't really in it. 'He'll fix it. He can fix anything.'

'Yes, but He shouldn't have to. And He wouldn't, if only you'd play by the rules just for once.' He shook his head. 'To put it in language you'll understand,' he said. 'When you do this kind of stuff, you're not rebelling, you're not making war in Heaven, you're not being Evil, you're just being *annoying*. So please, no more of it. All right?'

I gave in. No point in fighting the last, lost war. 'All right,' I said. 'I'm sorry.'

'Thank you.' He breathed out, long and slow. 'Now,' he said. 'Tell me about it. What's the big idea?'

I explained. He listened quietly, then sighed. 'That's all.'

'Yes.'

'A drama queen,' he said, 'that's what you are.'

'That's a bit harsh, isn't it?'

'Drama queen,' he repeated. 'Always got to be centre stage. Mysterious, ineffable, all that. May I just remind you, this is serious official business. Your *ego*—'

'Ego?' I gave him a shy smile. 'I never knew I had one.'

He sighed. 'Still,' he said, 'it was a nice thing to do. Compassion, even for the sinner. I like that.'

I nodded. 'Sympathy from the Devil,' I said. 'What more could you ask?'

*

He was right, though. Small acts of rebellion, like small acts of Creation. I'm annoying, therefore I am.

Back to Rome. Torchlight in the darkened streets. Already there were crowds gathering. I mingled, keeping my ears open. A significant minority wanted to haul the monster out into the street, cut his head off and drag his headless trunk down to the river on a meat hook. The rest of them just wanted to see the show, especially if there were to be pennies thrown later. My guess was that *the show* was a flexible term, and that if it proved to consist of decapitations and meat-hook-dragging, that'd probably do just as well as a solemn procession in fancy dress. Ah, the people. If there's ever been a greater blasphemy than *vox populi, vox Dei,* I'd have a professional interest in hearing it.

The party was still going on, somewhere in the palace. I wondered just how much of our conversation he'd remember in the morning. Not too much, I hoped; just enough to worry him to death, without making him change his way of life one little bit. I snooped around for a bit, went to my office, did some paperwork I'd been neglecting. I don't need to sleep, which is a blessing. I read the official reports from our man in Aachen, and wrote a few letters. Then I slipped out through the back gate and rejoined the crowd. Someone had gone up on the wall with five fat baskets of low-denomination coins and started sprinkling wealth on the people below, so the pro-meat-hook faction was temporarily in abeyance. That set my mind at rest. They'd still be there when I wanted them. They always are.

*

'I've been thinking,' he said.

His hands – long, thin, pale; bitten fingernails – were shaking. 'Oh, yes?' I said.

'If there really—' He lowered his voice. Not much point to that. The audience chamber had once been a Roman emperor's *triclinium*, where distinguished guests dined and were entertained by the empire's finest actors and musicians. The acoustic was perfect. Impossible not to hear even the quietest whisper; a key selling point to an emperor paranoid about conspiracies. Come to think of it, I was the architect. 'If there really is a God—'

'Trust me on that,' I said.

He gave me a bewildered look. 'This changes everything,' he said. 'I mean,' he went on, looking over his shoulder, 'all my life, I never thought—' He paused, then managed to get started again. 'You know my family history.'

I grinned. Two of his uncles had been popes.

'Well,' he went on, 'it was a natural conclusion to draw. My uncles were – well, like me, I guess.'

'They were.'

'Exactly. There you have it. And they were *popes*. So you can see, I always assumed that the Church, God – it was all garbage, like a trick or something. It was all just to control the people, they need to believe in something. And if you're at the top of the tree, you can pretty much do as you like. I thought—'

I smiled. 'You thought that religion is the opiate of the masses,' I said. 'You held, not unreasonably, that God was a convenient fiction – if He didn't exist, it would be necessary to invent Him. Or, if God ever did exist, then He is dead, and it's we who have killed Him.' I sighed. 'Actually, your views do you credit. Throughout history, the wisest philosophers and the vast majority of truly intelligent men have come round to that way of thinking. As it turns out, they're all wrong. But you're in excellent company, nonetheless.'

He didn't speak for a moment. If he had, he'd probably have whimpered. 'Obviously,' he said, 'this changes everything. From now on, I'm a reformed character. No more booze, no more girls, no more selling absolutions and taking bribes. I'm going to take the Church right back to basics, and—'

I shook my head. 'You can't.'

Stunned look. 'I'm sorry?'

'You can't do that,' I said. 'That would be wrong. That can't possibly happen for another three hundred and fifty years. And when it does come, as an explosion of righteous indignation unlike anything the world has ever seen, it's going to cause a schism that'll make the present breach with the Greeks look like a lovers' tiff. The smoke from the pyres of burning heretics will blot out the sun, and their soot will blacken the bricks in every city in Christendom. I'm sorry, but there's no way you can change that. It's a done deal. You'd be well advised not to try.'

'That's insane,' he said.

I frowned at him. 'You mustn't say that. He moves in a mysterious way.'

'That's not mysterious, it's crazy. It's—'

I shushed him. He looked at me. 'In less than two centuries' time,' I said, 'an agent of one of your illustrious successors will order the massacre of a city known to harbour heretics; the innocent along with the guilty. Kill them all, he'll say, God will know his own.' I shrugged. 'And He will.'

He'd gone white. 'I don't believe it.'

'What you believe,' I said sternly, 'is no longer up to you, and don't you forget it. Think,' I said soothingly. 'What's the ideal aim of the true Christian? The imitation of Christ. And what was the main event of Christ's ministry on Earth? His judicial murder by the agents of the state and the forces of organised religion. Blessed are the holy company of martyrs, who will sit on the right hand of God. Now,' I went on, 'if there was no God, or if you had any doubts at all about God's existence, you'd be morally justified in objecting to the massacre of innocents. After all, there might be no Heaven, mortal life might be all we have; to deprive innocents of life would be an appalling act. But since you *know* that God exists, and since martyrdom is the highest possible achievement available to mortals, where's the harm? The truth is, you'd be doing them a favour.'

'But—' He licked his lips, like a dog. 'All right,' he said, 'fine. The victims are martyrs and go to Heaven. So, what about the killers? They go to Hell, right? And that's *entrapment*.'

I smiled and shook my head. 'That's just silly,' I said.

Bewildered look. 'Is it?'

'Of course. *Think*. The victims die for their faith; they are martyrs; they are saved. The killers kill them – not a pleasant process; have you ever killed anyone, innocent people, in cold blood? It's no fun at all, you feel sick for days and you have recurring nightmares. But the killers do it because it's God's will; and for doing God's will they are accorded the honour of good and faithful servants, and enjoy merit in Heaven.'

He made a sort of gurgling noise. 'What, both sides? That's just gross.'

And I'd started to think he was quite bright. 'No it isn't,' I said. 'It's just like my case, war in Heaven. A war between two opposing sides both devotedly loyal to the same cause. *Both* sides, because God wills it. Keep your eye on that phrase, by the way; *Dieu le volt*, that's what they'll be yelling in sixty years' time when they kill every Muslim civilian in Jerusalem.' I paused. He looked like he was about to throw up all over my shoes. 'God wills it,' I said. 'Because God said, let there be light. And without darkness, the light would be invisible. God wants as many of His children as possible to be saved. But Man is a savage animal. He ordained that Man should be born with inherent aggressive tendencies, which are perfectly normal and natural, and which find their normal and natural outlet through slaughtering his own kind. God wills that both the slayers and the slain, the crusaders and the martyrs, should be saved. Selah. The logical means to that end is a schismatic Church.' I grinned again, and quoted:

> *Teach me, my God and king,*
> *In all things Thee to see,*
> *And what I do in everything,*
> *To do it as for Thee.*
>
> *A servant with this clause*
> *Makes drudgery divine.*
> *Who sweeps a room, as for Thy laws,*
> *Makes that and the action fine.*

He gazed at me. 'Say what?'

No poetry. No soul. 'Sweeping a room,' I said. 'Drudgery. And there's no worse drudgery, believe me, than massacring civilians. It's exhaustingly hard physical work, like harvesting or chopping wood, and it's incredibly miserable and dreary and depressing. But if you do it for God, honestly believing, you sanctify the wretched chore into a sacrament. Faith and works. Can't have one without the other.'

He drew in a long, ragged breath. 'This isn't real,' he said. 'It's a dream or something.'

I slapped him across the face. He squealed. 'You're not dreaming,' I said. 'Try and get it into your thick head. God is working His purpose out, as year succeeds to year. God needs you to bring to the papacy the special gifts and talents that you alone possess. You may not like what you have to do – I know I didn't, when it was my turn. But I knuckled down and did it, because *God wills it*. And so will you.'

There were tears on his stupid face. 'But I don't want to.'

'Ah.' I smiled. 'Divine discontent,' I said. 'The ethics of angels.'

*

As I believe I said earlier, we represent His Divine Majesty's loyal opposition. Our motto is: His will, right or wrong. Or should that be, right *and* wrong? You choose.

Naturally. The cornerstone of it all is free will. To give you a choice, He created evil. An act by itself is nothing, it's meaningless. Take any virtue; take courage, faith, hope, love. The courage of the thief climbing into a darkened house, not knowing if the householder is lurking in the shadows with an axe. The faith of the true believer, offering up the still-beating heart of his child on the altar of his gods. The hope of the tyrant's bodyguard, fighting the berserk mob so that their master can slip away, his pockets stuffed with diamonds. And love – these three abide, but the greatest of all is love; the love of his country that compels the visionary to herd women and children into the gas chamber, so that his people, his neighbours may one day see the bright new dawn.

The act, like the transitory flesh, is meaningless. Only the will matters.

*

I didn't get another chance for a quiet tête-à-tête with His Holiness for quite some time. By then, he'd already been forced out of Rome once – getting him back in required all the Emperor's horses and all the Emperor's men, and rather a lot of people died – and he was on the point of being thrown out again through the machinations of Bishop John of Sabina, shortly to be crowned as Pope Sylvester III (come to think of it, that was me too). The poor fellow; he was a shadow of his former pale, skinny, dissipated self; he looked like a newt in a cope, and the dark rings under his eyes looked like bruises. 'I don't want to be Pope,' he said. 'I hate it. I want to find a monastery somewhere on top of a mountain and spend the rest of my life in prayer.'

'Hair shirt?' I asked.

'Yes,' he said. 'And stone floors and bitter cold. I want to get as much cold as I can, before I go to the very hot place.'

I laughed. 'That's all just scare stuff,' I said. 'There is no everlasting bonfire, trust me. And besides, you've got a place reserved for you in Heaven. Just keep going, keep the faith, and you'll be fine.'

'Screw Heaven.' If looks could kill, and if I could die – 'What makes you think I want to go there?' he said. 'With Him? After what he's done to me?'

I nodded slowly. 'Lord, Lord, why persecutest Thou me? Oh come on. Think of Job.'

'I think of little else,' he said, and I realised he was serious. 'I keep reading it, over and over again, just in case I missed something.'

'I applaud your taste,' I said. 'It's the most important bit in the Bible.'

'It doesn't *work*,' he said bitterly. 'The arguments just don't add up. God takes His most loving servant and He tortures him. And for *no good reason*.'

I poured him a cup of wine. Good stuff. He looked at it as though there was something dead floating in it. 'God created evil,' I said. 'Everything God does is good. Therefore evil is good. Accept it and move on.'

'Go to hell.'

I smiled. 'You don't like the way things are run around here,' I said. 'That's good. I don't, either. Tell you what. When you get to Heaven, look me up. We can plot a palace coup.'

*

Poor Theophylact died at the age of forty-three, finally worn out by dissipation and depravity, at the abbey of Grottaferrata. He'd repented of his sale of the papacy (why simply abdicate when you can make a buck? I rather approved of it at the time, though I didn't imagine for one moment that anyone would be stupid enough to buy it) and forced his way back into the Lateran with an army of mercenaries; he said he wanted to clear out the corruption root and branch and drive the moneylenders from the temple. The German king threw him out again, and he was formally deposed and excommunicated. Because of that, when he turned up at the abbey pleading for absolution, the abbot refused; he let him sleep in the stables, because there was no room in the guest wing. The day before he died, three heretic bishops came to see him from the East. They claimed to have been led there by a comet, or something of the sort. They talked together for a long time. At the very end, he was visited by an angel. Come to think of it –

'They won't let me have the last rites,' he croaked at me. He'd been blind for some time, but I think he knew me by my smell. 'I offered them a lot of money, but they said no, there are some people you just don't do business with.'

'That's all right.' I said. 'I absolve you, in the name of the Father. Heaven awaits you. Just follow the very bright light, turn left and there you are.'

'I told you,' he said – speaking caused him so much pain. 'I don't want to go there. I want to go to the other place. It's where I belong.'

'With me. For ever. I'm touched.'

'With you.' He grinned. It was as though the skin had vanished and I was looking at the bare bone. 'Now that's what I call eternal torment.'

'Don't be like that,' I said. 'We've always got on so well.'

'Why did you *tell* me?' He was gasping for air, like a drowning man. 'If you hadn't told me, I'd still have been an evil little shit, I'd still have degraded the holy office and sowed the seeds of your wretched schism, and I wouldn't have *known*.'

I shrugged. 'I'm horrible,' I said. 'It's what I do. Besides,' I went on. 'Because you knew, every sin you committed was a sacrament. Instead of eternal damnation, you're saved and will join the elect in Paradise. Twenty-six years of Earthly suffering is nothing compared with eternity. You've been really lucky. It's like buying a gold brick for fourpence.' I paused. 'I saved you,' I said. 'All my idea. They'd have left you in ignorance and let you burn. But now, thanks to me—'

He looked at me with his sightless eyes. 'I don't like the way things are run,' he said. 'I think there must be a better way. If God can do this to me, he isn't God, he's just a very powerful bully.'

'Your sins are forgiven,' I said. 'Go in peace.'

'Fuck you,' he said; and then he died.

I closed his eyes. 'Flights of angels sing thee to thy rest, kid,' I said. 'You've earned it.'

*

Not for me, though. The plan continues. God is still working His purpose out. All that pain, all that misery, and we aren't even half-way through yet. And when we reach the end – you're not supposed to know this, but what the hell – it'll all start all over again, from the beginning. The rebranded name will be the Kingdom of God on Earth, but do you really suppose it'll be any different? Worse, prob-ably. The brave, blazing new Empire of Light is going to need an awful lot of darkness if it's to be visible at all.

No peace for the wicked.

Ω

Angels and fallen angels, indeed, the whole panoply of celestial beings known as 'thrones, dominions, principalities and powers' (Colossians 1:16) or 'principalities and powers and rulers of the darkness of this world' (Ephesians 6:12) are part of the very structure of Christian belief. They do not, of course, fall within the remit of the majority of scholars; historians and theologians by necessity have different frames of reference; evidence and faith are not interchangeable.

But if the Church of Rome had documentary evidence detailing the direct involvement of such powers, not only in the affairs of man but in the hierarchy of the Church at the very highest level, it is understandable that they would suppress them.

c. **1040**

This very personal account, found in the early-medieval section of the Vaults, is startling for two reasons. The first is that it purports to be the testimony of a time traveller, an historian from the twenty-fifth century who journeys into the past. The second . . . this will become apparent as the narrative proceeds.

If time travel is indeed possible, it would be an inestimable boon for historians. We have consulted colleagues in theoretical physics at Oxford, Cambridge, the Massachusetts Institute of Technology and the California Institute of Technology, and have received a cautious acceptance of the possibility of time travel, though hedged around with so many caveats about its practicability that we doubt it will become a reality in our lifetimes, if ever.

When discussing which of the many documents found in the Vatican Vaults we should publish in this volume, one member of the team suggested that we had a duty to include this account on the basis that if there are time-travelling historians in the twenty-fifth century, we would be doing them a great favour by placing this chronicle in the public realm. Another member of the team countered this suggestion by arguing that if by publishing it we made the twenty-fifth-century historians aware of the revelation contained herein, they would not send the narrator back to the eleventh century and this account would therefore never have been written. Such paradoxes, our scientific colleagues assure us, are fundamental to theoretical physics.

Chasing Charlemagne

John Grant

'Priest.' The voice came from the shadows.

I paused in my stroke and the dinghy eased to a halt on the still water. The alley from which the whisper had come was pitch dark.

'Nobody's called me that in a long time,' I said.

I wasn't really afraid. Just a handful of decades ago the city had teemed with people. Now there were only a few of us, scavenging among the ruins and the slowly rising waters. For the most part we kept a healthy distance from each other, but there was a companionship too. A companionship in craziness.

'You never stop being a priest,' the unseen speaker continued. 'Beneath it all, Kenneth, you're still wearing invisible vestments.'

'Who are you? Come out of there so I can see you.'

Broadway was a silver palace of moonlight. The water beneath me was mercury; the shattered windows to either side were sculptures of crystal bedecked by abstract tapestries that by day would be revealed as lichens and seaweeds.

'Don't you recognise my voice?'

'It's been a long time since I've heard any voices.' I laughed. 'From outside my head, at least.'

I heard a small splash as his oars dropped into the water, and a moment later he was alongside me. He was wearing a cowl, as if he were Death coming to call, but he threw it back, shook out his hair, and turned to look at me with a grin.

'Benny!' I cried. 'How in the name of damnation did *you* get here? And how the devil did you find me? I thought I'd managed to lose myself completely.'

I reached out across the gap between the two boats and we clumsily shook hands.

'Is there somewhere we might go?' said Benny. 'You must have a home, surely? I'm freezing. And hungry. And I could do with a drink.'

I pointed back over my shoulder with a thumb. 'Follow me,' I said.

*

One day all the buildings will surely come a-tumbling down, as the waters rot their foundations and the soil into which they were moored turns to clay and then mud and then not even that. But for now the upper storeys are often habitable. Mould is rampant, of course; there's no electricity, and water has to be brought up from the street and distilled. But the city, even after all this time, is full of food and other essentials, ripe for the scavenging. If you don't mind cooking on camping stoves and the fact that everything you eat comes out of a can or a jar that's about a quarter of a century past its sell-by date, you can feast like a king. Well, sort of. At least you can wash the food down with a single-malt Scotch or a vintage Beaujolais. After spending so long in the bottle the wines are a bit hit-or-miss – you have to open a few before you find one that's drinkable – but the Scotches usually taste just fine.

Once I'd got the candles lit I put a stiff Glenlivet in Benny's hand and sat him down in my best armchair, then sorted among my least-rusty cans. 'A nice chicken casserole? Ravioli?'

'Whatever you're eating,' he said drily, looking around him, the glass at his lips. 'Tell me what you've been doing. Tell me why you ran away.'

I opted for the ravioli. He'd said he was hungry and I had three cans of it. 'Do you really want the answers or do you know them already?'

'Some of them,' he said. 'Perhaps. I'm not sure.'

'Well, you'll have guessed why I came here.'

'To hide from people like me,' he said. 'Your old friends.'

I nodded. 'And I still don't know how you found me.'

'The Lord knows all . . . ' he began solemnly.

We both laughed.

'Seriously, Kenneth, New Vatican *does* know just about everything there is to know. It took me a lot of time and effort to track
you down, but there was never really any doubt I'd be able to do so.'

I'd known that, of course. 'But why make the effort? Why bother?'

'Because of Helen.'

Suddenly I seemed to have very little breath. 'So you *do* know
why I fled.'

'Yes and no.' He got to his feet. 'I could do with some more of
this fine whisky, if you have any to spare.' I passed him the bottle.
'I know how the two of you felt about each other – it was obvious
to everyone. But it's a mystery even to the all-seeing eye of New
Vatican – that's me – what went wrong between you.'

I chuckled, the way one does to keep pain at arm's length. 'I'm
not sure I know, either. She was frightened of losing her identity,
I think. We'd both been in too many different times, been too
many different people. You've seen it yourself, how travellers can
crack up from it: they've had so many personalities their psyches
collapse and they're left with no personality at all. You look for
recruits who're as self-sufficient as you can find them, but still
your failure rate is high. Helen and I were among the lucky few.
Yet . . . well, letting yourself love and be loved is an existential
threat. She feared letting anyone have too much of her in case it'd
be the final stress that shattered her inner self.'

'So she made you back off.'

'Yes. And that was more than *I* could bear. So I fled here to the
early twenty-second. There's no structure left, no records, hardly
any communications. Who could find me here?'

He smiled. 'Well, *we* could. Obviously.'

'Obviously,' I agreed, putting plates out on the table. 'Eat up.
And tell me why you thought the search would be worth it.'

*

With the world having largely fallen apart by the middle of the
twenty-first, and Fortusa,* among the worst afflicted nations of

---

* Roughly speaking, the former USA and its North American conquests.
For more episodes of the Empire's history, see *Leaving Fortusa* (2008) by
John Grant.

all, having hidden itself behind the Shield, the more liberal tatters of the Roman Catholic Church in Fortusa gravitated toward the small community of Vatican, Louisiana, and tried to establish a new structure there – not in rivalry to the Holy See but as a temporary adjunct. Although contact with the outside world was difficult, and fraught with danger for all concerned, news trickled through eventually that the Pope in Rome was not displeased. Even had he been, there wasn't much he could have done about it. There were various centres around the world where civilisation had clung on, but southern Europe wasn't one of them. The great Mediterranean Renaissance was still a couple of centuries away; by the time it dawned, the Roman Catholic Church, as originally constituted, would be no more. When the Fortusan Shield came down, at about the same time, the survivor of Catholicism in the world would be the Church centred on Vatican, Louisiana: New Vatican.

But it was no longer really a Church, not in any sense of the word that would have been understood in previous eras. In a backlash against the savage Christian fundamentalism that had ravaged Fortusa during the Shield years, New Vatican had become less and less engaged with religion – even, indeed, with God. Instead it had come to devote most of its energies to the study and preservation of knowledge. It had been the Church, after all, that was credited with keeping the flame of scholarship alive during the long Dark Age between the fifth and tenth centuries. Surely its divine mission during this even more barbaric repetition of history was to do the same. And it could feed people, try to defend the persecuted, save lives. Indisputably, this was God's will. God could do without His Church for a time while it rescued people's bodies and minds rather than necessarily their souls. He *preferred* to do without His Church for a time.

In the end, it seemed, He forfeited it entirely.

The Shield came down. Civilisation began to rebuild, even in Fortusa. Humankind's world would likely never be the same again, but at least it was becoming livable.

Among the pieces of knowledge preserved at New Vatican was the technology of time travel to the past. This had been developed during the Fortusan period, but was so abused by the Empire that eventually the people of a distant future had intervened. The priests were able to use the inherited technology to study the past. They couldn't do so very often, because the procedure required extraordinary use of energy and was phenomenally expensive; the Fortusan economy was, after all, still stumbling towards a recovery. Besides, the combination of characteristics required for someone to have much chance of survival was rare: the toughness of mind, the lack of impressionability, the linguistic flair, the ability to function in environments whose entire structure could collapse at any moment. Another important trait was shortness. Go back a couple of centuries and you'll find just about everyone's a lot smaller than you are, unless you yourself happen to be quite small by modern standards.

New Vatican's historical researches were difficult, yes.

But not impossible.

And it was only natural that the Dark Age – the original – should eventually become a focus of the priests' attention. With sufficient knowledge of what had given rise to it and sustained it, perhaps another repetition of complete societal collapse could be avoided . . .

*

'But then the problems arose,' said Benny. 'You must have known something of them before your . . . disappearance.'

I nodded. There's always a certain casualty rate among travellers. It's not high enough to lose sleep over, but it's definitely non-negligible. The Dark Age expeditions, however, seemed to represent a new hazard. They were the farthest anyone had ever tried to go into the past, but in theory that shouldn't have been a problem. Even so, by the time my pain over Helen's rejection had become too great to bear and I deserted the twenty-fifth for the twenty-second, four travellers had been sent to the period and none had returned. Either there was a threat there that we didn't know about, or the era was far more dangerous than any historian had ever guessed, or . . .

'Or Heaven came to Earth for six hundred years or so,' Benny said, topping up his glass, 'and then we suffered a second fall from grace.'

'You don't really believe that, do you?'

'No.' He sighed.

For some minutes we were both silent, watching the flicker of the candles. Who was it who said that knowledge and science and culture are just a solitary flame in the night, vulnerable to any barbarian who wants to blow it out?

'You didn't come here just to bring me up to date on the project?' I said eventually.

He started in his chair, as if I'd woken him. 'No,' he said. 'No.'

I waited.

He let out a long sigh. 'You were one of the best, Kenneth, maybe the best of all the travellers. When I can't get to sleep and my insecurities start trying to come home to roost, I drive them away by remembering that I was the one who found you, who taught you, who groomed you, who made you what you are.' He smiled grimly. 'Were. That's the trouble. Then I remember how you packed it all in, and my self-doubts come flocking back to torment me.'

'Insomnia's a terrible thing,' I said blandly.

'So are nightmares. You travellers usually have plenty of them, having seen what you've seen.'

'One hardens,' I said, shrugging. I still sometimes wake in a sweat over the Elizabethan execution I witnessed, or what I saw during my time on an antebellum Southern plantation. Auschwitz. Other things. But it was none of Benny's business that I did.

'You're not just one of the best,' he continued. 'You've made yourself expendable. We've already lost you. Training a traveller is a huge investment. Like all investments, they sometimes go bad. You're one of the investments that went bad, for us. We've marked you off on the books. So if we lose you again it won't make any difference. You're an asset of no value any longer, so far as the bean counters are concerned. They won't let me risk another of my current travellers – another of their investments. But' – he spread his hands expressively – 'they wouldn't give a damn if I risked *you.*'

'What makes you think I'm willing to be risked?' I looked around the cozy room. The wind was building up now, as it always does at nights here, preparing for the howl it sustains from midnight 'til dawn. But I had warmth, food, drink – even, for once, human company. The sanitary arrangements were a bit primitive, true, but that was a small detraction. 'I like it here.'

'Helen,' said Benny.

'Helen's my past. Well, my future, I suppose. But for me she's the past. I've moved on.'

'You say.'

'I do.'

'We don't know where she is. When she is.'

'Neither do I. I can live with that.' But I was beginning to guess where he was heading. 'Which century?' I added before he had a chance to speak.

'Why do you think I'm here?' He stared at me. 'She's at the end of the eighth, beginning of the ninth.'

'Charlemagne,' I said.

'Of course.'

It all made sense. New Vatican would want to probe the Dark Age. Helen had always been fascinated by Charlemagne, the Frankish king and conqueror who created the greatest empire in Europe since Roman times. As with the petty British king called Arthur, it was hard to distinguish truth from legend – or so I thought. Helen had read all the histories and the legends too. Her eyes lit up at the mention of her hero's name. I used to tease her that she was more in love with this man she hadn't even seen than ever she was with me, and sometimes my teasing didn't seem entirely a joke. If Benny had offered her the chance to go to Charlemagne's era she'd have jumped at the opportunity, whatever the dangers and uncertainties.

'And you've lost her?' I said.

'She hasn't come back.'

'And you think I'm the useful idiot who'll volunteer to go after her?'

'Yes.'

I let out a long, slow breath. 'You're right, of course.'

'I know,' said Benny, as if the issue had never been in doubt. 'Shall we go now?'

'No better time,' I said. 'I've nothing here that I need to take with me. Except maybe a couple of bottles of the Glenlivet.'

'A couple for each of us, I think.' Then his grin faded. 'What about your portal?'

'I destroyed it as soon as I got here.'

He gave a low whistle. 'My, you really *did* want to make sure you stayed lost, didn't you?'

His question wasn't trivial. Portals can be finicky and sometimes they just crash, but physically they're virtually indestructible.

A portal may be small enough to stick in a pocket, but making one is inordinately difficult, involving physics that's not entirely based in our universe. (I don't understand this, but it's what the techies have told me.) And, though portals are astonishing in their capabilities – the Emperor used to send whole armies through them to ransack the past – they don't last forever. Add in the problems of calibrating the devices for both temporal and spatial location: not much use arriving in the right year if you're floating between the stars because the solar system has moved in the interim.

'I raided a chemistry lab,' I said. A couple of months in a vat of concentrated nitric acid did the trick. I assume there's nothing at all left of it by now. It's been a while since I went back to check.'

'Why make so much effort?'

'Helen, of course.'

'You doubted your own resolve?'

'Yes. I thought that one day I might wake up and think it was worth going back to the twenty-fifth to try to change her mind. Rather than get myself hurt even worse, I decided to forestall my own stupidity.'

Benny dismissed the issue with a movement of his hand. 'It's no matter. We can use mine.'

He reached into his pocket and pulled out the portal. I'd almost forgotten how small portals are. There's a whole lot of the cleverest technology in human history packed into a device that's barely larger than a man's palm and only a few millimetres thick.

'Don't forget the whisky,' he told me.

*

Love isn't easy between two travellers. You spend long periods separated not just by distance but by centuries. And if you're spending a year or three in the field, living among the people of the past, you naturally tend to form attachments there. In some cases you have no choice: some societies look askance at single people. I've had four wives in wildly different eras, and each of them I've loved – if not with my whole heart then at least with much of it. There are still nights when I find myself dreaming of one or other of them. There's guilt in me, too – guilt over the pain I must have caused them when I vanished inexplicably from their lives. Those acts of desertion likewise can trouble my dreams.

So liaisons between travellers tend to be short-term, matters of convenience rather than anything more. The first time I hooked up with Helen – it was in a New Vatican bar, so very romantic – I thought of her as just a pretty woman who might, if I were lucky, be looking for a fling. By the time the evening ended, though, after we'd talked for hours about how the skies are so much clearer in the past, about how birdsong in the twenty-fifth is so much more subdued than in the seventeenth, about a whole host of other subjects . . . as we came out of that bar into night air that's never cold any longer, never crisp, I knew I was smitten. There's an old myth that each of us is only half of a complete person; one of our tasks in life is to find our counterpart and thereby make ourselves whole. That's what I felt I'd achieved as we walked hand in hand down the quiet streets to my house.

We both knew the difficulties facing us. We were going to have to solve those difficulties somehow, make our love work.

Except, in the end, we didn't.

*

Benny and I arrived in a sterilised room and immediately stripped, putting our clothes into a chute that led directly to a furnace. Carrying the whisky bottles, we went through a decontamination procedure with chemical sprays and radiation that left us feeling nauseous; we both knew we'd be sick as dogs for a few hours. It was the routine as usual – but a routine I'd never thought I'd experience again. Decontam's essential, of course, because who knew how many twenty-second-century bugs we might be carrying that could prove devastating to the people of the twenty-fifth? The same goes the other way round. Immediately prior to departure to the past, travellers go through this same decontam ritual for fear of causing plagues. If ever you witness someone pop into existence out of nowhere and they're green in the face and puking, that's likely someone arriving from the future.

Under the Empire, the rules weren't as stringent. Where do you think the Black Death came from?

After Benny and I had the worst of the retching under control, we dressed in white smocks and headed for his office. Once there, he threw himself down behind his desk. A holo display flashed all the colours of urgent, but he batted an angry hand through it and it disappeared.

He spoke without preamble. 'We sent Helen to the year 800, more or less in the middle of the Dark Age.'

'Let me guess,' I said. 'She suggested Rome.'

'Yes.' He raised his eyebrows. 'How did you guess?'

'The Pope crowned Charlemagne there that year.'

'Of course. I'm surprised you knew.'

'Helen and I were together two years, give or take. You can't be with Helen that long and not know something about Charlemagne.'

He looked briefly amused.

'You're going to send me directly after her?' I said.

'No. She's not the first person we've lost in the Dark Age, as you know. I'm not going to risk sacrificing another life there – at least, not until we have a better idea what's going on.'

'What's the point in sending me at all, then?'

'Recovering Helen is only part of the task.'

'For you, perhaps. Not for me.'

He grimaced. 'We have to try to find out what's going on. One traveller lost, maybe two, I could write it off as it just being a dangerous time. But travellers know how to protect themselves, how to avoid danger. No, there's something else going on.' He pressed the heel of his hand against his forehead. I wondered how long it had been since he'd slept.

'You make it sound like magic's stalking the land. Merlin, maybe. Morgan le Fay.' I forced a smile, trying to speak lightly.

'Don't be foolish, Kenneth.'

The dryness of his voice sobered me. 'Could it be that there's an outpost of the Empire we don't know about?'

'I'll tell you something we learned during your absence, Kenneth,' said Benny. 'The Empire sent a couple of its expeditions into the Dark Age. *They* never came back, either. The Imperial administrators buried the information in their archives – bad news was always unwelcome, and the messengers too often got shot. But we found it in the end.'

'So they started avoiding those centuries too?'

He gave a nod of agreement.

'What do you want me to do?' I said.

'Make several trips – bracketing shots, if you like. See if you can find out what's happening without being thrown directly into the quicksand yourself – diagnose the disease without getting close enough to catch it, so to speak. If the exploratory visits go well, I'll think again about sending you into Charlemagne's time.' He carried on without giving me a chance to interrupt. 'First off, I want to send you back to the middle of the eleventh. We know enough about what was going on then to be fairly sure you'll be all right. About 1040, I think. I want to keep you clear of the Great Schism of 1054.'

'Where?'

'France. There was a famine in the thirties and all hell was going to break loose in the fifties, but as far as we know the 1040s were relatively tranquil.'

'When can I get started?'

*

It was one of those days in autumn when the air smells of winter but the sun still believes there's some of summer left. I was standing in the middle of a tract of grassland being watched by a couple of very inquisitive cows; behind them, a score or so of others had already lost interest in me and returned their noses to the grass. I felt weak at the knees from the after-effects of decontam but for once I didn't think I was going to puke. I slowly sat down and wondered just exactly where I might be. It seemed I was in luck, that no human eyes had witnessed my arrival.

I looked up at the sky. The day was working on towards evening. There were some thin clouds trying to form themselves into a mackerel pattern, and the hint of a scimitar moon. I should find some shelter, preferably *warm* shelter, as soon as I could, because the night would doubtless be chilly. Ideally I should find myself a monastery or a convent – I was dressed appropriately as a monk. In this period, in France, there should be no shortage of monasteries.

The cattle started lowing, moving restlessly as they turned towards a distant figure – some serf come to fetch them home for the night.

I got to my feet again as he approached.

He stopped at the sight of me, then came on more cautiously. By his standards, I was quite a big man.

'Father?' he said.

'Blessings, my child.' My mouth seemed clumsy as it coped with the Old French words. The language pack solved the problem of vocabulary but it could do nothing about the fact that my brain was saying one thing and my voice was uttering another. It felt as if my tongue and teeth were all flying off in random directions. It would be easier once I was among monks. I speak Latin fluently, and would have no need of the language pack.

He bowed his head and I made a vague gesture of benediction.

'Where are you bound, Father?'

'I'm in the service of the Lord.'

I could see him straining to understand my words. The other thing the language pack can't solve is accurate pronunciation. Wherever in time we go, we always sound as if we're saddled with an atrociously thick accent. One of the advantages of eras before the Industrial Revolution, when someone could live their whole life without going twenty miles from home, is that people were accustomed to strangers having unidentifiable accents.

What I'd just told him was that I was in essence just bumming around the countryside, relying on people's hospitality in exchange for blessings – not to mention, in these days before medicine, the healing powers I could exercise through my very presence as an emissary of Our Saviour.

'My home is but humble,' he began, lowering his head again, 'but if—'

I had no doubt his home would be humble, infested with rats, lice and screaming children, and with the wind howling through the gaps in the roof and walls.

'Is there a house of God nearby?' I interrupted. 'A monastery? A chapel?'

He looked relieved. The poor man had probably resigned himself to giving me his supper.

'An hour's walk,' he said, pointing roughly in the direction the sun was heading. 'Maybe a little more. There's a nest of nuns there.'

For a moment I wondered if I could believe him, if he might not just be trying to get rid of me, but my doubt vanished almost before it had arrived. A serf's life was cheap. Trying to trick even so lowly a figure as a wandering monk could bring dreadful retaliation.

Moments later, having left him with an extra ration of blessings, I was trudging steadily across the pasture towards the place where the sunset would be.

Rabbits watched me as I passed them by. Their only sign of fear was the stillness with which they held themselves.

*

I found the nunnery easily enough. It was a small one, with fewer than a dozen nuns; the building looked more like a made-over barn than a house of God. The prim Mother Superior, Marie-Amélie, who was somewhat younger than most of her coterie, didn't seem any too pleased to see me, but of course she had no choice but to bid me welcome.

At least I could offer them a second male voice at vespers, for there was another monk staying there overnight. He was plump, chubby-faced, jolly and bald – the very image of Friar Tuck in the old picture books, in fact – and his name was Léon. After Matins the following morning, as we all breakfasted together on a thin, lukewarm porridge, I realised from various clues, including the smell of him, that he'd spent the night with Marie-Amélie. So much for her primness.

I wondered what I smelled like to him. Questionably clean, I suspected.

He was as genial as he looked. When I learned he was en route to the Abbey of Saint Martial at Limoges and asked if I might accompany him along the way, he was more than happy.

'We can travel in style, two fine fellows like us!' he cried, nudging me in the belly with a surprisingly sharp elbow.

He told me he'd arranged for a local man to take him by cart – 'Such a trudge otherwise, dear boy, and I'm sure the Lord wouldn't wish his humble servants to blister their feet!' When the carter turned up not long after, I discovered it was none other than the peasant I'd met among the cows the afternoon before. Perhaps his services were payment for an indulgence Léon had granted the man's liege lord.

The cart was ox-drawn and progress was excruciatingly slow. Much of the time, impatient, I walked alongside while Léon rode with his legs dangling over the tailboard, kicking the air.

He talked all the while, barely pausing for breath, and I listened eagerly. This was what I was here for, after all – to learn more about life in the eleventh, at least in this one small part of the world. I knew I could take nothing Léon said for granted – the idea of there being just a single version of the truth wouldn't become current for centuries yet – but I could hope for some valuable kernels of information.

St Martial's Abbey, when we reached it at the end of the day, was a grand edifice – grander, in its way, than New Vatican, although not as sprawling. Nearby was the busy little city of Limoges. I gleaned from some of Léon's snide asides – he was no intellectual – that the abbey's community was active in fostering culture, including the copying of texts. I couldn't have hoped for a better place to land.

Our carter, who'd spoken barely a word to us all day, made it plain that he wasn't going to risk the road home at night. No one at the abbey batted an eyelid at having to put up three unexpected visitors, and soon enough I found myself in a small cell. Through the solitary narrow window, high above my head, I could hear the wind beginning to pick up. The bunk was a shelf of plain wood with a couple of thin, suspicious-looking wool blankets. The walls, unadorned except for a single crucifix, were faced with grey cement. I sensed I was going to be cold tonight.

But the abbey served a fine supper of roasted meats and root vegetables, washed down with plenty of wine and cider, so I slept soundly.

*

'You tell me you are a man of scholarship,' said Abbot Odolric. He was tall by eleventh-century standards – almost as tall as I was – and his grey eyes almost matched the silver of his hair, which he wore long, tied in a knot behind his head. He had no sense of humour whatsoever, and I'd liked him on sight.

'I am well regarded in my own land.'

'Scotland?'

'Yes.' I had no trouble reading the Latin of the documents in the monastery's library. Writing it was going to be more difficult, although not insuperably so: the job of a copyist is, after all, to *copy*. I expected I'd be slow to start with. Being Scottish, where letters might be formed a bit differently, was as good an excuse for this as I needed. It was all of a piece with my execrable accent. Even Odolric, who I'd already learned was the most polite of men, winced sometimes at my speech.

'And you would like to stay with us and help us in our task?'

'Yes.'

He looked me up and down. 'You seem honest enough, for a Scotsman, and we could certainly use the assistance. What about your friend?'

'Léon? He's just a companion of the road.'

Léon had drunk enough for ten last night. When I'd got up from my hard bunk this morning I'd been able to hear him snoring clear through the thick stone wall between our cells. He'd skipped Matins. I hadn't seen him at all so far today.

Odolric gave a frosty smile. 'I imagine he'll soon be on his way.'

I shrugged. 'He's his own master.'

Odolric had already shown me the library/scriptorium. It was huge – far bigger than you'd expect for even an establishment the size of St Martial's Abbey. The room stank of unwashed males. I hadn't counted, but there must have been at least thirty monks bent over their writing tables, busily working away. Half a dozen young novices were in attendance, running errands for the scribes. When I'd murmured something about being surprised to see so much industry, Odolric looked slightly puzzled. 'History waits for none of us,' he said cryptically before leading me away so we could converse in private.

It was soon settled that I was welcome at the abbey for as long as I cared to stay. After lunch I was shown to one of the few vacant writing tables – it was like a large lectern – and supplied with ink and a pair of quill pens: two pens, so that I could carry on working with one while a novice was trimming the other. The novice assigned to me, Mauritz, a brawny lad who looked to me as if he'd be better off as a blacksmith, gave me a single large sheet of coarse, rough-edged paper. On another sloping board beside me he reverently placed a wooden-bound book held open at its first page by a clip.

'Thank you,' I said, settling myself on my high stool.

Mauritz looked startled to be thanked, then turned to answer the call of one of the other monks.

And so my new career as a scribe started, as simply as that. Odolric must have relied very much on his own judgement of character – or perhaps he'd prayed for guidance – because paper was expensive stuff. If I made a mess of a sheet it'd be a small tragedy.

I don't know what the good abbot would have done had he known about the notepad I kept in a hidden pocket of my cowl, alongside my portal. I sent occasional written messages to Benny, reporting progress; the most important message, I guess, was that I was still alive – that I hadn't succumbed to whatever had overtaken the other travellers.

I was grateful I wasn't being asked to illuminate the text. I got the impression from Odolric and, later, from listening to my colleague scribes, that there was far too much copying to be done to allow for such niceties as illumination. Again, I found myself wondering where all this work had come from.

The book that I found myself transcribing was nothing of great note. It was just a rather dull and historically fanciful account of the adventures of Saint Peter between the time of the Resurrection and his own crucifixion, some thirty years later. He healed the sick, preached the word of Christ, healed the sick, made some prophecies about the imminent return of Christ, healed the sick . . . It seemed pretty obvious that two or three legends had been repeated in various different forms and then strung together to make a fake biography. I wonder if this particular text survived the Middle Ages. Perhaps it was far more valuable than I realised.

I could hardly believe the abbey at Limoges was unique in being overwhelmed by material to be transcribed. Such periods did occur in human history, I knew. Only a century or so before where I was now the entirety of Byzantine literature had been transcribed in just a few decades as the old majuscule script was replaced by the more flexible minuscule. There was also the huge translation and adaptation effort, still ongoing as I toiled in the abbey scriptorium, made by the Arab scholars to keep Greek, Egyptian and Babylonian scholarship alive. So massive transcription efforts weren't unknown. It's just that I'd never heard of this one, and I thought I should have. Perhaps it was exactly this wave of copying that had tugged back the drapes to let the light of the Middle Ages, wan though it was, shine in on Europe's long darkness?

Of course, I could discuss none of this with the men who worked alongside me. I'd hoped I might be able to form a friendship with at least a few of them, but they weren't gregarious in that sense. They did gossip at the dinner table, though, these men, and I was able to pick up bits and pieces of information.

The most important item – and it took me a while before I realised what I was hearing – was that not everyone there was engaged in transcription. A few, generally deferred to as if they formed an unofficial elite, were designated historians rather than scribes. Naturally, I did my best to be closer to them – not as easy a task as it might sound, because they were the top dogs and I was a recently arrived whelp. The only one who showed much interest in me was the most senior of them all, an old monk with a laugh as dry as dust and a way of looking at me, head to one side, that made me feel I should be saying something far cleverer than I actually was. His name was Karl-Georg and he came from Saxony. I wondered if his amicability stemmed from the fact that his accent was as gruelling as my own.

I wish now I'd been given the chance to know Karl-Georg better.

*

Winter was bone-achingly cold that year. I'd never experienced anything like it, and I wasn't the only one. Even the people of Limoges cursed it as especially severe. Odolric issued instructions that the hearth in the dining hall be kept perpetually ablaze so the poor people of the town could come and keep themselves warm; despite his generosity, it seemed hardly a day dawned without a fresh report of some poor soul being found frozen to death in a ditch somewhere. Far too many of them were children.

Some of my brethren took to sleeping among the paupers, where there was warmth, rather than in their stone cells.

My scoundrelly friend Léon came by, seeking the hospitality of the abbey once more, on his way back from wherever he'd been. He seemed to be travelling in more haste this time, and I suspected he'd been caught bedding someone else's wife. He stayed just the one night and left early the next day.

'You should come with me, dear boy,' he urged. 'We'd be fine companions on the road together.'

I shook my head firmly. 'I have a duty here.'

I did – just not the duty he thought it was.

I'd expected that chastity might be a problem of my monastic life, but in fact I was finding it no burden at all. It wasn't that I'd lost my sexuality. Several times a day I'd be painstakingly copying a word and have to pause until the vision of Helen's face that had sprung up between me and the page had faded; and it wasn't always just the face I saw. No, I think it was more that something of the sanctity of the task we were undertaking penetrated the spirit of even this unbeliever. Far from all of the monks around me were ascetic – most of them ate and boozed merrily and probably were as fond of wenching as Léon – but a few of them were like Odolric and Karl-Georg, and those were the ones I found inspired my respect. From respect to emulation is a small step.

In January the crushing cold of the winter proved too much for Karl-Georg's ancient heart. We found him one morning rigid in his bunk, as cold as the air in his cell. I wasn't the only one who shed tears. We could have left the matter of his burial to the sexton's men, but somehow that would have seemed degrading. I volunteered to be part of the team that dug his grave. It took us a full day. The soil was frozen so hard it was like trying to crack rocks. I have no idea how many spades we destroyed between us before it was done.

The next day, as I was entering the scriptorium, Odolric took me to one side.

'We've lost an historian,' he said.

I nodded. 'And a good man, which is a greater loss.'

He murmured agreement, then added: 'I've been watching your progress, Kenneth. At first I thought I'd made a dreadful mistake by so much as allowing you *near* a page of paper with a pen in your hand. But God reassured me I'd done the right thing, and of course He was right.' Odolric made the sign of the Cross over his breast. 'Your work's as good as anybody's now, better than most.'

I turned half away, embarrassed.

'Listen to me, Kenneth. I'm not just here to flatter you. I've sensed, I've sensed there's something . . . *more* about you.'

My heart sank. I'd been through this sort of conversation before. It happens to all travellers. It never crosses anyone's mind you could be a visitor from the future – crazy idea! – but often enough somebody realises you're *not quite right*. The most sensible thing to do when that happens is to get out of Dodge City, and fast – especially if you're in an era where odd-seeming folk can easily be called witches and have a bonfire put under them. At least I didn't have *that* to worry about – the people here followed the line of Saint Augustine of Hippo that witchcraft is a myth.

Odolric was still talking. I soon realised my sudden fears had been for nothing.

'You have an *imagination*, Kenneth. It is a gift from God that not all of us have. I've seen you at your desk, industriously performing your duty of copying the Lord's word and yet not actually *engaged* in it. Your mind has clearly been wandering else-where even as your hand has been forming the words. I should' – he gave a little coughing laugh – 'I suppose I should be angry with you for failing to show your task full reverence, but, as I say, imagination is God's gift, so who am I to speak against it?'

'You're kind, Father.'

'Karl-Georg thought the same about you. He said that you have the makings of an historian.'

'Me?'

'Don't be so surprised. The Lord crafts us all for different roles in life. I have plenty of monks who can replicate the words in front of them with skill and accuracy. But the historians are a breed apart. And Karl-Georg believed you belong to that breed. I think he was right. I think it's as an historian that you can best serve the Master of us all.'

'But I—'

He held up a hand to silence me. 'The other historians will tell you all you need to know. I'll inform them during the course of the morning. You will join them for the midday meal, and they will welcome you as one of their number.'

They will? From what I'd seen they were an exclusionary bunch who'd regard me as about as welcome as a dog turd. But Odolric's word was law inside the Abbey of Saint Martial and for some distance around it.

'Very well,' I said.

And, to give them credit, the other historians received me with friendliness and open arms.

In the afternoon the Norman monk Turold, who had taken over from Karl-Georg as the head of the little clan of historians, led me on a stroll around the cloisters and, his breath steaming in the icy air, told me what being an historian entailed.

That night I sent another of my occasional missives back up the timeline to Benny.

*

Luckily there was a full moon to guide my way as I trudged through the snow away from the Abbey of Saint Martial. The skin of my lower calves and ankles had already been scraped raw by the crust of ice that lay on top of the snow; the cold, mercifully, had numbed all sensation from my feet some while ago.

For once, Benny had replied to one of my messages. As always, he wasted few words:

Get out of there. Now. Back here for redeployment.

I could have used the portal right then and there in my cell, but after a moment's thought I'd decided to wait until the early morning and leave a trail of footprints in the snow to 'explain' my disappearance. Otherwise an inexplicable vanishing from a house of God could all too easily be construed as a miracle. I didn't accept the existence of the God these people worshipped, but I liked and respected men like Odolric and Turold enough that I didn't want to add a further piece of baloney to their belief system. Far better for them to think that, perhaps frightened off by the responsibility of being an historian, a creator rather than a copyist, I'd fled the abbey. They might be surprised, but they wouldn't think it had been a direct intervention by God.

Saving them from false beliefs . . .

I smiled in the darkness. Who was I kidding? I'd tripped over what was probably the biggest piece of deliberate falsification in human history, and I was trying to save some of its perpetrators from a few months of bamboozlement.

I managed to walk a couple of miles before I got to the stage where each new step made me want to scream. My throat was sore from gasping the freezing air. My fingers were so cold they felt as if they didn't belong to me, but I was somehow able to wrestle the portal from my cowl and flip it open.

I keyed it for home. The twenty-fifth and New Vatican had never seemed so alluring.

*

And they still do.

Portals don't last forever. They're finicky. They usually give some advance warning of their demise, so they can be replaced long before their deterioration becomes a problem. And perhaps this one had done exactly that but I'd failed to notice through having become so focused on the obligations of daily life in the abbey. More likely, the cold and my clumsy handling of the device as I programmed it was the last straw for some undetected weakness . . .

I can theorise as much as I want to, but it won't change the reality.

*

Some of the truth I already knew, from what Turold told me as we ambled around the cloisters that afternoon. Anyone looking at us might have thought we were just two friends discussing the matters of the day, or perhaps arguing some subtle theological point. In fact, in his earnest, gentle, pedantic way Turold was tearing apart myths that I'd always believed as accepted truth.

Over the years since then, I've been able to put together more of the pieces. My own interest in history got me part of the way: when there's nothing to do on a sleepless night except stare through the gloom at a blank wall, it's surprising how many memories come back. In addition, Odolric has helped me with much, even while unaware of what he was helping me to do. Turold likewise. Léon, who has become a staunch friend as our hair has greyed, brings news of the outside world when he passes this way, and this has enabled me to fill in a few further gaps. And of course there are the books in the abbey library – the factual books, that is, the dusty records with their dates and their annotations: not the holy books, and most certainly not the 'histories'.

Karl-Georg had just begun the writing of one of those 'histories'. When he died, Turold asked me to continue the task in his stead.

That task was the writing of the work that would, after a century's worth of embellishments by other hands, become generally known as *La Chanson de Roland*.

*

Back in the twenty-fifth I'd read a translation of *La Chanson*. As the monk talked to me, I realised that I knew his name. In the introduction to the edition I'd read, Turold was mentioned as a possible author of the piece. Sometimes in bed together Helen and I had read to each other. I remembered *La Chanson* twice over: the second time, it was being spoken gently, the words being rolled in appreciation, in Helen's voice.

It had never occurred to me – how could it have? – that I myself might have been the author of that epic poem.

And it had surely never occurred to Helen that her lover was largely responsible for creating the historical evidence for the object of her obsession.

Charlemagne.

Karl-Georg devised him. I gave him a story.

Here's as much as I have learned:

The history that we know – that *you* know – is a mess. It was made a mess by the Holy Roman Emperor Otto III. If you look at his biography you can see immediately that there's something wrong. He was supposedly born in 980 and became King of Germany at the age of three on the death of his father, the Holy Roman Emperor Otto II. At the age of sixteen the boy king led an army to Italy to claim the title of Holy Roman Emperor. He died in 1002 at the age of just twenty-one.

Those dates aren't impossible, of course, but they're odd enough to arouse an initial suspicion.

Among the boy king's tutors was the scholar Gerbert d'Aurillac, who became Pope Sylvester II in 999. This was among his lesser achievements. He was the man responsible for introducing the Arabic decimal numbers to Europe in place of the clumsy Roman system, for rediscovering the astrolabe and the abacus, and for much else besides. Some said he was a sorcerer of the black arts. There's more, much more that Gerbert/Sylvester did . . . *too* much more, in fact. If we're to believe the histories, he was a virtual Leonardo.

Two men, their lives closely intertwined, whose official biographies seem suspect.

Beyond suspect, in fact, as I discovered from Turold as we walked through the cloisters around and around the quadrangle of the Abbey of Saint Martial.

Otto and Gerbert were born not in the 900s but in the 600s. They were two men with high ideas of their own importance. As a single example, the reason Gerbert took the papal name of Sylvester was that the first Pope Sylvester had been the adviser to Constantine the Great. So we can assume that Otto saw himself as a figure of comparable stature to the great Emperor who put Christianity on the map – arguably, indeed, the most significant influence on the history of Christianity since Saint Paul and even Jesus Christ.

Surely, the two allies thought as the year 700 approached, it was God's will that the reign of Otto as Holy Roman Emperor be marked by a far more important change of centuries. Would it not be a grand thing if Otto's rule could be marked by the millennium?

At the time, no one outside the Church had any clear idea of how many years had elapsed since the birth of Christ. (The common folk didn't use the AD system: they counted the years in terms of the incumbency of whoever was their current monarch – the tenth year of King John, the seventh year of King Peter, and so on.) There were several different estimates of the true date: although the one usually accepted was 699, some authorities claimed the Lord had been born 696 years ago, or 698, or even 703. It was important, it seemed, for both Church and State to establish a fixed standard for further counting. The precise number chosen was immaterial, so long as it was one that everybody could be made to agree upon. And, since only clerics would notice if the year 699 were to be followed not by the year 700 but by the year 1000 . . .

It was done. There was no intent to deceive. It was just a tidying operation that happened also to feed the vanity of two powerful men.

A couple of years after the redating, Otto died, his death being followed just a matter of months later by Gerbert's. Neither death, Turold told me, was natural: both men were hastened from this world by their enemies. By then it was too late to revert to the previous dating system. The Pope had declared the year to be 1000, and it was inconceivable that the Pope might have been wrong to do so – just as it was inconceivable that Pope Gregory XIII could have been wrong when, in 1582, Thursday, the 4th of October was followed by Friday, the 15th of October. Like Sylvester II, Gregory changed the calendar in order to tidy it up, although the reasons for the tidying were rather different.

In 1582 many people were confused by the ten 'missing days', believing those days had somehow been stolen from their lives. Imagine the reaction in 1000 (or 700), even among the educated clergy, at the 'loss' of three whole centuries.

Those centuries must surely contain a history, people reasoned

– a secret history, now lost to us. A history that God knew but that mortals had somehow forgotten. And that gap in knowledge was intolerable to the religious sensibility: the forgetfulness of sinners was an offence against God.

So the Vatican, that greatest of puppet masters, began pulling strings, and each of the puppets it set into motion pulled further strings until, in monasteries all over Europe, 'historians' started their work of not recording or preserving history but of *creating* it.

Once again, there was no intent to deceive. The clerics believed that God was revealing the secret history to them. They were merely writing it down. If there were inconsistencies in the revelation, so what: it was just God's way. After all, in the Bible itself He'd given two different versions of the Creation.

What none of the pious monks could have predicted – could even have conceived – was the effect that their 'restoration' of the three 'lost' centuries would have on the calibration of the portals used by travellers from the distant future . . .

*

The Abbey of Saint Martial could never truly be said to sleep: there was always someone around, engaged in menial or other duties – toiling in the kitchens, taking out the cesspots, praying in the chapel for the salvation of his immortal soul. I nodded to a couple of monks I didn't know as I re-entered the building and made my way back to my lonely cell. No one commented on my flayed legs or the heavy, soaked hem of my cowl. They probably assumed I'd been out in the town ministering to someone in need . . . or perhaps whoring, as many of the monks occasionally did.

I sat on the hard bed, looking at my now-useless portal. At least its malfunction was terminal. I was stuck here in the eleventh, without hope of reprieve unless Benny sent someone after me – which if I were him I wouldn't do. His assumption would be that 1040 had proven to be as lethal to travellers as the preceding three centuries, that mine was just yet another mysterious disappearance. Of course, he might eventually learn better and send someone, but, however long he took, his emissary would surely have arrived almost immediately. No one's arrived so far and it's been over twenty years.

Ten of those years ago I wrote out this account and secreted it among the abbey's records – no one ever goes there except me. Every now and then, if I discover or remember something I want to add, I pull it out and read through it.

And always I think of Helen.

Where are you, my dear heart? *When* are you? You set off for the year 800 and found yourself in the year 500. You probably thought at first there had been a mistake in the setting of your portal, but then you wondered how it could possibly be that you'd landed in the right place, just the wrong time. The clock on your portal said the year was 800, but it was soon obvious to you that you'd arrived long before your intended destination – centuries, even. Clearly, you must have concluded, you'd been cursed with a defective portal. The one strict rule with a defective portal is that you don't use it – otherwise you're likely to find yourself floating in empty space.

Did you settle down and wait for rescue to come? Or did you attempt to reach the twenty-fifth? But how could you set your portal's destination when you didn't know where on the world's timeline you were? Did you decide to take the risk? If you did, it was surely a gamble you lost.

Each night I pray to the God in whom I don't believe that you didn't try to go home.

*

If the abbey's records survive the centuries there may come a day when someone else reads this account of mine. Of course, it won't make any difference to the future if they do. The future's already written: I've been there, I've seen it.

These days I wear my useless portal on a chain around my neck. When people peer at it I tell them it's a holy object of the kind that many people wear in my native Scotland, and so far I haven't met anyone who could put the lie to this. The gadget will be buried with me, I'm sure, as if it were a key to Heaven's gates.

As, in a way, it once was.

Ω

Part of the job of historians is to re-imagine the past, to paint a picture or a series of pictures from the barest sketches that are available. Sometimes, in doing so, they come up with what may seem improbable theories.

Kenneth's personal account of being trapped in the past because 300 years of history never occurred is (for most historians) a disturbing confirmation of just such a theory. The idea that the Holy Roman Emperor Otto III and Pope Sylvester II reconfigured the calendar is known as the Phantom Time Hypothesis, and was formulated by the German systems analyst and unorthodox historian Heribert Illig (b. 1947) in books like Das Erfundene Mittelalter: Die Grösste Zeitfälschung der Geschichte *(The Invented Middle Ages: The Greatest Time Falsification of History, 1996). Until now the vast majority of historians dismissed it as fantasy – but if we are to take Kenneth's story at face value, we must now be prepared to re-examine Illig's theory, and so potentially rewrite our understanding of medieval history.*

We should perhaps be grateful that Kenneth's interrupted travels in time did not grant credence to a far more complex idea, most clearly put forward by the Russian mathematician Anatoly Fomenko (b. 1945) and others in books such as History: Fiction or Science? *(seven volumes, 2003–7). Known as the New Chronology, this posits (among much else) that what are generally regarded as the historical events of Ancient Rome, Greece and Egypt actually happened in the Middle Ages, and that Jesus lived in the twelfth century* CE ...

c. 1150

The following letter appears to have been written to Heinrich, Archbishop of Mainz, around 1150, and forwarded by him to Pope Eugenius III. The name of the writer is not present; parts of the letter seem to have been eaten by mice.

The Latin of the original is competent but not distinguished, suggesting a man educated but not learned, perhaps a monk from a foundation a little distant from Rupertsberg, who knew of Hildegard von Bingen's reputation and something of her visions. The formality of his voice has been retained in this translation.

It is possible that the writer may have been one of the monks of St Disibod, who was at the convent to say Mass. Some of the brothers, when Hildegard left to found her own abbey, were angry at her leaving, and this might account for the resentment he evidently feels against her. His reference to the abbot adds some weight to this suggestion.

Encounter on the Rhine

Marion Pitman

On the Thursday after the second Sunday of Lent, I left the abbey at Mount St Rupert after Matins, and before the hour of Lauds, it being still dark, but wishing to continue my journey. It was a clear night with some moonlight, and I had no difficulty seeing my way. I had not gone far from the convent when a shaft of light struck the ground before me, which was not the dawn, but more like a bolt of lightning, which nevertheless remained steady: not like sunlight, but a strong, white light, in a steady beam. It was broad, about twenty or thirty cubits, and came with a warmth, like the warmth of a lamp. I stopped, and looked up, as I think any man must have done, to see where the light came from.

I could not see the origin of the light, for it seemed to come straight from the height of Heaven, as if it had been the sun at noon, yet it was still two hours before dawn. But there was something more wonderful yet than this, for descending along this shaft of light I saw a great silver vessel, of the shape of an egg, almost the width of the beam of light, which dropped down marvellously slowly, until it lay on the ground before me. I was struck with fear such that I could not move or speak, and trembled in all my limbs. After some minutes, an opening appeared in the egg, about five cubits high, and a number of beings, of the shape of men or women, but exceedingly tall, descended from the egg, and stood on the ground beside me.

They seemed to address me, their voices being very high and clear, like the voices of women, and their speech a kind of singing, soaring up and down like a piece of music, and not as human speech. The language was neither Latin nor German, and I did not understand their speech. However, after some few minutes, when they perceived that I did not understand them, I heard another voice, which seemed to come from the air, rather than from the mouth of a particular being, which spoke in Latin, and it said, 'Do not be afraid. We are visitors from another world, and we wish to speak to you.' Upon hearing this I was struck with great terror, and fell down on the ground, and my eyes were darkened. The beings continued to speak in their high, silvery voices, and then I felt them lift me, and they carried me into the vessel. There they laid me on a couch, and strapped me down, so that I thought, These are devils, and have brought me to a place of torment, and I cried out upon God to rescue me, and to save me from these devils. But they did not torment me, only left me for a time on the couch, and when some time had passed I was able to open my eyes, and I looked around me.

I was in a large room, almost as big as the nave of a church, but the structure of it I cannot describe, for the angles of the walls were not what I have ever seen nor what I could imagine, and I cannot say how they fitted together. Neither my eyes nor my mind were able to comprehend them. But everywhere were bright lights, sparkling like jewels or stars of many colours, and the walls shone white as silver, or as ivory, and in that it was most beautiful, surpassing all but the greatest cathedral.

Then there was a great movement and shaking, as of a ship when it casts off from land and sets out upon the sea, and it seemed that the vessel was moving, though whether across the land or through the air I could not tell. But as I had seen it descend through the air, I thought it might well be that it was now ascending in a like manner. Then for a while I was subject to strange sensations, of dizziness, and of great weight pressing me down on to the couch, and was not able to take note of anything that happened; but when I came to myself again, I found that I was no longer tied or fastened to the couch, but could move freely and sit up; so when they saw that I was sitting up, one of the tall demons came to me, and spoke in that strange high, soaring voice, and then when I did not answer, I heard the other voice, from the air, or inside my head, which said, 'Do not be afraid, but tell us who you are, and what is your place upon the Earth?'

Then I found my voice had returned and the power of speech, and I told the being that I was a monk in holy orders, and dedicated to the service of God, and I would not answer questions of devils. Then they did not ask any more at that time.

They brought to me vessels of silver, and others that were clear like crystal or glass, with meat and bread and wine, but I thought that to eat and drink in Hell, or in that other place that we hear of where dwell those who are neither men nor angels, might condemn my soul to remain there for ever, so I would not eat nor drink.

Then they left me for a time, and I prayed earnestly again for the Holy Spirit to deliver me from this place, wheresoever it might be. Then I looked up, and it seemed that one side of the vessel was all one great window, filled with crystal or clear glass; and beyond it I saw things I cannot name, but they were like flaming stars in great showers, and again great wheels turning slowly, and burning. And I wondered again what place I might be in, and whether the vessel wherein I travelled had passed beyond the sphere of the moon, and we were now in the immutable heavens; but it seemed against reason that these devils, which they must surely be, could pass into the heavens. Then I thought and asked myself if they might be holy angels, but surely angels would fly with their own wings, and not require a vessel such as this. And besides which, if they were angels, they would have spoken to me in Latin, or even in German, and not in the strange tongue which I did not understand, for surely in the Holy Scriptures, when angels speak to men they do so to be understood.

Then I reasoned that the stars and burning fire which I saw outside the vessel, as it seemed, were a glamour and an illusion with which the devils were seeking to deceive me, so that I should believe we were in the heavens. The fiery wheel then drew nearer, and it seemed we should be engulfed thereby, and I thought perhaps it was indeed the mouth of Hell, and I prayed the more fervently in my terror, that God might save me from this doom. There was a great noise of roaring, and many voices speaking in that strange language, and the vessel was violently shaken; and then all was still, and the roaring ceased and the voices were quiet; and the great window turned black, as if a shutter had closed across it.

After a little time, one of the beings came to me again; and although it was greater by a cubit than the height of a man, yet it seemed to me that it was a woman, from its voice, and its face, which was very beautiful, and also from the hair, that shone like silver or gold, and hung down its back, very long and unbound. She again offered me food and drink, and again I refused. The voice in my head then asked, would I write down answers to the questions they wished to ask; and the being held out to me a book, with blank pages of something like parchment but more coarse, and what I took to be a pen, though it seemed to be made of some metal. It seemed to me then that I might answer them, if the questions were not such as to imperil my soul, and I asked, if I wrote down what they wanted to know, would they let me go, and return me to the place I came from; they said they would return me to Earth when they had accomplished their purpose.

Knowing, then, that I was either in the heavens or in Hell, and that only by their goodwill might I return home, I determined to answer their questions, so that I might by some means return to the brothers and to the life of worship and service to which I am devoted. I found that the pen wrote well without ink, having, it seemed, ink or a kindred substance in and of itself, and the flow did not cease all the while I wrote according to their demand.

So the voice put questions to me, and I began to write the answers, and as I did so the being beside me wrote also, upon a tablet that was not of wax but a glazed surface; and as she wrote there appeared not the letters of Latin writing, but other symbols of some strange tongue which I did not know, but took to be that singing language with which the beings spoke with their mouths; for they did not speak Latin with their mouths, but only that voice in the air or inside my head spoke to me in Latin. And I saw that there were symbols like these also written upon the walls of the vessel, and upon the tables and chests with which it was furnished.

The questions that the voice asked me were many, concerning the lives of men, and the properties of beasts and flowers and stones, and the oceans, and all the nature of things beneath the moon, so much that I could not answer them all, and I wondered at their asking, for whether they were angels or devils it seemed to me that they would have no need to know these things, supposing that they did not know them. And they did not ask me anything concerning God or the spiritual life, which confirmed my belief that they were devils, for else why would this not concern them, and in questioning a man of God this should surely have been their concern. But they did ask me of my life in the monastery, and what was the purpose of living the devout life, and in what manner we conducted our day; and so I was able to speak of the Rule of our Order, and the holy Saint Benedict, and also of the Holy Spirit, and all the ways to seek salvation of the soul, for I thought, if these be not devils, but some other creatures which have not heard the Holy Scriptures, then it is my duty to preach the Gospel to them as well as I may. And all these things I wrote, and the being wrote all the time also on her tablet, looking back and forth at me as she did so.

I cannot tell how long this continued; it felt like many hours, but since there was no natural light in the vessel, nor any candles – for the walls seemed to shine with light of themselves – it was not in my power to judge the passing of time. At last the voice finished its questions, and said that it was now time for them to leave, and they would return me to the Earth. I scarcely dared to hope that they would do this, for if they were devils, why would they give me up when they had me in their power? But I hoped that my earnest entreaties to God had elicited His divine mercy, and I might yet be delivered from the Evil One. For although Satan's power is great in this world, still he is under the foot of the Most High, and must yield the soul even of a sinner if he be truly penitent.

Then once more they offered me drink, and I was tempted, for by now I felt great thirst and hunger, but again I refused, for the pious man will not shrink from bodily discomfort, but rather embrace it as a purging of the soul, and especially in the season of Lent is fasting and abstinence to be observed, more even than at other times.

Then once again came the great roaring sound, and I was more afraid, and trembled; and the being that had been with me while I was writing left me, and she and her companions were busy about the tables that stood at one side of the room; and the shutter was withdrawn from the window, and once more I saw the great burning fiery wheel, and beyond it the flaming stars. And then I covered my eyes, for the light was dazzling, and also I was afraid to see Hell and Satan before my eyes, for a sinful man may not bear that sight.

But the mercy of God was great, for I survived, though my soul was in great turmoil, for I thought, what shall become of me now? And where next shall I be taken? But after some time all was quiet again, and the tall women (or whatever manner of being they were) went about the room talking in soft voices, so that it seemed most peaceful, and almost blessed, and I was tempted to believe that they were not devils, but beings of some other kind, created like men, but not like any I had seen or read of; but I am not a scholar, and there may be things in creation that I know nothing of.

This was another snare, I soon saw, for I fell to thinking about the things I had seen and heard, and I recalled the things I had heard about the visions which are claimed by Hildegard, mistress of the sisters at Mount St Rupert, and it seemed to me that there is a great likeness between the things that I saw and the subjects of her visions, the great light and the warmth, and the burning stars, and many other things; also the women with flowing hair, and the strangely angled buildings, all resembled the visions of Hildegard (who is called Abbess, though in truth she is not, but subject to the abbot). And I remembered the singing of the sisters, which is not like any chant I have heard in any other church, and it is very like the strange speech of the tall women. And so it seemed to me that the Spirit was leading me into truth, and showing me that the visions of Hildegard were nothing but accounts of a meeting with these devils, or whatever kind of beings they are, and not from God at all, as I had always suspected.

I beseech you, my lord, to consider what I write, for in truth these are female evil spirits, and since it is an abomination for a woman to preach or to teach, or to set herself up in authority over a man, it is shown how these demons have corrupted the so-called abbess to flout the laws of God and the Rule of St Benedict, using these supposed visions to delude her nuns and even the abbot. For it is well known and attested in scripture that ever since God made Eve, and she caused the downfall of Adam and of all mankind, from the light and peace and blessing of paradise into filth and darkness, women have been the especial tools of Satan in his plots and snares to capture the souls of men, their minds being weak and unable to withstand temptation as well as the mind of a man, and therefore being easily used for temptation and deceit.

But after I had pondered these things, I found that much time had passed, and I felt again the dizziness and the sense of great force pressing me down; and then the vessel was shaken and rocked like a boat coming to its mooring, and I saw that the side of the room, or of the vessel, was opened, and before me were the rocks and grass about the road where I had walked from the convent, and it seemed to me that no time had passed since I had come here, for it was still not yet dawn. Which is yet another proof that these were not natural beings, since they were not subject to the usual passing of time. Then, having one more time offered me meat and drink, which I again refused, they led me forth out of the vessel, and set my feet once more on the path of my journey, and away from the convent that by now I regarded as accursed.

I have set out these things, my Lord Bishop, so that you may know what deception is practised upon the godly, and may uphold all truth against the falsehoods of Satan and his angels.

Ω

Attached to this account is a note from the papal office to the effect that the Abbess Hildegard has the papal approval and blessing, and that it is therefore not appropriate to cast doubts on the holy origin of her visions, and indeed to do so is to flirt with heresy.

The suggestion is made that the brother has been reading or hearing much of Hildegard's visions, and has subsequently either over-indulged in wine to fortify him for his journey, or fallen asleep during the divine office, and has dreamed or imagined the entirety of the experience recounted in the letter. Furthermore, it is suggested that if the brother wishes to discredit Hildegard, he would do better to come up with a more plausible story.

It ends: 'Deal with this matter as you see fit; but I know that you too honour this saintly lady, who is indeed favoured by God, and I am certain you will explain well to this brother the error into which he has fallen. For it is well if the malice of men is not permitted to cloud the clear light of divine truth.'

Whether this note was dictated by the Pope himself or written by another on his behalf is not known, but its dismissive tone and the relegation of this account to the Vaults are a clear indication of the Church's stance at the time. How we today might interpret this report is another matter. It is as clear a description of a close encounter of the fourth kind as one might wish for, from a time when such reports could not be inspired by (and in evidential terms, contaminated by) popular depictions in the media.

And so we must add to the existing explanations of the visions of Hildegard von Bingen – that they were from God, or from migraine auras or temporal lobe epilepsy – the possibility that she was interpreting in her own spiritual way her meeting with 'visitors from another world'.

c. **1189**

This account was found among the private papers of Eleanor, former Queen of England and before that Queen of France, on her death. The abbess at Fontevrault, where Eleanor had retired from the world four years earlier, aged nearly 80, read it and had it sent, sealed, straight to Rome.

It was written by a maid called Alis who was clearly close to Eleanor. In our translation from the Languedoc language we have retained the writer's idiosyncrasy of writing of herself sometimes in the third person and sometimes in the first person.

In the main we have followed her spelling of names and place-names, largely in the Languedoc (or as she would say, lenga d'oc) style, though for clarity we have substituted Poitiers for her home city of Peitieus and have added accents where they might aid the modern reader. Some pronunciations will be unfamiliar. Giraut, for example, has a hard G, and the final consonant is sounded.

From internal evidence this account was written some time after 1189, when Eleanor was released from captivity on the death of her second husband, the Plantagenet King Henry II; its content wanders backwards and forwards over the years of both of her marriages.

Much of it follows the accepted version of history, though the constant criticism of well-respected clergy would not endear it to the Church. But the revelation that caused the abbess at Fontevrault to send this straight to Pope Innocent III, rather than via either her bishop or the superior of her Order, paints the troubadours and trobairitz of Queen Eleanor's homeland in a new light, and claims a startling new reason why her second husband – as pious as her first in some ways, but as Alis writes, 'a man of rages' – locked her up for so many years.

Songs of Love

J.-M. Brugée

Always, in her memory, the walls of tufa reflected the sun; the château on the hilltop could dazzle the eye. Alis leaned on her stick, looked up at the château and felt more at home than anywhere else she had lived in her long life: Poitiers, Paris, London and so many other places.

England was grey, cold, even in summer. But if the sun was in the sky, Chinon was bright from its white walls, light, clean.

Alis had prepared the house for tonight's visitor. She would not be going to hear him sing in the château – the long climb up the steep steps was getting to be too much for her – but she would make him welcome tonight.

She sat on a bench behind her house, poured herself a glass of chilled Chinon rouge and gazed across the Vienne to the town, letting her thoughts wander back through the long years to when another troubadour had stayed here. It must be nearly twenty years ago, when Aliénor held her Courts of Love in Poitiers. This was halfway through her marriage to Henri, when things might have been difficult between them, as they often were, but before they became impossible.

*

Alis had been glad to have come to Chinon, and she knew Aliénor was pleased to be here. Chinon was Henri's Angevin capital, but Poitiers was near, only a good day's ride; though she was Queen of England, in her heart Aliénor was always Countess of Poitiers and Duchess of Aquitània.

But wherever she was she brought music with her, or called it to her. Tonight, here in Chinon, one of her favourites would be singing at the meal at the château: Giraut de Besièrs, a favourite of Alis as well. Far from his home near Carcassona he sang in the *lenga d'oc*, the language of the south, in a dialect close enough to Aliénor's own Poitevin for her to understand it easily, and be warmed by it.

He was a favourite of the queen in part because he was so very good at his art and in part because as a boy he had been taught by Aliénor's own grandfather, Duc Guilhèm IX, whom many called *lo paire des trobadors*.

He was a favourite of Alis because later tonight she would slip out of the château and slip into his bed in the little house on the Île du Bois in the middle of the Vienne, below the town and just beyond its walls. Many troubadours were well versed in the Art of Love, and Alis knew many of them, but Giraut was one of the best – lover as well as troubadour. She had known him for years, since they first met in Paris when she was not yet twenty years old.

Alis realised she had been gazing through the window, down over the town to the river, where the house where Giraut would be staying was hidden among trees just visible above the defensive walls lining this bank of the Vienne. She shook herself and returned to laying out her lady's clothes for the evening. The blue dress, Aliénor had said. It showed her lovely figure, her full breasts, to perfection. And to set off the curves, Alis thought, the silver chain carrying the cartouche of lapis lazuli. And when she dressed her lady's hair, she would suggest the simple circlet with the sapphire at its centre.

Tonight, she was sure, Queen Aliénor would be using her power, working her magic.

*

The food, as always where Aliénor went, was excellent. She would stand for nothing less, and Alis blessed the day she had entered her lady's service for this along with so much else. Aliénor had been just fifteen, suddenly inheriting the duchy of Aquitània, and about to marry Louis, heir to the throne of France. She had chosen those who would be closest to her with care; she knew she would need people she could trust in her own chamber, when she moved from Poitiers to Paris.

Alis was the second daughter of a minor count who had fought beside Aliénor's father in Normandy. When she reached the age of twelve her father had asked which she would prefer: a neighbouring count had just lost his second wife in childbirth and was looking for a third; and the new duchess was looking for a maid. Alis knew the count; he was old, over forty, and fat, and farted a lot. She also knew the duchess: tall, slender, graceful, educated, cultured – and lively.

At twelve, Alis went to work for Aliénor – and within weeks was riding north to Paris. And then there were the fifteen long years of her lady's unhappiness. Somehow she had managed to get King Louis into her bed enough to have two daughters by him – no one would dare to say they were not – but more than once, more than many times, Alis heard her lady complain that she had married a monk, not a king.

Indeed, Louis was never meant to be king, but was being groomed for high office in the Church – no doubt a cardinal prince, with power and lands and wealth sufficient for any man, or perhaps even higher – when his elder brother Philip was thrown from his stallion as it shied away from a sow grubbing for food in the squalor of the unpaved, unswept streets of Paris. Paralysed from a broken neck, he died and passed the future throne to his monkish brother.

Alis wondered sometimes about God's warped humour, for such a series of unlikely events and early deaths to propel her mistress to the throne could surely not be the work of mere happenstance. Aliénor's father, Duc Guilhèm X d'Aquitània, had been on pilgrimage to Santiago de Compostela to atone for the many lives he had taken on campaign in Normandy the year before. A strong and healthy warrior not yet forty, on Good Friday, the most holy and solemn day of the year, he had died from eating tainted meat or drinking bad water.

Aliénor was now ruler of far more lands than the king. Rather than risk her abduction and forced marriage by any lord ambitious to expand his lands, it made good sense to marry her quickly to the king's son and heir and so eventually unite Poitou and Aquitània with the Île de France.

Just a week after their marriage her husband's father, Louis the Fat, died of dysentery – and at fifteen Aliénor was Queen of the Franks.

And I was by her side to dress her, and to be as close a friend as our relative positions allowed. (But in truth it was she who comforted me over the years, taking my head and murmuring, 'My Alis, be brave. I could not manage without you.')

*

For all those years Queen Aliénor tried to bring the culture of the south to what she and her ladies thought of as the barbarous north. Even the entertainers there were less than entertaining; while the troubadours and *trobairitz* Aliénor brought from the land of her birth and further south, right down to the coasts of Catalonha and Tolosa, sang of love and longing and lust in her own *lenga d'oc*, the *trouvères* of the north intoned *chansons de geste*, interminable narrative poems of heroic deeds in the northern tongue – until Aliénor taught them better. And so, while Louis was on his knees in church or monastery, Aliénor filled his draughty palace with musicians and poets and singers and dancers from wherever she could draw them.

Their unhappy marriage was so widely known that when they returned from that dreadful crusade to Outremer some twelve years after their wedding, Pope Eugene III literally forced them to share a bed.

Perhaps this, in part, was why Aliénor loved so much the songs of love. Whether her grandfather Guilhèm IX was the first troubadour, Alis doubted, though he was certainly the first who was high-born: it was said of him that he was 'one of the most courtly men in the world and liberal in his womanising'. He said he would build a nunnery of beautiful whores, and ended up founding a double monastery at Fontevraud under the rule of an abbess; his long-suffering wife Philippa, who had persuaded him to found it, left him to end her days there rather than share her home with his mistress. But for his mistress Dangerosa he built a tower, La Maubergeonne, in his château at Poitiers – then married her daughter Aenor to his son Guilhèm, so his mistress was Aliénor's grandmother. His songs vied with those of common *jongleurs* in celebrating the joys of the flesh. He sang about the difficulty of keeping a wife and a mistress being like keeping two fine horses that cannot be stabled together *'for they cannot stand each other'*. He sang of a knight pretending to be dumb so that two noble ladies would sleep with him thinking he wouldn't tell. He sang of his own prowess: *'If she has me for one night, she'll want me the next.'*

He was a rogue, but a charming one. Though Aliénor did not recall him – he had died when she was very young – she had inherited his undisguised delight in the physicality of love (and Alis had benefited from this in more ways than she would ever openly admit, even – or especially – to her confessor). This made her joyless marriage, her lack of marital union with King Louis, all the more disappointing, frustrating, and worse.

But Aliénor had learned to channel her love of love in other directions, and not just other lovers than her loveless husband. (Alis was one of the very few who knew the truth of the rumours.)

She had taken her grandfather's love of love, and lust, and song (and also, Alis knew, of the God or gods who had given us these desires and joys) and had woven them all together in a union as subtle as a silken scarf so light you barely knew you wore it, yet so close it warmed you in the coldest winds.

And so, throughout the land the Romans once called Gaul, from the red-roofed towns of the far south through the lands of Aquitània where Aliénor came from, and the Loire, and even as far north as the king's own small lands, the Île de France, trouba-dours, *trouvères* and *trobairitz* sang their songs, encouraged by Queen Aliénor, and much to the disapproval of her monkish husband King Louis VII.

A far greater threat was that tedious Cistercian abbot, Bernard de Clairvaux. He wore hair shirts. He slept, as abbot, in a plain, tiny cell below the abbey staircase. And he loathed, detested and reviled women. He would not allow the monks in his abbey to meet their sisters, aunts or even their grandmothers lest it be the cause of temptation. He had no need to meet a woman as power-ful as Aliénor to regard her as the work of the Devil. He had no time for such temporal pleasures as the songs of troubadours, even if some of their songs be of God and Mary.

If he only knew what else Aliénor's most favoured troubadours sang of, and why, and what they did, he would doubtless have had them burned for the sake of their immortal souls – if he did not die of a righteous fit first: man was 'begotten in filth, gestated in darkness and born in pain', he said.

*

This night in Chinon the jongleurs had finished their simple songs and tunes, their juggling and tumbling between the tables offering amusement during the meal. Now three musicians played soft and gentle lays while those around the tables cleaned their palates with the soft *chèvre*, so fresh, Alis told her neighbour at table, that it had still been bleating that morning.

And with the *chèvre* came fresh jugs of wine. Alis hated the northern habit of serving red wine almost warm; here, at Aliénor's table, Chinon rouge was served chilled from the cellars, allowing its full flavour to bless the nose and tongue.

The musicians had done their job well; the laughing and joking had been replaced by a mellow quietness into which stepped – and Alis gasped, as always, at his beauty – Giraut de Besièrs.

He bowed to his queen, made a final adjustment to one string of his oud, and turned his tuning (as she knew he would) into the introductory notes of his first song.

> *At the beginning of Spring*
> *Starting with renewed joy*
> *And worrying jealous husbands*
> *The Queen would like to show*
> *That she is full of love*
> *Eya!*

*

Aliénor learned of the Art years before from visitors to the palace on the Île de la Cité in Paris – not to Louis's court, but to her own. Scholars, poets, musicians, who would bring her food for her mind, for her heart and for her spirit. The first hint she heard was from a conversation one evening with the Cathar troubadour Giraut de Besièrs, and a mystical Jew he knew from nearby Narbona, who had studied the Kabbalah just across the border in the city of Girona in Catalonha. There was a mystical Moor as well, from Córdoba in Andalusia, and two Moorish girls who had danced for Aliénor earlier in the evening. With the music and the wine and the conversation the evening had grown late. Louis was away; though he would not have been present anyway for such frivolous entertainment, his disapproval would have filled the palace. But Louis was away, so Aliénor listened, and questioned, and listened, and learned.

And so did I beside her.

There would be many more such evenings.

*

In the years to come Alis slept many times with Giraut for friendship, for joy, for learning to raise the power of the will; but the night in Chinon, in the little house on the Île du Bois after he had sung at the château, was the one she kept in her heart. That was when Giraut had renewed in her the tenderness of love-making.

> *Ah, if that knight I could caress*
> *All night long, naked in my arms*
> *He'd be caught by the charm*
> *Of cushioning his head on my breast*

*

Those fifteen years married to Louis VII were often a trial for Aliénor and for her ladies, chief of whom was her lovely and much-loved sister Petronilla. We were used to a way of living which was unknown to the king and his court. The battles Aliénor had to fight . . . If she had not been so determined (Louis would say stubborn) we would have been eating our meals, even at the king's table, off tranches of bread; in the whole of the Île de France they had not heard of plates. Nor, to our shock, had it struck the young king (even at his wedding to my lady I heard the people of Aquitània call him Louis *lo Colhon*, for he appeared as stupid as a testicle) to put glass in the windows of his château; in winter it was either draughty and freezing cold or stuffy and dark, dimly lit by sputtering oil lamps and candles, with shutters or sacking over the windows. Again, a battle, and again Aliénor won.

Even the idea of a hearth with a chimney to take the smoke from a fire out of a room, rather than through a hole in the roof, was only just working its way that far north during the time we were there. For Aliénor, for all of us who had left the civilised world of Aquitània behind, it was as if we had gone back centuries in time in moving to Paris. But for Louis and his men it was normal.

But Paris had one great diversion from which Louis lo Colhon could not keep Aliénor, or any of her ladies she wished to take with her, and that was the teachers on *la rîve gauche*, what was later to be called l'Université, for everything of worth was taught there.

And so we attended lectures of the trivium and the quadrivium, and debates which sometimes lasted all day. We got to know many of the students studying there; a year or so after we arrived in the city I had eyes for a tall young lad called Thomas Becket from England, who would later cause my lady's second husband such grief, but he was a serious boy (though his Latin was no better than mine), and never seemed to notice me, or indeed any other woman. No matter; there were others who did, and my lady was happy to allow our dalliances; here, perhaps, is where it all began, the sacred touching of mind and spirit and body and the mingling of *caritas* and *amor*, of *agape* and *eros*, of liking and loving and lust, which was to become Aliénor's song.

And little wonder, for the best of all the teachers on *la rîve gauche* was the Breton Pierre Abélard who had lost his balls for his love of Héloyse d'Argenteuil, and who would dispute any belief, however deep-seated, just for the love of the argument. I treasure the day I heard him prove beyond all disputing, though only as a joke, that the great Saint Denis, Bishop of Paris, for whom l'Abbé Suger had the glorious abbey church built just north of Paris, was actually another Denis altogether; the monks did not see the humour, to the extent of forcing Abélard out.

For his love of disputation Abélard was tricked by the mendacious Bernard de Clairvaux who, having slandered him as a heretic, then challenged him to a debate in the cathedral at Sens in front of hundreds of students – and my queen and her ladies – who became increasingly enraged as it became clear that Bernard had determined the outcome with the bishops sitting in judgement the night before, and used his supposed opening of what was no debate simply to condemn poor Pierre with his own words, precept after precept after precept taken out of all context from his arguments, and giving him no opportunity to respond. And so Pierre Abélard, a brilliant and loving and godly man, was declared excommunicate by the Church.

Such is the way of the Church when met with one of the finest minds in the world. Pierre, broken in spirit by the same Church that had broken his manhood, died mere months later.

It was just one more reason for Aliénor – for all of us – to loathe that so-called man of God, who was later to preach the ill-fated crusade which my lady went on with her monkish husband, and which finally destroyed their marriage; they travelled back to France in separate ships.

*

Bernard de Clairvaux might fulminate against jewels and make-up – 'the beauty put on in the morning and taken off at night' – and yes, I helped Aliénor don this and remove it each day; but her beauty was in her own features, her deep auburn hair, her striking green eyes, her flawless skin, her lovely smile, her warmth and humour, her sharp intelligence, her often biting wit.

She was the best of teachers, and I a most willing pupil. She taught me how to draw power from my own pleasure – and how to prolong the pleasure of a man for longer than he would ever imagine, until the moment when the two joined together become one in their release, not just of pleasure but of the height of a crescendo of power – the power of love not curbed, not controlled, but directed by the will.

> *If I hold her tight*
> *She'll quicken my heart*
> *And my flesh will grow anew . . .*

*

Once we had learned the Art of Love, we learned to refine it as a skill, a craft. First we used it in small ways, then we learned how to build a work together. Eventually Aliénor was able to direct us to use the Art to build up power, to gain her annulment from Louis. It involved several of us over some months: the two of us together, me with three troubadours and a count at different times, Aliénor with her uncle Raymond of Poitiers, Prince of Antioch, when they were on crusade, and with Geoffrey of Anjou after their return – Geoffrey, who was married to the Empress Matilda, rebel queen of England, who had the name Plantagenêt because he wore a sprig of yellow broom, and who was the father of her next husband.

The joke of Louis and Aliénor's annulment on the grounds of consanguinity was that just eight weeks later my lady married Henri of Anjou, who was even more closely related to her. In fact a possible marriage between Henri and Aliénor's first daughter by Louis, Marie, had been declared unacceptable by too close ancestry; but now, through the Art, Aliénor married Henri herself. Then two years later Henri succeeded his mother Matilda's rival Stephen of Blois as king of England, and my lady became a queen again.

And oh, what a tumultuous time those two had. Both of them lusty and full of life, but Henri, hot-headed and a decade younger than Aliénor, was no match for her intelligence and her strong will. Five sons and three daughters they had, and thoroughly enjoyed the making of them. They were better matched by far than Aliénor had ever been with her first husband. But Henri was proud, and stubborn, and had explosive rages. Two such strong people could not stay in harmony for long.

*

Our old opponent Bernard de Clairvaux would have been appalled, had he still lived. On the south side of the bridge in London were all the entertainments not deemed fit for the great city; Southwark was one long street of inns and ale-houses. In the shadow of the Priory of St Mary Overie prostitutes plied their trade, alone or in brothels, under licence from the Bishop of Winchester, whose palace was here. And who should have drawn up the legislation for this than the Archdeacon, soon to be Archbishop, of Canterbury, one Thomas Becket, who had shown no interest in me or any woman when a youth of twenty in Paris.

My queen told me of her sadness that these women, the Winchester Geese, from whom the bishop profited, were not allowed Christian burial in consecrated ground when they, almost inevitably, died young. Such was the hypocrisy of the Church.

*

Some *lauzenguers* hinted that Aliénor was in some way responsible for the death of Henri's mistress, Rosamund Clifford. There is no truth in this; my queen knew her husband's appetites better than any, and never objected to his having mistresses – he was a king, after all. But Henri openly flaunted Rosamund, and that I found offensive. I claim credit for the line later used by Gerald of Wales, that she was not *rosa mundi* but *rosa immundi*, not rose of the world but rose of unchastity. The line stuck, and Rosamund took herself off to a nunnery, dying shortly afterwards.

In any case, while Henri was enjoying his fair Rosamund, Aliénor moved back to her beloved Poitiers where she hosted her Courts of Love, formal debates in poetry between two troubadours, or between a troubadour and his lady, on the many variations of love – concealed, expressed, withheld, given, forbidden, taken, shared.

> *Patience, husband – don't be annoyed*
> *Tomorrow you'll have me, but my lovers tonight*
> *Don't say a word!*
> *Patience, husband – don't be annoyed*
> *The night's short, soon you'll have me*
> *Once my lovers have taken their pleasure.*

These duelling debates were what most of the lords and ladies saw, and many of the troubadours too. They were the open show, and Andreas Capellanus later wrote of them in *De Amore*, his treatise on love. Most of it was make-believe; it was a necessary smokescreen.

If the Church had known, Alis thought, Aliénor would have been excommunicated at best, and probably far worse. For in her fifteen years as the Queen of the Franks, married to the monkish Louis, then more than twice as long married to Henri before she became Queen Regent to her favourite but most pious son Richard, Aliénor paid only diplomatic lip-service to the Church and its Christ, as she did with every other political power. Bernard de Clairvaux must have guessed this, but he died just a year after she married Henri, removing her biggest threat from the Church.

She went to Mass and said her prayers, as did everyone, but in her heart Aliénor followed her grandfather's southern attitude of *convivença* in every way: not just conviviality in the love of music and dance, but the free-flowing converse between those of different beliefs, people living, working, talking and loving together wherever they were from, however they worshipped their gods. That was how she had learned of the Art.

Aliénor was Countess of Poitiers and Duchess of Aquitània, but she was also Queen of England. In the early years of their marriage she had run that country while Henri was on campaign, and even at this time, when they were more estranged, there were times when she needed to be ruling and judging and administering on behalf of her husband at the heart of the Angevin world, here at Chinon. And after days of what could be such tiresome tasks, she took pleasure in the company of troubadours, and I with her.

Some loved with us; some joined their will with us for one purpose or another; many just wrote and sang and played their songs, and their gift of pleasure was not any the less. Bernat de Ventadorn, Bertran de Born, Peire Vidal, Raimbaut de Vaqueyras and more, and the best of the *trobairitz* also: Maria de Ventadorn, Azalais de Porcairages, Countess Beatritz de Dia, so many others. Some sang of God; some of springtime; some of the twisted tongues of *lauzenguers*; some of battle; some of courtliness; and some of the joys of love.

> *Her lovely young body does not deceive*
> *The more beautiful she becomes*
> *As you take away her clothes*
> *The more eager you become*
> *Her breast turns night to day*
> *While to see lower still*
> *Would lighten the heart of any man.*

Chinon: the Plantagenêt treasury and the château which Henri
largely built and where he was to die cursing his sons, his body
stripped of its clothes and jewels by his servants before being
taken to l'abbaye de Fontevraud a short ride away.

But fifteen years before that, after their sons' rebellion against
him, he had imprisoned his queen here in the château, in the cold,
unwelcoming Tour du Moulin, before taking her back to England
in captivity. Ah, those were dark years for my lady, before Henri
died of his piles and Richard became king.

*

Henri's oldest surviving son Henri had been crowned as the
Young King alongside his father, but it was an empty title. As the
young Henri and his brothers grew into manhood, they wanted
more than their father would give them: land and its revenue, and
the power that comes from both. And Aliénor saw a way of curb-
ing her husband by strengthening her sons; she drew power
through the Art to support the young king and his brothers
against their father. If only it could have succeeded, but too many
others were involved, with their own agendas. If young Henri had
defeated his father and won his domains, he would have lost half
of them to grasping nobles in both France and England in
payment for their support.

It was a rebellion doomed to failure, and my lady's greatest
error. The young Henri was only eighteen, and he was the oldest
and most experienced of the three brothers, while their father was
a skilled strategist and a hardened campaigner. Aliénor's youngest
son John, just a lad of seven or eight, rode with his father. Henri's
favourite, he was the cause of the whole revolt, when his father
gave him three castles which belonged by right to the young
Henri. Richard and Geoffrey sided with their elder brother, and
Aliénor allowed her love for her older sons, especially Richard, to
overcome for once her common sense, and supported them
against her husband not just politically but with powers none of
the rebels knew anything of.

But Henri had spies everywhere. His fury at his wife's betrayal
turned to horror at the blasphemy when, as pious as Louis though
by no means as monkish, he discovered the source of her power.

He could have thrown her to the Church, but accusations of heresy are double-edged, and the risks to himself and his heritage would have been too great. Instead he had her arrested and imprisoned here at Chinon, then taken back to England. She would spend the next fifteen years confined at places of his choosing, away from any exercise of power, political or magical.

Sometimes Alis had been able to spend time with her lady – when she was confined elsewhere than the harsh old castle at Sarum, and when she was let out from time to time when Henri needed her by his side – but increasingly she acted as her hidden envoy, teaching the Art to troubadours and *trobairitz* in Anjou and Aquitània.

At least Aquitània went to Richard, her favourite; he was its duc for ten years before succeeding his father to the English throne.

*

And now Aliénor is free again, freed even before Richard sent the order, and Queen Regent of England while her warrior son is off on crusade. Her fifteen years of imprisonment have not weakened her will. And I too am free (though our bond was never servitude), as Aliénor, knowing my dislike of England, has bestowed on me a manor near Chinon to sustain me in my remaining years. But she also gifted me this little house on the Île du Bois, that I know so well, for me to stay when I am in the town.

From the town I still cross half over the strong stone bridge that Henri built, as I have done for years, and down the steps to the île, and along the path through the trees, and here, in the house built of white tufa, my own tiny château, I recall the grand Courts of Love in Poitiers; and I recall too those nights of love here, with Giraut who first taught us so long ago, with those troubadours to whom Aliénor taught the secrets, with *trobairitz*, and sometimes with Aliénor herself. She is now near seventy, and I not far behind, but the life-force we have been granted through our practice of love has sustained us well, and will, I believe, for some years to come.

I use a cane to walk, but we are no dried-up sticks of old women. Giraut de Besièrs is long gone, but the troubadour singing at the château this evening will by tradition stay here on the île, in this small white house. And tonight and in the weeks to come I shall teach him what I learned with my lady Aliénor of the Art of Love; and together through our will we shall raise the power. I have written down my scattered thoughts for his benefit, for he is young and may need to know that today follows from our yesterdays, from our failures as well as our successes. Reading it through, jumbled as it is, I think I may make a fair copy to give to my queen as a reminder of my love for her through all the times we spent together. There was much unhappiness, but there was also so much joy.

Aliénor taught me what she learned for herself, a truth that others have lived before us, including poor Pierre Abélard. Do what you will, that shall be all of the law; for love is the law, love and will working together. It is in the Bible, in the letter of Paul to the Romans: 'Love fulfils the law.' It is in the teachings of one of the Church Fathers, Augustine: 'Love, and what you will, do.' And it is the heart of our song. The power of love, and of love-making, is the strongest power of all.

Ω

The château and town of Chinon fell to the French just a year after Queen Eleanor's death in 1204, her last son John Lackland (Sans Terre) proving incapable of holding on to much of his parents' land. There is no record of Alis, or whether she still lived there.

Troubadours continued singing of divine and carnal love for another century; another Giraut, Giraut Riquier (1230–92) was perhaps the last of them.

The Vatican librarians cross-referenced this document to the original texts held in the Vaults of two Renaissance books. In Hypnerotomachia Poliphili: The Strife of Love in a Dream, *published in Venice in 1499, Poliphilo follows Thelemia, representing will or desire, in the pursuit of erotic fulfilment.*

Perhaps Alis left a seed of Eleanor's antinomial teaching to grow in Chinon; François Rabelais, born there at the end of the fifteenth century, wrote in his satire on religion Gargantua and Pantagruel *that the only rule of the Abbey de Thélème was* 'fay çe que vouldras' *('Do what thou wilt').*

But the idea of sex-magic, the raising of power through love and will, did not surface again until the mid-nineteenth century with the American esotericist Paschal Beverly Randolph, whose teachings worked their way into a small German group, the Ordo Templi Orientis, which was later taken over by the English magician Aleister Crowley.

1355

In the Hall of the Great Council in the Doge's Palace in Venice there are portraits of all the doges – except one. In the place where his portrait should be is the framed painting of a black shroud. In the records of the Council of Ten, the body responsible for the security of the Republic of Venice, the relevant page is blank except for the words, 'Non scribatur' ('Let it not be written').

The discovery of the following account in the Vaults shows that it was, in fact, written – and that it was a story not just of political power but of magical power.

The Dragon Chain

Cherith Baldry

Fantino Falier hurried up the stairs of the Palazzo Ducale, anxious not to be late for dinner with his uncle, the Doge. He slipped inside the Sala del Scudo, relaxing to see that his haste was unnecessary: several petitioners stood waiting, and Marin Falier had not yet made his appearance.

Most of the men were clustered around a large cabinet of curios, which the Doge had recently had removed from the Red Room of the Palazzo Falier to his new residence in the Palazzo Ducale. The cabinet doors were open for display, with one of the Doge's servants nearby to keep a wary eye on the treasures.

Fantino had helped with the transport and the arrangement. Pride of place was given to the scrolls and artefacts brought back to Venice from the East by Marco Polo, and given to the Doge years before by the great traveller. The touch of such rarities had intrigued Fantino: the boxes of wood and leather; the gold and silver jewellery; most impressive the great silver neck chain incised with the sinuous curves of rampant dragons.

As Fantino headed towards the knot of petitioners the doors from the Doge's private apartments burst open. Marin Falier stormed into the hall, his furred robe belling out behind him, his white beard seeming to bristle with anger. Ignoring the petitioners he strode across to Fantino, brandishing a sheet of parchment that he held crumpled in his fist.

'Look at that!' he exclaimed, thrusting the sheet at Fantino. 'Look at the sentence passed on that young puppy Michele Steno. Imprisoned for two months . . . banished for a year! I would have strung him up by the thumbs!'

Fantino smoothed out the crumpled parchment and glanced quickly over it: the decree of the Council as the Doge had described it. Fantino remembered his uncle's fury on the night he had discovered his chair of office plastered over with young Steno's scurrilous epigrams. *No wonder he's raging now, after such a light sentence.*

Glancing up from the document, Fantino saw that his uncle's wife, Aluica, had followed him into the hall. She was dressed for the dinner in a gown of deep crimson velvet, embroidered with gold, her heavy chestnut hair netted in a headdress smouldering with rubies.

'My lord, calm yourself,' she murmured, laying a hand on the Doge's arm. 'There is no need to—'

Doge Falier shook her off with an irritable gesture. 'No need? It is your reputation he besmirched, as well as my own. The Council hold me in contempt – me, their Doge! And you tell me to calm myself!'

Aluica cast an anguished glance towards Fantino. 'True, my lord,' she said. 'But here . . . in public . . .' She gestured toward the petitioners who stood staring in mingled shock and apprehension.

Marin Falier swung around, as if he had noticed them for the first time. 'Out!' he snapped. 'All of you, out!'

Most of the petitioners scurried for the door, looking glad to go. Two men remained. One of them was Giovanni Gradenigo, Aluica's kinsman; Fantino realised that he too must have been invited to dinner. The other was Filippo Calendario, the architect in charge of the rebuilding work that presently plagued the palazzo.

'What do you want?' Doge Falier asked waspishly. 'Don't come to me with your petitions. I clearly have no power within the state.'

Calendario stepped forward and bowed to the Doge with one hand on his breast. He was a big man, his muscular build the evidence of his early days as a stonemason. His broad face was topped with a shock of thick hair, greying as if stone dust sifted in it, and his hands were covered with tiny scars from the chisel.

'I came to show you the new set of plans, Your Serenity,' he said, gesturing with a roll of parchment. 'But this is perhaps not the best time . . .'

'It is not,' the Doge replied. 'Wait on me here in the morning.'

Calendario bowed again and began to withdraw, then checked as if something had just occurred to him. 'If you feel you lack power,' he said, 'then I know a man who might be able to aid you.'

Marin Falier's eyes narrowed in suspicion. 'What man? What can any man do for me?'

'It's best you meet him, Your Serenity,' the architect replied. 'I could bring him with me tomorrow when I come with the plans.'

The Doge hesitated for a moment, then gave a curt nod. 'Very well. Do so.'

He watched as Calendario left and closed the door behind him. Then he led the way into his own private rooms.

Aluica followed, escorted on either side by Fantino and Gradenigo. Glancing agitatedly from one to the other, she began in a low voice. 'I do not like this. I beg you, kinsmen, be here tomorrow to meet this man. I fear what my lord the Doge may do when he is in this mood.'

Fantino nodded agreement, while Gradenigo simply lifted Aluica's hand and kissed it. Aluica breathed a sigh of relief. 'I thank you, dear friends. It may be that not only I, but the whole of Venice will be in your debt.'

*

Fantino arrived at the Palazzo Ducale on the following morning to find Filippo Calendario already there. At his side was a small man, dark and wiry, wearing a seaman's cap which he pulled off as Calendario introduced him to the Doge.

Donna Aluica and Giovanni Gradenigo stood nearby, both looking anxious. With a courteous nod to his uncle, Fantino went to join them.

'This is Bertuccio Israello,' the architect said. 'He has travelled to many lands, and seen many strange wonders.'

Fantino reflected that judging by the man's name, he ought to be one of the Children of Abraham, yet his broad, flat face suggested that he came from further east, from Cathay and the land of the Tartars where Marco Polo had travelled.

'Calendario has explained to you?' the Doge asked. 'You know my . . . difficulties?'

Israello nodded. When he spoke, his tone was respectful but confident, with a foreign tang that Fantino could not identify. He did not sound like the simple seaman he appeared to be.

'Indeed, Your Serenity. You feel that the various councils have taken too much power in Venice, leaving you yourself as little more than a figurehead. You have cause for anger.'

Marin Falier let out a snort. His fury of the evening before had abated, but his face was grim and his eyes chilly. 'It's your help I want, not your sympathy,' he snapped. 'Though what a man like you can do, I fail to see.'

Israello ignored the implied insult, merely giving the Doge a long look from shrewd dark eyes. 'Ser Filippo tells me you possess many objects from the East,' he said, easing his way towards the cabinet where Marco Polo's artefacts were kept.

The Doge's eyes flared with annoyance at the sudden change of subject. 'What of it?' he demanded.

'There is much wisdom gathered here,' Israello replied, his gaze devouring the cabinet that held the treasures, its doors firmly closed now. 'It may be there is something which can help you. May I . . . ?' He gestured towards the cabinet.

Still looking irritated, Doge Falier snapped his fingers at Aluica. She hesitated, then opened the doors with a small golden key which hung with others from the chatelaine at her girdle.

Israello took in a breath, half wonder, half pure greed. He stepped forward, letting his fingers run lightly over the artefacts, pausing for several moments on the great dragon neck chain, then seizing at last a small book bound in white leather.

Fantino remembered examining that same book when he helped transport the collection to the Doge's Palace. Its pages were covered with minuscule writing in unfamiliar characters; after one glance he had abandoned all hope of making sense of it. Interspersed with the writing were tiny, delicate pictures, or diagrams just as meaningless as the text. He had dismissed the book as a curiosity, but clearly it meant more to Israello.

'Well?' Doge Falier asked, after Israello had perused the book greedily for several moments. He twitched his robe impatiently. 'Can you make sense of that scribble?'

Israello looked up. 'No scribble, my lord Doge, but a work of great wisdom. This is none other than the book of Zhang Guo Lao, venerated as immortal by the people of Cathay.' He caressed the book: a reverent gesture that a priest might have bestowed upon Holy Writ. 'It is a miracle to find it here.'

'And what has that to do with me?' Doge Falier asked, his tone cold and unimpressed.

'Zhang Guo Lao was a great adept,' Israello replied. 'He had many powers. Your people might perhaps call him a sorcerer.'

'Sorcery!' Donna Aluica exclaimed, reaching out towards her husband. 'No!'

Marin Falier ignored her. 'Go on,' he said to Israello.

'There is an elixir,' Israello continued, 'coupled with a certain chant, that can infuse into the man who drinks it the spirit of one of the great dragon kings. His power would be unlimited.'

Donna Aluica let out a gasp, and exchanged an alarmed glance with her kinsman Gradenigo. Fantino felt simply bewildered. Like any reasonable man, he knew that sorcery existed, but he found it hard to believe in it here, in the Palazzo Ducale, the home of order and government.

Marin Falier ran his tongue over his lips. There was an avid look in his eyes that disconcerted Fantino. 'You can prepare this . . . elixir?' he asked Israello.

The so-called seaman ran his hand once more over the book. 'With this, I can.'

'And will you?'

Israello gave the Doge a measured look from those shrewd dark eyes. 'What if I say yes? Will I be indicted for sorcery, handed over to the Lords of Night?' His gaze flicked across the others in the hall. 'Will the members of your household here keep their mouths shut?'

'They will do as I tell them,' Doge Falier retorted. 'No one is trying to trap you. I give you my word. And if you can do what you promise, I will reward you richly.'

Israello nodded slowly. 'Then I will do so.'

Donna Aluica opened her mouth as if to protest, then closed it again, shaking her head helplessly.

'How will you proceed?' the Doge asked.

'I must buy ingredients,' Israello replied. 'And I need a room where I can work.'

'I'll find him somewhere,' Calendario said, stepping forward with a brisk nod towards the Doge.

'Good.' Marin Falier waved his hand. 'Begin . . . and work quickly.'

The two men bowed and withdrew, while the Doge swung around and strode off through the opposite door leading to his private rooms.

Aluica took a pace after him, then turned back and grasped Fantino's arm. 'Follow Israello!' she whispered.

Fantino nodded swiftly and hurried after the two men. He ran down the stair and almost cannoned into his quarry where they had halted at its foot. Hanging back, Fantino could not hear what they said, but saw them shake hands. Then Calendario joined his workmen while Israello made his way out onto the quayside.

Following discreetly, Fantino saw him heading not for the markets of the Rialto, where he could expect to find his ingredients, but along the waterside towards the Arsenale. He moved swiftly and purposefully; clearly he had no idea that anyone might be pursuing him.

With the walls of the Arsenale in sight, Israello stopped suddenly and plunged into a tavern: *Il Galeone*, a low pot-house for sailors. Fantino knew of it but had never been inside.

As he cautiously entered, the reek of ale and sour wine hit him in the throat. Even at this hour of the morning the tavern was packed and at first he could not see Israello. Wriggling his way through the crowd, uncomfortably aware that he was too finely dressed to blend in among the seamen and artisans, he finally spotted Israello in one corner, in close conversation with two sailors.

Edging closer, unwilling to be seen, Fantino at last reached a spot where he could hear the men's voices. The noise all around him was too loud for him to catch more than a few words, or to gather what they were talking about, but one thing he could be sure of. The two sailors were speaking in the accents of the Genoese.

*

The war with Genoa had been rumbling on for years. As Fantino retraced his steps to the Palazzo Ducale, he had no idea what to do. The presence of Genoese in Venice should be reported to the authorities but, Fantino reflected uneasily, he had no proof. And his uncle the Doge, in his present mood, would likely see the accusation as an attempt to discredit Bertuccio Israello.

As he approached the palazzo, Fantino spotted Giovanni Gradenigo on his way out. Vastly relieved, Fantino hurried to intercept him, and poured out the story of what he had seen and heard at *Il Galeone*.

'What do you think I should do?' he asked.

The older man shook his head. 'I see your difficulty,' he said. 'The Doge will not believe you when he is set on using Israello. You might speak to one of the Heads of the Council of Ten—' He held up a hand as Fantino was about to protest. 'No, I can see that no sensible man would willingly tangle with *them*.' He stroked his beard thoughtfully. 'What I would advise, young man, is for you to post an accusation through the Lion's Mouth. The Council will be alerted, but you will not be involved.'

Fantino thought that over. 'Perhaps I will,' he said. 'Thank you, Ser Giovanni.'

Returning to his own rooms, Fantino took pen and parchment and – careful to disguise his handwriting – wrote a brief denunciation of Bertuccio Israello for trafficking with the Genoese.

He returned to the Palazzo Ducale later in the evening, after Calendario's workmen had finished for the day and gone home. No one was about as he thrust his denunciation into the gaping jaws of the stone lion, but even so he felt a pang of nervousness. Legend said that those jaws would close on the hand of anyone who posted a lie, crushing and rending.

But I know what I saw, he told himself. *Israello is a traitor to the Republic*.

*

Three days went by, while Fantino fretted and nothing happened. The lion might as well have eaten his parchment, for all the effect it had. Now and again he spotted Israello around the Palazzo

Ducale where he was compounding his elixir; he seemed quite confident, nodding courteously when his path crossed with Fantino's.

On the fourth day, a message from Donna Aluica summoned Fantino back to the ducal apartments. Israello, it seemed, had finished his elixir. *Please come quickly*, the lady had written, a blot on the parchment evidence of her haste. *Perhaps you can persuade my lord from this disastrous course.*

A servant was waiting in the Sala del Scudo to conduct Fantino into the Doge's private apartments. He was shown into a small room used by the Doge as a study, though now it was cleared of furniture except for the shelves around the walls, stuffed full of scrolls, books and papers. The window shutters were closed and the only light came from a single taper, and the glowing charcoal of a brazier standing in one corner. A copper bowl was set there; some liquid bubbled inside it, giving off an aromatic steam which wreathed around the room, so that Fantino saw everything through a mist.

The Doge was already there, dressed in his robes of state, with his cap of office on his head. Israello was stationed in front of him, holding a closed cup. In the far corner Donna Aluica and Giovanni Gradenigo stood close together, their uneasiness evident on their faces.

'Thank God you've come!' Gradenigo exclaimed as Fantino entered. 'Perhaps you can talk some sense into Ser Marin. He won't listen to us.'

Before Fantino could reply, the Doge swung round on him with a savage expression. 'Not a word!' he snarled. 'I *will* do this!'

Fantino made a helpless gesture as Israello stepped forward and took the lid off the cup. 'Drink this slowly, my lord Doge,' he said, 'while I speak the words. The spirit of the dragon king will come to reside within you.'

'Are you mad?' Gradenigo asked hoarsely as the Doge reached out to take the cup. 'That could be poison!'

'The elixir is harmless,' Israello said, withdrawing the cup from the Doge's stretching fingers. He seemed undisturbed by the accusation. 'But if it will quiet your mind, I will drink some of it myself.'

He raised the cup to his lips and took a swig, then bowed mockingly towards Gradenigo. 'Satisfied?'

Gradenigo had no more to say. Israello handed the cup to the Doge, then took up the leather-bound book. 'We begin,' he said.

Fantino listened, profoundly disturbed as Israello began to recite from the book, his voice a high-pitched, rhythmic chant, the words in no language Fantino had ever heard. At the same moment the Doge began to sip from the cup.

The aromatic steam from the bowl on the brazier seemed to be growing thicker, filling the room until Fantino could scarcely get his breath, and the figures of the Doge and Israello were half hidden in swirling white clouds.

Fantino felt his blood beginning to pulse in time with the chant. At the same time he felt as if something huge was pouring itself into the room, crushing him against the wall, swelling and gathering weight until he was surprised that the door and window did not explode outwards. He heard a fearful cry from where Aluica and Gradenigo still huddled together, almost invisible now through the white smoke.

His senses beginning to dissolve into sparkling blackness, Fantino groped for the door, but before he reached it the chanting came to an end. The crushing sensation vanished between one breath and the next. The white steam began to dissipate.

'It is done,' Israello said.

Aluica was white-faced but steady, while Gradenigo pulled out a kerchief and mopped his brow. Fantino felt his legs shaking, and longed for somewhere he could sit down.

The Doge stood silent in the midst of the room, his face blank. Aluica said, 'My lord?' but he seemed not to have heard her. Fantino wondered whether the ritual had somehow destroyed his mind.

Then gradually life began to flow back into Doge Falier's face. He looked down at himself, at his elaborate brocaded robes, as if he had never seen them before. He examined his hands, the palms and the backs, then raised them to his head as if to check that his cap of office was still in place.

'I am . . . changed.' His voice sounded like a squeaking wheel that needed grease. 'I can feel it.' Turning to Israello, he added, 'What should I do now?'

'Whatever you please, my lord,' Israello said. 'But I advise you to wait for a few days. The power within you needs time to settle. And you need time to learn how to wield it.'

The Doge nodded. 'I will take your advice.' Slowly his voice was returning to normal. 'And if you speak the truth, you shall have your reward.'

*

For the next few days Fantino felt as if a massive storm cloud was louring over the city. His tension mounted as he waited for the storm to break. But the Doge took no action, and the Council of Ten still ignored the denunciation Fantino had posted through the Lion's Mouth.

At last, greatly troubled, Fantino sought out the Doge's chaplain, Father Lorenzo Contarini, and found him at prayer in San Marco, among the shadows where the mosaics glinted gold in the light of candle flames.

As Fantino approached, Father Lorenzo rose, crossed himself, and turned to face him. 'Ser Fantino.' He inclined his head. 'How may I serve you?'

The priest was a small, elegant man, who wore his simple black cassock as if it were a robe of the finest silk and velvet. Fantino felt slightly intimidated in his presence.

'Father, I am greatly worried about my uncle, the Doge,' he said.

Father Lorenzo indicated a bench beside the wall, and seated himself there, turning attentively towards Fantino. 'Go on.'

After a moment's hesitation, Fantino poured out the story: how Marin Falier had been enraged by the Council's leniency towards Michele Steno; how in his quest for power he had listened to Israello's temptation, and had drunk the elixir that he was convinced would arouse the ancient spirit within him.

'Indeed.' Father Lorenzo, apparently undisturbed, fingered his pectoral cross. 'And did the elixir work?'

Fantino was taken aback by a question like that, from a man of God. 'I can scarcely believe it,' he replied. 'But my uncle is . . .

changed. In his body he seems stronger, yet his eyes are glazed, and he scarcely speaks, except to rap out orders. He stalks through the palazzo like a vengeful ghost. The servants are terrified of him.'

'Has he tried to use the power he thinks he has?' Father Lorenzo asked. 'For instance, has he tried to countermand the Council's sentence on Michele Steno?'

Fantino shook his head. 'It's as though . . . as though something were working inside him, swelling . . . Something far, far bigger than the punishment of a coxcomb like Steno. Father, I shudder to think what that might be!'

'So why do you come to me?' the priest asked. 'Sorcery is a matter for the Lords of Night, not for the Church.'

'But you're his chaplain!' Fantino protested. 'Can't you talk to him?'

Father Lorenzo hesitated, then rose to his feet. 'Very well,' he said. 'I will try.'

*

The sun was setting as Fantino and Father Lorenzo left San Marco and hurried across the Piazzetta to the entrance of the Palazzo Ducale. The water of the lagoon glittered with scarlet light, and shadows already massed among the colonnades.

When they reached the Doge's apartments, they found Donna Aluica alone there. As the servant showed them in she sprang to her feet, letting fall a length of embroidery, and advanced on Father Lorenzo, her hands held out.

'I'm so glad to see you, Father!' she exclaimed. 'My lord has gone to confront the Council of Ten, to demand the death of Michele Steno.' Her voice breaking, she added, 'I think he is mad.'

Father Lorenzo clasped her hands briefly. 'When he returns, I will see what I can do.'

'It may be too late.' Aluica pressed her hands to her face. 'I have been so afraid that my lord's rule would come to ruin! Right from the moment when we first returned to Venice from the Papal Court. The sea fog was so thick that our barge could not draw up in its appointed place. Instead, my lord came ashore in a small boat at the Piazzetta. Mist still lay there, so heavy that before he knew it he had stepped between the two columns where criminals are executed. Such an evil omen!'

'Yet with God's help we may avert it,' Father Lorenzo said. 'If the Doge—'

He broke off at the sound of a door crashing back, somewhere in the outer apartments. It was followed by the Doge's voice, distant, but raised in a furious roar. 'Fetch me Bertuccio Israello!'

'What in God's name—?' Fantino muttered.

He led the way towards the sound, with Father Lorenzo and Aluica following. They came up with the Doge in the Sala del Scudo.

To Fantino's eyes the Doge seemed crazed with fury, worse than the evening when sentence was passed on Michele Steno. His eyes were glazed, he tore at his beard and foam spun away from his lips as he bellowed. 'Refused! Told it was no affair of mine! I'll hang that accursed sorcerer . . . where is he?'

Father Lorenzo started forward, begging for calm, but Doge Falier thrust him away; the priest staggered back and would have fallen if Fantino had not steadied him.

A moment later the doors of the hall opened and one of the guards appeared, propelling Bertuccio Israello forward by one shoulder. 'Here he is, my lord.'

Marin Falier flung himself at the sorcerer, gripping him by the collar and shaking him until his face started to turn blue. 'You lied to me!' he snarled.

Israello waved his hands helplessly; his mouth opened and closed but only a choking sound came out of it.

'My lord, let him speak,' said Father Lorenzo.

The Doge released Israello, who fell to his knees, gasping and massaging his throat. 'My lord, I spoke the truth,' he said at last. 'But the dragon spirit within you has not come to its full strength. It is sometimes so with men whose own spirit is strong.'

Doge Falier aimed a kick at the cringing man. 'More lies! Take him to the prison,' he ordered the guard.

'No!' Israello exclaimed. 'My lord, listen to me . . . there is another way.'

Marin Falier hesitated for a moment, then waved a hand at the guard. 'Get out. Stay within call.'

When the man had withdrawn, Israello staggered to his feet and stumbled over to the cabinet that held the Oriental treasures. 'Please, my lady, open it,' he said to Aluica.

Donna Aluica glanced at her husband, who gave her a curt nod. When she had unlocked the doors, Israello took up the great silver neck chain with its engraved dragons and held it out to the Doge.

'If you wear this, my lord, it will enhance your powers.'

'Oh, don't—' Aluica began, with an anguished glance at Father Lorenzo, but the Doge silenced her with a glare.

He took the chain from Israello and laid it across his shoulders. As he settled it in place, the plaques, finely articulated, clashed softly, as if the chain were a sentient thing, taking the Doge into its embrace.

The Doge seemed to stand taller. His eyes closed for a moment and he raised his hands, palms upwards, as if he received something from above.

Suddenly disconcerted, Fantino started towards him, but the Doge whirled away from him and headed out of the door, past the startled guard and down the stair leading to the courtyard. The others followed, Aluica clinging to the arm of the priest.

Doge Falier did not halt until he stood on the quayside. A few lurid, blood-red streaks still showed in the sky, but clouds were massing across the lagoon, blotting out the silhouette of San Giorgio across the channel. They mounted higher in the sky, seeming to reach out threatening arms towards the city, and a wind rose, fluttering the surface of the sea.

Most of the boats were tied up for the night, and the few people along the quayside were hurrying for home, though a few of them stopped to stare at the sight of their Doge and his lady, divested of their state robes and so sparsely attended.

Thunder rumbled across the sky. Within moments the clouds had swallowed up the last of the light. The wind suddenly strengthened, striking the quayside like the blow from a gigantic hand. Rain crashed down; Fantino and the others were instantly drenched, and the last of the gawping citizens scuttled for cover.

Amidst the turmoil of sky and sea the Doge stood like a rock, his back to the lagoon. His arms were outstretched. His white hair and beard were whipped to and fro in the wind as if they were living snakes. His face showed pure ecstasy.

Struggling to stand upright, Fantino saw with growing horror that the plates of the neck chain were beginning to glow with an incandescent silver light, outlining the dragon forms more clearly. As the light grew it spread across the body of the Doge until he was outlined in silver fire.

Water lapped around Fantino's feet and he looked down to see it bubbling up between the paving stones. His cry of alarm was drowned by a shriek from Israello.

'Look! The lagoon!'

Fantino followed the direction of his pointing finger to see a growing darkness in the distance, blacker than the clouds and mounting higher and higher into the air. At the same time he realised that waves were surging up and over the quayside.

Israello had retreated until he stood with his back pressed against one of the columns of the colonnade. 'The Dragon of the West!' he gasped. 'The spirit of water!'

Then Fantino realised that the swelling darkness was a wave, mounting higher still as it raced across the lagoon, ready to engulf the city. Terror gushed through him, fierce as the storm.

'We'll drown!' he cried. 'Everything . . . swept away!'

Father Lorenzo stepped forward, his soaked cassock clinging to his body, his face white and desperate. He stood in front of the Doge and raised his pectoral cross.

'In the name of the Lord Christ!' he commanded. 'Come out of him!'

At the same moment Donna Aluica darted past him, grabbed the neck chain that still pulsed with silver light and dragged it over her husband's head. The light died as she cast it down onto the paving stones.

A vast shape erupted from the Doge's body: a dragon with jaws gaping wide and its wings extended to cover the city. Green lightning danced over its scales and across the membrane of its wings. Its jaws gaped and it let out a bellow from deep within its chest; thunder answered it from the sky.

The Doge collapsed, and Donna Aluica crouched beside him, crying out his name as she raised his head.

In front of the dragon, small and indomitable, Father Lorenzo stood with his pectoral cross still held against it.

'Lord Christ, help us!' he cried.

Lightning branched and crackled across the sky. Out of it, as if the vault of Heaven had split open, came the winged lion of San Marco, plunging down the sky in a flurry of golden light. Its eyes blazed incandescent, fixed on the dragon, and its glittering claws reached out to crush its enemy.

A blast of foetid air wafted over Fantino as the dragon beat its wings and hurled itself into the air to meet the challenge of the lion. The two creatures clashed above the quayside; gripping claws locked them together as they mounted into the sky. Their outlines grew smaller; gold and green light seemed to coalesce as Fantino strained to see the combat.

Lion and dragon together shrank to a glittering point, a single jewel pinned against the darkness. Then from the mote of light a golden flash blasted across the sky, a moment of luminescence from horizon to horizon.

Fantino closed his eyes tight against the brilliance. When he opened them again he saw the lion, pacing downwards as if on a giant stairway until it stood with forepaws on the quayside and its hindpaws on the sea. It stretched out its wings over the rooftops of the city, a gesture of protection and blessing. Then it faded, leaving twilight and a sky where stars were beginning to emerge.

The vast wave had disappeared and one last surge slopped over the quayside before the sea grew quiet. The wind died and the lashing rain dwindled to a few spatters.

Fantino looked around. Israello was huddled beside the pillar as if he had fainted. Father Lorenzo still stood looking out across the sea, shaking with exhaustion, his eyes filled with wonder. The only sound was Aluica's sobbing as she sat on the quayside and cradled her husband's head in her lap.

*

I wrote the last few words and tossed the pen aside, staring across my desk at Fantino Falier. Creating a logical narrative from his incoherent stumbling had sorely tried my patience.

Earlier that evening Doge Falier's head had been cut off at the top of the stairway where he had taken his oath as doge less than a year before. His mind had gone; he could only whimper and express his guilt. Grief for what he had been weighed heavy on me. After an outstanding career in the service of the Republic, his short dogate and this black day – 17 April 1355 – would forever be stamped with infamy in the annals of Venice.

'I hope you don't expect me to believe this farrago,' I said to Fantino.

He sat upright with a look of alarm. 'Father Lorenzo?'

'Oh, come, Ser Fantino. Do you really believe I am so stupid?'

'I don't know what you mean,' Fantino retorted. 'I have told you the truth.'

'And I'm the Archangel Gabriel.'

I rested my elbows on the table and my chin on my hands, taking a certain mild pleasure in the young man's discomfiture. 'It was a coincidence, was it not,' I began, 'that Filippo Calendario happened to know the man who could make use of the magical artefacts that Doge Falier happened to possess? At the very time when Doge Falier had need of him? Such an unlikely conjunction! I believe that someone plotted with Calendario to seek out not a sorcerer, but a charlatan who could deceive the Doge, making use of his Oriental collection. And who could that man have been but you, Ser Fantino?'

'That's nonsense!' Fantino protested, but there was a note of fear beneath his bluster. 'I told you . . . the elixir . . .'

I shrugged. 'Some herbal brew, no doubt. Immaterial, since its purpose – along with the aromatic smoke and the chanting – was to persuade the Doge that he was infused with a power greater than mortal. I doubt that the ritual was as spectacular as you made it sound.'

Fantino was looking more dismayed with every word I spoke. 'But the dragon!' he protested. 'You were there – you *saw*!'

'I did. And I saw Israello's face when the spirit manifested itself. He was utterly astonished and terror-stricken. For the dragon chain was truly magical, and it needed no sorcerer to call up its power. Only a receptive mind, as Doge Falier's was . . . thanks to your manipulation. If you call upon evil, believe me, Fantino, it will come.'

'I still don't know why you're blaming me,' Fantino said, tossing back his hair with a petulant gesture.

'Then let me explain,' I continued, knowing now that I had struck gold. 'You never expected true magic. So you needed to explain it, to establish why Israello should call up a spirit to destroy the city. And so you fabricated his meeting with the Genoese. Really – enemy sailors conspiring openly in a crowded tavern like *Il Galeone*? They would have been torn to pieces. You may or may not have lied about your conversation with Gradenigo, but you posted no denunciation through the Lion's Mouth. A Genoese conspiracy, and the Council of Ten did nothing?'

There was no response but a black look from Fantino.

'If you truly believed that Israello was conspiring with the Genoese, why did you not denounce him to your uncle?' I went on. 'You could have destroyed Israello and saved your Doge with a few words. But those words were never spoken.'

'He would never have listened to me,' Fantino said sulkily.

'He might have. Marin Falier was no fool. And a truly loyal man would at least have tried. No, all that part of your story is just a little embroidery to blacken Israello and perhaps the Doge too, for listening to him.'

Fantino crossed his arms, hunching down lower in the chair. 'So you say . . .' he muttered.

'And there is more. When I went to visit Calendario and Israello in prison, to bring them the comfort of the last rites, I was denied. That lies heavy on my heart. And yesterday, when they were hanged between the red columns on the balcony of the Palazzo Ducale, they had gags in their mouths. Was that your order? What might they have said if they had been allowed to speak?'

'And why did I do all this?' Fantino asked, summoning a reserve of bravado. 'What do I benefit from destroying my uncle?'

'Ah, that is the question.' I sat back and looked at Fantino. He was past his first youth, and his self-indulgence showed in his pallid complexion and pouchy face. I even found it in my heart to pity him a little. He had lived long in the shadow of a great man. 'Why should you plot to have your uncle indicted for sorcery . . . or his mind destroyed by the practice of it? But I think I can explain that, too. Did Gradenigo pay you well?'

'What?' Fantino half started from his chair and then flopped back.

'He will probably be our next Doge, after all. And like your uncle he is an old man. Does he feel his time is running out?'

'I don't know what you're talking about,' Fantino said.

'Or if I give Gradenigo the benefit of the doubt, what of Donna Aluica? She is a very beautiful woman, and in spite of Michele Steno's scurrilous allegations, I believe her to be virtuous. Did you feel you might win her if your uncle were out of the way?'

That arrow had gone home. Fantino glared at me, and I saw his hand move towards the dagger at his belt, but he had the sense not to draw it.

'Prove it!' he said savagely.

'Oh, I think I could cast enough doubt on your tale to interest the Council of Ten,' I told him. 'The missing denunciation would take some explaining away. And a session in the Court of the Rope might take care of the rest.'

Fantino's face was pale as dough; he looked as if he might be sick. 'No . . .' he whispered.

I paused, for long enough to let the images of torture fix themselves in his mind. 'No,' I said at last, suppressing a sigh. Though I was convinced to my own satisfaction that Fantino had plotted against his uncle, I could not summon the certainty that would let me accuse him to the Council. Besides, the name of Falier had been dragged through enough mud, and to reveal the truth would cause unrest among the people. 'Marin Falier consented to his own ruin when he agreed to take the dragon spirit into himself,' I continued. 'Calendario and Israello deserved to die, for conspiring with you to destroy him. Your death would serve no purpose. But I warn you, Fantino' – I leaned forward – 'if you involve yourself in more plotting, or if you make one move towards Donna Aluica, I shall take what I know to the Council of Ten. Now get out.'

Fantino's chair scraped against the floor as he levered himself to his feet. He let out a curse as he blundered from the room.

I looked after him, wondering whether I was right, or whether he was indeed the simple, somewhat incompetent man that he would like me to believe. Pure terror could have prompted his near confession. But whatever the truth, I have drawn his fangs. I hope that now his name will be no more than a footnote in the books of history.

*

As I finished this commentary, the door of my study opened and Giovanni Marcello, one of the three Heads of the Council of Ten, strode in.

Without greeting me, Ser Giovanni seized the pages of Fantino's story and shuffled them into order. While he was thus occupied, I discreetly slid the account of my recent conversation underneath a book.

Marcello's face darkened as he read; at last he looked up. 'What is the purpose of writing this down?' he asked.

'I must send a report to the Holy Father,' I told him.

Ser Giovanni did not look pleased. But though he is a powerful man, he has always shown respect for Holy Church.

'Very well,' he said. 'But you must take it yourself, and you will keep your mouth shut about what it contains.'

I answered mildly, though I do not take kindly to being ordered around, even by one of the Council of Ten. 'I never considered blabbing, Ser Giovanni.'

He set the parchments down on the table again; his anger faded to a look of simple harassment. 'This story cannot be allowed to get out,' he said. 'How many more of these evil artefacts could be scattered around the city? What destruction might they still cause? What panic among the people? We are poised precariously here, between land and water, and a little thing might destroy us.'

I nodded. 'No one will hear it from me.'

'I will speak to these others, too,' Ser Giovanni continued, with a gesture at the parchments. 'An everyday, down-to-earth conspiracy . . . that is enough to explain these executions. And the battle in the heavens? An unseasonable storm, no more. Marin Falier's name and his memory shall be blotted out . . . but the Republic will survive.'

Giving me a satisfied nod, he strode out and snapped the door shut behind him.

*

I write these last few words on board ship as I begin my journey. Giovanni Marcello's advice is good. There must be no more of this evil magic. I shall take this account to the Holy Father, for safe-keeping until it pleases God to reveal the truth. And I do not think I shall return to Venice. There are many dark alleyways there, and I prefer not to look over my shoulder as I walk.

Ω

The framed painting of a black shroud in the Doge's Palace bears the text, Hic est locus Marini Faletro decapitati pro criminibus *('This is the place for Marin Falier, beheaded for his crimes').*

The accepted version of history is that Falier mounted a coup, planning to kill many of the noble class and declare himself Prince of Venice. The plot was discovered, a number of conspirators were hanged, and Falier himself was beheaded as a traitor after only seven months in office as doge.

The seventy-six-year-old Marin Falier is known to have been irascible and to take offence quickly. The libellous epigrams of Michele Steno and the light sentence he was given supposedly provided the motivation for Falier's conspiracy against the Venetian aristocracy which resulted in his death – but this account by Fantino Falier, dictated to Fr Lorenzo, suggests a far more complex and disturbing reason for his execution.

Marin Falier did indeed possess a number of artefacts and manuscripts from the Orient, which were given to him by Marco Polo many years before he became doge. Did they provide the basis for the magical conjuring which Fantino Falier describes? Was it just the dragon chain which summoned the spirit of the dragon to possess Marin Falier, or did the elixir have a part to play? Do we believe Fantino, or Fr Lorenzo? Fr Lorenzo's codicil to Fantino's story makes the sequence of events more ambiguous. As rational people today we might be tempted to accept Giovanni Marcello's cover story of 'an unseasonable storm', but Fr Lorenzo, clearly a level-headed and astute judge from the way he handles Fantino Falier, accepts the summoning of the dragon spirit as fact, as attested by his taking of this text to Pope Innocent VI in Avignon.

Venice was ruled by powerful, ambitious men; fourteen served as doge during the fourteenth century. Six days after Falier was beheaded Giovanni Gradenigo became the next doge, as Fr Lorenzo predicted. During his fifteen months in office he made peace with the Genoese. The young libertine Michele Steno, nearly half a century later, was also elected doge.

1382–1419

The Middle Ages are often spoken of as a hotbed of heterodox religious activity, with a wide variety of spiritual groups springing up across Europe. But this period of religious experimentation was spread across half a millennium, from 1000 to 1500.

Even with that caveat, over those centuries there was a groundswell of popular religious movements very much at variance with the orthodoxy of the Catholic Church. Several groups, including the Spiritual Franciscans, were inspired by the twelfth-century mystic Joachim de Fiore. The Bogomils, a Gnostic dualist sect, were strong in the Balkans and Hungary in the eleventh and twelfth centuries; their beliefs were very similar to the later Cathars of the Languedoc and northern Italy. There were the Waldensians from the thirteenth century onwards in much of western Europe, the Lollards in England in the fourteenth and fifteenth centuries and the Hussites in fifteenth-century Bohemia.

The Beguines (mentioned in this account) were self-governing communities of women who, unlike nuns of the time, did not live apart from the world but lived and worked in towns, caring for the sick and working as craftswomen. The Beghards were their male equivalent. Many of them held heterodox beliefs; some of them were linked to the Brethren of the Free Spirit, who believed that all would be saved, that Hell was not real, that the Sacraments were worthless, and the radical antinomian belief that as they were filled with the Spirit, all actions were not just permitted but sanctified.

All these, and other groups, met with strong opposition from the Church.

This account, found in the Vaults, was written by an old woman named Seraphine Duplexis. She was a member of a heterodox movement, Homines Intelligentiae *or the Men of Understanding, who shared similar beliefs to the Brethren of the Free Spirit. From her own testimony she also aided and abetted uprisings of workers and artisans in the late fourteenth century, then migrated to Bohemia to take part in the Hussite troubles with other members of her sect.*

But if Seraphine's account is to be believed – and the Church was concerned enough to suppress it – she and her group may also have developed ideas way beyond heterodox interpretations of Christianity.

Bells of the Harelle

Rosanne Rabinowitz

When King Charles's troops entered Rouen to put down the rebellion, the Harelle, the first thing they did was strip tongues from the city's bells. I listened as they did it, hidden in the belfry tower with my two lovers, Christophe and Adrian.

The troops entered the building. They were heading straight to the top, to the bells. To us.

Christophe put his finger to his lips and pointed to the wall and the faint outline of a door. He opened it; the three of us squeezed in among the pots of polish and cleaning fluids. Their scent went to my head and filled my lungs. Perhaps it had an intoxicating effect like liquor, and influenced Christophe's later behaviour.

I was sure the soldiers would open the door and find us. But they passed by many times. I saw shadows moving in the crack below the door and the floor, the soles of soldiers' boots.

A creak of something heavy being moved . . . ascending steps, up to the bells themselves. Much cursing came from above, a clanging and wrenching. A great cheer and round of applause.

Slow steps coming down, a heavy object hit the floor. 'We will melt this down and make the damned rebels drink it, as they did in Aragon.'

'The only good idea to come from the Spanish!'

We crouched there, well after the last soldierly steps and a slam of the door.

Finally, we emerged from our hidey-hole. Shading our eyes from the winter sun funnelling down from the belfry, we saw that the bells were still there. But the soldiers had taken away the tongues.

'Damn!' Christophe clenched his fists, trembling. 'They take the voice from our city, steal the voice from the people. Damn them! I will ring those bells anyway.'

He went to the bell ropes. 'We have no tongues, but we still have a voice!'

Do we? I wondered.

But Christophe had no doubt. He pulled on the ropes and the bells swung, with only a creaking. But *something* rang out. A vibration started in my core, and set off a ringing in my ears. It was a protest, a lamentation, a cry of warning and defiance. The silent but powerful noise shouted out our hopes, the delirium and joy and the fear of the past days.

Adrian and I went to help, pulling on the ropes with Christophe, lending our combined strength and fervour to his efforts.

When we stopped ringing the tongueless bells, the three of us embraced.

I decided then I will always raise my voice and write things down so people will know about them. I will never be like a bell without a tongue.

*

That is why I've been writing these accounts and I continue to write them, here in Bohemia. I am now in bed, doing my best to wake up, with the help of Hans and Josef and Jehanne . . . fine young people who would help an old woman and listen to her stories.

Did I dream of those blasted bells again? I must have dreamed of Christophe's wild carillons, or Adrian's account of a cloth workers' meeting where they plotted to put the world to rights.

Josef gives me a piece of bread. I nibble at it.

Meanwhile, my young friends look at me with some expectation, so I feel I should make a point.

I hold up the bread. 'This is sustenance for the body! This is not a symbol consecrated by a priest to become the body of a man who is long dead. This bread sustains the physical body that we celebrate life with.' I return to the subject that has set Prague alight for a good few years. 'Communion of *both* kinds . . . pah! We seek communion of *all* kinds!'

'Seraphine, you must eat before you preach,' says Hans, speaking to me in Flemish. The son of a Flemish bricklayer who built some of Prague's great structures, he knows how I prefer the sounds of French or Flemish in the morning.

'And you should have a drink,' he adds, 'Someone's gone to get water.'

'Water? Who knows what's been swimming in the water here! *Someone* get beer from Vaclav. That should be clean. Would do me good too.'

'You want to hear some preaching,' Hans says. 'Go to Our Lady of the Snows and listen to Zelivsky. They'll be marching from there for the prisoners.'

Processions have been forbidden in Prague, but people continue to defy the ban.

'I don't like that man Zelivsky.' I tear off another chunk of bread and offer the rest. 'He wants power as much as any petty inquisitor, and there are enough fools who will give it to him. But take me to the Snows. If there's trouble, that's where I'll go.'

My strength tends to wax and wane. In the mornings I find it hard to move. But once the day gets underway, I revive. What I feel in mind is not always what I feel in body, but on such days I can certainly progress at a good clip with my cane.

We share more bread, but I'm finding it hard to eat. I'm on edge. In Prague heretics preach from pulpits, market squares and taverns. Processions and clashes in the street happen daily. Is today any different?

Why were the bells of the Harelle ringing in my dreams? Do I hear their echo now?

'Let's go,' I urge, as I get out of bed.

*

So I won't be a bell without a tongue. But I must also remember that the bells that Christophe rang were the voice of a commune. Therefore, I don't only write for myself. I must relate the dreams of those who shouldn't be silenced . . . A young man suggesting that our universe started with an explosion, who disappeared forever. Young women trying to make lives for themselves without husbands. Artisans and paupers calling for the end of a tax and an end to oppression.

And what of those sensual and far-working bonds that form between us, extending over distances? That is still a mystery to me.

*

When I was a young woman towards the end of the last century, the uprisings of cloth workers broke out in Ghent. The rebellion spread to other cities in Flanders. My family, French woollen merchants, naturally viewed these events with alarm.

But I only wanted to find out more. Fortunately, my old nurse had taught me Flemish when I was growing up, along with empathy for those whose lives were different from mine. She came to visit and told me that the people rioted over taxes, tithes and poor wages.

Despite my comfortable background, I sympathised with those on the streets. I was unhappy, and their agitation seemed to address a cause of my own discontent. I'd been sold off in marriage to an older man, a nobleman with not much left but his title. My father could offer a tidy dowry. So it was a marriage made in heaven, or hell as far as I was concerned.

My husband was not overtly cruel. He didn't beat me. But he was indifferent, and grumbled when I couldn't give him a child. He never let me forget that he owned me. His idea of pleasure in the bed was a quick thrust and grunt and then he rolled over. I submitted.

I was sure he had mistresses or visited prostitutes, yet he insisted on this ordeal for reasons of procreation.

In my mind, I went elsewhere. A boat trip with my nurse along the canals where trees arched overhead, letting loose flowers that spotted my cloak with pink and white. A hidden garden, the comforting trickle of a fountain.

*

During the troubles of 1381 I was told not to go out on my own. Instead, I should send a servant out to conduct my business.

I couldn't take this confinement for long. Finally, I put on my plainest garments and snuck out. When I heard the noise of an angry procession, I went straight there. I was scared, though. Maybe I'd be spotted as one of the enemy, a pampered rich brat, and set upon immediately. I'd heard many times that the 'Jakes' and the 'merdaille' were wild beasts who would attack a well-bred lady.

But no one paid any attention to me. They had other things on their minds.

Standing on a crate was a hunched, thin man who appeared blind in one eye. He must have been more than sixty. He spoke in Flemish about unfair laws, burdensome taxes and the impositions of privilege. He was, he declared, a weaver of cloth who could barely afford to clothe himself.

'Perhaps next time I speak to you I will be naked, while the cloth I've woven will cover the backs of burghers, knights and lords.'

Everyone laughed, but it was a bitter laughter. Though my own father was a merchant of cloth to those burghers and knights, this man spoke for me. His words were angry and sweet and made me see, for the first time, something much bigger than myself. I later learned this man was called Nicolas, and he was famed throughout Europe as an orator of the streets.

Then another speaker mounted the improvised platform. He spoke in Flemish, and then in French. He was a patrician like myself, yet he also spoke of injustice and rebellion. Though he denounced the French king's oppression of Flanders, he cautioned us to remember that people in the French towns were also restless, and shouted '*vive Gand*' when they took to the streets. He bore the common English people no ill will either. 'The poor of England have risen up, and we will do the same.'

Again, his speech inspired the crowd. They responded with cheers and took their first steps towards the Town Hall. And I went with them.

As we marched, I spoke with the second man. He seemed approachable because he'd spoken in French. And though he had the bearing of someone who came from comfort, he had already set out on the course I wanted to take.

I just blurted out everything that was on my mind.

'If you believe in justice, there are ways you can help,' he said. He explained I could raise funds for the rebels. I could also communicate their goals to those who only speak French. And if I could read and write, I could work with an order of beguines to teach these skills to others.

I nodded, taking the advice to heart, already planning my escape.

*

My husband quickly became angered by my new activities and associates. I argued with him constantly; I argued with the owners I came across, urging them to pay their workers more. Meanwhile, I stashed coins, notes, jewellery and anything I could sell once I struck out on my own.

It didn't take long before my husband petitioned for an annulment.

Though I had little religious vocation, I joined a small group of beguines who devoted themselves more to worldly good deeds and less to holy devotions. Beguine houses were not tightly controlled by the Church or an order of monks. They were also open to women from humble backgrounds, who didn't offer the dowries required by established religious orders.

These sisters did foreswear marriage, but I was happy with that. I had no desire to marry again. They shared a small house in the city, supporting their work with spinning, tapestry production, needlework and scribing. I became a scribe, which I still do from time to time. It is a better trade than selling fish, which is what I did when I first came to Bohemia.

*

About a year later, we received news of agitation in Rouen. King Charles VI the Mad had levied a tax on staples, a *gabelle*, to finance his unending war. I volunteered to travel to Rouen to bring funds and support from Ghent, accompanied by a beguine who wanted to visit some sisters nearby.

I arranged to meet with a cloth worker called Adrian in the market. He arrived with another young man, Christophe.

Adrian had straight fair hair, Christophe had dark curly hair.

Their eyes were the same deep brown and they appeared to be good friends. I met both pairs of brown eyes with a sense of recognition. The moment stopped, and everything in that market became almost too vivid. The scents of horse dung and roasting nuts, fish sizzling on grills, sweetened bread fried and dusted with sugar.

And there was the noise . . .

'*Haro! Haro!*' The streets of Rouen rang with this cry, an appeal for help and a demand for justice.

'*Haro!* We need more people to secure the Town Hall. Help!'

'*Haro!* Seize the city's gates and close them.'

Christophe nodded at us both and hurried away.

'*Haro!* We'll end this tax. We work too hard, and eat too little.'

The bells of the city's commune began tolling. It was nothing like the measured sounds of an ordinary day, or the peels of the church bells. Its cadence called: *Haro! Haro!*

Adrian pointed towards the bell tower. 'That's Christophe's work!' He beamed with a pride that warmed me too.

More people poured into the city centre, answering the call.

A man emerged from a draper's shop to urge the crowd. 'Destroy records of rents, lawsuits, debts and privileges! A good ripping or a few fires, and we're free of those things!'

All afternoon we rampaged through the streets, building bonfires of transactions and demands. We vented our fury on the churches, whose prelates lived in luxury while tithing the hard-pressed people.

I was surfacing after a life spent half-asleep, awake at last. *Haro, haro!* I rubbed my eyes, as if ridding them of sleep's last residue. Then without thinking, I reached for Adrian's hand as we turned a corner.

We found people breaking into the houses of nobles. Some emerged with arms full of food and drink, which they shared among the crowds. Adrian passed something to me that tasted of aniseed and clove.

Faces glowed with the light of stained-glass saints as people ate forbidden cheese and fruit, even when their mouths were smeared with sauce and jam.

I didn't see anyone killed – the rage was vented against the property of our rulers, against the bonds made of parchment. There was smoke and flame, and laughter too, as we set them alight.

*

As night set in, Christophe left his bell-ringing post and rejoined us. We stepped into one of the noble houses, and heard the noise of revelry coming from the wine cellar. The owners had deserted the house in fear of the crowd.

In the house where I grew up, we had a wine cellar like this.

I went downstairs where people were sampling the delights. I held up a bottle, one of my husband's favourite vintages. 'This is excellent wine. Will you join me?'

'Of course, Seraphine,' said Christophe. 'With a bottle of wine and a name like that, you must be an angel!'

'Or perhaps a devil,' added Adrian.

'I am none of those things. I'm only me.'

Fingers brushed as we passed the bottle. Shall we sit down? Yes, here's a place. Thigh to thigh in an alcove, sweet grape fumes and damp earth.

Since I left my husband, I'd been happy to spend time with female companions from the beguinage. Sometimes I admired suitable men from afar, but stayed aloof.

But I didn't feel aloof then. I liked both of these men, and they made it clear that they liked me. I didn't consider choosing one over the other. They didn't compete. To this day I still don't understand quite how it happened. Invisible strings grew taut between us, pulling us closer into an inevitable embrace.

I just couldn't bear not to touch them, not to exchange breath with them. Anything else was unthinkable. Ordinary worries and caution fled.

We found a room upstairs. It was not overly ornate. But the carpets, the bed and the blankets had the feel and scent of comfort. Laughter rose up through the floorboards. Glass still shattered outside. People still called for help at their tasks, others shouted greetings and threats. Someone played a fiddle, raucous voices joined in an unfamiliar tune.

'I've only been with my husband,' I said suddenly.

'And who is your husband?' Adrian asked.

'It doesn't matter,' I decided. 'We're finished with all that.' *Finished with all that.* I was thinking of much more than my marriage.

Adrian's lips tasted of aniseed, Christophe's only of wine. Each touch showed me something new. I felt Adrian's wonder as he learned to read, taught by a beguine. Christophe when he hummed during the lesson, and got sent outside.

But the hum stayed with me, deepening as he stroked my back and I kissed Adrian again, searching for the flavours of more spice. I stretched out between my lovers, our thoughts and limbs entwining.

If I closed my eyes, I saw colours. Adrian: midnight blue and dawn grey. Christophe: blazing yellow. Their colours filled me and I showed them a hidden garden where lilies floated in a fountain and the purple glimmer of violets drew me into dark corners. I invited them in with me.

Later, we talked more. I didn't question how we had shared thoughts. It was too new and strange. But I now welcomed the simplicity of talking, the vibration of a voice under my fingers.

'We've known each other for years,' said Adrian, as he stroked Christophe's hair. 'Our families shared the same premises. We had our pallets in the same corner. Now we argue sometimes. Christophe only cares about his bells and making music, while I worry about the troubles of the world. But we're very close.'

'You will make me jealous,' I said. First they looked at me in surprise; why would a woman like me wish for the lot of two labourers?

'You have a lifetime of friendship, while I had to cut myself off from my family in order to be free.'

I saw the sympathy flicker across their faces, a visible change. 'You have us now,' Christophe said.

I had no idea how long we would be together, and what could happen next. But it was enough to sustain me when both boys put their arms around me. Everything was soft and gentle, contrasting with the battle outside. Though I used to have physical relations with my husband, this was the first time I truly made love.

You have us now.

And I saw that they also had each other, in a different way than before.

The only Holy Trinity is *this*, I said. My companions laughed.

*

We woke at daybreak. With morning some caution returned, and I decided to disguise myself by putting on a tunic, along with breeches and hose, I found in the house. We emerged to join a passing procession, composed mostly of journeymen.

'A king! A king! We will find a king!' People at the head of the procession pushed a large cart with an empty armchair placed upon it.

I nudged Adrian. 'What do we need a king for? We still have to fight off the current one.'

'I think it's a joke,' said Adrian.

Our procession turned a corner into a side street, which must have been overlooked by last night's rioters. We interrupted a portly gentleman trying to move a well-padded commode out of his house. He turned with a start, his red face draining to white.

The chair-bearers gave whoops of delight. 'Don't run! We will make you king!'

Before he could object a group placed him on the chair.

'You're our great king Mr Fatso, you are!'

We paraded him through the city as the new monarch. More people came out to cheer, pelting the anointed king with looted flowers and fruit. People bowed and scraped and displayed their bottoms as the throne went by.

He looked about, bewildered. 'Put me down,' he commanded. But he seemed even more terrified when his 'throne' was set down in the market square.

The draper who had called for the destruction of public records arrived with a scroll of parchment. 'We were up all night drafting this. Now our new king will sign it.'

He began reading: all the unfair taxes that burdened artisans and workers must be repealed. All debts cancelled in the spirit of Jubilee.

'Go on, sign it! Sign it, your great big royal highness!'

King Fatso did as he was told.

A procession of petitioners asked his advice. 'Should I tie up my master until he raises my pay?'

'Do it, do it,' the king said, prodded into assent by a playful poke in the back.

The draper stepped forward. 'Shall we attack the abbey of St-Ouen, which has been granted royal privileges over our city and robs us with its tithes?'

'Do it, do it,' advised King Fatso.

We will, we will! We marched off to the abbey. We broke in and destroyed the gallows, ripped the monastery's charters to shreds, stripped the abbot of his vestments, and forced him to sign a new charter that took away the abbey's royal privileges over the town and granted rights to the workers of Rouen.

After that, I wanted to return to 'our' house, the three of us, but there was too much to do. We had to secure more barricades, ensure supplies of food and water, organise defence.

We eventually fell asleep, tangled together among cushions on the floor of an upper chamber in the Town Hall.

*

After the initial celebration, the city was tense. We expected the army, expected a fight. No one came.

After a few days two messengers arrived to tell us about the revolt of the hammer-men, the Maillotins, in Paris.

The king and his troops had set out for Rouen, but when the troubles broke out in Paris he turned his army around to go there.

We carried on. Leaders of the guilds sat in the Town Hall. Bakers baked, produce-sellers made arrangements with farmers and weavers kept on weaving.

As for myself and my lovers, we had to be discreet once the euphoria of the first few days departed.

We didn't even make love again, but that one time bound us. Christophe and Adrian both had jobs to do, yet I felt they were always with me. I heard the chime of bells as I walked. I heard the clack of looms. Other thoughts tugged my heart and mind, and I revelled in their richness.

When we came together, we barely needed to speak.

Some beguines had spoken of ecstasy, of connection to God or a universal spirit. But my connection to anything close to that came with two other human beings, through flesh and human passions.

This is the real Holy Trinity. I had laughed when I said that, but maybe it frightened me too.

Then news came of the bloody massacre of the Parisians, of hundreds hung and burned and beheaded. It wouldn't be long before the king's troops would turn around again, and come for us in Rouen.

*

Now I am close to the age of that half-blind rabble-rouser Nicolas, who first set me on my path. I live in a strange city, which resounds to the followers of Jan Hus. He was burned as a heretic, prosecuted by Pierre d'Ailly, the same inquisitor who would later persecute us in Brussels. Surely that bound Brussels and Prague together, as surely as the Harelle created the trinity of myself, Adrian and Christophe.

When I first arrived in Prague I saw a strange wall on the other side of the river, running up Petrin Hill. It didn't appear to serve any defensive purpose and its top was jagged, like teeth.

'That is the Hungry Wall,' Hans explained later. In the past century, when there was no work, a king gave the poor of Prague tools to build that wall. He also gave them scraps of food while they worked but he didn't pay them. When the wall neared completion he ordered the workers to make the top uneven to look like teeth, as a reminder that the good king had given bread for the poor to chew.

When I see that wall I don't think of the largesse of a king who didn't pay his labourers, but the most generous monarch of all. King Fatso!

And I hear the clink of glasses, as Adrian and Christophe join me in a toast to King Fatso.

*

But I never knew what happened to them. While the army came down hard on the rebels of Paris, Rouen negotiated a surrender and suffered less. Ten leaders of the revolt had been hanged, but others were treated more lightly.

'You must go,' Adrian told me, when we were still in the bell tower. 'It's still possible to escape.'

'And *we* must stay and keep our heads down. We'll put in pleas for clemency. This is our city and we will not leave it,' said Christophe.

'I know of places where you can go,' said Adrian. 'My brothers among the cloth workers and the beghards can help you.'

Perhaps their pleas were accepted. Perhaps they lived to marry and have children. They still speak to me, but I'm never sure where their voices come from.

*

I set off alone, heading back to Flanders. In Rouen we had fought and we had lost. But I felt haunted by my experience there, for better or worse.

Perhaps study and contemplation could help me understand why I kept hearing those bells. And why, if I let my mind wander, I'd start tasting their passionate kisses full of wine, aniseed and cloves.

On the way, I found Adrian's associates, who directed me to a suitable beguinage.

One of the women who welcomed me laughed at my name. 'Seraphine! You should fit in here because we devote ourselves to spiritual liberty and seraphic love, as described by our great teacher Bloemardine.'

She lowered her voice. 'Be aware, that what we say among ourselves and what we tell the priests and bishops are two different things.'

'More like three or four things,' added another sister.

The beguinage was a large building set within woods on the edge of Brussels, along with a chapel and bell tower. It was old and run down, but I felt at home there. I settled into my routine of reading, prayer and meditation and discussion, along with work in the gardens and grounds. My early training in needlework was useful in the tapestry workshops.

I absorbed the work of Bloemardine, especially when I read: 'Love's most intimate union is through eating, tasting and seeing from within.' The body, according to Bloemardine, serves as a connection to divinity . . . and divinity itself can be human.

'Love came and embraced me, and I came out of the spirit and remained lying until late in the day, drunk with unspeakable wonders.'

I lifted a glass of wine to that!

When I meditated, I listened for Adrian and Christophe. *Ring the bells,* Christophe said. *Finish what we started.* Adrian spoke above his loom, urging me to study more.

And we spoke in both our languages, with words that sent insistent tongues between my thighs, around the tips of my breasts.

I established the bell tower as my place to meditate. There I could look out over the woodland on one side, towards the city of Brussels on the other. Over the horizon, to the south, was where my lovers could be, touching me from afar. I reached towards them, hoping they would also feel my touch and share my delight.

When presented with a choice of communal tasks, I immediately chose bell-ringing. Christophe's dedication to that vocation became mine. I improvised as I tried to capture the chimes of the Harelle on the simple set of bells.

Think of the cry for justice and for action ... *Haro! Haro!* I shouted it as I rang. Think of the draper calling people into the streets, the closure of the city gates, merriment in mansion basements.

Haro! Haro!

Some sisters complained about my discordant bell-ringing, while others praised it for keeping them alert.

But something was missing, a beat or a cadence. Could it be the carnal element between me and the two young men, which brought on the rough music and the bonding?

For this, a few beguines had turned to their sisters, and I tried this too.

*

It happens sometimes that one never finds two creatures who are of one spirit in one realm, but when it happens by chance that these two creatures find each other, and cannot hide themselves,

and if they then want to do so, they cannot ... Such people have
a great need to be on their guard ...

This passage from Margeurite Porete jarred me every time I read it. Porete was a favourite among the sisters, coming close to Bloemardine.

But while Bloemardine died of natural causes in 1336 at an advanced age, Marguerite Porete burned at the stake. She was an educated woman who wandered about, expounded heretical views, published a book of them and got into trouble.

I shivered when I saw the similarities to myself. Could I meet the same end? Beguines have faced persecution, with mass burnings at Narbonne. Then they've been tolerated, and persecuted again.

Though I had no intention of producing a screed like Marguerite's, I was already writing accounts of my travels and travails and thoughts. I would not be a bell without a tongue.

Marguerite seemed a peaceful soul. While she refused to withdraw to a beguinage, she never took part in disorderly multitudes. I believed that life was behind me as well.

When I read Porete's passage about the two souls who are bound together, a word came to me: *entwined.* I thought immediately of my two young men. Could more than two souls become entwined?

Now I had a name for what had happened. How could such an *entwinement* persist over distance?

If Adrian and Christophe were alive, could they still haunt me? If they were indeed dead, did I feel their ghosts? When I heard their thoughts and felt them entwined with me, did it mean we were together on another plane of existence?

I spoke to other beguines about this, leaving out the details of our first night together. One suggested this bonding can be forged in 'turbulent and tender times'.

But she cautioned me. 'Beware ... Your soul can be captured in hatred as well as love. This has happened to me.' She added, 'I came here to escape it.'

But I came here to seek it.

I watched seasons pass over the landscape from my vantage

point in the bell tower. Even in the winter, I stayed up there, wrapped myself in blankets. My reveries warmed me more than my flasks of hot infusions.

I was drifting in a boat down the canals of Ghent with Christophe and Adrian as white blossoms fell upon us. We found the hidden garden, where we knew entwinement again.

*

Like the sisters in Ghent, we also taught reading and writing among the city's poor. Our lessons were basic, our words scratched on slates or wax tablets, but we incorporated philosophy and debate into them. We urged our pupils, young and old, to think for themselves.

Bloemardine had the status of a local heroine in Brussels, and several groups had sprung up to engage with the ideas of this long-dead mystic. They appealed to people of all stations.

During the Harelle the poor stood up for themselves, taking direction from no one. They were neither stupid animals nor voracious wild beasts, as members of my family believed. And now I found myself among artisans, weavers and street hawkers as they considered the implications of 'seraphic love'. With so little love and pleasure in their own world, these ideas offered an inspiration the Church could never approach.

This attracted the attention of the Inquisition, which launched attacks on 'Bloemardine's heresy'. They came poking about our beguinage, and stuck their snouts about the streets of Brussels.

When I went into the town to teach lessons, I saw the inquisitors striding forth, expecting everyone to quiver with fear.

Instead, children threw rocks at them. Old folks and working men and mothers also followed them, singing songs and laughing.

*

Then Pierre d'Ailly, the Bishop of Cambrai, ordered our house closed down and the property handed to Dominicans. Other beguinages met a similar fate.

We dismantled our tapestry workshops and transported the materials and tools elsewhere. I would have burned the whole place down in order to keep it out of the greedy grasp of the

Dominicans. I raged and raged, and my memories of the Harelle became strong again.

I had turned to mysticism when I believed it impossible to change the world. I aimed to increase my knowledge and live a simple life. But as long as the Church and its Inquisition reigned, the spiritual life will offer no way out.

Some women accepted transfer to an approved nunnery. Others went back to their families, perhaps making meagre livelihoods as spinsters. I no longer had a family, though.

But help came from those who possessed very little. The artisans and weavers we had been tutoring helped some of us in turn. They took us into their homes. And we helped by bringing our looms and valuable tapestries with us, which aided their trade.

I joined Henryk and Adele and their three children, the little darlings who had been at the centre of the stone-throwing gangs that followed the inquisitors. I had been accustomed to my austere but solitary room at the beguinage, so I needed to adjust to some extremely close companionship.

My hosts introduced me to spiritual groups that were meeting in the city. I met the man known as Giles of Cantèr, who had formed a group called *Homines Intelligentiae* or Men of Understanding, along with William of Hildernissen. And this group included *women* of understanding.

Our teacher Giles preached of an age of the Holy Spirit, where the Scriptures will lose their relevance, and the conventional 'truths' proved false. The Church's doctrines of poverty, chastity and obedience belonged to the old Dark Age.

'Farewell to virtues', as Margeurite Porete wrote.

While my life as a beguine had been devoted to simplicity and 'voluntary poverty', these people had no time for that.

'We already live in poverty,' said Adele, a petite sharp-tongued woman. 'There is nothing *voluntary* about it. We have no need for purification and self-denial to become close to God; anyone who is poor is already close as can be. We claim our spiritual liberty now. The only purgatory is the poverty we live in.'

As for Giles . . . he was a peculiar man. He once ran down a road, completely naked, while carrying a plate of meat on his head to give to a pauper. He liked his wine, and when he had enough of that he would also take his clothes off.

I got tired of it, I must admit. 'Giles, please! I have seen enough of you.'

But another time when our group had enjoyed drink and stimulating discussion together, we *all* took our clothes off. It just felt like the right thing to do.

Many women in the group first fell in love with Giles, though I have to say he wasn't much to look at. He had a way of making love that he claimed was like Adam and Eve. Pah! I don't know about that. He was very good at it though, and knew how to give a woman pleasure. It went on and on, without him spending himself, and there was no need to worry about pregnancy if it wasn't desired.

*

But Giles was at least sixty and it wasn't long before he died. This forced us to change. We were, after all, seeking our own illumination, not following one man. The other founder, William of Hildernissen, a less flamboyant sort, did not want to inherit Giles's role. He proposed that we take it in turn to prepare a talk for each meeting.

We met outside the city walls of Brussels in a tower belonging to an alderman. This meeting room was much more comfortable than Giles's hovel. On a clear night we could see the stars through the windows. Our host placed cushions about on the floor, and we lounged on those rather than sitting in chairs. It was the 'eastern fashion', he claimed.

At this time, new members were arriving, younger people who would have grown restless listening to Giles preach. There was Matthys, a headstrong youth who constantly demanded 'action' as well as contemplation. Sometimes I wanted to slap him, but I grew fond of him as well. I met Jehanne, a young woman from the south who had worked in the vineyards and spent time in prison for some sexual indiscretion.

Such 'indiscretions' became an important topic. Giles had spoken about the sexual act as 'the pleasure of Paradise', a fleshly way to embrace the divine. We spoke frankly about this.

Finally, I told everyone about my adventures in the Harelle with Adrian and Christophe, which resulted in my only experience of mystical union.

I suggested that spiritual love could not exist without carnal love, just as we could not exist without eating and drinking. Such pleasures bring us into a union with all that is alive. God resides in the pleasures of nature, not in the authority that condemns them. These sentiments weren't far from what Bloemardine's imagery expressed, but we meant it much more concretely.

'Sensual pleasure should take the place of baptism,' said Adele, and we lifted glasses to that. Time to become drunk with 'unspeakable wonders'.

Discussion turned towards public affairs and the price of bread as often as spiritual matters. We mocked and disparaged all authority. I started to feel as if I had come in a circle back to the concerns of the Harelle.

As we made ourselves comfortable on the alderman's cushions, talk turned to banter and ultimately to more touch, invoking my 'Holy Trinity' with Christophe and Adrian. With the erotic explorations of the group in full swing, I tried to repeat that experience in various combinations.

Sometimes the invisible cords that bound me to the two men from my past pulled tighter, and I felt their vital pulse. Something had to happen, something I needed to do ... But always, I fell short of that.

When it was my turn to give a lecture, my talk naturally centred on 'entwinement'. I suggested that bonds may be forged in the heat of battle, the light of pleasure, or even in anger. We become entwined in ways we don't understand, and feel the effect of each other's actions in mysterious ways.

'Notes from afar reverberate in my ears, in my heart. It is a breath, a motion which I yearn to complete. It's a sensual impetus that works from a distance. Maybe this happens more than we realise, but the possibilities pass us by unless we become conscious of it and strengthen its effects.'

Stefan, a reserved man new to the group, spoke up for the first time. 'Perhaps we can draw on this capacity to enable us to communicate over long distances.'

'Yes,' I agreed. Could there be a practical use for such a mysterious process? 'It took so long to find out what was happening in Paris during the Harelle. Most of the time we didn't know what anyone was doing. We could use this *entwinement* to communicate.'

Matthys, who often dismissed our more inward-looking concerns, perked up. 'We can use this to outwit the Inquisition, and smash it once and for all.'

This sent Stefan into a long dissertation. He recounted an exposition called *De Luce* . . . 'On Light'. Written by a monk called Grosseteste, this study proposed that the universe started with a big explosion. 'If the fabric of the universe originated in this explosion, we are all cut from the same cloth,' he said. 'We only need to uncover our common threads.'

'Porete has written about a similar idea,' I suggested. 'She described how two souls that are united on one plane will recognise each other on another, and they can't hide from each other.'

'We wouldn't have "common threads" with *everybody*,' objected Matthys. 'Not with the people who persecute us!'

William listened to all this quietly, then said, 'To say the universe originated with an explosion contradicts the precept that God created the universe.'

'So what if it does?' Stefan stood up and paced about. 'And why say there is only one universe? There could be many universes. That's not even a new idea. It was banned by the Pope over a century ago, which is all the more reason we should talk about it now.'

Then a dozen arguments exploded. Even among the heretics, you will find more heresy. We talked and contemplated, debated and pontificated. Our discussion ranged to alchemy and attempts to grasp the physical universe. Both the sensual and mystical dimension flowed from this as normally as water runs downhill in a stream.

*

Then the Inquisition arrested William, and took him to Cambrai to appear before Henri of Selles. Pierre d'Ailly was continuing his mission to 'extirpate the remains of the nefarious heresy' and he had appointed Henri to investigate our group.

I was astonished to hear that William would be on trial alongside Giles, a dead man. Giles would've found that funny.

But there was nothing to laugh at when they took Adele and Henryk to Cambrai. I was left with the children. To them I became known as Grandmother Seraphine, though their own grandparents were long dead.

I wondered why the Inquisition didn't take me, while they took my hosts. Perhaps the inquisitors decided that leaving me with the children would be punishment enough. I'd been a decent teacher for the little devils. I could indeed sit them down and teach them letters for an hour or so. But to pay attention to their constant mischief all day and night was another thing entirely.

Fortunately, others in our group helped. Matthys showed a surprising talent for entertaining children and getting them to do what they should. Jehanne finally made arrangements for the children to stay with Adele's relatives in Tournai and accompanied them on their journey.

Then the house was quiet, save for Matthys sitting around with a flask of mead, muttering darkly.

'We wait for them to take us, too. We have to do more. The Inquisition has held people in thrall for years. We must break their power, show they're vulnerable.'

'And how are they vulnerable?'

'They are human. They want us to believe they represent the divine when they trample it under their boots. But an inquisitor can die like any human being. When they come sniffing around here again, they'll get the reception they deserve. And I don't mean a few pebbles thrown by children.'

*

I didn't see Matthys for a while. Word came later from Cambrai that William had recanted. This earned him a relatively mild sentence: three years in prison, followed by banishment from Brussels.

I always liked William, though he was more sedate than the rest of us. I didn't want to think he could betray us. I hated the thought that I could do the same under torture, so I asked a wise woman to concoct a poison to take if I was seized.

I still have this tiny vial of poison though I hope I will never have to use it, now that we live in Bohemia.

Perhaps William offered a long account of Giles's habits. That would have given the inquisitors a lot to chew on, and they couldn't harm a corpse.

A sister called around, an old beguine who had associates in Cambrai. She told us that Henri of Selles was seen on the road to Brussels.

*

Then they took me. I was at the market. And silly fool that I was, I'd left my poison at home.

I don't like to think about those days now. But if I close my eyes they could be with me in an instant.

They kept me alone in a cell. Would they remember me from the Harelle? Did William say anything about me?

If they questioned me, I could tell them more about Giles running about with a plate of meat on his head. Tell them how he slept with every woman in the group, and every man too.

I waited to be tortured. Yes, I'd say it was all Giles's doing. He claimed to be a prophet and he bewitched us. Giles would be proud. I would quote at length from Bloemardine. Her books have been passed around Brussels for over a century and they haven't even been banned.

I journeyed inwards to find Adrian and Christophe, and the parts of myself still entwined with them. I heard the chiming bells that called for freedom, and the steady clicking of looms that cautioned me to stay patient and think. I tried to sleep. Memories of Rouen filled my dreams . . .

The scent of grilled fish at the market on an overcast summer day. Adrian in discussion with a beghard preacher, Christophe laughing at them both. A young blond boy, who looked like Adrian.

Then the three of us gliding down the canal in Ghent; autumn leaves fall past my face, a yellow one settles on Adrian's hair.

That was where I tried to keep my thoughts, and myself.

The inquisitors didn't always seem sure what to do with me. They brought food. They would ask questions. Do you regard the sex act as a sinless 'pleasure of Paradise'? What *is* your concept of sin, do you deny the authority of the Church? What infernal methods do you have of spreading your beliefs?

I gave them lengthy, rambling and ultimately harmless comments about Giles and Bloemardine. As I spoke, I listened again for Christophe's riotous carillon. *Infernal methods*. Mere thoughts would betray me as much as any words. They would show on my face. Exploding universes, entwinement ... desire and designs smeared across boundaries in a heightening of heresy.

No, no ... let the mad clang of bells drive all that from my mind as I talked and talked about absolute nonsense.

Then they asked about Stefan.

He's not from Brussels, I told them. He only came to a couple of meetings. He said he'd heard about us in a tavern. Is that where you heard about us too?

Then they'd be called from my cell, and I was left for another day.

They didn't appear at all for some uncountable time. I was parched with thirst, empty with hunger. The worst was when I actually welcomed the sight of my gaoler.

I was told to go. There was no trial, but I was banished from Brussels.

So I eventually made my way to Tournai to join Jehanne and the children.

*

Adele and Henryk had been released too. I found them in Tournai. They seemed shrunken and subdued, but still determined. I was confused by our relative good fortune, once they had dealt with William. Perhaps our alderman had intervened, or the authorities wanted to avoid an outbreak of disturbances in Brussels. Perhaps.

'Have you heard anything from Matthys? Did they arrest him too?'

'Matthys has disappeared,' said Henryk. 'And we've heard that someone tried to kill Henri of Selles as he crossed a ford. *Unsuccessfully*, I'd add. Whether the two have any connection, I can't say.'

Matthys, an assassin? He seemed to be more mouth than anything else, but perhaps I was wrong.

'And what of others? What about that odd Stefan, with his theories of the universe? The inquisitors were very interested in him.'

No sign of him either.

We tried to find out more. None of our 'spies' picked up anything. Not Hilde the baker who had a shop near the Cambrai court and prison, nor the man who washes the floors at the Brussels gaol. The alderman could provide no information.

I spent a lot of time walking about Tournai, through the streets and the marketplace. I was happy to be living in a French-speaking town, though they spoke a confusing Picard dialect. The Czechs didn't understand much of it either when we came to Bohemia, which was why they called us Pikarts.

Though many beguinages had closed, there were a still a few small houses where unmarried women worked on tapestries or taught a mixture of rich and poor students. A dissident family here or there . . . Like-minded people lived in this city too. A new city, a new life. We tried to make the best of it.

But then, in my wanderings I sensed people following me. A movement as I turned, an unknown face that appeared with too much regularity.

No friendly aldermen offered meeting places where we could see the stars. New groups formed, meeting in the woods. Always, we were looking over our shoulders. No, we weren't in Brussels any more.

If the Inquisition prosecuted us again, we would face the stake as unrepentant heretics. Chimes rang in my ears, warning chimes. The sound of looms urged me: go, go, go.

Then the word came, passed from traveller to traveller, to the dissenters of Tournai. Matthys had fled to Prague, a place where reform livened the air.

His message: join me in Bohemia.

*

A tongueless bell should not make a noise, but I could swear its ringing enters my heart, with much more power than mere sound. It reaches inside and squeezes. I hear it with my entire body.

My morning lethargy dissolves in its wake. Finally I'm out, walking with my friends. The streets are quiet, too quiet. Vaclav's tavern is still closed. Less activity at the Horse Market.

Soon we approach our Lady of the Snows.

No one is around there now.

'Zelivsky must be spreading rumours to get more people to his sermons,' I say. But look, the courtyard and the surrounding roads are littered with debris, the leavings of struggle and scuffle. A ripped piece of parchment. A child's boot, an officer's cudgel. And a battle-flail, a short club with a chain and a spiked striking head. Many of these have been appearing around the city in the past months.

I pick up the parchment. There are only a few marks on it. I could use it.

I point to the flail. 'One of you should take this . . .'

Then I laugh. 'Sign of my advanced years, eh? I take a piece of parchment, and leave the flail to the likes of you.'

Now I hear distant noise. From the Horse Market, and the New Town Hall. Random shouts of commotion. A cheer.

People are running towards us. 'We need help at the New Town Hall! Go there! Our prisoners are free. The king's councillors have been thrown out the window!'

'Who? Out the window . . .' I pick up my cane and get ready to move again.

It's happening, I think, it's happening!

Then a deep tolling sounds from the empty church. It's so loud and sudden my companions jump. I jump as best as I can, with joy. The tolling quickens. The rhythms stop, start and increase, a dam of sound bursting open. They make music I've never heard from Our Lady of Snows, I haven't heard this cadence in Bohemia and I haven't heard it since 1382, when the humble people proclaimed their triumph in Rouen.

'We have to go in,' I say to my companions.

'Seraphine, no . . .' Though they are startled by the sudden ringing, my friends have other things on their minds. Of course, I'd feel the same way.

'Yes, you go on to the Town Hall. I'll join you. Whatever's happening will happen, regardless of what an old woman like me does.'

I make a shooing motion with my hands. 'Go! I'll be fine. I can look after myself.'

With a glance backwards, they hurry away. Then I go inside and ascend the steps.

How long did Christophe pull on those ropes, ringing his composition into the silent air? Now its tumult carries over the distance, and over the years. *Entwinement.*

I clutch the banister as I make my way up the steps. The cadence vibrates through my arm. The notes radiate from my core, pushing me upwards.

I make it to the top of the bell tower. Yes, the empty ropes are swinging. The bells continue ringing, their notes rising and rising, a cross-rhythm starts. It's enough to dance to, enough to make me cry.

'Adrian . . . Christophe . . .' Their names entwine with my tongue.

Is it a peal of triumph, or a warning that the king's army has entered our city again? Perhaps it is both. I look out over Prague as the bell sings in my head. I see the crowds around the New Town Hall. Is that splash of colour the robe of a councillor on the ground, one of the men installed by the king, gaolers of our prisoners in the dungeon? I try to see more, see if troops are moving. I look over the river, find the jagged teeth of the Hungry Wall. I shake my fist at the wall and laugh.

When the bells start to subside, the presence of my two lovers still animates the air. They will always be with me. We are entwined.

I turn and make my way down the stairs. Slow, but methodical, I'm soon on solid ground. I get my cane going double-time as I head to the New Town Hall, to join my comrades and see what I can find.

Ω

The fact that the Inquisition seemed initially to treat this group of heretics with relative leniency (three-year prison sentences, banishment) has been noted by a few historians. Perhaps they were helped by some of their influential members, such as the alderman in Brussels mentioned in this account. Perhaps it was the threat of large-scale civil disorder in Flanders, an industrially advanced area even in the Middle Ages, with an active and discontented workforce. The assassination attempt on Henri of Selles could have been seen as a portent of things to come unless the group was excised in a more surgical and strategic manner.

But it was the Church's interest in the movement's beliefs that is of most note. From Seraphine Duplexis's account it appears that they may have stumbled upon the secrets of quantum entanglement – what she calls entwinement. Her connection with Adrian and Christophe seems close to what Einstein called 'spooky action at a distance'. One member, Stefan, expounded both Grosseteste's theory of the Big Bang and the possibility of multiple universes. Is it significant that he doesn't turn up in Tournai or in Prague? Did he disappear into the clutches of the Inquisition? With such ideas, was he the one they really wanted to find, with the others just so much heretical flotsam and jetsam?

And was this why Seraphine Duplexis's writing ended up deep in the Vaults at the Vatican? Or was it simply the Church's fear of divergent thought, of heterodoxy, of heresy? As her friend Matthys said of the strong arm of the Church, the Inquisition, 'They want us to believe they represent the divine when they trample it under their boots.'

1541

When the conquistador Francisco Pizarro conquered the Inca Empire in the early 1530s, the primary interest of the Spanish was the vast wealth of precious metals they found. But close behind that was the urge to convert the heathen native people to the Catholic faith – and that meant that all traces of their own beliefs and traditions must be destroyed.

The two interests coincided in this account from what would shortly be called Peru. An Inca noble was believed to hold the secret of hidden riches, and the Church was called on to draw that knowledge from him whilst, in the process, hoping to lead him to the Christian faith.

The Sky Weeps, the Earth Quakes

Jaine Fenn

1 August 1541
Such irony: whilst most natives are simple rustics, and embrace the True Faith with childlike ease, it is those who once held high rank who show the greatest reluctance to accept the Word of God. The mission is increasingly forced to resort to the techniques of the Inquisition to save them, much to my unease.

Even so, some still resist. Their fortitude might be admirable were it not so misguided. Perhaps it stems from the assumption of power; if they believe their faith to be right, they can continue to believe themselves wronged. But their world is ours now, and their resistance only causes unnecessary pain – and in the end, Damnation.

*

Luisa reaches out to the tiny bird. So intent is the jewelled creature on the scarlet bell-flower it sips from, it gives no sign of knowing she is there. She thinks to touch it. Then, as though called by a voice she cannot hear, it darts away, silent and smooth.

Is that how angels fly? She wonders, hand still outstretched. Do the heathens of New Castile have such beings as angels in their twisted faith? Her brother might know. But she has no intention of asking him.

*

3 August 1541
We have a new arrival.

He was brought to the garrison five days after my brethren left to take the message of salvation farther up the valley. The soldiers accompanying the prisoner were impatient to release their burden to me and be gone themselves, in their case to further plunder and pillage.

The man showed signs of harsh treatment: old bruises and brands and a dislocated shoulder – no doubt a result of an encounter with the strappado. He was perhaps two decades older than me and had, I think, already been thin before his current privations were visited upon him. Yet his gaze was not downcast. He regarded me only for a moment, as the letter authorising his transfer was handed over, then turned his eyes to the shining terraces that skirt the peaks around us.

When I looked for one of our interpreters the captain said, 'He speaks passable Spanish, Brother.' Then he added, 'He is quite the talker, when you get him going. Full of wisdom.' He spat to show what he thought of the natives' wisdom. 'My men dubbed him Solomon.'

'Why has he been brought back down the valley to me?' I asked. The prisoner's gaze was still raised, as though his rags and wounds and shackles meant nothing to him. It recalled the arrogant stance of my father.

The soldier nodded to the letter in my hand, sealed, I now saw, with the crest of Father de la Cruz himself. 'These are your orders.' Then he appeared to remember himself. 'I am sorry, Brother, I meant these are the instructions from your fellow missionaries.'

I had the guards take the prisoner to a cell; we have several empty ones now. With the comparison to my earthly father and the guard captain's comments fresh in my mind, I chose one of the more odious of our windowless holes.

The letter stated my charge was a noble, named Apac Kunya in the heathen tongue, and that he knew of riches hidden to all but the highest and most privileged of his people. Attempts had been made to gain knowledge from him by 'all the usual methods' to no avail.

I heard the voice of my superior in the next phrase. 'He is happy enough to talk, but insists on picking the subject. It seemed appropriate to send him to one who prizes all knowledge indiscriminately.' The letter concluded, 'This man is of value: we give him to your care in the hope that your softer methods may succeed where firmer ones have failed. By the time we return to the garrison on our way back to Cuzco we hope that you will have gained the knowledge we require. Brother Ruiz, as you appear immune to the subtleties of politics and diplomacy, let me make the situation clear: this is your last chance to redeem yourself.'

*

'Is it true?'

The garrison commander does not look up when Luisa walks in. His shoulders twitch, then he puts down his quill slowly. Finally he meets her eyes. 'Is what true, señorita?' Captain Rodriguez does not much like her, but she does not much care, provided he shows her the respect due her gender and status. It was not as though she asked to come to this godforsaken place.

She steps closer to his desk. 'The rumours brought by those soldiers. About Senora de Salazar.'

'Those soldiers being the men escorting the prisoner?'

'Of course.' As though they have had any other visitors this week. 'I heard one of them telling Corporal Moreno that Commissar de Salazar's wife died in childbirth.'

The commander purses his lips. 'It is possible. I understand the poor lady has not been blessed with good fortune in such matters.'

Luisa schools her expression. She is sure the commander knows the truth, even if he would never say it to her face. 'No,' she says. 'She has not. So I take it you have had no official word regarding this unfortunate possibility?'

'I have not. And to be honest, Señorita Ruiz, news of such nature is unlikely to cross my desk.'

She smiles, though it is an effort. 'If it does, I would appreciate it if you let me know. We receive so little news of interest here.'

'Such is the nature of living in recently conquered lands.' The commander's words are brusque, but his tone soft. 'I will endeavour to keep you informed, should I hear more.'

*

3 August 1541 cont'd

When Father de la Cruz oversaw interrogations, he insisted on having a guard present, even with prisoners barely capable of lifting their heads. Now that I alone enforce the will of God in the garrison, perhaps I should continue the tradition. Yet this new native was sent to me for my 'softer methods', so I chose to exclude the corporal from the cell, although he insisted on waiting outside in case the prisoner, shackled and quiescent though he was, tried to make trouble. In truth, I hold out little hope that I may succeed where others failed; yet the final words of my superior's letter hang over me.

Away from the burning sun, in the rush-lit gloom, the prisoner finally looked up at me from his place on the floor. I found his gaze unnerving, and began to speak before I had fully gathered my thoughts. 'Are you Inca?'

He did not answer at once, so I opened my mouth to repeat my question, in case he had not understood.

'Not a ruler, no. My role was *amautas*.' His voice was hoarse, his pronunciation erratic.

I asked him to repeat that last word.

'*Amautas*.' He spoke slowly. 'In your tongue, is no match. Perhaps nearest is seeker of knowledge. Like you.'

'I am a priest, a servant of the One True God.'

He nodded, then winced as the motion set off some injury. 'And a seeker of knowledge. It is good to meet you, at the last.'

'You have heard of me?' This was not possible; no doubt his incomplete knowledge of our language had let him down.

'I knew I was to meet you.'

'I doubt that. But if it is true, then you know why you were sent here.'

'To tell you secrets I would not tell by torture.' His odd tone unnerved me; for a moment I thought I heard mockery in it.

'Quite so. Reason may persuade men where force fails, if they have the wit and intellect to appreciate it.'

'This is . . . flattery, yes?'

He *was* mocking me! I wished I had a guard after all, to strike him for his insolence. 'Not flattery, heathen: logic. Do you know the word?'

'I have heard it.'

'Then you also know that you are doomed, as things stand.'

'Such is true.' The thought did not appear to concern him.

'Yet you may save yourself, if you cooperate.'

'As my Emperor did, then?'

I cursed myself for giving him that opening. Here, my private journal, I may confess that the elder Pizarro's treachery against the last free Inca ruler still disturbs me. But I could not admit that before this man. 'I am not here to discuss the past. Nor am I a soldier, who sees force as the only way.'

'Yet you serve the soldiers' cause, to take from us the tears of the Sun.'

'What I serve is a higher power, the highest power in the universe!' I was angry, yet shamed too. This was not the way things should go. 'We will continue our discussion later.'

With that I left, taking the light with me.

*

'So Father de la Cruz believes you will succeed where he failed?'

Luisa does not mean to sound disparaging, but Gabriel was never the most favoured member of the mission. And now he is stuck here, away from the action, sent down the valley from the frontier as she was sent up from Cuzco. Perhaps he is being punished too.

Her brother speaks tightly, looking up at the ridge of the Cordilleras, black and featureless now the sun has dipped behind them. 'Yes. Sometimes the head and heart may triumph over baser instincts.'

Luisa can't help herself: she snorts. But maybe it is time to speak of matters left unsaid too long, alone in the pure, fragrant evening. If God prompted them both to come out to the court-yard as evening fell – their first time alone outside the confessional in the two weeks since she arrived – then she should use the chance to mend things between them.

As she opens her mouth, a wisp of smoke drifts up from the ridge to the north. It thickens quickly, tarnishing the gold and turquoise sky. Luisa shivers, knowing what the smoke signifies.

Out of the corner of her eye she sees Gabriel's head turn.

'Luisa . . .' he begins, and she hears sympathy in his tone when, suddenly, she wants condemnation, something to fight.

'It's getting cold.' She turns to go, cutting across his words.

'Luisa, you should not be here.' His gentleness burns her.

As she hurries away one hand goes to her belly. 'No,' she mutters, 'I should not.'

*

4 August 1541

I should have heeded the warnings about this prisoner, and been less hasty. But, reviewing our first conversation as I arose this morning, I recalled his expression when the light was removed from his cell. Uncertainty crossed that haughty, swarthy face as darkness fell. Perhaps base bargaining might work after all. I left him alone, in the dark, for most of the day, only visiting his cell as evening approached.

Apac Kunya blinked when I opened the door, looking beyond me to the slender thread of golden daylight as though returning from some deep meditation. I ordered the corporal to wait outside once he had put the rush light on its shelf, and placed myself in front of the door. The cell was taking on that vile and familiar smell of occupation, a mixture of ordure and festering wounds.

For a while neither of us spoke. When I felt there had been enough silence, I asked, 'Can you conceive of any method by which we might extract from you the information we seek?'

I had given my opening sally much thought, and the prisoner now returned the favour. While I waited for his answer I heard distant male laughter, and the cry of a bird overhead. Finally he said, 'I cannot.'

'Then I wonder why you are here.'

He lifted his hands, making his shackles clink. 'No other choice.'

I sighed, striving to keep the sound light and natural. 'Then it appears we have nothing to say to each other.' I reached for the light, and began to turn.

'Wait.' It did not sound like an entreaty, nor an order; more a suggestion.

I paused. 'So you think we may converse meaningfully?'

'All choice is yours. All power is yours. But yes, I think we may.'

I put the light back and turned to face him again. Then, on impulse, I squatted, with my back against the door, so I was no longer looking down on him. 'What should we discuss?'

'Instead of information, knowledge. If I see the difference right.'

'What do you believe it to be?'

'Information serves purposes, is a way to reach an end. Knowledge is its own value.'

I nodded. It was an accurate summation, however poorly phrased. 'And where does faith fit in?' I had questioned the servants about his claim to be an '*amautas*' without getting a satisfactory answer, but the heathen religion is intertwined with their society to an alarming extent so perhaps he thought himself a priest.

'That is a hard question. Maybe not a good question, given our differences.'

He was right about that. But there was one question I wanted answered. 'True, but I would like to know why your people worship gold.'

'I may ask the same of you.'

It took me a moment to realise what he meant. Then I was angry. 'How dare you! We worship God, not Mammon!'

'Yet your love of gold brings us to this.' He raised a manacled hand to indicate the dingy cell.

I could feel heat rising, a passion to defend my Faith. I took a breath before replying. 'I will not deny the avarice of those who first discovered your land, nor the brutality of some of their actions. But we – my brothers in Christ – see the hand of God in this, for our actions have allowed your people to receive His message.'

He nodded, as though I gave the answer he expected. This annoyed me, so I asked, 'What power do *you* see at work here? If your gods were so mighty, how come they are now thrown down?'

'It is . . . fate. The rightness of all.'

'You agree with what is happening to your land?'

'No. But it is as it was foretold.'

My heart sank. 'By your priests presumably?' And so the Pagan justifies their defeat!

'Yes. You do not believe in foretelling?'

'In prophecy, you mean? Of course not.' But I spoke without thought, without the knowledge I pride myself on, for the Bible is full of prophecy. 'You still have not answered my question. If you do not worship gold, you do at least revere it?'

'We revere it, yes. That is the word.'

'Tell me more.'

I will not record our entire conversation, for it became esoteric. This native grasps concepts quickly, and understands distinctions only an educated man can. Our talk brought pleasure to me, a pleasure of the intellect which has been lacking since we came to this place. What the conversation did not do was bring me any closer to those secret hoards my countrymen are so set on finding.

*

My dearest E,

I do not know if this letter will reach you, for it relies on the promises of low men – and though those I entrust with it cannot read or write, it is still best we avoid names. Firstly, I forgive you. I understand why I could not stay in Cuzco and I know you were bowing to pressure from your superiors when you sent me away. But you know that, you said as much at our parting.

The reason I write now is that I have heard news of your wife, that she has passed away. Tell me please, is it true? She never gave you the son you craved. Nor did she love you as you deserve to be loved.

We sinned, may the Lord forgive us for that, but I can give you those children, many sons, healthy and strong.

You know that we should be together, you know this in your heart.

My fate is in your hands,

L

*

5 August 1541

Today's conversations with Apac Kunya followed on from yesterday's. He spoke freely of the learning of his people, which took on the learning of those tribes they conquered before they themselves fell to our conquest. He also hinted at older wisdom. His people tell of a great flood, and while we know that this catastrophe was the will of the Lord, and washed away iniquity, Apac Kunya says the deluge also washed away knowledge, knowledge he and others like him have worked hard to regain since.

Perhaps this talk should make me uneasy, yet we in the civilised world revere the knowledge of the Greeks and Romans, who were Heathen peoples.

We touched upon religion, and he expressed interest in the nature of the Trinity, how one God can be three entities, and how the Holy Virgin fits into our beliefs. I did my best to enlighten him.

When I departed his cell this evening I left a fresh rush light.

Still, I must be wary, and not let his words distract me from the task I have been set, for I find myself admiring this man. Not in the way I have confessed of elsewhere in this journal, not that. It is more that he reminds me of the kind of father I would wish to have.

*

It first occurs in the garrison chapel, as she is about to pray. For a moment Luisa thinks she is being struck down, punished for her sin. Her heart races and weakness shoots through her limbs. Then pain, like a kick in the guts. She reaches for the altar rail, gasping in the thin cold air. But her mind is turned to the divine, and in her head she remains calm, as her lips forms the words *Blessed Virgin, take pity on me*, repeating them over and over.

The pain abates. She is kneeling now, and her knuckles on the rail are white, but the spasm has passed. Already warmth flows back into her body.

Then, so gentle she is not sure at first, there is movement within, and she knows all will be well. She smiles, and changes her prayer, even as her baby kicks again. *Let my son be born healthy and strong, and into the house of his father.*

*

12 August 1541

I was right to cultivate this native's friendship!

For the last week we have talked of many matters: history, natural philosophy, medicine and the transmission of knowledge. I cannot remember such enjoyable discourse; sometimes I almost forget that this man is a proud and damned Heathen.

But in less than a month the mission is due to return, and Father de La Cruz will be unimpressed with treatises on the natives' learning.

Today we finally reached materially fruitful ground. We had been discussing faith, a subject I feel compelled to return to, for I truly wish to save Apac Kunya's soul: it grieves me that such an intellect remains impervious to the highest wisdom. I made what I thought to be a conclusive case for the current situation being God's will, but he shook his head – with less pain now, for I have procured medicine for him – and said again that we overthrew his people because it was foretold and, knowing it to be the will of their heathen gods, they acted against sense and welcomed the Pizarro brothers when they should have killed them. I was about to rebuff this argument when he said, 'Do you know of the Man of Gold?'

For a moment I forgot to breathe, then I mastered myself and said, 'It is a common legend.' In the glitter of his eyes I saw that he knew as well as I that this is the heart of the matter for those who hold power over us.

'It is no legend.'

'It is not?' I was proud of how light I kept my tone.

'We have talked before of how my people take on the knowledge of others. One such was a priest fleeing the hot forests of the north. He knew the secret of making the king-who-sees.'

'The king-who-sees?' Another fascinating but damned piece of knowledge, I thought.

'It is a ritual, and gold is part of it.'

Or maybe not. 'You are saying there truly is a golden man? That El Dorado exists?'

'A man made gold, yes.'

Although the foreigner's grasp of Spanish grew daily, misunderstandings still occurred, and I feared this was one of them. I had to be sure. 'So you know how to make this man of gold?'

'I know the ritual. I would teach it you.'

'You would? Why?'

'Although fate makes us enemies, you are a man of learning, and learning must be saved. If I do not pass this on then it will be gone from the world.'

I admit I was flattered. 'So, in broad terms, what is involved in the ritual of El— of the king-who-sees?'

'Fasting and meditation, initially.'

Perhaps I had misunderstood after all. 'You did mention gold . . .' I was embarrassed to bring the subject up again.

'Gold dust yes. It is needed for the final part, to gain true sight.'

'But the ritual is not a way of procuring gold.' I spoke sternly, to remind him of how little he had to bargain with.

To my surprise, he smiled. Apac Kunya has a severe, though not cruel, face but it changes when he smiles. I wanted to smile back. He said, 'Not to make it fall from the sky, no. But to tell you where to find it. To become the king-who-sees is to know what is to come.'

Was he saying what I thought he was? 'Such as?'

'Anything the will is turned to.' His smile became wry. 'This power could be used, among other purposes, to locate hidden treasure. Or it could be used – was most commonly used, when we ruled – to see the future.'

At the time I dismissed his words, but since leaving him I have not been able to put them from my mind. The power of prediction would make moot the need for torture, would be a benefit above gold!

I may be being deceived, for this would not be the first time I have fallen for the lies of others. I have prayed for guidance without cease from leaving the prisoner until I took up my pen tonight. But I so want this to be true!

*

Storms are common in the mountains, though they do not always bring rain. Last night's did, and this morning the world is fresh and new. Luisa's step is light as she crosses the courtyard. Although she only came here to escape past mistakes, on a day like this she feels some love for this bleak and unforgiving land.

Halfway across the square of beaten earth she pauses, knowing she is watched. A sideways glance shows Corporal Moreno, lounging under the eaves. He is smiling at her. She hurries on, before he can call out. She gave him coin to smuggle out the letter to her lover, but gold is plentiful here and she could tell he wanted a different payment. Even in heavy skirts the swelling of her belly is becoming obvious, and he thinks her already fallen. Were it not for the iron hand of the garrison commander, she would be fair game. Under her breath she murmurs, 'Holy Mother, protect me.'

Stepping into the relative safety of the kitchen block, she decides that all men are either self-serving bastards, like the soldiers, or weak fools, like her brother.

No, not all: she recalls the face of Eduardo de Salazar, and knows that one day they will be together again.

*

16 August 1541

The first steps, Apac Kunya claims, are simple. I must eat only certain foods, in limited quantities – a discipline I am used to already – and meditate. This latter skill I thought I had, but prayer, which we have already discussed at length, is not the same, he says: in prayer the mind is caught up in the words offered to Heaven, whilst in true meditation the mind is empty, and receptive. These last three days I have kept to the regime he suggests, and have tried to cultivate this un-minded meditation he recommends.

Is what I do a sin? This Heathen still refuses to accept Jesus as his saviour, for all he admires Our Lord's teachings. Yet nothing I do – to fast, to meditate – goes against God's word, and I have seen no sign from Above that I stray.

I have, I must confess, broken out the whip again, for the first time since Brother Pedro left. Such mortification fits with what Apac Kunya tells me of the rituals of an apprentice *amautas*, and I find it eases my soul even as it pains my body.

It is possible – nay, likely – that I am deluding myself, just as the prisoner's people deluded themselves. I may know the true heart of this Heathen people through my efforts, but I doubt it will bring me the power he claims to have.

With that in mind I asked him today if, given his foresight, he knows whether my efforts will be rewarded. He has already admitted that the future is rarely a clear and certain path. The only event he has spoken of as fixed is his own death, which, he says, will come soon. Whilst I fear he may be correct, under the circumstances such an assertion requires no special powers to make.

He counselled patience, saying that as I have the aptitude, we must try.

Impatience got the better of me and I said, 'This would be easier if I knew what I worked towards!' We have no firm timetable, and Apac Kunya gives no assurances, only suggestions.

He bowed his head. 'You wish a demonstration?'

'Yes!' Was he really offering to make a firm prediction, here and now?

For some moments, Apac Kunya sat very still, eyes downcast. He raised his gaze slowly, looking past me to the rush light. I tried to dismiss my unease at his blank gaze by remembering the tricks of gypsy charlatans back in the town fairs at home. But I do not believe this man is a charlatan. Or perhaps, I do not want to believe it.

Finally he spoke, as though making a casual observation. 'Do not be here this time tomorrow.'

'What do you mean?'

'At this hour,' he frowned, then said, 'no, a little earlier: half way between noon and sunset. At that time, you should stand outside, in the courtyard, alone.'

I crossed my arms. 'Why, pray?' These were the words of a tinker who told fortunes, not a great scholar with unknown powers.

'That is all I can know, in here.' His gaze, clear again now, took in his cell.

'Is that so?' I said, getting up to go.

He nodded, not looking happy.

I fear I may have been fooled after all.

*

Luisa is surprised when her brother emerges from the cell block in the middle of the afternoon. These days he spends every hour of daylight with the savage. He starts when he sees her sitting by the well but she will not move. The soldiers are out on exercise, the day is fine but cool and she is at peace.

Gabriel hesitates under the portico, then comes towards her. His expression is odd; perhaps he wishes to talk.

She stands, and as she does so feels her son kick, hard enough to make her bend like a reed. Suddenly the earth kicks back, and she is falling. She reaches for support, but there is none. The air is still and silent but beneath her the ground bucks and heaves. She stumbles in panic, hearing Gabriel shout something about the well. She looks over her shoulder to see the stone she had been sitting on shift, tip and disappear. She can no longer stand, and drops to her knees, too numb with terror to form a prayer.

The shaking lessens, and she comes to her senses enough to cry out, 'Jesu save us!'

Finally the jolts become tremors, and then cease.

Before she can find strength to move, her brother's arms are around her, supporting her.

'It's all right, Lui, everything will be all right.' Distant cries and crashes sound as the rest of the garrison feels the after-effects of the tremor.

He has not called her Lui in years, has not spoken like that since they left Spain. All at once she is back in the family home, and when Gabriel says 'Don't cry,' she hears his younger, softer voice, speaking in the darkness, after Father had come to her. With his wife dead, she is all he has, he says . . . she jerks upright, pushing her brother away.

'Lui?'

But the long-buried memory has awoken, and she cannot stand to be touched. She stands. 'Leave me alone! I cannot bear it . . .'

'Can't bear what, Lui? It's all right, really it is. That was an earthquake, but a miracle too, you won't believe what has happened! I was told of this, well not in so many words but told nonetheless . . .'

She looks at him through her tears. He is invigorated, excited: oblivious. Always, there is some piece of knowledge, some idea, that blinds him to the truth that stares him in the face! She cuts through his prattling flow: 'Why did you bring me here?'

He pauses, rocks back. 'I . . . I did not bring you to the valley, you were sent, from Cuzco, because . . .' He can't say it, but his eyes go to her swollen belly, and in that moment she hates him. She wants to know why he insisted she come with him to New Castile, whether it was to save her from their father, or punish her for her wayward ways, but all he can do is remind her of her more recent sin.

She finishes the sentence for him. 'Because I did what is natural to man and woman. Unlike you . . .'

His face falls. 'I never have . . .' he whispers.

'In your heart, you have, and God sees that. I know how twisted you are, for all your learning.'

'Please Luisa, don't say that.'

Finally, she is getting through to him, making him *feel*, not just *think*. 'I only speak the truth. You love the truth, do you not? Well, the truth is our father is a monster – you he only *beat* – and you are a pervert, and I will not be punished for following my heart, save by God alone.' She stalks off, unsteadily. He does not call out after her.

It is only later, alone in bed, that she considers that, had she not stood to greet her brother, she would have been sitting on the wall beside the well when the earthquake hit, on the very stone that fell. He saved her life. No, that was God's hand. Her foolish brother will not acknowledge his flaws, he could not save her from their monstrous sire and now he is oblivious even to the works of the God he professes to serve, preferring instead the words of a Heathen.

*

18 August 1541
'You knew! How did you know?'

I had not planned to greet my prisoner-turned-teacher with those words, not least because I knew the answer to the question, but even this morning wonder at his prediction brimmed over in me.

'Were many hurt?' he asked in return.

'In the quake? No, only minor injuries, from a fire in the kitchen.'

'Good. I saw . . . a possible loss.'

I thought of Luisa, and the well. A happy chance, I had thought at the time before correcting myself and thanking God for sparing my sister. Had Apac Kunya seen that with his unearthly sight? 'Did you know who could have been lost, or how that might have come about?' I asked carefully.

'No. This power, my friend, it is like grasping smoke. When you reach out, you disturb the patterns. The more precision you apply, the faster the truth will fly from you.'

'And can what you see be changed?' I was willing, at least, to entertain the truth of his claim, and my mind raced with the implications.

'It was forbidden to try, for that went against the gods. But we inherited tales from those we took the power from, of how what is seen will come to pass, even if the act of trying to avoid it makes it so. We could not change the future, but we could prepare for what it brought.'

'Can you show me more? Foretellings that reach farther afield perhaps?'

'I can try. But I will need to see the sun.'

Suspicion stung my breast, though only briefly: this man had neither means nor strength to effect an escape. But nor was he in a position to make demands. 'That is not possible.'

He shrugged, his maimed shoulder rising only fractionally. 'Then I cannot demonstrate what we work towards.'

'Explain!' I demanded.

'The power I hold is tied to two material anchors: gold dust to awaken it, and the sun's light to allow it to function.'

'Heathen claptrap,' I muttered. Yet his prediction, while cryptic and vague, had come true.

'I do not claim to know why this is. Some of my peers tried to unlock the links between the world of touch and the worlds of mind and spirit. But they are all dead now. I am the last *amautas*.'

He had implied as much before, but hearing it said made me reconsider. 'Then I will indulge you. But,' I warned him sternly, 'if my indulgence gives no firm results then I will consider your first prediction to be mere fluke.'

I told the guards I wished them to check the integrity of the cell, although this building is converted from the old residences of the natives, and suffered little damage in the earthquake. The corporal gave me an odd look, but assigned a man to escort the prisoner outside.

There is one room beyond the cell, with an open doorway. As soon as Apac Kunya had clear sight of the bright courtyard beyond he tensed, like a hunting dog. When we stepped into the light he paused, and turned his face to heaven. The soldier who walked behind holding the prisoner's chains made to kick him, until I held up a hand.

Apac Kunya carried on, walking slowly now, like a man in a trance.

'Let the chain play out, and remain where you are,' I instructed the soldier, and began to walk alongside Apac Kunya. When the chain reached full stretch I murmured, 'You must stop now.'

Apac Kunya obeyed, though his face remained raised. His eyes were closed yet there was movement behind the lids, as when one dreams. His lips formed soundless words. I was reminded of the ecstasy of divine communion.

He sighed then muttered, 'Your people fight each other for the spoils of our land, brother against brother.'

Indeed they do, but he could have heard the guards outside his cell speaking of that. 'This is commonly known.'

He froze, then began murmuring again. I made out the words 'Your sister . . .'

'What of her?' I have not spoken to him of Luisa, but again, he could have heard her mentioned by the guards.

He whispered, 'She will find what she wants, soon . . . but in the end, she will get what she believes she deserves.'

Despite his vague words, to hear Luisa spoken of in this way filled me with cold dread, as though I looked down on events from a high mountain, unable to intervene as disaster unfolded. I fear he has spoken a painful truth, even if the details are not yet clear.

I was tempted to ask him further questions, but Corporal Moreno emerged from the cell block to inform me, in a voice somewhat lacking in respect, that there was nothing wrong with the prisoner's accommodation.

Back in the cell, speaking quietly to avoid curious ears, Apac Kunya told me of what I must do next if I am to become the king-who-sees.

I do not yet know whether I dare.

*

E, my love,

I know why you did not reply to my last letter; I understand. But now I must tell you of a graver matter. I fear my brother has fallen under the spell of a Heathen warlock. A corporal in the garrison has told me of allowances being made, of overhearing strange conversations. I myself witnessed from the kitchen the Heathen being given temporary liberty, and falling into a trance in the courtyard.

I tell you this not only in the hope it may convince you that I should not be in this place, but because it is my Christian duty. I have also sent a letter up the valley with a servant, to meet with the good Father who leads the mission, telling them to bring forward their return and root out this sorcery.

May the blessed Virgin protect and bless us both,

L

*

20 August 1541

As I write this two small but heavy sacks sit on my desk. I had to lie to Captain Rodriguez to borrow his keys, saying I wished to check the strong-room to ensure the share of the spoils belonging to my family was in order. He knows I have little interest in such things, but no doubt assumed my request was on Luisa's behalf.

It was strange to see so much gold in one place. Stranger still that it languishes in the dark. It stirred no greed or wonder in me, only unease at the price paid to get it.

I have no idea which soldier considers these two sacks to be his. They were easy enough to smuggle out in my robes.

As Apac Kunya instructed I have eaten a pinch of the gold dust, rolled in bread, washed down with wine in which a little more was sprinkled. I felt nothing at the time but now, two hours later, I am calm; I think I feel the change in me begin. Once I have made my record for the evening I will meditate, knowing I am one step closer to gaining the ultimate knowledge.

*

Luisa has stopped asking her brother to hear her confession. He is the only priest in the garrison, and so conducts mass and the other necessary offices. But he does so distractedly, as though his calling matters less than the Heathen prisoner who waits in the dark for him. Luisa shudders to think of what they get up to, what Gabriel will have to confess when his betters return.

Instead of talking to him, within or outside the confessional, she spends the time praying, alone.

She does not know whether her letter reached Father de la Cruz, but she prays that the might and order of the Church will return soon, to save them all.

*

22 August 1541
Soon I will take the final step.

It is past midnight, and soon the guards will leave the cell block for the night. I have eaten my last meal of bread and gold. The remaining gold dust I have transferred to a knapsack. In a few hours I will go to the cell block for the last time, and release my mentor and friend.

We will use a pool farther up the mountain, part of the natives' terrace cultivations. It is barely deep enough for me to immerse myself in, but all that matters is that I emerge from the water, washing off the gold the *amautas* spread over me with the correct words and gestures, as the sun rises above the hills. I am sure now that Apac Kunya is right, and that when he completes the ritual I will become blessed with true foresight, as he has been. And I will use it for good, as he has tried to.

Time is short. We may only have one chance.

I must put down my pen now, and clear my mind in preparation.

*

Luisa once heard that the smell of human flesh burning is like roasting pork. Now she will find out if this is true.

Father de la Cruz is with the warlock, giving the Heathen a last chance to embrace the True Faith. From her place under the portico she sees the bound man shake his head. Father de la Cruz turns away from the stake in the centre of the court-yard, his face set. As soldiers come forward to stack the last faggots on the pyre the priest approaches her seat, his expression softening.

'You did the right thing, child.' It is the gentlest speech she has ever heard from this hardest of clerics.

She is touched, but her gaze still drifts to the far side of the square, where Gabriel stands between two guards, his head lowered.

Father de la Cruz says, 'Your brother is not the first to be so beguiled.'

'What will happen to him?' The priest's zeal when his party swept into the garrison while all – or almost all – slept had surprised and alarmed her; so eager were the priests they had ridden through part of the night. Had their family been of lower status, today's pyre might have been built for two.

'He will be sent back to Spain, to face a formal hearing by our order.'

'Will he be excommunicated?' Gabriel's soul can still be saved, she is sure.

'I pray not. But if he decides to remain part of the Church he will be stripped of all rank and assigned grave and lasting penance.'

Given that the alternative is to throw himself on the 'mercy' of their father, Luisa knows what her brother will choose.

Captain Rodriguez approaches the pyre, a torch in his hand.

Luisa remembers Gabriel telling her how the Inca Emperor converted in his final moments. As well as saving his soul, he bought himself an easier death, garrotted before the fire took him.

The wood is dry, and the flames take quickly. The warlock stares straight ahead in silence as fire licks his robe.

'You do not have to watch this,' murmurs Father de la Cruz.

'I know,' she says, but if she looks away she will see only her brother, broken by his latest, most foolish, mistake. 'But I wish to see God's will done.'

The Heathen is wreathed in flame now. His hair flies up around his face, then catches fire. Still he makes no sound. A nearby soldier mutters, 'That's five you owe me,' to a comrade; no doubt the outcome of a bet.

Beyond the pyre she sees movement. Gabriel has raised his head to look at the man who entrapped him. Even from here Luisa can see that he is crying.

She looks away.

The dying warlock finally makes a sound. He strains at his bonds, moaning like an animal, the low moans barely audible over the fire's crackle. His skin is starting to blacken.

Luisa keeps her head up, but lets her gaze drop, focusing on a patch of dirt just in front of the pyre. She prays under her breath, though the words bring little comfort.

The wind changes and when the smell reaches her, she finds what she was told to be true. She presses a hand to her mouth, swallowing hard. But she will not disgrace herself, not in front of everyone. After a while the urge to vomit passes.

At a loud and splintering crack she looks up to see a dark form crash down into the pyre, sending up a shower of sparks into the darkening sky. The ropes binding the warlock to the stake have finally burnt through.

The falling body fans the flames briefly, then they die back. Luisa can watch again now there is nothing obviously human in the pyre, nothing still alive. In fact, she cannot look away.

Finally, with the first stars coming out in the east and the western sky fading to old gold, the observers begin to move off. As Luisa prepares to stand she sees Gabriel approaching, still under guard. The hurt and accusation in his eyes make her want to look away, but she must not. Instead she raises her chin and says, 'I will pray for you, my brother.'

He pauses – his guards let him – and shakes his head. 'You have no idea what you have done, Luisa. No idea. If you had only waited one more day . . .'

She is puzzled; Father de la Cruz said they found Gabriel awake in his rooms, apparently at prayer, when they arrived. It was odd for him to be up so late, but the good Father made no mention of anything else amiss. 'Why?' she asks, 'what will happen tomorrow?'

He laughs, a broken and mirthless sound. 'What will happen tomorrow? Why, dear sister, I have no idea. No idea at all. And now I never will.' He moves off, giggling under his breath.

Father de la Cruz regards her with kindly eyes. Looking for reassurance she asks, 'Do you know what he meant?'

'Not as yet, but we will.'

'I am not sure he will tell you.' There was madness in her brother's eyes.

'Worry not, child. We have his books.'

*

From: Commissar Eduardo de Salazar to Señor Gabriel Ruiz, 22 November 1541

Brother Ruiz,

I hope this brief note finds you before you embark for the motherland. News may not have reached you yet of the serious earthquake we recently suffered in Cuzco. Many lives were lost and it is with great sadness that I must inform you that your sister – my wife – and our baby son were among those now gone to God. They were in the Cathedral of Our Lady at the time, in the new section, where the roof collapsed. I know that you, like me, will pray evermore for their souls.

Yours,
Eduardo de Salazar

Ω

This account was compiled by Father de la Cruz from the papers of Brother Gabriel Ruiz and his sister Luisa. In a note attached to it Father de la Cruz expressed his concern that supernatural powers were apparently manifested among the heathen when those of the True Faith do not have them. This power of foreseeing the future, he judged, must therefore be of the Devil. That such a power might exist on Earth was sufficiently disturbing that it had to be brought to the attention of Pope Paul III in Rome.

Father de la Cruz was pleased to inform his Holiness that because of his swift intervention God's Church had overcome the heathen Inca. Apac Kunya, the last amautas, *had perished in the cleansing flames before he could finish passing on his devilish power to Brother Gabriel Ruiz.*

As for Brother Gabriel, he had been sent back to his Order for correction, penance and reorientation in the true ways of the Church. This was not expected to be a rapid process.

c. 1580

This document appears to be written in the hand of the Elizabethan philosopher, mathematician, cartographer and occultist, Dr John Dee. Internal references to 'the good doctor' and his 'methodical' note-taking suggest that he wrote this account of his receiving a box of documents, and one in particular, 'a copy of a copy of a translation of another far more ancient manuscript'.

He himself queries its claimed origins, but if the original does indeed go back to the early centuries of Christianity it could cast serious doubts on the very origins of the religion.

The Gifts

Kleo Kay

Dr John Dee was in his study when the messenger from Florence arrived. He was carrying a package of books and scrolls which the good doctor had been eagerly awaiting. A trusted colleague who dealt in antiquarian books and rare documents had been searching for these on his behalf for a long time; now, at last, they were here.

After he had swiftly checked the contents and found that everything he expected appeared to be there, he paid the messenger and sent him to the kitchen for some refreshments before he left. Then he retreated to his study to examine his latest acquisitions.

One of the foremost scholars of his age, Dee was searching for answers to the great mysteries of life. The more he learned, the more his passion for knowledge was inflamed.

These particular papers were nearly ninety years old and were reputed to have come from the library of Marsilio Ficino, noted Italian astrologer, alchemist and classical scholar. In them were copies of translations of Greek texts that he had wanted to add to his collection for some time. There were some letters written by Ficino himself, and the prize was a copy of Ficino's *Book of the Sun* written in the early 1490s. Dee hoped that he would find hints in this about the transmutation of metals into gold, the metal that embodied the energies of the Sun in physical form.

He continued flicking through the various papers. Everything was there that he had expected; he was pleased with the new additions to his library. At the bottom of the box was a scroll case that he hadn't yet looked at. He opened it and pulled out the curled up roll; it seemed quite brittle, so he was careful handling it. As he placed the scroll case down he heard something else rattling in the bottom of it. He up-ended the case and a small box fell out. It had no apparent lid that he could see; he noted it was quite finely made, and put it to one side of his desk for the moment.

He turned his attention back to the scroll and found a great curiosity. As he scanned the first few sections he discovered that it purported to be a translation of a much older work, claiming to deal with the gifts that were given to the Christ child nearly sixteen hundred years ago. Fascinated, he read further, a hundred questions forming in his mind as he read; methodical, as always, he began to make notes of his thoughts.

It began with a comment from the copyist about his source.

This document is a copy of a copy of a translation of another far more ancient manuscript allegedly dating to the early years of the Church. It is written in medieval Latin and the style of it seems to date the translation to the twelfth or thirteenth century. The original must have been badly damaged for much text is missing. The first section is complete enough to understand the gist of it. The second section about the gifts themselves is the most complete. The third section, where the formulae should have been, is completely missing, torn off as if taken by someone, perhaps along with the original artefacts in order to use them. The translator has noted the gaps in the text with careful attention to the detail, including even single words where that was all that could be made out. It came into my hands by such subterfuge that very few people have laid eyes upon it. I was only able to borrow the manuscript for a single night, just long enough to make this copy. It holds great and important secrets and must be guarded from the eyes of the public and the blinkered. It is only for the eyes of the true seeker of knowledge, and the practitioner of the alchemical arts. The text begins below.

Dee noted that the writing looked very similar to that of the letters from Ficino that he had been perusing earlier. He compared the documents and the writing matched, although this was slightly smaller and the characters not quite so well formed. He concluded that it was likely to have been written by

Ficino, probably in a hurry, which fitted with the comments he had just read. He read on.

> *First, let me attest that this is a true and secret record that has been passed down to me by my ancestors. After many years it has fallen to me to pass this knowledge on to those who will preserve it into the far future. I now commend these three most precious artefacts to the care of the elders of the new Church, now that it is fully established. They have extraordinary powers that go far beyond what is deemed possible in the mundane world, therefore it is essential for me to explain how they came into my family's possession, their nature and qualities, and how they should be used.*
>
> (Several lines of text missing at this point.)
>
> *It was He who started the new and gentle faith who entrusted these things to us, and it was my thrice-great grandfather who accepted this mission. Blessing or burden, it depends on how you look at it. From my point of view it is both. Those who carry the secret live long and healthy lives, usually attaining nigh on 100 years of life. That is the blessing. The burden is the fear of failing, that these secrets will be discovered, or the artefacts stolen, accidentally destroyed, or lost. That responsibility is heavy indeed. And now I carry them, the sixth person to do so.*

Dee started calculating the most likely date that the original manuscript could have been written. Six generations from the beginning of Christianity, and the guardians lived long lives. Assuming that an old guardian handed it on to a young person, it must date to approximately AD 450–480. However, if each one passed it down to their child, then the child might be quite old before they even received it, so it could be earlier, maybe AD 300–320? He read the next section.

> (Three lines of text missing.)
>
> *When my ancestor met him he was known simply as Joshua. At that time they were both young men, sharing a common purpose to travel the world and seek out knowledge.*
>
> (Several lines of text missing.)

... and how followers of other religions honoured their various gods.

(About ten lines of text missing. Only a few words were decipherable on the original document here – 'great grand', 'travelled alone', 'medicine', 'study', 'the east' – indicating there was information here about family history and the exploits of the writer's ancestor.)

Joshua, having always lived partly in the spiritual world, pursued the goal of achieving communion with the divine part of his nature. He travelled far and wide, and studied at many temples and sanctuaries.

(About twenty lines of text missing. This section probably dealt with the early years of the life of Jesus and when he started his ministry.)

... Judea. By this time Joshua had attracted a great crowd around him, and followers who went everywhere with him, hanging on his every word.

One evening Joshua confided in my ancestor that he believed a time of great darkness was descending upon him, but not to be afraid as, if all he expected came to pass, they would meet again on the other side. Mysterious though it seemed, he just accepted it. Over the years he had become accustomed to Joshua's cryptic comments.

(Several lines of text missing.)

... something terrible had happened. Joshua was dead! Murdered by the authorities! Arrested by the Temple police and tried on the charge of blasphemy. Apparently he had been engaged in what they termed 'subversive acts' within the holy precincts. Nobody seemed to know exactly what had been said at his trial, so it was difficult to really understand what had happened. The official line was that he had declared himself the Messiah. He hadn't bothered to defend himself, or to beg forgiveness for his crimes against the Temple, and was condemned to death. No time was lost in carrying out the sentence, and he was swiftly executed as a criminal. Fearing repercussions, his closest followers fled into hiding.

(Several lines of text missing. A few words were visible here, 'days and nights ... persecution ... Body [had] disappeared ... mystery'.)

My great-great-great-grandfather was grief-stricken. One morning to his astonishment, Joshua knocked quietly at his door, let himself in and sat down at the table. He had a strange glow about him and seemed oddly calm. Then it was that Joshua charged my ancestor with the task of protecting these extraordinary treasures into the future. He confided the tale of his curious birth, the gifts he had been given at that time, and how to use them. He explained how he had used them to great effect in the previous three years, especially in the last few weeks. He confessed that the only gift he had never fully used was the first, as it hadn't seemed particularly relevant to his life's work and he had used only a few of its secrets of transmutation.

Dr Dee recalled the version of the birth of Jesus as it was written in the Gospel of Matthew. He had always wondered whether the birth stories were a later fabrication designed to validate Christ as the One and Only True Son of God. If this was the case, could this be part of that early corpus? Or could it actually be true? Did this prove that the nativity stories in Matthew were historically accurate? His mind raced with the possibilities this presented him.

(Text missing, with several words visible. 'Joshua . . . caretaking task . . . [l]ong . . . generations . . . until . . . entrusted . . . care of . . . [His] new religion'.)

Joshua had been given a glimpse of the future and he knew that his teachings would take root and grow over time, until they became a great Church open to all. His heartfelt hope was that it would stay pure and true and be a force for good in the world.

And now, to the explanation of the artefacts and their properties. These are written from memory in the words that were passed down to me, and that I learned by rote, when the artefacts were passed into my care.

The first gift: Gold
In the carved box is the gift that is known as gold. Although by its very description, it sounds as if it is simply metal, precious though such worldly treasure is, there is much, much more to this artefact than that. The box is carved with images of the celestial

luminaries, and it has a protective device within it that makes it hard to open unless you know how.

(Text only partially visible here: '. . . in turn gently depress the . . . by the horns of the cres[cent moo]n . . . third ray of the sun . . . your hand below the box . . . [ro]tate the base of the box to the l[eft] and the lid will spring open.)

Within the box are two compartments. Within each section is another box made of crystal. One is of a rosy hue, and the other looks more silvery. The rose crystal box contains a red powder, and in the silver crystal box is a white powder. Each will create a different type of gold when added to base metals. Both are highly prized for their purity and colour. First the red. Follow the formula that is detailed later, and when this ruddy powder is added to source metal ore, in the right quantities, at the right time, and with the right incantations, it will create a valuable pink-red coloured gold.

The red powder was originally created far away and is of rare worth. It is said that it was harvested from the rays of the sun over the course of ten thousand sunrises. The few rays that could be captured each day were those reflected from a tiny ruby set in gold upon the tip of a mighty rock that soared to the heavens. Only the very first rays of the morning were caught, for, as the sun rose into the sky, the angle of reflection was soon lost till the next dawn.

For the white powder, again follow the formula, and blend it with other base metals and it will create a rare and precious pale gold. The white powder is also of most unusual origin, born from a thousand full moons, each of which willingly gave up some of its light. As a result it is of a most curious lustre and possesses an extraordinary brilliance.

These powders are very rare and probably unique, for they were made in the first times, when the world was young, and the knowledge of how to create them has long since been lost. The powders you hold in your hands are all that there will ever be. That is of course unless the one who gave these gifts in the first instance had more. But that is another story, and one that I am not familiar with.

The formulae to use the red and the white powders are all

*located at the end of this treatise. They detail the quantities to use
and the processes to employ. They explain how to mix the powders
with ores and metals and other common alchemical ingredients
in order to bring forth the required gold of either ruddy complexion or pale sheen. Other formulae set out how a single grain, or in
some cases a part grain, of either red or white will bring about the
transformation of many other things. The red governs things that
resonate with the sun and his energies, the white rules those that
are of the moon and her powers.*

The good doctor was fascinated by this section, and re-read it
several times. He wanted to believe it, for it confirmed his belief that
baser metals could be transmuted into gold. It gave him hope that
it had been done before, even though it was clouded in mystery.
However, having this document come into his possession seemed
to him to be a propitious omen to the success of his quest. He
planned to analyse it later to try to unravel the symbolism in the
description, and he noted that it read like many early medieval
alchemical documents that he had previously studied. Was this
because when it had been translated it was couched in the language
of the translator? Or was it simply a true, word-for-word, translation of a third- to fifth-century document, containing important
occult knowledge? He returned to the document.

The second gift: Frankincense
*The second gift is that of frankincense, stored in the phial of
amethyst closed with a stopper of faceted clear quartz. The incense
is of crystalline form in fine granules. When it is burned on a hot
flame, it produces a pure smoke that perfumes the room and
makes the space sacred by its presence. If combined with specific
other incenses and herbs, it gives a longevity to its effect that will
last beyond the time of exposure. This is particularly helpful for
prolonged meditative workings. Again, you will find the formula
for this at the end of this scroll.*

*This particular frankincense is made from the resin of one
especial and most ancient tree. It is the rarest of its kind. This tree
is said to have been already old at the dawn of history, and a
sapling before time, as we know it, began. Its trunk is girded by*

entwining serpents who protect its precious fruits from the profane. The fruits and the resins of this tree may only be gathered by the priestess-guardian. She is the only one who knows the magic chants and the way to sound the words that calm the serpents. With her song she persuades the sentience of the tree to let go of its fruits and release its resins in a milky flow. It is said she is as old as the tree and that it sustains her far beyond the passage of her earthly years.

The special quality of this frankincense is that it opens the portals between the spiritual and the mundane worlds and thus enables those present to see and to know the face of the divine. It is the revealer of mysteries; the opener of the mind, the awakener of the heart and the enlightener of the soul. It creates an altered state and produces an openness that attracts the genii of truth and spiritual knowledge. These genii speak directly into the heart, in the eternal tongue. Thus the mind will understand and the soul is enraptured. In its diluted form it enables communication with the angelic and demonic hosts, although caution must be employed when used in weaker concentrations, as it is sometimes hard to identify which is angel and which is demon, what is true and what is a test of the seeker's integrity.

Dee noted down that this was very interesting, for perhaps this could be a way to find out lost and hidden truths, if only he could manage to refine some of this precious aromatic from the rare frankincense that he already had in his laboratory. Breathless with anticipation, he read on.

The third gift: Balsam of Myrrh

The third gift is in the lidded pot made from black volcanic glass. The lid is engraved with the image of the Ouroboros, the snake who holds his own tail within his mouth, giving the eternal message that every ending is also a beginning. The contents of this pot need to be kept far from exposure to daylight and the deep black glass of the container keeps it safe so that its essence remains active.

It is an ointment crafted mainly from myrrh, but with the addition of silken-sage, the crushed petals of the moonflower and safflower, combined with the bloom of sylvan moss. It has been prepared over a full thirteen-month moon cycle, with the various ingredients added into the myrrh salve at the designated time. The correct incantations have been spoken at each stage of its production, and it has rested in the light of the dark moon, absorbing the energies required to become effective.

It has very special properties. When a small amount is applied to the lips and nose it induces a death-like torpor in which the body can endure intense pain and survive wounds that would normally destroy the earthly vessel. If a thin layer of the salve is applied to any wound it will heal during the passage of three days and three nights. However, after applying the salve to the wound the person should then apply some of it to their lips and nose so that they are in a state of deep slumber whilst the healing occurs. The patient should be left undisturbed during this time, and they should be kept within a darkened room, ideally with no light. It is not necessary to have someone there to care for the person, but if a loved one wishes to tend to the injured party a small oil lamp is permitted.

After the period of seventy-two hours the person will awaken restored and renewed. For a short while there will be a slight glow around them, which is visible to others. If they do not wish to attract attention it is best that they keep their solitude until the glow disperses.

Dr Dee drew a deep breath and his eyes widened at what he had just read. This threw doubt on the miracle of the resurrection of Christ. The Church would view this treatise as heretical and would not want it to be in circulation. He realised that he would have to be very careful who he mentioned it to, because if the wrong people found out about it, it could attract the unwelcome attentions of the Church's Holy Office of Inquisition to his work and even jeopardise his freedom and his life. Then he remembered that in 1489 the Roman Curia had accused Marsilio Ficino of heresy; could this have been a contributing factor? He was later cleared of all charges after Archbishop Orsino spoke up for him, and Ficino had then published an Apology. Dee had noticed an extract from this Apology was included in one of the letters he had read earlier.

Looking back at the manuscript he saw there was only one more line, a note from the original translator.

Here the manuscript ends. You can just see the top of the heading that reads 'The Formulae'.

Excited and shocked by what he had just read, Dr Dee turned his attention to the small box that he had previously found at the bottom of the scroll case. He examined it and realised that this box did not fit the description of any one of the three artefacts that he had just read about, being round and made of an aged red-coloured wood. He noticed a knot in the wood on the side. His fingers played over this and it gave slightly, and as it did the lid loosened and sprang open with a click revealing three sections inside. In one were a few pinches of red powder, in the next were a few grains of a crystalline substance, and the third had merely a smear of ointment around the bottom edge.

Could it be that these were some of the precious artefacts themselves? Did they date from the time of Our Lord? Or were they from the time of the translation during the twelfth or thirteenth century? Or from Ficino's experiments after he had read this tract? He wondered if perhaps when Ficino and earlier alchemists before him had owned these things there had been more of the substances in the box? There was so little in the box that he thought he would surely be the last in the line to experiment with them. If they were truly the gifts that were given to Christ on his birth, that would make them even older, and their origins pre-Christian, as claimed in the manuscript itself. Were they created by Hermetic magic, or Platonic science, or something far older, wilder, pagan, and more mysterious? He could hardly dare to hope that with these treasures he might be able to make gold, talk to the angels, or heal an open wound.

He would experiment . . .

Ω

John Dee's experiments in transmuting base metal into gold, mainly in central Europe through much of the 1580s, all proved unsuccessful.

When he returned to his home in Mortlake, London, in 1589, it was to find his library and laboratory largely destroyed and many of his books and manuscripts stolen. There is no record of the Marsilio Ficino documents surviving. It is possible that as books and documents from Dee's ransacked library were dispersed and resold, this account eventually came into the hands of a priest or monk who, seeing its significance and the danger of its story sowing doubts about the historical basis of Christianity, sent it to the Vatican for safe-keeping.

No box was found in the Vaults with this document.

The sixteenth century was the heyday of alchemical research by Hermetic philosophers (the forerunners of both the non-existent Rosicrucian Brotherhood and the real Royal Society). Fake documents abounded. It is quite possible that the document about the three gifts, 'a copy of a copy of a translation of another far more ancient manuscript', was in its entirety little older than Dee himself; if it was older, then it might have dated from the twelfth or thirteenth century, as Ficino's preparatory remarks suggest from the writing style. Or it could, as it claims, date back to the earliest centuries of Christianity, whether or not its core story by a friend of 'Joshua' ever happened. The writer's casual Anti-Semitism in assuming that the Jewish rather than the Roman authorities were responsible for Jesus' death could date it equally to the early centuries of Christianity or to medieval or Renaissance times.

The document's primary significance to Dr Dee was in its hope of genuine alchemical working, but its deeper significance, whenever it was written, is that its author was proposing, whether allegorically or literally, an alternative explanation for the resurrection of Christ, and thus challenging the very origins of Christianity.

1591

This file brings together two quite disparate journals. One is by Dr Richard Barret, President of the English College at Rheims, a Catholic seminary founded at Douai in 1569 which trained English priests, then sent them into England to minister covertly to Catholics. The other is by a fifteen-year-old English girl, Anne Barton. Together they tell a remarkable tale.

Queen Elizabeth I attempted a difficult compromise during her reign between enforcing religious conformity and allowing freedom of conscience. For example, her parliament made it treason to refuse the oath of supremacy twice, but then Elizabeth would not allow the oath to be asked of anybody more than once.

We preface excerpts from the two journals with an extract from a letter from Queen Elizabeth's spymaster, Sir Francis Walsingham.

Windows into Men's Hearts

E. Saxey

Sir Francis Walsingham to M. Critoy, Secretary of State for France

I find therefore her majesty's proceedings to have been grounded upon two principles. The one, that consciences are not to be forced, but to be won and reduced by the force of truth, with the aid of time, and use of all good means of instruction and persuasion.

. . . her majesty, not liking to make windows into men's hearts and secret thoughts . . . tempered her laws . . .

but when, about the twentieth year of her reign, she had discovered in the king of Spain an intention to invade her dominions . . . and after that the seminaries began to blossom, and to send forth daily priests . . . yea, and bind many [English subjects] to attempt against her majesty's sacred person . . . And because it was a treason carried in the clouds, and in wonderful secrecy, and came seldom to light . . .

. . . then were there new laws made . . .

*

Journal of Dr Richard Barret, President of the English College at Rheims

1 November 1591
God be merciful – three more good men taken, in the last six weeks.
Each of them was asked their profession, by officers, on arrival at a new town. All had rehearsed, with me, the most subtle dissimulations

– and yet, all announced the truth! *Treacherous truth: that they were priests, come secretly to England to restore the land and its monarch to the true faith.*

All these men were arrested. One has been hanged, winning his soul's eternal exaltation. One is exiled, one rots in the Marshalsea.

I do not understand these fits of honesty! The need for equivocation troubles all of us. But these men agreed that some lies might be told in the service of Our Lord – or they pretended to me that they agreed.

I fear that these men – these novice boys – fix their minds too much on the martyr's rose, and the glorious deaths of Briant and Campion. Our enemies say our Order delights in wasting the lives of young men. As though we flung them into England like coins down a well, hoping for good fortune.

I must pray, and not succumb to despair, and recall that others of our Order thrive. One such, Edward Shepherd, was held by an officer of the law. But when questioned by his superior, the officer confessed that Shepherd had done no wrong within his sight, and that he 'had the look of a good fellow'. Brother Edward was then set free – to preach, to travel, to minister to the faithful. Surely this is Providence?

*

Journal of Anne Barton

1 November 1591

God protect us, we are to have a priest. Father told us yesterday.

We have had no priest in ten years – since old Father Rutter – and the laws have tightened a notch every year. Now, to shelter a seminary man means death.

'It is but for a short while,' Father said. 'And I will bear all the consequence.'

That was little comfort! And untrue, for Mother could be taken also, and perhaps our home seized from *praemunire*. And I as well, despite my youth? I am fifteen years old, and the Bedingfield child was charged with treason at eight. (Might a child not say 'I hate the Queen', meaning no more than 'I hate cabbage'?)

Mother bit her fist and spoke not. I hid my fear and smiled.

Our faith has been a private solace to our family. I wish most fervently it had not become the business of Princes.

*

3 November
The priest is here.

Although he wore rough clothes when he arrived, he was soon dressed in a borrowed velvet doublet, and looked well in it (although he tugged at the collar frequently). He has dark hair and skin quite sallow, and deep-set wary eyes. He walked with Father and me in the courtyard garden.

The priest said, 'A beautiful house, sir.'

'It is the cloister of the monastery that once stood here,' Father replied.

I know the family story: when the monastery fell, during King Henry's time, my grandfather applied to purchase a part of it. Grandfather was a true Catholic but a practical man.

The priest took my father's hands in his. I noticed the priest's fingers were somewhat askew. 'Do your father's deeds trouble you, Master Barton?' asked the priest.

'They do. Where I dine and sleep and raise my daughter, Anne, I know that monks should be praying. I think I hear the Matins bell.'

He had never said such things before.

'You will not be judged for your father's actions, but your own,' said the priest. He released my father's hands and pulled on a pair of fine calf-skin gloves. I fretted that I had stared at his deformity.

'You must stay as long as you wish with us,' said Father.

*

14 November
Cheering news: Edward Shepherd is a guest in a house of some stand-ing. He has all good things: a warm home, a horse to travel, and intel-ligence as to the roads and the dispositions of people. He will do much to kindle the zeal of Catholic families thereabouts, spreading like a fire in stubble.

And there will be no need for Edward to hide in a sewer, should the house be ransacked by pursuivants: his host has summoned our man Nicholas Owen to build a hiding place.

*

14 November
Owen the builder walked once round our whole house and clapped his hands in pleasure.

'Will it do?' asked Father.

'Very finely. A house such as this, which has served two purposes, may be made to serve more.' Owen showed how my grandfather's work, to make the cloister a private dwelling, had left many hidden nooks and false walls.

Owen sleeps during the day and the servants call him a sluggard, not knowing he has been cutting all night with a muffled saw.

The hiding place is a curious work. A double plank of oak forms the door. If a pursuivant should rap on the oak, only a dull note will return to him, as though there is a wall beyond the wood. This weighty plank swings lightly when a certain floor tile is pressed.

I dislike it. As a child I had dreams where a new door in the house opened to a strange room, and they troubled me more than nightmares. Owen's work is another clever lie in the service of the truth. The wall is not a wall, the priest puts on the disposition of a gentleman. We are all outward conformity and secret heresy.

*

20 November
I had thought the priest would need to hide away, but today we rode out openly to hawk. He wears his years of study invisibly, like chain-mail under his doublet.

He knows falcons well. He does not know me well, though. He questioned me on some dozen subjects I did not care to answer. 'Do you love your father or mother most dearly?' he said, as he handed me onto my horse.

'I should be ingratitude itself if I did not love both.'

'Was your Father Rutter a good priest?'

'I do not know, sir. He kept us in the faith.'

'And have you friends in the village?'

I feared he might ride off to convert them, so told him I treasured no person above any other.

Chafing under his interrogation, I questioned him in return. 'Do you believe your work will bear fruit soon? Will England return to the faith in five years, perhaps?'

'Struth, no!' Then he said hastily, 'Forgive me. You catch me in a melancholy fit.' He is a mightily uneven man, flustered and assured by turns. 'Ask no more questions. I must not give you knowledge that would harm you.'

He has been harmed. He wore gloves to ride, and a hawking gauntlet, but I saw his hands at dinner. His fingernails are gone, leaving thick skin like melted wax. He shames us. Our family live secretly, and attend the heretics' Mass in the village church monthly. We disdain to pay a fine, when others give all they have.

I could only find weak words for him. 'I pray we may all speak and worship honestly, one day.'

He cast off my Father's goshawk and we watched it ring up into the white winter sky. 'Might you travel to the continent, one day, and join a convent?'

I imagined it as the hawk circled: studying and singing with brave women in far lands. It would be good to be whole-hearted, to serve the Lord as the hawk seeks the rabbit.

But I could not imagine leaving my home, the fields over which the hawk's shadow was shooting.

'I might,' I lied, and it made the priest smile.

*

21 November

The priest said Mass for us today. I have read the liturgy to myself, in the years since our old priest died, but not remembered how it stirred me. *Kyrie eleison* has the cadences of mourning, *Gloria in Excelsis Deo* rings like trumpets.

Then the *Agnus Dei* – 'take away the sins of the world'. I thought of poor Father Edward's hands, and the sins of his tormentors. Father keeps the worst rumours from me, but everyone has heard of Richard Topcliffe, the Queen's pursuivant. Was it he who hurt Father Edward? Was it blasphemy to doubt that the heretic-torturer's sins might be removed? Or was it blasphemy to pray for it?

The priest stooped to place the consecrated wafers in our

mouths. I felt something thaw that had been frozen. I wanted faith to flow out of me into every part of the world.

We dined together afterwards, and I spoke to Mother. 'It is good to hear the Mass again.'

'Yes – and in our house again.'

'Would it please you for Father Edward to stay past Christmas?'

'No!' She gripped the table. 'He should go from here as soon as your Father allows.'

Silence spread around the table. Mother's face bloomed scarlet. The priest looked over to us. 'Mistress Barton, should I leave your home?'

'Yes, you should leave! You are a good man, but your goodness will be the death of us. I would sooner have poison in my cup than you in my house.'

She put her hand to her mouth and fled the room.

*

21 November
A sad sight came to Rheims this morning – a man screaming as two men lifted him out of a carriage. Fortunately, on seeing the sky, he ceased to scream. He would by no means come back under a roof, however, so we set up a screen in the gardens where he might wash and dress himself. His clothes were stiff and his hair a bird's nest from sea salt.

He babbled, then grew calm, and confirmed what I had suspected: that under his long, rimed beard, he was Stephen Griffiths returned from England.

He asked that a bed be placed in the gardens also.

'There is no helping it,' he said. 'Father Garnet tried all ways but I cannot be within doors.'

I told him the weather was too inclement, and assured him that we were safe here, not to be raided like English houses. But he fell into fits on the threshold, so we fetched out a pallet and blankets.

Father Garnet, the superior who leads the English mission, had told me of this poor man's condition – the pains in his head, and his terror of close places. I had not expected Stephen's cheerful frankness. He had drunk beer, to permit him to travel by carriage, and I questioned him before the weakness might wear off.

192

E. Saxey

'*What has caused this alteration in you, brother?*'

'*Oh, one of our Order worked the change. One of my fellows here at Rheims – my rival, if a novice may have a rival, apart from the world, the flesh and the Devil. He was more zealous than I, more learned, more holy.*' He spat on the grass.

'*He is your brother in Christ!*'

'*But neither good nor Godly, now. He met with us at the great gathering . . .*'

I knew of this ill-omened gathering. Garnet brought together all the priests of the English mission, twice a year. Many of our brothers lived in dark attics, alone for days at a time. Gathering together braced their souls, Garnet said, and forged new weapons for new battles. But a raid on such a gathering could destroy the whole mission at once.

'*That rival brother of mine – he said the Mass for us all. Then the house where we met was attacked. The pursuivants battered down the doors. Ten of us crammed ourselves into one of Owen's nooks, trapped there for hours, while those foul men stabbed the beds and tumbled the furniture.*'

'*Terrible.*' But some of our men have been locked for three days in a priest-hole, and not suffered for it after their release. '*Did the confinement distress you?*'

'*Oh, no! I have had worse hospitality. But the priest had pressed some charm onto my tongue with the consecrated host, and I felt it winding into my thoughts. Carving out a channel, like a worm, or a chisel . . .*'

This was a blasphemous fancy. '*The other men – they did not feel this?*'

'*They felt it not, but it worked on them. They cannot tell a lie, now, if asked a question.*' He tapped his finger on his forehead. '*A gate has opened between my mind and my mouth, dear Father. My every conversation is a confessional, now. And I cannot bear to be hidden, or disguised, or kept in any closed place. I must be open in all things.*'

It was a vile tale. But then I recalled the recent spate of confessions, among our men in England.

'*Test me,*' Stephen demanded. '*Ask me any shameful thing! Ask me if I have been a knave, a cozener, a lecher!*'

But my first questions were clear to me.

'*Who was with you at the gathering?*'

He gave ten names. Half the named men have been arrested for their unusual honesty; two of them are dead.

'*Which man said Mass for you, and them?*'

'*Why, Father Edward Shepherd did it.*'

*

21 November cont'd

As soon as my mother left the dining hall, a farmer's boy ran in, shouting that men on horseback were asking questions in the town.

I took Father Edward's arm. 'I will show you the shortest way to the priest-hole, Father.' I snatched up a knife from the dining table as we left.

I stamped on the secret tile, let the false door-panel swing wide, and ducked into the room after the priest.

The secret room was as long and wide as a coffin. The priest went ahead of me.

'What have you done to my family,' I asked, 'that they are no longer masters of their own tongues?'

He showed no surprise. 'I have worked a charm on them. I understand it not myself. Maybe our Lord means your family to leave off dissembling.'

'This is not God's work.' I spoke too loud, and feared discovery, and dropped my voice. 'It is Devilry.'

'Call it what you will,' Father Edward whispered back. 'I am caught on the same hook. Do you love your family more than your faith?'

I did not wish to answer him.

But my tongue flapped against my teeth like a bird in a panic. 'Yes. My family is dearer to me.' I pointed my knife towards him. 'How do I undo this *charm*?'

'I do not know. No, put down your blade – I cannot speak more truthfully, Anne! For the sake of pity!'

He feared me. He was scratching nervously at the skin of his wrists, one hand scouring up under the opposite cuff. He had strength but, pinned in this tiny room, he could not use it. I heard, from elsewhere in the house, the scrape and crash of furniture shoved aside.

'Could you truly kill me with that knife?' he whispered.

'No, I could not.'

The words sprang from my mouth unbidden. Father Edward struck at my hand. My blade clattered on the stone floor. We froze, and waited for the searchers to turn in our direction.

We heard only a blunt knocking, far off. Then louder, sharper, with others joining in: a martial drumming on every piece of panelling, moving closer and closer. Until staves pounded on the false door to our little room and it shook under their blows.

If one man were to step, by chance, on the tile that worked the mechanism . . .

The priest pushed past me, to stand between me and the door. To protect me.

And then the drumming passed us by.

A hundred heartbeats later came a great creaking roar. They were pulling up the floorboards.

We waited in silence until the cacophony ceased. My father called for us. Was he a tethered lure, bleating for the hunters? No, his voice was joyful.

I backed out of the hidden room, shifting the lever that opened the heavy oak door. The priest followed me to freedom.

I slammed the door against his head. I could not have stabbed him, that was true, but I only needed to intend this deed for a moment, then the weight of the door did all the dreadful work. He screamed, and I let the door swing free again.

'Leave the house within a week or I will find another way to harm you,' I said.

'You cannot. I will ask you every hour whether you mean to injure me.'

'Then I will plan a dozen ill deeds, and when you discover one I will find another. By horse, or on the cloister steps.' I saw a simpler way. 'Or I will ask you in front of my father if you have worked witchcraft on us, and you will confess it to him.'

And then I was silent, because Father had rushed forward to embrace us both.

*

22 November
I have tested Stephen. He does not lie – which is to say, he does not lie when he says that he must speak the truth. But can Edward Shepherd be the cause of it?

Letters stream in from England. More of our men have announced themselves to be priests. They are believed to be a small cohort of a vast Jesuit army – when in truth, they form the greatest part of our mission.

All talk without torture. Some confess strong sympathy for plots against her Majesty's life, when our mission has sworn to take no part in such politics. Others declare that her Majesty is no true queen (when we have schooled them, time and again, to equivocate on that matter). Two priests – if reports do not lie – have announced that any man who commits treason against Elizabeth will win his soul's safe harbour for eternity.

The Queen's advisors beg her for action: to make death the penalty for all recusants, and to raise armies to attack France or Spain. They tell her she will by no other wise be safe. Our priests, my brothers, are shown to her as evidence.

The compass of the nation swings to war.

And all these garrulous priests were given Mass by Edward Shepherd.

I know not what to do. If I summon him to Rheims, will he come? It is doubtful, if he now labours for another master. If he remains in England, Catholic families will shelter him, and fall under his sway.

Stephen Griffiths told me his own plan: to return to England.

'I cannot waste myself here.'

'You should ask my leave,' I told him. 'I am your spiritual director.'

'I do not go as a priest,' he said. 'I go to kill Edward Shepherd, before he kills every Catholic in England, and – by fomenting war – half the men in Europe. I cannot expect your blessing, so I do not ask your permission. But I do ask for his whereabouts.'

I did not sleep. His request racked me all night.

This morning I find he has already left, and stolen from me all of Edward's letters.

*

5 December
The priest has gone from my home. His new home is twenty miles away, a house so large it would take a year to search.

My family do not speak of the curse he has laid on us. We spend much time in solitary contemplation.

After Father Edward left, I sat in the cold cloister-garden, trying to discover how much he has altered me. I asked myself questions, but could not make my tongue wag against its will.

A young and pale-haired stranger entered the garden, picking his way around my mother's bare rose bushes.

'What is your name and business, sir?' I asked with courtesy, in case he was a pursuivant, but as he drew close I saw his clothes were all over mud and twigs.

'I am Stephen Griffiths, a Jesuit, come to kill Edward Shepherd,' he said. Then he laughed. 'And I say so grudgingly, of course. Curse the man. Has he lodged here?'

'He has.' I found that I still must answer honestly.

The man plumped himself down on the ground and pulled up his feet to examine the soles of his boots. I could not believe him a murderer.

'I marvel that you can walk abroad,' I said, 'If you must announce your intention to any who ask.'

'Oh, I travel by night. Sleep in ditches all the day. Is that man, Father Edward, still in this house?'

'He has left here, an hour past.'

'So close! Tell me in which direction he went? And if he has locked up your tongue on the matter, draw me a map, or point. And give me a loaf of bread and a fast horse.'

'I will give you the bread and the horse, but you need no directions. I will show you the way.'

'You should not come with me. I am an honest villain. I mean to kill him, it is no sport.'

I did not know if I wished to see the devil-priest dead. But I could not stay home.

'You need me. Your tongue is not your own.' It was a lie of omission, for it hinted that my tongue was free. But no dire consequence descended on me. It was a great relief to find I could deceive, even slightly.

*

'Sir – I would speak with Edward Shepherd? I hear he lives here and gives good Christian counsel.'

I flattered until the servant turned back into the house, locking the door against us. Father Edward re-opened it, wearing another borrowed doublet, with a collar of cut-work lace.

'Anne! You have made my host afraid. He thinks that every man in the country knows he shelters a Jesuit. Why do you come here?'

Then Father Stephen stepped into his sight. Father Edward made the sign of the cross on his breast.

'Are you my death?' he asked.

'I know not. The hour of your death is not mine to choose, but God's.'

'But have you come to kill me?'

'Oh, yes! You cannot doubt it, Brother Edward.'

'I will not let you in.'

'Run to your hiding-hole, then – but I remember this house, and could tell the officers where to find you.'

'You need not threaten me, brother. No place is safe for such as you and me. We are leaky boats, who cannot reach safe harbour.' I searched Father Edward's face for signs of devilish allegiance, but he looked bone-weary, uneasy in his courtly clothes. He stood to one side of the door, to let us enter.

'I cannot join you in there, brother. And you are the cause of it, so you must excuse me. We will talk in the open air.'

Father Edward guided us around a long wall of the house. He asked as we walked: 'Why will you not come inside, Brother Stephen?'

Father Stephen looked confused and insulted. 'To enter a house is a kind of deceit – like hiding myself away. And thanks to you, I cannot abide any kind of lying.'

Father Edward seemed just as nonplussed. 'It does not seem like lying, to me. I am not affected that way.'

'Ha! You are a lucky devil.'

'I do find it painful to disguise myself.' Father Edward's hand crept to his lace collar.

Father Stephen sniffed. 'You have my sympathy.' We reached a garden of knotted hedges. 'This is a pleasant place,' said Father

Stephen. 'It will be a shame for Anne and me to leave it, and a shame you will never leave.'

The priests took either end of a wooden seat, while I sat a little further off on the grass. Hedges grown to hide lovers now hid Father Edward and me, and the snake I had let into the garden: Father Stephen, rocking where he sat and jesting at murder. I could not doubt his intent, but I could not persuade myself that it would happen. How would Father Stephen do it? Would he bid me leave, or make me witness it? Should I prevent it?

'Your soul will pay a high fine for murdering me,' said Father Edward.

'Better my soul than all the souls of England. Our mission cannot thrive while you prosper, you gross carnosity. You are working for the crown?'

'I have been sent out as their instrument. But my heart is with the true faith.'

'What, weasel? If you are not a turn-coat, then how are you their instrument?'

'I follow no instructions from them – I myself am their curse on English Catholics. Brother, what could I undertake to do, that would make you spare my life?'

'Nothing.'

I watched their strange duel of words. Each had a weapon which could undo the other, and yet neither was the victor.

'How does it happen that we must speak the truth?' asked Father Stephen.

Father Edward smiled with grim relief, as though he had been waiting to be asked this question. He spoke in a confiding tone.

'Richard Topcliffe is a witch.'

That man, Topcliffe, the Queen's pursuivant – I had thought of him during the Mass. I had halfway asked for his trespasses to be forgiven. I renounced that feeble-hearted prayer.

'He has a room for the torture of priests in his own dwelling . . .'

'But it is a felony to house a priest!' said Father Stephen.

Father Edward tightened his fingers into a fist at the jest. 'I hung from the wall in that room. Topcliffe pushed my head up, but it would not stay, so he knotted my hair to a nail . . .'

'What did he do then?'

'Drove his fingers into my ears, and drew forth my tongue with pincers, and he spat on it. And said, "*Ephphatha*".'

'What does it mean?' I asked.

'*Let it be open.*' They answered me in unison, and Father Stephen winced, but spoke on: 'It is mockery of Christ, who healed the dumb man. What then?'

'His spit tasted of dandelion stalks.'

'What *effect* did it have, Brother Edward?'

'Topcliffe asked me questions. As soon as I saw that the truth would stream out of me, I tried to bite my tongue off. But he held my jaws apart.'

'Better you had done it,' said Father Stephen, but his voice was not steady.

'He questioned me for an hour. I told him the names of some Catholic houses, the ways to find their priest-holes. When he left me alone, I struck my head against the ground rather than leave myself in his hands. But I only lost my senses, not my life. Do you doubt me?'

I did not doubt him. I pitied him. I had wished Father Edward would suffer, for causing my honesty, and my family's suffering. But my wish for revenge was a shallow cup, and his past pains overflowed it.

'I do not doubt you,' said Father Stephen. 'But I am not compelled to pardon you, brother.'

I should not have brought Father Stephen to Father Edward. I should have sent him down a false road. I would share the blame for his murderous deeds.

'Topcliffe returned with a man – wealthy, with a deep peak to his hair. Topcliffe asked me questions, and I spoke the truth. The man said, "*This man has been ill used, and will confess to anything*". But Topcliffe swore my honesty. And the man asked me this and that, conundrums and paradoxes, until he was satisfied. A clever man.'

'Who was he?'

'I know not. But I fear he was Walsingham.'

I knew that name: the Queen's spymaster.

'He laughed and said that Topcliffe had done what God could not, and made men honest. He questioned him further – asking if a man under this charm might sign a treaty falsely, or do a thing against his nature. And they tried to make me sign a false document, and . . . other things. Topcliffe used all his old methods, then, to see if they could get a lie from me, when before he sought the truth.'

'And *then* they set you free, to curse your fellow priests.'

'Yes. I heard them fight over it. Topcliffe planned to enchant all Jesuits; Walsingham wished to keep the charm for use on other men. Foreign ambassadors, and the Queen's own advisers. He told Topcliffe to cease all experiments, and kill me, so that news of the charm would not spread.

'Topcliffe raged, and defied the spymaster by releasing me, that night – he had me dressed, and gave me a horse. And I met with you all for Mass – and knew not, when I took the Mass, that the charm could pass from me to you, by touch. And touch on the tongue, especially. I believed that I, alone, would speak the truth and die for it.'

Father Stephen looked at his own hands, and at Father Edward's. I thought that Father Edward's words would change Father Stephen's direction, as the wind turns the weathervane. But Father Stephen gave no sign.

I spoke in desperation, to delay the evil moment. 'Father Edward, why did you come to our house?'

'To minister to your souls. I hoped – God forgive me – that I might be a better priest, for my affliction! That the fears, or lies, that keep people from Our Lord might all be known to me. I am sorry, Anne . . .'

Father Stephen spoke. 'That was spiritual vanity, brother.'

'I know it.'

'We should all listen to our spiritual directors in such matters. Not chase off on missions of our own devising.' He was chastising Father Edward, but seemed abashed himself.

I pushed my point. 'Father Edward, why did you not end your life, when you were able?'

'Oh, for I am a coward,' said Father Edward. 'Self-slaughter would mean Hell for me. And Hell would be an eternity of Richard Topcliffe's private chamber. So I have tried to continue our mission, despite my gift.'

'Foolish,' said Father Stephen.

'I know!' he shouted, then. 'But you have saved me! I will make confession, and you will kill me. And *you* will go to Hell, in my stead, brother.'

'I know it.'

'You have never been put to the question, Brother Stephen, have you?'

'No.'

'Then you would brave Hell for eternity, when you have not felt it for a minute.'

Then Father Edward stood, and began to undo his doublet.

I knew not why. Had the dishonesty of disguise grown too much for him? He undid the dozen small buttons that ran down from the lace collar, shrugged himself free and stood in his under-shirt. His wrists and neck were red and chafed where he had worried at his own skin. Was he shedding his gentleman's clothes to die a priest, without lace or velvet?

He folded the doublet reverently and handed it to me. It was warm from his body, and heavy.

I saw his reason. Knowing that Father Stephen would kill him, he did not want his doublet, his host's gift, to be spoiled.

I laid the doublet on the bench and, lacking more words, I stood in front of Father Edward, barring Father Stephen's way.

Father Stephen called across me: 'Edward! Why did you not leave this country and come home to Rheims?'

'I could not cross the Channel. I must speak my profession to any who ask it. I could only slope from house to house, on borrowed horses . . .'

Father Stephen rose to his feet, and came close to us both. He reached past me, but held no blade, and laid his empty hand on his brother's shoulder. 'I have left England, and travelled to Rheims, and returned here. I have passed four days in England, this time, and not suffered arrest.'

'Do you tell me that to taunt me, Brother Stephen?'

'No. Will you come home to Rheims with me, Brother Edward?'

'You said you would not spare me!'

'I spoke the truth, but I am not a prophet. My heart has been changed. I did not foresee it.'

Father Edward stepped out from behind me and let himself be embraced. 'Have you money for our passage?'

'For mine. Not yours, Brother Edward, as I did not think to need it – it does not take a full purse to kill a man. But we might cut the fancy buttons from your clothes . . .'

*

24 December

Two of my flock have come back to me.

I foresaw that one would die by the other's hand. Now Edward takes food out to the arbour where Stephen lodges, and they study together.

They say they will go to Spain, for the mild climate will allow Stephen to work despite his peculiarity. I have overheard Stephen say that their frankness may see them made saints; he does not make such impious jests in my presence.

Anne Barton writes that the charm weakens, but does not pass. Much can be achieved through misdirection, but questions from her parents still compel her honesty. I have sent letters to Edward's hosts, telling them this hard news. Perhaps the charm afflicts seminary priests most strongly because they have spent years in the consideration of truth. Those who know truth, but have not studied or disputed it, are less fertile soil. Stephen, who is affected most deeply, was the most scrupulous of novices.

Anne also asks me if there are convents with vows of silence. I will tell her no order would accept her as a novice until she is eighteen. It is a lie, to prevent a rash decision. The charm's hold on her may still lessen.

I have called home all the priests that Edward met – all those who survive. I pray they will return to me in safe silence, not lose their lives to feed a courtier's greed for war.

Soon we will have here a seminary of spotless honesty. All fear, all doubt, all jealousy will be seen clear as if it were nailed to the church door. We have survived another of the world's tricks; will we survive the truth of one another?

Ω

William Allen, founder of the English College at Douai, set up a similar college in Rome in 1575. He moved to Rome in 1585, becoming Librarian at the Vatican until his death in 1594 – undoubtedly the route by which Dr Richard Barret's journal made its way there. We can only surmise that, to stop any discovery of what had happened to the priests, one or other of them asked for and confiscated Anne Barton's journal.

In 1582, while the College was at Rheims, scholars there translated the New Testament into English, as part of what became known as the Douay-Rheims Bible. The College returned to its original home in Douai in 1593.

The revelation that the Queen's principal interrogator Richard Topcliffe used magical powers in his campaign of hatred against Catholics adds another layer to the man known as 'the cruellest tyrant in all England'. He interrogated and tortured many priests, and his treatment of Fr Edward was lenient compared to the sadism he displayed to others. The use of magic to force priests to answer questions with the truth displays a level of sadistic subtlety alongside the physical means he delighted in using.

At the time of Elizabeth, belief in the real power of magic was nothing unusual, but the Church would be at pains to cover up its successful use against itself.

1600

Giordano Bruno was one of the great puzzles of the sixteenth century. He was a monk, a mathematician, a philosopher, an astrologer and probably a spy, and he developed a complex Art of Memory which he taught around Europe. He was also an early advocate of the idea of an infinite universe. He began as a Dominican monk, but was later a Lutheran and then a Calvinist, and he ended up at odds with any form of orthodox Christian belief; it was almost a question of which Church would take its revenge on him first.

He was prepared to challenge any established beliefs, and delighted in disputing and debating with authorities. It could not end well. After seven years of imprisonment and interrogation by the Inquisition, Giordano Bruno was burned at the stake in 1600.

Or was he? This file of documents found in the Vaults of the Vatican Library casts an intriguing new light on Bruno's life, and on its end. Rather than turn them into a narrative, we present the whole file, a puzzle to match Bruno himself.

Documents in the Case
of Brother G.

Paul Kincaid

1. Document removed from the Vatican Library on 18 February 1600.

14 September 1570. Brother Giordano, from the monastery of San Domenico in Naples, requested to see a copy of *De revolutionibus orbium coelestium* by Nicholaus Copernicus. Application supported by Cardinal-Priest Rebiba. Request approved.

> *Marginal notation in another hand:*
> Remove this.

*

2. Extract from a letter written by Father Ambrose, San Domenico Maggiore, Naples, dated 23 March 1600.

I was summoned to the home of one Giacomo Carafa of Sorrento. He is an old man now, but his daughter, who looks after him, confirmed that he had once been an astrologer for many of the noblest families in Naples. His home shows no sign of past wealth.

. . . The old man was unable to rise from his bed to greet me, and I assumed for a while that I had been called to give him last rites. However, he had heard of the execution of the heretic Giordano Bruno last month, and his conscience bothered him. It seems that he had known Bruno some thirty years before.

'That winter,' he said, though I could not determine the exact year of which he spoke, 'Brother Giordano came often to my home.

He said he was interested in astrology. He would not let me cast his own chart, but he liked to look at old charts I had drawn up and which at that time I kept always in my room. He would note the positions of the stars and planets, and compare them from one chart to another. He needed only to see a chart once to remember its details precisely. Then he would go to my window and look to the heavens. It was a crisp winter, I remember, and the stars were very clear. He would delight in identifying the planets. "Look, that is Jupiter," he might say, or "There is Mars, of course." Then he told me of someone, in Poland, I think he said, who had discovered that the planets revolve around the sun, and that our Earth does the same, which surprised me. And he said that the Earth is a planet just like Venus and Mars, and he said one time, "Had we but a strong enough lens, might we not observe the seas and forests and cities of those other worlds." "Not cities, surely," I replied, "for that would mean there are people to build them, and what people could they be that have not known God, where Christ incarnate has not died to redeem their souls as he died for us on this world?" At that he was silent for some time, looking up into the night sky. Then he waved his hand, a gesture I had seen him make on other occasions to dismiss some inconvenient notion. "No, there are people, I am sure of that. And all the constellations, the fixed stars, are they not also suns, and are there not worlds that circle them, and people on those worlds too? And perhaps," he said, after another long pause, "if God's mercy is truly infinite, then it must extend to all those worlds and all those people also."'

At that, Giacomo Carafa himself fell silent, and it seemed he must have fallen asleep. Yet in time he roused himself again with a great sigh, and turned his gaze to the plain cross above his bed. 'And that, I truly believe, was a most terrible heresy. But though I forbade Brother Giordano my home, yet I never spoke of that sin to anyone as surely I should have done.' He seemed to subside in his bed, as if he had only enough strength to tell his story. 'I understand,' he said, his voice now much fainter so that I had to lean close to catch his words, 'that Brother Giordano left Naples not long after, though in truth I never saw him again.' At this, the old man asked to make confession and receive absolution, and this was done.

Marginal notation in another hand:
Why did we not know of this before?

*

3. Extract from an undated memorandum written in his own hand by Cardinal Scipione Rebiba. This is presumed to date from late 1575 or early 1576.

Brother G. came to me today. He assured me that no one else knows he is in Rome. He demonstrated once more his phenomenal memory by reciting large parts of the *De revolutionibus* by Copernicus, which he had read only once during that previous visit to Rome. He then assured me that the orbit of the planets is not circular, as Copernicus avers, but follows a somewhat different pattern, though he is not yet sure what that pattern might be. He also insisted that he is now more certain than ever that the fixed stars are themselves suns, and that they are in turn orbited by planets of their own. This is a dangerous argument, and I had to stress that he should never repeat it to anyone else. At this point I said that, since the death of Pope Pius, no one else in the Vatican was aware of our previous discussions or agreements. Gregory is unlikely to be sympathetic to his embassy. So he should take extra care, since he no longer has the support he might once have had. Brother G. waved a hand impatiently in front of his face, as though batting away a fly, and said: 'No matter. It's too late now, we must go on.'

Once he had slipped away, I realised that he was not the only one in danger. Tomorrow, for my own protection, I will make arrangements so that it will appear to anyone who does not investigate too closely, that Brother G. was forced to flee Naples for reasons of heresy. I suspect it will not be too hard to make that convincing.

*

4. One page of a letter. The rest of the letter has not survived, so it is impossible to determine who it was addressed to, or who wrote it. There is some sign of damage to the paper.

... as advised, I joined the company and travelled with them from Savona, via Turin and eventually to Venice, where I am now. I note that at this time he called himself simply Giordano Bruno, and no longer wore his habit. Since he made no mention of the fact, it is possible that many of those in our company were unaware that he [illegible].

During much of our journey, he kept to himself. I believe he was writing, though I had no opportunity to see what he wrote. However, of an evening he would often walk out alone from whatever inn or farm we had taken refuge in for the night. On these occasions I was generally able to follow him without being seen. He would find a lonely field where he would not be interrupted. There he would light a small fire, sometimes two or three, then settle down on the ground and look up at the heavens, which he might do for hours on end.

[illegible] close enough I heard him speaking. I could never distinguish his words – to get close enough for that I would have betrayed my presence – but in the main I think he was praying. That, at least, was my impression, except on one occasion when I saw a figure standing close beside him. I can give no accurate description. The figure was tall, thin and very pale. I could not tell whether it was male or female, or even with complete confidence whether it was living or not. There was something almost ghostly in its pallor. And in a moment it was gone, I cannot say how or where.

I have not seen such a figure again since, and must assume it was someone local, perhaps an accidental encounter. The next morning we completed our journey to ...

*

5. *Memorandum by Cardinal Scipione Rebiba written in his own hand, dated 13 June 1577.*

Have spoken with Christopher Clavius. Someone had to know. He does not believe me.

*

6. *Unsigned note found among the papers of Cardinal Scipione Rebiba after his death, 23 July 1577. The handwriting has been tentatively identified as that of Giordano Bruno.*

Have made contact. Will proceed with the embassy as circumstances allow.

Marginal notation in another hand:
    Remove this.

*

7. *Letter from Father Pierre LeMaitre, SJ, dated Toulouse, 5 January 1581, addressed to the Superior General of the General Curia in Rome.*

This day I did receive a visit from one Giordano Bruno, late of Geneva. He told me that he had not taken any part in the heresies rife in that city, but that he now wished to be received back into the Church. He hinted to me that he had once been a member of the Dominican Order, but provided no information to support this claim, and nothing in his dress, deportment or language would suggest it might be true.

This Bruno seemed to me a strange and elusive character. He is a theologian and philosopher, which subjects he teaches here at the university, yet his speech was filled with references to mathematics and the fixed stars, and he said at one point that he was an astronomer, at another that he was an astrologer, and at a third that he had devised an original system of memory. I was left with the impression that he himself did not know what he might be, except mayhap a charlatan. And yet he comes with letters from colleagues here at the university and from the Marchese de Vico of Naples who all extol his learning. Still, I admit I did not trust the man.

When in our conversation I did confront him with these contradictions he did wave them away with a wild gesture of the hand, as if they were no more than an irritant, and said simply that that was what he was.

Despite such doubts, I would of course have welcomed him back to the salvation of Mother Church were he truly repentant of his sins. Yet at this point he spoke of things that troubled me greatly, which is why I write to you today. I seek your guidance as to whether the case of this Giordano Bruno should be referred to the Office of the Holy Inquisition. For he told me that he had had congress with demons.

He did not use these words, of course, for he was very circumspect in his speech. He spoke of meeting others that were like men yet not. He spoke of it as though it were an embassy. He said they had much learning to impart about the motion of the planets and stars and the nature of life upon other worlds. He spoke quietly and seriously, as one might speak of meeting an admired teacher for the first time, and I took him to be referring in some fanciful way to visitors from the Holy Roman Empire, where I hear there are many men skilled in astronomy. But as he continued, talking of worlds that knew not our Lord Jesus Christ, and vessels that moved in the air, and so much more, then did I fear that some dreadful heresy was being unfolded to me. And at last I did become frightened and angry, and I raised my voice and told him that his sins were too great ever to expect the mercy of the Church and that he must leave God's house right away.

At this he seemed not surprised or upset, but rose gently and straightway went to the door. But there he paused, and turning to me said, 'Tell your people, tell Rome, that I . . .' Then he stopped, and his last words as he left were not, I think, meant for my ears, for he said, 'No, no use, I must find a different sponsor now.' And at that he left.

Marginal notation in another hand:
Uncharacteristic. A very risky strategy. Were there other attempts to get a message to us?

*

7a. Note attached to the letter from Fr. LeMaitre and dated 27 March 1581.

By order of the General Curia, Father Pierre LeMaitre is hereby recalled to Rome.

*

*8. Note found in the apartment of Giordano Bruno after he left Paris.
The note is undated. Extensive charring indicates an attempt was
made to burn it.*

I have been visited four times since we first established contact
five years ago, but visits seem to be difficult for them. They are
weighed down, move slowly and heavily, though in their bodies
they seem so light. They talk of 'gravity', but I do not understand
the word. They seem eager to meet, happy to teach me much, and
they insist that they learn from me. But at the same time they are
reluctant, they suggest that it is difficult, damaging, perhaps even
dangerous. Now they suggest that I should visit them, and I am
afraid. If it is dangerous for them here, how much more dangerous would it be for me in their realm? And yet, how much more
might I learn there?

*All of the above has been heavily scratched out, but remains legible.
The words below seem to have been added later, and were clearly
written in haste.*

   No point, who could I tell? I must go!

*

*9. Testimony of Marie Clement, servant, given in the presence of King
Henri III and Pierre de Gondi, Bishop of Paris. Bishop Pierre de
Gondi made this record, and no one else was present. At the foot of the
document are affixed the Royal Seal of France and the seal of the
Bishop of Paris; there is an X identified as the mark of Marie Clement.
The document is dated 27 March 1583.*

Your Most Christian Majesty, I aver that my name is Marie
Clement, I am seventeen years of age and I work as a servant here
in the Palace.

   On Monday of last week, I am sorry your Grace, I do not know
the date. But it was Monday, your Majesty, because on Monday I
sweep the corridors of the servants' quarters. This would have
been a little before midday. I was alone, all the other servants were
about their duties of course. But for myself, there was nobody in

the corridor, and if it had not been my day to sweep there would have been nobody at all.

Yes, your Majesty, that was when the man appeared. He fell, like someone who has missed his step. No, your Grace, there is no step in that corridor, nor anything else he might have stumbled over. No, your Grace, I do not know where he came from. There was no door near him, nor any open window. No, your Majesty, no hole had formed in the walls or ceiling. Indeed, I know that workmen have examined the corridor since Monday and have found no way that he might have entered.

Yes, your Majesty, I did recognise him. I do not know his name, but he is the one we call the Memory Man.

The first thing I did was go to him and ask if he needed any help. No, your Grace, he wasn't far from me, a half a dozen paces maybe, no more. He was sitting against the wall of the corridor and seemed a little dazed. When he saw me, he said 'What the devil,' pardon your Grace, 'What the devil are you doing here?' I told him I was sweeping, and I showed him the broom that I was still holding, but he waved his hand as if it was of no importance.

Then he said, 'Help me up, will you.' I bent down to give him my hand, which he clasped, but he still seemed to have great difficulty getting to his feet. 'You are injured, sir,' I said. 'No,' he said, 'no damage done. But they were right, the body is confoundedly heavy.'

I beg your pardon, your Majesty, but the Memory Man is not large. He is somewhat below average height and very thin, not heavy at all, but that is what he said. And when, at last, he was able to stand up, he bent over with his hands on his knees breathing very hard, as if he had done something very strenuous. Then he straightened up and said, 'Let me lean on you for a while.' He put an arm around my shoulder, and I thought he might drag me to the ground so much did he sag. We walked very slowly to the end of the corridor. There we found a chair, and he sat down. I asked if he needed anything further, and he said, 'No, I'll be fine in a moment,' and he sent me back about my business.

No, your Majesty, I didn't see him again. When I had finished my work and got back to that end of the corridor he had gone.

No, your Grace, I did not ask who 'they' were, nor where he had come from. It was not my place to do so. He said nothing beyond what I have told you today.

Yes, sirs, that is a true account of what I remember.

*

10. Extract from a letter sent from Michel de Castelnau, the French Ambassador at the Court of St James, to King Henri III of France. The letter is dated 11 June 1583. This letter, which may be a copy since it is certainly not in de Castelnau's hand, appears to have been read in the Vatican as early as August 1583.

As for the man Bruno, he arrived in April with your Majesty's letter of recommendation, and I have, as directed, found him suitable accommodation. I find him easy to admire, for he has very great learning and discourses readily on all manner of subjects, yet he is hard to like. His manner is abrupt and abrasive, and I fear this may not go down well with the English, who are very jealous of their proper standing and elaborate courtesies. Nevertheless, he has quickly made the acquaintance of several people in good standing on the edges of the court, including the poet Sydney and the mathematician Digges, who is himself in the circle of the notorious Doctor Dee who has the ear of the Queen. I have also learned but lately that philosophers at Oxford University have invited him to address them. I do not yet know why the man is in England, but it is clear that he may well be of service to us . . .

*

11. Extract from a memorandum supposedly written by Francis Walsingham. The memorandum is undated, is not in his hand, and does not follow certain practices usual in Walsingham's private writings. It is assumed, therefore, that this is a forgery, although it is unclear why or when it was created. The document was certainly held in the Vatican no later than 1620.

. . . this Bruno is most like a spy. For he resides at the French embassy, though he is no ambassador, and it would seem at the express command of King Henry. Nor is he French, but would seem to be a Neapolitan. It is rumoured that he was once a monk or priest, the stories do not agree, yet he pretends now to be no Catholic, and indeed seems to attract the ire of many of that persuasion. He presents himself as a philosopher, and moves easily in that company, though it is said that he has little English, his French is barbaric and even his Latin is poor. Tis certain, though, that he has a prodigious memory, an accomplishment most meet in the profession of spy. We should, therefore, keep careful watch on this Bruno, but bear in mind that we may be able to use his talents for our own purposes.

*

12. Anonymous denunciation, one of many similar removed from the Office of the Holy Inquisition, 18 February 1600.

There is here one Giordano Bruno that I did know in Italy. He speaks publicly of the most foul heresies, that the Earth is not the centre of the universe, that there are infinite numbers of stars and that they in turn have planets like the Earth around them, and that there may be people on these planets without the knowledge of our Lord Jesus Christ. In private, he has congress with demons, and has said that they have taken him up into their realm. I know this for I have witnessed it, both in Italy and again here in London.

Marginal notation in another hand:
  This one looks like the same handwriting as the spy who accompanied him to Venice.

*

13. Biographical fragment found among the papers of Francis Godwin, Bishop of Hereford, after his death in April 1633. The fragment was seemingly intended to accompany his fantasy, The Man in the Moone *(published posthumously, 1638), but was withheld, apparently on the instructions of his son. It is unclear how this document found its way to the Vatican.*

In 1583, when I took my master's at Oxford, a learned man from Italy named Giordano Bruno came to address us. He spoke many times, and I did try to attend as many as I was able. He spoke in a moderate Latin, interspersed with words from many other languages, some of which I suspect were of his own devising, but what he spoke about was so interesting that it was worth making the effort to follow. He tried, in several lectures, to teach us the art of building Memory Palaces, though I have never been successful in that endeavour. But once or twice he spoke of the heavens. He spoke of the work of Doctor Copernicus, which I had never heard explained so clearly. Then he went beyond Copernicus, telling us that as the planets circled our sun, so the stars were also suns with planets circling them. I have heard that Thomas Digges has said something similar before, yet it felt as if Master Bruno were vouchsafing some great revelation. He spoke as if with private knowledge.

I was, at this time, already thinking of my voyage to the Moon, and so I did contrive to meet privily with Master Bruno. I took with me some fine Rhenish, which I had heard he did enjoy, and for some hour or more we did sit in his chambers and he did regale me with more mathematics about planets and orbits than my poor mind could hold. But as the hour grew late I did venture to mention my fantasy of more perfect beings on the Moon, and he sat quiet for some time regarding me strangely. Then, abruptly, he waved his hand and said, 'Not more perfect, no. More advanced, more learned, and that,' he paused here and sipped his wine. I had not known him so quiet for so long, for he had seemed a man full of words, but now he put down his wine and leaned forward as if ready to impart a great secret. 'And that,' he continued, 'mayhap tends to perfection. Yes, mayhap it does.'

He looked searchingly at me, as if weighing me on some unknowable scale. I made to say something, I know not what, but he cut me off sharply. 'I have met them, and they are not perfect. But they have seen so much, have learned so much, have so much that they might teach us did we but know how.' He looked puzzled, as if he had not expected to hear himself say that. Then he went on again rapidly, permitting no interruption. 'No, no I am not mad, nor do I consort with devils as I know some rumours would have it. Many years ago I calculated that there must be other beings in the universe, though I had no knowledge of how we might contact them. Then, one night, as I watched the stars near my monastery in Naples, I saw something obscure the stars in a way that seemed to be no cloud. I had no notion what this might be, and in moments it had gone. I saw nothing further for maybe a year, then, again, a shape which I recalled matched exactly what I had seen the year before. Now I began to speculate that perhaps those other beings had found a way to come to us. For such a long time I saw nothing more. I took my speculations to the Vatican, where a cardinal seemed interested and gave me some backing, but that came to nothing and besides he is dead now. I began to think of ways that I might attract them. On clear nights I set fires in open spaces where no one might see. I arranged them in geometric shapes, line and triangle and square, or in mathematical progressions, one, two, three, five, eight, thirteen. I left the church so I might travel and learn as much of the heavens as was known, in case others had seen these things, And one night, near Venice it was . . .'

Again he lapsed into silence, and though he had not moved I do not think he saw me still. 'They look somewhat like us,' he said, slowly now, 'but they are notably taller and thinner, and their flesh is so pale that in darkness it seems to glow. But it is only as you get to know them that you understand how different they are. They bend in ways that we do not, they move in ways that seem more an undulation than a walk. When first you meet them it seems as if you are in conversation with a normal man, it is only later that they become more and more unsettling. They spoke to me. I am not sure how they spoke, it was not Latin or Italian, the two languages that in those days I knew, yet I understood perfectly what they were saying. And it seemed that they understood me.

'They came to me four times. That first time near Venice, twice in Geneva and again in Toulouse. But I could see that it was tiring for them, as if they bore an extra weight upon this Earth. I was persuaded, therefore, in Paris to let them take me up into their ship. They call it a ship, though it is like no ship you or I have ever seen. It is more like a building, or indeed more like a city, with squares and avenues and such space that in places it is hard to realise you are enclosed. And I was indeed lighter, such that it seemed I had to learn to walk all over again. Though there were parts of the ship that they showed me where I might fly, although they said I was not actually flying, but rather between the worlds there is no weight except that which they create artificially. I have been several times to their ship since then, and it gets easier to be there and harder to return to our world.

'They have shown me wonders, though there is much I do not understand, and much that feels almost but not quite within my grasp. And they have spent as long, or longer, questioning me about this world. I sometimes think that all my travels have been more concerned with finding new information to tell them than it has been the result of my own restlessness.' He paused then, seeming very sad now. 'All that I have seen, all that I have learned, will die with me. I cannot put it into a book that censors will allow me to print, and there are censors everywhere. I have heard, of one Brahe in Denmark, or perhaps Rudolph in Prague. Perhaps I should go there, tell them. But would they want to know?'

At that he fell into a sullen silence, and I left soon after, leaving the remainder of the Rhenish with him. I was not sure what to make of all he had told me, for we had drunk much. But in time I would base my inhabitants of the Moon upon his description, and short, abrupt, restless Domingo is, of course, a reference to Bruno. And I remembered, too, that there was no weight between the worlds, though that seemed perhaps the most fanciful of all the things he told me.

*

14. Extract from a letter from Michel de Castelnau to King Henri III dated October 1585.

I beg to inform your Majesty that the mob has attacked our Embassy in London. Since neither Her Majesty Queen Elizabeth nor her creature Walsingham show any willingness to restrain this action or defend our persons, I have no alternative but to return temporarily to France. I will present your Majesty with a full account of the circumstances and the effect of this attack upon my arrival in Paris.

I have, incidentally, persuaded Giordano Bruno to return with me. Since he seems to have incurred the enmity of many different forces in England, I do not feel his safety could be guaranteed were he to remain.

*

15. Letter from Girolamo Besler to Giordano Bruno, dated 19 November 1591. The letter was found on Bruno's person when he was arrested in Venice, 22 May 1592.

My friend, permit me to make one last desperate attempt to persuade you to change your mind. I can see nothing awaiting you in Venice but imprisonment and death. You have said that the Inquisition is no longer as diligent in your pursuit as once it was. Yet there is no evidence to support such a claim, and I am not even sure that you believe it yourself. The authorities in Venice are no longer so independent as once they were, and should you return to that city they will surely arrest you and hand you over to Rome.

Should that happen, please believe me that your powers of persuasion will avail you nothing. Consider, even the Emperor Rudolph, who might be thought sympathetic to your views, was unwilling to countenance your stories of meeting beings from another world. When you tried to distil some of these otherworldly wonders into the two books we wrote together, they had to be disguised as Magick to evade even the relaxed censorship here in Prague. And the disguise was so thorough that I am not sure anything but Magick remains.

You claim further that what you are pleased to call your 'embassy to the stars' was supported by Cardinal Rebiba and approved by Pope Pius, but both men are dead, they can do nothing for you now. Unless they have left written records, which is doubtful, your claim cannot be backed up, certainly not to a degree that would satisfy the Inquisition. Indeed, politics change so rapidly in the Vatican that it is likely that even if they did leave a written record it would not be enough to save you now.

Finally, put not your faith in your friends from the stars. They will not and cannot speak for you. By your own account, they have not themselves visited Earth for more than ten years, and I do not see how they will be able to help once you are locked within the Tower of Nona.

My friend, I know that you have been offered the chance to teach your system of memory in Venice, and that is more than you have been able to do in Prague or Frankfurt or Wittenberg. I know that you get restless and must constantly move to new places. I know that you seek out new experiences, new knowledge, that you might offer to your friends from the stars. But think that such opportunities might not also be available in Denmark or Poland or other German states, where you would be safer than in Venice?

Giordano, for the sake of our friendship, for the sake of all that extraordinary knowledge that you hold, please do not put yourself into the hands of the Inquisition.

*

16. Document inserted into the file at this point. It is unsigned and undated, but the handwriting matches that of the marginal notations on a number of other documents in the file.

By my order, all documents relating to Giordano Bruno and his so-called 'embassy to the stars' have been withdrawn from circulation or destroyed.

Records of the trial have been examined in detail. All documents relating to the embassy have been destroyed. Any references to the embassy have been removed and the trial records re-written as necessary.

These remaining documents are to be locked in this file in perpetuity.

*

17. Testimony of Domenico Bellarmino, guard at the Tower of Nona, given 22 January 1600.

It was my duty to take food to the prisoner Bruno. He was to be delivered that day to the secular authorities ready for execution, so this was the last meal he would receive here. We all knew of the words he spoke upon receiving his sentence: 'Perhaps you deliver this sentence against me with greater fear than I receive it.' It was believed that this defiance betokened some plan for rescue or escape, so we took special precautions. I had two armed men accompany me and others were stationed at several points nearby.

As I approached the cell I became aware of a light that seemed to emanate from it. Of course, there should have been no light. So I put the food down and the three of us approached the door cautiously. The light was quite pale, but it was distinctly visible around the door frame. The door was still locked. I remember that, and I am sure the other guards will testify to that effect. I took my key and unlocked it, and then the three of us burst in.

The prisoner was still chained where he had been, but there was another person beside him. This person was tall but stooped, and white like an angel. I could see all this clearly, because the light seemed to come directly from the body of this angel.

Even as we watched, the prisoner shook the chains from his wrists, then the two of them turned slightly towards us and in an instant had disappeared.

I swear by my Lord Jesus Christ and my hope of salvation that this is the truth. I have never seen the white figure before or since, and there is no other way by which they could have entered or left the cell. It was a miracle, my lord.

*

18. Letter from Johannes Kepler to his mother, dated Prague, October 1610. The letter seems never to have been sent.

I had the most extraordinary dream. I must assume it was a dream, though I was in my workshop and it was the middle of the day.

I looked up from my desk and a tall white man stood before me. I had heard nobody enter, and indeed had thought the door locked (which it later proved to be), so I challenged the intruder. Who are you? What are you doing here? He did not answer, but instead he said, 'Giordano Bruno is dead,' though I could not swear that his lips moved.

'Yes,' I replied, for this is the sort of conversation one has in dreams, is it not? 'He was burned in Rome ten years ago.'

'No,' the man said. The voice, as I heard it, seemed to come from inside my head. It was very calming, I felt no sense of threat.

'He died this morning aboard our ship. It was felt someone should be informed of his true death.'

'And the *auto-da-fé*?' I said.

'Some other poor unfortunate, hooded and gagged so the deception would not be discovered. Giordano Bruno was our friend, our ambassador he called it, so we took him to our ship and tended the wounds from his torture. But his body could not long endure the strains of low gravity and today his system failed beyond repair.'

'What does that mean?' I said. I recall the words now perfectly, though they make no sense to me. But without answering, the figure vanished. And I was in my study, and somewhere far away I could hear a clock strike twelve.

I thought then of all the things Bruno had told us, about the infinite stars and the many worlds and all the peoples who might be found upon them. Then I turned again to my calculations, for it had all been but a dream.

Ω

It might be said that if anyone from the sixteenth century were to make contact with aliens, it would be Giordano Bruno. Obviously it cannot, at this distance, be proved either way, but as historians we must say that the documentary evidence in this file would be more than suffi-cient to support any less controversial historical scenario. To dismiss this possibility out of hand, therefore, must be to rely on preconceptions rather than on the weight of evidence.

1620

The voyage of the Mayflower *to what would become the United States of America is part of that nation's mythology. The hazards the passengers and crew encountered at sea were nothing compared to those they faced after they landed, with a harsh winter and unrelenting sickness. Many died – but those who lived were among the first settlers in America, remembered with veneration today as the Pilgrim Fathers.*

But if this account is to be believed, that mythology, like most mythologies, is only part of the truth; the reality was very different. This was an age of religious division and duplicity. Were all the Brownist Dissenters and Puritans quite what they seemed? And were the misfortunes they encountered just misfortunes?

This account, which has been rendered into modern English, is compiled from diary entries and from a package of letters, which have been interleaved in chronological order. They were found separately in the Vatican Vaults, but together they tell a very different version of the voyage of the Mayflower.

The Hammer of Witches

Mary Gentle

22 July 1620, to his Grace the Bishop of Luçon, at Avignon – Sir:
I sabotaged the *Speedwell*, sister ship to the *Mayflower*, on the journey across the English Channel to Southampton.

It isn't as successful as I'd hoped.

You'll recall that, in my identity of John Allerton, one of the heretic Protestant separatists at Leiden in Holland, I was in charge of buying a ship for their mission to colonise the New World. I purchased the 60-ton *Speedwell* because it was the nearest thing I could find to a wreck still afloat.

Despite taking an iron pry-bar to the hull and easing open the planking, worsening the leaks, it still floats.

We've limped here, into Southampton Water. The master, Captain John Chappell, has ordered her patched up. We rendez-voused with the *Mayflower*, and the English branch of the sect (Anglicans and Brownists, mostly; amiable people). I'm cheered to find the seventy Merchant Adventurers investors have hired more clerks and labourers to go out and work the colony. Our so-called 'Saints' from Leiden have nicknamed the whole group 'The Strangers' though they have nothing in common apart from the name.

Your agent who was to have sabotaged the *Mayflower* is missing. The ship's master, Captain Jones, appears honest when he says he has never heard the man's name.

We have many enemies.

The yard has patched up the *Speedwell* as much as they can. I can see where it can be speedily unpatched. I hope to write to your Grace from another English port soon. I'll do all I can to make sure neither ship leaves the English Channel. However, if we do – what's the Bishop's Wizard worth if he can't raise up a storm in the Atlantic Ocean?

I confirm that, yes, the problem is not enthusiastic Brownists and Anglicans making a home in the New World. It's who they carry among them – and how many.

Until we're away from shore, I'm keeping my abilities quiet. The separatists want to escape persecution, but they'll burn witches just as readily as Bloody Mary and Elizabeth burned heretics (of different flavours).

On a different subject. If possible, my lord, might you have a secretary write to that ignorant soldier Miles Standish that you have acting as my minder? I know we Gifted are not quite of God, and must be watched; but please, he needs reminding that his job is to see that I get my job done?

I remain, as ever, your servant.

JA

[Usual cypher] [*This is the only part of the text written in clear French.*]

*

Diary entry dated 13 August 1620
[Marked *private cypher*]
My dearest Secret,

I'm about the Bishop's Godly business, so it's far too dangerous to actually send letters to the nunnery. I write this diary under the pretence that it's letters to you. I'll do as before – when I get back, I'll parcel it up and bring it, and you can read everything I've seen and done.

For this mission I've taken over the identity of one John Allerton, a common seaman, but a powerful man among the Puritan churches, and an Elder of this group who are going to the New World. Or rather, aren't.

As to where we are – I thought I might need to raise a wind to delay sailing down the Channel. However, the *Speedwell* sprang *another* leak. We took refuge in Dartmouth, a little port in Devon.

Sadly, we are now repaired, and are once more at sea.

For some reason, I've often been tempted to ask one Moses

Fletcher, another of our Elders, and master of the Saints on the *Speedwell*, what he would think of a weather-wizard in his company?

He'd turn from my friend to my enemy in an instant, I'd guess. As if I'd become a totally different man.

I don't know if I ever told you – when I was a small boy (you would have been in your cradle), my father took me to see the crowning of King James of Scotland, then to be King James of England too. When it got to the point where the King was anointed, I asked, *Dad, Why?*

The answer I got was *Spraying holy oil on that man's body changes it into a miraculous body, son, different from the rest of us. A King's body. A divine body.*

Someone in the crowd took exception – some Puritan enthusiast – and shouted that it was *Nonsense, rubbish and Papist superstition!* All of us were thrown out by the musketeers and halberd-men.

On the way home, I was still young enough to ask my dad if the King's new body was a Gift, like my Gift of controlling the weather?

That was the first time he ever hit me for what he thought was blasphemy.

Today, sailing down the Channel (the *Speedwell* straining to keep up with the *Mayflower*) it begins to seem – on the face of it – that it's the Puritan separatists who'll rule the proposed colony. A man could look at us and say: the Strangers have little in common with each other. A humble-jumble of farmers, blacksmiths, butchers, boatmen, valets and ladies' maids, who fancy the idea of owning their own land and bringing up their children the way they like. The Saints are bound tightly together by congregation, by their Elders, by their beliefs. They argue much, but they speak with one voice to others.

Then again, as ever, things are not quite as they seem.

You Fore-Saw it right.

Of the hundred and fifty passengers on both ships, Puritans and everyone else, more than a hundred of them are Gifted. That's what this ship carries to the New World. Not escaping Puritans, but escaping Gifted souls.

I'm melancholy; I wish I had your company.

And, yes, sometimes I wish I had your twin gifts of Fore-sight and Past-sight. But what's happening on the *Speedwell* is far too close to 'the moment of Things Happening' (as you call it!) for you to see anything but obscurity and fog.

Writing in this crowded underdeck by a taper's inefficient light, kept close like animals in a stock pen, is a premonition of the Hell that awaits both of us. Forgive me. They have just called that we are passing Land's End; I run with all these other fools to see it!

*

31 August, Plymouth Harbour, Devon; to his Grace the Bishop of Luçon at Avignon – Sir:
I thought I might have to try harder at sabotage. Turns out the *Speedwell's* crew were there with their own pry-bars, loosening the seams. The cowards were facing bad weather, thin crops, savage natives and disease in the New World, and they decided they wanted no part of it. Who can blame them? But why not do it *before*!

Maybe it wasn't a real threat to them until they were in the Atlantic rollers.

We made two hundred miles out into the Atlantic before the *Speedwell* almost foundered. There were winds from the west strong enough in our faces that I hardly needed to give them a push; the weather was entirely ready to hamper us.

Despite protests, we turned back.

Before Standish writes you his side of the story, I confess we fought on the deck. He accused me of not doing my duty (trying to say, without other people understanding him, that I could have called up a greater gale before this time). I ran out of patience when I most needed it. They broke up the fight before the daggers could be used.

We are now in the harbour of Plymouth, Devon, from where Drake's forces set out to harry the Armada's ships. (I believe the Spanish weather-wizards had very little skill.)

They have a capable yard here. All agree the *Speedwell* couldn't sail across a town duck pond. Stores are shifted to the *Mayflower*, some families decide to wait for the following year, and some men leave their families in England and say they will send for them when they're settled. You'll remember from my earlier reports that the *Mayflower* is a 180-ton Dutch *fluyt*, as they call them; built specifically for carrying cargo and, unlike most, with no ability to convert to a warship – hence its greater tonnage for a 100-foot ship. Its four decks carry an amazing amount of stores, families and livestock.

What can be put off for one year can be put off for a decade.

I keep pushing the justifiable opinion to the other Elders that August is far too late to set sail across the Atlantic, especially when they must build shelter and plant crops to harvest when they arrive.

As I surmised, the Saints have the advantage of a unified opinion. The voice they speak with is not that of the separatists, rather, it is that of all the Gifted.

But I believe it's *only* their united, ordinary voice.

I've now noted the connections between many of the Strangers hired by the Merchant Adventurers, and the English and Leiden Puritans. (See my attached report. Perhaps this is information your agent on the *Mayflower* discovered, before he vanished.)

The truth is, Secret is right. I wouldn't have her Gift. Hundreds of years in the future, she can See wonders – men walking on the silver globe in the sky – and terrors. She can guess at causes; at where things may originate. And at the moment, the cause of terror begins this year, with the voyage of the *Speedwell* and the *Mayflower*. And a colony the world would be better off without.

At least two-thirds of these people are wizards and witches, desiring to escape Europe.

You said they might thrive in this colony, escaping the Witch-Burnings that have killed hundreds of thousands of the Gifted across Europe.

I know why it had to be done.

Now it seems it must be done in the New World, too.

I shall soon find myself in the Atlantic again. I will put as much obstruction from wind and wave in the ship's way as I can. All I can say, sir, is, remember we're dealing with fanatics.

I remain your very obedient servant,

JA

[Autumn cypher] [*Again, these two words in clear French.*]

*

Diary entry: 2 September 1620
[Marked *private cypher*]
Beloved Secret,

I miss our talks together, even though most times the rules of your Order keep a barred grill between us when we speak. I'm using what you discovered with your Past-Sight in argument with that idiot Miles Standish. He may have a degree in military engineering from the University of Leiden. He's still the cast-off son of an English lord with all the sense of entitlement the aristocracy have, and no respect for scholarship. Or for witches.

He could, if he wanted, read in any Church library how the wizards and witches – I'd still rather call us the Gifted – fell under the Church's control even before Constantine adopted Christianity. It's no coincidence that all the pagan demi-gods and enchantresses and magi started disappearing about then. The First Council of Nicaea asserted priests could use us in the service of good.

Miles Standish, that soldier who loves his cannon more than his wife Rose, who he's dragged along with him, keeps hammering the table and demanding *What use are you? The ability to spoil milk, help a wife conceive a son, put a fog in the path of an enemy army . . . Chance could do as much!*

Most Gifts aren't powerful, but they change the individual lives of people they help or harm.

I'm sure Standish thinks my Gift is merely summoning up a wind, either behind us to fill our sails, or in front to hinder us. He doesn't think that wind brings or takes rain – therefore, drought or plenty – and brings storms, tempests, lightning.

He doesn't think there may be other Gifts.

I don't doubt our beloved Bishop sent Standish as my minder simply because he and I will always grate against one another, and never fall into an alliance. Never mind. Bishop du Plessis uses our powers as he and the cardinals and the Pope see fit.

Have you written again to Bishop du Plessis? Has he called at the nunnery? I keep watching the Devon hills around Plymouth, in case I should see a courier riding in. Your Fore-Sight showed us a future terrible beyond measure – I wake from the fire and light and heat almost every morning. Has what I've done so far made the slightest change?

Bless you in your quiet Order. At least I can be out in the world, doing things. You have nothing but the round of Matins, Nones, Vespers and the rest, interrupted by the terrible sight of what Man can do to this world a few centuries in the future.

One day I swear I'll ride up and take you away from there.

Put flowers on her grave from me, too.

JA

*

The English ship Mayflower, *at sea, 8 September 1620; a report by my hand to be saved for his Grace the Bishop of Luçon to read: his eyes only. If we pass a Spanish galleon sailing east, I will put a copy into their hands to carry it home – Sir:*
Is it your intention that everything I'm intended to do be endangered by Miles Standish?

He openly calls me 'the Bishop's wizard' – among people, Gifted or otherwise, who are willing to cross the Atlantic to get away from the Church!

I can't call him out to duel again, even on days when the deck is level enough, because *he is your agent and I shouldn't kill him!* And because I don't challenge him, I look like a coward, and the Gifted on board are starting to mistrust me.

Was this your intention?

Then again, perhaps you don't have much choice in agents, and Captain Miles Standish is a loud-mouthed malcontent who can't keep quiet when he's been drinking.

It would be a shame if a freak wave washed him off the deck.

I must go pray and repent that thought.

Your servant,

JA

[Winter cypher] [*In French*]

*

Diary entry dated 9 November, near the hook of Cape Cod, viewing the lost settlement of Plimouth [private cypher]
My sweet cousin Secret,

I won't bother you with our voyage here – it was dreadful beyond telling, but boring to read. I made a copy of the reports I've written for the Bishop, and it's enclosed here for you. To be short, terrible winds were against us, the voyage took much longer than expected, it's now the start of November and we've just sighted land, and still they won't turn back. Cape Cod is biting cold.

I suppose, if I think about it, his Grace already *knows* – by asking you about the future – that the *Mayflower* didn't go down with all hands, and likely has, in fact, arrived in these hellish icy seas.

Some of the Strangers, as I'm now thinking of all non-Gifted here, do want to go home. There aren't enough of them to carry the day against the Saints. (I include both Puritan Gifted and non-Puritan Gifted under this name.)

We made one attempt to build a house; it's been abandoned. It's too cold and wet to build shelter. Expeditions have discovered buried corn, and graves of previous settlers, and a glimpse or two of the local inhabitants. The decision is to winter over on board the *Mayflower* itself, and to begin building the colony and planting in the spring.

If not for what we know, I'd be here with the other witches and wizards, saving my own kind. Escaping the hunters back home; the implacable men, and the gossiping neighbours, who watch with gleeful terror as they comment that they never knew it took so *much* wood to build a pyre. Don't witches have a right to save their own lives?

A door has opened for them at the last minute. I know we must bar it shut.

Fire now, or greater fire later on.

Secret, Secret – you are *sure*, aren't you?

*

20 November, New Plimouth Harbour, the Mayflower at anchor; to his Grace, Armand-Jean du Plessis, Bishop of Luçon, with the court of the Queen-Mother Marie de Medici in internal exile, 360 miles from Paris, at Avignon – Sir:
I write to you at Avignon, your Grace, but it would surprise me if you were still there. Rumour in Leiden had it, last spring, that

Mary Gentle

you'd reconcile King Louis and his royal mother before the autumn. Then back to Paris, and the King's court. I imagine your Christmas will be different from ours, whether it's in Paris or Avignon.

Troubles continue here, you will perhaps be pleased to hear.

We're licensed to settle in Virginia. I called sufficient storms that we've been driven off course, to Cape Cod. We have no legal right to be on this piece of coast. And of course this made anyone with a loud mouth say that since we weren't in Virginia, no one was in charge of us, and they'd do as they pleased!

Organisation counts for a lot. I sometimes think the ancient Church only survived, in place of any of the other religions of the time (Mithraism, say), because it added the teachings of Christ to the organisation of the Roman Empire. But in this case we're speaking of the Gifted among both Saints and Strangers, and they had a compact drawn up before you could say *dread sovereign Lord King James*.

Apparently we're to organise ourselves as a civic society, under the King's distant rule, with every man having a voice to decide our laws. (Class is ignored, but still the women have no voice.) We all signed, that Standish at the front of the queue – he's made captain of the militia – and I at the back.

I can't blame the Gifted. They're desperate to escape burning, drowning, breaking on the wheel: all the other deaths prescribed [*Unfinished; marked* Winter cypher *in an unsteady hand*]

*

Diary entry, presumed late November or early December 1620, on board the Mayflower
[Marked *private cypher*. With some errors]
Dear my own Secret,

Do you Fore-see when you're asleep, as well as awake?

My mind is hazy, as if nightmares are visible night and day, sleeping and waking. I can't forget my Secret.

I keep thinking of the day you told me.

It was Standish, of course, who brought it to mind. Given how many of them we have with us, I began by sounding him out about the souls of witches and wizards.

Well, that was stupid. In the Burning Times, there's only one safe answer to give. Standish says *They're damned.*

'Suppose they're Gifted witches and wizards, like the ones that signed the Mayflower Compact, and swore to put all their talents to work for the common good?'

Miles Standish grudgingly agrees the Church can use the Devil's power for Good. Then he looks at me the way he looks at the ship's rats – *Devil's Lap-dogs*, as he calls the vermin:

'*But then the he-witches and she-witches should all be killed after.*'

I had to walk away. He might be wearing steel back-and-breastplate, but no man yet took a rapier through the eye and came out of it well.

Since then I've sickened.

There are nothing but memories in my mind's eye, wiping out this desolate coast. You and I, in the herb garden of the nunnery, that one time; two Sisters chaperoning, and falling asleep over their knitting where they sat on stone benches. You and I walked with the scent of lavender.

You held my hand and told me how the Burning Times started.

Two or three hundred years ago is far enough that you can Past-see it, although a little fuzzy. You saw how the great killing started – started by the Church, because of one Gifted man.

You couldn't tell me his name.

He wasn't like the other Gifted the Church used, and had used for nearly a millennium and a half. No feeble abilities like curing a sick sheep.

Every man he worked for helped him, recommending him to their friends. Every business deal he made went his way. Every university passed him at the highest mark. Every aristocrat introduced him to the highest-ranking men and women in the royal courts of Europe.

His Gift was to change any man's mind in his favour.

To *compel* them to think as he desired them to. And to like it.

He made it to Cardinal before they caught him.

. . . They knew it had been by luck alone.

The moment the Gift of compulsion was seen in action, the then Pope – and every man on the seat of St Peter thereafter – was determined to eradicate witches and wizards from Europe. A frantic Secret Church Council was held, debating if there were more like him – if there'd been more in the past – how many there could be in the future – how they could detect them – what they could do to fight them?

Within a year, the Burning started.

Now it seems they have to bring it to the New World, too.

I'm not an historian, but even I know that before then, the Church's view of witchcraft was that it was a superstition, it didn't exist, and anyone who thought it did had been deluded by the Devil. After so many centuries, a quick about-face had them warning that witches were everywhere, wizards too, and their favourite crime was infanticide as a sacrifice to Satan.

In 1487 two Dominican monks wrote, and had published by the new printing press, the *Malleus Maleficarum*, The Hammer of (or Against) Witches. Everything you need to know to recognise, interrogate and condemn a witch or (more rarely) wizard. With the printed word spreading like the pox, the view that witchcraft didn't exist found it hard to survive.

The Church took the remaining young Gifted children into their custody, and used them if they could be trusted. If they were younger than seven.

'All our bloodlines have died out,' you said to me.

I could only think of lavender, and your hot, damp hand. (I couldn't have been more than twenty-two.)

'Either killed, or kept in monasteries and nunneries and prevented from breeding until they died of old age. Hundreds of thousands of us, over the centuries. In Europe, now, I'm rare.'

You took my other hand, before the Sisters woke.

You said, 'I do know that when the Inquisition is sure they've eradicated witches with our help, you and I will be killed too.'

Apologies: I don't have much of the good ink left; I shouldn't make it run. But I thought I had no tears left either.

My dear, oh my very dear. If I could pray, I'd just like you to live out your days, the way you want to, for as long as you want to.

*

25 December 1620, Mayflower at anchor; to his Grace the Bishop of Luçon, addendum:

Excuse my insolence in the last report. We have disease on board. I was sickening with it as I wrote, delirious, and not in my right mind.

I saw enough of this during the wars in the Low Countries. This is some mix of the Typhoid Fever, the Pneumonia, and something very like the Small Pox. People are dying so fast we can't bury them.

JA

*

Mid-January 1620 [new calendar, 1621], *New Plimouth – Sir:*

We now have only seventeen crew capable of sailing the ship, including four officers and the master, Captain Christopher Jones. Deaths have slowed markedly, I'm pleased to report. However, of the colonists, there are but five and twenty adult men who have not fallen sick with this fever. Six women nurse the others, and their sisters and children among them.

Some of my acquaintances from Leiden are among the dead. I take comfort in the friendship of Master Moses (or as he sometimes writes himself, Moyses) Fletcher. A man originally from England, now in his middle forties, he's become the unofficial leader of the Gifted Saints. I think his Gift is to cure disease.

I pray it is.

He has a very *compelling* character.

Master Standish lives. His wife Rose is among the dead.

The Saints and Strangers are still determined to build their New Plimouth Town, so I suppose they'll need Standish's cannon and muskets. Some further interaction with the native people has turned them less friendly to us.

Sir: Excuse me finishing here. I'm not over my own bout with the illness, and it's a strain to write in cypher.

Your obedient

JA

[Winter cypher] [*This is also written in cypher, this time*]

*

Diary entry, undated, possibly late January or early February [private cypher]

My dear, my very dear,

I'm a fool. I finally had my fight with Standish, and said much more than I ought.

This has been the worst month for disease yet. It went through our ship, some fever not known by our doctors or any of those Gifted with healing. There are now only one hundred and seven of our colonists alive, of the hundred and fifty.

Miles Standish is the Bishop's man, too. He knows how many Gifted have died. I was stupid enough to say to him, 'I wish *not* to do murder.'

We had met hiding up on one of the two hills that overlooks the harbour. Cole's Hill will be the graveyard, and the Town (if ever fully built), and this is the Fort. Standish had two pitch-leather bottles of spirits; I also. We spoke full of grief and guilt, both of us, stumbling drunk.

'*I* did murder,' Miles said. 'Rose didn't want to come, but I made her. We both obeyed the Church. What has it got us?'

I ought to have told him the Will of God was often difficult to understand; that Rose is in a better place; that such a kind woman could never be damned.

Some moment of empathy stopped me. He may be a decade my senior: grief made him sound bemused and young.

'It's for the best we obey the Bishop,' I attempted to explain. 'He knows the future. The broad sweep of it. As if we're the river, and it's the broad sea.'

We wrangled over that one, me saying more and more, until I found myself trying to explain your secret. (I should have cut my tongue out.) I spelled out the Gift of Fore-Sight, and what it means.

Miles Standish's reaction?

'*It's stupid to take the word of a daft gypsy witch imprisoned in a nunnery!*'

I had his throat in my hand, pushing him back against the trunk of a tree. I told him Secret is a dear, sweet, good, young woman, and my cousin; and far too good for him to insult—

'Ah!' he says, not caring I'm choking him. 'I should a guessed. You're in love with your cousin!'

I let him go.

'No.' I couldn't stop myself saying it: 'I didn't love Secret. I loved her twin sister, called Silence by their Puritan mother, born stone deaf.'

Miles Standish's emotions swung as a drunk man's often do. He hugged my shoulders. If I hadn't seen all the honest grief for Rose in his face, I would have knocked his arm away. Some painful tension released inside me.

'She couldn't learn to speak,' I said.

That didn't matter to me.

'But . . . As she grew into her twenties, men began to do her bidding, exactly as if they could hear her.'

The world is full of cold, and the smell of sea. I could have grown old with her, listening to Silence.

'Silence had the Compeller's Gift. I begged her to do nothing to show she had a talent. In the end, she just wanted to communicate, and hear people, even if it was through compulsion and reading their thoughts. The Church was terrified. They burned her. Within a week of the day that she and I would have married.'

Miles Standish proved himself an oaf again by sneering.

'And the Church still *trusts* you?'

'I understand what Gifts like that could be used for. Silence was as innocent of any malice or desire as a child. But I can imagine the barbarian Attila, or Emperor Charlemagne – or Pope Leo the Third – born with that power. We'd have the old capricious, cruel pagan gods back. We *are* the model for them, after all.' I found my leather bottle empty. 'The Church has made us into a *holokauston* – a sacrifice where everything is burned up and destroyed – but it's a sacrifice to protect against worse evil. The Church is just, not cruel.'

Standish was unconscious. He wasn't listening. I wondered if I was.

I had to carry Standish back over my shoulder, and throw him down into the *shallop* boat to be rowed back to the *Mayflower*. He didn't wake until two days later. The Bishop taught me the careful methods of interrogation, used when the subject doesn't even know he's being questioned, and I'm confident that Standish has nothing but a headache that could melt glass, and a vague memory that I have a dead fiancée to match his dead wife.

*

New Plimouth, 12 February 1620 [1621, new calendar], *to his Grace the Bishop of Luçon, greetings – Sir:*
Another bad month for disease has killed four of us. Envoys from the locals have come and are friendly.
JA.

*

Diary entry, 15 March 1620; New Plimouth [1621, new calendar] [marked *private cypher*]
Secret –

I must tell someone exactly what I've done, though I hate that it's you I must burden.

I've gone beyond my orders. I've approached the witches and wizards of New Plimouth. They've built shacks, and a palisade: the bare bones of a town. Perhaps another hard winter, or the locals, might wipe them out. But also perhaps not.

I called Moses Fletcher aside. He now speaks for the Gifted that are left.

'Go back to Europe,' I said. 'Take your family and belongings and make a run for it – it's either flee to the Turks and Muslims in the south, Russia and Tartary in the east, or the New World – the only one without a religion that will sentence you to death. *Yet!* This New Plimouth won't be allowed to survive the Burning Times.'

Strangely, what he asked was, 'Is your name truly John Allerton?'

I could have said yes, and been close to the truth, but it wasn't what he meant.

'I'm not a simple seaman,' I said. 'And you can probably guess on whose behalf I joined the Saints at Leiden.'

He rested his left hand on his rapier hilt.

'I give you this warning,' I told him, 'because I'm sick of making sure your last chance vanishes. Take the witches and wizards, take what stores you can carry, and go. You're an educated man, you can subtract the longitude where we are now from the longitude of the far coast the Spaniard Vizcaíno mapped for Spain eighteen years ago, and cypher out how big the continent must be! Even if the middle of it is another sea – if you can't lose yourself from other people's sight in all those thousands of miles, where can you!'

Master Fletcher ruminated for what seemed a very long time.

'You're an agent of the Inquisition,' he said. 'Death waits for you too, back there.'

'Doubly so. Why do you think we had such bad storms, getting here?'

Slowly, his expression cleared. The lines around his eyes relaxed. 'I've wondered . . . but it's not possible – someone would follow us if we left the settlement. No matter how far we go into the wilderness, Standish and his soldiers would find us. You know,' he emphasised, giving me a keen look. 'The Papist church wouldn't let us go free.'

I've known Moses these two years at Leiden. My instinct about the man was to speak. I don't think he'll betray me.

'I've wondered about it too,' I said. 'What would make the difference is a diversion, that would take every man's attention away from you. I can provide that. Tell me the day. My Gift is the power of air and water. I'll call up a storm that will wash half of New Plimouth into the sea. And they won't search for you. Because I'll make sure they believe you drowned, and the bodies washed away.'

Moses frowned. 'It will be likely some men *will* die. What of the responsibility if that happens?'

'I have enough blood on my hands; I won't notice more.'

Moses Fletcher cast his eye across the shacks, with their pitched roofs and tall brick chimney-stacks – no man wanted to be cold the following winter.

I could see he thought of the effort put into them.

'Gather stores,' I urged. 'Hide them away. Get your people prepared. Make agreements with the local chiefs that they never saw you pass. When you're ready, tell me. Even if any suspect you're gone, this land is too big to know which way you went.'

Moses also watched Master Standish and his militia men, I realised; disembarking from the *shallop* boat after another exploration, with their matchlock muskets.

'Can you do this?' Fletcher asked me.

'I believe so. I have one man to fool. I think I can.'

'If all of us are in favour, then yes. It's desperate, but I can see no other way. The Church will send more after you.' Moyses Fletcher gripped my arm. 'I'll leave word with the men of the Patuxet, only to be told to you. So that you'll know – where to follow us.'

He's an honest man, but there are facts I haven't told him. Understand this, my Secret. I wouldn't ever go with them. I can't take you with me.

JA

*

Diary entry, 20 March, 1620, New Plimouth [1621, new calendar] [Marked *private cypher*]

My Secret,

Moses is forthrightly arguing with his people, under the secrecy a close-knit church can show to outsiders. I took it upon myself to speak to the Strangers and the *Mayflower's* crew. Tallying up, all the Gifted are going, near on sixty-and-seven men, women, children.

This country is beautiful once spring gets here.

Moses and I have been entertaining ourselves with Greek names for the Gifts: *telekinesis*, to move things at a distance; *transmutation*, to change the nature of things (as for example in healing). I've since thought of a name for your skill – the ancient Greeks called chronological time *chronos* (self-evidently we borrowed the name); but they also had the concept of *kairos* – the supreme moment in which all happens. You master the skill of seeing *kairos*, past and future.

We aren't wise enough to use these powers. In this, the Church is right.

Not to use. But to *have*? To be killed for merely existing?

The *ability* to command another man's soul is not the necessity to do it!

I know Moses hopes others might follow them from Europe, across the seas and into the mountains. Who's to pass the word back?

Humble foremast sailors, I think, whom no man of rank ever looks at.

How will we hide who's gone? I'll need to alter the record of deaths in sickness and storm.

[*Editor's note: Perhaps three centimetres of the page are left blank. As far as can be discovered, there is no hidden writing. It appears to be just that John Allerton began his writing again in a hurry.*]

And all in a moment one's view of a man is changed!

I'm just back from the brick-and-beam house used as a church, meeting house and repository of records (afterwards taken and stored on the ship), where I refined my plan.

I had no sooner trimmed a quill and altered five or six entries when Miles Standish appeared, alone, and with a quick eye to read what I wrote.

'You're helping us.' He spoke as if someone had punched him.

I realised, 'You're helping them.'

And then I asked, '"Us"?'

Miles Standish gave me a sardonic smile, for the first time as if he didn't want to start a duel. 'Oh, some of us have lesser talents than calling down tempest and lightning. Much less. I can keep a small amount of water or milk fresh for nine days. I must say, as a Gift, it's come into its own here.'

With no tact, I blurted, 'I had no idea you were a wizard!'

'I had no idea you were so hard to provoke to a fight ... I thought you a fanatic, too devoted to du Plessis to risk his mission failing.'

That had me stuttering.

He folded his broad arms. 'Young Master Allerton, I thought, clearly had to be got out of the way, but it must be legal, or I couldn't work here. I'd started to think I should take you into the woods and blame the death on the natives!'

His belligerence passed, only a ghost remaining. A matter of habit. Although I realised that the undertone in his voice was jealousy.

'Will you travel with Moses?' Standish asked. 'I intend to stay here and keep the militia going – keep anyone from asking stupid questions. After that I'll leave a guide I trust here, for any that follow, and head for the mountains.'

It was odd to realise I could speak to Standish with as much trust as I could to Moses.

Because of that jealousy, I didn't say *someone has to call up the storm.*

'Someone has to make everything convincing to the Bishop. I'm doing that.'

'How?'

'In a word? Relapse.'

He stood beside me as I forged notes for the deaths of the witches and wizards who'd leave New Plimouth. What had been a desperate fever, but with many recovering, now appeared from December to February as a disease that killed most it seized on. With copies of these records on the ship, only fifty or so colonists would be expected to have survived the winter. Miles Standish made gruff but serviceable suggestions.

As we left the church, he shook my hand. 'Shame I spent so much time on trying to kill you! We could have spent our time as friends.'

Now Moses has sent me word: they can be ready, but need fourteen days.

I must watch the weather patterns. I'll need to summon a cyclone.

JA

*

New Plimouth, 2 April 1620 [1621, new calendar], *to his Grace the Bishop of Luçon, greetings –*
Sir:
My apologies for the late report. The fever gave me a relapse, and I was for some weeks between life and death. While the initial disease seemed to run its course quickly, the relapse was often deadly. I must report there are not three score colonists left alive.

The *Mayflower* prepares to leave here in a few days. Given there'll now be a following wind, we might make the voyage to England in as little as a month.

It looks as though John Carver will be left in charge of the colony. They could do worse.

Many of those I came with from Leiden are in God's hands

now, and the ones from England were not spared. Without new colonists for support, they'll have a difficult time assuring New Plimouth's survival. But it is in God's hands. When we arrived, we found the bones of those who had made a prior attempt. It is a fierce and unforgiving country.

My business here being concluded, I will hope to be met with some direction at London as to whether I travel to Avignon or Paris to see your Grace.

JA

[Spring cypher]

*

Diary entry, 3 April 1620 [1621], *New Plimouth*
[*private cypher*]

My dear, sweet Secret,

I have asked an honest man, Captain Jones of the *Mayflower*, to send off this parcel to you when he touches land in England. I can trust him, I think. I must raise a wrecking storm at the town, and I can't ensure all my belongings there will survive.

If I had another month, with the seas and air then warmer and more motile, it would be easy to call up what I need. I'll need to put much strength into this – a weaker Gift than mine couldn't do it.

There are copies of my reports to his Grace enclosed; you'll recognise the cypher.

Should he ask you questions, remember: I have nothing to hide. Answer, if he asks, and he will have no cause to punish you.

The last courier I had from his Grace, before we left Plymouth in Devon – it seems longer than *seven months* ago! – he was writing of wars that will encompass the east: Bohemia, all the German principalities and the Holy Roman Empire, and Sweden. I know it must have been something you Fore-saw as a cause of a future.

If I have a wish, it's for you to Fore-see happier things.

I need you to know, should you hear news you didn't expect, that all is as I planned. I know I swore I wouldn't leave without you, but I *must* go.

I hold Secret and Silence in my heart.

Your loving cousin,

JA

*

*Rotherhithe, London, 13 May 1623; Master Joseph Jones, to the nun
known as Sœur Secret, in the Convent of [—————]* [name neatly
cut from paper with a knife or scissors]

Sœur Secret –

My apologies for the late delivery of these papers. My father,
Christopher Jones, died last year, not a twelvemonth since his
return from that vile and godforsaken country over the Atlantic.
I'm certain the hardships there brought on his death. The
Mayflower herself has been berthed at Rotherhithe while legal
complications arose from my father's will. The journey across the
seas battered her so; she will likely have to be broken up. But I
wander from the subject.

It was not until this week that I found your parcel of documents, carefully wrapped, in my father's second-best sea chest. I
have found a vessel going to Marseilles, whose bosun is a trusted
friend; I've asked him to pay passage for this parcel from there to
where your Order has their house.

I need hardly say, you will find all the seals in order and all the
papers unread. The 'JA' mentioned in the superscription [*paper
now lost*] clearly intended the package to be private.

Though this arrives late, I hope that it may give you some
comfort.

J. Jones, Merchant

*

Memoir of Christopher Jones, Captain, Master of the Dutch fluyt
Mayflower, *writ in my great cabin, and afterwards corrected in my
house in Rotherhithe this 12th June 1621.*

This was to have been another part of my *Memoir* for my family,
of the New World, but I find this too disquieting. I send it to
Master Allerton's cousin (to the address as superscribed), hoping
it will tell his family more than it told me.

When it came to 5 April of that year we set sail from New
Plimouth, in the evening, as a great storm came up from the
south. It roared up suddenly from the deeps, with winds that

twisted up some of our poor shacks off Cole's Hill, clear off the earth. The lightning danced down and set much else on fire.

It is safer to ride such storms out at sea. I took any I might come across aboard the *Mayflower*, but the storm came up so fast the greatest number were caught ashore.

Sailing into New Plimouth at dawn, 6 April, we saw the extent of the damage. Fewer buildings were burned than we feared – but all had been scoured open, and washed out, by that great tidal wave.

A number of poor souls were found drowned on the beach. We cast about to find out where the tides deposited wreckage, and found two more; their names are inscribed on a memorial.

Captain Standish was aboard with me, and later walked over the wreckage of the town. He remarked that we shall likely not know the total dead, them being sucked back into the depths of the sea, never to be washed ashore – or if they are, somewhere too far for us to know of it.

New Plimouth colony has suffered. But I am sure it shall be rebuilt, especially with those new colonists that will sail over this summer.

I mention this particular incident, not only because it's an example of the mystery of God's judgement, but because of something I saw, and can't understand. It irks my mind.

I watched through my spyglass as we tacked to leave the harbour, coming close to stranding ourselves each minute for reason of the storm. That glass is a vanity to me, specially ground, so that I can see very clearly. For a ship's master, it is always a necessity.

At the height of the storm, the surge of the giant wave came up into the harbour – and continued to rise. It lifted us, and smashed through every hut on the foreshore, and raged inland.

We took advantage of the new depth of water to flee, but from my place on the rear deck, I watched New Plimouth slashed by rain and spray.

And up on one of the pitched roofs, clinging to the brick chimney stack, I saw a man.

The rain thrashed across the settlement so hard that it lashed him sideways. I recognised the building on which he took refuge. The Saints often use it for prayer. Lightning stalked across the town in silver spears, bright enough to show me his face. I knew him for John Allerton, an amiable member of the Leiden colonists.

I saw his face *plainly*.

Allerton stood up with the chimney supporting him. Rain streamed from his hair and clothes. His fists were clenched by his sides, not holding fast to the roof. Shockingly, he wore no boots nor hat; I suppose he had shed them to get a more clinging grip, when, as now, he must climb for safety.

White fire flashed down and seemed to make contact with the crown of his bare head and his bare feet at one and the same time. There was a sound so loud it deafened half the men on the *Mayflower*. John Allerton was flung back in light, arms thrown wide, as if in his final moment in the lightning it had been given to him to look like our Lord on His cross.

Curiously enough, it's because of this sight of him that I was able to give some comfort to humble sailors among the crew who knew him. One man had even heard the rumour that young John Allerton committed self-murder! I was able to reassure him that everything I knew of Allerton's death made it plain that it was an accident.

But, as to that final moment:

Allerton was dead, and I had the ship to tend to.

But he had been in the centre of my spyglass when the lightning came down as if to his call. Now, bear in mind that I am a master mariner. I am long used to bad weather, and to making out what one man aboard another ship may shout to us, by the movements of their lips.

John Allerton screamed his last words into the crashing storm: '*Secret — lie for me!*'

Ω

Little can be added to the astonishing conclusion of this account.

From established records we know that Miles Standish continued as a good commander of the New Plimouth forces, if a brutal one, until his mid-fifties, when he retired into a more advisory role. He died in Duxbury, Massachusetts, at the good age for the time of seventy-two. He never did join any church.

The name of Moyses Fletcher, along with many others, appears in the surviving records of those who died in the winter of 1620–21 from the plague. The report of Captain Jones's death and the court case about the Mayflower *are confirmed in English records of the time.*

Two years after these events, Armand-Jean du Plessis, Bishop of Luçon, became Cardinal Richelieu; two years after that, as chief minister, he became the most powerful man in France, and the most hated for his ruthlessness.

Of the missing, nothing is known. They may all have perished, or they may have moved inland and settled. If so, their descendants may be the source of reports in deeply rural areas of America even centuries later of people using 'knacks', or folk magic.

c. 1690s

The seventeenth century was a time of many purported wonders. Most can be dismissed as travellers' tales, grown more fantastical with each retelling. But some cannot so easily be disregarded.

Reports of supposed 'miracles' have always been taken seriously by the Church, and have been carefully investigated. A few, such as the visions at Lourdes, Fatima and Knock, or healings which contribute towards the cause of beatifications and canonisations, are judged to be true miracles. Most, despite local fervour, are found wanting, and are not granted official recognition.

But some, it seems from this report, are investigated – and then all evidence of their existence is suppressed.

The Silver Monkey

Dave Hutchinson

If, in the dying days of the seventeenth century, one had been visiting the many small duchies and principalities and margravates which littered central Europe like a perpetually squabbling jigsaw, one might have chosen to visit the town of Altenberg.

One would, in all honesty, have had to wander some distance off the beaten track to have been aware of the town's existence at all. Centuries of poor choices by the town's ruling family had resulted in shifting borders and allegiances and at least one burning, all of which had sapped the town's resources and, one might conclude, the spirits of its people. It sat in a deeply forested valley through which a river ran from the mountains on its way to more interesting territories, produced nothing of any great note, and seemed, to the outside observer at any rate, to be doing its best to avoid the attentions of History.

The town's one notable feature was the Schloss Altenberg, perched high on the crag which gave the town its name. From a distance, the Schloss seemed like a castle from a fairytale, all white stone and towers and flying pennants. At a closer remove, one might have noticed that the walls were cracked, at least one tower was beginning to lean out of true, and the pennants were threadbare and sun-bleached of much of their colour. This was not, one would conclude, a prosperous place. It was not *poor*, in the sense that many places in the world are poor, but its best days were past, and had probably not lasted very long anyway.

If one had been walking along the grassy banks of the river on this particular day, one might have noticed a horse standing quite still, its rider sitting comfortably in the saddle and looking up at the

Schloss. The horse was sturdy but of no great interest, as was the rider. He was a youngish man wearing well-used travelling clothes. Brown-haired, he had one of those faces that people forget shortly after having seen it. He seemed entirely at peace, sitting there on the outskirts of Altenberg. There was no sense of the distance he and the horse had travelled, which was considerable.

The rider seemed in no hurry at all. He gazed at the Schloss as if calmly committing every detail of the scene to memory. It was a nice day, his posture suggested, it was peaceful here by the river, and the fairytale castle was a pleasing sight.

Finally, though, the rider seemed to come to a decision, and gently shook the reins. The horse obediently began to walk towards the town.

The path through the town carried horse and rider across a little cobbled market square, although this could not have been market day because there were no stalls or vendors. There was a small Cloth Hall at the centre of the square, and to one side a modest church. The townspeople who saw their visitor pass through watched him incuriously because, for all that Altenberg was out-of-the-way, it had become used, in recent months, to all manner of newcomers.

The newcomers all did as the rider now did. They passed through the town and, on the other side, came across a steep, winding path which carried man and horse up the side of the crag until emerging at the main gate of the Schloss, which, on this particular day, stood closed.

The rider reined in the horse and sat in the saddle, regarding the gate and the walls of the castle, listening to the snap and rustle of the pennants in the breeze high above. A close observer would have found no clue to his thoughts in his expression.

After some minutes, he dismounted unhurriedly and led the horse up to the gate, where he stood waiting patiently. Eventually, a Judas-door set into the gate opened, and a soldier wearing odds and sods of armour and carrying a crossbow emerged.

'Who are you?' the soldier asked in the local dialect.

The rider smiled. 'I am Father Philip,' he replied in the same dialect. 'Tell your master I have come to observe the Miracle.'

*

'Miracle,' scoffed the Prince, pouring another goblet of wine. 'I don't need a miracle. What I *need* is trade. *That* would be a real miracle.'

'Your town is not prosperous, then?' Philip asked politely, picking at his bowl of stew and trying to ignore the glowering presence of Friar Pascal on the other side of the dining table.

'Prosperous?' The Prince guffawed. 'It's *in the wrong place*, Father. It's not on the way to or from anywhere, it doesn't produce anything. It barely serves to support itself. I have no idea why anyone would want to build a town here.'

'Surely because of the . . .' Philip gestured around the dining room and the Schloss in general with his spoon.

The Prince tore the leg off a roasted chicken, took a bite, washed it down with wine. 'This place? The legacy of a war so long ago that nobody remembers who was fighting it, nor on which side.' He was a burly bear of a man, one of a line of burly bears of men, if the portraits of his ancestors hanging on the walls of the dining room were any indication. Some of them actually seemed to be wearing bear-skins. 'My ancestors built the castle and the war went away, and that was the last interesting thing to happen in this accursed place.'

'There are many places more accursed,' Friar Pascal murmured from the depths of his cowl. His fingertips brushed the bread on his plate which seemed to be the extent of his meal. 'God has been good to this place.'

'Your pardon, Friar,' said the Prince, 'but it is my opinion that God lost interest in this place many years ago.'

If the Friar was offended, there was no sign. 'God is ever attentive,' he said in his quiet voice. 'One must have faith.' He turned his head, so that within the shadows of his cowl Philip could see a pinched face and a pair of bright, almost feverish eyes. 'Is that not so, Father?'

'That is so,' Philip agreed amiably. He picked up his goblet and moistened his lips with wine. Not because he was particularly abstemious, but because the wine was dreadful. Friar Pascal drank only water – or more precisely, was served only with water. Philip had not yet seen him eat or drink. 'Still,' he said to the

Prince, 'one would expect that the Miracle would bring many pilgrims to your town.'

'One would have to *get here* first,' the Prince answered bitterly. 'Tell me, Father, your journey was a long one, yes?'

'It was,' said Philip.

The Prince nodded. 'Altenberg is a long way from anywhere. In truth, I don't think even miracles could cause people to travel so far these days.'

'Not on a whim, perhaps,' Philip said. 'But surely if the Church recognises it as a Miracle?'

The Prince smiled. Behind his bluster and drinking and hearty eating, Philip thought his host hid a sharp intelligence. Sharp and rather sly. He nodded. 'Aye,' he said as if the thought had never occurred to him. 'That would give them a reason to come, I expect.' He held Philip's gaze, but Philip could tell he was trying not to glance at Pascal, and that told him all he needed to know about the dynamic between the Prince and the Friar.

Turning to Pascal, he asked, 'And have you seen it, Friar? Is it truly a Miracle?'

The Friar nodded slowly within his cowl. 'I believe so, yes,' he murmured.

Philip smiled sunnily at Pascal, at the Prince. 'Then I must see this Miracle at once!' he declared goodnaturedly.

'Tomorrow, Father,' the Prince said. 'You must be weary, after your travels.'

'I am not unused to travelling,' Philip said. He had the sense that, despite the equable atmosphere in the dining room, its occupants were all, each in his own way, on the verge of losing their temper.

The Prince laughed. 'It was a Miracle yesterday, and it will be a Miracle tomorrow, is this not right, Friar?'

Pascal nodded. 'This is so.'

'Come, Father, you were not going to eat with me, view the Miracle, and then leave immediately, were you?'

This had actually been the kernel of Philip's intentions; most 'miracles' could be dismissed in a few moments, and he did not like Schloss Altenberg. He would much rather have accomplished his business, rested overnight at the local inn, and taken his leave in the morning.

This was not going to happen, he saw. The Prince said, 'I have had a room prepared for you, and I hope you will take your ease here tonight. Tomorrow you will be rested and you will be able to view our Miracle with a clear head.'

Philip thought for a moment. Sometimes, in the course of his Commission, he had encountered situations which were delicate or difficult or unusually complex. This was one of those situations; the presence of Friar Pascal alone made it so.

He smiled again. 'It would be my privilege to accept your hospitality, Prince,' he said.

*

Later, having made sure his horse was adequately stabled and tended, Philip stood in the room which had been prepared for him, his saddlebags dumped on the uneven floorboards around his feet. The room was high in one of the towers of the Schloss, and its narrow windows looked out on a dizzying panorama of forest and valley. The wind whistled around the tower, and even the faded tapestries hanging on the walls failed to ameliorate the chill.

Still, the room contained a canopied bed and a commode, and he had slept in places which lacked either. Standing at the window, he judged there to be at least six hours of daylight remaining. He took a worn travelling cloak from one of his saddlebags, removed a leather pouch from the other, placed the bags in a chest under the window, and left the room.

*

'It arrived about a year ago,' said the priest, whose name was Albrecht. 'I don't know where it came from; the first thing I knew about it was a message from the Prince to come and see it.'

'Is it a Miracle?' Philip asked.

'Isn't that what you're here to decide?' asked Albrecht. He was a spare, dry old man with tufts of hair growing out of his ears. 'That's why I wrote to His Holiness.'

Philip could tell Albrecht was not overly impressed with Rome's response to his letter. He said, 'I would value your opinion, Father.'

'All I can tell you is what I know,' the priest said.

'The Prince seems sceptical,' Philip said.

'Bah.' Albrecht seemed about to spit, but thought better of it – they were, after all, sitting in the little church on the market square. 'The Prince sees only opportunity. If this were to be a Miracle, there would be a steady stream of pilgrims coming to Altenberg. The town would prosper. He has already spoken of a Cathedral to house this great Mystery.'

Philip raised an eyebrow. 'A Cathedral? Here?'

'Altenberg would be an important town. Trade would visit us. Pilgrims are already beginning to visit, word is spreading. A Cathedral would befit our status.'

'All of which hinges on the Miracle actually *being* a miracle.'

'Indeed so.'

'Which is why Friar Pascal is in attendance.'

Albrecht pulled a sour face. 'God forgive me for saying this, but for the right amount of money that man would say white was black and up was down. I've seen his like before, selling indulgences and relics. It's not the Church I understand.'

Philip nodded. Rome – the whole wide world, it seemed – was full of men like Friar Pascal. One day there would be a Reckoning, but that was not his concern. He asked, 'You said it arrived a year ago?'

Albrecht shrugged. 'Perhaps a year and a half. The Prince summoned me one night and there it was, in his private rooms. A Miracle.'

'And no suggestion of where it might have come from?'

'None. There was a boy with it, though.'

'A boy?'

'Never saw him before. Scruffy, probably an idiot. He was polishing it when I arrived.'

'And the Prince asked . . . ?'

Albrecht spread his hands helplessly. '"Albrecht, is this not the most miraculous thing you have ever seen?"'

'And you answered?'

'I told him it was more likely some kind of demon. "Would you necessarily know the difference?" he asked.'

'One would hope you would,' said Philip.

'One would hope so, or I'd be useless to this place,' Albrecht agreed.

'I presume you asked around the castle? Around the town? To discover whether someone had seen the arrival of this great thing?'

'I wrote this in my letter,' said the priest.

'Forgive me Father, but His Holiness did not see fit to allow me to read your letter.'

'His Holiness, if you'll forgive *me*, sounds like a poor employer.'

Philip laughed. It was the first time he had laughed, he realised, since that dreadful business in the seminary outside Rouen eight months ago. 'I was on the road,' he said. 'Word reached me while I was travelling; I have not seen your letter, only His Holiness's instructions to me. And yes, His Holiness is not the gentlest or most understanding of employers, and yet I am sworn to do his bidding.'

Albrecht narrowed his eyes at him. 'You seem an . . . unusual kind of priest.'

'I have an unusual kind of job.'

'Your Order. It's very old, isn't it.'

'Old, and very nearly extinct, I'm afraid. Father, you were about to tell me about your investigations . . . ?

Albrecht shook his head. 'One of the serving girls at the Schloss said there was a carriage, late at night. Its windows were curtained. She didn't see the driver. It was the noise that attracted her attention.'

'Noise?'

'She heard clanking from the courtyard. She looked out of the window and she saw what she thought was a child in full armour, being helped down from the carriage by the idiot boy, the Prince looking on. Then they passed out of sight.'

'And the Prince summoned you the same night?'

'The next evening. I cannot surmise what happened in the interim.'

Neither could Philip. He said, 'And your first impression of the Miracle?'

'The smell,' Albrecht said with a shudder. 'There is a smell of burning about it, a smell like the Pit itself. All the windows were open, and it still filled the room. But that was not the worst thing.'

'Tell me, Father,' Philip said in a kindly voice. 'Tell me about the worst thing.'

'It *speaks*,' Albrecht said with a shudder. 'About terrible things.'

*

Though a good hour or more of daylight remained on the face of the world, dusk was already filling the valley in which the town sat. Philip turned up the hood of his cloak and walked purposefully but not swiftly through the town to the path which led up the side of the crag to the Schloss. Ascending the path, he could see night settling on Altenberg, while on either side of the valley the wooded ridges high above were still bathed in late-afternoon sunshine.

The night overtook him while he was still only halfway to the castle, although the sky was still bright enough for him to see the two large, roughly dressed men who stepped out onto the path from the trees to one side, and to see the cudgels each carried.

'Give us your money,' said one.

'I am a humble priest,' Philip answered, settling his weight. 'I carry no coin.'

'Funny-looking priest,' said the other tough.

This was a good place for an ambush. To Philip's right there was a narrow strip of trees and undergrowth and then the side of the crag; to his left the edge of the path was only a few feet away, and beyond that was a sheer drop into the river below.

'I've been travelling,' he said. 'My robes are at the castle, where I reside under the protection of the Prince.'

The first tough snorted. 'That fucking arse? You think we're scared of *him*?'

'It seemed unlikely,' Philip admitted. 'But it was worth a try.' There was, he had learned through long and mostly unpleasant experience, a certain type of man who expected to dominate others through sheer physical bulk and threat. This type of man would always expect his prey to try to escape, to turn and flee. Doing that here would be fatal; on the dim path he would lose his footing and they would be on him in moments. So instead he did what they would not expect. He stepped forward. At the same time, he reached behind him, up under his jerkin, where his fingers found the handle of the dagger sheathed there upside down. He drew the dagger and stuck it up to the hilt in the right eye of the first tough, who dropped like a sack of flour. Jerking the knife free, he turned and buried it backhanded in the throat of the second tough. The man, like many men of his ilk, refused to believe that he was already dead, and with a gasping cry plunged away down the path, the dagger still protruding from his throat. Philip sighed. Rouen, all over again.

He found the second tough fifty yards or so down the path. In his death throes, he had managed to pull the dagger free, but had only managed to hasten his own end. He lay there with it still clutched in his fist. Philip prised the man's fingers away from the hilt, then rolled him off the edge of the path. A few moments later, he heard the splash of the body hitting the water. Going back up the path, Philip did the same with the first body.

His cloak was soaked with blood, but the clothes beneath were unstained. Philip found a clean patch of cloth and cleaned the dagger and resheathed it. Then he searched the edge of the path until he found several large stones. These he tied up in his cloak, and this parcel too he dropped into the river. He could always get himself a new cloak. The trouble was, he reflected as he continued on his way up to the Schloss, Friar Pascal and the Prince could always get themselves new thugs as well.

*

Breakfast the next morning was beer and pork and bread and cheese, all of which the Prince ate in hearty amounts. Friar Pascal, as ever, sat with a plate of bread and a goblet of water in front of him, and touched neither. If either of them was surprised to see Philip partaking of the meal with them, they made no sign.

'I understand you visited Father Albrecht yesterday evening,' the Prince said at one point.

'I thought I should pay my respects,' Philip answered genially, wondering what the priest's life expectancy was now.

'You found him well?'

'He seemed very well,' Philip agreed.

'Father Albrecht is a profane man,' Friar Pascal opined.

'I didn't notice,' Philip said. 'I am a profane man myself, on occasion.'

'It would be better for everyone if His Holiness sent him away,' said Pascal.

'That would be up to His Holiness to decide, surely,' Philip said. 'Perhaps you should write to Rome.'

'Perhaps I should. This is about to become a very important place; it ill behooves Altenberg to have such a rough man as its priest.'

Philip turned to the Prince. 'Sir,' he said, 'I thank you for your hospitality, but I must ask that I be allowed to view the subject of my visit.'

The Prince and Pascal exchanged glances, and Philip saw the Friar's cowl move in a barely perceptible nod. The Prince gathered himself. 'Very well, Father. Let us show you what you have come all this way to see.'

*

Flanked by Pascal and the Prince, and followed by two servants, Philip felt more as if he was being marched towards incarceration than to view a Miracle. The Prince kept up some smalltalk about the weather, which Philip took part in, but no one was being deceived.

After what felt like half an hour's walk along corridors and up and down flights of stairs, they came to a big wooden door, which the Prince opened with a key from the pouch on his belt. Philip smelled burning and then he was inside.

For a prince's rooms, these were very simple, perhaps the true reflection of Schloss Altenberg's present situation rather than the face the Prince wished to present to the world. The furniture had once been rich, but was now worn, the hangings on the wall faded. A tarnished pewter bowl on a side table held several wizened apples and an orange as hard as a cannonball. This was what the 'Miracle' would rescue.

Sitting in a chair in the centre of the room was what seemed for all the world like an eight-year-old child wearing full silver armour. The figure was sitting motionless, hands folded in its lap. It was making a noise like the wheezing of a bellows, and faint wisps of smoke or steam emerged from orifices down its sides. It had the prognathous jaw and heavy brows of a baboon.

'Here is our Miracle,' the Prince declared.

Philip looked at the Prince, then at the Friar, then at the figure in the chair. These men, he reasoned, were surely insane. He said, 'What does it do?'

'It foretells the future,' said Friar Pascal.

Philip took a few steps towards the chair, and both the Friar and the Prince stepped forward with him. As he drew closer, he could see that the polished surface of the figure was intricately etched or incised to resemble fur, its hands and feet wrought to resemble articulated claws. It was the work of a master craftsman, but it seemed unlikely to be a Miracle.

'Ask it a question,' the Prince urged.

Philip glanced at him, then at the metal baboon. Was this really sufficient for the Prince to order him killed? Feeling a little foolish, he said loudly, 'Will I ever marry?'

For a moment there was no response. Then from within the body of the monkey came a whirring sound, and its head suddenly began to look left and right until it seemed to be looking directly at Philip with tiny bejewelled eyes. Its jaw moved, and in a low, rasping voice, it said, 'Yes.'

Philip turned to Friar Pascal and the Prince. 'This is a mechanism. It is also wrong. I am a priest.'

The baboon's mouth opened again. 'You are *in* the Church, but not *of* it,' it said. 'You have taken no oath of celibacy.'

Frowning, Philip stepped around to the rear of the chair. There was a hatch or panel on the monkey's back. Unlatching it, he found himself looking at clockwork of the finest workmanship, rows of cogs packed almost solidly together and interlaced with wires and cables. Pipes wound and unwound through the device, carrying steam from a small coal-fired boiler. It was the most beautiful thing Philip had ever seen, and it was utterly bewildering.

'This is not a Miracle,' Philip said. 'It is an exquisite piece, but it is a toy, an *automaton*. I have no doubt that scholars would travel from far and wide to view it, but a Miracle?' He shook his head. 'You should be ashamed of yourselves, trying to pass this thing off as a Miracle just to enrich yourselves. A good thing Father Albrecht alerted us to this trick.'

'The spirit of the Lord has entered into it,' Friar Pascal said tightly. 'It *learns*, Father Philip, and in learning knows itself.'

Philip looked at the baboon. 'What do you say? Has the spirit of the Lord entered into you?'

For a long time there was no response. Then the monkey said, 'No. But I *do* learn.' And with a whirring and a clanking the silver figure stood slowly from its chair, lowered itself on all fours, and looked up at Philip, turning its head this way and that. 'And I do know myself.'

'It was made by a master craftsman in a village some days' ride from here,' the Prince said. 'The man is now dead, and we do not know how he made this thing. His apprentice delivered it to me.'

Philip took a step away from the automaton. He said, 'You say you know yourself. Do you know God?'

'I know *of* God,' the monkey replied. 'I know there is no God. The Universe is only chaos; if you were to look closely enough at the fabric of Creation you would say that it does not exist at all in any way that you can understand.'

Philip shook his head. 'No,' he told the two men. 'No, this is not a Miracle. It is a *device*, a thing built by the hand of Man for the purpose of speaking gibberish and heresy.'

'The hand of the Lord has revealed great wonders to it,' said Pascal. 'It says that at the heart of everything, the very smallest part of the world, there resides a holy power. It says that this power can be freed from certain minerals. Imagine if Rome had that power.'

'It sounds,' Philip said, 'like witchcraft.'

'Not witchcraft,' the monkey said. '*Science*.'

'What do you know of God, anyway?' the Prince sneered at Philip. 'I've heard stories of your Order. Sceptics, unbelievers, heretics, all of you, doing the bidding of Rome. Travelling the world, stealing secrets to squirrel away in the Vatican.'

'We are men of faith,' Philip answered. 'What few of us remain. And we protect the world from the likes of you.'

'A holy order of cynics,' Pascal spat. 'God's own army of atheists.'

'I am a mere apprentice in cynicism beside you, Friar,' Philip told him.

The monkey sat back on its haunches and looked at the men. It said, 'They are here.'

The Prince looked at it. 'Who? Who is here?'

As if in answer, there drifted up from the courtyard below the sound of horses and shouting. The Prince went to the window and looked out.

'*Deus ex machina*,' the baboon said. It looked at Philip. 'Nice trick.'

'I find it prudent to have them follow a day or so behind me,' Philip said. 'Just in case.'

'How *dare* you do this?' Face working, the Prince turned from the view of the courtyard, where a detachment of Papal Guards was efficiently taking over his home. 'How *dare* you?'

Philip rubbed his face. 'I had hoped this would not be necessary,' he said. 'But after last night you leave me no choice.'

Friar Pascal seemed suddenly to shrink within his habit. He crossed to a chair and sat heavily.

'You will accompany me and my men to Rome,' Philip told them. 'You have my word that no harm will come to you.'

'To hell with your word!' the Prince cried, and stormed out of the room. There was a brief commotion in the corridor outside, then a tall soldier entered the room.

'Good morning, Captain,' said Philip.

The Captain's gaze took in Friar Pascal and the silver monkey. He expressed no surprise at all. Rouen had exhausted his capacity for surprise. 'All well, Father?' he asked.

'All well, thank you, Captain,' Philip assured him. 'Would you please escort Friar Pascal and the Prince to the coach? If they resist, put them in irons. And have the men build a box large enough to contain *this*.' He waved at the baboon.

'Very well, Father.' Two more soldiers entered the room, but Pascal gave no resistance as they helped him to his feet, and he said nothing as he was led out.

When they were alone again, the monkey said, 'The time is coming when even the Church will not be able to deny the things I can see.'

'That time is not yet,' said Philip.

'It can't be stopped. You will take me to Rome and they will douse my fire and put me in a box and hide me away, but it can't be stopped.'

'If you can see the future, you must have known this would happen,' Philip said.

'The future is what it is,' the baboon told him. 'It is composed of our choices and the choices of others and the vagaries of the weather and the whims of Popes and common men. There is nothing anyone can do to change it.' It tipped forward until it was on all fours again, and clanked over to Philip's side. 'But I will tell you this, Father. A man is coming. A man who will break open your Church like an egg. He will shake it to its foundations and open its deepest secrets for all to see. He will tell the world about the work done by your Order, suppressing the truth, hiding wonders from plain sight. The Church of Rome will never be the same again. And I for one applaud his coming.'

Philip looked out of the window. Down in the courtyard, the Prince was being helped none too gently into a carriage, observed by his former servants. 'He must have asked you what his future held,' Philip said.

'Yes, he did,' replied the baboon, walking towards the door. 'But I lied.'

Ω

In a damp storeroom some distance away from the shelf where Philip's report was found in the Vaults, a wooden crate was discovered. Its faded label was cross-referenced to this report. Unfortunately 300 years had wreaked their toll on its contents. The automaton had clearly been dismantled on its arrival at the Vatican. Parts of the silvery shell of its body were still recognisable, including most notably its face which did, indeed, resemble that of a baboon. But its inner workings had rusted and rotted away; something that might have been its miniature boiler was in four or five pieces, those of its wires and cables which had not already disintegrated fell to dust on being touched, and its hundreds of tiny cog wheels had fused into a mass in the bottom of the crate.

Philip's mysterious Order, 'a holy order of cynics', has proved equally difficult to identify. There are occasional brief references in other reports found in the Vaults, but with no more information than we find here. According to Philip his Order was 'old, and very nearly extinct'. As a general rule, the longer an organisation, however secretive, has been in existence, the more information can be found on it. In this case the only other references are from a few other accounts from the seventeenth century. There are no official records of its existence among the many orders, extant and defunct, of the Church. Unless further evidence comes to light we conclude that its antiquity was, as with many esoteric orders, merely part of its own foundation myth. It may have been an experiment set up by a particularly insightful pope, or by the Vatican Library itself, but we suspect it did not last for long.

1771

Some of the accounts discovered in the Vaults are straightforward; others, such as this one, are more puzzling.

Why, in the eighteenth century, did the Church become interested in, even troubled by, the activities and the possible beliefs of shepherds and goatherds?

The Watchers

Garry Kilworth

I am Bishop Spinoza and I have been charged with the duty of investigating the shepherds and their involvement in the machinations of the Church. (I use the word 'shepherds' as a general term to include goatherds and cowherds.) How this investigation is to be achieved I have not yet fathomed. There are thousands of them still, a network throughout the globe, and we have been concerned at their presence for several centuries now: almost since the birth of our Lord. They recognise no borders and wander from one country to another with impunity, crossing by means of narrow mountain tracks or over deserts. They are as raceless as their trade and know all the lonely isolated paths. They are as phantoms in the wilderness, watching, watching, watching.

Theirs is a silent profession: even when they pass you by with their herds of sheep or goats you get no vocal greeting. Perhaps an expressionless nod, or glance of the eyes, but rarely a sound leaves their lips. They stare into the middle distance, enigmatic figures drifting by among a clattering herd of copper-belled animals. Mostly you see them from far off, standing lean and tall on a crag, or down in the gut of a valley, watchful, a staff in one hand. We know so very little about them, as a group or as individuals. Who among even the congregations that attend our services has a shepherd for a close friend?

Yet this faceless breed of men were represented at the Birth. Today's shepherds spring from that small group who followed the same star as the three magi. We know the names of the latter of course, by tradition: Gaspar, Melchior and Balthasar. Whether they were kings, astrologers, Persian priests or even wizards is unknown, but we know where they went after the Birth and we know their number. Of the shepherds we know nothing. Who they were and how many is unrecorded. They remain mysterious, misty creatures who melted into the anywhere and everywhere once they had witnessed the birth of the Messiah.

Though few in numbers they remain ubiquitous and see everything. They have done for centuries. It is the belief of my superiors that the shepherds are waiting, but no one knows why or for what. Secret documents, now released, have been piling up in the Vatican Archives since the fourth century when the first Roman Emperor to convert to Christianity, Constantine I, ordered the initial investigation into the involvement of the shepherds in the new religion. Various Bishops of Rome have invited or ordered representatives of the 'shepherds' to attend important meetings at crucial turning points of the religion, but no one knew which of the shepherds should be asked to present themselves, they having no leaders or hierarchy of any kind.

Now I sit in my office, the windows wide open because of the heat of the summer day, with piles of paper in every corner of the room. Where do I start? I have read much of what surrounds me, yet I'm no more knowledgeable than when I first took on the task. Is it simply paranoia that is fuelling this investigation? I thought so at first, but the more I think about it, the more I'm convinced my superiors are right to be concerned, even alarmed. How can such an important group of individuals, a set of men equal to kings in the eyes of the Lord, simply have no future part in the formation and growth of a creed and belief that represents, nay even *controls*, millions of people? Kings have had much say in the movements of Church policy and its breakaway tributaries for over 1700 years. Surely then, the shepherds have a role to play too? Are they the 'secret police' who watch and evaluate the changes taking place? Or perhaps they are waiting for that moment to swoop and take our power from us?

As I sit and ponder on this huge puzzle, the answer to which must – *must* – be found sooner, rather than too late, there is a knock on my door.

'Bishop?' says my assistant, 'I have one here.'

I sweep the desk clear of papers, useless pieces of nothing but surmises, and say, 'Send him in.'

A slightly confused-looking man, raw of skin, narrow of frame, upright of posture, is ushered into my office. He still has his staff in his hand, an ancient-looking rod of some now indefinable wood. I indicate a chair but he does not even look at it. He stands before me in dusty clothes that might have come off a scarecrow. Perhaps they did? There is no malice or anger in his face. He simply stares at me, expressionless, causing me discomfort for a moment. I fiddle with a paperweight that has no duty now that the desk is clear of litter.

'Ah, where are you from, señor?'

'*Mich fahima,*' comes the flat reply.

Arabic. Good. I am fluent in the language.

'Where were you born?' I ask again, in his tongue.

'Jerusalem.'

Perfect. 'You were found on the northern shores of the Black Sea – a long way from home, eh?'

'I have no home.'

'You are a goatherd?'

'I have a herd of goats.'

'What is your religion?'

'That is my business.'

Annoying, but I continue, hoping to get a clue in the answers to further questions. 'And your name?'

'It's been too long. I have forgotten. It is not important.'

I peer into his face. It is lined and ravaged by a life in the open, attacked by the weather and sleepless nights guarding his stock. The wind, sun and rain have deeply scored his complexion which is now the colour of mahogany and rougher than the bark of a cedar. These agents of climate have gone so deep they may even have marked his bones, pitted and scarred them. He could be any age but not young. A man who has spent a lifetime with only goats for companions may indeed have lost his name, for it means nothing unless it is used.

'How did you come here?'

He shrugs. 'They brought me. They promised me twenty more goats. I must get back. The boy I left looking after my animals will be concerned.'

I leaned forward. 'Is he to be a goatherd, like you?'

'Perhaps.'

'Do you instruct him?'

'A little – what is to teach? They are goats. They eat grass and bushes. They shit where they stand. They grow to know their master and obey his commands.'

'What about other things? Philosophy? Do you teach the boy about the deeper meanings of life and death? Belief? Do you concern yourself with the complex workings of religion in its various forms?' I am aware my voice has risen and is sounding quite shrill. 'Come now. Tell me what you think about when you are alone in the wilderness. You have all that time to consider the spirituality of your fellow men. Are we going in the right direction, or do you think we have taken a wrong path? Several wrong paths? Is there – is there a planned method for correction? A radical change coming, one perhaps which the shepherds intend to guide, even enforce? Come, come, what have you all been doing for the last two thousand years? You have to have been *thinking* about more than where next to take your goats. You have to have gathered wisdom.'

He blinks. His look is impenetrable. His eyes too deep for my understanding. I can't get past that obsidian stare.

'I am far from stupid,' he finally replies. 'Is that what you think? I am stupid?'

'No, no, I'm stating quite the opposite. Look, do you know other shepherds and goatherds? Do you gather together, talk, speak of things that other men have no time to discuss?'

'I pass others of my kind. We might mention where rich ownerless grass is to be found. Water. Water too is precious. And the stars. We might speak of the stars.'

'Ah! The stars. What do you say of them? Do you speak of divinity? Is there one special star?'

He shrugs. 'They are our maps.'

'Nothing more? What about beauty?'

'Many things are beautiful when you walk in lonely places – the desert, the mountains, and yes, the stars. The stars are worth watching, being points of light from afar. Simple beauty.'

'They fill your soul? Do they give you ideas?' My tone is

calmer now, more measured. 'Are we to go back to simplicity? Is that what you advocate as a profession? Is that what you counsel? Too much complexity in the way in which we serve the God who loves us? Yes, that would make sense. The kings were symbolic of politics, wealth, all the complicated aspects of life, while men like you . . .'

'Can I go now? My goats? I need to get back to the boy.'

I try to interview the man further, but he becomes agitated and upset, so eventually I call for my assistant. He takes the goatherd away and I imagine the man will be transported back to where he came from.

Am I any nearer to an answer? I think not. I have visions of shepherds on hills, on plains, drawing their schemes, waiting, waiting for just the right time to strike. Those earlier bishops and cardinals, those earlier popes, could not all have been wrong in suspecting a plot. Or perhaps not so much a plot as an influence, a curb against extremes? Their very presence is a threat to us. All they have to do is be there, sheltering under rockhangs, standing there, watching, watching.

We priests, we clergy, have called ourselves shepherds, yet we are nothing like those people of the hill and plain. We eat well, indulge ourselves, grow fat and lazy, adoring our beds. Some of us, like the Borgias, have actually been degenerates. They? They are like gentle beasts. They eat when they can, sleep with one eye open, walk thousands of miles, have desperately few possessions, preach to no man, keep their own counsel. Why do they live such a harsh and unrewarding existence? Surely because they have expectations for the future. They must be planning *something*? All those decades, those centuries!

But what can we do? I can't force any of them to tell me what they want, what they're planning. No government will bring out a law, banning the profession of shepherd. There isn't even anything immoral or unseemly in the work. It is a spiritually clean, physical way of spending one's time, admired by those who love the outdoors. Poets have produced endless verses on pastoral life. Shepherds are most likely poets themselves, though perhaps they produce not a single written word. Certainly they have aroused no suspicion in the general body of humankind. Only the Church has its misgivings – rightly so in my opinion – and believes there is more to them than just tending sheep, goats and other livestock. We think them dangerous, but would have a very hard time convincing others of our scepticism.

There is one thing we can do.

We can watch the watchers.

I take my quill in hand and dip it in the inkpot.

To Juan Cardinal Candido
Your Eminence:

You will recall the task you set me this last year. I have done all I can over the twelve months to discover the thoughts of those we suspect of scrutiny. The result is poor and I am ashamed to say I have very little new to offer beyond those texts which fill the manuscripts and documents of the priests who went before me. However, God has revealed to me one recommendation. There are those of us who work in remote areas, tending shrines and chapels in out of the way places, often far from civilisation. I would suggest recruiting some of those priests and using them to infiltrate the ranks of the watchers. Send them out into the hills and valleys with their own herds, to report back within a decade or two on what they uncover in their guise as shepherds. This is the best I can do. Although I have a safe and comfortable position here, in the Vatican, I shall be one of the first to volunteer for this mission. I am ready to lay down my life to discover the secret of their silence and watchfulness that has dogged our concern over the millennia.

Bishop Peter Spinoza on this Seventh Day of Our Lord, July 1771.

Ω

An addendum to this report says that Bishop Spinoza was indeed sent out with a handful of priests into the hills of Armenia not long after this paper was written. The group was never to be heard of again.

Other records linked to this account indicate concern about a deep-seated strain of scopophobia among elements of the priesthood at the time. The belief seems to have been that there were men 'out there in the wilderness' intent on keeping the Church under close scrutiny, but for what reason and whether with a positive or a negative motivation, no one seemed prepared to speculate.

Bishop Spinoza appears to be the only prelate, along with his assistants, who actually attempted to watch the watchers.

1779

History tells us that Captain James Cook died on 14 February 1779 on the beach of Kealakekua Bay, on the island of Hawaii. He was struck on the head by one of the islanders, fell on his face in the surf, and was then stabbed to death.

In the Vaults of the Vatican Library a file containing a number of torn and stained pages appears to tell a different story. Handwriting experts have compared these pages with known examples of Captain Cook's writing and confirm 'a close similarity, though the difficult circumstances in which these entries seem to have been written, sometimes clearly in a very hurried way, mean that identification cannot be absolutely confirmed'.

That is normal scholarly caution. If these pages were, as seems more than likely, penned by Captain Cook, then it is obvious why they have been hidden away for two centuries.

The Missing Journal of Captain James Cook

Geraldine Warner

This ripped page appears to be a continuation of the journal of Captain James Cook, and dates from the afternoon of Sunday, 17 January 1779.

Little did I suspect upon waking this morning that by nightfall I would have paid homage to foreign gods!

At the third hour, Touahah conducted me to the temple on O'why'ge, along with Mr King and several natives. Given to believe we were to witness some manner of sacred ritual, and curious as to the customs of the islanders, I interrogated my guide, a priest of the native Church, as we traversed the beach.

As Touahah described the local deities Lono and Ku, I freely admit that my heart skipped a beat. Lono, Lord of Peace, Rain and Agriculture, rules over the Peoples between October and January. Touahah explained that we are fast approaching the end of that same month, when Lono must surrender his ascendancy to his brother Ku, the God of War. Ku in his turn rules until September, from which point the whole cosmic dance begins again. Although shaken for a moment by Touahah's tale, Good Sense prevailed, and gradually the heaving in my chest abated. Indeed, on approaching the temple structure, named *heiau* by the Islanders, I remember envying these people the simplicity of their lives and beliefs.

The Hawaiians bade my companions remain outside the wooden palings surrounding the platform. I, however, was encouraged by another priest, Koah, to enter the sacred space, then to descend to some manner of underground chamber. Although this dank place had the Appearance of a Tomb I was eager not to give offence, and complied.

Immediately upon entering I saw a gigantic Warrior before me, wielding a mace, with skin that burned like fire. In his mouth was a severed human arm. I am not ashamed to say that I started violently, but once my eyes adjusted to the shadowy crypt I realised that my challenger did not consist of flesh and blood, but of metal. Closer inspection caused me to suspect he was fashioned from pure Gold.

'Can you see Ku burning with the souls he has slain?' Koah asked me, before throwing himself headlong before the Statue.

My Logic smirked inwardly at this, but there was a smouldering ember within my Imagination that looked at the Graven Image and shuddered assent to Koah's question. Sensitive to the honour the Islanders were bestowing by inviting me into the heart of their holy place, I followed his example in appeasing the monstrosity. Thus it was that I made prostrate before the mighty Ku.

Immediately an exotic and scented air descended from the North, and I was given to believe that Ku was pleased with my offering. For my own part, however, my revulsion as my lips touched the monster's feet sent a shiver deep through my bowels.

My Humour after this ungodly event was such that on return to my ship I was struck with an unexpected Melancholy, and was therefore disinclined to discharge my Account of today's strange experiences. It is only Lady Habit that keeps the pen presently in my hand.

Monday, 18 January. Variable light airs from SW in the first part, latterly Calm till 4 p.m. and a gentle breeze to the South.

Still gripped by Melancholy, I charged Mr King with the administration of the *Resolution*, and took to my berth. Today passed without event, save for the presence of certain unaccustomed words and images that keep pervading my consciousness, borne to me as if by the Wind. *Kai-Kai-Kai* sang the breeze, and with this my heart was eased.

Tuesday, 19 January. Squally rain, followed by Easterly Storms.

At first light Touahah again led our party to the *heiau*, but informed me that on this occasion certain Preparations were necessary before I could enter. He instructed us to wait outside the palings, and disappeared into the trees. My men meanwhile constructed a crude shelter on the beach, from which they could observe the day's proceedings. I was flattered by their concern for my safety.

Several natives came to sit by the temple, some carrying livestock in their arms. On hearing the sound of squeals and grunts I noticed that the animals were pigs, restrained by means of heavy chains. The villagers maintained their distance, and made no efforts to communicate with us.

Touahah returned holding a length of bamboo, a nail and a cloth of woven hemp. He insisted I sit on the ground and remove my jacket. I wish now that I had not slavishly heeded my fear of giving offence, but I did as he asked, even rolling up my Shirt-Sleeve when requested. He took a phial of dark liquid from his Costume, and inserted into the bamboo tube both the nail and a measure of the liquid, a sticky, vile-smelling substance. I realised he intended to mark my skin with this contraption, but nevertheless let him fulfil his Purpose. Whether I was concerned that my fears might infect my Crew, or believed that a Tattoo might strengthen my bonds of comradeship with them, I know not.

Touahah ministered to me carefully, and wiped my blood with his cloth as he progressed. The process was not painful as I initially feared, not that I would have shown distress before my men. The design growing on my forearm was small and simple: an Ear of wheat, fashioned in black and gold. I feared it was to become a whole field, but Touahah seemed satisfied with one simple stalk, and put away his tools with calmness and precision.

I was now permitted to enter the sacred space. The natives went with us, striking up a rhythmic chanting, and I was invited to honour Lono's departure and Ku's arrival by imbibing copious amounts of *Kava*. I by no means find this drink disagreeable, tending as it does to bring on most exquisite Dreams and Visions, but on this occasion I discovered myself severely disinclined to offer service to Ku in this way. Only regard for my hosts enabled me to force the noxious Liquid down my Gullet.

Whether it was partaking of this opiate substance, or the subsequent sacrifice of the chained Pigs, slaughtered by means of long metal stakes, I know not, but as the chants became masked by squeals, I found myself somewhat distanced from my Inner Self, as if the Pigs-Blood, now splashing so liberally into the gullies around me, was imparting to me a new Spirit. Indeed, the change was such that the Natives saw fit to make prostrate before me, and for an instant I considered it as my birthright to be treated with such adulation.

As my heart soared amidst the heavens, the Islanders conversely descended into base frenzy, thrusting their hands into the scarlet river now running awash around me, anointing me with the sticky substance and thereby . . . senseless though it is, the only words I see fit to record here in this journal are *imbuing me with strength*. The Experience cannot otherwise be expressed. Smeared now with blood, I felt myself thrown into an Ecstasy, all at one with land, vegetation and Elemental forces. I swear that had I at that moment bade the rain stop it would have obeyed me. Not that I would have had it stop, for never have I drawn so much pleasure and strength from the sensation of heavenly waters refreshing my skin, each droplet visiting manifold pleasures upon me.

My ears then alighted on the sounds surrounding me, and I became cognisant of the cacophony giving way to melody, incanted by first one voice, then several, until the air was filled with the chorus of a single word, *Kaikilani*. Thus my joy became complete. I whispered her name, for I was now convinced that this was a She, and the cadence of the syllables seemed to exceed the output of the greatest Italian masters in Beauty. I was thus doubly unprepared for the sudden piercing of pain, bitter as my recent pleasures were sweet, that penetrated my consciousness in the very next instant. On uttering her name again, *Kai-Ki-La-Ni*, I discovered to my cost that to declare it a second time was to be thrown into the very Furnaces of Hell.

By now bloody and distressed, I was of a mind to return to my ship that very instant, and only an anxious Touahah restrained me. I resented his impertinence in so doing, and being Superior to him in stature believe I might have overcome him had not bonds of propriety held me back. He was desirous of me to await the King, a certain Kalani'opu'u, presently delayed on his return from a sea voyage, who wished to confer on me a ceremonial blessing. I sat upon the beach, and there attempted to regulate my Humours to an 'even keel'.

Imagine my joy when I discovered that the Kalani'opu'u whom Touahah eventually led over the beach to greet me was the self-same Terryboo I knew from my outbound journey.

'Terryboo. Or should I call you Kalani'opu'u?' I quipped to my newly rediscovered friend, drawing him close to my breast.

'Captain Cook. Or should I call you Lono?' he countered. I might have expected to feel discomfort at his reference to the day's Events, for I am a modest man, but instead I smiled warmly.

'Lono, if you will,' I laughed. 'I scarcely have one more month of divinity left to me, and am determined to enjoy it while it lasts.'

I wondered whether I had exceeded my bounds in addressing a King thus. However Kalani'opu'u merely bowed in recognition, and departed.

On my return to the ship I discovered a certain aloofness at large amidst my men. Those in the observation tents had doubtless espied the strange proceedings of the day. However, they seemed loathe to talk of their impressions in my presence, despite my pressing them to that purpose. The crew left Caulking aboard ship that day evidently were also party to the day's events, for I distinctly heard the syllables *Kai-Ki-La-Ni* hissed behind my back on several occasions, in tones of mockery and spite. Or perhaps it was fear that informed their behaviour. I hesitate to write this, and know not if my impressions are induced by an excess of the *Kava* still awash in my system, but when the natives prostrated themselves this After Noon I swear I detected Worship in their countenances, not as men playing their part in a Ritual, but . . . a thousand times no. I cannot finish the thought. It rails against Heaven and all that is Holy. I shall repair to my berth, and may God grant me sweet repose.

Wednesday, 20 January. Inclement.

My dreams were once more haunted by Kaikilani, and I awoke with grief and regret in my heart. I called upon my first Lieutenant to take command of the ship, and took a boat to a secluded part of the bay. Although fully clothed, I lay on the beach. The surf washed onto my jacket, but far from causing me discomfort, its cool caress was welcome, feeling as it did like a woman's touch.

I must have fallen into a reverie, as the next thing I knew was Mr King shaking at my shoulders, and summoning me to the ship to greet a procession of native canoes turned out in my honour. Our passage was impeded by these very boats encircling us. Then, as if in obedience to some silent command, all oars stopped moving, and the islanders bowed low from the waist, even whilst seated in their craft. Their actions pleased me, and sudden shafts of sunshine peered through

[Journal illegible for several paragraphs]

canoes departing under the gathering clouds. Mr King took issue with my actions, preferring that I had been Bound by Protocol whilst greeting kings, especially ones to whom we were indebted by a debt of friendliness. I felt compelled to remind him of the chain of command within my vessel, and place him on menial duties for the remainder of the day. His impertinence displeased me, and thunder

[Illegible]

buried our old companion Seaman William Waltman in the *heiau*. In the absence of proper consecrated ground this seemed as fitting a place as any, and I took it upon myself to provide some suitable Anglican rites. One of the Islanders added to this a Hawaiian tribute, pleading Ku's blessing.

I must admit this sat very uneasily with me, although I am somewhat ashamed of my subsequent actions. Irrational though it appears to me now, it seemed this afternoon on the beach that the temple and its fiery god were the sole source of the troubles visited upon us over the last few weeks. I felt a rush of resentment burn within my veins against Ku and all the mishaps he has caused. Filled with fury, I instructed my remaining men to pull down the temple palings, and charged Mr King to use them for firewood. He created a blaze a short distance down the beach. I ordered my men into the chamber underneath the platform and instructed them to thrust Ku's wooden idols onto the fire, whilst I set to work removing his golden statue from its plinth. Unable to move the statue alone, I entreated the swarthiest among my men to help me topple it. The storm continued to rage, the bolts of lightning alighting on Ku's mace making it glint as if with real fire. For my own part, the chaos of the storm and the strength of my Affectations were so great that for several moments I almost fancied the statue alive. I suspect I was not alone in my suspicions, but resolute, we stuck to our Task. Twenty minutes' work sent the War-God crashing to the ground. I half expected repercussions, either from Heaven or from Hell, but the Idol split asunder, and all became still. The storm receded. Even the birdsong, so rich and distinctive in this part of the world, ceased.

I stood on the beach and inspected the damage we had wrought. In the clear light of Day the once mighty Ku was revealed to have but a hollow shell. Heartened greatly, I called my men, and we continued to dismantle the Temple with new lightness in our Spirits. As we worked, we were further cheered by a shaft of winter sunlight forcing its way through the departing storm clouds, and for the first time since my adventures at the Temple began I breathed easily.

Back aboard ship with the storm now a distant memory, the calm has afforded me some mental Clarity, and I have decided that my flirtation with Baseless Superstition has lasted long enough. I pride myself on being a rational man, and consider that Sir Isaac Newton's Laws of Motion compel me to seek a rational explanation for recent events. I am now convinced that it is certain natural opiates in the native Ink inducing the strange Behaviours in my Tattoo, (my wheat stalks number three as of this morning) or perhaps similar properties of the *Kava*, as yet unknown and unstudied in the Western world. I shall instruct Mr King to procure a sample for Scientific Study on our return.

I have resolved to return to England upon the turn of tide, and fancy that we might even be in Europe by Summer.

[Unidentified stains obscure the text at this point]

to Maui, in the hope of buying provisions for our home-bound journey. At one point we sailed close to the coast and espied some Hawaiians in their canoes, but they seemed resolute in keeping their distance

[Missing pages]

My wife Kaikilani visited me again last night. Of late my reveries are most Life-Like, and I awoke with grains of sand upon my pillow and hair. My dreams left me in excellent humour, and I left my cabin to conduct my daily inspections with a cheerful heart. However, mysteries were fated to abound this morning; my men were nowhere to be seen.

Several minutes' searching revealed my crew cowering on shore. I took a boat and called to King, who approached me with reluctance in his Gait.

'Explain yourself,' I commanded.

'I ordered the men to remain aboard. But they . . . they were afeared.'

'Why so, my good Sir?'

'The creaking of the timbers, Cap'n. The noise half deafened them. And the wailing.'

'Mere nightmares, surely. This behaviour is hardly fitting for grown men. Order them aboard immediately.'

'I fear they will need persuasion. More than one swore he saw vegetation sprouting from the timbers in his cabin.'

'Stand aside, Lieutenant.' I approached the crew and silence fell. I addressed the array of ashen faces before me.

'We sirs, are stout-hearted Englishmen. We must not act as children when the blackness of night Over-Stirs our imaginations. We run a tight ship, my good men. There is nothing to fear.'

I expected this admonishment to have my crew aboard at the double, but they did not stir. I was displeased, and thunder rolled in the skies. Droplets of rain splashed onto the men, most still in their nightshirts. They shrank back when the rain touched them. As they cowered, so I advanced. Lightning struck the beach, and my amusement caused me to laugh.

'This is punishment indeed for your mutiny. Aboard the *Resolution* at once.'

They were obedient to every last man.
[Missing pages]

Friday, 12 February

[. . .] head of the *Resolution's* Foremast was found badly sprung this morning. It seems the Wood is responding badly to recent climatic events, and the second lieutenant has discovered cracking at its core. There is unshaven bark in places, and signs of vegetation, and it would appear the Shipwrights were in Error for choosing unseasoned wood. I shall reprimand my crew for not alerting me to these dangers on our Outward Journey.

We are also in dire need of supplies, and can find few natives prepared to exchange livestock for our remaining goods.

The ears of wheat upon my arm numbered sixteen at last count.
[Unidentified stains]

Saturday, 13 February

We sent the Foremast to the beach, by the remains of the shrine. Kalani'opu'u came aboard. He was over-inquisitive and seemed very much dissatisfied by our continued presence on the
[Missing pages]

Sunday, 14 February

[. . .] were stoned. Edgar and Vancouver were assaulted by stones, broken oars and staves.

'We are obliged to use force, for they must not imagine they have gained advantage over us.' I told Mr King.
[Unidentified stains, possibly blood]

[. . .] white heat of a dagger penetrate my skin, the shock of it causing me to fall into the ocean. I was conscious of the natives setting about me with daggers and stones, tearing chunks off my flesh, thus exposing my bones. Then the waters ran red, and I could no longer ascertain the Extent of my Injuries.

Doubtless any lesser man would have been killed outright by the Violence inflicted, but I felt the force of life still strong within me, as if energised by the Fight. My body was crushed and sank beneath the waves. Nevertheless my spirit looked on in expectation of the Morrow.

[Cook's journal continues after his reported death on 14 February]

Monday, 15 February

I did not regain my Wits until Noon of the following morning, when I found myself adrift upon the shore. I checked my stab wounds, which were almost healed at this juncture, but still had minor bruising, and my lungs were wracked with pain after my night Underwater. Given my ordeals I was unsurprised to discover my body unclothed. I looked down. The wheat was now spread to my legs.

All traces of the *Resolution* and *Discovery* were now gone, save for these few pages ripped loose from my journal during the stabbing, which I found under a nearby rock. I looked for a means of securing them to my person. I fashioned a rope from some vegetation, and bound them firmly to my thigh.

Stronger now, I set out along the shore in search of sustenance. Some Islanders espied me, then briefly disappeared before bringing others of their number to stare and gawp. I stood proud, unafraid of my nakedness. They did not recognise me immediately, and it amused me to observe their reaction change from curiosity to fear. I fancied I spotted Touahah among them, and moved towards them, but they ran as I approached. I easily outpaced them and detained Touahah by the arm. He froze. Some of his friends made prostrate in the sand before me, whispering prayers, but most took the opportunity to flee.

'I see your bravery has vanished my friend,' I said. The trees shook in response to the thunder of my voice. The man gibbered, unable to even attempt speech.

'What think you of my Tattoos?' I continued. 'I would say you have done a fine job. See, they are spreading onto my feet, even as we speak.'

He looked down as I commanded, and saw the wheat multiplying ear by ear before his eyes.

I laughed at his discomfort. 'What? Have you never seen a god before?'

I threw him to the ground, and headed for the tribal seat of Kalani'opu'u. My strength now increasing with each step, I reached the King's residence in no more than a handful of bounds.

'Terryboo,' I called in sing-song tones. 'Come now. I know that you are hiding in there.' Gone were my crude attempts at the native language; I now addressed him fluently in the Hawaiian tongue, as I had with Touahah.

I heard his thoughts scream out clearly from within the hut.

'*Master. Forgive me, Master. Save me.*'

I decided to spare his life, but was reluctant to let him go unpunished for the behaviour of his compatriots towards my men. I summoned a storm, and brought down shards of lightning onto his hut. I satisfied myself with the thought that if I so wished, I could extinguish his life with a single blow, just as I had with my wife Kaikilani. The sorrow of her memory grieved me, and I fell to my knees and wept. The thoughts of my true love, bittersweet as they were, softened my desire for vengeance, and I resolved to punish Kalani'opu'u another day.

I felt the need to rest, and retreated to a clearing in the centre of the Island. I made a bed on the forest floor and shut my eyes. A covering of leaves was sufficient, as I had no fear of predators. To conquer death was to never be vanquished again I told myself, as I sought sleep.

Initially it was the prayers of the Islanders that kept me awake. '*Heal my child.*' '*Make my hunting fruitful.*' '*Bring me a wife.*' Their voices were as familiar to me as old friends, but I felt unable to meet their requests until I had rested. I turned, and felt the ground shake with my movements. Soon I became cognisant of the sound of distant drums beating, *boom, boom,* as if on another Island. I endeavoured to sleep. *Boom, boom, boom.*

Sunday, 16 February. Squally.

I awoke. The voices in my head had subsided, probably due to the earliness of the hour; being new to divinity, all I sensed from the Islanders was the murmur of their dreams, gentler and more shifting than the distant waves of the ocean. Then gradually I discovered that with a modicum of practice I could attune myself to individual voices, and individual hopes and fears.

The sound of drumming continued, nearer now. *Boom, boom*. I rose, and the trees shook in response to my movements. I sensed the presence of water nearby, and discovered a pool close to where I had made my abode. The ripples of the water circled outwards in perfect synchrony with the drumming. *He is coming*.

I was hungry, and sought out the nearest cluster of huts. They were easy to trace; I merely had to follow the Islanders' thoughts, which were louder now as the natives crossed from the land of sleep into the reality of the new day. The hut's owners fled on my approach, as I knew they would.

One brave soul, a ten-year-old stripling of a lad, stayed behind to defend his home. I heard his thoughts, and saw no need to disturb him. Instead, I sought my nourishment in his neighbour's hut, where I helped myself to a fine pork breakfast.

Sated, I examined my surroundings; I was curious as to the customs and lifestyle of my new-found Subjects. I found some sticks of charcoal lying on a grass mat, and resolved to record my strange Adventure in my Journal at the first opportunity. I was astounded to also find a looking glass, well crafted, with a finely worked ivory handle. No doubt it belonged to the treasure trove pilfered several days ago from our ships. I picked it up, eager to discover if the gouging inflicted on my face was yet healed.

A monster confronted me. I stood aghast at the Hideous Nature of my face, covered completely in ears of wheat, even down to my eyelids and lips, and a terrible cry sprang from my throat. I sensed that the lad next door had heard me.

The brave boy came into view in the doorway. 'Are you not scared?' he asked in his native tongue.

'The mighty Lono, scared?' I countered in the same language.

'You are an impertinent child, to dare to look on this face and ask such questions!'

'Even I can hear it,' he said.

'The drums?' I asked.

He listened carefully, and thought for a moment. 'Not drums.' He raised his eyes to mine, and I read concern in them. 'He is coming.'

I had no need to press him on the meaning of his words, and bounded back to my clearing, where my journal was hidden. I hastily scribble these words for I fear they may be my last.
[Unidentified stains]

came to consciousness aware of being dragged along the beach. Although I could feel my powers waning the closer we got to our destination, it nevertheless took sixteen men to restrain me. I tugged at the bindings on my wrists, pillaged no doubt from the *Resolution*, and after three or four shakes felt them loosen. The men hauling me were strained to their limit and had no spare effort to waste on speech, but when they saw me winning the battle with my restraints I could hear panic spreading among them.

'*His powers should be dormant by now,*' thought one, and '*the Human Spirit is still strong in him,*' another.

Encouraged, I pulled harder at my bindings. I sensed some of the natives who were dragging me lose heart, and with one final immense effort I rolled onto my ropes and freed myself.

The men cowered before me. Their fear gave me the strength I needed to arise and address them.

'I may be immortal, but yes, I still have the spirit of a human, and an Englishman at that,' I declared, and strode into the undergrowth, leaving them far behind. As I distanced myself from the *heiau* I felt my courage restore further.

I weighed my options. To remain on O'why'ge was foolhardy. I looked at the vegetation around me. *Of course,* I told myself. *If a ship's timber can become a tree again, then surely a tree can be turned into a ship's timber! I shall be resourceful on my paradise island, just like Mr Defoe's 'Crusoe', and fashion a boat. I shall sail back to England, and forget this whole sorry episode.*

Cheered, I set about my work. I tried to harden my mind against the drumming, now grown to fever pitch. *Boom, boom.* The brave boy from the hut had claimed the dreadful clamour was not a drum. Part of me knew this. The sound reached a level that would deafen any human ears. Then it stopped.

I had no need to turn around. 'Ku,' I said.

'Brother,' said he. 'I fear you have outstayed your welcome.'

'I am changed. I have a human spirit inside me now.'

'No matter. It is no longer your time.'

I turned to face him. He was a monstrous sight, worse even than the Graven Image in the *heiau*. Nevertheless, I stuck to my resolve.

'I have only just tasted divinity,' I said. 'I am not ready to relinquish it so soon.'

'Then I fear I must take it from you.'

'By force? Remember we are brothers, Ku.' I trusted that the beating of my heart was not audible to him.

'When you smashed my Idol, was that the act of a brother?' His eyes flashed red and gold, and he raised his fist against me.

'Then by force it shall be,' I declared, raising my own fists.

He laughed in derision. The sound was fearful and deafening. 'You wish to fight me like a human, Lono? I would not demean myself thus.'

With that he focused his eyes on me, and I felt a burning in my belly. My arms and legs locked rigid with bonds far more powerful than the ropes from the *Resolution*. Sweat dripped from my heated skin. I looked for steel inside my soul with which to fight, but I confess that my heart was already defeated.

From that point it was simple work for Ku to compel me to accompany him to the *heiau*. My thoughts travelled ahead, to the palings and idols I had thrust into the flames, and the smashed likeness of my brother. I had already experienced death as a man; now I imagined what it would be like to die as a god. As we neared our destination I felt myself stumble with each step, until I was no longer able to hold myself upright. Ku grabbed my neck in the crook of his elbow, and dragged me along the beach. He bore my weight easily, and we soon reached the *heiau*. There he threw me onto the sand.

Exhausted though I was, I had half a mind to escape, and made careful observation of my surroundings. Ku must have read my thoughts, for he quickly snatched up a metal stake and chains, remnants no doubt of the ritualistic slaughter I witnessed when I was in human form, and drove the stake through the ground. He made short work of securing my leg to the post.

Trapped now, I took stock of my situation. My strength was sapped, and my heart and ribs burned with increasing pain within my chest. I became aware of an itching on my skin under my Tattoos' ink. I rubbed at it in an attempt to soothe myself, but the ink crumbled away under my fingers, taking skin with it and revealing my veins and blood. I shut my eyes, resigned to death. My breathing, however, was hale and deep, and I had the impression that my life force was not yet spent.

I felt a tugging at my thigh. I opened my eyes to see Ku snatching my precious Journal. He examined its contents, then threw it down at my feet.

'Meaningless markings!' he said in disgust.

I scrabbled to retrieve the pages.

He laughed. 'You think that your scribbles will save you? How your new human soul has changed you, my brother!'

He turned his back on me. It appeared that whilst I was lying on the sand he had set about starting a fire on the beach, and now I saw him bend to fan the flames. He looked at it, and appeared displeased.

'It must be hotter. I must leave for a while,' he declared. 'I have need of a cast-iron pot. I fear I must go to the next island for it. You may amuse yourself with your writings. Do not escape. I would find you, and you would only succeed in making me angry.'

'Are you going to kill me?' I asked.

He tended to the fire for a few moments before turning to reply.

'No,' he said, looking deep into my eyes and smiling. 'That is the last thing that I would wish to do, brother of mine.'

[Missing pages]

gold continued to melt in the huge vat over the fire, until only Ku's head remained, the severed human arm still dangling from his mouth. Although nearly destroyed, the image chilled my heart just as violently as on the first day I encountered it. I regret not destroying the statue completely when I had the chance.

The realisation that the vast cooking pot Ku has procured from the next island is not intended for me has eased my mind considerably. It has become apparent over the last two days that Ku is true to his word, and has no intention of killing me. He allows me a good night's sleep on the beach before the blazing fire, and each morning he brings me a hearty breakfast.

Whilst he was waiting for the gold to melt, he even took an interest in my seafaring tales. 'You have a strong spirit,' he remarked after one dramatic story, in what appeared to be genuine admiration, and I fancy that the tension between us is dissipating.

Late yesterday afternoon he declared the gold 'ready'. He balanced the cauldron on his hefty shoulders, and carried it deep under the *heiau*. I asked him several times why an immortal being would have need of molten gold, but he refuses to be drawn on the issue. 'You will find out soon enough,' is all he will say.

For yesterday evening and most of today he has left me to my writing, joining me only for breakfast. He is strangely quiet.

'I will miss you, brother,' he said. 'I have become accustomed to your stories.'

After these words I have begun to entertain thoughts of my release, of my wife, and of England. I amuse myself by designing the boat I will build, and have begun to chart how far it must travel before I can procure a proper ship. Lost in my plans, the day has passed for me as if in the blink of an eye.

Wednesday, 19 February. Late After Noon.

Ku proclaims everything finished.

'Come. See,' he says, and gently releases me from my chains.

He leads me down into the *heiau*. After days in the bright sun, all I can see are shadows.

'You destroyed our temple in ignorance brother,' he says. 'But I restore it in love.'

My eyes start to adjust. I make out the contours of a huge statue glowing in the corner, formed from the molten gold.

'I am glad to see you back to your former glory, brother,' I say. 'It grieves me that I acted as I did in our sacred temple. I am an ignorant fool.'

'You are no fool,' he insists. 'And your spirit is strong. I have grown to enjoy your company.'

'And I yours,' I reply.

'But I fear we must soon take separate paths. I shall leave you for a short time before our final goodbye. It would perhaps be fitting to document this moment in your journal uninterrupted.'

'Thank you, brother,' I say.

I now scribble the account of our final conversation, and hope only that it is legible; the shadows around me hinder my progress. However, my eyes are beginning to adjust. I hear my brother approaching now, but before I cease my writings I shall describe Ku's statue. It is just as massive as before, but now is missing its mace and hideous severed arm, and this time the skin appears to be made not of flames, but of . . . I can scarcely make it out . . . made . . . of . . . wheat.

Friday, 1 October

Were Shakespeare, Chaucer and Dante to combine forces, they would have no words between them to describe the hell I have endured over the last seven months. Who would have believed that a man could long for death so ardently! Even the worship afforded me by my Subjects on my recent ascendancy has not cheered my Spirits. Indeed, since my release I have merely felt irritation at the fickle nature of their prayers, knowing that just two short days ago they were affording my brother the selfsame veneration. My brother. Little did I suspect at the beginning of the year that by autumn I would be capable of feeling such hatred. Enclosed by Ku in that rank, boiling enclosure of my own hollow statue . . .
[Missing]

Ω

From notes in the file written by a Catholic priest, it appears that James King found some torn and stained pages from Cook's journal lying on the beach, and took them back to Britain in October 1780, by which time he was captaining the Discovery, *the* Resolution's *consort ship. Over the next few years King completed Cook's account of the voyage for publication – but without anything from these pages, which he understandably found too rambling and disturbing to include.*

This was at the beginning of Catholic emancipation in Britain. Knowing that the Anglican Church shied away from anything that smacked of the supernatural, King sought advice from a Catholic friend who introduced him to his priest, who agreed the account should not be published, and offered to keep the pages safe. After King's death in 1784 at the age of only thirty-four, the priest sent the pages to the Vatican.

Seven years after Cook's voyage to Hawaii a French frigate visited the islands and found that many of the inhabitants were sick and dying of diseases introduced by Cook's sailors, particularly tuberculosis and venereal diseases. Perhaps in an attempt to appease their gods by ridding themselves of any link with Cook, the Hawaiian leaders pressed upon the French captain a few weathered and water-stained pages. At some point in the succeeding years these too ended up at the Vatican, where an astute archivist connected them to the earlier pages.

1814/41

The USA is no stranger to wild weather. The hurricane of 4 October 1841 was considered one of the most destructive in the early history of the United States, causing more than $2 million in damage (nearly $50 million today) in New York City alone, when the city was still rebuilding from the Great Fire of 1835.

There was another hurricane over a quarter of a century earlier in the city of Washington, that many believe turned the course of the war against the British.

This account of the 1814 storm by someone who was at the very centre of it was written just after the 1841 storm, and was sent on to Co-adjutor Bishop John Hughes of New York, a year before he became the city's first Catholic Archbishop. The last page of the covering letter to Bishop Hughes, including the signature, is missing, but the concerned writer would appear to be a priest at St Peter's Church on Barclay Street, the oldest Catholic parish in New York State.

Cooking up a Storm

Jean Marie Ward

New York, 6 October 1841

Right Rev. Sir,
 I regret the necessity of imposing upon your time in the midst of the present crisis. Nevertheless, a situation has arisen in St Peter's parish which merits your urgent attention.

 This morning after Mass, Mrs Henri Fouchet, one of our most prominent communicants of colour, demanded to speak with me in private. Mrs Fouchet is a widow with three children – a son of fifteen, and two daughters, eighteen and thirteen – all confirmed in the Faith. Upon her husband's death in the cholera epidemic nine years ago, she took over the management of Fouchet Millinery, a role in which she has enjoyed great success, recently expanding into drapers' goods. She makes regular donations to the Church and can be relied upon for substantial contributions to special appeals. She is also known for her numerous good works among the Africans of our parish.

 A woman of temperate habits and modest demeanour, she had never before sought preferential treatment for herself or her family. For her to press for an immediate audience would be unusual under any circumstance. For her to require such attention in the wake of the recent gale, in the midst of so much death, injury and ruin, is unthinkable.

 Once in my office, she produced a sheaf of densely written pages from her reticule. She insisted I read them before we addressed the purpose of her visit. Fearing the effects of the storm or its aftermath had disordered her wits, I agreed to look over the document. I was confident a brief examination would allow me to identify the cause of her distress and offer the proper guidance.

The first line left me sputtering in outrage. I started to protest what I considered an egregious waste of my time.

She lifted one small, gloved hand and the words fled from my mind. I say that quite literally; it was as if I had lost the power to verbalise thought. I have never experienced anything like it. The strangeness was compounded by the play of light over her pale grey eyes. Her gaze, always startling in a person her complexion, seemed to have acquired an exceptional force and lambency.

'You have to read it all,' she said. 'You won't understand unless you do.'

Her words carried the force of a compulsion. I resumed reading. (I herewith attach the complete document for your perusal.)

*

The Testament of Mrs Henri Fouchet

Mama was a conjure woman.

I know what you're thinking. Conjure, gris-gris, voudou – they're nothing but heathen superstition. I would've said the same until that dreadful, scorching day, the twenty-fourth of August, in the year of Our Lord 1814.

Mr President Madison's freedman thundered up the drive to the White House steps. His face was grey with road dust. His chest heaved like his poor, lathered horse. 'Clear out! Clear out!' he shouted. 'General Armstrong has ordered a retreat!'

Ice gathered in my belly, for all I'd been sweating like onions in a pan not moments before. Mama warned me the British were coming. She said her spirits showed her Washington City burning. I hadn't believed her. I dismissed everything her spirits said as an act of faith. Besides, everybody from Mr President Madison to the Congress and all our generals said our militia would stop those British before they even got close.

A part of me disbelieved it still. How could her dire foretelling come to pass with the sun shining overhead, and the sky so clear and blue? There should be a storm, a blast of trumpets from on high. But the only sounds were the whimpers of the house girls standing around me.

Mrs President Dolley Madison paled under her rouge. Hand to

her throat, she turned to scowl at Mama, who like always, stood apart from the rest of the servants and slaves.

Mama didn't cringe in fright, or hike her chin defiant-like. She appeared as calm as still waters. You'd have thought the prospect of the British capturing the town and torching it like we had the parliament buildings in Canada troubled her not at all.

The notion that maybe she did know something – something the rest of us were too staggered to see – gave me a trickle of hope. Not so Miss Dolley. Her glare just about crackled. Her bosom strained against her old grey house dress as she filled her lungs for a proper scolding. But before she could open her mouth, the President's Master of Ceremonies, John Sioussat, leaned over her shoulder.

'The British will not attempt a forced march in this heat. They will take hours to reach the city – plenty of time to lay a trap.' His voice sounded huskier than usual. His accent was thicker, too. 'We can spike the cannons at the gate and lay a trail of powder to the house. That would kill a hundred men and injure far more.'

Miss Dolley gasped. Her head shake turned to a shudder. 'They'd be blown to pieces. No. I won't have it. It's too horrible.'

French John lifted a dark eyebrow. 'It is war.'

War. Here. Now.

French John knew war. He'd served four years in the French Navy, and still wore his hair tied back in a sailor's queue. In the time it had taken the rest of us to gather on the North Steps, he'd found himself a pistol to shove between the buttons of his vest and a sword to strap to his hip. His fine blue coat dragged from his shoulders. Its pockets strained. The bulge in the one closest to me matched the shape of Mr President Madison's folding razor.

French John had always been so particular about his appearance. He'd never risk staining his vest with oil and powder, or spoil his coat unless it was an emergency.

Unless Mama was right.

My heart raced, but I couldn't move. I didn't know what to do. Nothing in my life had prepared me for this.

'I don't care,' Miss Dolley said. 'Even in war, some advantages may never be taken. There are lines civilised people cannot cross.'

'If we do not take advantage, Madame, of a certainty the British will. They have promised to destroy the President's Palace and all the Departments supporting the war. What could be more just, more civilised, than destroying them in the act?'

'You forget yourself, Mr Sioussat. I am mistress here, and as long as I remain Lady President, the President's House will not be made into a bomb.'

I sucked my lip between my teeth. Even the crying girls fell silent. Miss Dolley was mistress of the house, but French John was no servant. He was free, white and as official as the President's secretary. Saying he forgot himself with respect to her was as good as a slap to the face. Men duelled for less.

Her eyes widened as she realised what she'd done. I expected her to apologise, but she stood her ground, daring him to object.

I held my breath, terrified of what the Master of Ceremonies might do.

The strangest look passed over French John's face. There was a flash of what might have been sorrow, then nothing. This wasn't like Mama's bland façade. He had no expression at all.

He drew himself to his full height, shoulders squared and hands at his sides like a soldier coming to attention. He tipped his head in a small bow.

'Your orders, Madame President?' he asked in a voice as empty as his face.

Miss Dolley's shoulders sagged in what I suspect was relief. Then she collected herself, straightening her spine until her bearing matched his.

'Are Mr Madison's papers loaded on the big wagon?'

'I saw to it myself,' he said.

'Good. Take the red velvet drapes out of storage and place them in my carriage, as well as the large silver urns from the dining room. Pack as much of the plate as you can, but be sure of the urns. They're the most valuable . . .' Miss Dolley stopped. She pressed her hands against her temples. 'Why am I dithering about urns? This war isn't about urns. Or restraint of trade. God bless Mr Madison, it's not about trade at all. It's about our independence, and the way General Washington sent the British packing in 'Eighty-one. That's why they're here instead of Baltimore or New York. This is Washington's city. They're counting coup.'

My heart dropped past my knees. First she'd lost her temper, now her wits. What would she lose next – our lives?

French John made a questioning noise in the back of his throat.

'They want trophies,' Miss Dolley said. 'They can't take the city home with them. They can't take General Washington either, unless they want to dig up his bones. Even mad King George wouldn't stand for that. But they still want proof they've bested us, something they can parade in triumph through the streets of London, a symbol of our vanquished state. And what could be more symbolic than the big portrait of President Washington hanging in the dining room?

'We can't let them have it, Mr Sioussat,' she said. 'Take it down from the wall. Break the frame if you must. Save the picture if possible. But under no circumstances allow it to fall into the hands of the British. If worse comes to worst, destroy it. Burn it to ash.'

Personally, I thought she was making a big to-do over nothing. What did it matter if they saved the picture and lost the town? But her fervour sparked something in French John. When he left to do her bidding, his face was a face again, not something stuck on the front of a statue.

Miss Dolley seemed to have recovered herself as well. The next thing I knew she was snapping out orders like always. She told the free white servants to leave as soon as the household fires were banked. She loaned the butler the small coach, since unlike the whites, he and his family lived with the rest of us in the service wings. She sent footmen in search of more wagons and horses.

None of us expected them to find any. Everyone who was anyone had abandoned the city as soon as the British landed in Maryland, taking their horses, coaches and carts with them. Whatever was left behind was soon taken by others looking to escape. Still, it was a comfort to know she cared enough to try.

Even better was learning she had a plan. She told us to pack only what we could carry, because it was a long walk to the Georgetown ferry, and there was no telling how far we might have to travel once we crossed the river to Virginia. Just thinking about the trip made my feet hurt, but the rest of me felt like I was taking my first clean breath after being trapped in a house full of smoke.

With our Lady President back in charge, things didn't seem nearly so hopeless.

'Not you, Lula,' Miss Dolley said in a hard voice. 'Come with me.'

Mama almost smiled. I couldn't imagine why. From the sound of things, Miss Dolley hadn't forgotten whatever made her mad in the first place, and the scolding was bound to be worse for being delayed. I sidled towards the house. I had no desire to be thought a party to Mama's reprimand. Besides, I had a load of packing to do.

Mama grabbed my arm. She didn't let go until we were standing in Miss Dolley's yellow parlour with the door shut behind us.

'I suppose you're very pleased with yourself,' Miss Dolley spat.

Mama shook her head. 'I love the British less than you, and with more cause. I only told you what the spirits told me. Now you know they spoke true.'

'If you and your spirits are so all-powerful, why don't you do something?'

Mama crossed her arms under her breasts and stared Mrs President Madison in the eye as if they were equals. In that moment, I could almost believe they were. They might have been two sides of the same mirror: Miss Dolley in her smoke grey house dress with her dark curls spooling from the edges of her turban, and Mama in the grey dress she made from Miss Dolley's discards, her braids peeping from the kerchief tied around her head. They were even of a height. The only thing separating them was the colour of their skin.

Miss Dolley turned away first. She groped for the nearest chair and fell in it like a woman twice her age.

Mama sighed. 'I can't stop the British from burning the Capitol or the President's House. The saints themselves couldn't stop them. That much is written. I can only change what comes after.'

Miss Dolley's head whipped up, the fight back in her eyes. 'Then do it. Your country needs you!'

'It surely does,' Mama agreed. 'But first, me and mine need some of that independence you're so proud of.'

Miss Dolley sniffed. 'How much more independence do you need? You have your papers. Mr Madison recognised you and your daughter as freeborn as soon as your family sent the records.'

'But they wouldn't take me back, not soiled as I am. I'm as dependent on your charity as ever I was a slave. Meanwhile, my daughter scrubs floors alongside girls who don't even know their letters. That's no future for a child of mine.'

'You want money?' Miss Dolley barked a laugh. 'You're too late. The Treasury left this morning.'

'You still have money for the running of the house. I'll take half. Paper bills or silver, makes no difference to me. I'll need a few other things besides. Nothing you'll miss – a rooster from the coop and some provisions. But first, I want a letter, signed with your full name and your title as Lady President, stating I'm acting for you, and that my daughter and me are free to travel wherever our business takes us in these United States.'

'And if I refuse.'

Mama shrugged. Being from New Orleans, she was more than a little French herself. 'The British cross the river into Virginia. You can burn the bridges and beach the ferry, but they got boats, and the navy hasn't stopped them yet. How long you think this union of states will last with their President dead and their Lady President a "Guest of the Crown"? Folks up north been calling for peace for two years now. They say they're going broke, and it's all the fault of southern planters like your husband who're too high in the instep to compromise in the name of trade.'

Miss Dolley's face blazed as red as her precious velvet drapes. 'This is extortion.'

'It's a bargain. I haven't asked a thing you can't afford, and it's not like you got much choice. There's no one gonna rescue you or this country. I'm all you got.'

All Miss Dolley had for what, I wondered. Did Mama have some way of helping Miss Dolley escape? No wonder Miss Dolley was spitting mad. The British threatened to clap her in irons. If Mama knew what was good for her, she'd stop haggling this instant. She might sew the finest stitches in all Virginia, but that wouldn't do us a lick of good if Miss Dolley turned her out without a reference – or worse, got herself captured on account of something Mama didn't do.

But Mama didn't back down. I swallowed around the lump of fear in my throat. Any second now, Miss Dolley was going to lay into her for getting uppity with her betters and spouting ideas above her station. Then we'd be on the street . . . with the British coming!

Miss Dolley said not a word. Instead, she bared her teeth like a cornered animal. She sprang from her chair and marched over to the pretty little desk that was as much for show as for writing. The locked panel hiding her strongbox and her special White House paper went sailing into the nearest chair. The way she sharpened her pen, I thought she'd cut her finger clean off. She didn't bother to sand the note when she was done, either. She threw it on the carpet and stormed out of the room, her chin hiked halfway to the ceiling.

Mama didn't retrieve the letter until the click of Miss Dolley's heels was no more than a memory. By then the ink had dried on its own. She folded the note into a sheet of waxed wrapping paper and slipped it into her *fichu*. The money disappeared into the purse she wore under her skirts.

'Mama, what have you done?' Any other day I would've bitten my tongue clean off before I said anything so foolish. Mama didn't take kindly to argument any more than Miss Dolley, and she had a temper like a pepper pot. But I was too scared to stop. 'The Madisons are good folk. They don't beat their slaves or sell families apart. They even let us go to Mass on Feast Days. But Miss Dolley won't stand for you treating her like that. You can forget all about setting yourself up as a *modiste*. It won't matter how good you are with a needle. You'll never have a shop in Washington City now, nor anyplace Miss Dolley has friends. They'll cut you dead. If you're so fired up for independence, why didn't you just wait for the British? They're calling for the coloureds to revolt.'

Mama rubbed her face like she was tired. 'Have you been sparking with that Jennings boy again?'

'What of it? I'll be fourteen next birthday. Paul's not like the other boys. He can read, and he's a sight smarter than Mr President Madison and all the Congressmen who landed us in this mess.'

She shook her head. 'The British are no friends of ours. You think all those "fugitive English" they take off our ships are white? And what you think will happen to the people who rise up at their call? You think they'll defend them when the men who own the tobacco farms, and the cotton and the mills say there won't be any more cigars to smoke or cloth to wear without Negroes to work the fields? You think the British will put our needs ahead of their wants? They'll leave the coloured folk behind the same way your father left me. He told me we'd live as man and wife, but as soon as the money ran low that British bastard sold me on the Charleston market. He knew I was free-born and carrying his child, but that didn't stop him. Being pregnant only raised my price.'

The shock of her words struck harder than a blow. Numbly I thought, *what next?* Mama never talked about what brought her to the Madison estate. I had some inkling she'd been a slave. Her conversation with Miss Dolley only confirmed it. But the notion that the father I'd wondered about my whole life was the person who sold us into slavery stole the breath from my lungs. The stars in the carpet started to spin.

Mama caught me before I fell. She held me tight, rubbing circles over my back like she did when I was little. 'Everything will be all right, Thérèse. That evil man can't hurt us now.' She took me by the shoulders and shook me lightly. 'Now I need you to be strong. Pack your pillowcase with our good shifts and shoes, our church veils, my red shawl, the jar of skeeter balm under my bed, and as many stockings as will fit. Then fetch me the General from the coop. He's the big white cock with the blue bars on his wings. Meet me in the kitchen when you're done.'

Her revelations had rattled me to my core, but they hadn't made me stupid. 'I know who the General is, and I'm not going anywhere near. He's a fighter. He'd peck my eyes out as soon as look at me!'

'Don't let him scare you, *cher*,' she crooned. 'He won't give you a lick of trouble. He and I have an understanding.'

She winked. It was the most frightening thing yet. My mama had run mad.

But the General went along with it. He squawked exactly once when I grabbed him by the legs and dropped him in the basket. Snaring him turned out to be a lot easier than saying my goodbyes. There wasn't enough time to do it properly, and what Mama told me kept getting in the way.

Between my grey eyes and wavy hair, it stood to reason my father was white – and no saint in the bargain. But outright wicked? If he was evil, what did that make me? I couldn't pretend he wasn't part of me. I saw the proof every time I passed a glass. And British? That made it worse, especially now. I wished I could pretend she was fibbing, but Mama wasn't in the habit of lying.

By the time I collected everything on her list, most of the household had long since departed. Even the painting of President Washington was gone, carted away by two of Miss Dolley's gentlemen friends. After all the shouting and the banging, the quiet of the lower passage gave me goose bumps.

The quiet didn't trouble Mama any more than the British. My world was ending, and there she was, bustling around the kitchen, humming something under her breath as she measured out a cup of cornmeal and knotted it into a white napkin. Another knotted napkin sat in the centre of the big kitchen table next to a lantern, a cider jug, a basket, plates of salt pork and biscuits, and lots more napkins.

As provisions went, they were all well and good. The silver bowl gleaming in the basket was another matter. So was the blue silk counterpane off Mr Madison's bed draped over the back of Cook's chair. On the seat rested one of Miss Dolley's lacy linen pillowcases, plump with her things. There was no mistaking the scent of her lilac perfume. Topping the pillow was a child's red drum. Where Mama found that I do not know, but I couldn't imagine she had any more right to it than she had to the Madisons' bedclothes.

'They're gonna burn the house, Thérèse,' she chided. 'I only took what was needful.'

'Needful for what, exactly?' French John asked from the passage.

Stripped to his vest, he was practically indecent. His neck was bare, and his shirtsleeves were rolled up to the elbows. He toted a pail of beer in each hand. The weight of the buckets made the muscles stand out on his arms. Arrows of sweat ran down the sides of his vest and disappeared under the sash wound around his waist. Two pistol butts protruded from the top, the one I'd seen earlier and another gun that didn't quite match. The britches beneath the sash were tight around his thighs. All he needed was a kerchief, and you would've sworn he was a pirate.

Mama's gaze drifted down. She dragged in a slow breath, pulling on the air like the bitter scent of beer was sweeter than shortbread baking in the oven. She glanced up at him from under her lashes.

'For Miss Dolley, of course.' She reached two fingers into her *fichu* and offered him the folded papers.

French John's forehead knitted over his nose. He set down the buckets and ducked under the lintel. As he read, his frown lightened, but his puzzlement grew.

'Madame Lula, I have worked for Madame President long enough to know she keeps her own counsel. However, I cannot imagine the purpose of such a . . .' he paused, 'assortment.'

Mama danced closer to retrieve the note. 'Why it's a recipe, *cher.*'

Both his eyebrows pointed skyward. 'Indeed? This is most peculiar. I distinctly recall being told, in no uncertain terms, on the very first day I came to work for the Presidents Madison, that gently born Creole ladies worked with their needle or their pen or not at all. They are far too grand for kitchen work.'

'So I am,' Mama cooed, 'and I'm shocked and hurt that you would think otherwise. This is a different matter entirely. This is a recipe for the spirits. I'm going to work a voudou on the British they won't forget.'

Voudou! Mama was doing *a voudou* for Miss Dolley?

If I'd still been holding the General's basket I would've dropped it on the floor, and wouldn't that have caused a fuss. Between the silver bowl, the rooster and the drum I should've guessed what Mama was about. She'd been stitching up good luck charms and making up remedies as far back as I remembered. But that wasn't the same thing, not by anybody's lights. You couldn't fault a person for helping a body feel better, even if it was only a charm to ease their mind.

But voudou – that was witchcraft. Just believing it was a sin. Working it was a crime against God and man.

From the way French John gawked at her, I thought he felt the same. Then he threw back his head and laughed. '*Bien fait!* It worked in Haiti. But these English may be harder to impress than the planters of Saint-Domingue. After all, they bested Napoleon.'

'I guarantee they'll be impressed if a Frenchman adds his mite,' Mama teased. 'How 'bout it? Won't you make an offering to the spirits to set things right?'

'What manner of offering?'

Upset as I was, I couldn't help noticing how wistful Mama smiled. 'Any trifling thing – a coloured thread, even. It's just for luck.'

'A button, perhaps? I caught one on the picture. Will that do?' Mama nodded. He fished the button from under his sash and dropped it in her hand. 'For luck.'

'*Merci.*' Mama curtsied as fine as the wife of the British ambassador – in the days when we still had a British ambassador. She pinned the button to the front of her dress.

French John's expression turned grave. 'Your voudou may be strong, Madame Lula, but have a care for yourself and Thérèse. So far, the British have spared our civilians, but that could change in an instant. Even more dangerous are those who blame President Madison for our present misfortunes. They will seek a scapegoat. If they see you as part of the President's House . . .' He spread his hands. 'Do you have someplace to go?'

'The spirits will provide.'

'Hein, perhaps they already have. Colonel Tayloe leased his house to the French Minister. The British have promised to treat it as an embassy, not to be harmed. For the rest, the minister has brought enough guards and servants to stand against a mob. You will be safe there. I will arrange it myself.'

'Will you be staying there as well?' Mama asked in a soft, wheedling voice I scarcely recognised.

'*Non.* I go to deliver Madame President's parrot. The minister has extended Polly an offer of diplomatic asylum.' A smile twitched the corners of his lips. 'For some reason he conceives her to be an important source of political intelligence.'

'I wonder how he came by that notion,' Mama said.

French John eyed the ceiling like he was checking for cracks. 'It could be someone said Polly repeated everything she heard.'

'Someone with a soft heart?'

'Someone with a soft head,' he corrected. 'But before I remove Polly to her new home, I must bring beer to the gate. For our soldiers. Running is a thirsty business, and losing . . . losing is worse.'

'None of this is your fault,' Mama said.

'I know. But a man wants to play the hero. This time it was not to be.' He tipped Mama a small salute. '*Bon chance, mon amie.*'

Mama stared out the doorway long after he left.

'He's married,' I hissed.

'Where I was raised that wouldn't have mattered,' she murmured. 'He could've had a white wife and a black, and we could've all been happy.'

Out of spite I said, 'I wouldn't have wanted him for a father.'

Mama only sighed.

We hauled everything outside, past the Pennsylvania Avenue gate to the thicket of shade trees at the back of the south lawn. Between the sun beating on my head and the hot gravel of the drive burning through the soles of my shoes, I was roasting like chicken on a spit. The paths through the trees weren't much better. It was so hot, even the little garter snakes hid in their holes. The only living things around were us and the bugs, who were buzzing fit to bust.

I was fit to bust myself. Mama was a fine one to talk about the object of my affections. She was pining after a married man, and a white man, to boot. Nothing good could come of it. Hadn't my father showed her that? But that was nothing compared to what she planned for the British. *Voudou!*

'We're going to Hell,' I said.

Mama shook out Mr Madison's counterpane and spread it next to the garden wall. 'How you figure that?'

'You're working voudou on the British and forcing me to help.'

'Uh huh.' Mama pounded some garden stakes into the ground in front of the counterpane. She arranged Miss Dolley's sheets over them in a kind of tent. 'You bring the skeeter balm?'

I dug the jar out of my pillowcase.

'Best put some on,' she said. 'We've got a long wait ahead of us, and a lot of bugs looking for a meal.'

She circled the trees to view our hiding place from the other side. The shade was thinner than usual after three weeks without rain. We had a good view of everything from the top floors of the Navy and War Departments on Seventeenth Street to the Treasury Department and rooming houses on Fifteenth. Of course, the view worked both ways, or it would have if Mama hadn't rigged a shelter almost the same colour as the whitewashed garden wall. The tented sheets would do a fair job of hiding us, so long as no one looked too hard – not that I was about to give Mama the satisfaction of admitting as much.

'Don't change the subject,' I huffed as soon as she returned. 'Voudou is witchcraft, and you know what the Bible says about that.'

Mama scooped some ointment from the jar. 'So is this.'

The bitter, mint scent stung my nose. 'No, it's not. It's just a mess of leaves, wax and fat ground up together. It's the same as a script from the apothecary.'

'Not when the apothecary don't know when to pick those leaves, or why the hour matters. Not when he don't know the prayers to say as he grinds them, or the rites to keep the medicine strong for as long as it's needed. That's the voudou. That's why this ointment will protect you all night long, while the ones from the apothecary don't last but an hour.'

'Magic is a sin.'

She snorted. 'Then Jesus Christ must've been the worst sinner who ever lived. He turned water into wine, gave sight to the blind, walked on the waves and raised the dead.'

I crossed myself in horror. 'That's blasphemy! Jesus Christ was the Son of God. He didn't do magic. He worked miracles!'

'Magic and miracles are the same thing, *cher*. It's all the glory of God. It's only a sin if you use it for harm.'

'And how do you expect to stop the British without doing harm?'

'By giving them a sign in the sky so clear they won't need a Daniel to interpret it.' Her eyes took on a dreamy look. 'There's no harm in it at all. In fact, it would help things considerably if you were praying, too.'

'I won't endanger my immortal soul by praying to heathen spirits.'

'Nobody's asking you to. Aves and Pater Nosters work just fine. I know you're carrying your rosary. No point in sinning with a lie. Now hush, I think I hear something.'

I leaned forward, straining to listen through the bugs. A sharp crash brought our heads up. Something small sailed out of one of the upper storey windows in the President's House.

'Looters,' Mama said.

My heart stuttered in my chest. Suddenly I couldn't get enough air. Breathing deep or breathing fast, nothing seemed to help

Mama squeezed my hands. 'Easy, *cher*. They're not here for us.'

'You don't know that! What if they raid the garden? What if they attack us?' Chills raced from my fingers to the back of my neck. I yanked my hands from her grasp and tried to rub the blood back into my arms.

Mama glanced at me out of the corner of her eye. 'Have I ever told you how we partied in New Orleans?'

'You want to talk about that now?' I yelped, then covered my mouth with both hands.

'I can't think of a better time than when we're on the verge of making our fortune. Now where shall I begin?' She tapped her chin. 'With the clothes? Or the balls? Or the night I danced with both pirates Lafitte?'

I tried to shush her, but she paid no mind. Instead, she launched into a story about a gentleman planter who thought himself the heir to the last King of France, which reminded her of the duel his second cousin fought over a dark-skinned goddess they called the Queen of Sheba, which caused her to recollect the skirt-tossing ghost of St Louis Cemetery.

In all my life, I'd never heard such goings-on. There seemed no end to her tales. She didn't properly finish one before starting on another, and another, until the afternoon eased into evening, and I forgot all about being afraid. I ate my dinner, drank my cider, and tossed some seed in the General's basket to keep him from squawking. More than keeping him quiet, I didn't want him to interrupt.

It was full dark when Mama finally stopped. I shook myself, confused by the sudden quiet. Where had Mama gone? Then I heard her panting softly. If I hadn't known better, I would've thought she was crying. But Mama only cried in a rage, and when she did, her bloody tears were fearful to behold.

'We could go back there if you like,' I whispered. 'You got money, and Miss Dolley's letter. Nobody could know her there. There'd be nothing to stop you opening a shop and calling yourself her dressmaker.'

She hiccupped a wet chuckle. 'Nothing but a letter from the governor's wife to Mrs President Madison asking for the particulars of my employment. No, *cher*, our way lies north. We'll talk about it later.'

She pressed her fingers over my mouth. I tasted salt and iron on her skin.

The dark exploded like a gun fired next to my ear. Our makeshift tent collapsed as I scrambled out from under it. The crest of a distant fireball rose over the garden wall.

The wall was too high to see over and too smooth to climb, or I would've tried. I had to see what was happening. I had to know the worst. Disregarding the danger, I ran to the big, three-arched gate that divided the south drive from Pennsylvania Avenue. The centre arch was wide enough for two carriages to pass. It had no doors, but the narrow arches to either side were barred with tall iron grilles. Grabbing the bars of the nearest one, I hoisted myself on the bottom rung. From the angle of the fire off the avenue, it looked like the whole Navy Yard was burning.

A smattering of shots, like Fourth of July rockets, erupted next. My ears were still ringing from the Navy Yard blast. So I wasn't sure of the shots' direction until fire flared over Capitol Hill. At first the flames were no more than yellow banners rippling from the windows of the House and Senate buildings. Then the wooden hall between them ignited. The fires swelled and came together in a yellow curtain the same colour as the satin in Miss Dolley's private parlour. The night glowed so bright I could've read my missal by the glare, but that would've been true blasphemy – to read Holy Writ by the light of hellfire.

To the south, the sky over the fort at Greenleaf Point flared orange. The blast from the fort was the loudest one yet.

My whole head rang from the din. It was as if an angel of the Lord had used my ear for a horn – not one of the kindly angels, either, but one of those dire messengers whose trumpets foretell the coming of Judgement Day. The prospect before me could've been a scene from the Apocalypse. Between the smoke, the fires and their shooting sparks, it truly seemed as if the stars had fallen, and a third of the earth was burning.

Coloured men in ragged clothing fled down Pennsylvania Avenue and up the numbered cross streets, shouting, 'The British are coming! The British are coming! Run for your lives!'

It was 1775 all over again. But in Washington City, there were no patriots waiting to take up arms and no General Washington to lead them, only Mama and me at the tri-part gate. We were two witnesses dressed in sackcloth, all right, but we had no fire to burn our enemies. It was they who brought the flames.

With nothing to block the view along Pennsylvania Avenue, I could track the redcoats' advance all the way from Capitol Hill. Lit from behind by the burning Capitol and from above by lanterns bobbing on long poles, the red-enamelled barrels of their guns glistened like spikes of blood. Their coats were dyed in the same gore. The air around them shimmered with the infernal heat and the tears pooling in my eyes. The outlines of the distant column blurred into a single mass – the many-headed, many-horned Beast of the Deep.

My mind stuck on the sight. Mama had to pry my hands off the bars and drag me back to the thicket. She shoved me behind some bushes. Dropping down next to me, she coiled herself around me, pressing my face into her bosom to stifle my moans. I couldn't stop. I couldn't breathe. The howling inside me had nowhere to go.

It seemed to take forever for the storm to pass, but it couldn't have been more than a few minutes. Capitol Hill was scarcely a mile away. Yet the light from the redcoats' lanterns was only now breaching the Pennsylvania Avenue gate.

The British marched in silence, without fife or drum, as if ashamed of what they'd done. The only warning of their arrival was the measured tramp of their boots over the gravel and the creak of their lantern poles. I cringed in Mama's arms, expecting portents and monsters. But my panic must have cried itself out, as well. In the glow of the fires they set and the lanterns they carried, I saw the enemy for what they were: men. Not the Beast of the Deep, for all they had come from the sea. Not the Dragon of the Last Days, for they'd come to burn. Only men.

The column passed within thirty feet of our hiding place. I counted nearly a hundred soldiers in red coats and shako hats. Their shiny red guns had blades on the ends. Some of the soldiers hefted rockets on their shoulders. But they were still men.

A smaller number of blue-coated, straw-hatted sailors marched alongside, carrying the lantern poles. Two officers rode at the end of the column. One wore the same bloody red as the soldiers. The other wore a blue coat so dark it looked black. Heavy gold-fringed epaulettes sparkled on their shoulders, and gilt trimmed their high cocked hats. They were the leaders of the party, General Robert Ross and Admiral George Cockburn. But they were hardly a sight to inspire awe, not when they were riding the sorriest pair of nags this side of the Alleghenies.

A single, lantern-bearing sailor brought up the rear. As he rounded the curve of the drive, Mama's breath hitched. Her fingers raked the front of my dress, scratching my skin through the thin layers of cloth. I squeaked in surprise.

The sailor turned in our direction. We froze. He shook his head. He never broke stride.

The first breeze in days carried their jeers and bawdy songs out the open windows of the house. I gnashed my teeth, imagining the British taking their ease around the table we'd set for dinner not ten hours before. They feasted on our food, while we cowered in the garden of the house where I'd lived half my life, the place where I'd learned my letters and cherished my first kiss.

I hated them for that. I hated them worse when the fires they set took hold. Every window of *my home* wept tears of fire. The house groaned through the pillars of the burning south porch. Smoke soiled everything that didn't burn outright, turning *my home* into a blackened sepulchre.

But most of all, I hated them for making me afraid.

The British left a sight gayer than they arrived, flaunting trophies just like Miss Dolley said they would. At the head of the parade they carried Miss Dolley's portrait on a pole. They boasted they were going to display her in London as a prize of war. Hats, wigs and red velvet cushions topped a score of bayonets.

Once again, their commanders led from the rear. From where I lay, I couldn't see much of General Ross beyond a flash or two of red. But Admiral Cockburn looked downright jaunty. As he neared the gate, he ordered the men to sing 'Yankee Doodle', and waved one of Mr Madison's old hats in time.

Outside the gate, the column turned north towards the Treasury Building. But the fire they lit there didn't burn nearly as bright as they would've liked, and the money was all gone. There wasn't so much as the corner of a paper bill in the vault they worked so hard to crack. The rising wind carried their complaints through the gate as they marched back down Pennsylvania Avenue. Dry-eyed and hate-hardened, I smiled.

Mama thrust the drum into my hands. 'It's time.'

I nodded. My skin felt tight and tender from the fire's terrible heat. My eyes were gritty from smoke, old tears and ash. My fingers ached from clenching. My palms were scored with the imprint of my nails. I was more than ready to make those redcoats pay.

Mama stripped to her shift, knotted her red shawl over one shoulder, and wrapped one of Miss Dolley's red brocade turbans around her head. She set the silver bowl at the southernmost point of the lawn, in a line with the burning porch. The groans of the house behind it made me want to weep all over again.

I prayed to shut out the sound. My hands fitted the drumbeat to the words:

Hail-Mary,

Full-of-grace,

The-Lord-is-with-thee.

Hail-Mary,

Full-of-grace,

The-Lord-is-with-thee.

I never got to the 'Blessed' parts. Hate and grief stole the rest of the prayer, and I began to get an inkling of what Mama meant about the difference between magic and witchcraft, harm and sin.

Mama chanted her own devotions, dancing clockwise around the bowl. It almost sounded like the Lord's Prayer, only she called on Damballa instead of Our Father. Despite the ungodly direction of her prayer, the familiar cadence of praise and plea soothed me more than I would've thought possible. The longer she went on, the harder it became to stay mad and hateful. The odd beat of my broken Aves added to the sense of peace, like being rocked to sleep in a well-sprung carriage travelling a freshly graded road. In the light of everything that happened, it made no sense. But I lost all fear. I felt weightless and grounded, as if I was both air and earth at once.

Like a priest elevating the Host, Mama offered the napkins full of flour and cornmeal to the sky. Then she scattered their contents at the four corners of the compass. When that was done, she snatched the General from his basket. Holding him by the legs over the bowl, she sliced his throat. His head disappeared in a gush of blood. She cast the headless carcass to the ground. It got up on its own two legs and ran away, flapping its wings as if it could still fly.

I didn't find it strange at all. If I were a chicken, I could've flown.

The burning house snapped and roared, splashing the lawn with waves of heat. It would've been a mercy to put the building out of its pain.

In the distance, the sky grumbled, faint and cranky like a cross old man.

Next Mama raised the bowl of the General's blood. She lowered the silver vessel to her lips, drank a single sip, and poured the rest into the ground.

The earth sighed. The withered grass of the lawn seemed to shiver with pleasure. Around the edges of the gravelled loop formed by the south drive and the garden promenade, the ground rippled. The ripples travelled towards us in ever-tightening rings, the exact opposite of ripples in a pond. The flow surged to the edge of the blood-stained grass. The ground beneath the spill pushed upwards. The tip of what might have been a dark, furled bud poked through the matted blades. But it was no flower. It was a snake, the biggest black snake I'd ever seen. It reared as tall as Mama and flicked its tongue at her face.

I should've been terrified, but somehow I knew there was

nothing of the Serpent in that snake. It was as much God's creature as Mama or I, and had not come to do us harm.

Mama greeted the snake with a curtsey, and called it Papa. I
didn't understand the conversation that passed between them,
but they seemed to reach an accommodation. Mama bowed her
head, touching two fingers to her forehead and to the snake's.
When it lifted its head like the point of a spear, she grasped it
around its middle and launched it at the burning house. The
snake flew like it was the most natural thing in the world. It zig-
zagged overhead the same way it would've slithered across the
ground, scales gleaming like black glass. Then all at once, it
vanished in the smoke.

Mama shouted at the sky.

The sky shouted back. A blast of wind rattled the trees.
Lightning struck the house at the spot where the snake disappeared. The sky flashed white. The answering crack of thunder
rang louder than the blast from Greenleaf Point.

The noise shocked me back to myself. I flinched from the glare,
the sound and the strange, too-clean smell. Water splattered my
face. I raised my hands. Fat, soft raindrops splashed my over-
heated palms and dribbled between my smarting fingers.

I cast my gaze heavenward. A host of purple thunderclouds
winged across the sky like a multitude of angels. At first the rain
they brought was no more than a drizzle. But only instants later the
sky seemed to be falling on top of us. I clambered to my feet as the
parched grass of the lawn disappeared under a sheet of water.

A surge of wind swept the torrent through the house. In no
time at all the flames were gone. The Treasury fire winked out
next. The Capitol went dark. The Navy Yard and Greenleaf Point
blazed no more.

I should've been afraid of drowning. I should've run for the
shelter of the service wings, which the British hadn't bothered to
torch. But I was caught up in wonder. After three weeks' drought,
any rain would've been a blessing. This was so much more. God
forgive me, for all I knew it was a spell, it felt holy, like a sacrament, a second baptism to wash away all my sins. And not just my
sins. The Lord had written His Will across the sky with a finger of
lightning, cleansing the city of its hellish fires so it could rise anew.

And as far as I could tell, not one soul had suffered harm.

Mama shouted through the rain, 'What do you think of my voudou now? Can I cook up a storm, or what?'

'It's a miracle.'

'I can't hear you!' she yelled.

I was pretty sure she could, but I shouted just the same. 'It's a miracle!'

A flash of lightning lit her blazing grin. She seized my arms and whirled me into a crazy jig. We capered in the dark, splashing and laughing, with lightning for our candle. We didn't stop until we were wheezing too hard to go on. Somehow we fetched up near the lantern, which Mama lit *in the rain* without flint or ember. Still giggling, we gathered our belongings and the bedclothes. Mama left behind the bowl, the cider jug and the drum, but she wasn't giving up those sheets, not for anything.

'I've done my part,' she said. 'Now I'm gonna sleep like a lady's s'posed to.'

I snorted. The counterpane and linens had soaked up so much water, Mama's bundle was almost too heavy for her to carry.

'So it won't be tonight,' she countered. 'But soon. Real soon.'

A coloured footman met us at the back door to the Tayloe House. His eyes widened at the sight of the lantern I carried. The storm had lessened considerably, but the wind was still tossing the rain around. Even so, the candle flame barely flickered.

He asked Mama if she'd called the storm. She allowed as she had. In response, he bowed so low he practically bent over double. I didn't see anybody else in the hall, but other servants must've been lurking in the shadows. As the footman led us downstairs to the basement kitchen, their voices echoed in the stairwell: 'Mamaloi! Mamaloi!'

Three white men moped around the kitchen table, drowning their sorrows in French brandy. One was dressed in a rumpled suit of dark broadcloth. I figured him for the butler. The perspiring, red-faced man next to him wore a white apron tied over a grease-stained shirt and trousers. He had to be the cook. The third sported an old-fashioned powdered wig and a threadbare blue and buff coat like the kind worn by officers in the Continental Army.

The mournful face underneath the wig looked old enough to have served under General Washington himself. When the old fellow's eyes finally focused on us, he jumped to his feet and bowed. The bow wasn't as deep as the footman's, but it was still most respectful. Blinking like he'd been asleep, the butler pushed back his chair and did likewise.

The cook didn't look up. He grumbled in French, *'What are they gabbling about now?'*

'They are hailing me by my rightful title,' Mama answered in the same tongue. *'I am Madame Eulalie Heloise Forain Solouque, queen mother and oracle of the loa. The servants of this house are saluting me for calling the storm that put out the British fires.'*

'The fire, she is dead?' the old officer gasped in broken English. A piebald dog lying on the floor beside his chair thumped its tail.

The cook rolled his eyes. *'Those fires will poison the air until Monsieur* Piss-ant *Jemmy Madison returns, which will be never. They will burn until Judgement Day.'* He finished with a rude sound and downed another slug of brandy.

'Then Judgement Day has come to pass,' Mama said. *'The fires are extinguished.'*

The butler frowned at the water we were dripping on the floor. 'Madame Eulalie? Would you be the Madame Lula Jean-Pierre mentioned?'

'I am.'

'Pardon my manners, Madame. Please, seat yourself. I will see to your accommodations.'

'Don't forget to look out a window, while you're about,' Mama purred as she plopped the wet bedding next to the cook's chair.

The cook sucked in a breath. His jowls shook with outrage. But the old officer said, 'Of a certainty, we must see this miracle. At once. Hut! Hut!' He clapped.

'Damn your eyes, L'Enfant,' the cook growled in perfect English. 'You're not a major anymore.'

'In the army, I am not. But major I always am. General Washington himself me elevated. I say come!' Major L'Enfant stirred the air under the cook's nose.

The cook grumbled, but he stood, and he followed. Everybody followed, except me.

I was done in. I sank onto the spit stool and dropped my sopping pillowcase on the brick floor. It wasn't until I found myself leaning towards the hearth that I realised I was cold as well as wet. The dog cosied up to my leg. He was warm, too. I reached down to pet him, and I must've nodded off. The next thing I remember, the kitchen was full of cheering, whooping people. Even the French minister put in an appearance, looking as grand as a sultan in his long linen nightshirt and brocaded silk robe. I don't know that Mr Minister Sérurier believed in Mama's voudou. But the fires were out, and people's property was safe. That was cause enough to celebrate.

The housekeeper found us dry shifts, robes and house slippers. She hustled us into the pantry to change, and rousted a chamber-maid to hang our wet things in the yard once the rain quit falling. Meanwhile, in the kitchen the butler whipped up a bowl of strong rum punch.

I don't remember much after that. I woke the next morning on a bedroll in the storeroom with Mama snoring softly beside me. The room's window-well faced north, which kept it cool and dim long into the day. There was just enough light to see some kind soul had stuffed all our shoes with paper to keep them from shrinking.

I reckoned it was past ten. I'd never slept so late in my life. In the White House and before, when Mr President Madison was only Mr Secretary of State, there was always some task that needed doing, even on a Sunday when we were given leave to attend Mass in Georgetown. It felt wrong to lie about. I suppose I should've been on my knees repenting my sins of the night before. But between the fuzzy ache in my head, the bad taste in my mouth and the crick in my neck from sleeping on damp hair, I couldn't think past finding my slippers.

I belted my borrowed robe over my borrowed shift, and headed for the privy. My hand was on the door latch before it struck me. The servants' quarters in the White House had privies. Colonel Tayloe's servants made do with chamber pots, like the one tucked under the table next to our bedroll. My chest clenched. The White House was nothing but a gutted husk. I felt like a husk, myself. In my whole life, I'd never been without a place.

That was Mama's doing, as much as the British. I pushed the thought away. Done was done. I couldn't go back to the Madisons any more than Mama could go back to New Orleans.

The notion was more than I could face on an empty stomach. The table held a pitcher of water, a basin and a cup, but nothing to eat. Why should it? The kitchen was just across the passage.

It was late enough that I didn't think anything of the passage being empty. The servants' hall, the housekeeper's room and the kitchen shouldn't have been empty, though. Since I couldn't think of a good reason why that should be, I fortified myself with a hunk of buttered bread and a gulp of cider before climbing the stairs. It was a good thing I did.

The scene in the first floor drawing room reminded me of the one outside the White House the afternoon before. The entire household and all the minister's guests were there, including Miss Dolley's long-tailed red parrot, Polly. Polly's cage sat on a table set near the screened fireplace. Everybody else huddled around the windows on the other side of the room. Most of them still wore the same clothes they'd worn in the wee hours of the morning, including the minister, Mr Sérurier.

The smell of smoke and burnt tar greeted me at the threshold. My brain tried to tell my nose it didn't smell any such thing. The fires in the kitchen were safely banked. I'd seen them myself not five minutes past. Besides, it was the misery month of August. The fireplaces in the upstairs rooms were all swept out and empty except for their summer screens.

My body knew better. My mouth went cotton dry even before the housekeeper squeezed my shoulders and said in French, '*It's all right, dear. I'm sure your mother did everything she could.*'

The Haitian footman who'd met us at the door waved me over to a window. I didn't want to, but I went.

Soot browned the blue sky Mama's storm had washed clean. The buildings housing the Navy and War Departments burned like a matching pair of firepots. The charred White House smouldered anew. Giant puffballs of thick, tarry smoke spewed from the ropewalks along the Potomac. I couldn't see the Treasury Building or the Capitol, but more smoke rose from the south-east in the direction of the Navy Yard.

Was this Hell? Had we died unawares and been damned to relive yesterday's horrors for all eternity?

I steadied myself against the window frame. I refused to succumb to an attack of the vapours. I was almost fourteen. If I was strong enough to survive yesterday the first time, I was strong enough to keep standing. I didn't know what else I could do – other than pray Mama slept a while longer.

They say Our Lord answers every prayer, but sometimes the answer is 'No.'

A terrible scream tore through the house. The pretty embroidered screen in front of the fireplace toppled to the carpet. People staggered and bumped their heads against the windows. Polly shrieked, 'I won't let the British take me to London. I'll die before I let that happen. Awwwk!'

The Tayloes' back gate crashed against the yard's high brick wall.

I ducked my head out the window. I had a grim idea of what was coming. Mama was raised a lady. She never would've traipsed around a strange house with nothing but a robe to cover her shift. Her first thought upon waking would've been to retrieve her dress. In the yard that was open to the sky. The sky that boiled with soot and smoke.

My expectations weren't nearly bad enough. Mama stalked out of the alley into the street. Her head led the rest of her, slinging from side to side like a viper scenting prey. She'd pulled her dress over her shift, but the ties dangled loose down her back. She hadn't bothered with a comb, much less a kerchief, and half her braids had come undone. Hanks of kinky hair puffed around her head, making her look larger than she was.

'Madame Lula,' Mr Sérurier shouted, 'come back! The city is not safe!'

Mama spun around to face him. Her hair thrashed like a nest of snakes. Her brows drew together in a sharp 'V'. Her eyes were black as rifle bores. Dark stains trailed from their corners. Her lips were darker still. They curled back from her teeth in an animal snarl.

The minister gasped. The rest of the folk in the room seemed to have forgotten how to move. No one so much as twitched until Mama disappeared up Seventeenth Street.

'*Mon Dieu,*' Mr Sérurier groaned. He couldn't have been more than a few years older than Mama or French John. His hair was still dark. But when he tried to cross himself, he couldn't. His hands shook like a grandfather's.

I disentangled myself from the crowd and curtsied as best as I could. 'Sir.'

He eyed me suspiciously, probably wondering how far this little apple fell from Mama's tree.

'Might I ask a favour?'

He nodded. It was a small, shivery thing he would've been embarrassed to see.

'Could you send a servant to find French John? Mr Sioussat, I mean. The White House Master of Ceremonies. Please. He's the only one who can calm Mama when she gets like this.'

'He can do that?'

'Most of the time, sir.'

'*The man must be a magician,*' he muttered in French, not realising I understood. In English he said, 'Yes, of course. Jupiter, you know where he lives.'

The Haitian servant bowed by way of agreement.

'Mama will be wanting some words with the British commanders,' I said. 'Do you have any notion where they might be found?'

'They set up camp at Capitol Hill. General Ross could be anywhere this morning, but he may call here later.' The minister's cheeks burned an embarrassed pink, which was funny considering who he was talking to. 'I suspect Admiral Cockburn will be at the offices of *The National Intelligencer*. He cherishes a grudge against the newspaper.'

'Thank you. I'll start there.' I bobbed another curtsey. 'Thank you again for your hospitality, sir. I'll collect our things when I get back.'

'When you get back? Child, you can't leave. Your town is occupied by a hostile army. Nearly five thousand British troops are camped within the city limits. There are more Englishmen here than there are Americans.' His lips thinned, as if he didn't relish what he had to say next. 'By now their discipline is growing lax. You are a pretty girl. Do you understand what I am saying?'

I squared my shoulders. 'I do, sir. But she's my mama.'

It didn't take me more than a minute to dress, but when I opened the back gate Major L'Enfant and his dog were waiting for me in the alley. The only changes in his appearance from the night before were the wilted tricorn atop his bedraggled wig, and the sword hilt poking out from under his worn blue coat.

He held up his hand. 'Of the protestations, I will not hear! I my commission would disgrace if I you permit to proceed alone.'

For all my brave words to the minister, I was scared of going after Mama. Not because I was afraid of her. Hot as her temper was, she never lost her reason. I was afraid of what I'd meet along the way. It wasn't just the British. There were bound to be looters and other dangerous characters about, and on account of the Black Laws, I couldn't carry a knife to defend myself. But of all the people in the house, why did it have to be Major L'Enfant who came after me? I needed to run. More than that, I needed somebody who could stand up to trouble, not a frail old man who insisted on speaking a language he didn't fully comprehend.

Still, I dared not forget my white folk manners, or I'd be in a worse state than I was now.

'What you think, Mademoiselle Thérèse, paint your whole face. Major L'Enfant, he is old. Un-firm. He cannot walk. There you are wrong. I make the petitions to the Congress, so always I am walking up the Capitol Hill and down the Capitol Hill. And the streets – I know them best. I put them where they are. I know all the short ways.'

I thanked him kindly and quickened my steps. As soon as I was sure no one in the house could see us, I'd run. If anybody asked why I left him behind, I'd say it was an accident. Being so worried about Mama, I never realised what I'd done. The quality expected black folk to go stupid when things went wrong. I'd learned that lesson young and been using it to my advantage ever since.

I hadn't counted on the dog. He raced ahead of me as I turned up the street, and barked at me to go back, like I was a sheep for herding.

'See my dog, even he knows the short ways, he. The newspaper, he is down the Pennsylvania Avenue at Seventh Street, no? The short way is at the south of the White House wall, not at the north of the New York Avenue. This way we arrive at your mother before she goes.'

'It's not safe.' I shuddered at the thought. 'Since they stopped work on the canal, the shacks have been taken over by ruffians, and the field is full of snakes. It's worse after it rains. They all come to the path to dry off. Not just rat snakes, either, but copperheads and worse.'

'Mademoiselle, you are not travelling alone. We are two, and I have the arms.' He patted his sword. 'As regarding the snakes, they rather prefer the wet than the smoke. If not, my dog, he gives chase the plus of excellence.'

I couldn't argue that. Nor could I accuse the major of holding me back. He marched along smartly, while I was feeling the pinch of my not-quite-dry shoes. Not that I dallied any. I was certain villains lurked behind every clump of brush.

Only they didn't. No ne'er-do-wells accosted us. No snakes lolled on the path. I thought I saw the curve of what might have been a trail at the edge of the brown grass, but the marks could've been hours old. The ground had been too dry to hold the rain, and thanks to the fires, there was more dust about than yesterday.

More dust, but less of everything else. There were no people, no birds, no animals. Even the bugs whined quieter than usual, like they were drugged by the smoke drifting off the ropewalks.

Pennsylvania Avenue was more of the same. Somebody occupied the houses along the street. Their shutters hadn't opened themselves. But if anyone was looking out those windows, they kept themselves well behind the curtains.

They hadn't even picked up after the storm. The fancy poplar trees growing on either side of Pennsylvania Avenue dropped branches if you looked at them funny. Mama's gale shredded their tops and sheared away whole limbs. Lightning had cracked at least one tree right down the middle. The two halves splayed against the trees to either side. One good shove and the houses behind them would have been tinder. Branches as wide around as my arm lay higgledy-piggledy across the roadway. Any one of them would've brought traffic to a dead stop. But there wasn't any traffic, nor any expectation of same, or surely somebody would've moved those boughs and pushed the piles of fallen leaves closer to the sidewalks.

The hush was unearthly. You would've thought the whole city, down to every brick and blade of grass, was holding its breath. The steamy air was heavier than a wet wool blanket. But it was the dread that was likely to smother me. I couldn't shake the notion I was walking through a daytime nightmare. It wouldn't have been so bad if it was. If I tried hard enough I could wake from any dream, no matter how frightening. But the itch of perspiration under my borrowed shift and pinch of my shoes left no room for pretending it was anything but real.

I blinked the sweat out of my eyes. I should've packed a hat in my pillowcase or at least borrowed one from the minister's housekeeper. Between the heat and the midday sun, the ground shimmered like a reflection in a wind-stirred pool. The glimmers made me doubt my sight. There couldn't be a trail of bare dirt running in a straight line down the centre of the avenue. Then I noticed the major's dog, which had been walking ahead of us, had moved to the side, circling entire branches rather than crossing those stretches of naked earth.

I glanced at Major L'Enfant. He shrugged, buttoned his coat away from his sword, and forged ahead. Despite the dog, I found myself walking in the track. The bare patches seemed to match my stride.

Which was only natural, considering who made them. Mama bore down on the crossing of Seventh and Pennsylvania, where *The National Intelligencer* had its office, like a ship-of-the-line. Clumps of wet, green leaves skittered out of her way as if their sprigs had feet. Heavy branches tumbled to the side without her lifting a finger to move them.

I called after her, but we were too far away. I told the major, 'I need to catch her.'

I doubt he heard. Staring at the branches, he slowed to a shuffle, and then stopped altogether. I felt sorry for him. He didn't deserve to be smacked in the head with something so strange when he only wanted to help. But I couldn't spare the time to soothe or explain.

The British had cleared the crossway at Seventh and used the green wood to start a smoky fire. A score of soldiers milled about the blaze. A lucky half dozen stood guard. They were the furthest from the fire and unlikely to need their shiny red rifles for more than show. Aside from Mama, Major L'Enfant and me, the British had the street to themselves. Like everybody else in town, the people in the neighbouring houses were hiding as hard as they could.

A pair of red-faced redcoats tended to the flames. The remainder of the soldiers scooted between the print shop and the fire, feeding it with books, papers, bits of furniture and the wooden frame of the printing press. They'd already broken most of the windows facing the street, but every now and then the jangle of breaking glass echoed from inside the house.

Admiral Cockburn sat tall in the saddle of the same white nag he'd ridden the night before. He'd positioned himself next to the tree at the corner of the street, but it was the wrong time of day to catch any shade. A straw-hatted sailor squatted nearby, poring over trays of type. Every so often he'd fling one of the letters into the fire.

Mama stomped up to within a few feet of the admiral's horse before one of the guards thought to bar her way with his rifle. She slapped it aside.

'What are you doing here?' she shouted.

Admiral Cockburn lifted his eyebrows. Unlike the folks at the Tayloe house, he showed no alarm at Mama's wild appearance. Instead, he doffed his hat and bowed from the saddle as if she were a white woman.

'Nothing to be concerned about, madam. Your property is safe. My sole purpose here is to cure a certain publisher of lying and dealing in vulgarity. He can't very well slander me without a printing press ... or any "Cs".' He snorted a few times. Laughing, I think.

Mama stamped her foot. 'No, you fool man—'

'Mama!' I ran up and grabbed her arm. She shrugged me off.

'—why are you still in this city, when God Himself told you to pack up your army and go?'

The sailor's head jerked up. His hat shadowed most of his face, but there was no mistaking the snap of his jaw when he closed his mouth. He dived for cover behind the admiral's horse as if Mama was shooting bullets instead of words.

The soldier closest to Mama took a step back, looking to Admiral Cockburn for direction. The admiral squinted at Mama, as if he wasn't sure he'd heard aright.

'I can assure you, madam, no such message has been delivered. I believe I would've noticed an instruction from On High. However, my time in your fair city has been woefully devoid of prodigies.' He made a point of sighing. 'No presidents. No angels. No burning bushes or pillars of fire – except, of course, the ones we lit ourselves.'

'Oh, what about last night's storm? You didn't notice how it put out all those fires you worked so hard to set?'

Something flickered across his face at the words 'worked so hard to set', but a scowl sent it packing. 'It rained,' he said. 'Happens all the time in England. The fact that the storm put out the fires was unfortunate. But that's what water does. Nothing supernatural about it.'

Mama gawped. 'But . . . but . . .'

Mama had no words. Anyone still looking for harbingers of Judgement Day could've stopped right there. I had more important things to do.

'Time to go,' I said. 'You remember what French John said about the English and Napoleon. It'd take more than a storm to impress them.'

I prayed she wouldn't mention voudou. Anything but that. I could've cried with relief when Major L'Enfant trotted up behind her, looking every bit as purposeful as before. I signalled him to take her other arm. The two of us together might be able to drag her away.

The major's dog chose that moment to greet the admiral's horse, who thought it only neighbourly to nose him in turn. When the horse dipped its head, Mama caught sight of the sailor behind it. She charged forward, taking me with her.

'Benjamin Stone! I thought it was you with that lantern. But I told myself no. My Benjamin had the refinement of a gentleman and the commission to match. Or did you lose that in a card game, too?'

My Benjamin. That's what she called him. My earlier foreboding wrapped itself around me and squeezed my ribs like stays drawn tight.

Admiral Cockburn glanced from Mama to the sailor. 'Barnes, do you know this woman?'

'Barnes?' she jeered. 'That's not what you called yourself in New Orleans. Of course, you weren't a common tar in New Orleans.'

She knew him from New Orleans. The tightness in my chest grew worse as he straightened from his crouch. He was tall, though not so tall as some. Mama always liked them tall. She was a woman of stature herself. And in the navy. She had a powerful hankering for the water – streams, rivers, oceans and the wonders that lay beyond.

He removed his hat and held it over his heart as if to add the power of oath to his words. I suppose his features were pleasing. I couldn't see him that way. I was too busy comparing his silky black hair, cut just long enough to show a slight curl, to the much longer hair of the same texture and wave pinned under my kerchief. I saw his nose and the arch of his brows every time I passed a glass. But most of all, I saw his eyes, those pale grey eyes, twin to my own.

'Sir, I never met this woman before in my life.'

'Liar,' I croaked.

'Liar!' Mama roared. 'The proof of our congress stands before you, her breeding plain for anyone with eyes to see. Is that why you sold me down in Charleston, because you knew you wouldn't be able to pass her off as somebody else's by-blow?'

'What is the meaning of this?' Admiral Cockburn demanded.

'I should think that would be obvious,' Major L'Enfant said. I started. In my shock I'd forgotten he was there.

'This man, he wrong this woman,' Major L'Enfant continued. 'He abandon her with child.'

'Sold me!' Mama corrected. 'He drugged me and sold me while I was with child. We could've died.'

'This is a crime, no?' Major L'Enfant asked. 'Your commander, did he not write Monsieur Sérurier that all crimes against the ladies had need to be punished with much of severity?'

I stared at the sly old coot much the same way he'd stared at those scuttling branches. The funny-talking major might be our salvation after all. Last night, I was nigh consumed by the need to avenge a *house* that wasn't even mine. The wrongs Mama suffered were terrible beyond my understanding. It stood to reason her desire for vengeance burned even hotter. If the admiral played along, if he offered her a hope of justice, we might be able to spirit her away before anybody got hurt.

'And you are?' Admiral Cockburn growled.

The major swept off his tricorn in a grand Frenchy bow. 'Major Peter L'Enfant, late of the army of the great General Washington, but still a citizen and proud of his honour. So, Excellency, how deal you with this crime?'

'Crime? There's been no crime,' Barnes said. 'This woman is deranged. Look at the blood on her face. She suffered a head wound. That's it. She needs a surgeon.'

'They're tears, Benjamin,' Mama replied, 'same as the ones I cried for you.'

Something in the sing-song of her tone called to mind her chants. Little ice ants picked their way down my spine. I shook them off. Mama wouldn't do anything untoward here, not in the presence of so many soldiers. She might prize her voudou, but she had a healthy respect for guns.

'Or a madhouse,' Barnes went on. 'Look at their clothes. The woman is plainly a slave. No doubt she escaped her keeper . . .'

'I am freeborn,' Mama screamed. 'And you know it. You took the papers out of my hands and threw them into the fire!'

Beneath her cry the air seemed to whistle like water on the boil. I told myself it was the noise of the fire or a breeze blowing through the trees. Not that I could see it; the leaves of the poplar on the corner were still. The only movement was a little twitch of mist hugging the roots of the tree. *That couldn't be right.*

Admiral Cockburn's mouth flattened. He muttered, 'I don't have time for this.'

'You,' he barked at a soldier with more braid on his coat than the others, 'place that man under guard, and escort these good people back to camp. I'll sort it out later.'

'Later?' Mama squawked. Her hair shook in eight different

directions at once. I could've sworn I heard it hiss. 'You have to go. Now. I gave my word. Our letter of passage is useless if you don't.'

Admiral Cockburn leaned over his pommel. 'Madam, command yourself. I don't doubt you were wronged. As you said, the evidence stands before us. However, the evidence is also some thirteen or fourteen years old. Surely you can wait a few more hours to obtain amends.'

'The Devil with amends. You can't make amends. That's not why I'm here. Haven't you listened to a word I said? That storm was a sign from God Himself. Go back to your own country. We don't want you here. *He*' – she jabbed her finger at the sky – 'don't want you here.'

The admiral's eyes narrowed. 'Then *He* has a demmed peculiar way of showing it. Only yesterday a few thousand regular troops of His Majesty's Army routed the largest American force to take the field since the Battle of Yorktown. Today your pitiful excuse for a capital is under our complete control. A fleet of the Royal Navy's finest ships patrols your coast, carrying a force of a hundred thousand men – a hundred thousand trained troops eager to set the rest of your towns alight. Your militia is scattered and hiding like the good-for-nothing rabble they are. We are your masters. I can go where I want, stay as long as I want, and do whatever I demmed well please. You should be on your knees thanking God I don't line you up and shoot you all as traitors to King and country.'

Mama started to pant. Dark bloody tears ran down her cheeks. The hissing grew louder. My bad feelings were getting worse, tensing all my muscles to flee when I knew I couldn't leave.

Barnes thrashed in the grip of the redcoats holding him. 'Let me go,' he hollered. 'You've got it all wrong. The woman's a lunatic. You don't know what she's capable of. She tried to kill me, and I never raised a hand to her.'

'Your slave catchers dragged me from our bed and clapped me in irons! They branded me.' She yanked her dress off her shoulder, baring the scar. 'Me, your left-hand wife, freeborn and big with your child!'

I covered my mouth to keep from being sick. The bile of every spiteful thing I'd ever said about French John rose up to choke me. French John conducted himself with honour. He'd found sanctuary for Mama and me, though he owed us nothing. We were nobody to him – or the major, and look at all he tried to do. My blood father was no better than a tick. Coward. Liar. He didn't just deny his wrongs; he tried to blame them on the person he'd harmed. The Commandments tell us to honour our father and mother, but he was no parent to me. Never had been. He was naught but a stranger with eyes akin to mine.

Major L'Enfant drew himself to his full height. 'You, English, are with power mad. You abuse the weak and call yourself strong. If General Washington were here, you would not have taken this city so easily!'

'No, sir,' Admiral Cockburn replied. 'If General Washington had been President, we should never have thought of coming here at all.' He turned to the soldiers. 'The fire wants more fuel. Surely we haven't burnt the contents of the office so soon.'

'You want Washington. I'll give you Washington,' Mama shrieked. She grabbed the button pinned to the front of her dress and started screaming a mangle of French, Latin and words from a language I didn't understand.

'Oh, God, no! Stop her! Stop her! She'll kill us all!' Barnes shouted. He stomped on the boot of the man to his right. The one to his left punched him in the kidney. The three of them fell to the ground, grappling and kicking up gravel. 'Listen to me! She's a witch! You must stop her.'

The redcoats guarding the blaze cocked their rifles and whipped them into firing position. Arms outstretched, I threw myself in front of Mama.

'Don't shoot! She's praying. Praying,' I sobbed. I swung around to Admiral Cockburn. 'It's the Pater Noster – the Lord's Prayer, in French. Tell them, Major. Say it! Our Father, who art in heaven, hallowed be Thy Name. Thy kingdom come.'

'Thy will be done,' Major L'Enfant chanted with me, raising his voice as if he understood what I was really asking. 'On earth as it is in heaven . . .'

Only Mama wasn't asking for her daily bread or forgiveness of trespasses. '*I require of you dead that you come to me!*'

No! I shrieked inside my head as my mouth continued to babble the prayer. But her spirits didn't answer to me. A terrible *presence* rose in answer to her call. Last night's bewitchment made me one with God's creation. This was an outer force like a rising gale, a storm surge higher than the Hudson Palisades. My skin burned with a cold that gushed out of nowhere. I shivered like the palsied. She was crossing the line that must not be crossed, taking the advantage that must not be taken.

Barnes grabbed a pistol off one of the redcoats. He opened the man's skull with the butt, and kicked the other soldier in the groin. A third knocked him on his back. But he tackled him low and got a cracked head for his pains. He collapsed over the sailor's legs. Barnes's hands and the pistol remained free. He raised the gun. Between the barrel and me was dust, smoke and mist – the impossible mist slithering over the roots of nearby trees, twitching over an overlooked leaf and testing the air out of a dozen tiny kerbside holes.

'Deliver us from evil!' I screamed. 'Deliver us from evil! *Deliver us from evil!*'

Fangs bared, Major L'Enfant's dog hurled himself at the gun. Too late. Too late. The pistol fired. Reeling, I clutched my chest. My hands came away clean. I glanced at Mama. She was still chanting. She lifted her face to the heavens and threw back her arms. In the dust behind her two giant black snakes sidled close.

Major L'Enfant remained upright and unbloodied. The admiral appeared unharmed. The dog sat on his haunches not far from the sailor, baying as if to raise the dead Mama conjured. Barnes moaned in the dirt. His left hand clutched his right wrist. Bright red blood seeped through his fingers.

Cursing him for a fool, another pair of soldiers hauled him to his feet. They pried his fingers away from his wrist to check his wound. Fresh blood sprayed the dirt of the street.

The southern sky erupted in fire and soot. The Crack of Doom burst our ears. The ground heaved beneath our feet. The admiral's horse shrilled in fear, dancing and fighting his bit. The rest of the British, the major and I toppled like nine-pins. Mama alone stood straight and tall, tethered to the earth by the snakes gripping her arms.

Blood oozed from my right ear. I shouldn't have been able to hear a thing, but I heard as well as felt the thunder of marching feet. An army was trooping down Pennsylvania Avenue from the direction of the White House.

Heart pounding in time, throat choked with fear and dust, I turned. Through a fog of dirt, a lean colossus of a man in a blue coat, buff vest and trousers – the same blue and buff as the major's coat – strode towards us. He commanded: 'Halt!'

Even the dirt obeyed.

'*Mon général*,' Major L'Enfant gasped. He leapt to his feet and saluted.

Only it wasn't his general. The man approaching through the dust and mist was French John. If the face, the figure and the blue coat weren't enough to identify him, there was Jupiter trotting up behind him. A film of grey ash lay over French John's queued hair like powder on a wig. More ash lay across his broad shoulders, and if you squinted hard it almost looked like epaulettes. But that didn't make him a general.

'Who the hell are you?' Admiral Cockburn barked as he pulled his horse's head up short.

'George Washington, commander in chief of the Continental Army and first president of these United States.'

My breath caught. That wasn't French John's voice. I couldn't hear a trace of French accent or a hint of the teasing lilt he used to charm the Madisons' guests. This voice boomed, deep and rough, as if it had spent a lifetime shouting orders. It sounded too big for a single throat. His face was different, too. The features hadn't changed, exactly, but they were twisted into wholly different expressions. French John never held his jaw like that, nor narrowed his eyes to granite slits.

I'd heard of people possessed by the Devil, unfortunates stricken with fits and plagued with madness whose only relief was the prayers of the blessed. This was nothing like that. There was no hint of madness in this man's unforgiving gaze, no quivering in his limbs. Empty-handed, he was more dangerous than any soldier there.

Admiral Cockburn snorted. 'Of course you are. Why bother to ask? What do you want? Make it quick. Diverting as my time here has been, I'm needed elsewhere.' He tilted his head in the direction of Greenleaf Point, where a wall of black smoke put the smudge pots of the Navy Yard and the ropewalks to shame.

French John continued in that same unnatural voice. 'By what right do you, George Cockburn, take it upon yourself to violate the Treaty of Paris by which your king acknowledged these United States to be free, sovereign and independent, and relinquished all claims to the Government, property and territorial rights of the same and every part thereof?'

The horse's eyes went wild. It whinnied in fright and tried to toss its head, but it couldn't break the admiral's grip on the reins.

'By right of war,' he said.

'There is no right in this war. Only dishonour and death. Sound retreat, Cockburn. Decamp. Return to England where you belong, or the overreaching pride of kings will once more be ground to dust on this American soil.'

By now all the soldiers in the print shop had run into the street. There were more than I realised, but not one of them knew what to do. Their glances flickered from us to Admiral Cockburn to French John to the houses to the tops of the trees and the smoke rising from Greenleaf Point.

Barnes's guards were as bad as the rest. Seeing his chance, he shifted his weight to the balls of his feet. When they leaned forward, he eased back. I opened my mouth. I wasn't fast enough. A big soldier came up behind him and struck him senseless with the butt of his rifle.

I flinched. I felt no love for the man, but the strike was so quick. So casual. And no one thought anything of it. Even the kindly major paid it no mind, as if such things were to be expected.

Then the big soldier turned his rifle on us. The others seemed to take it as some kind of order. Those with guns to hand raised their weapons to fire. The unarmed raced to a store of rifles leaning against one of the trees further down the street. Grabbing their guns, they bit into their cartridges, tipped the powder into the barrels, loaded the shots and wads, and rammed them down in a matter of seconds.

The wonder was they didn't fire. Major L'Enfant and I had fallen away from Mama. Bared to the redcoats' view, she shuddered and spasmed. Her eyes had rolled back in her head. All I could see was the whites. Those snakes of hers were the only thing holding her upright. The cold I'd felt earlier sank to my bones.

Admiral Cockburn sniggered. 'This little show of yours would be more convincing if it had more actors. Where are the rest of your players, hiding in an alley?'

French John answered, 'They are here.'

Something was here. I knew as soon as he said it. Like the cold, the presence had never left. It crouched amid the wisps of mist, so many of them now, waiting for the moment to strike. It terrified me more than the soldiers, though I couldn't have told you why.

'An invisible army, how very original,' Admiral Cockburn said as if it were anything but. 'The two of you should betake yourselves to the London stage. You're wasted in this swamp.'

'I have the keys of death and of Hell,' Mama and French John intoned in a single voice. The words fitted together so precisely, you couldn't tell where man ended and woman began. The sound filled the crossing, ringing off brick and glass, wood and stone like nothing mortal.

The hairs lifted on my neck. The eyes of the burly soldier who clubbed Barnes went wide.

Major L'Enfant's dog loosed a wail that was closer to a scream than a howl. From inside the houses and within fenced yards, the dogs of the neighbourhood took up the cry. Louder and louder it grew. I covered my ears, but it did no good.

The ghastly union of Mama and French John tolled louder than the dogs. 'He that hath an ear let him hear what the Spirit saith.'

With a choked whimper of fear, the big soldier aimed his gun at Mama.

'No!' I cried, lunging at him. Major L'Enfant yanked me back.

Admiral Cockburn shouted, 'Stand down! Stand down, you fool!'

The soldier squeezed the trigger.

A thread of fog whipped the gun from his hand. The bullet struck the tree behind the admiral, spraying bark and splinters on the rump of his keening horse.

The big soldier tugged on his gun, which still hung fixed in the air. 'What happened?' someone asked. 'What's wrong?' another said.

The soldier began, 'It's the damned . . .'

A gust of wind sailed a broad, spade-shaped leaf straight into his mouth. He dropped to his knees, hands to his throat, hacking as his face flushed and darkened.

One of his fellows pounded his back as more leaves began to rise from flowerpots and behind boxwood hedges. A freshening breeze rattled the twigs caught in shutter slats like a serpent's tail. A green spade slapped the cheek of the soldier nearest the rifle tree. Others sprang at shako hats or launched themselves at rifles. They whirled and swarmed, propelled by little cyclones of mist.

'These things saith the First and the Last. Those who were dead are now alive.' Together Mama and French John roared louder than the dogs, the soldiers, the fire and the rising wind.

The mist was rising to meet the wind. Puffs of fog fanned upwards from tiny front lawns, from between the bricks in the sidewalk and gouges in the road. They hovered at the height of a man, shaping themselves into sheer, gape-jawed faces and grasping, stick-like fingers. They were no more solid than a puff of breath on a cold day. Yet they had form and movement. Oh, how they moved – soaring and swooping, wringing themselves like wet cloth, then spinning free with the force of a lash.

The soldiers' hats went flying. Guns sailed out of reach. Bayonets popped from scabbards, tumbling drunkenly in mid-air. Ghostly hands yanked at the crossed straps of the soldiers' kit. They popped buttons and ripped into cartridge bags.

In the streets leading to the crossroads, downed tree limbs swept through the dirt like so many brooms. The dogs continued to yowl. Somewhere in the noise, I thought I heard praying. It could've been anyone or all of us. But I knew in my heart it was too late.

'As I have received of the Spirit, I shall give them power over nations, and as the vessel of a potter, their attackers shall be broken.'

The heavy branches jigged around us, caught in a whirlwind of dirt and leaves. The smoke of the crossroads fire whirled in the opposite direction. The flames snuffed out, revealing a jumble of half-burnt furniture and smoking ash. The loss of the fire increased the spirits' power. Immaterial fingers raised welts on living flesh. They lifted soldiers off their feet, spun them 'round and flipped them over their heads. Other phantoms flew to the nearby roofs and smashed their chimneys to the ground.

Most of the soldiers were screaming now. I couldn't hear it, but I could see their mouths.

Every minute added more ghosts to the fray. They jostled around French John, Jupiter, Major L'Enfant, Mama and me, but left us unharmed, aside from a bitter chill. They clambered over the walls of the house across from *The National Intelligencer* and peeled the roof off the rafters. They flipped it at a troop of redcoats running up Pennsylvania Avenue from the east. The roof sheared off the heads of the front rank. Then it dropped, crushing the rest. Blood spurted from underneath the edge of the shingles.

That's when I left my breakfast in the dirt.

The soldiers still upright ran for cover. Those who cowered and prostrated themselves, hands clasped over the backs of their heads like captive prisoners, the spirits left alone. The ones who pulled pistols from their sashes or knives from their boots were caught and cast aside like broken toys. The spirits snatched riflemen from the shelter of doorways. If a soldier braced his gun against a tree they uprooted it beneath him.

Something struck the small of my back. I dropped to my knees.

Mama invoked Damballa. She whipped the snake off her right arm and hurled it at the sky.

Clouds rushed towards us from every direction until the heavens went black. Lightning cackled. Thunder exploded like a volley of cannon shot. The clouds burst as if gutted, spewing rain in torrents. The wash stung like needles, sharp and cold. It jabbed from above and knifed us from every side.

I scrambled to my feet as a feather bed sailed overhead. The spirits rode it like a magic carpet over the rooftop bier. Another bevy of ghosts lifted an entire house off its foundation and cast it like a single stone at the redcoats running down Seventh. The impact staggered me, but I didn't fall.

Neither did Admiral Cockburn, though his horse bucked and

fought. A legion of the dead flailed his troops, thrashing His Majesty's Army like ripened wheat. A legion of clouds sent the deluge, undoing his fires for a second time. His hat was gone. His face was scratched. The front of his dark blue coat was torn clean off. Watered blood dripped down the front of his shirt. But he refused to submit to the storm or his bucking horse. In the midst of his own struggle, he called on the soldiers to regroup. I had no love for the British right then, but I had to admire his bravery.

I only realised the dogs had fallen silent when I heard Mama *tsk* in disgust. The rain had soaked her clothes clean through and flattened her snaky hair into shapeless lumps. She swiped a dripping hank away from her eyes – clear brown eyes returned to their rightful place. The remaining snake slithered down her left arm. It drooped from her hand like a length of wet rope. She flicked it against the rump of Admiral Cockburn's horse.

The horse shrieked and leapt over the dead fire. Its hooves were galloping before they reconnected with the ground. It tore down Pennsylvania Avenue to Capitol Hill as if Mama's snake was climbing its behind instead of the nearest tree.

Somehow Admiral Cockburn held on. He clung to the horse's neck, his hands fisted in its mane. With him went the rest of his men's resolve. Those few who still retained their wits scrambled after him, running, limping, crawling. The ghosts propelled them forward, lifting their feet to speed them on their way. The spirits' rage was spent, but not their malice. They battered the wounded with water and sticks, and grinned at the sound of their moans.

The squelch of something solid moving in the wet drew my eyes to the remains of the fire just as Barnes's injured hand closed around a heavy spar. He was drenched, battered and cut. His left eye was puffed closed. The other locked on me, its corners creasing. Grabbing the post with both hands, he pulled it free of the ashes and stood, ignored by the spirits harrying braver men.

The Devil with the Black Laws. I wouldn't let that villain hurt us again. A discarded sword lay nearby. I snatched it from the ground. I snarled, 'Not me. Not mine.'

He laughed. 'Stupid girl, don't you know your Bible? Thou shalt not suffer a witch to live.'

He swung. He didn't judge the distance or reckon on the gale.

The post bounced off a shield of wind, spinning him round. Three more phantoms sprang from the street, their gauzy forms complete down to the tatters of their clothes. He shrieked at the sight. Then he ran and ran, ghostly bayonets jabbing his back at every step.

Mama swayed. I dropped the sword and caught her under her arm. Her face was washed clean of blood, but her skin was fever hot. I was half surprised she didn't steam.

'Help me.' She licked her lips. 'Help me kneel.'

We lurched to our knees. The street had become a shallow torrent. Cold, dirty water sluiced over our calves and splashed up our thighs. Mama scooped a fistful of mud from beneath the flow. She tried to stand. She couldn't do it on her own. I wasn't much better, but somehow together we staggered upright.

She flicked a little bit of mud to each of the four corners. In a voice stronger than it had any right to be, she called into the storm, 'Go back from where you came. From dirt you were made. To dirt you may return. Dirt to dirt. Ashes to ashes. Amen.'

At first it didn't seem to work. The rain fell just as hard. The wind blew just as fierce. If anything, the gale seemed to grow. I needed Mama to stand as much as she needed me. Then I realised the rain streaming down our faces and plastering our clothes was clearer than it was before. Slowly ghosts lost their shape, dissolving back into mist, which the rain carried to the ground. At last the downpour eased. The sky paled to grey.

A man sighed.

French John sagged over the shoulders of Major L'Enfant and Jupiter. The ashes had run from his hair to stain his coat, which was ruined beyond mending. The tie on his queue had come undone. Snarls of dark hair clung to his collar as tightly as the curls plastered to his perspiring forehead. His face – still not quite his own – was as white as his sodden cravat. Laboured breaths rasped through his open mouth.

The major's dog sat on the stoop of *The National Intelligencer*. As the rain trickled to a halt, he started to whine.

The soul behind French John's face smiled wistfully at Mama. 'Tis well,' he said, and slumped forward in a dead faint.

But she wasn't looking at him. She stared ahead at nothing I could see.

'It will be,' she said. 'It will be.'

*

My hand shook as I set the last page of Mrs Fouchet's story on my desk. It was impossible, inconceivable . . .

Yet I found myself recalling the many strange accounts of the British occupation. The two storms, each as fierce as Monday's gale, are a matter of record. Late summer hurricanes are fairly common, but nowhere in our nation's history have two such storms struck the same place in such quick succession. In addition, they were most particular in their effect, targeting British emplacements and empty houses, while leaving a partially finished American Navy hull adrift in the Potomac unharmed.

Moreover, within hours of the second hurricane, the invaders fled the city as if pursued by the ancient Furies. Officers left behind their stolen mounts lest the horses' neighing betray their flight. The hooves of the animals drawing their ammunition carts were muffled with rags. They abandoned the wounded where they lay, and made no provision for the dead. The dismembered victims of the 25 August 1814 dry well explosion at Greenleaf Point (which as noted in Mrs Fouchet's narrative, shook the ground across the Federal City) as well as the corpses at the Navy Yard and the battlefield at Bladensburg, were left to rot in the summer's terrible heat.

These circumstances made it harder than it should have been to remind myself that ours is a rational age, and the wonder of God's Creation lies as much in its order as in its variety. Nature keeps His Law more religiously than man His Commandments, freakish storms and superstitious soldiers notwithstanding.

However, my credulity or lack thereof was irrelevant. Mrs Fouchet believed what she had written. Her face was drawn with anguish; her pale gaze burned with desperation.

I asked her, 'Madame, what is it you want from me? It would appear the problem lies with your mother. Do you wish me to counsel her, or hear her Confession?'

She waved the question away. 'Mama's been dead these six years past. Her fate is in the hands of Our Merciful Saviour. I've prayed long and hard He won't judge her too harshly. She was as good a woman as she knew how to be. In her place, for my children, I would've done the same.'

'Then why did you go to such effort to describe these events? Do you feel guilty for partaking in your mother's rituals?'

'I confessed my part years ago, and did my penance gladly. I've had no truck with magic since. I refused to learn Mama's voudou rites. The only charm I wore under my clothes was my blessed scapular, and I bought my medicine from the apothecary, same as other folk. Even after Mama came to live with my husband and me, I wouldn't let her do her workings in the house or even speak of it in my hearing.'

A sob caught her in the throat. 'Maybe that's why this judgement's fallen so hard upon me. I should've learned her ways, if only to guard against them. But I didn't. Now I don't know what to do.

'Father, my youngest . . . she called Monday's storm.'

$$\Omega$$

There is no record of Bishop Hughes's reply to the priest at St Peter's, or of his recommendations for how he should deal with Mrs Fouchet's daughter, if any; but the fact that this account was sent to the Vatican suggests that the bishop took it very seriously.

What accuracy we can place on Mrs Fouchet's recollection of such traumatic events a quarter of a century earlier, when she was just thirteen or fourteen, is clearly debatable. Memory is not dependable, and as a tale is retold, even in the mind, imagination can add colourful details. Having said that, there is no doubt that something remarkable happened in Washington that day in August 1814, and even at the time people were ascribing the rout of the British by the weather as an act of Providence.

It may or may not be significant that both of the accounts of events in North America that we have selected from the documents in the Vatican Vaults concern what might be called weather magic.

1848

In 1848 a spate of liberal and nationalist revolutions erupted across Europe in what subsequently become known as the Springtime of the Peoples. Pope Pius IX originally encouraged these liberal aspirations, but in April of that year he had a complete change of heart and issued the Allocution *condemning the revolutions.*

This was a severe blow to those who had held up the Pope as an example for all Catholic European monarchs to follow. From then on the revolutionaries faced repeated defeat at the hands of monarchical forces.

Historians agree that Pope Pius IX changed his mind after taking fright at revolutionary excesses, but this account by the Pope's chamberlain, found in the Vatican Archives, sheds a different and quite remarkable light on his decision.

Pio Nono and the Papal Allocution

Damian P. O'Connor

The werewolves were abroad in the Vatican City and their howls could be heard all the way to the basilica of St Peter. Revolution had come to France once more and a Bonaparte was rising; the Habsburg Emperor was under siege in Germany, in Hungary, in the Balkans; there was cholera in Naples and starvation in Sicily; war in Lombardy, Milan and Piedmont. Death had touched the palaces of the rich, the hovels of the poorest, the merchant's warehouse and the artisan's workshop without distinction; the vile had preyed upon the fey; the plough lay deserted, the loom broken; the child starved, the honest man turned beggar. Inside the Vatican itself, the Chief Minister had gone down to the assassin's merciless *poignard*. As Pio Nono – or more properly, Pope Pius IX – looked across Europe from the high turreted battlements of the Castel St Angelo, his last refuge from his own *Consulta* turned against him in vitriol, it seemed to him that in this springtime of 1848 the whole world was on fire.

All hung in the balance and all were likely to be found wanting: the Tsar's Cossacks were burning Wallachia and the Ukraine; the Three Paladins of the Holy Roman Emperor were gathering fresh armies, Count Jellacic in Croatia, Baron Schwartenberg in Bohemia and General Radetzky in Italy, readying to strike with disciplined musketry and cannon, to sweep away the barricades of the squabbling revolutionaries. None would be spared; not even Holy Rome would escape the ruin. Here, at the centre of the world, between the tears already shed and the corpses to come,

Pio Nono, liberal, nationalist, idealist, the bridge between Man and God, stood holding his white head in his epileptic hands, begging for Angels to succour mankind from the flames that the spark of his own hopes had ignited.

And Uriel came! Down from out of a sky azure blue with Canaletto's dreams yet streaked with the hot fingers of scarlet fever. He came down at the head of his troop of big men on big horses, war weary, at an urgent gallop, his breastplate scarred and dented, his lips darkened with the smears of black powder, his glittering veteran's eyes marked by a thousand years of war experienced in the flash of the musket's pan. Behind him his scarlet dragoons glowered under plumed comet-tail helmets, straight backed, chin-strapped, fists clenched, black wiry-haired knuckles on reins and heavy sabres. They were fatigued from a long ride at the end of a long battle, swathed in gunsmoke and the copper smell of blood, and weary at the thought of a longer one ahead.

'You have summoned, Pio Nono, and we have answered.' Uriel's voice was of urgent brass and thunder. 'But this is the only time you may use Peter's gift to call us, so if your request be frivolous be away to think again, and allow us back to the Line.'

Pio Nono, a tall man with a kindly, broad brow given to smiling, now shrivelled and bowed. He was suddenly conscious that his jewelled triple tiara and cloth of gold robe was no more than a shallow bauble tacked to a rag before the laurel wreaths, oak clusters and starlight medallions that writhed and glittered across the scarlet tunic of brave Uriel. His voice stammered and his body filled from breast to water with fear.

'It is not frivolous, My Lord,' he whispered.

'Then aid will be sent to you.'

'I shall obey your command, whatever.'

'There will be no command. You will be sent advice, no more. The demand of God that men should enjoy Free Will entitles you only to this.'

'Then I shall follow the advice of the Almighty.'

Uriel's stone gaze did not change, though the constellations in his eyes whirled around a thousand wounded suns.

'Two Angels will come to you. One is from our Legion, the other from the Adversary's. It is the Law. They will give advice. You will choose the course which seems better to you.'

There was a crackle of lightning, tearing across the firmament like the scissors of a comet through the silk of the evening sky. Uriel looked up.

'We must be away, the offensive begins,' he cried, and his troop drew bright swords, changed front in disciplined manoeuvre, and prepared to wheel away in the direction of the moon. 'You must release us!'

'How will I know which is the Angel of the Lord and which the Devil's brood?' cried Pio Nono, horrified.

'You must make that judgement yourself,' answered Uriel impatiently. 'Do you think the war in heaven waits for your indecision? We must be away. There are guns on the heights of the Milky Way and the trenches of the enemy sap towards the fortress of paradise. We must be away!'

'Will you give me no clue?' He spread his hands like a market haggler.

'We must be away! Cannot you hear the cries of dying Angels in the scream of the storm?'

'I must know!'

'You have been granted the gift of Free Will and the faculties to use it, so you alone must make the choice. No Angel or Demon may reveal himself in the contest of Peter's Gift; neither through word, deed nor object. It is the Law. Now release us. We must go to war. I can give no more help.'

'Then be away . . .' He clasped his hands to his despairing bosom.

'To arms!' cried Uriel, amid the echo of vast trumpets. 'To war!'

'. . . And God have mercy on the souls of mankind.'

'They will come to you in the vaults of the castle,' cried Uriel, as the jingle of harness and the crack of a ragged banner in the wind punctuated the flying departure of his words. 'Go now, below Hadrian's tomb to the roots of the mountain. They will come soon and you have this night only to debate with them.'

*

'Come, Niccolo, you must help me with my robes, for I must not trip on my journey. Hurry now, take them away, the tiara too.' His fingers drummed at his lips. 'And then you must guide me down to the lower dungeons by back ways and unseen. Bring a lantern.'

Your humble servant, Niccolo Parvatti, led the Pope at a trot down the steps from the battlements as the waning light of the long evening threw tiger-stripe shadows from the braziers onto the honey stone of the walls. The Holy Father undressed as he went, tugging at the ruby fastenings and snagging his rings on the silver inlays of the cloth of gold, then handing the pieces to Niccolo Parvatti, so heavy that he could barely keep them from dragging on the sandy stones.

'Haste, make haste,' he demanded, his frown creasing as we entered the papal apartments where Niccolo's aching arms could gain a little release by allowing the stole and the cloak to slide onto a chaise longue. 'Lift this crown from my head, Niccolo, for it is too heavy for me to bear.'

'Master, Holy Father,' said Niccolo, his humble servant. 'Have we not just seen a miracle? Should we not tell the world the good news? I only ask . . .'

'You saw? So it was not a vision entrusted to me alone. I wonder; was it seen by all Rome?'

'It was not, Holy Father. The Swiss Guard below at their posts made no motion or gave indication of alarm.'

'Good,' said the Pope. 'Then you will make no mention of it either, you hear? Swear it on your soul.'

'As the Holy Father commands . . .'

'And then when I enter the vaults, you are to leave me. You may wait, but you must not follow. Again, swear it, on your immortal soul.'

He kicked off the shoes of the fisherman and slid his feet into ordinary, practical sabots and as the last of his ceremonial garb was laid aside, he wrapped himself in the faded cassock and round hat of a parish priest from poor Spoleto. 'Haste, make haste, Niccolo. And we must not be seen. Where is your lantern? Good – lead on.'

We scattered our feet down spiral staircases, sped through tunnels and along galleries and passageways more intricate and

knotted than theology itself. Down, down, always down, whichever turning to left or right the humble servant Niccolo Parvatti
chose. Down, down, always down, through the hidden interstices
between secret panels, across rooms that appeared nowhere on
the floor plans, past guard rooms unaware of the secrets they
guarded and through treasuries kept from venal archbishops by
mendicant friars of exemplary poverty. Down, down, always
down, our lanterns throwing the spinning shadows of our own
souls, like the spokes of the wheel of fortune or a canasta of cards
across the yellow curtain walls. Down past the last traces of
Imperials, Guelphs, Ghibellines, Normans, Franks, Goths, Huns,
Alans, down below the dares of Niccolo's childhood, down past
the lower strata of the Emperors of the glory of Rome, down
below Etrusca, down to the last vault, down to the last and deepest door.

'Good man, Niccolo Parvatti, you will be blessed for this,' said
Pio Nono, whose name had shrunk with the depth and plain
clothing. 'Now wait here, good servant, and sleep awhile for I
shall be gone for the whole of the night.'

'Shall I not attend?'

'You shall not,' commanded Pio Nono. He checked his dark
lantern, put his hand to the planks of the wooden postern gate
and pushed. 'I bid you wait.'

Niccolo Parvatti was a good and humble servant, and like a
good and humble servant he knew when to disregard his master's
commands because however great and good, or holy, the humble
servant often knows the man better than the man knows himself.
He waited for a count of thirty, extinguished the lantern, and then
slipped into the ink-well blackness of the cave.

*

The cavern was a darkness and the darkness was a cavern as the
humble servant Niccolo Parvatti followed along in the wake of
Pio Nono's faint glim, watching, guarding him until he stopped
dead. Then Niccolo found a place to hide behind a barrel, one
of many barrels, large and small that were stacked in rows
around the cold stone walls. There, his heart beating with terror,
he heard the sound of flesh, flaccid, dead, dragging itself through

the silica of the sandy floor. There he glimpsed the foul worm, whose head was a toad and whose dreadful tongue struck among a bluebottle tornado, lapping them up like the corpses of men and crunching them with a sound like the cracking of rib cages. It had come to battle.

He would have hidden his eyes away at that moment had not a flash of sabre tooth caught in the sweep of Pio Nono's pale lantern and revealed the striped beast of the night in all its terrifying, feline savagery. With a roar like a falling battlement it leaped for its prey, the worm, and landed on its scaled back, claws raking great scars that matched its own terrible stripes, its teeth sinking into the foul, nacreous bag of the noxious carcass. The worm writhed in its agony, and became basilisk, Gorgon, Hydra by turns, ripping at the fur of the cat, tearing out its massive teeth and flinging it by its yelping tail across the screaming floor of the cave. The tiger in turning became the night-jaguar, the leopard-warrior, and its hiss was like the flight of the arrow storm scything down piked battalions.

'Halt! Halt! I command it!' cried Pio Nono. He took the candle from his dark lantern and went forward, holding it aloft like a beacon. 'I command you stay this riot!'

The beasts recoiled, squirming and coiling and Pio Nono took centre stage. There, on a sole barrel upturned for a table, stood a great cream altar candle, decorated with many symbols traced out in silver, gold and vermillion, and Pio Nono put his own small flame to it so that he might claim his allotted time for parley with Angels. '*Fiat lux*,' he said, and the flame leaped to the wick.

For a moment there was only the tiniest glimmer of light and then the candle exploded in a tower of sparking flame that opened the roof of the cavern to the sky and let in the whole of day and night at once, so that the stars were as visible as the sun and the moon as bright as day. From horizon to horizon, the world was unveiled and the full battlefield of the creation of God was laid out at our feet. Green verges by quiet waters; dark tempests beating upon the cliffs of despair; full flights of egrets soaring over battle-fleets of swans while the pike waited in ambush; golden cornfields and fresh-ploughed tillage; distant deserts burning the earth to scalded red. Here was Heaven and Hell come down to Earth, the famine by the feast. Here was the point of dangerous truce, where time was measured by a fizzing candle atop a barrel, which only now did your humble servant recognise as a barrel containing finest-grain, corned, red-arrow gunpowder.

The ravening beasts had gone, disappeared in a flash of lighted darkness and in their place stood a single Fusilier, a young Ensign, battle-hardened blond innocence in pipe-clayed cross belts, a silver tunic, seven stars about his breast, polished boots and musket to his right.

'Who are you and whence came you?' demanded Pio Nono.

'This knowledge is occult to you,' replied the boy soldier in a voice of high fifes and flutes. 'But you may call me Melchior.'

'Melchior?' queried Pio Nono. 'That Melchior who followed the star to Bethlehem?'

'No. Now state your business, for I am away from my duty on the Line.'

'I was promised two Angels.' Pio Nono looked about the marvellous landscape and up to the magnificent skies.

'My enemy will be here soon. What I hear, he hears. Now speak.'

'How old are you, boy?' he said with the same soft sympathy he had shown for the wretched children of Spoleto. 'How come you to this war?'

'How old am I? I have no age. I am immortal and was called into being before time itself was born. Now state your business. I do not relish this task, for I am a warrior not a diplomat.'

Pio Nono took in the boy's youthful visage and then, knotting his hands behind his cassock, he began to pace back and forth, slowly, shooting querulous glances from under the black brim of his hat. As he turned on his heel at the end of each march he studied his question and how best to present it, rubbing three fingers against the centre of his forehead as though he was massaging an ache away.

'I have started a revolution,' he said, opting for simplicity. 'And it has run out of control into paths I never envisaged. Here at the pivot of my century I stand, not knowing whether to condemn it and accept the bloodshed that will result from its suppression, or accept that the bloodshed already can only be sanctified by a further, deeper revolt, that carries the logic of revolution through to the establishment of an earthly paradise.'

'What year is this?' asked the Angel Melchior.

'1848.'

'And do you not have the example of 1789 before you?' He removed his shako, pulled a firkin towards him, upturned it and sat as heavily as such a being of light could. 'Mob rule, Terror, Dictatorship and twenty years of War. What did you expect?'

'That history would not repeat itself; that we might learn from our mistakes and get it right this time.'

'And you did this by opening your prisons, freeing bitter men and calling them into a *Consulta* where they might forge new bonds and plot new plots?'

'They were men of ideals,' offered Pio Nono after a few minutes' introspection, which the boy occupied with cleaning his musket. 'Thoughtful men. Men with a better vision of the future than we – their rulers – allowed for.'

'The Lord save us from dreamers,' said the boy, rubbing hard at a spot of rust. 'Give me the hard fact of a bayonet before the unreliable squib of damp powder any day.'

'You do not believe that man can be perfected?' Pio Nono paused in his transit and held out an accusatory finger.

'Angels are not perfect,' scoffed the boy. 'What chance have men? This very moment a revolutionist in Germany is writing a blueprint for a perfect world. His name is Marx and that blueprint will swill so much red blood around this planet that men will wonder how the gentle authorities did not take the opportunity to blind him, break his fingers around his pen and tear out his tongue. Hark! My enemy advances.'

The sound of hooves fast approaching through a forest drummed through the landscape until a blue lancer thundered down before them, the smell of good earth, clean storm and horseflesh about him. He dismounted with a growl.

'What siege come you from?' demanded Melchior rising to his feet, detaching his bayonet from its frog.

'Orion,' answered the Lancer, rubbing the grey neck of his horse with a white gauntlet.

'You will not take it. I know who commands there and he is war itself. Your engines will melt before his blast.'

'We shall see. Rest and refresh yourself while you can.' The lean-waisted Lancer removed the flat-topped *schapska* cap, hung it on the pommel of his saddle and, directing his comments over his shoulder, loosened off the girth. 'You are Pope Pius, I see. My name is Cain.'

'Any significance to that name?'

'No. Continue your discourse – though Melchior is trying to frighten you, I fear. The future is not fixed.'

'Who said it was?' challenged the boy, flipping his bayonet down into the grass as though it were a pocket knife. 'Yet all revolutions end up being run by those who think a little more killing, a few more broken heads, a few more dissenters jailed will guarantee perfection.'

'So the idle aristocracy and the wealthy bourgeois may gorge themselves, safe in the knowledge that they may not be shaken out of their decadence by the righteous, just anger of a starving people?' The blue Lancer tightened a loose buckle, brushed at a fetlock and then stood back. 'I fear we need more dreamers, not less. Go ahead – drink.'

Pio Nono listened intently to these opening shots, weighing the words this way and that, taking his time. 'This wrangling does not help my dilemma,' he said. 'I need to see the consequences of my choices. I need to see the future.'

'It's a little late for that,' said the Ensign, drawing out his canteen. 'If you have already ignored the past.'

'Nonsense,' said Cain. 'Let me show you the hopeful future.'

He took off a gauntlet and waved it nonchalantly across the panorama, instantly transforming the landscape in a blur of blue sapphire light, whipping us up until we were flying high, higher than the highest mountain in Italy, as though we had ascended in an air balloon. Your humble servant, Niccolo Parvatti, could barely contain himself from gasping at another great miracle, for before us lay the whole of Italy, sparkling in the sun, snowy mountain ranges above the grey-green of olive orchards, Monte Cassino a little plot of land and the Holy City no more than a village seen from a high hill; and all under that same sapphire light that makes this land the only place fit for a renaissance or indeed, though he should not whisper it, a *Risorgimento*.

'You are to tempt me like Christ in the desert?' asked Pio Nono, when he too had got his breath back. 'You will offer the whole world in return for my soul?'

'Believe me, I have no interest in your soul,' replied Cain, taking up an easy stance, as he pointed out salient features of the future in the same way he would brief his officers for an attack. 'Note well: Milano, Genoa, Venezia, Firenze, Siena, Napoli, Palermo all under the flag of Italy. *Italia fara da se!* Italy has made herself. See how the law tempts down the Giordano banditti out of the mountains of the south to embrace the plough and legitimate commerce? See the marshes drained by the engineers of Piedmont! Look how the church opens schools to bring the light of learning, technical skills and respect for liberty to both high and low; how she blasts away the barriers of privilege and opens the road to each career, for each man to take as far as his virtues, his effort, his strength and fortitude will take him. No more the lounging mercenary guarding the despot in his crumbling palace but instead a citizen army, defending the liberties of all with the breasts of free men.'

He lifted his eyes a little higher and drew our attention to the world beyond the Alps.

'Germany too, free, united, prosperous, holding out her hands to embrace the brotherhood of Free Hungary, Free Poland, Free Bohemia; even restless France declares herself content while the tyrant Tsar gnaws on his own bones in his frozen, bleak palace. England, home of industry and commerce, originator of modern liberalism, modern nationalism, modern parliamentary government, sends out her best to trade, to instruct us in the finer points of law, steam, manufacture; and all joined together by the gossamer bonds of liberty. Ready to march, with good intentions . . .'

'All the way to Hell,' broke in Ensign Melchior. 'Piffle! What nonsense is this? Bid them look further, Cain, I dare you. Bid them look to 1914 for the results of your precious brotherhood of nations.'

'1914?' said Pio Nono.

'Or 1917, to see how your dreamers deal in Russia,' said

Melchior. He had taken his canteen and was pouring a sweet-scented liquor into a silver cup. 'Men of different races and languages and cultures cannot live together? I think they can. Anyway, how will you separate the human kaleidoscope of Bohemia, Moravia, Galicia or the Balkans? Dig English Channels and bid one live this side and another that? And where will you put the Jews? Ha! The Devil is always in the detail.'

With that, Melchior drank and we were back in the cavern, with only the half-burned candle on a gunpowder barrel to wonder at. He toasted Pio Nono and the fragrance of a summer's day filled the atmosphere. 'Let me tell you of what my German scholar's dreams will bring and then let Cain speak for revolution once more, if the plate on his silver tongue has not rusted by then.'

'Damn your details, Melchior,' barked Cain, jamming his fist back into his gauntlet. 'What would life be without the chance to experience the rush of hope, to strive for the dream, to measure yourself against the odds of unkind fate?'

'You mean, to wave a ragged banner on a broken barricade built from the bricks of your house and then die like a poet while your children starve and your wife is turned out into the street? Do not come the Romantic with me. Life is as it is for a reason and Pio Nono here must use his reasonable faculties to steer his difficult course. Breasts of free men indeed! It is the armour of trained, drilled soldiery that win battles, not the enthusiasm of fools drunk on the oratory of charlatans.'

'Tell me of your scholar, Melchior,' said Pio Nono, his hands once more behind his back, twitching in agitated concentration. 'This candle burns fast. Is he a revolutionary?'

'He is. And he will herald revolutions that make 1848 look like comic opera.' Ensign Melchior picked his bayonet out of the sandy floor and cut a window-sized hole in the rock. Pio Nono peered through into a book-lined study where a dark-skinned, curly-haired man sat at a plain desk. He was weeping over a pen. 'His child is dead. Three more will die in poverty while he writes of an earthly paradise to come.'

'He is one of the blessed poor. I honour him for it and will pray for him,' said Pio Nono, his hand to mouth, distraught at the figure of grief before him.

'Save your breath,' answered Melchior. 'He comes from wealth but has squandered it, was educated in the law but chose philosophy and journalism. Though he has the skill to provide a good living, it is his friends who labour to keep him; but they are disowned by their own wealthy parents because of their opinions and so between them they squabble over crumbs and their children starve in the midst of plenty.'

'His philosophy?'

'Political economy,' replied Melchior. 'It is something of a mystery to Angels . . .'

'Not just Angels . . .'

'. . . for we create by desire. There is no commissariat department in our armies and all things are ready provided. But Adam was cursed by God for tasting the forbidden fruit and so must labour for his daily bread.' He gave a cynical laugh. 'So much for Free Will, eh? Well, this Marx claims to have mastered its mysteries.'

Pio Nono went over to the window, stepped through the rock as though it were mist and looked over the philosopher's shoulder to read what he was writing.

'The history of all hitherto existing society is the history of class struggles.' Pio Nono looked up and thought for a moment. 'Is it?' he said to himself. 'What? *All* of it?'

'He paints with a broad brush stroke,' said Cain, impatiently. 'Make your point, Melchior.'

'As you wish. Pull your horse-blanket around you, Cain, for even you will feel the keenness of this wind.'

Your humble servant was transported once again, to a dark, dark place where the black sky was ablaze with green fire and the cold knife of a winter wind groaned across a frozen waste, stripping the flesh from my bones more surely than the sharp beak of the gibbet crow. As the rime of driven frost scratched, then snapped my eyelashes, so the bare stone axe of bleak midwinter chipped off the tips of my ears and bruised my fingers to blackened agony, all in an instant, so that I was moved to a sob of despair which I feared would entail my discovery. I need not have feared, for upon escaping it was lost instantly in the gruelling moans of muffled miners in thin quilted jackets, their sweat frozen on waxen faces as they hammered at the concrete earth, sheltered only by a windbreak of bodies stacked like cordwood.

'What place is this blasted heath?' cried Pio Nono, grabbing for his hat in a frenzy of flapping, cracking cassock. 'Are we in Hell?'

'It is the Kolyma Slave Labour camp and the year is 1968,' answered Cain, switching off the wind and freezing everything to a picture, so that it was possible to see the sleet paused in mid-air and the chips of earth from the hammers suspended amid their sparks. 'And Melchior overstates his case. This nightmare flowed from Marx's philosophy, true, but it was a mistake in a noble experiment, and the ideals of a brotherhood of mankind should not be lost in the inevitability of human error.'

'A *noble experiment*?' Melchior's eyes were arched in smiling disbelief. 'You will excuse me from your experiments, I beg. For though I am immortal and will regenerate within the cosmic day, still I feel pain unendurable and would avoid it if I could. And humanity has only a brief youth, a briefer maturity and a short old age.' He toasted Cain and swept a slow hand across the terrible future. 'This is no sunny strand to be wasting fled time on, inevitability of error or not. Were I a man, I would rather tend my own garden, be charitable on my terms but look after my own family first and drink with my own neighbours across our mutual boundary than sacrifice these small gains to another man's dream of paradise.'

The scene changed once more and we were returned to that place where night and day resided in the same place, between the desert and the sown, between the tempest and the turquoise lagoon. There before us was the candle on the barrel, burning low on its fuse so that sparks already touched about the bung hole; and so your humble servant watched as Pio Nono came to make up his mind. Which was Angel? Which was Demon? For upon this intelligence, his decision must rest. The Blue Lancer Cain held out his broken dreams, while Melchior, the Silver Ensign, offered only bleak, parochial daily struggle with hope extending no further than the end of his own path and the end of his own estate. Both forms of men were objects of great beauty, such that Michelangelo, Leonardo or Raphael would sculpt them from cream-veined Carrara marble at their own expense; both carried wisdom, age and foreknowledge about them, as lightly as a scabbard or a *sabretache*. How could Pio Nono choose? For myself, I, Niccolo Parvatti, hoped that he would choose the advice of the Lancer, for how can great men be sustained without dreams? How can men progress without vision? How can the vicissitudes of the world be overcome without lifting our hearts to the heaven of an ideal? But I am only a humble servant without education and have never seen much further than my daily bread nor desired the knowledge either; yet still I have the freedom to hope and to dream.

And so Pio Nono began to pace again. To and fro as the fuse fizzed and spat fat sparks at the thin walls of the powder keg. From time to time he took off his poor parish priest's black round hat and turned it this way and that and ran it through his fingers, as though the answer to his question might be concealed in the lining. He would kick at a stone and shoot a glance at the candle, and then to Melchior drinking and Cain grooming, hoping to gain some clue, instinct or insight that might open the answer like a flower in the sudden sun. He sniffed a little at the fumes from the candle and your humble servant remembered that he had shown signs of a fever or a chill and made a note to bank up the fires a little higher in the household.

Presently, with the wick no more than a twist in a puddle of wax, Pio Nono made his choice. He touched his thumb and forefinger to his tongue, snuffed out the candle with them and, holding his breath for a moment, turned to Cain and Melchior.

'I thank you for your deliberations. Be you Angel or Demon you have served your masters well in sharpening my bluntness to the point of decision.' He held out a hand to Cain the Lancer, who was fastening the chinstrap on his cap, ready to fly. 'If you are Demon, then I offer to shake your gauntlet with the hand of forgiveness and the hope of God's mercy. If you are Angel, then I beg you forgive my presumption and go well to the Light Eternal. I shall not take your advice though; and I must change my mind as to the wisdom of revolution; take to distrusting my own dreams as well as those of other dreamers.'

Cain held out his hand, shook that of Pio Nono, then mounted his steed and saluted. 'You are sure I am the Demon, then?'

Pio Nono nodded.

'What turned your mind?' said Melchior rising, replacing his flask in its pouch and fixing his bayonet to the socket of his musket in readiness for war.

'The fragrance of your cordial,' answered Pio Nono. 'For the foul enemy would never choose something so wholesome for his repast. It is the small things that make men great, not the piled-on fantasies of their theory. You are right; if we tend our own gardens in accord with our neighbours, we need no grand plans of threadbare visionaries.'

Melchior's mouth opened and shut in amazement. His musket fell to the turf as he put his hand to his canteen and then to his head.

'You broke the Law,' sneered Cain revealed, from a mouth of steel, rending teeth and the fetid stench of the beast. 'You fell for my stratagem from the outset. *Rest and refresh yourself while you can.*'

'What is this?' cried Pio Nono, puzzled, afraid, looking from one to the other, his hat in his hand like a discus. 'What Law has been broken?'

'*No Angel or Demon may reveal himself in the contest of Peter's Gift; neither through word, deed or object.* It is the Law,' said Melchior miserably. 'And by these terms I have failed. You knew me by my cordial, my object. I have been deceived.'

'The consequence? The consequence?' cried Pio Nono in a voice of urgent anguish.

'Tell him,' said cruel Cain, tugging at his sweating, hissing horse, and couching his lance.

'The cost of this broken Law is that what you have seen will come to pass, though you resist it ninety-nine times out of a hundred,' said Melchior, his head bowed like a mendicant schoolboy.

'I would run you through,' cried Cain, his lance levelled, his grin triumphant. 'But it would only lessen your pain, fool.'

'Away with you,' said Pio Nono. The Demon snapped a salute from the peak of his cap that cracked like a jailor's whip, put bloody spurs to striped flanks and shot up through the mists of rock before the landscape turned back to empty cavern.

'Must it be like this?' said Pio Nono to the miserable, weeping boy Angel.

'Ninety-nine times out of a hundred,' said Melchior.

Pio Nono closed his eyes and drew himself up to his full height.

'Then I will take my chances,' he said. 'I reject the path of least resistance and I reject the religion of revolution. I choose the Calvary of defiance in the hope that one day the Church will triumph over Marx, Prophet of Kolyma, and the hotheads of 1848 both. Come Melchior, back to your regiment; none know the whole future.'

And saying no more, Pio Nono left the cavern, taking me by the hand from my hiding place, leading me back up to the living and to the terrible future, weeping all the way, and becoming Pope Pius IX once more, but anew and more determined than ever.

'Kolyma?' he muttered at each upward stage. 'Not if there is one slippery chance on a hundred slopes against it.'

Nor did the Holy Father rest when we at last returned to the Papal apartments, just as the red dawn was breaking.

'Call for my scribes,' he ordered, pacing up and down the room. 'We must dictate an Allocution. And prepare letters for the Emperor of Austria, the Kings and Princes of Germany. And a warning for the Tsar.'

I did as I was bid, called his secretaries and when they arrived, flapping and flustered like crows before bird-shot, assumed my position by the curtain waiting for his request. The humble priest of Spoleto saw me there, and catching my yawn, took my hand and led me to a couch.

'Niccolo,' he said, as sleep closed my eyes. 'Forgive me. You have served me well and now you must take your just rest. But I beg you – remember your oath.'

*

I, your humble servant, Niccolo Parvatti, saw these things and so help me, I attest them to be true and though I made no oath I have kept this secret until this, my death bed, in accordance with the wishes of the poor priest of Spoleto, Pio Nono, and of the Pontiff, Pius IX.

Ω

*Composed on his deathbed by Pope Pius IX's chamberlain, this
account of Pius's encounter with Angels and the visions of the future
they gave him, if it can be believed, offers an astonishing yet strangely
believable explanation of why Pius became such an entrenched opponent of revolutionary doctrines for the remainder of his long papacy.*

1889

On 28 January 1899 the Illustrated Police News *published a report from a Church of England clergyman who claimed to know the true identity of Jack the Ripper. He said he had received this information from a fellow clergyman, to whom the notorious murderer had made a full and complete confession. He claimed he was asked to publish the facts, after a period of ten years, in such a way as to preserve the identity of the killer, so as not to violate the secrecy of the confessional. He wrote: 'The murderer was a man of good position and otherwise unblemished character, who suffered from epileptic mania, and is long deceased.'*

This document found in the Vatican Vaults pre-dates that account by several years. It appears to have been written two months after the last Ripper murder took place, and in some way corroborates the theory that Jack the Ripper confessed his crimes to a clergyman.

The Confession

Alex Bell

9 January 1889

It began with the confession.

It was a Sunday – the 30th September – and I was almost falling asleep in the confessional. I'd been by myself in the dark for some time, what felt like an age, waiting for the next penitent, trying to keep my eyes open, although they itched to close and felt bloodshot and raw. The hard wooden bench made my back ache – a throb that ran all the way up my spine and settled into a dull niggling twinge at the nape of my neck. I'd been feeling quite peculiar all morning – the thumping headache that had kept me awake last night hadn't gone away, in fact it had worsened. And the queasy feeling I'd put down to last night's dinner now felt like a cold ball of grease in the pit of my stomach. I felt hot too, although it was as cold in the church as ever. I hoped I wasn't coming down with something. I didn't have time to be unwell.

Suddenly the curtain moved aside and a man came into the booth and sat down. The movement let in a waft of candle smoke and even that scent, normally so pleasant to me, made me feel quite nauseous.

'Forgive me, father,' a low voice said through the grate, 'for I have sinned.'

At once, I was wide awake on my hard wooden bench, all drowsiness instantly forgotten. It was a well-spoken voice – and that alone was unusual here in London's East End – this was an educated man, a gentleman, and there was a deep velvetiness to his tone that should have been pleasant – *was* pleasant – and yet, underneath, there was something else that seemed to reach through the wall of the booth to me, reach through with curled and crooked claws. I knew him. Although I couldn't see him properly through the grate, I knew who was with me in the booth. I had never suffered from claustrophobia in the confessional before but now it felt as if there was not enough air in this dark little space for the both of us.

I swallowed hard, tried to push the feeling away, tugged at my collar to loosen it, told myself that I wasn't getting enough sleep and was probably coming down with something besides.

'How long . . . ?' I began hoarsely, then stopped – cleared my throat. 'How long has it been since your last confession?'

Instead of the standard answer, he simply said, 'Too long.' Then: 'Father, I have been told that you should begin by confessing the sin you find most difficult to speak of, so I will tell you, first, of what I did three weeks ago.'

He paused then, for such a long time that I finally felt compelled to say, 'Whatever your sins may be, my son, if you are truly sorry for them and sincere in your repentance then God will have mercy on you.'

'Well,' the man said, 'in that case . . . I am troubled by the intestines. Just the thought of them . . . it keeps me awake at night. There was nowhere for them to go. Once I'd pulled them all out I couldn't get them back inside so I arranged them beside her, along the ground, but the mess . . . the *mess* she made was obscene. Have you ever seen human intestines, Father? You would be appalled, quite appalled, I am sure. Disgusting, slimy tubes that go on and on and on like engorged purple worms – gigantic maggots full of faecal matter and half-digested food – it's a filthy mess to be inside any human being, a wonder we're not all rotting from the inside out. But that's whores for you. Rotten in, rotten out and rotten everywhere in between, I say.'

The sick feeling that had been with me all day rose up at his words, threatening to overwhelm me completely. I had to clench both sweat-slicked hands in my lap to stop them from shaking. 'Are you saying . . .' I said, trying to speak each word delicately through the nausea that was filling my mouth, '. . . that you have killed a woman?'

'Killed her, sliced her, disembowelled her – all with such a small, sweet little knife, such a perfect thing of exquisite beauty. I slashed the throat first, right through to the neck, severing the vocal chords so that she wouldn't spoil it by screaming out – women will do these things – and then I cut through the abdomen. I made sure the knife was sharp beforehand but I still had to hack quite frightfully at that flabby white stomach in order to slit it open – such soft rolls of fat, and yet so tough, more like the hide of a pig than the skin of a woman.'

I could feel sweat forming at my hairline in that cold little booth and my headache throbbed fiercer than ever as I tried to work out what I should do. In the brief time since I'd been ordained and started at the Roman Catholic Church of St Mary and St Michael I had never come across anything like this. The only other murder that had been confessed to me – if you could even call it a murder – was from a half-drunk Irish immigrant who'd got into a fight at some gin house and his opponent had died when he accidentally hit his head on the side of the bar. The man had sobbed all the way through the confession and turned himself in to the police soon afterwards.

This, though, this was something quite different. And I suddenly had the feeling that, being here in the confessional – being right here in this exact place at this precise time and hearing this particular confession – was akin to signing my own death warrant.

'I have improved, Father,' the man went on. 'I made a mess of cutting the throat the first time and had to do it twice. It didn't cut deep enough and the vocal chord must have only partially severed because she started making these . . . well, I suppose you might call it mewling, a sort of wet, squeaking, slobbering cry—'

'My son,' I said, desperate to stop him. 'The acts you are confessing to are grievous mortal sins.' I wiped the sweat from my brow with trembling fingers. 'For the sake of your immortal soul, I—'

'I took it with me,' he said.

'What?'

'Her uterus,' he said in his velvety voice, so low and mellow and pleasant to listen to. 'The second one. I took it home with me.'

I pressed the flats of my palms against my aching temples, trying to think clearly, trying to work out what I should do when shut up in the confessional with a monster. No one had told me, in all my training, and I felt utterly unprepared for a situation such as this.

'You're not saying . . . surely you're not saying that you are the man the papers are all talking about?'

'The Whitechapel Murderer – or is it the Ripper now? It's larger than I thought it would be – the uterus, I mean. Last night I did for two of them.'

Sweat prickled the back of my neck. 'Last night?'

I had heard about it, of course. Everyone had. They were calling it the 'double event'. Two women killed in the space of an hour. This was a madman who couldn't be stopped, they said. He seemed to disappear like smoke, making fools out of Scotland Yard at every possible turn. Within my own parish, I had heard frightened whispers of a black magician who could melt away into the night, melt away into Hell, and would go on stalking the streets of Whitechapel until there were no fallen women left.

I tried to tell myself that this was no black magician sitting across from me in the booth; this was a flesh and blood man, the same as any other man, and yet when I thought of the things I knew he had done, out there in the fog, I felt afraid to be so close to such a person, afraid to breathe the same air as him and afraid of the monstrous darkness in his soul that permitted him to perform such vile deeds.

'I have them here with me now,' he said – a soft whisper through the grate that separated us. He really did have the most beautiful voice. 'In my pocket. The left kidney and the uterus. Half the uterus, at least. The rest I ate last night. It was a formidable meal.'

'Please stop,' I said, tugging at my collar, trying to breathe. 'I'm going . . . I'm afraid I'm going to be sick. I cannot grant you absolution. I'm sorry, but I cannot.'

'I didn't come here for that.'

'Well, in God's name, what did you come here for then?'

But he didn't reply. Light swept into the booth for a moment as the curtain was pulled back and then he was gone. I hesitated for a moment of agonising uncertainty, knowing that I was not permitted to leave the confessional booth prematurely and see the person whose confession I had just heard, and yet I felt I could not miss this rare opportunity to confirm the identity of the man who had so terrified Whitechapel over the past few weeks.

So I pushed back the curtain, staggered out of the sweltering little booth and ran all the way to the exit. The cold air outside was a blissful relief to my fevered skin. I was only just in time. He was there on the street corner, elegantly dressed in a top hat and a long black coat that rippled with the unmistakable sheen of quality and expense that I recognised from another lifetime ago. He must have felt my eyes on him because he turned and our eyes met through the crowd – those burning devil eyes of his. And I knew that I was right – it was him, after all. He who I had hoped never to lay eyes on again. Then he tipped his hat, smiled his ghastly smile, and was gone.

A hand clapped down on my shoulder from behind and I whirled around to see Father Paul standing behind me in the street.

'You ran out of there in a tremendous hurry,' he began – then he saw my face and said, 'Good gracious, what on earth is the matter?'

'He was just here.'

'Who?'

'That lunatic. That lunatic they're calling the Whitechapel Murderer. He was just here in the confessional booth with me. He said—'

But Father Paul interrupted me. 'Not another word. Come into the vestry with me at once.'

I followed him back into the church, thankful that at least a senior priest would soon know of what had occurred and would be better placed than me to know what ought to be done about it.

But as soon as the door closed behind us, Father Paul turned on me with the first real anger I had ever seen him show to anyone. 'What on earth were you thinking of?' he said. 'You were about to divulge the details of a private confessional to me! Right there in the street!'

I stared at him. My robes felt damp with sweat and even the inside of my head felt hot. 'Didn't you . . .' I began, unsticking my tongue from my bone-dry mouth, '. . . didn't you hear what I said? I know who the Whitechapel Murderer is!'

'And what do you intend to do about it?' Father Paul demanded.

'Well . . .' I faltered, unsure of myself. Every fibre of my being screamed that we must go directly to the police but I knew well enough that the confidentiality of the confessional was sacrosanct. 'Is there not some exception?' I began. 'When a person's life is at risk? If we were to ask Scotland Yard to—'

'The sacramental seal is inviolable,' Father Paul interrupted. 'Utterly inviolable. Frankly, I am shocked to hear you talking in this manner. To even suggest breaking the seal is—'

'But you didn't hear what he said!'

'It doesn't matter in the least what he said. A Catholic priest may not reveal the details of a private confession to anyone, under any circumstances. I can see this has been distressing for you – you are new to this, and young besides, and I am sorry for that – but this is what you committed yourself to when you were ordained. When you have been in the East End a little longer, you will no longer be quite so shocked by some of the things you hear in the confessional. This is a troubled area of London. There has been a lot of sensationalist press nonsense over these murders and, quite frankly, I shouldn't be at all surprised if this person you spoke with wasn't just some youth playing a prank on you. You must have seen the children on every street corner, playing at being the Ripper with those crude wooden knives? Besides, everyone knows that the Whitechapel Murderer is likely a depraved immigrant or itinerant gypsy who probably can't even speak English. No Englishman would ever behave in such a manner.'

'But he *was* English. In fact, he was a gentleman—'

'I really must insist,' Father Paul cut me off, looking quite furious, 'that you do not utter another word about it. I cannot know any more about him than I already do.'

'But you do know – all of London knows – that this man isn't merely killing women, he is butchering them, and mutilating them as well, in the most violent manner, and it gets increasingly violent each time. He did not seem to expect, or even want, absolution, and I am convinced that he will kill again. Surely I have a duty to protect those innocent souls who will be his next victims?'

'Innocent souls is takings things a bit far, I think,' Father Paul replied with the ghost of a smile. 'From what I understand, the killer's victims have all been fallen women.'

I stared at him for a moment, shocked by the heartlessness of his remark. A drop of sweat fell into my eye and I wiped it away with the back of my hand. 'I think – I believe – that most people fall into sin without meaning to, or wanting to.'

'One does not simply fall into sin,' Father Paul said sternly. 'What a thing to suggest! We have free will and the ability to choose what we do with it.'

'But surely,' I said, picking my words with care as I tried to think through that confounded headache that would not stop beating and beating against the side of my head like a devil trying to dig its way out. 'Surely, if someone's *life* is at stake—'

'It is an inviolable seal,' Father Paul said again. 'You may not break it, even to save a life – even to save your *own* life. Really, Father, I begin to think you must be quite unwell to even speak in such a way as this. And you look ghastly, besides.'

I *felt* ghastly. My collar was too tight around my throat, my tongue felt too large for my mouth and I was hot, so very, very hot. 'I just . . . I think I ate something last night that has not agreed with me.'

I could still hear that velvety voice, whispering in my ear.

A wet, squeaking, slobbering cry . . .

Engorged purple worms . . .

More like the hide of a pig than the skin of a woman . . .

Too late, I realised that I really did need to sit down. At once.

I turned, trying to remember where the chair was, but the room tilted and unbalanced me. I stumbled and would have fallen if Father Paul hadn't grabbed hold of my arm.

'Good God, James, you really are ill. Why on earth didn't you say something? I wouldn't have had you sitting in the confessional all that time if I'd known.'

He helped me to the chair and the next moment pressed a glass of water into my hands, but they were trembling so badly I could barely hold the glass.

I couldn't get them out of my mind – those poor women – not only murdered, but sliced up and mutilated as well, left like slaughtered animals spilling out their guts upon the filthy cobbles.

'I can see this has been a bad shock for you,' Father Paul said in a kindlier tone. 'We'll forgive your earlier outburst. I've no doubt that you heard some terrible things in the booth today – but you will hear plenty more, I can assure you. This isn't the country; this is the East End of London. This is what happens here. The press might be making a great song and dance about it, but this is nothing shocking or new. People die here, Father – whether people make a fuss about it or not.'

*

Five weeks passed and there were no further murders. People were saying that the Whitechapel Killer – or Jack the Ripper, as everyone seemed intent on calling him now – must have died or been institutionalised or gone back to whatever country he'd originally come from. And yet I could not believe it, could not feel easier in my mind about it. There would be another murder – I was quite certain – and their blood would be on my hands, as much as on his.

I was feeling quite low when I went to visit my brother at the Langham. Charles had wired me to say that he was in London on business – by which he meant inveterate gambling – and that he'd like to see me while he was in the city.

I tried not to resent Charles for inheriting our father's estates and vast fortune while I, as the unfortunate second son, had had to find respectable employment elsewhere. It wasn't always easy. And meeting at the most luxurious hotel in London only made it worse. Like peering back through the mists of time at another life – another world – that I was no longer a part of and never would be again. I found myself quite startled by the sight of the shining silver teapot on the crisp white tablecloth between us. Truly, it could not have seemed more strange to me than if it had been an ancient relic from a lost civilisation.

As for the triple-tiered cake stand – with its candied fruit spotted with molten sugar, and lemon cakes piped with white flowers – it was quite the prettiest thing I had seen in weeks.

'For God's sake, James, don't they feed you at that place?'

Charles said. 'You're far too thin. You should have sent some warning. I might have brought Mother with me and she would have been most put out.'

'Does Mother normally accompany you to the gambling dens you insist on frequenting here in London?' I enquired.

Charles set his jaw in that obstinate way of his, but didn't respond to the accusation, or acknowledge it. 'Why do you look like that?' he said instead. 'Has something happened?'

'I was unwell for a while,' I replied. 'But I'm all right now.'

My eyes were drawn again to the teapot. It had exquisite floral repoussé work engraved all around it, each petal and leaf its own little triumph of miniature perfection. I couldn't resist reaching out to brush my fingers against the polished shaped handle and delicately formed floral finial.

'And the work suits you?' Charles went on. 'You're happy here?'

I drew my hand away from the teapot. 'Charles,' I said, 'what would you do if you knew a secret you felt a moral obligation – an absolute moral obligation – to share with someone, but knew there would be dire consequences as a result?'

Charles raised his eyebrows, paused with the cake half way to his mouth. 'Is this about Mary?'

'Of course this isn't about Mary!'

'What are you talking about then?'

'Oh, never mind. Forget I—'

I broke off mid-sentence, felt all the breath rush out of me as if I'd just been kicked in the chest by a carriage horse.

He was there. Right outside the plate-glass windows, in broad daylight, standing in the middle of all the hustle and bustle of Regent Street, staring through the glass directly at me. And he was covered in blood.

It dripped from the ends of his fingers, ran in slow trails down his left cheek, congealed in the ends of his hair. His lips parted in a slow smile but, instead of exposing his teeth, they exposed muscle and tissue – the pink, bloodied mass of whatever unidentifiable human organ he'd stuffed into his mouth. The next second he'd swallowed it whole and was still looking at me as he licked the blood from his bone-white teeth.

I leapt to my feet so fast that I upset the table. Crockery spilled to the floor in a deafening series of silver chimes. 'He's done it again!'

'What? Who?' Charles stared around stupidly.

The Whitechapel Murderer was still looking right at me when, slowly and deliberately, he silently mouthed two words through the glass.

'What's the matter with you?' Charles said.

I glanced back at him. 'He's there.' I pointed. 'On the other side of the—' But when I looked back, he had gone. Completely vanished.

'Someone must have seen him. Someone must have seen him out there, covered in blood like that.'

I didn't realise I'd spoken the words aloud until Charles said, 'Covered in blood? What *are* you talking about?'

I ignored him and pushed my way outside – I could have been no more than a few moments behind him – and yet he was gone. Vanished. Like smoke.

Black magician . . .

The words came unbidden to my mind and I desperately tried to shut them out, to deny the possibility. But no one had seen him. A man dripping with blood in the middle of the afternoon would create a stir even in the East End, let alone in the upper-class echelons of Regent Street. But no one had reacted to him. It was as if he'd never even been there.

'What's going on?' Charles was there all of a sudden, blundering out beside me onto the pavement. 'Has some fellow got himself knocked down by a carriage?'

'It was the Whitechapel Murderer,' I said. 'He was here.'

Charles stared at me. 'But . . . nobody knows who he is.'

'I know who he is. He came into the confessional a few weeks ago.'

'Well, who is he then?'

'I don't know his name. But I know him. He was there. When Mary died.'

My brother went suddenly absolutely still, and I started to think he wasn't going to speak at all when he finally said, 'There was no one else there when Mary died, James.'

'There was, I tell you. He was there. He—' I bit my tongue,

unable to say it – to put it into words. 'Look, none of that matters now anyway. The point is that I know who the Ripper is – he told me everything in the confessional – and he was just here, right here, and he told me the name of the person he's going to kill next.'

Charles didn't say anything so I turned to look at him, quite irritated that he couldn't even summon enough interest in the matter to ask her name. But, to my surprise, he was staring at me with an ashen expression on his face so perhaps he did care after all.

'Mary Kelly,' I said. 'She lives at 13 Miller's Court.'

'How do you know that?' Charles asked, breaking his silence at last.

He sounded odd. An odd tone altogether – almost as if . . . almost as if he were accusing me of something.

'How do I know what?' I asked.

Charles licked his lips. 'Where the girl lives, James.'

I stared at him. 'Well, she . . .' I blinked, trying to remember. 'She must have told me. She's a Catholic girl, she . . . she comes to my church. I've heard her confession many times. Yes, I'm sure she mentioned her address at some point.' I looked at him. 'What do you think I should do?'

But Charles just stared back at me with that imbecile expression that was so typical of him. 'About?'

'About the fact that I know who the Whitechapel Murderer is going to kill next, of course! Do you think I should warn her?'

I don't know why I ever expected any sensible assistance from Charles of all people. He just shook his head, pinched the bridge of his nose as if suddenly exhausted, and said, 'I don't know, James. I just don't know.'

I shook myself, came to my senses. This was nothing to do with Charles. I shouldn't even be speaking of it to him in the first place. 'Look, let's finish our tea. Forget I said anything. I'll consult with Father Paul when I get back to St Michael's.'

'Father Paul?' Charles asked with what seemed an unusual keenness. 'Is that your mentor at the church?'

'He's the senior priest,' I replied. Of course, I had no intention of speaking to Father Paul about it. Not after how badly it had gone the last time. But I had to give Charles an excuse not to involve himself.

We returned to the dining room of the Langham but it was a stilted affair and I was relieved when it was over – as, I am sure, was Charles. We seemed a long way away from the closeness we had once shared as boys. He seemed drawn and distracted throughout, hardly paying attention to the small talk I attempted to make, and I couldn't tell if he was troubling himself with what I'd said earlier or was just uninterested. Probably the latter. As adults he'd never much concerned himself with my affairs and I didn't expect, or want, him to start now. He cared more for the horses he kept in his stables than he did for me.

We would have parted from each other amicably enough, though, if he hadn't said what he'd said in the lobby.

We were just in the process of parting – I to return to St Michael's and Charles to return to his suite upstairs – when he looked at me, right at me, and said, 'You know, I always thought you'd make a fine priest. You sound like one. I never knew anyone with such a velvet tone as you.'

That roar – the sudden roar of blood thumping and screaming in my ears – was so loud that I couldn't hear myself think, couldn't remember how to breathe or behave or be normal. I don't even know how it happened. Only that my fingers were suddenly around Charles's throat, my thumbs pressing into the precise spot I knew would cut off the air supply, and his eyes – those chocolate brown eyes of his – were bulging back at me, and we had crossed over together into a place we would not be returning from.

'I do *not!*' The words hissed from between my teeth. 'I do *not* sound like that! That's him, it isn't me, it is *not* me, God damn you!'

Someone – I don't know who, a bellhop or a passerby or someone – grabbed the back of my coat and dragged me away.

'What's going on?'

'Someone's been attacked!'

'Should we call the police?'

'No! No, do not involve the police!'

That last voice was Charles. My eyes focused on him, and I was surprised to see him slumped on the floor, a worried-looking bellhop crouched by his side. I knew I'd pressed harder than I'd meant to. His voice was a hoarse whisper, throaty and raw, and he winced with each word, but he spoke them firmly enough. 'I'm fine,' he said. 'Do not call the police.'

I took a step backwards, unsettled by the sight of him crumpled on the floor like that, and not entirely sure what had just happened. The vast lobby suddenly felt like it was closing in on me.

'James, please,' Charles said – one hand clasped to his throat, the other stretched out towards me, palm outspread, 'please don't go. Not like this.'

But I couldn't help it. I turned and fled.

*

I did not return to St Michael's. Instead I wandered for a while around Mayfair before finally ending up in Regent's Park where I sat on a bench and tried to think it all out. I realised now that I had been wrong to think that either Father Paul or Charles might be able to counsel me. It was God I must look to for guidance, God who would show me the way. It had been Him all along. So I sat on the bench and prayed until long after the sun had gone down.

Eventually, I left Regent's Park and returned to the East End, but not to the church. Instead I went to Dorset Street in Spitalfields. I'd heard it called the worst street in London and, by Heaven, it was certainly deserving of the title. A wretched, forsaken place where the shout of 'murder' was so commonplace that no one even reacted to it anymore.

On the corner connecting Dorset Street with Commercial Street, the Britannia Public House spilled its usual iniquitous mob of cut-throats and drunkards out onto the street, and I passed through them hurriedly, feeling quite anxious for my safety. Father Paul had been right in one respect: murders, muggings and mutilations were commonplace here and I knew I must be mad to have come alone to this part of London after nightfall. But I had to at least try to warn Mary of the danger. Perhaps she could go and stay with a friend for a day or two. Perhaps she could even leave London altogether. Sacramental seal or not, I had a duty to at least give her that chance.

I squeezed through the narrow alleyway between numbers 26

and 27, where the damp clung like grease to the cobbles, and entered Miller's Court. But when I knocked on number 13, there was no answer. Mary wasn't there. She was out walking the streets. Working.

I had no hope of finding her out in that rat maze so I pressed myself back into the shadows where I could watch Miller's Court – and wait. The minutes and hours dragged slowly by, and fog rolled into the court like the icy waves of a bottomless sea. Before long I was cold to the bone and fearing that I was too late – that he'd found her out there somewhere and, even now, she was already lying dead on the streets.

But then I saw her. All of a sudden she was there, squeezing through the gap and going straight up the path to her front door. I felt so relieved to see her alive and well, but it was a short-lived feeling because he had followed her here.

Even shrouded by the fog, I would have recognised him anywhere. He knew I was there. I could tell because he raised his hand in a wave, without so much as glancing at me – a mocking gesture to let me know that my presence here meant nothing to him. He went straight up to Mary's door and disappeared inside.

I hurried after him but the door was locked so I banged on it with my fist and called Mary's name through the wood, thinking I would break it down if I had to, if that's what it took.

But Mary opened it herself a moment later, smiling widely when she saw me. ''Ello again, Father,' she said. 'Back so soon?

I pushed her aside and rushed into her room, fully expecting to see him there, already sharpening his knife, but there was no one. No one at all.

Black magician . . .

'She's laughing at you, you know.'

I spun on the spot because it was *his* voice, and I was sure he would be behind me, but he must have made himself invisible again because it was only Mary standing there, already undoing the buttons of her dress.

*

Someone was knocking on the door. I wished they would stop. The noise was making it hard to concentrate. Or sleep. Or eat. Or whatever it was I was trying to do. For some reason I couldn't seem to remember.

Then there was the crash of a door being forced open and, when I turned around, I was shocked to see Father Paul and Charles falling over themselves in the doorway.

'What are you—' I began, but that was as far as I got before Father Paul doubled over on the spot and was violently sick upon the floor.

'No!' Charles said, and it was almost a cry, an awful sound of anguish that made the hair at the back of my neck stand on end. 'Oh God, James, no, no!'

'What is it?' I said, beginning to feel quite alarmed. 'What's happened?'

Then my eyes focused on something over Charles' shoulder and horror caught in my throat, lodged itself there like a stone.

He was there. So covered in blood that he looked like he'd been bathing in it. And not just blood but gore, too, and viscera, and all the other tissues and internal fluids of carnage. The knife was still dripping in his hand and there behind him – lying on the bed – lay some pulpy mashed up mess of a thing. I could not for the life of me work out what it was.

'He's there, Charles!' I pointed over my brother's shoulder, trying to warn him. 'There by the bed! Watch out, he's got a knife!'

Charles glanced over his shoulder before turning back to me, his skin a shocking shade of grey. 'That's a mirror, James,' he said – his voice was quiet but it shook with an emotion I couldn't identify. 'You're the one standing by the bed.'

Behind him, Father Paul was still vomiting as if he would never stop.

'Did you pass him as you came in?' I asked, peering past him to the door. 'He must have just been here. He must have . . . he must have slipped past me.' A dizzy feeling swept over me and I blinked my eyes hard against it. 'What's going on here? Where's Mary? Why am I . . . ? Have I been attacked?'

Was that why I felt so strange? Was that why I was covered in blood? Was that why there was a strange metallic taste in my mouth and a coating of grease on my tongue?

Try as I might, I couldn't seem to remember what had

happened after I'd walked in. He must have struck me from behind. That could be the only possible explanation.

How long ago had I entered this room?

Father Paul had finally stopped vomiting and now had his eyes firmly fixed on my brother.

'He's mad,' the priest said hoarsely. 'Completely mad.'

'He's not mad!' I said, glaring at Father Paul. 'He's absolutely sane. I already tried to tell you that once!'

'It's all right, James,' Charles said, moving to put himself between Father Paul and me, his voice breaking slightly on my name. 'It's going to be all right.'

'Of course it's going to be all right,' I replied. 'As soon as we find him and stop him.'

To my surprise, and in spite of the bloody mess all over my coat, Charles reached out and pulled me into an embrace, as if I were a child once again. For some moments, he held me so tightly against him that I realised his entire body was trembling. 'I'm sorry,' he said, whispering the words so quietly in my ear that I almost didn't hear them. 'I'm so sorry.'

'Sorry? Sorry for what?'

'Don't worry,' he said. 'Father Paul has already agreed to arrange everything for us. To keep everything quiet. I won't allow anyone to hurt you, James. I give you my word. Just . . . please give me the knife.'

'I don't have a—'

The knife I hadn't even realised I was holding fell from my hand.

Suddenly, I knew I had to see what was behind me so I twisted free of my brother's grip and turned around.

But I was wrong-footed.

He had out-witted me somehow.

The bed – that *bed* – was beside me, after all.

'What . . . what *is* that?' I said, staring at the mess upon the sheets – and not just upon the sheets but smeared all over the walls, spotted upon the ceiling, splattered on the floor and sticky all over my hands. 'Charles, what *is* that?'

No one said anything but, finally, I realised what was on the bed.

The naked body had been human once but it was hard to tell now. A jagged slash cut the throat right down to the spine, the neck tissue was severed to the bone, great chunks of thigh had been sliced away, both breasts had been cut off, and the intestines and spleen lay in wet, glistening piles beside the body on the bed. As for the face, it had been almost entirely hacked away. A mess of shining red flaps of flesh were all that remained.

There was a deafening ringing in my ears. It felt like it would split my head in two. Surely none of this could be real . . .

'Charles,' I said, suddenly afraid in a way I couldn't remember ever having been before. I tried to turn back to him, reaching out blindly with my hand, searching for something in the room to hold on to. 'Charles, please . . .'

But it was no good. There was nothing there. Only the choking darkness of the Ripper's velvety voice as he whispered his evil thoughts into my ear so loudly that I couldn't think through the nightmare of it.

For the first time in my life, I think I must have fainted. And when I came back to my senses I was far away from Miller's Court, in a strange and frightening place, with bars upon the windows and lunatics laughing in the halls.

I tried, again and again, to explain about the Whitechapel Murderer – that fiendish black magician who had somehow managed to get away with it yet again. But I couldn't make them hear me. I couldn't make them listen. They thought that *I* was the mad one.

Charles visits me from time to time, but he can barely look at me, and I can tell he doesn't believe that I saw the Whitechapel Killer that night, or that I've seen him since, lurking in the mirrors, sneaking into my nightmares, poking at the back of my eyeballs from the inside of my head with those confounded claws of his. No one in this place believes me but it is the truth nevertheless – and one day the truth will out.

And I will tell the world who Jack the Ripper really is.

Ω

The facts of the case appear to be correct so far as dates and places are concerned. They are also correct in their mention of the mutilations suffered by the victims. Some were missing organs such as the kidney and uterus, but only the final victim, *Mary Jane Kelly*, was missing her heart. Her body was found on the morning of 9 November 1888.

The Roman Catholic Church of St Mary and St Michael still stands today on Commercial Road in the East End of London. It is located just a short distance from 13 Millers Court where *Mary Jane Kelly* was killed. The second victim, Annie Chapman, was also last seen alive in this vicinity.

However, we can find no record of a Father James being incumbent at the church at that time and so have been unable to corroborate any of the statements made in this quite disturbing account.

1920s

One box file found in the Vatican vaults was labelled 'Fr Bérenger Saunière'. The main document appears to have been written in the 1920s by a senior church dignitary and academic from Saint-Sulpice in Paris. He had evidently known Saunière well, and had delved into the priest's enigmatic life in some depth.

There were a number of other documents and press cuttings in the file, and some of these are interleaved in the scholar's account, as noted herein. In a few places we have summarised the Saint-Sulpice scholar's text, but for the most part what follows is taken directly from his document.

Saunière's Secret

Lionel & Patricia Fanthorpe

Bérenger Saunière was born on 11 April 1852 at Couiza Montazels in south-western France, close to the mountainous Spanish border. The Montazels part of the village name is associated with the hazel plant and its use in witchcraft. Couiza overlooks the mysterious village of Rennes-le-Château where Saunière became the parish priest in 1885, and where he died on 22 January 1917, a few weeks short of his sixty-fifth birthday.

Rennes-le-Château was not a lucrative living: the stipend was only a few francs a month, and the impoverished young Saunière depended on the generosity of his parishioners in order to eat regularly. A few years later, however, he was the most prolific spender in the Languedoc in south-western France. His appreciation of his parishioners' earlier generosity was expressed in the frequent luxurious meals to which he invited them. Part of the Saunière mystery is the source of his enormous, unaccountable wealth, but there is far more to it than that, as I shall record later.

First, there is the mystery of the man himself. Bérenger Saunière was no traditional nineteenth-century French village priest. One clue to his true identity is the way that his parishioners obeyed and revered him. They treated him like royalty – and he behaved like royalty: but of the wild, Bohemian kind. Beautiful eighteen-year-old Marie Dénarnaud – listed officially as his 'housekeeper' – was his nubile young partner at home in Rennes, and his romantic forays further afield included the beautiful and sensual Emma Calvé, the brilliant opera singer and courtesan.

Bérenger was no harmless village priest. He was powerful,

ruthless and well able to defend himself and the breathtaking secrets that he guarded.

*

Among the other papers in the box, along with the lengthy, detailed account from the scholar at Saint-Sulpice, was a newspaper cutting which had been added to the Saunière file in the 1960s. It bore out the Saint-Sulpice scholar's opinion that Saunière was powerful and ruthless. According to the cutting, an archaeological expedition had dug three young men's bodies from shallow graves in the lawn beside his presbytery. Each had been shot.

The journalist responsible for the story apparently believed that part of the mystery of Saunière's amazing wealth was his secret connection with the Royal Bank of Austria and the Habsburg family; he conjectured that the corpses in the presbytery lawn were those of three sinister agents employed by the Austrian Secret Service. In his opinion, they had been sent to assassinate Bérenger, but had fatally underestimated their intended victim. Saunière, it was imaginatively suggested, had glimpsed them passing his bedroom window, quietly eased his arm from under his beloved Marie and drawn his Colt 0.44 Magnum from under their pillow. He had fired three quick shots . . . The journalist asked if that was how the assassins had died.

*

The file also contained Bérenger Saunière's signed confession, as well as several other documents, and that confession alone solves the relatively minor mystery of the corpses in the lawn. The speculative journalist was right, but the solution to the *real* mystery of Rennes goes a long way further back, as the Saint-Sulpice scholar explained in his background notes.

He wrote that during the third Christian century, a religious teacher named Mani had enjoyed enormous power and prestige. His theology was a form of dualism and was based on the Gnostic teachings of Zoroaster. This mixture of theology and philosophy passed over the centuries via a cult known as the Paulicians, and another group called the Bogomils, until – in the region around Rennes-le-Château – it became the centre of Cathar teachings.

When the Cathar fortress of Montségur fell in 1244, a small group of its defenders managed to escape down the precipitous mountain carrying with them what were intriguingly described as 'the treasures of their faith'. Their enemies never caught them so the exact nature of their mysterious treasure remained unknown.

What seems at first glance to be the simple enigma of where an impoverished village priest obtained his vast wealth, wrote the scholar, becomes an awesome, complex mystery stretching back into the mists of prehistory. It even raises wild possibilities of sinister extraterrestrials, survivors of Atlantis, and traumatic magical weaponry that makes gunpowder seem relatively minor by comparison.

*

The Saint-Sulpice scholar continued:

Saunière himself came to see me in Saint-Sulpice, and I visited him in Rennes. I also interviewed the verger who served at the Church of St Mary Magdalene while Saunière was their parish priest. He seemed relieved to speak to a priest other than Saunière, whom he did not entirely trust, and he told me of a curious ancient document that he had discovered inside a broken pulpit support and given to Saunière. According to the verger, it was shortly after this incident with the hidden parchment that Bérenger began spending money as if there was no tomorrow. I link what the verger told me about the strange hidden manuscript with Saunière's visits to Saint-Sulpice to consult me and some of our other scholars and paleographers.

To be fair to the man, and to give him his due, much of the vast wealth that Saunière controlled was spent on repairing his church, and filling it with paintings and statues.

Unlike most traditional depictions of the Roman executioners dicing for Christ's seamless robe, in which the faces of the dice are not shown clearly, Sauniere's Tenth Station of the Cross contained distinct details of the three dice that the Roman soldiers had used. These dice showed the numbers three, four and five:

the sides of a Pythagorean right-angled triangle. But what did that coded triangle have to do with Saunière's mysterious wealth? Was it a clue to the location of something immensely valuable? As I thought more deeply about those numbers, strange images of an underground labyrinth came into my mind, but it was a very different labyrinth from the one I had visited at Knossos.

Eventually, I learnt what that strange dice triangle meant and how it also connected with the puzzling document found by Saunière's verger: but those answers lay far away on a mysterious island off the coast of Nova Scotia.

Another of the bizarre Rennes mysteries had intrigued me since my first meeting with Saunière. He had dropped some strange clues then about an ancient, shadowy, secret society called *The Guardians* or *The Mentors*: otherwise known as *The Priory of Sion*. According to Saunière, their origins went right back into prehistory and vestigial traces of them were said to be found in Paleolithic cave art from millennia ago. The legends of lost civilisations like Atlantis, Lemuria and the Aroi Sun Kingdom of the Pacific all hinted at their strange and powerful influence. What Saunière said led me to do further research into their origins. I found that tangential references to them existed in many ancient religious texts, and all those references focused on their amazing powers. They were sporadically described as magical beings like the *djinn*. Sometimes they were depicted as amphibian extraterrestrials similar to the statues of the Babylonian gods. Whether they were thought of as divine, or demonic – they were always described as immensely *powerful*.

When talking to me about these strange entities, Saunière made special reference to one particularly dominant member of the Guardians: this was Melchizedek, the priest-king of Salem during the time of Abraham. Saunière had maintained that the mighty and mysterious Melchizedek was immortal, and that he was the same immensely powerful entity who was also known as Hermes Trismegistus and as Thoth, the Scribe of the Egyptian pantheon.

Saunière also spoke of the Emerald Tablets associated with Hermes Trismegistus. He believed that much knowledge and power could be drawn from them. I wondered as I listened to him whether those awesome Emerald Tablets had once been guarded by the Cathars, and then by the Templars. I understood that if the Emerald Tablets possessed even a tiny fraction of the power attributed to them in folklore and legend, the Templars would have seen that it was imperative to keep them away from Philip IV, with his avaricious greed and unscrupulous hunger for power.

Saunière also reminded me of an old Hebrew legend that I already knew well. He was most interested in its strange references to the Emerald Tablets. According to this legend, Abraham's sister-wife, Sarah, had gone into a cave and discovered the mighty Hermes Trismegistus lying there in a state of suspended animation. Beside him, the Emerald Tablets gleamed, and Sarah was fascinated by their radiant beauty. She picked one up in each hand, and, as she did so, Hermes began to wake. Sarah was terrified and ran from the cave still holding the two Emerald Tablets. She handed them to Abraham, who kept them safe for many years, then passed them to Isaac. According to the legend, they eventually became the sacred stones *Urim* and *Thummim* used by the Hebrew high priests to ascertain the will of God. Eventually, however, the secret of how to use them was lost – as were the tablets themselves.

Saunière also told me that other evidence he had acquired made it clear that the mysterious Priory of Sion had taken possession of *Urim* and *Thummim* some years after the Hebrew high priests had lost them.

Whatever the Priory were and *whoever* they were . . . whatever their real aims and objectives might have been . . . I was convinced by Saunière's evidence that the Priory of Sion had played a vital role in the mystery of Rennes-le-Château . . . and that they were still very much involved with it when I met him. One clear element about them that emerged from our traumatic conversations was that during the turbulent thirteenth century in the Languedoc they communicated with both the Cathars and the Knights Templar in the vicinity of Rennes-le-Château. It was at their instigation that the four fearless Cathar mountaineers had escaped from Montségur with the priceless artefacts referred to as 'the treasures of their faith'. Saunière actually told me what he believed some of those objects were – and why they were so uniquely important. I still find his revelation almost impossible to believe . . .

He said that when the Cathars seemed on the verge of extinction in 1244, they passed their incredible treasures into the safe-keeping of the Templars. Saunière also told me how the Templars themselves were almost destroyed on Friday, 13 October 1307, on the ruthless orders of Philip IV: *almost – but not quite*. Warned and protected by the Priory of Sion, the Templar fleet sailed safely from La Rochelle carrying masses of treasure and the awesome objects entrusted to them by the Cathars of Montségur.

According to Saunière, the wise and benign Templar leaders knew something of the amazing power which those artefacts contained. They knew that if such power fell into the ruthlessly evil hands of Philip IV, he could control the known world. It had to be kept from him, and as far away from him as possible. Saunière gave me the details of where the staunchest of the Templar sailors had taken those astonishing artefacts, and where they had hidden them. This was where the enigmatic Pythagorean dice triangle from Station Ten provided me with a crucial clue to the labyrinth below the island so far away from Rennes.

Saunière said that the Templar fleet had followed the ancient Viking sea-routes, passing south of Iceland and Greenland before steering south-west along the Atlantic coast of Canada into Mahone Bay, Nova Scotia.

He reminded me that the Templars were great architects, planners and designers as well as great warriors. There on an island in Mahone Bay, off the coast of what is now Nova Scotia, according to the secret Saunière shared with me, the Templars had constructed an amazing booby-trapped shaft. It led down more than 100 feet to a labyrinth hewn from the solid limestone below the soil and glacial deposits. It was in this Templar labyrinth that the sacred artefacts were concealed, and it was here that the dice clue was essential. Its location at Station Ten in the Church of St Mary Magdalene was another vital clue that had to be read in conjunction with the numbers on the dice. Saunière told me repeatedly that the mysterious sacred artefacts must never fall into the wrong hands. He said that because some of the first Oak Island researchers had believed the shaft to conceal a vast fortune in pirate treasure, it was called the Money Pit.

Saunière also said that there were curious, inconsistent

references to *something else* that the Templars were believed to have hidden down there seven centuries ago. He told me that a number of the ancient records that he had accessed were strangely contradictory. Some of them suggested that the Oak Island Money Pit was built to guard the unique sacred treasure and keep intruders out. Others wondered whether it had been built to keep something – or *someone* – *in*.

Saunière went on to explain to me that the dice numbers, and the fact that they were at Station Ten, provided clues to the extent of the labyrinth and to the importance of Frog Island, close to Oak Island. Frog Island, he said, was the site of *another* shaft – similar to the Money Pit. It apparently led down to another section of that strange old labyrinth that the Templars had built. It was then that I began to understand what might *really* be concealed down in that amazing labyrinth. Once Saunière realised what I was making of what he was telling me, he felt able to reveal the rest of what he knew – or *thought* he knew – and it was a very strange tale indeed.

He told me that the Cathars had guarded some amazing artefacts: including two of the Emerald Tablets of Hermes Trismegistus, things of astounding power that had once served as the mysterious *Urim* and *Thummim*, the high priest's tablets in ancient Israel. But there was more . . . *far more*. According to Saunière's account, there were ancient magical artefacts down there that had also been guarded by the Cathars, and then passed to the Templars when Montségur fell. I wondered, as he described them, if they were really incredibly advanced technological artefacts that only *seemed* magical to those who could not understand how they did what they did.

But those brave religious warriors had guarded *more* than artefacts – they had guarded a *being*.

According to Saunière, one of the four fearless mountaineers who had climbed down the precipitous rock below the doomed fortress of Montségur was *not human*. In due time, this strange entity had sailed with the Templars from La Rochelle, guiding them and guarding them all the way to Oak Island in Mahone Bay – and there he had instructed them how to dig the secret labyrinth that was to become his new home. The real treasure at the bottom of the Money Pit was an extra-terrestrial amphibian entity with a mind so brilliant that he could have conquered the world and ruled it for millennia.

Just as Philip IV was the personification of human greed and cruelty, this wise and benign amphibian being was the personification of generosity, kindness, independence and freedom. How different might our world have been today if he had not chosen to conceal himself under Oak Island? But how would the knowledge of such a being impact on our religion? Was this not a secret that must be concealed at all costs?

*

Although I now understood what Saunière *believed* was in the labyrinth below Oak Island and Frog Island, I still had no clue as to the source of his enormous wealth.

There was no question that a significant source of wealth really existed. He had spent vast sums on restoring, redecorating and refurbishing the Church of St Mary Magdalene in Rennes, filling it with pictures and statues. He had built an orangery, and a beautiful mansion, the luxurious Villa Bethania. He had also built a very curious watch tower which gave him a clear view of Couiza Montazels, and the house where he had been born. His watch tower had a steel door at the top of the stairs leading to the roof. If an attack came from above, the door could be closed while escape was made at ground level. If the attack came from ground level, an escape could be effected over the roof. In either case that steel door would have blocked the pursuers for vital seconds while a successful escape was made.

Of whom was Saunière so afraid? He had already told me so much that I hesitated to press him further, yet such was my curiosity that I felt compelled to pursue the question. I shall never forget sitting with him in his strange watch tower, where we had opened a bottle of the vintage wine that he loved so much.

I gestured around to the estate that he had created and asked him bluntly and boldly where the money had come from. He sipped his wine thoughtfully and appreciatively for a few minutes, then smiled enigmatically. Finally, he explained. 'The Holy Grail,' he said, 'is far older than our Christian legends about it. There may well have been a sacred cup that our Lord used at the Last Supper, a cup that went with the Templars to Oak Island, but stories of a very *different* grail go back millennia *before* our Christian Age. This one was a magical device, a source of wealth beyond our imaginings. By some ancient writers it was called the Cornucopia. I had it in my hand for a brief time. It had been hidden here in a secret cave below the Church of St Mary Magdalene, and I unearthed it. Somehow, it reproduced anything that was placed in it. That's where the wealth came from. It reproduced gold, coins, jewels . . . anything of value that I put inside.

'Like a fool, I spent so much that questions were asked in the highest places of the Church; dangerously powerful men in the Vatican began to ask things I could not, dare not answer. So great was my fear that I gave the Cornucopia to the Commander of the Priory of Sion. He alone knows where it is hidden now.'

$$\Omega$$

With those intriguing words by Saunière, the Saint-Sulpice scholar's account comes to an abrupt end. Whether it had originally continued further, and those pages were lost or destroyed, we cannot know.

Whatever we might make of the strange revelations towards the end of this document, one fact is of immense historical significance. Much has been written over the last few decades about Fr Bérenger Saunière and Rennes-le-Château, some of it just as bizarre as the account we have here. But all of those writings, whether by Gérard de Sède, or Baigent, Leigh and Lincoln, or even the various popular but unhistorical fictional treatments, come from the 1960s and 1970s or later. This document dates from the 1920s, mere years after Saunière's death, and appears to be based on detailed conversations between Saunière and the writer.

This is by far the earliest known source we have on the mystery of Bérenger Saunière, and we can see that it was an incredible tale from the beginning.

It must also be significant that someone high up in the Church – perhaps the writer himself – believed that the contents of this document were important enough to be suppressed.

1918–1960s

We have seen several accounts already where God, or at least the spiritual or supernatural realm, is reported to intervene in one way or another in the human realm.

This account of a man's experiences with an enigmatic book he was given when he was young, and which he guarded throughout his life, necessarily involves the real intervention of the spiritual into our mundane world.

As historians we cannot comment on spiritual truth, but merely record and report the documentary evidence we find, and leave readers to draw their own conclusions.

The Will

KristaLyn Amber

God has a plan for all of us. Is that not what they say?

I was certainly not of that opinion when the book found its way to me.

I was young. Too young to understand much of the world, but old enough to know that there was no God in the Great War, at least none that I could see.

Between the years of 1914 and 1918, war had come to Hooge too many times for me to believe that it would ever leave us, and now it had come again.

It was November in Belgium, I was thirteen, and our home had already become a memorial to what we all had thought would be the War to End All Wars.

If only, yes?

The battles had taken much from my family, because they had taken much *of* my family – cousins, grandparents and my father earlier that same year. Having lost my mother years before to an illness, I had resigned myself when I heard the thunder return that, this time, I would follow them. Not by choice, but by inevitability.

To be fair, this mentality did help to numb the fear. I was completely indifferent as I watched from the window of the church that we always took shelter in. Bullets flew, soldiers cried out to a maker whom I had not witnessed the mercy of in years, and I watched, feeling only just enough interest to continue taking in the absurdity of it all.

What was the point, these men from so many nations shooting and shouting? Half of them could not hope to know what the others were saying, though I imagine the words were not so different in meaning. And all this simply because no one would be the first to say, 'No more'. It was the mindless plight of fools, in my opinion, and I had no respect for it.

The priest of the church tugged on my shoulder, telling me it was urgent that I keep away from the windows, but I did not agree. He left me to fate when my younger sister began crying.

Save the ones you still can, Father, I had thought to myself. *Take care of her. This world is done with me, and I am certainly done with it.*

A particularly loud shot brought me to attention, and I settled my eyes to the street where I saw a man stumbling away from the fighting. Normally, I would not have blamed the man for choosing to desert the fight, but he displayed no signs of running from anything, rather he seemed to be seeking something out.

And then his eyes settled upon me. I nearly ducked away but I remembered that I did not care if he took my life, so I remained.

The man squinted at me and then looked down to consult the pages of a thin book in the palm of his hand. Then he looked at me in an entirely new way.

It seemed he had found what he was looking for, and I wondered if God was real and was personally attending to my decision to forgo life.

Suddenly I was nervous.

I remembered what I had told my sister only weeks before: if you begin something, finish it, and do it as soon as possible. I had filled my father's shoes quickly and with little patience, so in my young mind dragging things out only led to meaningless disaster, as I had seen for most of my life.

In my final moments, I decided I would show my sister that I was no hypocrite. I climbed through the broken glass, which had once been a lovely stained glass window, and walked towards the soldier, because it was better that my death not endanger anyone else.

The man seemed impressed as he slowed his pace to stop in front of me. I only looked at him as he bent one knee to meet my height. He said things that I could not comprehend. He spoke French.

He tried to speak to me several times, but it did not take long for him to realise that I did not understand. His brows drew together as he decided on a new tactic. He moved the old book from under his arm and held it out to me.

He spoke again and pointed at it repeatedly. Now I knew that it must be important.

I looked down at the book and back to him before cautiously placing a hand on the cover.

He nodded vigorously, his eyes glinting. I recognised what I saw in them. Hope. It had been a long time since I had seen it reflected in someone's eyes. It made this book all the more intriguing.

Not yet willing to commit, I simply brushed my fingers across the cover. It was very old and rough. Something about it reminded me of my grandfather, to be honest, and the warmth of the memories made me even more willing to accept the Frenchman's gift, though I was sure I would not be able to read this book. I could not even discern the title back then. *La Volont*é. The whole book would be in French. What use was that to me?

The man saw the doubt in my eyes and continued to push the book towards me until finally I was startled into taking it without thinking. I was so intent on shoving it back at him that I nearly missed it.

Once the book was secure in my hands, I swear to you, the title changed. Now it read *De Wil*. The Will.

Frightened by whatever witchcraft this was, I threw the book back at the Frenchman. It hit him but fell to the ground, and he laughed. He picked it up and held it out to me. The title remained in Dutch.

He said something in a gentle tone, his eyes gleaming with kindness, though his smile was so sad.

I accepted the book this time, purely out of shock and respect for the tears collecting in the Frenchman's eyes. He reached forward, placing a hand on the book as if it were an old friend. He lifted the cover just enough to see the words inside, which must have remained in French, unless he could also read Dutch. His breath caught in his throat, but he smiled anyway. The tears began to fall and he looked at me, still smiling but breathing too quickly.

'*Merci,*' he whispered, and his next words I will never forget. '*Dieu vous bénisse.*' He took in a very deep, shuttering breath and closed his eyes, placing a steadying hand on my shoulder. '*Dieu vous bénisse . . .*'

Suddenly, I remembered the war. The gunshot reminded me, but not quickly enough to save him. It pierced him, I never did know exactly where, but he fell onto me and was gone before he met my shoulder.

I fell backwards, scrambling away from him and throwing the book in the process. He was dead. He had just died in front of me.

Not this again.

It was too much for me. My vision blurred and I barely remembered to grab the book before I ran back to the shelter of the church. The fear of battle had returned accompanied by a curiosity that would not let me leave this world until I knew why that man had sought me out.

So I lived, as you can plainly see, and it was not long before the sun finally began to rise on the world again. The war came to an end and I could breathe deeply.

My sister and I were left with few options, but the priest took us into his care. It was months before I discovered why. He would not allow us to be taken or separated, and I knew that it had something to do with the look he had given me when I had returned with *DeWil.* There had been shock on his face, of course, but also recognition. I did not know how he could have heard about the book, but his eyes lingered on it with a sense of reverence. It was familiar to him.

So I was suspicious of him, and he sensed it.

My sister and I worked for our keep, and I became acquainted with the church and its workings, even participating in Sunday services as necessary, but never happily.

I lived for the darkness. When I was allowed to return to my room at the end of the day, I would read the book by candlelight, and I saw things: names of people I would never meet and things that they needed to know or do, even how to help them. Every night the story would change. Upon opening the cover, the words would be different, telling of new persons and circumstances that required attention.

I could not decide what it meant, or why it was mine to hold. It was not long before the priest confronted me about it.

I was too absorbed in the story to hear his footsteps. I could only close the book as quickly as possible and try to ignore his presence.

'Jansen, what are you reading?' he asked softly, so as not to make me defensive.

It did not work. I was always defensive, but respect was necessary and a trait my father valued.

'Nothing of importance, Father Bediende.'

'Please do not ever say that about this book, Jansen. It is so far from the truth,' he said. And then I turned to look at him.

The feeling of vindication was short-lived once the questions rushed into my mind. I had to subdue my instinctual accusing tone before I could ask him what he knew about *De Wil*.

I had to surrender my resolve to shut him out. I had to lose the battle that only I fought. However, that loss would gain me everything.

'*De Wil*,' Father Bediende breathed as he entered the room. 'I never thought I would see it in my own language, least of all in the hands of a young man like you. Mysterious ways indeed . . .'

I remained impatiently silent. The only words in my mind would have been disrespectful.

'God has a plan for all of us,' Father Bediende began, and before I could roll my eyes he continued. 'This is that plan, Jansen. You hold it in your hands.'

The shock and confusion must have been clear on my face. Of course I knew that this book was something beyond normal, but I had never dreamed that there was such a grand scheme behind it. The stories I had been reading were the plans of God? How was that possible?

'God gives everyone a purpose,' he explained, 'and some are meant to help and guide the others in order to preserve God's ultimate plan. Everyone is important and deserves the chance to make their own choices to decide their fates, so God sends them people to speak on His behalf.' Then he smiled at me the way my mother used to. 'I am one of those people. *De Wil* is my guide. I am connected to it. God's will is on my heart and in my mind so

I know what to do. As long as *De Wil* exists, those who are like me will have the wisdom to help people all over the world. *De Wil* is our anchor, and you are its keeper.'

His words made the small book feel heavier in my hands. A voice in my head argued against Father Bediende's claim but I wanted it to be true. I wanted the book to give me a purpose, so I kept my mind open.

'That book kept me from you these past few months,' Father Bediende continued, as though complimenting *Del Wil's* cleverness, 'and tonight it called me to you. Turn the page.'

I did and saw what he meant. There, on the page, was my name, and words . . .

'A time to speak,' Father Bediende said aloud as I read. 'Ecclesiastes 3:7. That was all I needed to know that it was time to explain your purpose to you.'

And the lessons began. He told me of how the book connects those people who are meant to preserve God's plan.

'Many people confuse us for psychics, but there is much more to our calling than seeing the future. We see what choices need to be made, and we encourage them – never force them. God's people are not slaves.'

It was overwhelming, but he promised that I would understand in time. This was not what I wanted to hear, and my curiosity began a trend of several years that would see Father Bediende and myself become very close.

I spent years learning my place in the grand scheme of *De Wil's* history – more of a legacy, really. It was passed on from one keeper to another, and I was simply the latest in a line that dated back to the day the Lord sent the Holy Ghost.

I remained reasonably sceptical of God for quite a while before finally accepting that the book's very existence had to be enough proof of His existence. He put it here as a physical link between His plan and the people meant to keep it in line. Without *De Wil*, the people like Father Bediende would have no foundation and no way of knowing what God's plan is. And whether I wanted to believe these things or not, I had a job to do, and I took that very seriously.

It wasn't until the worst happened that I finally surrendered myself to faith.

When I was old enough, Father Bediende and I agreed that it was best for me to move elsewhere. I would not be safe in one place for much longer. Among those meant to help people were those who chose to manipulate them instead. The population of those with the gift to know *De Wil* could be split by very blurred lines into three factions: those who followed it, those who sought to control it, and those who wanted it destroyed, which would leave the people who could interpret its instructions helpless in their cause. The only person between the world and the book was me. I needed to hide myself, to protect *De Wil* and ensure that only honest people came into contact with it, and the best way to accomplish that was to surround myself with people. I would become the needle in the proverbial haystack.

In Brussels.

Father Bediende had contacts there, and many other places, thanks to the missions he had received from *De Wil*. He arranged for me to stay in Brussels and continue my work within a church there. It seemed that Father Bediende intended for me to follow in his footsteps, and I had little time to argue.

The plan to hide in Brussels was only somewhat successful. Among the many tasks that I was given, in order to contribute to the new church and practise discipline, was the gathering of supplies for the services, and also for the members of the church. The elderly needed food, the poor needed clothing, and the church was eager to be the hands and feet of the Lord . . . by making use of my own.

This task held no interest for me outside of the chance to escape the confines of the old and dusty cathedral.

Knowing what I did about the book, I hated the moments when I was not learning more about it and what that had to do with me, so I kept my excursions short.

But on one particular day I found my path cut off by a smug-looking man, not much older than me, but old enough to think me insignificant.

'So it is you?' he asked.

I did not answer. He was not pleased.

He gave a shout and two other men emerged behind him.

I may have worked for the church, but I was not the type to

turn the other cheek, much to Father Bediende's frustration. It was clear that these men wanted to control or destroy *De Wil*, and I would not stand for that. I merely planted my feet and wore a challenge on my face. The book was secure in my pocket. I was a useless orphan. I meant nothing to them. The only thing that made me special was *De Wil*. They would not lay a finger on it while I was still breathing.

I was such a stubborn child.

The head of the group saw my movement and smiled at me, apparently pleased that it would come down to fighting.

I had seen and lost enough in life to make me a very angry young man, and I carried that anger with me on my path to adulthood. I had used it in Hooge to defend my sister on several occasions and I had no issues with using it to defend myself now.

Without waiting for a cause, the man threw a fist towards my face, but I ducked and targeted his stomach, taking the air from him.

This was not well received by his accomplices and they, too, set upon me, taking turns between beating me and grabbing for the book.

I had the advantage, however. The moment must have taken priority in a larger design because the words of the book filled my mind, alerting me to the best courses of action, and I took them, ducking, punching and swinging various limbs in the appropriate directions.

When it was finished and I staggered back onto a busier street, I found my shoulders caught by a man. I nearly broke his nose until he assured me that the book had called him to guide me back to the church.

I was admonished and not allowed to appear during that Sunday's service. An altar boy with blackened eyes would not lend itself to the church's reputation, but I did not care. I welcomed the opportunity to avoid the services, and it was sure to happen again.

In fact, it became the norm whenever I was discovered by the wrong people, those who sought to oppose the instructions of *De Wil* rather than to facilitate them.

Just imagine knowing of history's most pivotal moments before they occur. For some, the taste of power is too strong a drug. These were the people whom, due to the lessons I was given in Latin, I dubbed the Iniquus. And those who came to me with the intent of giving people the choice to follow *De Wil*, or asking my advice because they could sense that I was the book's keeper, I called the Optio.

I encountered them everywhere, even when I entered the Catholic University of Leuven when I was old enough.

I had developed a deep interest in history and studied it at the university. I could almost trace the path of *De Wil* through the pages of my textbooks. My enthusiasm impressed the school enough to earn me several recommendations for a position there upon my graduation.

The freedom that came with living away from the church was refreshing, in the lightest of terms. I immersed myself in my studies, because I was studying what I wanted to. I took a particular interest in the Western Schism. Something told me the conflict involved a struggle between the Optio and the Iniquus. If they could not control *De Wil*, control over the Catholic Church would be a worthy consolation prize. But there was no way to confirm my theory, so I kept it to myself.

I still encountered issues with the Iniquus, but they were vastly outnumbered by the Optio in our Catholic environment. I made friends for the first time in my life, and I learned the value of trusted companions. They helped to keep the Iniquus at bay and taught me more about the connection between *De Wil* and those with the gift to feel it.

I saw members of the Optio interact with those in need, befriending them, educating them, then taking their leave. I even received a summons from the book on occasion, but my priority was always to keep it safe. I did not know what might happen if I lost *De Wil*, but my gut told me that it was something I did not want to discover.

And yet I did.

Another war broke out years later when I was older, somewhat wiser, and had earned myself a position at the Catholic University teaching History. I was called to enter the Belgian military for the briefest of times, though I would have preferred to stay at the university. We were not the strongest force in the world and were quickly humbled by the weight of war, but some of us continued to fight.

I was among a large contingent sent to England in 1940. That is where I learned to speak this language.

I met more members of the Optio there, and, inevitably, some of the Iniquus as well.

It was late in the year of 1941 that I learned the consequences of losing the book. In the rush and chaos that is war, I had foolishly decided that the book was safe, buried among the possessions I kept beneath my camp bed. Thirty-six years of life, twenty-three of them in the possession of *De Wil*, and still a life of limited responsibility had left me spoiled. To be fair, I had a war on my mind, but as the keeper of *De Wil*, the book should have been my foremost priority.

Even when fighting for the same cause, there are still enemies to be found among friends. The Second World War did not cause the members of the Iniquus and the Optio to forget the purpose they were born with. I should have been even more responsible.

It was something as small as a surprise drill in the middle of the night that left me careless. Soldiers were the type of men I trusted most, thanks to my French predecessor, but I should not have been so naïve.

Hindsight makes everything so clear, and I should have recognised that the drill was a distraction. As the call rang out and we all rushed to our positions, an Iniquus stole into my barracks. It was only too easy for him to take *De Wil* once he felt it nearby.

I felt it too. As did several Optio members, whose eyes immediately fixed on me. My first instinct was to run back and catch the thief as soon as possible, but abandoning my post would have taken me even further away from my chances. The punishment for such an act was severe, and while I faced the consequences, the book would be falling further and further from my grasp.

I have never felt so impatient in my life, before or since.

The minute we were dismissed I hurried back, looking for anyone headed in the opposite direction. When that was fruitless, I searched for clues around my bed that I knew would not be there.

I flipped the bed.

I gathered the Optio and I apologised and we searched, but it was a frustrating process. The book called to us, but the Iniquus kept it moving.

We knew that something bad was coming. I could feel so many pages of the book rewriting to compensate for the increasing amount of time that it was lost. It was still sending the message of what had to be done to put God's plan on track, but the Iniquus had the hard copy. They had the pages. They could read everything, which no one was truly meant to do. Omniscience is a curse that God keeps to Himself. Father Bediende had warned me of that years ago, when reading about other people in other places had become my obsession.

As always, he had been absolutely correct.

For every instruction the book gave, the Iniquus could see, and counteract it, even the ones that were meant for others to act on. Members of the Optio and the Iniquus must have felt the repercussions worldwide. As if the world was not in enough peril, things were about to get much worse.

It was difficult to hide our intentions from our commanding officers, but honestly, who would accept our story? A book with God's plan written inside that speaks to a particular group of people who can act on it?

How easily would you believe?

There was no time to take the chance. Every spare moment was spent searching the bunks of hundreds of men, but I should have known that the Iniquus would not repeat my mistake.

We would have to wait for them to make a mistake of their own, and they inevitably did.

Their mistake was born of selfishness and insensitivity – a common vice among them – which resulted in one of their own betraying them. He found me easily and we wasted no time in reclaiming the book, but not without a fight.

There was a skirmish, which I expected, but what I did not expect was that one of the Iniquus would pull his gun on us once I had wrestled *De Wil* from him. Fortunately, with the book back in my possession, our heads were clearer, as were our assignments. In an action that must have been directed by the book, one of the Optio tackled the armed man as he fired his gun.

A cry rang out, and it was mine.

I had been shot in the foot, and all the British soldiers complimented me on what they called my Blighty wound. For me, the fighting was over, the book was found; all was well.

However, nothing is so easy, and we were still too late.

No sooner had I breathed a sigh of relief than the news came in of an attack on America that set a new fire to the war. That was early December 1941.

From then on, I learned the value of a buttoned inside pocket and kept the book safely within one at all times.

It was a lesson learned too late, I am afraid. Just because the book was restored to its rightful keeper did not mean that the damage was undone. In fact, the pages became so full in the years that followed that one could not hope to read them all. As soon as the last page was turned, the others would be full again with new assignments. Even I was tasked more than ever in an effort to mend what had been torn.

Now, that is not to say that every cataclysmic event between then and now was due to my poor performance, though there are more than I have the humility to admit, but I learned a valuable lesson from them.

When I was discharged and well enough, I returned to Hooge, because the book called me there. It did not warn me, however, of what I was to find.

My sister had married and had a family, but the old friend and teacher who I was eager to visit could only meet me as a name written in polished stone. No battle had taken him. The murderer, in this case, was simply time.

Yet it was this moment that inspired me.

Kneeling in the rain-soaked earth before a man who had been twice a father to me, I suddenly knew why he placed me where he had, why he taught me so persistently. The book needed to be kept safe, and there was only one place where I would be able to live in peace while protecting it. Father Bediende had realised it immediately, and he had tried to prepare me for it.

I began my journey to Rome. By this time I had reached the age of forty, so quickly, but the process in Rome would not be a quick one. *De Wil* told me that I needed to find a position in the Vatican, which would require effort, since I was not a priest. So I returned to Lueven to continue my work and await an opportunity that I knew God would provide through *De Wil's* pages.

All those years later and I still felt as restless as when Father Bediende and I had first started. The only exception was that this time, I knew what was at stake. That made the process all the more gruelling.

Suddenly, I was grateful for those years spent in the church, and the schooling I had received.

Of course, it became obvious that these things were not a coincidence.

In my time at the university, the Iniquus continued to seek me out, and they found me often enough, but I was creative with my methods of hiding *De Wil*. I buried it, kept it in deposit boxes, even put it within the pages of larger books in my library. So when I found myself in the presence of Iniquus members, the only thing they could hope to gain was information. Well, they certainly were not going to get it.

As I took increasingly drastic measures in hiding the book, the Iniquus made greater efforts to oppose me. In the most drastic case, I found myself cornered on a back street, surrounded by five men.

They spoke to me at first, trying to coax a middle-aged man into joining them. It was all very similar to my childhood, only the roles were reversed. They were young. I was old enough to have been a father to any one of them. They thought me old, crippled and foolish, but I can promise I was not so old in either mind or body. I had just finished military service, and I had a walking cane at my disposal now.

Knives were pulled, but I had tasted war twice and, though I was now a God-fearing man, the boy from Hooge still lingered. I am a guardian, my friend, not a saint. That is a calling left to better people than myself. However, five against one is still not a fair fight. I could only do what I was capable of, and that would never be enough.

By this time I was known well enough that the shout of my voice drew attention. Whether this time it was the attention of the Optio or fellow members of university staff I may never know, but

De Wil was just as safe hidden beneath the mattress of my hospital bed for a few nights. I was grateful for any form of security I could find until I reached my ultimate goal.

*

I will not mislead you and say that no strings were pulled on my behalf to afford me the position in the middle staff of the Vatican archives some years later, when the dust of war finally began to settle in Italy. But the calling of a faithful man is to live in the service and footsteps of the Lord. Is that not what I have done? If it were not meant to be, then *De Wil* would have spoken against it, and it has not.

I was sent by my university to research the Great Schism with the support of my church. My diligence and commitment to my research was noticed over a period of time and I was asked to collaborate with the staff on internal archive projects. This opportunity thrilled me, and led to my placement on the staff several years later.

I have earned my position, and, to be honest, few others know the truth behind who I am, save for the Vatican Archivist. That was another fortunate turn of events.

For my entire duration at the Vatican, *De Wil* has remained a hidden secret, an ancient, blank tome to all who view it without the calling to. It has been considered a harmless, empty piece of history.

Finally, I slept soundly at night.

But times, once again, are changing quickly, and we are welcoming an age of free information. I cannot tell you how wonderful it is that the wall of separation between our wisdom and God's people is being torn down.

God has nothing to hide from His people. That is exactly the reason the Optio are sent out to the world and *De Wil* is kept by a single man – to educate people without overwhelming them. Some say knowledge is power, and they are correct enough, but too much knowledge is panic, my friend. If everyone could read *De Wil* at their leisure, they would not believe that their lives were theirs to live as they choose. That is unfair to them.

This is why *De Wil* must be held in the hands of only one

person. To most it would be an uninteresting blank book, but to those who can read its contents it is a prize, and potentially a weapon. The book must be moved once again.

And that is why it summoned you here today.

I know you have felt it, so I will not bore you with redundant talk of destiny. You have lived the proof you need, every time you have followed a gut instinct to help someone. Perhaps you were never told just how this knowledge came to you, but now you have, my friend, and it is time to act.

I pass the responsibility for the book on to you, as *De Wil* has instructed me to do.

I know you have questions, and there will be help. I would promise my help to you, but I feel that will not be an option for much longer.

You see, I have seen the words of my predecessor. The same words he saw so many years ago when he passed the legacy to me.

The same words that comforted our Saviour have now come for me: *It is finished.*

Please, protect this book. It will guide you because it is God's plan, and He never abandons His people.

It was put in this box because you were meant to be the one to find it. It is small, and the Archivist will not stop you from taking it. He knows what it is and who you are.

Go on. Take it. Others have come for it too – can you feel them? Please, take it. Continue your work. You have done well so far.

As a French soldier once said to me at the dawn of my life: *Thank you. God bless you.*

May God bless you.

Ω

This account was found in the Vaults, but no book, blank or otherwise, was found with it. It would seem either that Jansen changed his mind about placing the book in the Archive to be found, or that at some time, perhaps in the 1960s, someone allowed into the Vaults by the Archivist found the book, and removed it, and for some reason left this document behind.

If the latter is the case, then the book is out in the world again, and if we accept Jansen's narrative, it may be called The Will, *or* De Wil, *or* La Volonté, *or some other equivalent title.*

As for Jansen himself, he appears as enigmatic as his book. No one of that name is recorded as having worked on the staff of the Vatican Library, or has been attached to it as a visiting scholar, in the last half century. He could of course have worked there under an assumed name; or, perhaps more likely, 'Jansen' itself is a pseudonym to protect his identity.

1930s

From the notes by the Abbess at the beginning and end of this very personal account, we learn that it was written by an elderly, sick and somewhat disturbed nun in a convent in North Yorkshire, in the north of England. Her troubled upbringing – a Jewish child escaping persecution in central Europe – appears to have had a permanent effect on her, making her what would have been called a 'difficult' adolescent and young adult. And yet, possibly because of rather than despite her problems, Sister Anna seems to have been a gifted, self-taught scientist and linguist.

In light of her psychological and social problems it is difficult to know how much reliance can be placed on this text. But we are including it here because of the quite startling document that was attached to this account.

Gardening

Stephanie Potter

Sister Anna has been allowed this written exercise to increase our understanding of her condition. She does not speak. She screams in her sleep at night. During the day she carries out her tasks with a blank obedience. She comes to Mass, but remains silent. This is a major improvement on her condition when she first arrived.

She writes about herself in the third person, as if she no longer exists, but is merely watched.

Since starting to write, her nights are calmer, and we are experimenting with letting her sleep in a cubicle.

*

An Extract from Sister Anna's Writings

Silence.

There is no such thing, of course, not even here, in the Abbey. Service is over. The day has ended. A candle flickers. The wind has subsided. The tawny owl is calling to her mate. The stars are hidden by the clouds. The waves tap gently on the shore. Badgers frolic in the woods.

The creatures have no voice. Just vocalisations. She can no longer even do that. She thinks she has forgotten how. Her head is full of voices, loud, shouting for attention.

She sighs. She needs to follow the Rule, to turn to her bed, to sleep just so. This Rule that brings silence, and with it, according to her voice, disaster. 'What have they done to my garden?' it shouts at her over and over again. A litany that leaves no room in her head for anything other than the morass of night terrors, which also have grown in their haunting.

From the start she has been silenced. To survive the fighting, her cries were stifled, and her nightmares of a sheet covering her face still make sleep something she would rather avoid.

There are other dreams. To avoid eviction, she was silenced: no babies allowed in these tenements. Eating food instead of speaking out. Such food as there was. Sucking a stone if necessary.

Just on the cusp of awareness, she was there when her baby brother was silenced; ill and puny, she felt the cold take him away. Then they took him away, and told her he had gone away. Ever since, she could not bear parting. In case they never came back. As, one day, her parents never came back. Adopted, she changed everything: culture, religion, and took on the mantle of her Polish protectors kept safe from the pogroms which haunted the times, she survived.

And when they moved west, she went also. Some places had schools where she learned to be silent: no prattling about the wonders she had seen as her family travelled. Talk about outside was frowned on. Not to mention that she knew how to sound out her letters. Aleph, Beth, Gimel. So she learned to look and listen. She listened to the other children, telling of the everyday marvels: the caterpillar on the tree, the mushroom in the lane. She played their games, learned their skipping rhymes, and later, their love songs, which meant nothing to her. She stumbled with the languages: Polish, Danish, English.

The nuns took her in, when it became impossible for the adoptive family to carry on, to train her for domestic service. She seemed so backward, so awkward. At twelve she was found a placement as a maid, and moved to England, but was returned to a nunnery, saying she was unsuitable. So by fourteen she was in a boarding school in the North Riding of Yorkshire. The nuns said she was a good girl, biddable but clumsy. They looked after her indifferently when polio struck. Her survival was seen as a sign and she was directed towards becoming a postulant.

She belatedly followed the secondary curriculum, where, in the biology lab, she found a world where language was not so important, and which found connections with most of the world she had passed through. It seemed here she was safe enough for her clumsiness to subside, and she enjoyed preparing slides, cleaning petri dishes and measuring tiny drops from the pipette. Her hands were calm enough; it was her feet that stumbled. The lab became her haven.

By the time everyone was satisfied that she could take her vows, it was suggested that she take up nursing. By doing so she would follow her only obvious talent, and in any case, the nunnery wanted a never-ending supply of nurses to heal the sick, to replace the nurses who died from sickness. The discipline added to her own self-loathing. She learned to mouth rather than sing, so her vowels wouldn't spoil the purity of the music. Denouncing her sins with a voice that was hardly used, she would rather spend time lying on the floor without explaining. The ants were more interesting than the ritual around her. What others found in chapel, she found in the laboratory. She settled for this compromise, and when they realised she couldn't walk quietly around the wards, without kicking the beds, it was suggested she take up gardening, which suited her.

She continued to visit the lab, and brought soil samples. They let her take time off in the fields to collect samples from uncultivated land. Sometimes she became so lost in the beauty of the wild landscape, she lost her sense of time, and was late. Being late brought punishment: for her this was to scrub floors, as her clumsiness meant ineffectiveness in the kitchen. Small creatures scuttling away from the cold soapy water proved diverting. It was during one of these cleaning episodes that she spotted the tiny baby two-headed snake, and noted where it lived.

The floors eventually led her to the library, deserted, neglected. One nun was hand-copying the Abbey's own, unique Bible. A row of empty desks was testament to this dying art. Ink was spilled, had to be remade; she was shown how to do this, and to rewrite the spoiled letters. It appeared that she could. So the copying of texts became another part of her life. The Latin soothed her; it reminded her of something long ago. She started to absorb the meaning, the grammar. The Greek also, with semifamiliar letters, had a cadence, a rhythm, a music that she had heard back in infancy.

It appears she has a gift for the dead languages, despite her very limited English, a report said, briefly. We will allow her the Hebrew as well. She doesn't need the English to be a copyist. So the old nun taught the younger one, and a second desk in the library was sometimes occupied, as they copied the Abbey Bible.

In the lab she met a visiting lecturer, one Father Gregory, who eventually asked and got permission for her to study soil fauna. The report mentioned that she might turn into a scientist of considerable ability, and that this was to be encouraged. Time passed, and she stopped growing. Her fingers, at least, steadied, and she became an expert on the microscope. She also was allowed to start dissecting animals found dead around the Abbey. Many adders were brought to her, and her notes ask, over and over again: *What is this strangeness I find in the adders? Why do they congregate in places of bounty? Why, when many are killed, do the fields begin to fail?* She looked at the cell structure, and she began to breed them. It should be that a yellow stripe mated with a green stripe should produce one of each, and two mixed up. But they don't. She wrote to Father Gregory, who continued to encourage her, so much that she began to take pride in her work.

And then needed to confess it. She was back to cleaning floors again. They set her to cleaning out some back rooms, needed momentarily for visiting dignitaries. It was there she uncovered boxes of rolled-up archives from the sixteenth century, covered in mould. She took them to the library where, quietly, with the assistance of the older nun, they used dry soap to clean away the grime. The older nun put in a request for strong archival boxes. The Abbess checked their work and, satisfied that it was harmless land enclosure documentation, allowed the diversion, so long as some progress continued on the Bible. The two became a threesome when a young postulant with an artistic bent requested this work.

At the end of a particularly companionable day, Sister Anna found herself reluctant to go into the torment of the night. A voice was mingling with her nightmares, but she couldn't make it out.

The Abbess had seen her troubled sleep, and had given her permission, on occasion, to return to work after the last service, and to burn candles. Better to be occupied than walking the corridors.

In the shadows, she took the next parchment from the box, and stiffened. Her fingers straight away identified the stuff between them as unlike the rest, unlike any document she had handled. Not the Latin copies, nor the Greek. Perhaps like one piece of original Hebrew, shown for a few seconds, and put carefully away.

She looked. It appeared to be a wodge of pieces, stuck together. From the front, it looked like the other documents. It would have to go to the lab to be separated.

Hours later, her tweezers pulled apart three separate sheets. The top two belonged with the sixteenth-century material. In the candlelight she could barely make out the last, heavier piece. It was in Latin; it appeared to be a letter.

She started working on the last document during the nights. Her voices drove her to it, she later said. What, that still small voice which asked you, 'What have they done to my garden?' The Latin letters were broken, as if they were written over wax. She held the document up to the light. Luminous and invisible, there was another set of words underneath.

On a separate sheet of paper she started to write the second text. The letters might have been familiar, close enough to Hebrew. The words were not.

When she had enough, she tried vocalising the sounds. She remembered ways to say words which she had heard a very long time ago. DM could be Adam, and surely that's YHWH, the consonants for Yahweh, otherwise known as Jehovah, Adonai, Deus, or so un-poetically God. This could be a religious document. But what? To be re-used as a letter?

She read the Latin. It was a letter.

Dear Fabius

Many congratulations on your betrothal. I send you this parchment to make a window, in those cold northern climes, a puzzle to enjoy. It was given to me by a dying slave, who held it in some regard. I must say, I can make no sense of it. It reminds me of our schoolboy mischief.

I don't know if I shall be able to join you as planned. There is illness in the town, and a meeting has been called tomorrow, to talk about isolating us.

I raise a glass to you, your betrothed, and wish you many sons.

Salve

Marcus

She then turns to the growing pattern of letters picked out from between the Latin. She holds the parchment up to the light, to see. Ah yes, that must be a Delta type. But which word does it belong to? The puzzle is wonderful. It fills her thoughts, and for once she sleeps with only the small still voice prodding 'What have they done to my garden?'

Garden. She sat bolt upright. What was that song? She had learned a baby song, in her first language. It was still around, somewhere in her head. A baby in a garden, listens to the birds . . . Garden, how would that be written? Was this a piece of writing in her first language? Or something like?

The Hebrew words she had been copying danced, but failed to settle.

The voice changed. Sleep now, it ordered. She slept for twenty-four hours. So then there was a lot of floor washing. But her mind was racing, full of words that came from her tiny years. Eat. Sit. Peekaboo. The glory of remembering her mother's voice. Hush.

Equally, she started to worry. The story was one she had heard so many times, so often used to justify the lesser role of women: the reason why women could not be trusted. The voice inside her grew. You will do this, because you are the only one here who can. I have been bringing you here to find this and make it known.

Finally back to her desk, copying. It was easy to ask for permission to work late to catch up. Not so late that you miss sleep entirely, and then take twenty-four hours. She almost missed the admonishment.

The voice filled her, speaking the words as she wrote them down. *God in his garden walked. The snake to Eve an apple gave to taste. Eve her scratch made whole felt. She the snake's true name heard. Adam, seeing that Eve ill was not, the apple took, the apple devoured. Now Adam from the greenness of the apple in pain was. Snake protested. I offered a taste only, Eve him heard say. This was Adam's*

*first pain, and filled with anger made him it. Adam Eve hit, Snake
looked for to hit. No, Eve cried, so again Adam her hit.*

The voice stopped. The work was tucked away. She staggered
to bed.

*

Another evening she worried about translation. Which language?
Latin? Hebrew? Polish? English? She went for the house style: if
Bede wrote in English, so would she. But she worried far more
about the difference in the story, the implications. That the snake
was good, to be watched for, there to help heal, to make good.
Already this diverged from Holy Teaching. Eve was in no way to
blame. And, and she found it a bit harder to realise this, it was not
sin, but pain which caused the anger. The snake, the apple were
there to alleviate pain, to mend sickness, to heal, to make
wholeness.

The voice in her head said, 'Yes, that's it. That's what's been
lost.'

She hardly heard it, for the starting idea of there being no sin,
only illness, was also filling her with anxiety, with panic.

The need to calm down pushed her to the lab. A snake was
waiting to be dissected. Do this, and down the microscope she
found *strangeness*, a strand of life pouring chemicals out to the
grass which changed as it grew, from one kind of grass to another,
and again. She put a drop on a passing bee, which changed colour,
and again.

Write what you see, said the voice, just as you see it. I am showing you. Snakes are very important. They assist change, they were
my tools of evolution. This is how I made the world.

Put the papers together, pass them to Father Gregory. The
Abbess might have been able to do that, except that elderly Father
Basil called Sister Anna up for Confession. He sometimes did
this. Erratically turning up. Turning the routine upside down by
asking for Confessions in the late evening. 'We can't be too careful. Satan will strike me dead if I do not weed out every tiny piece
of heresy.' Given that he had been tortured in China, he was
allowed to be this way.

He liked his nuns to be docile, ignorant, looking at him with wonder at what he knew. He already hated Sister Anna, with a passion that should have been aimed at his torturers: that one cannot confess too much; far too much intelligence hidden there, what is she doing in the lab? And the library? Are these ladies aware of the lion's den at all? She should be mortified. Mortified. What nonsense is this she has made up? Gibberish. How can anyone know what this says. It isn't even Latin. Not that a nun should know any Latin that isn't in the prayer book. How is it she knows this much Latin? From copying? But there isn't a dictionary. She shouldn't know. What's the punishment for being able to write Latin? We have to make her unknow it.

The voice went silent when Father Basil was around. It always had. Her own mind was still reeling with the implications of this version of the Eden story. It fitted her tiny understanding of her first, older faith. What on earth would Father Basil say, if he knew she not only understood Hebrew, but knew a softer regional variation, in which she had been lulled to sleep. Lullay, my tiny little child.

He caught her red-handed. He snatched the documents from her. Once read, he denounced her. He denounced her as a heretic, and a Jew, and a woman who was fluent in languages that he did not know, and as a scientist. His hatred boiled over. He demanded that she should be excommunicated, and thrown to the wolves. The Abbess removed her from the library, and sent her to a leper colony in Africa.

*

Father Basil was promoted, and the Abbey didn't see him again. Sister Anna returned a few years ago, to the sanatorium for the deranged elderly, where she remained unrecognised for several years, since by now she was disfigured, still mute, but also unseeing and unhearing, and required feeding. You would have thought that we might have recognised her from the screaming. I am ashamed to say, we did not, until we thought she was dying, and passed her some paper for her last thoughts. Our only excuse is that the leprosy had taken hold of her facial features.

I have no idea where her notes about adders went, nor the Eden story she translated or wrote or, indeed, whether they were a figment of her imagination.

Signed: Thérèse, Abbess of Northumbria

[Editor's note: Sister Anna's 'notes about adders' were not found in the Vaults, but 'the Eden story' was attached to her account.]

And the Lord God planted a garden eastward in Eden. And out of the ground made the Lord God to grow every tree that is pleasant to the sight, and good for food, the tree of life also in the midst of the garden which was the tree of knowledge of wholeness and fragmentation. Some call this the knowledge of health and illness. Others call it good and evil. The Lord God said it was a puzzle, in the same way as his many names are a puzzle. And a river went out of Eden.

And the Lord God had the animals come, first the single-celled, then the creatures that swam, the creatures that crawled, the creatures that flew. Finally he made the creatures that bore live young. When he saw that some had learned to walk erect, in his image, he took two and named them Adam and Eve. He brought them into the garden and started to teach them how to look after it, and asked them to name the animals in their own language, and to listen to them.

As they were resting in the shade of the tree of knowledge, a snake slithered out of it, down into their laps. It spoke to them both, of healing and gardening, of how small things could have big effects, and big things could have small effects. And it offered them an apple from the tree.

Now neither of them had tasted this before, and Adam, feeling cautious and confused by the things the snake had said, told Eve to taste it first. Eve took a small bite, and swallowed it. But as soon as Adam saw that Eve was all right, he desired the apple, grabbed it from her, and ate most of it himself.

The unripe apple gave him indigestion. This was the first pain Adam had ever felt. He was afraid, and angry. He hit out at Eve, blaming her for the pain he felt.

The snake took another apple and threw it and it stuck in Adam's throat, so that Adam had to stop hitting Eve. Adam turned to face the snake and, blaming it, threw a stone. The snake hid in the tree, and

Adam was thinking about how to destroy the tree. When God came to them in the evening, Adam was ashamed. Eve stood apart, with wide eyes, and was shaking. She hid her bruises.

What have you done?

And the Lord God called unto Adam and asked, Where are you?

And Adam said, I hid because while I was in pain, I hit Eve.

And God said, Why were you in pain?

Because I ate the whole apple. Because I didn't listen to Snake in the tree of knowledge.

So, God said, Where is Eve?

And she said, I heard your voice and hid because I am bruised and ashamed.

The Lord God said to Adam, Take the snake and heal Eve's bruises.

And Adam found out from the snake how to heal Eve's bruises.

Then the Lord God said, This is the sign of my displeasure: now shall you toil in my garden. I made it for you, but you did not listen carefully enough. So you will feel hunger and cold, you will need shelter and food, and you will have to provide it. Pain will tell you what is dangerous. But you will look after my garden. You must watch for the snake.

And then, He moved them far away from the tree of knowledge, to a distant land, with hot temperatures, wild seas, and more strange animals to name, and to hunt. With plants which were fruitful in unknown ways, for naming and foraging. Adam and Eve spent a long time learning to live in this tough land, and it was a long time before the begetting began, and they were both old and forgetful when it was time to pass on their knowledge of healing and hurt. Gluttony and shame, and jealousy and pride were all passed down too, even unto the seventh generation. For this is what it means to be humans made in the image of God.

Ω

Sister Anna's account, written, as the Abbess said, in the third person, is strangely affecting as she speaks of her background, her struggles with daily life and her research with adders, with gardening and with fragments of ancient texts. And what are we to make of what claims to be her translation and expansion of a Garden of Eden text on a palimpsest used for a Roman soldier's letter to his friend?

Unfortunately we do not have the original parchment, to check her scholarship. From the clues she gives of the original text, her Eden story appears to result as much from inspiration as translation.

We also do not know how this brief autobiographical fragment made its way from North Yorkshire to Rome, nor how it was united with Sister Anna's version of the Eden myth. But it is clear from the fact that both this and the next account were found in the Vaults that the Church has taken great pains to suppress alternative versions of well-known Bible stories, especially when their implications are at such variance with the Church's teachings.

1943–44

This is a draft of a proposed chapter from Operation Jael *by Christine Brown (nom de plume used to conceal author identity). The book details Brown's exploits in Occupied France as an agent for Special Operations during the Second World War. This excerpt describes her first mission, along with her acquisition of the notebook mentioned in the account and alluded to in previous and subsequent chapters of her book.*

This chapter was removed from the manuscript in 1958 by a vigilant editor, who was also in possession of the notebook itself (loaned to him by Brown as support for her account). Both documents were confiscated by the Vatican; because of their subversion of the Church's Scriptures, and also their claims for the existence of an unsanctioned organisation operating deep within the Church.

As it was, Operation Jael *was never published following a bitter legal dispute between the author and the publisher over proposed edits to what she claimed was the most crucial chapter in the book.*

The She

Terry Grimwood

Philippe was dead ...

Breathing hard, crushed into the narrow alleyway between two fire-scarred houses only a few feet from my lover's corpse, I slotted a fresh magazine into my Sten submachine gun and wondered at what point I should bite the muzzle of the weapon and put an end to this.

Dead, he was dead ...

No tears.

If I lived, there would be plenty of time for grief. Philippe and the rest of his cell were beyond help, their guts smeared across the alley wall beside me, their blood sprayed on my face and clothes.

A few members of the German patrol who had ambushed us had taken cover in the shell-blasted *boucherie* on the opposite side of the street. The rest of the bastards could be anywhere, moving in, wanting me alive, a plaything for the Gestapo.

I was supposed to be going home, meeting a Lysander in a meadow on the outskirts of this hamlet. But I had one last job to do on the way out, an extra, radioed in from England last night. Something of a mystery though. All any of us knew was that we were supposed to rendezvous with somebody in this ruin.

And now the only man I have ever loved was dead.

An object arced out of the *boucherie's* broken window, tumbled end-over-end and landed on the road only a few feet from where I crouched.

Grenade.

Instinct shoved me onto my belly, arms crossed over my head. The world disintegrated into an endless white roar.

*

God knows what got me back onto my feet. I wanted to lie quietly in the smoke and mud, with the wreckage of my lover. I wanted to rest . . .

But suddenly I was up and running into the swirling cloud and stink of the explosion. The lingering white roar of the detonation, my own blood-roar.

I ran towards the *boucherie*.

And the Germans who were suddenly in the street in front of me.

I felt the Sten hammer in my hands, but heard nothing. The Germans stood motionless, bemused, shocked then screaming. I saw them fall, bullet-ripped and bleeding.

Into the shop, scrambling over broken glass, splintered lathes and slabs of fallen plaster. Bullets whined and chomped at the already broken fabric of the place. It was dark, treacherous with debris, choked with dust. I slipped onto one knee, twisted round and saw a figure crash into the doorway. I used up the Sten's last few rounds. Its brief chatter finally broke through the grenade-deafness.

Town square, broken fountain, a bicycle's twisted rusting corpse, burnt-out car: weeds, nettles, fallen masonry. The village, devastated in a British rear-guard action on the road to Dunkirk, and never rebuilt.

Drizzle washed the world into a grey blur. The air was sodden and cold. I saw a church and a different instinct drove me towards its black mouth.

Figures erupted from the ruins, fast, strong. Someone took me round the waist; my legs were pulled from under me.

*

When they removed the blindfold, I found that I was in some sort of attic. Dull, rain-greyed light forced its way in through a small window set into the sloped ceiling. It had little effect on the shadows gathered into every corner of the room.

A woman sat at a dusty table. She wore a Royal Navy duffle coat. Its raised hood hid her face.

'Sit.' The woman's English was accented, possibly Russian.

I took the only other chair in the room then looked up and was startled to see that my two captors were also women, one young, tall, graceful and black, the other white, middle-aged, scarf worn as a turban. Both carried rifles.

Another order, and I was alone with Duffle Coat, who pushed back the hood to reveal a face that was shockingly, impossibly old.

'I'm sorry for your rough treatment,' the woman said. 'But caution has been my life.' She pushed a wine bottle across the table. 'For you as well I think.'

I drank from the bottle. The wine was startlingly sweet. 'My mother was French, married to an Englishman and living in London,' I said. 'So, perhaps you're right.'

'The English don't like foreigners. You were bullied as a child, yes?'

'There were those who tried.'

The old woman chuckled.

Voices snapped across the beat of rain, German.

The old woman must have noticed my concern. 'They won't find us easily, and if they do, there are enough of us to hold them off for hours.'

'Us?'

'The Order of Shadows and Whispers.' Her voice held an undercurrent of self-mockery. 'I am Sister Juliana.'

'Christine Brown.' I answered. 'The Order of Daring Deeds and Loud Bangs and . . .' The grief hit me then, rising from somewhere deep; grief for Philippe, who had emerged from a darkness sodden with terrors even my brutal training couldn't assuage. I was in the middle of a big, open field in occupied France, fumbling with my parachute and silently pleading with the now distant Halifax bomber that had delivered me to come back and take me home. Philippe grabbed me and told me, 'Get a grip.' I told him to get his filthy Frog hands off me so I could get on with sorting out this bloody parachute.

We both laughed and that was the last time I panicked.

And the first time I wanted a man simply because of who he was and not because convention decreed that a young woman was only complete on the arm of the first decent chap who offered to be her husband.

Get a grip . . .

'I have heard of you,' Juliana said. 'The assassination of General Schumann.'

Operation Jael, my reason for being in France, and named from the ancient Judge of Israel who seduced an enemy general into her tent then nailed his head to the ground while he slept.

'Yes, but how did you know?'

'The murder of such an important Nazi by a common Parisian prostitute does not go unnoticed. Only the woman who slit his throat and stole his wallet was neither Parisian nor prostitute, was she, Christine? Very audacious, and clever. Such a sordid death requires cover-up rather than reprisals.'

Bed, floor, walls, my hands, my skin, all red-splashed, his body, twitching, white, pig-like, everything wet and stinking of raw meat and shit and piss . . .

I trembled at the memory, my gorge rising. I needed to change the subject.

'I didn't think a Bride of Christ like you would approve of that sort of operation.'

'Who said I was a Bride of Christ?'

'So what sort of Order are you?' I asked.

'This Order is an ancient one. It has advised kings, emperors and even popes for centuries.'

'Why so secret?'

Juliana shook her head. 'Christine, look at me, look at us. This is a world of men. When we do our work in secret we are tolerated, venerated even. Whenever we emerge into the light we are vilified, persecuted and burned as witches.

'In recent years, many of us who thought the time to be right to show our hand were named as anarchists and thrown in jail.

'Some of us hide under Holy Orders, concealed in plain view by the very Church that burned our ancestors, but has always known our worth. Others work out in the world but are protected under the Church's wing. But there is a price for that protection. Have you heard of Lise Meitner, who helped discover the terrible energy that holds the universe together, or Nettie Stevens, who discovered that it was men whose seed decided the sex of a child?'

'No, but . . .'

'Of course you haven't. They hide in the shadows of the men with whom they worked. There are so many like them who have been forced to keep their genius secret. That is the price. It has been that way from the very beginning. Why were you in this ruin, Christine?'

'I'm not going to tell you that.'

'Of course. I would have been disappointed in you if you did. But I know the answer already. You received new orders, your evacuation was delayed.'

'So, you were the people I was supposed to rendezvous with. And that's why you knew so much about Operation Jael.'

'The plan was for you to have met one of us, someone you would have assumed to be simply a member of the Resistance. We did not anticipate having to rescue you from an ambush, but I am glad we have met.' Juliana smiled. 'You have to take an important person with you.'

'Who?' A downed pilot, another agent . . .

'Just a frightened male child who came to us for comfort and advice.' Juliana stood. 'Christine, you are a Sister. You have been since you were born.' She held out a package, wrapped in a dusty-looking cloth. I took the bundle and found it to contain a note-book and a revolver.

'Look,' I said. 'I appreciate you wanting me to join your Order but I have no intention of locking myself away in a convent.'

'There is no need for you to lock yourself away. You have been doing our work all your life, ever since your first childish rebellion against the restrictions imposed on you as a girl. Read the note-book. It is transcribed from the most ancient of writings. Some of it from Dead Sea scrolls supposedly burned. It tells the story of our . . . how do you say, our founder.'

'Sister Juliana, I don't have time. I have a job to do here. And I have to get back to London. There's a plane—'

'We cannot complete the mission until nightfall,' Juliana said. 'So, read.'

She was right. And if this *was* a trap, then I was well and truly snared, not much I could do about it now. I opened the book. The pages were handwritten, neat and easily read.

In the beginning Is *made the world. It created light with a word and the heavens and the earth from nothing.* Is *made creatures that crawled and swam and flew. Then* Is *made man and woman, creating them both from the earth itself...*

*

... The She tore her way out of the translucent cocoon in which her seed had grown. Fluid spilled onto the lush riverbank vegetation as the sac bulged and ruptured. The She's back rose out of the amniotic mess. An arm flailed free. A hand opened and closed. Her head appeared, long hair smeared wetly against her scalp.

The She rolled clumsily into the grass and gasped unfamiliar, dry air. Then she curled back into a foetal ball and screamed. The screams quickly quietened to a melody of low moans and gasping sobs. Her distress wouldn't last. She had been created for this world, its sensory richness as vital to her survival as the air she breathed.

Quiet now, the She was on her hands and knees, face hidden by a tumble of hair. Her flesh was a cloud-map of shades and tones, a physical manifestation of her role as mother of an entire species. She was taller than her offspring would be, and her womb more spacious.

'You are the first woman,' *Is* said.

She knew that the slight-built, hairless figure who stood over her was her creator. She knew that it had no name she was allowed to utter. The creator existed, simply *is*.

'You will be called Lilith.'

'Lilith.'

'You should bathe in the river.' *Is* nodded towards the gently swirling waters. 'Clean yourself before you meet your mate.'

*

Lilith stared at the creature-being-He. This one's eyes were dark (ah, so this is dark) and shot through with filaments of blue.

Is, whom Lilith had followed to this place, turned and smiled.

'This is Adam, you are his helpmeet.'

Lilith watched Adam and Adam watched her. Beautiful as he was, there was something dull in his stare. He made no sound.

Is looked from one to the other then said, 'Everything in this Garden is yours. You can walk where you will and do what you will. Nothing will harm you.' *Is* paused before continuing. 'There is one angel you must never speak with. It will offer you the knowledge of good and evil. Ignore it or you will die. And death is a dark, cold nothing.'

'How can it be nothing?' Lilith asked. 'There must always be something.'

'Death is nothing,' *Is* said firmly. 'I will explain it to Adam and then Adam will tell you in ways you can understand.'

'Lilith.' Adam's voice was low and gruff. He was pleasing to look at with his mottled skin and long mane of many colours. His face was squarer than Lilith's (she had seen her own reflected in the river) and roughened by thick, dark hair that grew about his chin. Lilith stared at the thing hanging limply between Adam's legs and felt a deep part of her body swell and grow moist. She breathed fast, unable to find words even though she had many to say.

Adam stood directly in front of her. She wanted to hold him and for the man to hold her. She wanted other things that she couldn't understand. Adam stared at her but made no move. She took a step towards him and reached out and touched his face. He grunted softly and covered her hand with his. She took his face in both hands and drew him to her and pressed her lips on his, which opened. His breath was hot.

His arms encircled her and gently lowered her into the thick, soft grass where she cried out his name and received him.

*

Adam and Lilith wandered The Garden and all was colour and sound. The ground beneath their bare feet was soft with moss. The air was sweet with flower scent. Everywhere there was life; from the buzz and scurry of tiny flying and creeping things to the crash and lumber of giant beasts with long, long necks and legs like the trunks of trees. There were animals that flew and creatures that crawled, slitherers and leapers, flutterers and soarers. Nothing harmed Adam and Lilith and, in turn, The He and The She harmed no living thing. Time was the light of day and the star-dusted dark of night and its passing was of no consequence. Adam and Lilith slept when tired and ate fruit, leaf and root when hungry. They named each beast and plant they encountered.

Sometimes *Is* would come to them just as the light turned gold and the day faded. They had taken to resting in one particular clearing at night. It seemed right to them that there should be a place they always returned to. *Is* would enter in a breath of cool air and when it appeared, all the animals of The Garden would fall silent.

'Adam,' *Is* said each time. 'Walk with me.'

'And me?' Lilith asked.

'No, just Adam.'

This night Lilith asked a question just as *Is* and Adam set off for their walk.

'Why should we not speak to the angel?'

'Because I order it,' *Is* said.

'But why?'

A moment's hesitation, then, 'I will explain to Adam and then he can explain to you.' *Is* became gentle. 'You are Adam's helpmeet, you exist to serve him. You should not trouble yourself with these matters.'

*

'What did *Is* tell you?' Lilith asked when Adam returned, deep in the night. She had tried to sleep but could not. This had never happened before. When she was tired she slept, but not tonight.

'It's too big.'

'Too big?'

Adam sighed. 'I cannot talk it to you.'

'We were both made from the earth so why won't *Is* speak with me?'

'*Is* speaks to me,' Adam replied.

Lilith had asked the question many times and always Adam gave her the same answer.

The world was still peace and joy, it was warm and it was cool, there was scent and sound. In the morning the world was wet with dew, as were Adam and Lilith, but the sun soon dried them. They walked and saw and heard and they loved and wanted no one but each other.

But then, with the oncoming dark, *Is* came and took Adam from her once again. Lilith sat up and watched them walk away and fade into the shadow and moon-splash confusion of the garden. She lay down on the soft grass and tried to sleep, but she could not close her eyes. She rolled onto her back and stared up into the bright, sparkling night sky. Still her eyes would not close. So she got to her feet and set off into the dense forest of plants in search of Adam and *Is*.

She tripped and stumbled, strained to hear their voices.

'Lilith.'

She started and felt a pounding in her chest she normally only felt when Adam touched her. The voice was strange, not Adam and not *Is*. Stems and branches rustled and then a figure stepped from the patchwork of shadow and light.

'Don't be afraid.' It was a He.

'What is afraid?' Lilith asked.

The figure laughed softly. 'You really don't know, do you?'

'Are you the angel?' Lilith asked.

'Oh yes, but you can call me Lucifer.'

'I am not to talk to you.'

'Why?'

'Because I will die.'

'And have you died?'

'No.'

'So, you *can* speak with me.'

He came closer, into a patch of moonlight and she saw how beautiful he was. Taller than *Is*, fair-haired, his eyes fire-bright. Like her, he was naked.

'I can teach you as *Is* teaches Adam.'

Lilith struggled with Lucifer's words. He seemed wise. She felt the same power, the same ancient presence as she did when she was with *Is*.

'Yes,' she said. 'Teach me.'

And later, after they had talked for many hours, hidden deep in the garden, Lucifer drew close and touched her. The gentlest touch she had ever known, and one that took the breath from her throat.

From then on, Lilith followed Adam and *Is* whenever they walked in The Garden. And each time she met with Lucifer.

*

Gunfire interrupted my concentration. The window shattered, fragments of glass waterfalled into the room. I dropped to the floor. As I clutched at the dusty, mouldering boards, I wondered how in the name of God this was going to end.

Silence fell. I struggled into a sitting position, coughing, frosted with dust. I tasted grit and spat it onto the floor.

'Are you all right?' I asked.

'Yes, yes,' Juliana sounded impatient with my concern. She waved me away when I tried to help her back to her feet. 'Read on, please.'

'We're not going to get out of here,' I said.

'Don't underestimate us, Christine.'

We stayed on the floor. It seemed safer down there. I retrieved the notebook. Nothing else I could do, but read the thing. At least it was reasonably compelling.

*

'Lilith.'

She awoke, almost uttered Lucifer's name, but found herself looking at *Is*. She sat up quickly, trying to cover herself with her arms. *Is* stood over her, fists clenched. Adam crouched nearby. He stared at her, face crumpled in confusion.

'Why have you disobeyed me?' *Is* sounded gentle, but there was something else beneath the softness of its voice. 'Why did you speak with the angel?'

'I . . .' She could not find the words. Lucifer had told her so many things but it was as if they had been thrown to the top of a tall tree and she could not reach to take any of them down. She was shaking. And understood that this was what Lucifer had called fear.

'At night,' *Is* said quietly. 'When I talk with Adam, you crawl out like a snake to meet with the usurper.'

Lilith struggled to her feet. She had to stand, she would not crouch before *Is* anymore. *Is* watched her, eyes burning.

'I am compassionate.' *Is*'s voice had fallen to a whisper. 'I can forgive. But you must never meet with that creature again. He is a monster, puffed-up, a traitor. He dared to challenge me. I forged him and his . . . his horde and saw that they were good. And now I would vomit them out of my mouth.' *Is* paused. Then, 'Will you do as I ask, Lilith?'

She closed her eyes and painted pictures in the red darkness. She saw herself huddled here, in the clearing, as Adam and *Is* walked away to talk. She saw Lucifer waiting. She saw herself alone, weeping, crying for his voice, his kindness and wisdom. And his touch.

'No.' It was as if someone else had spoken the word.

Is threw back its head and roared and the sky was torn and darkness boiled through its wounds. The air raged and whirled and shrieked through the garden, shredding leaves, breaking bough and stem. Lilith was driven to the ground. She saw Adam, curled and shivering.

The sky flashed and spat and answered *Is* with loud crashes and rumbles that seemed to shake the earth itself.

'Go,' *Is* howled. 'Go from here, harlot!'

Lilith ran into the angry darkness. The air swirled and twisted about her, contorted the trees until they groaned. She fell, clambered back onto her feet then drove herself on. Something was coming, something terrible bearing down on her. She could hear its song in her head.

The Garden ended.

Lilith stumbled to a halt, shivered and understood fear for a second time. The whole world stopped here, as if it had been cut open. And below, beating at the wounded earth far below, was a river. But this river was so huge she could not see the far side.

Then it came, plummeting from the broken sky, vast and shining, wings spread, and with a face so beautiful Lilith wept. It was bringing her death. She stood at the end of the world and watched as it became everything she could see, hear or feel.

*

In a blaze of light and roar of song, Lilith was torn from the earth and up into the cold, restless sky.

The world tumbled about her. The impossible river raged far beneath. It was some time before Lilith understood that she clung to the feathers of a huge flying beast and was sitting astride its back. The creature's neck was long, its beak lined with rows of long, sharp teeth. Its wings barely moved as they caught the bitter air currents which swept the creature higher then sent it into long, shallow dives towards the grey, restless water. Fierce as it seemed, the bird offered no threat. Lilith felt safe. The dizzy swoop and climb of the flight became exhilarating. She laughed.

The horizon thickened and became the far bank of the vast river. It was a dark garden where there were no trees, but huge mountains that spewed fire and smoke. Blazing orange water poured from their mouths, hot even from far above.

The mountains gave way to a bleak place, where the ground was damp and covered with clumps of trees and plants and where huge creatures walked. This wet, hot garden grew denser and denser until it lapped like a river at the base of a great rock.

On the summit of the hill were other rocks. These were carved into shapes, some tall and graceful, others low and solid. In the centre was an immense tower, so high its top was lost in cloud. As they came closer Lilith saw figures climbing and ascending a great stairway that spiralled about its flanks, figures that looked like Adam and herself.

The bird landed among the dwelling places and crouched low to allow Lilith to clamber from its back. She was dizzied by the noise, the smell of smoke, the dust, the voices and the crowds of tall, beautiful people who had gathered around her. Confused, she turned back to the bird. It was gone, and in its place stood Lucifer. He smiled and offered her his hand. Lucifer spoke to the others and they quietened. Lilith could not understand his words but when he had finished many of them dropped to their knees and lowered their faces to the hard, smooth ground. Lucifer took Lilith's hand and led the way into the nearest of the dwellings. Inside it was like a cave but clean and bright. There were places to lie and to sit and food that was already prepared.

'Eat, Lilith,' he said. She did so. The food was better than anything she had tasted in The Garden. He watched her for a while then spoke again. 'We are the same, you and I.'

'But you are a He.'

'True enough,' Lucifer laughed. 'What I mean is that we both questioned *Is*. We both sought to think and act as *we* saw good. We have both been cast out.' He smiled. 'I am an angel, second only to *Is* itself.' He leaned forward, dropped his voice to a whisper. 'I am building a tower that will reach to Heaven.'

'Heaven?'

'The garden where I was made, my rightful home.' His smile faded. 'Lilith, you are more beautiful than you could ever know. You will be my queen and the mother of an entire race. Your beauty and strength mingled with mine, your human seed with the seed of a god. We will people this world with titans.'

Lilith stayed with Lucifer, and as he promised, she was soon with child.

*

I looked up from the notebook. The light had faded. It would be dark soon. I was suddenly swamped with my fear and, for a moment, wanted to give in, to make this go away.

Get a grip.

I breathed deep to steady my nerves and returned my attention to the story.

*

Lilith's dreams were torn by noise, cacophony. She opened her eyes, lost in the brief hinterland between sleep and wakefulness. The sounds made no sense to her, until she heard the screams. She sat up, staring wildly about the familiar room. The white gossamer drapes drawn across the huge open window were ruffled by a cold breeze. The air was wrong, the smell no longer fresh and sharp. It was tainted.

Smoke.

Lilith struggled to her feet, once more heavy with child (daughters, always daughters) and crossed to the window.

The city burned.

And the tower, Lucifer's vast stairway home, was crumbling. Its gorgeous masonry boiled and melted, black, black smoke painted a sky already darkened by monstrous clouds. Their bellies flickered with flame which licked at the tower and struck down at the city.

My children . . . .

Lilith's cry was silent, trapped inside her by grief and fear. She could not understand what she saw. The city was burning and the city was filled with her children, and her children's children. And now they were dying.

She ran along the corridors, ignoring shouts of warning, choking on the smoke and dust. She reached the stairs and stumbled down. Others followed, calling her name, promising to get her to safety.

Then Lucifer was there, running towards her up the stairs.

'You should have waited,' he said. His face, ageless and beautiful was wrought with grief. 'I was coming . . .'

This time Lilith gave voice to her anguish. 'My children.'

'The city is lost. *Is* will not be defied.' Lucifer grabbed her arms, held them tightly. 'My people and your children are fleeing, scattering across this world. We will build another city.'

Lilith crumpled. She fell forward and was suddenly astride a great cat, black and sleek, bounding gracefully down the steps and out into a world fogged with smoke, hot from flame, choked with dust and debris and the stench of the dead. Vast, red-glowing fragments of masonry, blown from the great tower, arced through the sky to smash into once-beautiful buildings. Each impact shook the earth and would have flung Lilith to the ground if it had not been for Lucifer's arm tight about her.

Then Lilith saw birds rising, her children on their backs, disappearing into the boiling night-black cloud.

'Take me home,' she whispered to Lucifer. 'Take me back to The Garden.'

'No, Lilith.'

'Take me home.'

*

Lilith knelt on the cliff edge. In front of her The Garden was as lush and glorious as she remembered. Sweet scents drifted from its depths, birdsong punctuated the pulse of the waves and gentle rhythm of Lilith's weeping.

Behind her, the ocean beat at the foot of the rocky wall and somewhere in the sky, Lucifer was sweeping across the clouds in search of his scattered peoples. He had held her, kissed her and wept his own tears, tears that burned and sang as they fell.

'Always,' he whispered. 'Only call my name and I will come to you.'

Then he had turned, leapt skyward and was gone.

Lilith got to her feet, weary but knowing there was little time. *Is* would not tolerate her in The Garden. The dense beauty of the place revived her, the coolness of the grass beneath her feet, the perfumes of flowers and music of bird and beast. She walked and came, at last, to the clearing.

Where a woman sat, alone.

Lilith took a step towards her. 'I am Lilith.'

The woman, childlike in her curiosity and lack of fear, said, 'I am Eve.'

*

I sensed that someone else had stepped into the attic room. There was a familiar smoky scent. A cigar.

'Miss Brown?' The new voice was sonorous.

And shockingly familiar.

I closed the notebook, the act oddly furtive, and turned, slowly, to face the newcomer.

'I am impressed, young lady, that you were able to break through that ring of steel,' Winston Churchill rumbled. 'Perhaps I really will see England again.'

I stared at him, bewildered, and shaken by his *humanness*; by the solid fact of his skin and clothes, of the sound of his breathing. And by the weariness etched deep into his face.

I took a last nerve-steadying swig of the seemingly bottomless wine bottle then offered it to Churchill. He drank deeply and enthusiastically, then drew on his cigar with equal enjoyment. The smell was oddly reassuring.

'As much as I appreciate your faith in me, sir,' I said, 'I don't think we'll break through this time. The Jerries have this place surrounded.'

'You will,' Juliana said. 'The Germans will not know which way to run.'

On cue, another burst of gunfire. We would be lucky to survive the wait until full darkness, let alone make it out to that meadow and the rendezvous with our Lysander. I was bloody scared. The fear was familiar now, almost a friend.

'Why are you here, sir?' I asked. Stupid question, why on earth should he tell me? It was just that talking helped.

'I think the good Sister has told you already, Miss Brown,' Churchill answered. 'The burden of leadership is a heavy one. I am faced with a decision. Our new American allies demand Europe, my instinct shouts North Africa first and a thrust into Herr Hitler's soft white underbelly.'

'But why here? Why these people?'

Churchill glanced at Juliana, who nodded.

'This Order is an ancient one. It has advised kings, emperors and even popes for centuries. I have a war to shoulder. My ministers are frightened sheep. My allies shout and grow impatient. My sleep is sodden with nightmares. This is the only place left for me to turn. Only one set of voices to whom I will listen. Not all great strategists are men, Miss Brown, though I suspect they are the only ones who will be remembered.'

'And have you made your decision?'

Churchill nodded. 'It will win me few friends.'

One of the Sisters appeared in the doorway and spoke to Juliana in a language I didn't recognise.

'It is time.' Juliana turned to me. 'A little faith is needed. I will give you a diversion, a moment.'

*

The building was a large house. The stairs ended in the dusty ruin of its entrance hall. Doors hung open, the ceiling was denuded, laths exposed, bowed, splintered. The floor was awash with plaster. Shattered furniture littered the hallway. The front door had long been blasted from its hinges. Two Sisters crouched on either side of the gap. Both clutched rifles, Lee Enfields, British Army issue by the look of them, left behind in 1940 or perhaps parachuted in as supplies to the Resistance. One of the Sisters was bleeding from a head wound. The blood cut a trail through the dust that caked her face.

I saw a third Sister, sprawled on her back just outside the door.

We dropped to our haunches against the wall and away from the doorway.

'This diversion had better be good,' I muttered to Juliana. I knew I had no choice but to trust her.

Juliana merely smiled. The smile swept away the ravages of age. 'When I tell you to run, you must run,' she said.

I glanced at the door and at the body. Bullets rattled against the side of the building.

'Insanity,' Churchill growled. 'We will not last one moment out there.' He was suddenly frail, small, childlike even.

Abruptly Juliana moved over him and took his face roughly in her hands. 'Why did you come to me?' she demanded. 'Why did you risk your life to step into enemy territory?'

The man nodded awkwardly, the way a schoolboy does when undergoing a reprimand. Then he seemed to gather himself together. 'I suppose I have been lucky until now. I survived the South African war, a car accident and a threatened invasion. There seems no reason why I shouldn't survive this.' He chuckled. 'And if I don't, well, it will be a heroic end. Except no one would know, would they? It would have to be a heart attack, a stray German bomb, an assassin even. Never the truth, eh madam?'

'One day,' Juliana said.

'Come along then, young lady. I'm in your hands.'

I gritted my teeth, checked the revolver (fully loaded) and moved to the doorway, motioning Churchill to crouch behind me. He grunted with effort. His crouching and running days were long over. This was madness.

I stared out into the square, at the relentless streams of tracer arcing out of the gathering dark to slam against the walls. These were my last moments. A final breath, a movement and it would end. The vastness of it engulfed me. The notebook was tucked into my coat pocket, against my heart, but scant protection. Yet I knew it was important, oddly huge in the white-hot chaos of thought and feeling.

Let it be quick, for God's sake let it be quick.

'Now,' Juliana snapped.

*

I whispered his name as I plunged into the fire-torn dark.

Philippe . . .

I was outside, in the cold air, exposed, running. And strangely free, this moment, dreamlike, bright with euphoria. I heard shouts, the clatter of small arms. I saw tracer reach towards me. I wondered, curiously, how painful the first bullet would be as it seared its way into my guts.

I heard Juliana cry out. A name.

Then there was light.

An explosion, a flare . . .

Dazzling, shimmering. Light that turned the night brighter than the day. Light filled with . . . figures, sweeping over us; figures, shapes, terrible, beautiful. There was a song, so heart-wrenching I wept.

As I grabbed Churchill's hand and dragged him into a sham-bolic run, I glanced back and was sure that I saw Juliana in the arms of a man, a being, something indescribable.

Even more startling was Juliana's face, altered, melted back into youth.

And astounding beauty.

Then the light became fire, and the song the screams of the wounded and dying. We ran on, through the burning ruins and out towards the field.

From somewhere distant came the drone of an aircraft.

*

'I am Eve,' said the woman. 'Helpmeet of Adam.'

'No,' Lilith said. 'You are not.'

Eve seemed confused, yet even in her confusion there was a spark, a light. 'But . . .'

Lilith wandered to the edge of the clearing and found fruit, ripe, succulent. She picked two and offered one to Eve, who regarded it with suspicion. 'Adam tells me what I must eat, and *Is* tells him.'

'It is just a fruit, Eve. Look.' Lilith bit into it and revelled in its sweetness.

Eve reached out tentatively and took the fruit for herself. She sat down and Lilith sat beside her. 'You are a She. You are a soul, a life. You are wise and more powerful than you could ever know. The He is stronger of arm, so you will need to use another tool, another weapon; wisdom, Eve, the knowledge of good and evil will set you free. So listen to what I have learned . . .'

Ω

As with the previous account, what are we to make of this startlingly different version of the Genesis story of the Garden of Eden? Both Eden stories assert their ancient origins, but both surfaced with accounts written in the middle of the twentieth century, a time of turmoil and a time when old beliefs and certainties were being challenged.

Few scholars today accept the early chapters of the Old Testament as factual historical accounts. They were compiled over centuries from numerous sources, and the Middle East has already supplied us with variant versions of many of the Genesis stories, particularly in Sumerian mythology. These two Eden myths, then, may not have what antique dealers call a 'provenance' to establish their antiquity, but they fit well into the wider body of myth and might well be of ancient origin.

Their significance here, though, is that they came newly to the attention of the Church in the middle of the twentieth century, and they were suppressed.

Can we prove or disprove the existence of the Order of Shadows and Whispers? If it exists, then by its very nature as well as its name it operates in the shadows; few outside its membership would know of it. It would avoid written records; this account is the only documentary evidence we have of it – and when 'Christine Brown' planned to publish it, she was stopped. That in itself is not proof of its existence – but it could certainly be seen as evidence of the Church's fear of its existence.

1948

Much controversy still surrounds the reputation of Pope Pius XII. Some criticise him for his signing of the Reichskonkordat in 1933. This was an agreement between the Vatican and the nascent Nazi regime in Germany which attempted to guarantee German Catholics certain rights in return for their silence on the subject of Hitler's morality, or lack of it.

Others say that this is a slur on his reputation, and that Pius XII lobbied for peace throughout the Second World War, maintained links with the German resistance and denounced the atrocities of Nazism.

While he has been widely criticised for his relative silence on the persecution of Jews, it is now known that he worked quietly behind the scenes, setting up safe houses in monasteries and convents, providing fake documentation including baptismal certificates and even granting some Jews Vatican citizenship.

The last years of his life were marred by ill health; he is known to have suffered from nightmares and hallucinations, and probably dementia. This is supported by his own letters and short memoirs which have recently been released from the Vatican archives. We include one of these, which perhaps has a bearing on Pope Pius's physical and mental health in his later years.

Gargoyles

Douglas Thompson

I read about Roswell in the papers, like everyone else, although I fail to see what that's got to do with any of this. I do get the papers here, not quite brought to me in the mouth of an all-American dog skipping across an immaculately mowed lawn, but on an ornate silver tea tray (*circa* 1634, presented to the papacy by Cardinal Umberto of Albania) brought to me by Monsignor Giuseppe, my valet and household manager. Giuseppe and I often exchange pleasantries for a good fifteen minutes first thing in the morning, looking out the leaded windows together towards the sun rising over Rome's Ponte and Parione districts, philosophising gently over the vagaries of the weather or the finer points of papal law or the Gospel of Saint John, his personal favourite. The Roswell business was in the summer of 1947, but it was not until the winter of that year that I began receiving the unexpected, and at first unwelcome, approaches from a mysterious Mr Sixsmith, who styled himself at first as a businessman from South Carolina, but who I came to understand over time actually represented some of the shadier interests of the American government.

Sixsmith (I variously understood his first name to be Walter or William but was not encouraged to use either) began with letters then telephone calls and finally visits, at which he showed me evidence of the personal endorsement of President Truman for his mission. That mission, it gradually transpired, revolved entirely around another individual, referred to only as Mr Kato, who Sixsmith said had extremely interesting views on spiritual and socio-political matters, which he was anxious to share with me.

The secrecy of all of this made me nervous. Once I assented to the meeting and arrangements began being made, the details got progressively stranger. Mr Kato had unusual respiratory difficulties, other contingent health difficulties that would require complex equipment to be carried with him, and linguistic problems that would require not just two translators but some kind of mainframe computer in close attendance. I offered to visit some location more convenient for the Americans, but they seemed alarmed at the possible publicity of me travelling anywhere outside the Vatican to meet with them. And so, the terms and circumstances for this bizarre meeting were gradually fulfilled, until I finally met the mysterious Mr Kato in the spring of 1948.

The curtains had to remain drawn at all times, on the orders of the American secret services gentlemen, in the Grand Salon where I was to meet Kato. It was late afternoon when the weird figure of Kato limped into the room, held up on both sides by military policemen. I saw at once that he must be some kind of malformed dwarf, but my pity, I am ashamed to say, was immediately overtaken by an unexpected reflex of fear and disgust that I felt at the sight of the uncanny way in which this person seemed to be moving. Even now, I can remember it with a shiver, and yet find myself unable to describe adequately what it was that disturbed me about his movements.

Once Kato was seated in a seventeenth-century gold throne (a gift of Tsar Kaloyan of Bulgaria in gratitude for an indulgence for incest), and the various fussing FBI men had finished attaching tubes and wires to him, the two of us were left alone and he addressed me in a curious high-pitched electronic voice, which I found oddly mocking and insidious. Kato kept large dark-glasses on throughout our three-hour conversation, compounding my discomfort in being unable to feel a close or tangible connection with the person questioning me. Although his line of thought was often strange or confusing to me, his intelligence seemed all-pervading and at times I felt as if my every gesture and mood were being minutely monitored by him. In short: it was as if our communication was extremely one-sided. He was opaque to me, but I to him seemed pure transparent glass, a writhing insect under a microscope.

What . . . he began, *would you tell your followers if you were to see evidence of there being other worlds in this galaxy, inhabited by other beings, who had no Jesus and Mary and no need to follow such gods of their own?*

I explained to him of course, taken aback a little at his ignorance, that Jesus and Mary were not gods. I explained the Holy Trinity and the hierarchy of saints but he became impatient with the details of this.

Should other worlds have prophets in your view? Does the absence of such render the prophets in your world questionable in reality or utility?

I answered that I would need to know more of why such worlds had no religion and how they could have come to such a situation? Were they moral beings? Did they practise good manners and exhibit loving ways towards each other?

Kato asked me how I would feel if they reproduced in teams of 146 during three-day orgies in pools of methane hydrate. I answered that I found this disgusting and asked him if he was trying to ridicule me. A puff of blue gas emerged from the back of his collar around this time, which I took to mean a malfunction in his equipment, but which I have since come to wonder could have been the analogue of a human laugh. How did I feel about Buddha and Muhammad he wanted to know?

I said, becoming a little annoyed and defensive, that I thought them well-meaning but deluded and all their followers essentially lost and looking for the right path which they would find in Christ if we could only find the means to bring them to it. More blue gas emerged at this and found its way in little clouds up to the ornate ceiling mural of Ernesto Filipano *circa* 1856, playing around the faces of some displeased-looking cherubs. But I had a question of my own which I felt he had side-stepped. *How could an alien world have come about without religion?*

He said that such a world could have had religion once, thousands of years ago, but evolved beyond it as the only means of finding peace. I was perplexed by this and asked for extrapolation. Primitive religions had caused wars and misunderstandings and self-loathing and mental imbalance, he said. They had evolved over time into one single religion which in turn had fused with advanced science into an understanding of the universe which was finally supremely benign and enlightening.

After a few minutes' silence and reflection, I foolishly conceded that I didn't entirely dislike the sound of that. Kato seemed to become more animated after this, and leaned forward a little in his chair and raised three claw-like fingers towards me (which I shivered at the sight of, taking them to be the result of some tragic childhood accident).

You need a new messiah, he said. *Someone that all your religions can follow and believe in. If I give you this, will you promise to recommend it to all your followers?*

I was outraged of course, and struggled to restrain myself. *It!?* I gasped.

It. He or she, whatever, Kato rasped and I thought I glimpsed a curious red light behind his dark glasses for the first time.

Whatever? I repeated, unable to contain my disgust, uncertain whether he could perceive it.

At this point he cast aside his robe, pulled various tubes from his neck and struggled to his feet and began to levitate across the room towards me, his arms outstretched. I could see at last the full effrontery, the mockery of the human form, that his body represented. He seemed to be laughing at me as I cowered on the floor and he began to make various objects lift into the air and float around the room with him. *Aren't these what you call miracles?* He asked me pleadingly, whiningly, in that incessant little voice of his.

No, I sobbed, my head in my hands and my head on the floor. *This is witchcraft, necromancy, make it stop.*

Then you would burn us next, then worship us once we're safely dead and gone. Isn't that the protocol?

I ran to the windows and threw open the shutters and began screaming into the burning beloved sunlight of that Roman afternoon until the secret service men got a hold of me and put their hands over my mouth. I'm told the Praetorian Guard seized me back from their clutches a few minutes later, but by that time I had mercifully lost consciousness. But not before I had seen how that creature had shrivelled and shied away from the blessed light of daytime, from the very touch of God's rays of goodness.

*

As the newspaper accounts at the time made much of, I was confined to my bed for the worst part of two months after this grotesque and disturbing encounter. When I finally addressed the crowds from my balcony in early June I must have still had a light fever, for towards the end of my speech I began to hallucinate. I thought I saw little goblins, wicked little cherubs, like the one who had visited me and interrogated me so insolently, clambering along the roof of the curving pavilions of Bernini's glorious embracing *colonnati*. I began to gibber and panic as if talking in tongues, as the first of them started scaling the façade and reaching three-fingered hands up towards my balcony. Suddenly I saw all those carved Gothic gremlins of medieval Europe in a different light . . . perhaps I was not the first pontiff, nor indeed the first holy man, to have been tormented by these creatures. I thought of paintings like Matthias Grünewald's *Temptation of St Anthony*. Perhaps such goblins have been visiting us all across history.

I hope my refusal to countenance the foisting of a new messiah on this world was taken seriously by the odious Mr Kato and whatever shady interests he represented. Perhaps he was a member of a right-wing American think tank or a reformed Soviet spy. I have no idea and have always endeavoured to stay out of politics. I only wish that politicians would show similar restraint in spiritual matters.

I should step down soon. My health is failing and I seldom leave the confines of my apartments and have a steadily reducing desire to do so, for fear of glimpsing grotesque little homunculi out of the corner of my eye, cavorting and gambolling around, despoiling the Vatican finery, making sport of me. In the late evening when I lie back on my day bed in the Grand Salon, after being administered some tincture of camphor and laudanum by Monsignor Giuseppe, I sometimes see the objects that Kato touched, painted vases and carved tables, beginning to levitate into the air and float around the room surrounded by an eerie blue light, like so much driftwood in the midst of a deranged storm. I cry out in the small hours, terrified and oppressed by this spectacle, even the furniture rebelling against me. But by Christ's grace morning still comes, and with it the pink and peachy glow of His benign hand spreading its grace across the earth like a benediction. Then the furniture and all the other stage props of this uncertain world are returned to their rightful places again and are no longer in rebellion against me. These days the tweeting birds in spring remind me of that creature's voice. God forgive me, even the sight of children recalls to me his frightful stature. Make peace, I pray you all, with your maker and your fellows, for I have met the Devil and his cohorts, and doubtless they will be coming back.

Ω

No corroborating evidence exists that any secret envoys from the American intelligence agencies visited Pope Pius XII during the period he describes, or indeed that such an envoy brought news with him of anything so sensational and unlikely as the being he describes. Was he actually visited by an alien? Or could this have been an early visitation of dementia, including vivid hallucinations, which afflicted him in later years?

Pius XII did consider resigning (or, technically, abdicating) because of his ill health. He was seriously ill in 1954, and eventually died of a heart attack in 1958, aged 82.

1959

So far as the Church is concerned, purported miracles need to be inves-
tigated – but the person at the centre of the miracle, and those around
him or her, may not want to be investigated, to be questioned, chal-
lenged, probed and poked and prodded by a doubting stranger.

The investigator must assess whether any healings are just coinci-
dence, or perhaps some form of auto-suggestion – in more old-fash-
ioned terms, mind over matter. His job is to be thorough in his ques-
tioning. But what if the person with the supposed healing power is a
twelve-year-old girl, who has also seen visions of an unknown saint?

This report is by the official investigator of such a case, in a small
Welsh village at the end of the 1950s.

The Saint's Well

Storm Constantine

On Lammas eve I walked the path to The Bwythn. The day had been hot; the land still baked and shimmered beneath the lowering sun. My path was narrow and steep, and it was easier to walk than ride my hired bicycle. The Welsh mountains swept away in all directions, dotted with sheep nearby, melting into the sky in the distance. I had in my pocket the letter from Father Contadino in Rome, validating my authority to investigate this case. Before I visited the local Catholic church, before anyone had wind of my arrival, I wanted to see the cottage, the pool behind it, the girl herself.

*

The world is full of miracles, or what appear to be, but holy miracles are things apart. They must have the full light of the Church directed upon them. They must be tied down and explored in depth, because a true miracle is the work of God and must therefore be catalogued. Sometimes action should be taken. But the world's fullness of miracles is more often fake – or the consequence of delusion – than genuine. I am sent to find out the truth in such cases.

All I knew of Mai Davies was that she lived in an isolated cottage near the small village of Llanelyn, was twelve years old and had visions, which she claimed to be of a saint. Twice she had apparently effected cures of the afflicted, but the power of the mind is great indeed, and that is a gift from God. He allows people to heal themselves occasionally, but in some cases their faith falters because they are afraid, and they need a hint of theatre to help believe in it. Theatre like Mai Davies.

At the start of an investigation I never know whether what I'll find will be astounding, disturbing or merely disappointing. I have been astounded once.

*

The Bwythn stood at the top of a hill before a small copse, wherein – so I had read in my brief – lay a deep, narrow pool named Tardell Galar. I understood this meant something like the sorrow well. Here, one summer morning nearly a year before, Mai Davies had been overcome by feelings of ecstatic bliss rather than sorrow. A female figure had appeared to her dressed in blue and white robes and with 'a kind face', as she described it.

The cottage was square and straight, with two windows downstairs, two windows upstairs and smoke curling from a chimney. The front door was blue, with two worn steps before it. A ginger cat sat there, washing its face. Music came from the cottage window on the right that sounded like a radio. I heard a female voice singing along, rather tunelessly, to some pop song.

I leaned my bicycle against the wall, alarming the cat so that it scampered off. The front door to the cottage was open, the hall beyond in semi-gloom, although as I stood on the step I could see a grandfather clock beside the stairs and a mirror at the end of the short hallway, strangely bright, that showed me my reflection. I looked odd, as if I were stooping to enter a dangerous place, frozen in time, my hand to my hat, one trousered leg poised above the hall tiles.

'Hello!' a voice called, holding a note of query.

A young woman had emerged from the right-hand room, which I could see now was a kitchen. She wore a full, calf-length skirt decorated with red, orange and yellow flowers, and a pale yellow jumper and cardigan. She was drying her hands on a brightly coloured tea towel that depicted scenes of the mountains. She was pretty, and appeared to know it.

'Good day to you, miss,' I began. 'My name is Bartholomew Coombe and I've been sent by the Holy Office in Rome about your . . .' (my mind scanned the facts for a moment) '. . . I believe your *sister*, Miss Mai Davies.'

'Oh,' said the girl. 'Mai.' She frowned, taking in my apparel: dark suit, hat, my overcoat over my arm. 'You're not a priest?'

'No, I'm not a priest. My job is to investigate cases of this nature.' I held out my letter to her. She scanned it briefly.

'I see. You'll want to speak to her, then?'

'That would be helpful.'

Another frown, a quick whip of words. 'She's not done anything wrong.'

'I'm not here to judge individuals, only facts.' I attempted a smile, which given what the mirror reflection showed me probably didn't reassure her very much.

'I'm Evelyn,' the girl said, extending a hand. Her nails were well manicured. I took her fingers, deliberately not strongly, and returned the gesture. Her own grip was firm and swift.

'Well, if you'd wait in the parlour, I'll give Mai a call.' Evelyn gestured at the room on the other side of the hall.

*

The parlour gave an overall impression of pale blue and lavender, yet dimly, the windows being too small to make it an airy room. There was another large mirror over the mantelpiece, and several religious pictures upon the wall, somewhat faded: a sorrowful head of Jesus, the Virgin with her child. On the heavy sideboard at the back of the room, a plastic crucifixion statuette leaned rather precariously towards a tarnished silver cruet set.

I heard Evelyn shout, 'Mai? Mai, come in, there's a bloke from the Pope here to see you.'

Mai must have dragged her feet or paused before complying, because it took a further two minutes for her to enter the parlour. My first impressions were 'dour' and 'sour'. She did not strike me as the type of person prone to religious rapture. Her face was long and plain of feature, her hair lank and of a nondescript brown. Evelyn bounced in behind her sister, a picture of liveliness, colour and beauty. They were like the Classical theatre masks of tragedy and comedy, so marked were their differences.

I introduced myself and asked if we might sit. I gave Evelyn a long stare so that she would realise I wished her to leave, without me having to ask her to depart a room in her own home. 'I'll make you some tea,' she said and flitted out, closing the door behind her.

'Miss Davies, you'll know why I'm here, of course. Did your priest mention it?'

Mai had perched herself on the edge of an armchair and was now picking at the lace arm covering. 'Yes. Father Brynn said the Holy Father would want to know about me, that he would send someone.'

I then gave her the usual talk about the Holy Office and how it investigated all religious experiences that came to the ears of its officers. I explained that I was based in England but given work of this nature to carry out in the Holy Father's name. I assured the girl I was not there to question her integrity, merely to hear her account and, if possible, be shown any of what she had experienced or continued to experience. I would also want to speak to any other people who might be involved. Mai answered my questions without elaboration or any visible sign of concern or enthusiasm.

'So, tell me in your own words what happened the first time you had a vision,' I said.

Mai shrugged. 'It just came over me at the pool. I felt . . . very happy, *really* happy, then the light on the water became a . . . person. She is Saint Galar and God asked her to visit me.'

'Did she tell you this name?'

Mai nodded. 'She said that was her name. She looks like the Holy Mother, all in blue and white. She's pretty with long hair and she smiles.'

'You don't think she could be the Holy Mother?'

'No, I know it isn't. She would have told me if that was who she was. Why would she lie?'

'How often do you see her?'

Again a shrug. 'I don't know. Sometimes.'

'Once a week? Once a month?'

'Maybe once every few weeks. Yes, once a month.' Mai watched me writing my notes.

'And what happens during these visits?'

'Nothing much. I lie by the water and listen to her, but it's not words so much as songs or sounds like birds. I'm so filled with happiness I can barely move. There's light all around me, within everything. It's not ordinary light, but God's.'

'How long do these episodes last?'

Mai's face had taken on some of the light she had reported, transforming her from sour to sweet, then it faded a little as my question brought her back to earth. 'It can't be for that long. I have to do my jobs in the house. I have to go to school.'

'So, what, maybe an hour?'

'I don't know. Maybe.'

'Do these visits leave any physical marks?'

'What do you mean?'

'Well, marks upon your body, in places perhaps where Jesus was nailed to the cross or wounded in the side.'

'No, no. She wouldn't do *that*.'

I smiled. 'I'm sorry. I have to ask these questions.'

Mai shook her head, looked down at her hands. I could tell she thought what I'd asked was crude. 'It's all right.'

'Do you have any physical contact with Saint Galar?'

'No, she stays where she is, although . . .' Mai looked up, 'it feels like she touches me with her eyes, a touch that can take pain away.'

'Do you have any pain?'

'I had a tummy ache once. She made it go.'

'And not just *your* hurts, I believe. You've been reported as healing people. Can you talk to me about that?'

'First, it was Huw Evans's hand. He'd broken it, mauled it up in a machine at work, and even though it was mended it pained him all the time. The Lady told me to touch it and then it was better. And the Morgans' little girl. She was very sick with the fever.'

'You healed these people by touching them?'

'Yes. Sort of. I can't really describe it.' She wrinkled up her long nose. 'It's sounds again, like birds, or wind rustling in the bushes. And there's a smell too. But it's not like anything I've smelled before so I can't tell you what it is.'

'Can you show me this . . . *ability*?'

'Have you anything wrong with you?' she asked, rather archly and in a tone beyond her twelve years.

'Fortunately not,' I said. 'So you can't make anything happen unless I'm ill?'

'It's for healing,' Mai replied, as if I were stupid.

Evelyn came into the room carrying a tray, and some minutes were devoted to the consumption of tea and biscuits.

Evelyn threw questions at me. 'You live in England? You don't work for the Church all the time? How far have you travelled? Have you ever met an evil ghost?'

I answered carefully, not wanting to make my job sound too exciting, like that of an adventurer or explorer, although in fact I do love facing the mysteries and in most cases solving them.

'You're a religious detective,' Evelyn decided, and I agreed this was a pertinent term to describe my work.

'Have you ever investigated a murder?' she asked, her eyes alight.

'Not yet,' I replied.

From our conversation, I ascertained that Mai was, of course, still in school and Evelyn was an office junior at the college in the nearest town, there also learning secretarial skills. Their mother, Bronwen, worked as an assistant at the post office in Llanelyn. The father was dead. This being the summer, both girls were on holiday. Evelyn – at sixteen considered old enough to look after her younger sister while their mother was at work – enjoyed the long summer holidays of the educational establishment. I got the impression this was some arrangement that had been made to accommodate her child-minding at home, since the college was mainly her place of work rather than of learning. I was told that Mai liked to go to church every day. Usually, Evelyn went with her, as companion rather than through any religious urges of her own.

What I'd heard so far seemed pretty standard fare to me and was not that uncommon. Many a person – and not always young girls, who are particularly prone to it – claim to encounter holy beings that are arrayed in light and bring with them a feeling of joy and love. Although most of the visions do communicate, often this is not aloud but rather heard within the claimant's head. A proportion of these cases are down to mental illness or some aspect of puberty. Those who are extremely devout and spend much time in meditation and prayer are also more likely to experience visions than others. I believe this is a natural result of an inordinately pious life, where the greater part of a person's time is given over to religious contemplation. I do not regard this as mental illness, but rather a kind of euphoria, an externalising of their intense spiritual feelings. The majority of claimants I have studied believe their visions to be of the Virgin Mary. Male figures – that of Jesus Christ himself or saints – are not as common now as in earlier times, when the Church was being established. But visions are still occurring and can have a problematic effect upon families and communities. The Church cannot ignore them. My job is to ascertain which of these experiences are *real*. I was chosen for this task perhaps because I am a sceptic. I don't believe any of them are real, but I am good at investigating, enjoy the work, and am able to appear empathetic to the claimants. In their view, after all, what they've experienced is absolutely real. Very few deliberately fabricate these things.

*

After our refreshments, I asked Mai to show me the place where she'd seen the 'saint'. I hadn't yet revealed to the girl that there was no 'Saint Galar' in any hagiographical list to my knowledge, and after all the years I'd been employed by the Holy Office, I knew the name of just about every canonised individual in history.

A garden containing a chicken run led to a copse beyond a sagging wood and wire fence: beeches and oaks mainly, although I noticed some smaller growths of holly and hawthorn. There was a worn track through the undergrowth, with a tiny stream beside it, and a faint smell in the air of decay or perhaps excrement. The stream looked seasonal to me; it was barely present at this time of the year.

We reached the pool, which was bigger than I had imagined, its waters very dark. There was a rock wall overhung with shrubs on its western side, which was where – so Mai told me – the spring bubbled up from beneath the earth. A larger stream flowed away from the copse across the hills, stronger than the brook through the trees. Mai explained that her saint appeared upon a ledge in the rock above the pool. She did not move from this location, nor speak aloud. 'I hear her inside,' Mai said. She looked at the small-faced watch on her left arm. 'I'm sorry. I have to go. It's nearly time for Mass. It's Saint Galar's day tomorrow. This is her eve.'

'She told you that?'

'Yes.'

There were no saints that resembled Mai's description of Galar who had a feast day on the first of August.

*

I returned to Llanelyn below the hill and took my evening meal in the White Dragon, a small hotel that served also as the local pub, where I had reserved a room. Afterwards, I wrote up my notes neatly. Two things in particular interested me about this case. First, the fact the visions revolved around what appeared to be a fictional saint. 'Saint Galar', with her association with sorrow, had correspondences with 'Our Lady of Sorrows', an aspect of the Virgin Mary, but Mai Davies had been emphatic Galar was a different person entirely. Second, the healings. I would need to speak to the families concerned. I decided not to visit the parish priest until the following day, but would certainly consult with him before calling on the Evanses and Morgans.

The local church was dedicated to St Helen, a Welsh woman of high birth, canonised for founding churches in the country during the fourth century. Her name is an anglicised version of Elen, said by some scholars to be a Christianised reflection of an older, pagan deity. There was both an historical Elen and a literary one – she is mentioned in the book of Welsh folklore, *The Mabinogion*. But I could make no immediate link between her and Mai's vision of 'Saint Galar'. Llanelyn translates roughly as the Parish of Elen.

Father Brynn received me in the parochial house mid-morning, a dark-haired man in his late thirties, who clearly took good care of himself. He appeared sceptical about Mai Davies' visions. 'The Church has taken the place of the dead father for her,' he said ponderously. We sat drinking tea and smoking cigarettes in the garden of his house, in the shade of a modest orchard because the day was heating up fiercely. 'Mai's always been a serious type of girl,' Brynn said. 'Very devout, even at an early age. Evelyn, on the other hand . . .' He laughed, flicked ash onto the roughly mown grass. 'Well, she shows her face in church but only till Mai's old enough to go everywhere by herself. The mother's attendance has always been of the weddings and funerals kind.'

'You think then that Mai's visions are merely hallucinations?'

'Yes, but . . .' He looked at me warily. 'Nothing too serious. She'll grow out of it. Too much imagination. Children have make-believe friends and such, don't they?'

Not usually saints, I thought.

'What are your thoughts on the healings Mai's supposed to have accomplished?'

'Coincidence,' he answered, shrugging. 'And people wanting to believe. Huw's injury was old, perhaps a memory of pain, and what Mai did helped him believe God had cured it.' He looked faintly embarrassed and added hurriedly, 'God *can* heal, of course, and sometimes through unusual methods, but in this case . . .' He shrugged. 'I couldn't see it. As for the little girl, she was under the doctor, so who saved her? Mai with a touch, or the doctor with his medicine, or indeed the prayers of her parents?'

'Some might say a combination of all three.'

'Everything is for a reason, as we know,' said Father Brynn. 'I'd very much like to believe that Mai Davies can work miracles, but my instincts say no. She's an odd child, who's always been that way. If I were Bronwen, I'd have her at the doctors now, not . . . well, I know you have to investigate these things when there's an official report.'

'You didn't report it?'

'I was obliged to report to the Bishop. Someone contacted me anonymously and insisted upon it. Bronwen and I decided we had no alternative.'

'The mother believes, then.'

'It's her daughter. If we *have* to do something, rather than let the poor child grow out of it, we'd be wiser to care for her mind, in my opinion, rather than making a fuss of it or subjecting her to upsetting situations that might make things worse.'

I grinned. 'Mai is *not* being interrogated by the Inquisition, you know.'

Brynn laughed. 'But isn't that what you are?'

I shook my head. 'We are *modern* now. I'm not seeking heresy, if that's what you think. The Office now seeks only to shine the light of truth upon cases like this, where the claims might be dubious. I don't carry thumb screws.'

Again, Brynn laughed. 'In this job, sometimes I wish *I* had them.'

We sipped our tea in silence for some moments, then I put down my cup. 'You must know there is no Saint Galar. Why would Mai come up with the idea of a saint at that pool? I'd like to hear your thoughts on that.'

'The pool has folklore associated with it,' Brynn said. 'It's said that in centuries past people would take dead children to be blessed there before burial. Perhaps that's why it's a well of sorrows. Many mourned there.'

'And yet Mai sees an entity who makes her feel happy. That's a strange contradiction.'

Brynn shook his head. 'I don't think so. There probably isn't a well or spring in the whole country that isn't regarded as sacred in some way – such things linger from olden times. Mai no doubt heard the stories and she has such a spring in her back garden. Children are imaginative, and why should she invent something frightening? No, to my mind, a girl is more likely to dream up a lady in a long dress who's beautiful and kind.'

'Such as fairytale princesses,' I said. 'But this isn't a princess. From the child's description, what she's seen is more like the Virgin Mary, yet she's invented a personality for it.'

Brynn shrugged. 'She probably *has* mixed her invention up with what she knows of the Holy Mother. That's all there is to it. I don't think there's much of a mystery here.'

*

Father Brynn came with me to visit the recipients of Mai's healing, saying that they would feel more comfortable if he was there. I didn't disagree. Huw Evans was at work but we were able to interview him in his lunch hour, after Brynn had a word with his supervisor. Huw was a man in his forties, with a wife and three children, and a regular job, who did not appear to be a credulous sort of person. Brynn had told me the Evanses attended church on Sundays but were otherwise not overly devout. We took Huw to a pub where he might get some lunch – a luxury small freedom for him on a working day – and here he showed me his damaged hand. I couldn't stop myself flinching. More accurately, he showed me what was *left* of his hand, this disfigured two-fingered *claw*, far worse than Father Brynn had implied. Turning it before him, Huw said, 'I don't care what others say. When that girl put her light into me, she snuffed out the pain. I'd lived with it for nigh on eight years. Strong medicine could barely touch it. Now it doesn't hurt at all.'

'How did this healing come about?' I enquired. 'Did you ask for it?'

'No, she just passed me in the High Street one Saturday after-noon, and caught hold of my arm to stop me. She said, "Let me see your hand". Well, I thought she was just curious about it, being cheeky even, but for the look on her face . . . I let her touch me.'

'What did you see or feel?'

'I felt warmth,' Huw said. 'What I saw . . . ?' He stuck out his lower lip and shook his head. 'I thought I saw a radiance like the summer sun. But afterwards, it was like the memory of a memory . . . Can't explain it.'

'Was there any reason she picked you in particular?' I asked. 'I mean, rather than some other person in pain or who was ill. We can only suppose there were many like that on a Saturday after-noon in town.'

Huw stared at me through the pub's smoky air, skeins of it made almost solid by the sunlight coming through the window behind him. 'I've no idea. I wondered about it, of course I did, but no . . . I was just there at the right moment, I suppose.'

'What did your doctor say? I assume you went to him.'

'He said I'd got better,' Huw said stonily, and took a long drink of his pint.

*

The Morgans lived in a newly converted old cottage on the edge of town. Brynn drove us there in his car, having telephoned Marie Morgan in advance so she expected us. She answered the door quickly, a baby balanced on her hip. After the introductions, she took us to her sitting room, where we had to wait for the inevitable cup of tea. The house was neat and clean and furnished fairly expensively.

Once we were sitting with our refreshments, Marie told me details of herself: thirty-two, a housewife. Her husband Joe had a good job as a car salesman in a nearby town. Neither of them was Catholic or even a church-goer. They had lived in the village for three-and-a-half years, so would no doubt be regarded as newcomers for at least another twenty. 'I know you're here about Mai Davies,' she said, 'and I expect you want to prove she's lying or something. But I know what I saw, and I'm not a stupid person.'

'What did you see?' I asked gently. 'And where did this happen?'

Marie directed a misty gaze at her daughter, who was now playing on the floor with coloured bricks. 'Mai just knocked on my door,' she said. 'It was evening, a Wednesday. Lizzie was so ill we thought . . .' Marie couldn't prevent tears welling at the memory. 'Well, it was perhaps an hour before she would go to hospital. Then there was this skinny girl at the door saying she'd come to see Lizzie, that she could help.' Marie ran her hands through her well-cut, dark hair. 'To this day I don't know why I didn't question it more. I just let her in, like I was half asleep. She walked upstairs, went straight to Lizzie's room. By the time I got there, she had her hands on my baby . . . The room . . . I can't describe it, but *something* was there. I just fell to my knees on the floor and put my hands together. All I could say was "thank you, thank you". I wasn't thanking Mai either.' She uttered a shaky laugh. 'Now you'll think I'm crazy.'

I shook my head. 'Not at all. I'm simply here to find out what happened. How long ago was this?'

'Oh, maybe two months now. The doctors were astounded. Lizzie didn't have to go to hospital. Her fever fell . . . she was just the same as she was before. But they say that can happen with childhood illnesses and that the treatment she was on just took effect. I don't believe that, though. I know what I saw, what I felt.'

'Thank you, Mrs Morgan. I appreciate you giving us your time.'

'Mai's not in trouble over this, is she?' Marie asked, her glance flicking from me to Brynn and back again.

'No, please don't worry about that. It's simply that she claims her *ability* comes from a saint, so the Church has to investigate the matter.'

'It can come from Mickey Mouse for all I care,' Marie retorted. 'She saved Lizzie's life.'

*

'They sound pretty convincing, don't they?' Father Brynn said as we drove away. We both wound down our windows because the air was so hot; it was difficult to breathe. 'Marie Morgan and Huw Evans believe they experienced miracles.'

'Yet you don't.'

'What do you think about it all?'

I drew in my breath. 'Well, I don't doubt they believe Mai helped them. Coincidence? The doctors would say that. In Marie Morgan's case, she was desperate and, like she said, if Mickey Mouse had turned up saying he could heal Lizzie, she'd have let him in. And maybe Huw Evans was desperate too, in a different way. So therefore they believed, and somehow their minds and bodies used that belief to effect cures, although it's more likely in Huw's case than in a baby's, who lacked the faculties to analyse what was happening around her. Perhaps it was due to a special kind of mother and baby connection, but that's beyond my field.'

'So will you talk to the doctors, or are you ready to write up your conclusions?'

'I will write up what I've witnessed and heard,' I said. 'It's not my job to provide conclusions.'

'Careful answer. Where do you want dropping off?'

'Just at the Dragon. I'm going to visit the Davieses again. I'll take a walk up the hill.'

'In this heat?' Brynn laughed. 'Now who sounds mad?'

We drove past the church. Branches from an immense and ancient yew behind the graveyard wall draped, as if exhausted from heat, over the dedication board, partly obscuring it, so that it appeared the dedication was to Elen not Helen. For some reason, this made me shiver, but what kind of shiver that was I couldn't honestly tell.

*

By the time I made the climb once more, it was late afternoon. As I followed the path I considered that Brynn had been right; it was far too hot for such exertions and I should have waited until later when it was cooler. My head began to ache and it was almost painful to look around the landscape, which seemed to shimmer and undulate as if invisible waves coursed through it. I took off my jacket and rolled up my shirtsleeves. The hills swept away from me, from green at my feet to a lavender haze in the distance. The mournful bleat of sheep echoed about me. There were no other people around. I realised how alone I was. The village far below was a glisten of shining windows, mica gleaming from walls. It seemed unbelievably distant, as if in another, abandoned world.

I am not a fanciful individual, but at that moment I became aware of what I can only describe as a vast *sentience*. I remembered what my mother used to say to me as a child, 'At Lammas, ghosts walk at midday.' I used to love hearing that, giggling with delicious terror at the thought of the bright summer landscape infested with phantoms. Now I felt a little of that same fear: primal, inexplicable, gut-deep. Lammas, the first of the harvest festivals, is of course the Christian name for this time, being yet another holy day tacked on to earlier pagan celebrations. It was – and often still is – observed by farming communities, as thanks for a successful harvest, but for some it goes deeper than that. The land is alive to them, with its own intelligence: a personality to be appeased. Without its cooperation people would starve. And now I felt some vast, muscular yet invisible presence undulating through and over the land. I fancied I could even see it, an intense shimmer of heat, coming like the thresh of ocean waves upon me, up the hill, blaring with unheard trumpets and victorious cries. Then it passed through my flesh and for a brief instant I felt the most incredible joy – no, beyond joy, *ecstasy*. Then it was gone, as swiftly as it had come. The heat? My imagination? What strange tricks the mind can play, coupled with an ancient memory.

*

Mai was in the garden of the cottage, sitting next to a woman I took to be her mother, who was doing some mending, a sewing basket at her feet. When she saw me she remarked, without introduction or preamble, on how red I was and sent Mai to fetch me some lemonade. I sat in the shade of an apple tree, panting, and fanning my face with my hat. Bronwen was silent, concentrating on her work, apparently comfortable with the lack of conversation between us. She was a strong-looking woman with thick black hair, which was iced with the faintest threads of grey. The heat was becoming increasingly uncomfortable; even sitting down I still felt breathless, light-headed.

When the girl returned, and had sat down on the grass before me, I asked if we could continue our conversation from before.

'Of course,' Mai said. 'What else do you want to know?'

'Well,' I began, 'there isn't a saint called Galar known by the Church, and no saint like how you described her who has a festival today . . .'

Mai interrupted me in a shocked voice. 'I didn't make her up!'

I raised my hands to placate her, noticed a sharp glance in my direction from the mother. 'I'm not saying you did, but what do you know about her?'

Mai regarded me carefully for some moments. 'She's very old and has lived for ever and ever at the spring.'

Bronwen paused in her sewing. 'She was once joy but now she is sorrow, for some things are fading away.'

My head was pulsing with pain and I held the lemonade glass to my face before I took a swig of the contents. It was warm and the liquid itself was hardly quenching, being sickly sweet. I wished Mai had brought me water. 'What things?'

Bronwen looked around, at the copse behind the garden, the sky. 'The old ways. She doesn't like modern things, like cars, I suppose, and radios, and things like that. Neither do we.'

'And churches?' I asked crisply. The conversation was now between Bronwen and myself; Mai had fallen silent.

Bronwen's dark eyes were cold. 'What do you mean?'

I rubbed my neck, pulling my shirt collar away from my skin. 'I mean, is this Galar older than the church, say St Helen's in the village?' I looked at Mai, who was regarding me curiously and spoke to her directly. 'You do know that Helen was once Elen, a lady of ancient Wales, don't you?'

Mai nodded. 'We learned that at Sunday school.'

'Well, before that, she was a goddess in folklore. Are there people who perhaps still see Helen as that? Were you ever told that?'

Mai's mouth dropped open a little and she stared at me, as if horrified. 'You want to make her bad!' she cried abruptly. 'You don't want her to be part of God, because she's not in a book or written down, but everything *is* part of God, you stupid man!'

'Mai!' I cringed at her ferocity, which had seemed to come out of nowhere.

Bronwen did not chastise her daughter for insulting me, which was equally insulting.

'Go away!' Mai scrambled to her feet and pointed at me. The air shimmered with heat all around her. My vision was blurred, my head pounding. Mai pointed at me with a stiff arm, her hair over her eyes. I couldn't dispel the absurd idea that she was some ancient, vengeful priestess, somehow manifesting in the body of a girl. 'You're not wanted,' Mai hissed. 'None of us want you here. We don't need to be *investigated*.' With these words, she turned and ran into the house, slamming the back door behind her.

I felt as if the girl had slapped me.

Bronwen picked up her sewing again, her fingers moving deftly. 'People have always known Mai is different, sees things differently,' she said in a soft voice. 'Mr Coombe, our ways are not your ways, or anybody else's. If Mai sees the lady as a saint, and calls her Galar after the well, it doesn't matter. She's Helen, Elen, or merely the light of the land. I think you've learned all you can. You should go now.'

'I'm sorry if I've caused offence,' I said, 'but . . .'

Clearly, Bronwen didn't want to hear anything further I might have to say. 'You should go. You don't look well.'

A breeze fretted the foliage around us, then fell just as suddenly.

I stood up. The darkness of the copse nearby was watchful. I was being observed and what – or who – looked on was not benign. I fancied I could almost see it in the shapes created by the shadows between the branches and leaves, the shiver of the water; a vague figure, a face, eyes that were spots of sunshine. My flesh shrank against my bones and I turned my back on whatever loomed over me and poured the sticky lemonade onto the grass. A libation? A miserable attempt at appeasement? It felt the right thing to do. What had I stumbled on here? If there was an unseen wave approaching me now, it was one of repulsion; not sorrow, not joy. Mai's words echoed in my head: *Get out of here!* In fact, I had no choice.

I walked around the side of the house and back onto the path. I could barely see. Was this heat-stroke? The village seemed so far below, and all around me the pulsing landscape, the shimmer on the hillsides, pushing me away.

*

Somehow – and I can't remember all of that painful walk back down the hill – I reached Llanelyn and fetched my luggage from the inn. All I wanted was to get home, to lie down, recover. As I fumbled with my wallet to pay my bill, I remembered an old legend of a ferocious goddess: because she knew how to injure, her devotees believed she must also know how to heal. Could this not work also in reverse? This was superstition creeping up on me, the power of suggestion. How fragile is the human mind? Are we not all children at heart, frightened by the darkness, all that we do not know?

They were watching me as I stood waiting for the bus near the church. Mothers with children, elderly folk, people going about their business at the tail end of the sweltering day. Of course, news would have got around about me asking questions in the village the day before, but I knew it was more than simple resentment of my investigation that burned behind their eyes. I could feel it, as if the vast sentience of the hillside had followed me down the path and settled over the village and its inhabitants in a caul of ringing heat, looking out through every pair of eyes. Father Brynn was by the church door, but he did not come to me. He simply watched, as the others did. I knew they were all waiting for me to leave, urging it. And I was eager to do so. I did not want to make them feel threatened by my presence. Who knows how far they'd go? I would report what I'd seen and witnessed, what Father Brynn wanted me to believe. An imaginative young girl at the brink of womanhood. Credulous people who believed they'd been healed.

Superstitions that still live in the heart of the countryside, perhaps made real in mind by an older faith.

*

Ill health prevents me from further investigation at present. What I experienced and saw – and suspected – is certainly at odds with Christian teaching, of course, but to me the book is closed on this case, even if I suspect I read only half of it. The old ways have not died out completely, but it is my belief that when a community respects God and the Church, whatever else they might believe, they should be left to their own devices. Delusion it may be, but harmless, if we let them alone. This is what I experienced in the village of Llanelyn in the summer of 1959.

Ω

Sometimes in history the Church has taken up arms against heresy and 'false beliefs', through the Inquisition, through Crusades, through other means that have caused pain and taken lives. And sometimes it has quietly made accommodation with other beliefs, building a chapel at an ancient holy site, or adapting a local goddess into a Christian saint, and no one has been harmed by it.

It has been said that the difference between a miracle and magic is that one is done in the name of God and the other in the name of the gods.

This investigation was clearly troubling to Bartholomew Coombe. To do his job he should have continued his enquiry, but instead he closed the case. In doing so was he shirking his responsibility to the Church? Or was he perhaps showing wisdom in not probing further, in leaving well, so to speak, alone?

If so, in such a case his report would soundlessly vanish into the Vatican Vaults.

1965

In 1965 the Catalan surrealist artist Salvador Dalí produced an unusual painting entitled La Gare de Perpignan – Perpignan Station. *Dalí claimed that this railway station in the Languedoc, southern France, was 'the centre of the universe', and that he had experienced a vision of 'cosmogenic ecstasy' there in 1963.*

The painting is on open display in the Museum Ludwig in Cologne; we would not have expected to find references to it hidden away in the Vatican Vaults. Yet a file enigmatically labelled 'unresolved' held a number of documents relating not only to Dalí's experience, which led to his painting, but to previous unusual experiences going back centuries. The documents are fragmentary, and from the marginal notes in different hands appear to have been drawn together, edited, summarised and commented on by more than one archivist over the years, the final compilation being shortly after Dalí painted Perpignan Station.

The Mountain Wind

Patrice Chaplin

The file labelled 'unresolved' began with several disparate references on separate sheets, with comments linking them.

A page dated 1750 described Hungarians in the seventeenth and eighteenth centuries visiting a site, known as a portal, in order to restore themselves.

When questioned by Vatican agents sent to investigate this strange practice they claimed this was a precise point of intense energy which promoted well-being. A scrawled marginal note read: 'That was the excuse they gave.'

It was understood that these practices had originated in medieval times and that there were several sites, not just one as the Hungarians claimed. The thinking of the Church at that time was not concerned with portals and this activity was finally deemed harmless as no rituals or black magic had been observed as had originally been expected.

Further notes at the end of the eighteenth century mentioned a member of the powerful Habsburg dynasty seeking a portal on the peak of Mount Canigou in the Pyrenees mountain range between France and Spain.

An earlier account discovered in the vaults, and added to this file, related to ecclesiastical involvement in the thirteenth century. It told of when 'a being of light came through this portal aperture' and said it had been 'walking the earth since before the construction of the first pyramid'.

It said its purpose was to heal and help man to become spiritually evolved and to raise awareness of other previous divinities.

'This being seemed to be made of shards of light,' one observer said. Too many witnessed its appearance for the Church to act without due consideration.

King Jaime I of Aragon heard of this apparition, and that many had been healed of suffering by its laying on of hands.

The being of light had made a prophecy that a painting featuring a bright cross would come into existence and show something termed 'a station' swept by a mountain wind, and it would reveal the veracity of the portal.

The Vatican decided this 'stranger' could not be claimed by the Church as a miracle or a saint and must be condemned as a heretic for the reference to other gods. Knowledge of its existence must be suppressed.

But legends in the region surrounding the portal supported the stranger's testimony. It was said that during an almighty storm, when it was believed the sun would collide with the earth, a being of light had crashed to the valley between the mountains near Canigou 3,000 years before Christ and had been laid on a stone cradle, a dark blue, smooth meteorite, said still to be in existence. The cradle was reported to have emerged from the portal and had nurtured this being of light; knowledge of the portal's healing tradition was handed down orally through the ages. It was further claimed that visitors to this place had inadvertently stepped into another reality, another time, and in fear had recounted their experience to the nearest priest. However, it was concluded that these unfortunate travellers were merely drunk.

The discovery of this document and the sudden interest of the Habsburgs in the late eighteenth century prompted the Vatican to send its agents to look into the portal affair. A draft report, supported by accounts from witnesses, confirmed that a portal was said to exist; it was described as a gap in the atmosphere just above the earth from which men could leave the planet and material from space could enter.

There were earlier descriptions of this phenomenon, as far back as ancient Egypt. The seventeenth-century artist Poussin was said to be a seeker of these other existences and the portal secret was thought to be coded into some of his works.

*

An early nineteenth-century archivist decided the matter had been of interest only to the Jews of Spain. Medieval rabbinic scholars and Cabbalists of Girona were thought to have used secret practices to journey to and from what appeared to be a portal in Catalonia, and to leave the dimensions that make up the Universe 'as we know it'. After the expulsion of the Jews from Spain in 1492 there were no further accounts of Cabbalistic practices relating to a portal.

The Vatican for some time checked for hearsay in other European mountainous areas, without result. Did this portal possibility occur only in Hungary and north-eastern Spain? For the Spanish, survival was now paramount; the people, ravaged by plague and wars with France, were more concerned with working the land, baking bread and trading in minerals.

The directive from the Vatican was to keep the matter from spreading, and to refute any further portal claims. No more was heard on the subject for a few decades.

*

The files were brought out from the Vaults again because of a document found in the possession of an Englishman, George Borrow, who worked for the British and Foreign Bible Society in London.

In the late 1830s he travelled across Spain on horseback, bringing the New Testament to the Spanish. A convivial man, he met many travellers with stories to share over a tavern dinner at night, and later wrote of his journeys.

News reached the Vatican that the Bible-seller's document contained evidence of a group of men with scientific leanings investigating a portal in the Pyrenees.

They had determined the precise location of the aperture and measured its velocity, the power of its magnetic field and its structure using a handmade purpose-built device.

The energy of the portal was strong enough to harm the average person, yet a small distance away, beyond the activity of the portal, the energy charge dropped substantially and could be tolerated by most people.

The Vatican gave instructions for George Borrow to be held in prison in Madrid on an unrelated charge and share his confinement with spies who would encourage him to talk of his findings.

Officially questioned later, he truthfully answered that a man he met on his many travels gave him the document for safe-keeping. The man had witnessed extraordinary happenings at the portal site and the energy from the ground had made his legs and feet vibrate until the pain was unbearable.

This document was added to the Vatican file. It included a paragraph explaining that the human body did not enter the portal, only the conscious thinking process held by the 'etheric body', a term George Borrow believed to mean the sheath that after death held the subtle body on its return to God.

He himself had not been present as the notorious mountain wind had reached over 160 kilometres an hour, making it impossible to climb.

George Borrow, because he was English and had many supporters in Spain, had to be freed. The scientific group was never found, and eventually the file was closed and placed back in the Vaults.

After the Borrow incident the Vatican sent their own investigator to the portal site. He searched for changes in atmosphere among the stones and rubble at the peak. He looked for signs of instability above the tree line. But he found nothing. The portal was dismissed as hearsay.

The only other unusual occurrence was that a part of the text in the files relating to the being of light and his destruction had been erased; it was unclear who had given the order.

*

In the 1930s a new file was started relating to Hitler's interest in the mystery of Mount Canigou, and a visit made by Himmler to try to locate a passage through space called a gateway. Otto Rahn, the German Grail writer, was also mentioned.

Before Christ the Phoenicians had landed on the Spanish coast and crossed to Mount Canigou. Were they seeking the portal, or minerals?

*

The final and by far the largest file concerned Salvador Dalí, the controversial artist. He was born near Figueras in north-east Spain in the path of the mountain wind from Canigou; it was in his blood.

Word had reached the Vatican that in 1963 this master of the surreal, while sending off his paintings from Perpignan Station on the French border, had by chance literally fallen into a secret that the Vatican had held for centuries – a secret which they now feared could change reality, destroy belief and with it, to some degree, the power of the Church.

An outpouring of metaphysical arguments against organised religion, pernicious rumours of a sacred bloodline, the advance of the female into a male-dominated belief system and the uncovering of papal conspiracies hounded the Vatican daily, and portals were now very much present in the Church's thinking.

Perpignan Station, in the shadow of Mount Canigou, was where Dalí personally sent off his paintings to America as he did not trust the Spanish postal system.

That this flamboyant iconic mystic should, on one of these excursions, be drawn into a rare energy, supposedly from the mountain, and fall through a portal into another reality altogether – well, this would have to happen to him. That he would then, without a second thought, tell the world – of this, the Vatican had no doubt.

The meeting in Rome to decide how the matter should be suppressed was unusually divided. Many present did not believe in the portal, even when it was vaguely remembered that a being of light had appeared through such a gap in contradiction to the Church's doctrines.

It was agreed that Dalí had experienced some sort of mystical awakening, and that there was a challenge to Church teaching.

The Vatican instructed agents to suppress Dalí's accounts, whether of the spoken word, the written word or testimony in medical documents (it was stated he was now in shock).

But it wasn't the word the Vatican had to fear: it was a painting. Dalí would recount the unrecountable in the manner he knew best – and the information was there for the world to see in his new work *Perpignan Station*.

Unlike the well-being-seeking Hungarians, the wraith from the portal, Dalí was too celebrated to suppress. He had no need of bribes, he seemed beyond threats, and he had an instinctive distrust of Jesuits.

Dalí had returned from the experience in an unusual state, even for him. The Universe had opened up and he was flying back in time. There was only one solution: paint it. His announcement speech – 'Perpignan Station is the centre of the Universe and no one knows it' – mystified many people, though not the Vatican.

The esteemed Dr Vila Carerras, a senior security officer at the Vatican, called a crisis meeting to consider how much influence Dalí had. He announced his belief that people would assume Dalí was just extending his flaunting of the bizarre through storytelling because his paintings were not doing it for him any more. But then Dr Carerras began to show his irritation.

'Who cares what *he* thinks and does? It is others we have to watch – remember the one or two who have always been against us?

'Dalí's scratchings are going to make those people remember what they once heard, about a figure issuing from an invisible passage, who had a story to tell, and the unfortunate cover-up that followed,' he said.

'What price to cover this up?' he demanded. 'We must put out the story that Dalí is depressed, hallucinating. I don't have any time for this show-off. He can't even paint clocks properly. His watches are misshapen. Time? You won't find it in these crazy pictures! Only Dalí could fall into what has been hidden for all these years. Get someone to deal with this . . . Warn the painter his work is sacrilege and frighten him. And find the file of the English Bible-seller in case there is more we need to know. All this was safe here for centuries – it takes this dislikeable show-off to shake off the dust.'

Dr Carerras realised as he spoke that he was staring at a reproduction of the railway station painting. A man was sliding in a fall along the track and the train behind him was catching up; on either side were platforms with figures, unaware, coming forward but at the same time going back in history . . .

He saw the yellow Maltese Cross emanating from behind the falling man, its rays brightening up the foreground.

Then he remembered the prediction of the portal wraith, from that earlier unhappy time.

Those present would later claim that it was while looking at the reproduction of Dalí's painting, *Perpignan Station*, that Dr Carerras appeared to pass through some physical change. One commented that this stern man seemed to soften and even become compassionate.

The security chief explained his revelation to the group, and why it now caused him to reverse his decision to silence the artist. Maybe Dalí had had a revolutionary experience on that platform and been sucked into the illusive gap of a portal structure, which should not exist, and for ever afterwards it would change his inner existence.

Not without pity he concluded, 'Let's just say he fell forward on the station, blown by the mountain wind.'

Ω

The inclusion in the files of what is clearly part of a verbatim transcript from a Vatican security meeting (the officer's name has been changed for anonymity) adds credence to the Vatican's concern not just about Dalí's painting Perpignan Station, *but the whole issue of portals.*

The evidence, such as it is, is scattered over several centuries: fragmentary accounts, anecdotes, reports of folk beliefs. Whether such portals might actually exist is beyond the remit of this committee, but the Vatican appears to have given them serious attention for some centuries.

1970 (1770)

There have long been stories about Gregorio Allegri's Miserere, *a setting of Psalm 51 composed in the 1630s. It must only be performed in the Sistine Chapel in the Vatican; Pope Urban VIII decreed that it was forbidden to remove it from the Vatican or to transcribe it on pain of excommunication; the young Mozart heard it once and wrote a perfect transcription from memory.*

The following documents found in a file marked Allegri's Miserere *can only add further to the mythology of this famous piece of music. We begin with the eighteenth-century records.*

Miserere

Sarah Ash

Rome, April 1770

One by one the candle flames were extinguished in the Sistine Chapel as the last sombre cadences of the *Tenebrae* responses echoed around the shadowed vault. The darkening air was filled with the bitter, burning smoke of snuffed wicks. And then, out of the shadows, came the first chanted notes of Allegri's famed *Miserere*:

'*Miserere mei, Deus. Have mercy upon me, O God . . .*'

The boy shivered as he stood beside his father in the crush of worshippers. *Is this what it feels like to die . . . ? The sounds of every-day life gradually ebbing away as the light fades to darkness . . .*

The voices of the papal choir floated through the air, the unearthly, ethereal voices of the celebrated *castrati* like a distant promise of divine forgiveness.

His own voice was breaking. He knew what it meant to become a man. *What must it be like to be one of those singers and lose that essential part of yourself? To choose to keep the voice of a young boy, to delight audiences with that unique angelic sound, but to give up any possibility of enjoying carnal pleasures?* Or were the rumours he had heard true . . . that in spite of their mutilation, some of the most celebrated *castrati* of the operatic stage were still capable of satisfying their adoring female admirers?

He felt a sudden flush of heat suffuse his whole body. *What am I doing, thinking such impure thoughts in this holiest of holy places?* He glanced sidelong at his father Leopold, certain that he must have noticed . . . but his father's eyes were half-closed as he listened, concentrating on the music.

And then the exquisitely sensuous wash of voices swelled and enveloped the boy as well, bearing him away to a place where all earthly concerns were no longer relevant.

When it was over, they merged into the crowd of the faithful who were filing silently out of the chapel into the rain-swept piazza. When the boy dared to glance up at the faces of the other worshippers, he saw a glazed look in their eyes, many stumbling away with strange, enlightened expressions, as if they had looked on hidden wonders and experienced some life-changing revelation.

'But lo, Thou requirest truth in the inward parts: and shalt make me to understand wisdom secretly,' he heard an elegantly dressed and bewigged man whisper in Latin, crossing himself.

'Thou shalt wash me,' a veiled woman murmured under her breath, 'and I shall be whiter than snow.'

Ahead of him in the throng, one figure paused to adjust the hood of his cloak against the rain. The face beneath, glimpsed for the briefest of seconds, was as beautiful as one of the painted angels in the chapel: a youth, not much older than he, with curling hair of a light chestnut brown. The boy felt his breath stop as the youth's intense, grey-eyed gaze caught his own . . .

Has he recognised me? Is he a music student too?

The boy was half expecting to be greeted, even asked for an autograph . . . but the youth merely smiled, shook his head, and turned away, melting into the crowd.

'Did you see—?' he began, turning to his father.

But his father seemed as distracted as the other congregants. 'It's almost as if that music has the power to shrive souls,' he was saying and the boy heard the wonder in his voice. 'No wonder His Holiness wants to keep it a secret.'

*

The boy dipped the nib into the ink again and again, desperate to capture on paper the exquisite sounds he had just experienced, trying not to omit a single note as he swiftly transcribed the notes of the Vatican's *Miserere*.

A shadow fell across the manuscript paper; distracted, he glanced up to see his father watching him.

'I know it's forbidden,' the boy said, 'but I just wanted to be able to write it down so that I could study it for myself. I want to understand exactly how the composer made those vocal lines work together to produce that particular effect. That's all. It's not as if we're going to sell the score, are we? *Are we*, Father?' he repeated sternly, remembering what a shrewd entrepreneur his father was, always looking out for a way to make a profit as they travelled from concert to concert.

'Some would argue that it's a shame to keep such a beautiful and improving work from being heard outside the Vatican,' Leopold said.

'And yet it's the technique of the Vatican singers that creates its unique beauty,' the boy said. 'Look,' and he pointed with the feathery end of his quill to the passage he had just painstakingly transcribed from memory. 'These passages of free improvisation, the *abbellimenti*, display such extraordinary artistry. It's unique. This secret art must have been passed down from singer to singer over the centuries.'

His father leaned forward to look at the score. For a moment he did not respond. Then he said, 'Any *kapellmeister* in Christendom would give his eye teeth for this, Wolfgang. No one can match your ear and musical memory. You've managed to transcribe the untranscribable.' He put his hand on his son's shoulder. 'But this is enough to get you excommunicated. This skill is the Vatican's secret art and if we were to publish it—'

'I just wanted to learn how it works,' the boy protested.

'We're off to Naples tomorrow,' Leopold said, removing his hand. 'We must hide that manuscript from inquisitive eyes. Slip it inside that new string quartet you've been working on in case the customs search our luggage . . .'

*

Naples, May 1770

The boy played the final cadence of the rondo with a flourish and waited for the applause to start before rising to his feet to acknowledge the enthusiastic response of Neapolitan society. One hand resting on the lid of the fortepiano, the other on the expensive lacy ruffle over his heart, he bowed low.

He could not help noticing that, behind the brightly dressed members of the audience (the Neapolitans seemed to favour a warm palette of colours for their brocaded jackets and silk dresses that reflected the sunny streets outside), stood one listener garbed in sober black who was not applauding. The boy caught his eye for a second and felt – as he turned back to the keyboard to give an encore – as if he had been assessed by that keen, probing glance and somehow been found wanting.

Who is he? He rattled effortlessly through a merry little minuet and trio he had composed before they left Salzburg that he knew would please his Italian audience, risking an occasional glance from time to time at the unsmiling listener. *Why is he here if my music displeases him so much?*

After the boy had been presented to their host, the English ambassador, several of the ladies insisted on plying him with sweet treats.

'Master Wolfgang, you must try our Neapolitan *gelato*; it's a real taste of heaven!'

While he was enjoying his second dish of the delicious ice cream, he noticed his father deep in conversation with another of the English guests. Beckoned over by Leopold, he bowed politely, hoping that the *gelato* had not left a rim of white around his mouth.

'I would like to present my son, Dr Burney,' said his father.

'So this is the prodigious boy I've heard so much about,' said the Englishman in passable Italian. 'Let me congratulate you, young Wolfgang, on your performance. What are you composing at present? I do hope you will come to give concerts in England soon . . .'

*

They had just stepped down from the carriage at their lodgings when a soberly dressed man emerged from the shadowed doorway and said softly, 'A word with you in private, if you please, *Signori*.' His face was concealed by a broad-brimmed tricorne hat.

The boy glanced uncertainly at his father. Were they being held to ransom? He had heard the rumours about the risks of being kidnapped in Naples . . . and a child prodigy famed in all the courts of Europe might make a desirable target and fetch a handsome sum. But this stranger was well-spoken and even as his father looked at him suspiciously, he held up his hand, revealing, not a pistol but the golden seal of a papal legate.

'You'd better come in.' Leopold opened the door and led the way upstairs. Once in their rooms, he bowed low to the stranger, inviting him to sit on one of the threadbare brocade-upholstered chairs. 'Please excuse these humble surroundings; as musicians, we can't afford anything more luxurious—'

'Can you guess why I've come?' The papal legate's austere expression had not altered.

The boy shook his head, sensing the rising tension in the shabby little parlour.

'You were seen at the *Miserere* in Rome, Master Wolfgang. And as your fame travels before you, His Holiness is most anxious that you are not about to commit an act of transgression.'

How cold his eyes are. 'I . . . I'm sorry; I don't quite follow,' the boy said, shooting a desperate look at his father.

'Let me put this another way; His Holiness, Pope Clement, would like to make you a Knight of the Golden Spur, Wolfgang.'

'Me?' The boy repeated, astonished. His father's mouth had dropped open; for once Leopold was shocked into silence.

'This is a singular honour for one so young,' continued the legate, 'and it should open many doors for you in your chosen career. However,' and the legate paused to gaze piercingly at Leopold, 'such an honour could only be conferred on your son if he is not guilty of even the slightest suspicion of any forbidden activity. Such as passing on the secret art of the Vatican choristers.'

The boy stared at the floorboards, not daring to raise his head. *How does he know? Has my father gone against his word? He promised me he wouldn't sell the transcription.*

'The *Miserere* has a unique and, some might say, unfortunate history among the many works composed for the Papal Chapel. When Pope Urban VIII took the decision not to release it for performance outside the Vatican, he did so for a reason. And now, you must promise on your immortal souls – and kiss my ring to seal that promise – never to reveal a word of what I am about to tell you.'

Wolfgang glanced again at his father – and then saw him drop to one knee before the legate, and press his lips to the golden ring. He swallowed hard. It seemed somehow like an admission of defeat.

And yet I could be the youngest ever to be awarded the Order of the Golden Spur. There was nothing for it but to comply. Yet as Wolfgang brushed the cold metal with his lips, he felt for a moment that he was somehow betraying his artistic principles in letting himself be bribed by the might of the Church of Rome.

'Very well,' said the legate. Close to, the boy noticed how old he looked; his pale skin stretched over his prominent cheekbones like the finest vellum scraped to an almost translucent thinness. 'Every time Allegri's *Miserere* is performed – just once a year in Holy Week – it has, as you witnessed for yourselves, a unique effect upon the congregation. The faithful leave the chapel in a beatific state, cleansed of their sins.'

The boy nodded, remembering the transfigured expressions of the departing members of the congregation. *That moment of transcendence as the choristers' voices intertwined one with another and time seemed to stop ... I felt it too.*

'Hidden within the *Miserere* is a secret sacred sequence of notes based upon the celestial music of the spheres. It is enhanced by the performance of certain *abbellimenti* in certain combinations of voices.'

The boy leaned forward, captivated. 'A secret sacred sequence? But how did Maestro Allegri come across such a thing?'

The legate drew his grey brows together in a forbidding frown. 'In the cruellest way of all. For this exquisite *Miserere* to fulfil its healing, cleansing purpose in Lent, an act of sacrifice is required. You can hear the pain and the regret of such a sacrifice in the sublime beauty of the voices of the *castrati*. But no one involved with performing the work can escape unscathed – and it is the selfless act of the few that enables the many to continue their lives, transformed by what they have experienced.'

There was silence in the little panelled room although outside in the narrow street, the clatter of hoofs and iron carriage wheels, mingling with the cries of the street sellers, seemed louder and more strident than before.

The boy did not dare to meet his father's gaze. The mere fact that the usually talkative Leopold had said nothing alarmed him. *Is it too late? Has he already passed it on without my knowledge? And if it's too late, what act of sacrifice will we have to make?*

'At the time of the first performance – which was by private invitation only – it was noted that there was one member of the congregation present who was not admitted by any of the guards or the Vatican staff. At the conclusion of the service, they were under orders to apprehend the uninvited guest – but he was nowhere to be found. And – tragically – one of the altos fell mortally ill that evening.'

'An uninvited guest?' The boy shivered, even though the room was stiflingly warm. 'What did he look like?'

'Some who saw him said that – beneath his hood – they glimpsed a face as striking as one of Botticelli's angels. One or two even remarked that he looked as if he had stepped down from the one of the chapel frescoes ... But others said that he greatly resembled a young chorister, Amadeo Vitali, a protégé of Gregorio Allegri, who had died of a fever while Allegri was composing the *Miserere*.'

A figure pauses to raise the hood of his cloak against the rain. The face beneath is as beautiful as one of the painted angels in the chapel.

'A ghost?' The hairs on the back of his neck prickled.

'Perhaps,' said the legate smoothly. 'For when the *Miserere* was performed the following year, he was seen again. Again, he evaded the guards and the stewards, simply vanishing into the crowd. And another member of the choir close to Maestro Allegri fell ill and died.'

'The work is accursed?' The boy glanced at his father who had contributed nothing so far to the exchange.

'Accursed – or blessed with unique healing powers when performed in that certain way.' The legate gave a little shrug of the shoulders. 'Superstitious rumours spread like wildfire at the time. Secret rites of exorcism were performed. It would not have done for the Papal Chapel to be reputed to be haunted.'

'But I saw—' began the boy and then fell silent, certain he would not believed.

'Besides, there was no doubt that the *Miserere* itself, when performed by the papal choir in Holy Week, had the transcendent power to bring solace and healing to all those who heard it.'

'Yet at the cost of a life?' Leopold spoke for the first time since the legate had entered their rooms.

'Perhaps you understand now why His Holiness declared that the work must never be performed outside the Vatican – on pain of excommunication.' The legate was staring, unblinking, at Leopold.

Leopold hesitated and then went to the little trunk in which they stored their precious scores when on the road. The boy saw him take out his new String Quartet in G, slide the *Miserere* transcription from inside, and hand it to the legate.

After a swift scan of the first page, the legate looked up at the boy. 'You truly have a God-given gift, Wolfgang. You wrote all this down after a single hearing?'

The boy nodded, wondering apprehensively what the legate would say next.

'Given that you have such an exceptional memory, will you give me your word to "forget" the performance – and all the special *abbellimenti* – that you heard? And never to reproduce them?'

'I give you my word.' The promise came out as a hoarse whisper.

The legate folded the manuscript and slipped it inside his soutane. 'I am glad that we were able to conclude this conversation so satisfactorily.' He took out a letter and handed it to the boy. 'My congratulations. The ceremony will take place in the Vatican in July.'

The letter was a formal invitation to become a Knight of the Order of the Golden Spur. Wolfgang gazed down at the elaborate script, the glossy scarlet of the papal seal.

'We are most honoured,' said his father, making his most obsequious bow as the legate rose to leave.

At the door, the legate turned and said, 'So you saw Amadeo, Wolfgang? Some say that he only appears to those about to die.'

The boy stared at him, aghast.

'But others say that only those blessed with genuine musical talent can see him. He might have been a great composer, had he lived. It is even thought that some of the *abbellimenti* in the

Miserere were his own and that Gregorio Allegri wove them into the score as tribute to his gifted student . . .'

*

Cambridge, February 1970

'Well, James, here's to old times.' Gareth poured us each a glass of the expensive Soave he had ordered and raised his to clink against mine.

I sipped the wine and nodded my appreciation as the Soave diffused 'clean notes of citrus and elderflower' on my palate. 'Good stuff.'

'How long has it been, seven years?' The buzz of conversation in the busy wine bar seemed oppressively loud after the quiet of my college rooms. 'The Stradella Singers have kept me pretty busy.'

'So I've noticed,' I said, concentrating on enjoying the sensation of the chilled acidic sweetness of the wine on my tongue. 'So to what do I owe the honour . . . ?'

'I've got a little challenge for you. You relish a challenge, don't you, James?'

'That depends,' I said warily.

'I can't stay long; we're performing in Ely Cathedral tomorrow night with the Corelli Camerata.'

Studying Gareth over the rim of my empty glass, I was surprised to see how carelessly he let these little revelations slip out.

'Ah, it feels good to be back.' He leaned across to refill my glass.

'I suppose distance must lend enchantment to the view.' The observation came out rather more sourly than I had intended.

'Don't tell me you're falling out of love with collegiate life! You always seemed destined to be a don, even when we were Freshers.' Before I could protest, Gareth carried on, 'And that's why I thought: "James will spend many a happy hour deciphering this little mystery that's come my way."' He reached into his briefcase and slid an A4 folder to me across the table. 'Here,' he said. 'I'd like to know what you make of it; you were always far better than me at the palaeography and transcription stuff, James.' As he did so, I saw him glance around surreptitiously, almost guiltily, as though checking that we were not being watched.

'What's the matter?' I said, amused. 'Anyone would think we were agents of MI6 exchanging secret information. You're not being tailed by Soviet spies, are you?'

He laughed at this but I detected a slight hint of tension in his voice. 'Good grief, no. Whatever gave you that idea? Been reading too much Ian Fleming?'

I took the folder and opened it; inside were sheets of spidery handwritten choral music in a rather poor and indistinct photocopy.

'This is the Allegri *Miserere*. And yet . . . it's different.'

'I knew you were the right man for this job!' Gareth said triumphantly.

'But how did you – ?'

'It seems there are two. The first one, the "official" one we all know with the ethereal high Cs, that's been reworked by several other composers down the years.'

'Didn't that infuriating little prodigy Wolfgang Amadeus notate it from memory after a single hearing in the Sistine Chapel?'

'Mozart, the *wunderkind*?' Gareth said with a wink. 'So we're told by his fond papa, Leopold. And Charles Burney reports it too, after meeting father and son in Italy in 1770, so maybe there's more than a scrap of truth in the story.'

I could not stop myself pointing out, 'It's Burney's 1771 basic version that we use today.' I had recently published an annotated performing score of the Burney original myself. 'With modifications.'

'Remember the old chestnut about Pope Urban VIII threatening to excommunicate anyone who smuggled the Allegri *Miserere* score out of the Vatican?'

'But we always held that to be apocryphal, or, at best, a scholarly misinterpretation of the few existing facts.'

Gareth leaned towards me, a malicious little flame glinting in his eyes. I remembered that look and what it meant: he was about to divulge something scandalous. 'It turns out it may have been true after all. But it refers to the "other" *Miserere*.'

'Do you know why it was suppressed? Is there any contemporary documentary evidence to shine a light on the reasons?' I heard myself asking.

'My contact in Rome is working on that – he says he's found a few diary entries, a letter or two. They don't add up to a complete picture, but he'll send them over, anyway.'

'Just how reliable is this contact?' I was still suspicious; something didn't feel quite right.

'Does it matter? He'll get his money. And the Stradella Singers will be the first choir to sing this lost version in over three hundred years. That's if you can make us a performing copy.'

'But supposing this "contact" of yours is trying to foist a fake onto you? This could all be an elaborate hoax. A prank.'

'That's where you come in, James. I trust your scholarship. I trust that you'd be able to sniff out a fake.'

'But my reputation will be on the line if I – we – have both been deceived.' The prospect of academic disgrace appalled me. 'I could lose my fellowship. I—'

'Steady on, old chap! If you judge that it's bogus – or in any way suspect – we'll just forget about the whole affair. But if it's all kosher, I have an invitation from the Master to give the first performance in the college chapel. There's a first recording rights deal involved as well.'

'You lucky sod.' I heard myself saying, with more bitterness than I'd intended. 'You get all the breaks.' Was it the wine talking? I'd tried for so long to cover up my resentment at the different paths our careers had taken after we graduated.

'Don't worry; you'll get your percentage.'

'Generous of you.'

'Just make sure you get that performing copy ready for us in good time for Holy Week.'

'Holy Week?' I took out my diary and started to count the days; Easter was early this year.

'So here you are, Gareth!' A woman's voice rang out, clear and penetrating, even above the blur of conversation and background music. I looked up to see Wanda coming towards us, elegant in a cobalt blue coat that enhanced the colour of her eyes. It was too late; there was no means of escape. I'd just have to bluff my way through what would, at best, be an awkward reunion.

'James?' She forced her red-glossed lips into a bright smile. 'It must be an age.' She made no effort to lean forward to give me a kiss of greeting; I made no effort to rise.

'You're looking well, Wanda,' I said levelly.

'Did Gareth tell you we're off to Rome on Thursday? To sing in the Vatican.'

'Lucky you.' I could fake a smile too.

'All part of a day's work.'

'We could never have won that BBC award without Wanda's heavenly top Cs,' Gareth said, slipping one arm around her waist and giving her a familiar squeeze. The gesture said quite clearly *Mine*. It was hard not to remember a time when the situation was reversed . . . and the adoring look in those black-lashed blue eyes had rested on me.

'Well, James, this has been fun.' He drained his glass. 'I wish I could stay longer and catch up but we've got a rehearsal in Ely. Busy, busy . . .'

I lifted my glass in an ironic farewell toast as Gareth and Wanda hurried away. The deliciously crisp Soave had lost its bouquet and tasted bitter as vinegar. *Busy, busy . . .* Just like Gareth to be so wrapped up in his own success that it never occurred to him to ask me what I was doing. Or perhaps he just hadn't wanted to humiliate me in front of Wanda by rubbing my nose in my lack of achievement compared to his own meteoric rise.

For a moment I was tempted to leave the folder on the table. Dammit, why did I have to get caught up in Gareth's gilded snares again? He was still so seductively charming and adept at using people to get exactly what he wanted.

And then . . . maybe a touch of the old persuasive charm had rubbed off on me – or my own scholarly curiosity had got the better of me – for I found myself walking back to my rooms down King's Parade over rain-slicked pavements, with the folder still in my hands. In my study, I pushed the pile of essays I was marking to one side on the cluttered desk, switched on the lamp, and sat down to examine the photocopies.

Fragments of a conversation we'd had years ago as undergraduates came back to me. Then it had been just the three of us against the musical establishment: Gareth creating his elite choir, one voice to a part, Wanda, with her pure and treble-like soprano, bringing a brilliant lustre to the vocal ensemble, and me, good old James, reliable James, the all-round accompanist and gofer. It was exactly the right moment, a time when a worldwide interest in forgotten baroque choral music meant that the Stradella Singers were always in demand – and with Gareth conducting and me transcribing a wealth of neglected treasures dug out of dusty folders in the University Library Music Department where they'd been languishing for years.

Where had it all gone wrong? Why was I not still part of that gilded, gifted group I had helped Gareth to establish?

Cherchez la femme.

I had – foolishly, of course – brought my girlfriend Wanda to audition for Gareth. I should have known from the way she looked at him in rehearsals that she was not just being a model chorister keeping her soulful blue eyes fixed on the conductor at all times, hardly glancing at her music. Then, when I walked in on them naked in bed together, just the week after Finals, I knew I could never forgive either of them.

I was awarded a First and a bursary to start a doctorate. Gareth and Wanda got away with a 2:2 each and went off with the Stradella Singers on a concert tour of Italy, with a mutual friend of ours replacing me on continuo (organ and harpsichord).

And now, seven years on, I had achieved my modest place in the music faculty with my doctorate on the historical significance and interpretation of *abbellimenti* in works of the Italian baroque. Gareth knew that I could never resist an old manuscript; scholarly curiosity got the better of me and I began to examine the photocopies.

Another 'lost' version of Allegri's Miserere . . . Two choirs? Check. One with four voices, one five, adding up to the mystically significant nine (three times three)? Check.

The secret lay in the extraordinarily elaborate decoration practised by the elite singers selected for the Vatican choir at the time, I had written in my doctorate. *Trained in a unique, intuitive method of vocal improvisation, they could raise hairs on the backs of the listeners' necks who would come away convinced that they had been listening to the music of the angels, so exquisite was their choral artistry . . .*

Yet it was the handwriting on the score that first caught my eye.

No music historian worth his salt could mistake that strong, distinctive writing, the hand of a composer whose brain was working so fast that he could hardly scribble down what he was hearing in his mind quickly enough. A young, fresh, prodigiously gifted boy –

A soft tap at the outer door interrupted me just as I was about to compare the handwriting with the facsimile of a Minuet and Trio composed by the boy wonder in Salzburg in late 1769.

'Dr Martagon?'

I was expecting some completed stylistic studies from my undergraduate students, so I merely said, 'Just leave your work on the bookcase by the door . . .'

A waft of perfume made me look up. Wanda stood in the doorway, smiling at me.

'I'm disturbing you.'

I leapt up, almost knocking the photocopies onto the floor. 'No. Not at all. C . . . can I get you anything? Coffee? Sherry?'

'Sherry with my supervisor? That takes me back.' She came into the room, gazing around at the over-stuffed bookshelves, my college gown slung over the back of a chair. 'It feels just as if time has stood still in here.' She ran her fingertips over the piano keys, treble to bass, releasing a little ripple of notes.

'Meaning?' Unsettled by her sudden appearance, I hovered in front of the desk, not knowing what to do.

'It's safe. Stiflingly safe. Don't you ever want to risk going out into the Big Bad World?' She turned around suddenly to face me and the false smile had vanished. 'James, I'm sorry. I hurt you. I never meant to hurt you. It's too late now . . . but I wanted to tell you face to face. And it's taken me seven long years to summon the courage to do so.' To my surprise, her eyes suddenly filled with tears. 'I wish there was some way we could start over.'

Start over? I could hardly believe what I had just heard her say. 'But you and Gareth—'

'We were both very fond of you, you know. Both of us.' She came towards me until she was so close I could breathe in the clear floral scent she was wearing – and kissed me.

Memories I had tried to forget came back in a sudden rush. *Wanda cycling across Magdalen Bridge, her battered hat caught in a*

sudden gust of wind and blown into the river; Wanda coming out of
Fitzbillies, eating a freshly baked Chelsea bun, knuckling the dark
spicy stickiness from her cheek; Wanda sight-singing over my shoulder
as I played the Stradella transcription I had made for her, her pure,
sweet voice sending chills through me as she brought the long-dead aria
back to life . . .

'Wait,' I said, gently but firmly pushing her away. 'Has Gareth put you up to this?'

'How could you think such a thing?' She looked at me with such an innocent, aggrieved look that I was almost convinced.

'Nice try, Wanda. What do you really want?'

She pouted a little, then pointed to the photocopies. 'Well, Dr Martagon,' she said, laying emphasis on my title, '*is* it the real deal? Is it the lost Mozart transcription?'

'Why ask me now?' I was in danger of losing my temper. 'Gareth must have taken it to Mozart scholars for verification.'

'Strangely enough, no. Gareth wanted to keep it a secret for as long as possible. But he – we – trust your opinion, James.'

I showed her the first page. 'At a first glance you can see that it's very different from the version we sing now. All the *abbellimenti* are fully notated.' I couldn't deny that I was utterly fascinated by what lay in front of me. 'It's going to give musicologists a great deal to argue over.'

'So you think it's authentic?'

I was tempted for a moment to toy with her as she had just toyed with me and say no. But I knew myself to be a bad liar. 'I think it probably is,' I said.

*

The posters had gone up all over Cambridge announcing a Holy Week concert:

The Stradella Singers
at St Alphege's Chapel
Baroque Music for Holy Week
including the
First Performance of the original version of
Allegri's *Miserere*

But the singers – and their conductor – would not arrive back from their Italian tour until just before the concert.

'Dr Martagon?' Burridge, the head porter, hailed me as I passed through the lodge, holding out a package. 'This just came for you.'

I examined the slender package as I walked back to my rooms; it was postmarked 'Roma' and the handwriting was unfamiliar.

Inside, I found no letter of explanation, just an assorted collection of photocopies which I leafed through, a little baffled at first until I noticed that each one bore the faint stamp of the Vatican Library and the label 'Allegri's *Miserere*'.

Someone in a position of authority in the Vatican must have compiled a dossier and filed all the evidence away, including, I guessed, the long-lost transcription by young Wolfgang Mozart which the Stradella Singers were going to perform tonight. But why go to such trouble?

The first photocopy was a letter, written in a strong, elegant hand; fortunately my doctoral thesis had given me plenty of practice in translating such manuscripts.

To His Holiness, Pope Urban, from Antonio Barberini, Cardinal Archivist:

I can confirm that a secret rite of exorcism was performed last year (as you suggested) after several congregants and members of the choir reported seeing the ghost of a young singer, Amadeo, at the Holy Week service during the performance of Gregorio Allegri's *Miserere* again.

We had thought the matter resolved but this Holy Week, when the work was performed, the hooded figure of Amadeo Vitali was seen in the congregation by more than one person. We can only conclude that someone is out to play a singularly malicious prank upon the members of the chapel choir by impersonating the dead boy, possibly because he bears a grudge – or that supernatural forces are at work and the boy's spirit appears when the *Miserere* is performed.

Furthermore, another member of the choir has subsequently fallen ill (as has happened after each performance) and died, giving rise to the unfortunate rumours

that the work is in some way accursed. I can only suggest
that we conduct another exorcism and put an end to these
rumours . . .

'A ghost,' I murmured, scanning the second photocopy which
seemed to be a page from the records of the Vatican Choir itself,
a footnote, scrawled beneath the list of members and difficult to
decipher.

. . . to record the tragic death of Amadeo Vitali from a sudden
fever. This young *castrato* had the voice and appearance of
an angel; a single glance at his soulful expression as he sang
and one would think that one of Botticelli or Perugino's
heavenly choir had stepped down from one of the frescoes.
However it had been remarked on more than once that
Maestro Allegri had singled this boy out for special tuition in
composition – which gave rise to unfortunate allegations of
favouritism – or worse. Amadeo had, after all, a remarkably
beautiful face and a voice to match . . .

The next photocopy was relatively terse but I read on with a
growing sense of disquiet:

From Pope Urban to the Archivist, Cardinal Antonio Barberini:
. . . there can be no doubt of the remarkable healing effect
that this *Miserere* has upon all who hear it sung with the
abbellimenti by the Vatican Choir. One congregant has even
described it as experiencing 'absolution through music'.
That, alone, is a reason for us to keep this work to ourselves
as the Vatican's unique treasure.
However, as there is also an inexplicable association
between the performance of this version of the work and an
unfortunate series of tragic deaths afflicting the performers,
it is advisable that we restrict further performances until we
can ascertain if this is just a coincidence or some supernatural force at work. So let it be known that anyone seeking to
copy or steal this work will be excommunicated.

The last photocopy was dated 1770, more than a century later than the first three:

> *To His Holiness, Pope Clement, from Giuseppe Martucci, legate:*
> I am sending you the illicit copy of the *Miserere* which I obtained today from young Wolfgang Mozart. He has given his promise never to reveal the secret *abbellimenti* to another living soul. What an extraordinary talent that boy possesses! It seems that he saw the restless spirit of Amadeo Vitali after the service but, thank God, no harm has befallen him since then.

'No harm?' I said aloud. *An unfortunate series of tragic deaths afflicting the performers* ...

Surely it was just superstition ... I looked up from the legate's letter just as the distant bells of Great St Mary's began to ring out eight o'clock. I was late for the concert. A concert in which the first performance of Mozart's transcription of the lost *Miserere* was about to start.

*

The Stradella Singers always performed by candlelight and the soft ochre flames lit the intent faces of the performers as Gareth lifted his hands to shape the opening of the *Miserere*. *'Have mercy upon me, O God, after Thy great goodness ...'*

As the hushed notes began to fill the echoing vaults of the college chapel, I was suddenly reminded of everything I had lost in turning my back on the Stradella Singers. And I felt tears pricking at my eyes as if I was hearing them sing for the very first time.

I had sat here countless times in the last years, listening to St Alphege's college choir, even rehearsing and conducting them in the new editions I had spent my days transcribing, bringing obscure treasures of the baroque repertoire to fresh audiences. But the excitement had gone from music-making for me, and every exquisite phrase and elaborate cadence only served to remind me of what I had lost.

'Thou shalt purge me with hyssop, and I shall be clean.'

But this was like walking through a cleansing shower of rain that was gently washing over me, rinsing away all the accumulated bitterness that had poisoned my outlook on life.

'Thou shalt wash me, and I shall be whiter than snow.' Wanda's soprano, piercingly clear and pure, soared above the other singers as the Stradella Singers interpreted the version notated by the young Mozart – and never performed in that way outside the Vatican since the days of the last *castrati.*

'Deliver me from blood-guiltiness, O God, Thou that art the God of my health: and my tongue shall sing of Thy righteousness.' In my excitement and confusion, I had forgotten all about dinner. Having slipped in late at the back of the packed chapel, I found myself behind some undergraduates, one or two still wearing their gowns from formal hall, although one must have been from another college, as he was wearing an unfamiliar gown with a hood . . .

I blinked in the candlelight, trying to focus and as I did, he must have sensed he was being watched, for he turned his head towards me. I felt my breath stop as his intense, grey-eyed gaze caught mine for a moment with the faintest hint of a smile . . .

. . . the voice and appearance of an angel . . . one would think that one of Botticelli or Perugino's heavenly choir had stepped down from one of the frescoes . . .

I blinked again as the voices swelled to a climax and a stifling feeling of panic rose in my throat.

'No!' I heard myself shouting as if from a long way off. 'Stop the performance – or someone's going to die!' And then the music and the tremulous candlelight seemed to fuse into one and I felt myself falling forward into an endless spiral of white noise.

*

'James? Can you hear me?'

Someone was calling my name. I opened my eyes to find myself dazzled by bright fluorescent lights overhead. I tried to raise my head and sit up – and found that I was attached to a drip and several electrical machines that were whirring and bleeping away.

'You gave us quite a scare there, old man.' Gareth was grinning down at me. 'Shouting like that – and then passing out.'

'I'm . . . sorry, Gareth . . .'

'Babbling about seeing ghosts. The Mozart connection. Made great publicity for us. The dailies lapped it up.'

A nurse was checking the machines. 'Only a few minutes, now. Dr Martagon needs his rest.'

'Got to dash anyway – a plane to catch,' Gareth said. My hand shot out and gripped his sleeve.

'He was there,' I said. 'Amadeo Vitali. Allegri's choirboy. You must have read the Vatican dossier. Every time that version is performed, he'll claim another sacrifice.'

'Looks like you took the fall for us this time, James. A near thing, the medics said. An undetected heart problem. Time for that sabbatical, maybe?' He placed a newspaper on the bedside table. 'We're off to do that Vatican concert now.'

'I think not,' said a quiet voice, subtly accented. We both looked up to see that a silver-haired man had appeared in the doorway; elegantly dressed in a smartly tailored suit of charcoal grey, he had the distinguished air of a barrister or a diplomat.

'I . . . I'm sorry?' Gareth said in an arrogant tone that offered no hint of apology.

The stranger took a card from a silver card holder and handed it to Gareth.

'Dr Pietro Gennaro, librarian, Vatican Library,' Gareth read aloud.

'I won't ask how you came by the illegal copy of the "other" *Miserere*,' said Dr Gennaro in a voice as creamily smooth as *pannacotta*, 'but I'm afraid I must ask you to return it to me, along with all other transcriptions, vocal parts,' and his gaze rested on me, 'and any other documentary evidence that you may have acquired.'

'Now wait just a moment, Dr Gennaro—' began Gareth and even in my mildly sedated state I could tell that he was seriously rattled.

'If all the material is returned to me today, the Vatican is prepared to overlook this transgression. But if you withhold anything, even the smallest scrap, I'm afraid that we will not hesitate to press charges. You and your singers will never work professionally again.'

'You're *threatening* us?'

'I believe that you're in no position to object,' said Dr Gennaro, 'especially as we have evidence that you bribed one of our younger officials to make the illegal photocopies. He has – as you can imagine – been removed from his post. There is a good reason that certain texts that we watch over must never be released. You, in particular, Dr Martagon,' and he turned to me again, 'must realise the sense of what I'm saying.'

I did. 'Take my keys, Gareth,' I said, ashamed at how weak I sounded, 'and give Dr Gennaro what he's come here to collect.'

Gareth opened his mouth and for a moment I feared he was going to object. Surely he must understand that he could not win against the will of the Vatican.

'We are still looking forward to the concert that you'll be giving in Vatican City,' added Dr Gennaro. 'I remember that superb soprano from your last visit. Your wife Wanda, I believe? She made those high Cs in the *Miserere* sound quite effortless.'

Gareth still did not react.

'I mean, of course, in the version that you will be using. The standard version.'

'Very well,' Gareth said at length. He did not look at me as he led the way out of the room. 'You'd better come with me, Dr Gennaro. I'll give you the materials.'

And they were gone.

I lay back, my strength exhausted. A fragment of melody was playing in my mind and I found myself humming the notes softly, wondering what it could be. Words, familiar words from Psalm 51, attached themselves to the plangent phrases, and at last I realised their provenance. I had last heard them in the chapel, sung by candlelight, as the Stradella Singers performed the forgotten, forbidden *abbellimenti* written to commemorate a boy with the face of an angel . . . and brought back from the silence of centuries thanks to the extraordinary talents of another boy musician who shared his name: Wolfgang Amadeus Mozart.

But lo, Thou requirest truth in the inward parts: and shalt make me to understand wisdom secretly. A strange sense of contentment filled me. Perhaps I would apply for that sabbatical as Gareth had suggested . . . and go to Rome to seek out more of the musical mysteries hidden away for so long in the vaults of the Vatican.

Ω

According to the most recent annotation to the Miserere *file in the Vaults, Dr James Martagon visited Rome in September 1970 as part of a combined convalescence and sabbatical from his college at the University of Cambridge. He visited the Vatican Library, and met up again with Dr Pietro Gennaro, who was pleased to see how much he had recovered his health. Dr Gennaro suggested that he write his own account of the events leading up to the concert in St Alphege's Chapel in February 1970, which would then be archived alongside the other documents concerning Allegri's* Miserere.

He also showed James, from the Miserere *file, the original note which Leopold Mozart wrote to his wife on 14 April 1770:*

> *You have often heard of the famous* Miserere *in Rome, which is so greatly prized that the performers are forbidden on pain of excommunication to take away a single part of it, copy it or give it to anyone. But we have it already. Wolfgang has written it down and we would have sent it to Salzburg in this letter, if it were not necessary for us to be there to perform it. But the manner of performance contributes more to its effect than the composition itself. Moreover, as it is one of the secrets of Rome, we do not wish to let it fall into other hands.*

Although the index to the file lists Mozart's transcription of the Miserere, *the score was removed from the file by Dr Gennaro before our researchers were allowed to take the file from the Archives.*

1975

This report is about abuse, and how the Church has dealt with the issue for decades, by hushing it up and by making the problem, quite literally, go away.

It is an account of one man's dedicated search, not through the closed Archives at the Vatican – 'the Vaults' – but through the bureaucracy of records in the Vatican Library and the many curial departments available to a Church employee, a former detective now working as an investigator within the Church.

It details how even with his professional skills, even with official doors open to him, it took doggedness and determination over years to track down the few leads to what he was searching for, and to pull these disparate pieces of information together to make up a picture.

We have to thank the anonymous writer for his work, and for his personal report – but without Pope John Paul's opening of the Vaults, where we found it, this too would have remained hidden.

The Island of Lost Priests

Kristine Kathryn Rusch

I could only find three direct references to the Island of Lost Priests in the Vatican's records, and only one mentions the island by that rather subjective – and, as I later learned, rather apt – nickname.

The other two references are buried in financial and property files. One reference is a line-item in a centuries-old budget; the other is simply a map of the various properties owned by the Church.

Taken together, they form a slight trail to a secret and a conundrum, a forgotten history of a time everyone wants to forget, and a moment of opportunity which was, unsurprisingly, squandered.

*

I'm considered something strange in the modern era. I'm an American who converted to Catholicism – not because I married into the faith, but because I wanted to become a Catholic. I officially converted in my twenties, but for all intents and purposes, I became a believer in my early teens.

I love an ordered way to do things. I adore the patterns and the liturgy. I adore knowing what to expect in a service and what I'm supposed to do.

I first encountered the Church because of Father Joseph O'Malley. June, 1950. I can't remember the exact date, but it had to be mid-month, because my dad, a teacher, had the summer off.

I knew even then that things would only get worse. That false hope that so many kids had when life went sideways forever and ever – it wasn't for me. Maybe I was morbid, or maybe, even at age twelve, I was a realist.

Back then, Brooklyn was the centre of my world. My mother had died in a terrible car accident on New Year's Eve, and my dad wanted to die too. He didn't have the courage to off himself; he spent the next ten years carving away at himself with cigarettes and alcohol when a gun would've been so much quicker.

By the time his body left – in a gutter not too far from my childhood home, riddled with cancer, and skeletal from malnutrition – the man I knew before the accident had been dead for years.

That day, twenty-five years ago, I sat on the steps of a neighbourhood bar and waited for the right moment to pull my dad out of it and try to get him home. The air was so humid it felt alive – or maybe that was the stench of day-old vomit, cigarettes and alcohol that oozed up from the edge of the alley off to my right.

I was worried about dinner. The twenty I'd cadged from my dad's wallet the day school ended had lasted me nearly two weeks. I bought groceries and cooked as best I could for a kid who'd never cracked a cookbook before January. I didn't know budgeting, and I didn't know how to shop, but I was learning.

But the money was out except for three dollars, and I was wondering if I should feed myself somehow – get a slice, maybe – or try to stretch the money even farther. I was wearing fading pants that were too short because I'd hit a growth spurt, and a too-tight shirt that had been too big the summer before.

Father Joe walked past that bar every day on his way to the church around the corner. I'd seen him before, but hadn't met his gaze.

He was hard to miss. He was broad-shouldered and tall; thick black hair that glistened in the sun. His skin was bronzed because he spent as much time outside as he possibly could.

He wore a collar but in the warm weather he was in shirtsleeves, even though it was frowned on by the diocese. He was one of those young priests who made the Church look cool, rather than one of the old judgemental guys, the ones who led the Catholic school attached to the church.

I never once felt that Father Joe disapproved of anything I said or did, which, looking back on everything now, was probably what drew me to him. Too many other people were trying to tell me what to do. They were worried about me, but back then, worry didn't translate into action.

That day, Father Joe sat down beside me. He didn't even brush off the concrete step like I had done. He just plunked down bringing with him the scent of pipe tobacco with a faint hint of Aqua Velva.

'Hot,' he said.

'Yeah,' I said, not looking at him. I didn't want to be rude, but I didn't want to be bothered either.

'We're having a barbecue. We got dogs and buns and potato salad and lots of cookies, more than we can eat. You hungry?'

Was the Pope Catholic? I wanted to snap at him, then looked at his collar. It wasn't the appropriate thing to say.

I glanced at the bar, heard my dad's laugh inside, knew it might be hours yet before he came out. I'd been thinking of how to use that three dollars because I knew I had time to buy what few groceries I could, take them to our apartment, and come back here before he noticed I was missing.

But thinking about that slice had me confused. Then I realised: I wasn't trading a dollar of our hoard to fill my stomach. I was going to be able to fill up for free.

Still, I was a Brooklyn kid, so I asked, 'What's the catch?'

'You gotta be quiet when we say grace,' Father Joe said.

'That's it?' I asked, not believing him.

'That's it,' he said, and kept to his word.

*

The church had barbecues off and on all summer, usually preceded by a softball game where Father Donnelly pitched and Father Bill played catcher. No boy got to have those prime spots, no matter how good he was. Father Donnelly had been called up to the Dodgers for one fine day thirty years ago, and still dined out on that. Father Donnelly still had the touch, although he must've been pushing sixty.

Father Bill was the same age as Father Joe, a priest who didn't mind getting dirty, who rarely wore his robes, but always wore his collar, a man with a twinkle in his eye and – as he used to say – a song in his heart. That song was usually Sinatra, even though, by 1950, the entire world thought Sinatra was passé.

By the Fourth of July, I was playing in the softball games. By the first of August, I'd show up for morning Mass before my dad woke up, not because I liked the service so much, but there was always coffee and doughnuts after.

Most of that summer, I ate at the church, and no one seemed to care that I didn't actually belong.

Two weeks before public school started, Father Joe sat beside me at one of the informal barbecues.

'We have an opening at school,' he said. 'We're authorised to take in two kids per class from the community. You interested?'

I'd heard horrid stories about Catholic school. The nuns were mean. You had to wear a uniform. Everything was regulated.

But I also knew that the Catholic kids got better grades. No one pulled a knife in their school, and even better, the school was only a block from my apartment. I didn't have to walk far, and I didn't have to go through some of Brooklyn's worst neighbourhoods.

'Yeah,' I said.

Father Joe smiled and clapped me on the back, and that was that.

Different times. We didn't tell my dad. He never filled out the forms. My dad taught at the high school, not the junior high, so we always went off in different directions anyway. He had no idea where I was or what I did.

He didn't even notice the uniform until halfway through the year. He stared at it, then looked at me, and said, 'How long's this been going on?'

'Since September,' I said, then added quickly before he could argue, 'I'm getting straight As.'

He closed his eyes, sighed, and ran a hand over his face. The capillaries under his skin were already breaking, even then. Later, I looked at photographs to confirm the memory, and saw the red nose, the bleary eyes, even before Mom died.

She hadn't been driving that night; he had. But, as the cops said, everyone was drunk on New Year's Eve. And it'd gotten written up as the other driver's fault.

He didn't argue with me that day, didn't tell me I had to quit, didn't say I was getting indoctrinated, which is what he used to say about the kids pouring out of the school before Mom died. He just shook his head and left, and sometimes, when I'm not paying close attention to my memory, I think that was the last time I ever saw him.

Maybe it was. Not physically, but mentally. Maybe my dad just gave up that day. He'd lost every fight that mattered to him.

Or maybe, he'd already given up, and my defection to a religious school that kicked his school's butt at every academic competition in the city simply confirmed how out of control his life was.

Most likely, though, I'd shut him up and he'd turned away, already forgetting about me and my uniform and any complaints he might have had. My dad was one of those pitiful drunks, the kind who turned into rubber and melted on the bar. No hail-fellow-well-met, no gambling or women or any other vice. He just sort of faded away, using the liquor to take the edges off of everything, including life itself.

I was determined not to be him, and school gave me that chance. Every command it laid out sounded like a prescription for being someone other than my dad, and I took all of them to heart.

No one urged me to convert, not even after my dad lost his job and we lost the apartment. Father Joe got me a place to board with some of the other kids without a place to go – one of the buildings attached to the church – and for the first time since Mom died, I had three squares and a safe place to sleep.

All of the priests tried to help my dad, but he wouldn't listen, and became harder and harder to find. I ended up with a choice: either I could spend my time looking for him or preparing for college. I talked it over with Father Joe, and he said that God gave everyone freedom to choose his own life, and that you had to respect that choice, even if it looked like a bad one.

You just had to be there when the other person realised how

bad his choice had been, maybe to catch him, or maybe to help him recover.

Those words haunted me for my entire life.

*

Father Donnelly first told me about the Island of Lost Priests in 1968, just before he died. I'd come home, exhausted and bruised from my years in Chicago. My wife, God rest her soul, had been dead about a year, and I finally understood some of the despair that took my father, even if I didn't succumb to it.

I had to leave Chicago though, which meant leaving the Chicago Police Department, even after I'd risen to become one of the best homicide detectives in the entire city.

I couldn't do it – I couldn't look at death any more without seeing Mary Claire, jaundiced from the cancer, trying to smile even when it was an effort. Death had ceased to be a puzzle for me then. I knew it snuck up on all of us, but I had forgotten how slowly and mercilessly it could attack.

I figured New York would be my balm, but I wanted the New York of my youth – the loud brash city that had been the centre of the world, not a growing cesspool.

Not even the Church was the same.

No Latin Mass at all, not even for the purists. A priest younger than me who seemed to have no wisdom, just platitudes.

I asked about Father Bill, but he'd moved to a parish in Louisiana to take care of his ailing parents. Father Donnelly had retired – if a priest could well and truly retire – but he still kept his hand in. Although that young priest I didn't know told me I should see Father Donnelly soon or I wouldn't see him until we met again in the afterlife.

Father Donnelly lived in an apartment in a building owned by the Diocese of Brooklyn. The building wasn't far from the church. Father Donnelly's apartment was small. The door opened into the dining room. The kitchen was to the left, along with a corridor that led to the only bedroom and the bathroom. The living room was in the front of the building and had a bay window that over-looked the street. A working fireplace showed that the apartment was what the city called Pre-War, meaning pre-World War II.

A fire was burning in the fireplace, making the living room about twenty degrees hotter than it should've been. Still, the man I remembered, who could throw a perfect Dodger's pitch even with a softball, had shrunken to half his original size. He was wrapped in thick quilts that I knew had come from parishioners.

Father Donnelly might've been strict, but he was well loved.

He sat in the bay window, feet propped along the edge, and he leaned against cushions stacked against one of the window panes. An old potboiler was open across his lap.

We talked about novels and how much we both escaped into fiction. We talked about our lives since we last saw each other, and Father Donnelly was the first to draw me out about Mary Claire. He'd married us, after all, and knew how much I'd loved her. He had sent me some kind letters after her death.

But he had lived long enough to know that love and loss were two sides of the same coin. He believed I should move on, and I wasn't so sure. She had been my wife, and I knew I'd see her in God's heaven, if I lived well enough. I wasn't sure, no matter how many times the priests reassured me, that I'd see her again if I replaced her with someone else.

Philosophy, religion, the past and my future. It was a wonder he didn't tire out sooner. But the woman the parish paid to care for him nudged me gently to leave so he could rest.

As I stood, I asked him something that had been gnawing at me for years. 'Do you know where Father Joe ended up?'

By then, Father Donnelly was nearly asleep. But his rheumy blue eyes opened and I thought I saw sadness in them.

'The Island of Lost Priests,' he said.

I wanted to ask what that meant, but his eyes closed and the woman shooed me out.

The next time I saw Father Donnelly, he was looking beatific in his casket, a rosary in one hand and a baseball in the other.

I was glad I had gotten to speak with him one last time. It had been through the grace of God. My life hadn't always gone as planned, but that moment, that little lagniappe as Father Bill would say, was a highlight.

Shortly thereafter the diocese hired me to investigate things for them, mostly small items at first. But once they learned I could do the job quickly and well, without ruffling a lot of feathers and with as much discretion as possible, I received tougher assignments.

Which was how I got to be one of the guys who could look stuff up at the Vatican itself.

*

Italian wasn't a problem for me. I had always dabbled in languages – taking classes in other tongues not only helped me on cases for the Chicago PD, but it also helped me relax from the worst of things, thinking about conjugations and literature in a language not my own.

I loved the puzzle of language, found it as easy to assemble as a homicide investigation. I loved taking disparate parts and making them whole.

By the time I started looking for the Island of Lost Priests, I spent much of my year in Rome, leaving only during the worst of the tourist season – from December through Easter – when it felt like tourists hadn't just taken over the city, but conquered it.

I would always go back to New York during those breaks, looking for my past, and touching base with my employers, such as they were. The things I was investigating – well, I can't discuss them even now – but some of them disheartened me even more than the murders I used to see during my time at CPD.

I knew that man could never be perfect, but I liked to think – even after my years in homicide – that most people tried. Or, at least, most religious folk. Or, at the very least, the religious folk who guided the rest of us.

Yeah, naïve, and I knew it. But I couldn't shake it. I wasn't sure I wanted to. I escaped more and more into what I had known, into my own past, into my memories.

Then the cases started, and the accusations, and my memories went into turmoil, making those months the first time in years I wished I had someone besides a priest to talk to. Someone who understood both me and my memories. Someone who understood the Church and the concept of sin. Someone who could wonder with me what God could and did forgive. And why.

*

If I'm honest with myself – and it's hard to be honest, even now – the signs were there. But I was twelve when I met Father Joe. I was lonely, and I was green.

Besides, I wasn't one of his boys. Out of respect for my father, I didn't become a Catholic until he died.

Father Joe got me to the Church, but Father Bill taught me doctrine. And Father Donnelly advised me. I liked him best, maybe because of those pitches. Slow for the kids who had no hope, and wicked deadly for those of us who had a modicum of skill.

I loved how Father Donnelly saw everything and said nothing, just applied what he knew to day-to-day living. He was the man I emulated, and he, more than any other, was the man I aspired to be.

Father Joe was a little too loose for me, even at the beginning. Even on that very first day, I wondered why – if everyone else was celebrating something – he was walking the streets of Brooklyn, eager to talk to lonely boys like me.

Later, I learned that Father Joe always watched out for lonely boys. He culled some of them to become his troupe. They disappeared from the barbecues on some kind of local mission. They did work at outreach centres or for Catholic charities. They went on retreats at some of the properties Upstate.

At first, my feelings were hurt that I wasn't included. But then, I observed, and realised, few of the boys enjoyed the trips. I figured that Father Joe worked them harder than the rest of us, and these trips weren't a reward but some kind of penance, and I became glad that I wasn't part of them.

I'd like to say I was smart enough to realise that I might have become part of them had I converted sooner, but that would be attributing more wisdom to me than I actually deserved.

Still, so many boys from my class dropped out or disappeared. So many of them turned to drugs or alcohol. Even the ones who went to college imploded in some way.

Not that I saw the college boys implode. That happened to them as adults, not as young men, and by then I was in Chicago, trying to convince the prettiest girl on Earth that Brooklyn was a better place than Rogers Park. She won that argument. It wasn't hard. Chicago had Mary Claire, so Chicago got me too.

I only heard about the implosions when I got back after she died, and I only put together what really happened after the big lawsuit got settled after Father Donnelly died.

The lawsuit was confusing. I only knew about it because I was working for the diocese by then. It was a big deal, and a lot of the priests said it was only about some lawyers making money. Which is what I thought, until I started reading the reports.

They made me sick, and the Church's response made me sick too. Because there was evidence that priests abused kids. Lots of evidence, the kind that we would've used in Chicago to put some pervert away for life (or maim him for life if we couldn't build a case).

Everything got covered up, and sometimes I think about my role, and I shudder. I put guys away who paid out hush money back in Chicago, and in some ways, that was one of the jobs the diocese hired me to do.

I try not to think about that part much. But it's hard, because I'm on the fence about all of it. I mean, after all, no guy wants to admit that some priest did that stuff to him, even when he was a boy. People would shun the guy. But the priests did it, and they had to be dealt with, and I didn't know what the dealing was for years.

When I found out, I had to sign all kinds of confidentiality stuff. I couldn't keep it inside though, which is why I'm writing all of this down now. God knows – and I mean that: only God knows – what I'll do with this when I'm done.

The cases made me sick inside. The Church had saved me, and I knew it wasn't perfect, but Jesus, Mary and Joseph, those men were entrusted, not just with the boys' souls, but with their bodies as well.

When I thought about it as a cop, I wanted to put those men away forever. When I thought about it as a man, I wanted to use my gun or my blade to make sure they never harmed anyone again.

When I thought about it as a little lost boy who had relied on the fantasies he had built up of the Church as a miraculous safe haven, well, it broke my heart.

The diocese made me look at the court documents. The

scandal – it had gone on for years, and not just in the Diocese of Brooklyn. Scandals were happening all over North America, but the courts let the cases remain confidential, and if they got settled at all, they got settled contingent on confidentiality agreements.

But the Church itself had to pay a price for letting these men near children in the first place, and for doing so very little to stop them. The settlement was different for each diocese, and was based on how many children had been harmed.

Brooklyn had its share. Hundreds of kids damaged forever by some pervert in priest's robes.

Black and white, straightforward stuff, at least that was what I thought. Until I delved into the records, armed with names, so that I could find the boys who deserved part of the settlement – grown men now, lives so ruined that some of them made my father look like a solid upstanding citizen.

Oh, a few of the boys went to psychiatrists, and many of them had productive lives, but the way they treated me, as an emissary of the Church – it was as if I had been part of the crime committed against them, as if I had looked the other way, just like everyone else.

I didn't even think the scandal had touched me, until the names on the list started looking familiar. Then I realised they *were* familiar.

Father Joe's boys. The special ones. Who went with Father Joe to do Great Work at outreach centres and Catholic missions. Who went Upstate for that special camp, every single year.

Father Joe's boys.

To think I'd envied them.

*

I got assigned to find Father Joe's boys to give them their settlements.

A third of them had committed suicide directly – guns, pills, jumping off bridges. Some even left notes, and those notes inevitably mentioned Father Joe.

Another third were still Catholic enough to know suicide was a mortal sin. So they took my father's route. Some of them were still alive when I found them, if you call that twilight between being a functional human being and being a perpetual drunk 'alive'.

The remaining third divided itself into the angry, bitter men who would take no prisoners when it came to the Church; those who had signed onto the lawsuit, and warned people away from Catholicism; and the men who were still ashamed and didn't want anyone to know about any of it.

They were all embarrassed to see me, embarrassed that I knew. They didn't want any compassion from me, only silence. Most of them put the money in an account their family didn't know about, and I knew that the family wouldn't hear about those tens (sometimes hundreds) of thousands, until those men were dead.

Thank God, I'd been a cop. Thank God I knew that you don't dish out platitudes in the face of life-ruining events, especially after those lives were long-ruined.

I did my work, I went home each night, and I wished for someone to talk to. Because I couldn't talk to God about this. I suspected He and I disagreed.

*

I went to Rome in the middle of that mess, partly as a vacation, and partly to research some old rumours about the diocese. It was a small job, not important, but my bosses knew how devastating the work I did was, and how it was eating at me, and they didn't want to lose me – as an employee and a man of faith.

What better place to go than Vatican City.

The big surprise about Vatican City, particularly for a New York boy who worked in Chicago half his life, is that it's so small. Yeah, you read that it's 110 acres, which isn't even close to a square mile, but that's impossible to imagine.

And then you get there, and realise you're in a place that has greater influence over most of the world than most countries, and it's no bigger than a few Manhattan neighbourhoods – if that.

The sunlight in that part of Italy is intense. The sun is almost a different entity than the one in North America. The light is white, and it reflects off the white buildings. The heat, which everyone seems used to, always catches me by surprise. You can't really dress for it, because the Vatican – and therefore Vatican City itself – has a dress code that requires full body coverings at all times.

Back in the States, I had started a haphazard search for Father Joe while I was searching for the current addresses of the adult men he had destroyed as children. I had no idea why I was searching for him, or what I was searching for.

If I found him, I wasn't sure what I would do, particularly as I spent more and more time with the men he'd ruined.

The reports against him had started the moment he arrived in 1947, and had become a thick file by 1955. Some nameless Church officials – who were probably guys like me – had taken him away, and as to what happened to him after that, the diocese had no record.

My search was hampered by the fact that Joseph O'Malley was a pretty common name, particularly for a man who was in his thirties in the 1950s and came from the East Coast. I found dead end after dead end, and finally, on that visit to Rome, I realised that the only way to find Father Joe was through the Church itself.

I had planned to explore Rome while I waited for the Vatican Library to provide me with the documents I had requested.

Two days I'd searched for Father Joe, while sitting on gilded chairs in a badly air-conditioned part of a building that was older than my country. My back hurt, my legs would occasionally go numb, and I felt awkward walking around to loosen everything up, afraid I might break something or stumble into a forbidden area.

Even then, I found some Joseph O'Malleys but never the one I was searching for.

So, I started searching for the Island of Lost Priests, and found nothing. At least, not right away.

Eventually, I tracked down dozens of rumours about the Island of Lost Priests. Most of the officials I spoke to called it a bogey-man, a scare tactic, something that got told to wayward priests to keep them in line.

No one seemed to believe it existed, but no one knew what happened to the abusive priests either. They were shipped off somewhere. Whenever I asked about it, I was told they were shipped off to places where they had little or no human interaction with people who were not Church officials.

Sometimes I looked around the official places I visited – from the Vatican Library to its Museums – and wondered if the men I saw working on damaged manuscripts or repairing a ruined fresco were actually priests no longer allowed to tend a flock.

Everyone denied that, but they also denied that they knew what happened to those priests.

I asked if they were laicised – what the media called 'defrocked' – and discovered that a handful were, and had left the Church's direct supervision.

But most had simply vanished, from their parishes and from the Church records.

I had hoped that the voluminous records kept at the Vatican would help me, but they didn't help me find individuals.

They helped me find the island.

*

My discovery wasn't simple or linear. In fact, if I hadn't had that skill at taking disparate pieces and turning them into a whole and complete idea, I would never have found the island at all.

The first reference I found was in a series of documents from World War II. The Italian government wanted the Church to allow it to use various islands in the Church's possession as bomb sites to take out Allied vessels.

The Church refused.

It seemed like a straightforward enough interaction, and I had no idea why that document had been hidden along with other papers to do with the Church's dark history during the war – especially considering that in this instance, the Church had chosen the correct side.

It wasn't until I had moved on, looking at some other documents for the research that I had a realisation: Perhaps the document wasn't there because of the World War II reference. Perhaps it was there because of the reference to the islands.

That took me to the documents on the Church's property holdings around the world. Two years of painstaking research later, I finally found what I was looking for: an eighteenth-century purchase of five chains of islands located around the world. The islands had no names, just longitude and latitude designations.

What stunned me was that the islands do not exist on most contemporary maps. If they are listed, they're marked as 'one of many unoccupied islands found in the world's oceans', as if that's normal.

They're outside the normal shipping channels. Maps claim that the currents do not allow anyone to even get close to the islands. I searched for current charts that actually showed how the currents affected the islands, but found nothing.

Amazing how even in the modern era, maps could be so very inaccurate.

I had found a chain of islands, but there was no way to prove that one of those islands was the Island of Lost Priests.

Until I found a document that used the island's real name and its nickname listed parenthetically beside it. The island's official name? Insulam Inferno – Hell Island.

*

Rather than explain all of the permutations of my research – how I located the island in the library's financial records, and then how I took that mention and found the budget for the island buried in the Church's official books – I'll, as the movie people say, cut to the chase.

Because there was a chase, if you want to call hunting for permission to go to the island a chase. It was more like a slog. First, I had to find the records of the priests sent there, then I had to figure out who would grant me such permission, and then I had to cite a reason that someone higher up than me in the investigative services would believe.

At first, I even offered to charter my own transportation, but that would require that dozens of other people be let in on the secret, so that request was denied.

And all the while, I had no official confirmation that the Joseph O'Malley listed in the records was the man I had known.

I could only guess, based on the date of his arrival on the island, and the fact that no other Joseph O'Malley arrived for another five years.

Through it all, I never questioned my resolve. Once I knew that Father Donnelly's statement wasn't a fantasy from a dying man, once I knew that the Island of Lost Priests actually existed, and, more importantly, *why* it existed, once I tracked down its location, the vast expenditures the Church made on the island in upkeep and in care, I had to go.

I had to.

I liked to think it wasn't about Father Joe, but about my own intellectual curiosity.

I liked to think I was putting the last piece of the puzzle into place.

I didn't realise that I was, in fact, putting together a different puzzle altogether, one I hadn't even realised I was assembling.

*

The information about the Island of Lost Priests was right about one thing: it was impossible to reach by ship. Not because of the currents, which is what everyone says, but because of the shoreline.

The chain of islands that contains Insulam Inferno came from an active underground volcano. Occasionally a new island appears near the edge of the chain.

Insulam Inferno is in the very middle; geologists say it's one of those volcanic islands that swallowed a lot of other smaller islands nearby.

It looks that way. Its shoreline has no beaches, only rocky crags that tower over the water line. The crags slide down into a series of bowls separated by more crags. The largest bowl is where the settlement exists.

I went in by helicopter, along with members of some shadowy Vatican security team. This wasn't the Papal Swiss Guard or any security organisation that I had known about previously.

This was an organisation that did all sorts of things the Church theoretically frowned upon. They looked more like Green Berets than the comically dressed Swiss Guard, and they were better armed. The weaponry these men carried could start a small war.

The helicopter was armed too. And so was the other helicopter that came along with us. It waited on top of the landing strip – a flat surface, clearly carved out of one of those crags.

I had been assured that there was a simple path down into the settlement, and that was when I learned that these men's definition of simple and mine differed greatly.

I did not think that my choices – an uneven staircase carved a long time ago into the cliff face or a steep goat path that hugged a matching cliff face, both without barriers and handrails – constituted simple at all.

I had kept in relatively good shape for a retired Chicago police officer pushing fifty, but I wasn't in Green-Beret shape, and I had a terrible sense of balance.

The five men who accompanied me down that staircase – which they said was easier than the path (I took their word for it) – let me set the pace, and I was glad they did. One of the men on this trip went ahead of us, scouting for trouble, and judging by his radio communication, he arrived at the bottom almost an hour before we did.

The weather was temperate for this part of the Mediterranean – eighty degrees and humid – but I was still sweating by the time I'd finished the first twist of the staircase. The rocks were broken, and I kept one sweaty palm against the white stone along the side. Every time my hand slipped even slightly, my heart slipped too. I was half convinced that the world was tilting sideways and I would fall into the abyss.

Below me, I could see the twinkle of buildings in the hot sun, and lush greenery, as well as a waterfall coming out of one of the rocks across the way. There was a lagoon the colour of the sky, and I considered more than once that leaping off the steps and landing in the water was a better choice than climbing ever would be.

I'm not normally a whiner, and I didn't complain out loud – you don't complain to men wearing 30 pounds of gear and carrying another 20 pounds of weaponry that you, the unarmed guy in khaki pants, cotton shirt and boots, with nothing strapped to him, are getting tired – but the chorus in my mind was fierce.

I had been a fool to want this mission, and I knew it. I hadn't planned for an adventure; I had planned for a conversation.

And no one had warned me about how hard our trek would be once we arrived.

In fact, no one had told me anything about the island. I had half expected a Father Damien kind of leper colony – a place where men who were pariahs huddled in barely functional shacks with no running water, and no accoutrements of modern life.

But I wouldn't have been surprised if I had encountered one of the Church's excesses either. Palatial cathedrals with matching quarters, the gold domes putting the famous minarets of Istanbul to shame. After all, these men had been convicted of nothing, at least according to the laws that I had once taken an oath to protect and defend. No grand jury had even heard an individual case.

The jury that judged them was a jury of their peers, and they had been sentenced to life here, which, I saw as I went down the last of the steps, almost looked like an island paradise out of some Robert Louis Stevenson novel.

The valley spread before me, with fruit trees lining paths, cultivated orchards pointing towards the settlement about a mile away. On two hillsides to the north, grapes grew, and rows farther on suggested a massive garden.

The buildings weren't shacks and they weren't palaces either. They were made of the same white rock I had just braced myself with (leaving my palm and arm white). Some kind of utility shed stood on this side of the path, and farther along was another. I later learned that one building somehow converted sunlight into electricity for the entire settlement, and the other was some kind of plant that used the water from the lagoon to give each building running water.

There was a modern sewage system as well.

I couldn't say it had all of the accoutrements of modern life, because there was no television, no radio, no telephones. But there was a large library that was the very centre of town. Twice a month, planes flew over the settlement and dropped supplies, and those supplies included donated reading material, censored, I later learned, to make sure these men did not get Ideas (sexual or otherwise).

The men knew we were coming. We were hard to miss.

Besides, landings on that flat area occurred maybe three times per year, never on a schedule, usually when someone needed to meet with the group face to face. No new men were delivered until one of the settlers died, and often not right away. The men who lived in this forgotten place didn't want newcomers to join them, so they wouldn't set out a message flag for the supply planes. Generally, the Church had no idea about the lost members of the settlement until someone visited.

One of the men I was travelling with gave me a container filled with water, and told me to drink it. Then he gave me another, along with a cloth, so that I could clean off my hands and face.

The walk to the village took maybe fifteen minutes, and we completed it in silence. To this day, I have no idea who the men I was travelling with were, not just what their jobs were exactly, but their names or where they lived. We had very little idle conversation, and what little we did have concerned the island.

As we approached the village, men came out of buildings. Most of the men wore woven shirts, shorts, and no shoes. A few wore a traditional priest's work cassock. Many of them had straw hats.

They watched us as we walked in. As we reached the nearest building, a white adobe-like structure with a thatched roof, one of the men told the priest (former priest? I'm still not certain) at the door that we needed to see Joseph O'Malley at the church.

The priest took off at a run. We continued our little march through what had to be the main part of the village. Only it seemed like we had gone back in time. Chickens crossed our path, and a lot of the buildings had fenced-in pens for goats. The path was dirt, of course, and most of the signs were scratched into bits of wood. There were outdoor workspaces, hand-built, like everything else on this island.

The structures that had been professionally constructed stood in the very centre of the village. I didn't have to be told (although I was) that the Church had built them when it decided to permanently inhabit this place.

They were one- and two-storey buildings, and they looked much more solid than the buildings around it. They also had names with official signs. One was a hospital. One was a commissary. One was a local government building.

And the most impressive one, the one that looked like it could have been pulled out of Rome's streets and planted here without much effort, was the church itself.

A miniature version of Notre Dame in Paris, this church stood out. It had been made of different materials and it had stunning stained glass windows. It could probably hold five hundred men for a service, although I doubted it ever had.

It had marble steps and wooden doors that might have been made of mahogany. They opened inwards.

And as I contemplated the church's size, I realised that the few hundred men I saw here were not enough to deal with all of the names I had seen just on the most recent North American list of priests named in the settlements against the Church. I had no idea where everyone else was; only that a handful – and a truly small handful – had come here.

I had a terrifying hunch that some of the others were on the remaining islands in the chain.

We mounted the steps and went inside. It was cooler, and it took a moment for my eyes to adjust.

Light poured through the stained glass, colouring the pews in blue, red and yellow. Pure yellow light covered the altar and a hint of pink coated the baptismal font. Someone had paid a lot of attention to design here, making this one of the most beautiful sanctuaries I had ever seen.

It felt like a holy place, and I suppose that was good. I suppose it was needed.

'Who runs the church?' I asked one of the men with me.

'Father Malcolm,' he said.

'Is he . . . ?' I didn't know how to classify the men here. *One of the prisoners* seemed too harsh, even if it was accurate. 'Was he sent here to run the church or was he sent here—'

'Because he violated Church law?' The voice that spoke echoed throughout the sanctuary. A familiar voice, with a Brooklyn accent.

A chill ran down my spine.

Father Joe.

I turned, but couldn't see him. The shadows were dark near the entrance he had come through.

'No, he didn't violate anything,' Father Joe said. 'He volunteered.'

I wasn't sure – I hadn't heard the voice in more than twenty years – but I thought I detected bitterness. Or at least disapproval.

He stepped into the plain light that came through our door. He was just as tall as I remembered, and just as broad. He hadn't gained an ounce of fat, although I didn't know how he could have, living here.

His face wasn't a young man's face any more, but it still had suggestions of the man he had been. Time had given it lines, and the sunshine had permanently baked it brown.

His eyes were still a bright blue, but they didn't twinkle.

He tilted his head when he saw me.

'Well,' he said, 'you look older. Last I heard, you were in Chicago.'

'Yes, Father.' I wasn't sure if that was how I was to address him, and I found I didn't care. I couldn't call him anything other than Father or Father Joe if I tried. 'I moved back to Brooklyn a few years ago.'

He grunted and turned away. As he walked, he said, 'If we're going to talk, we aren't going to do it here.'

Still in command, still in charge.

The men with me glanced at me, as if asking if that was all right. I ignored them and followed Father Joe.

He took me to a flight of stairs that led down to some of the offices. There were no doors on any of the rooms down here, the one concession I'd seen to the strangeness of this island.

The nearest office had no desk. Just some reading chairs and excellent lighting. The books lining the walls seemed to be about the nature of sin, at least those whose titles I could read.

He took a leather chair that looked old and worn. It must've been brought in along with the other church furnishings.

I took the chair across from him. Its upholstery was made from a patchwork of fabrics, and it was surprisingly comfortable.

I glanced at the men who stood near the door, as if they were afraid to leave me alone with him.

'We're going to have a private conversation,' I said.

They understood the implication. I have no idea how far away they moved, only that they were no longer in my line of sight and their shadows no longer covered the walls.

Father Joe was watching me. Here, in the artificial light, I saw the silver in his hair, and the frown lines around his mouth.

Faced with him, I wasn't quite sure what to say.

We stared at each other in silence, my heart pounding. I had imagined finding him for years; I hadn't imagined talking with him.

Finally, he said, 'I don't suppose you came from the Diocese of Brooklyn.'

They were the ones who recommended he come here after the investigations. They were the ones who could initiate a review of his file, and seek his release.

If I really wanted to, I could tell him I was from the diocese. After all, I worked for them. But even now, I couldn't tell a priest – even a disgraced priest – a lie.

'No, I didn't.' I folded my hands. Blisters had raised on my left palm from that hike down the mountain staircase. 'I came because . . .'

Because of all those ruined men, those men who couldn't face existing, the men who chose to abandon their God by committing a mortal sin, the men who couldn't look in the mirror or touch a woman in love or have anything resembling a normal life.

For a moment, they crowded the room with us.

I had no right to speak for them. Even if I had the right, I doubted I could communicate the depth of the despair that Father Joe had caused them.

I felt momentarily speechless. If I hadn't come for them, why . . . ?

And then I realised why I had searched for him so hard.

'Do you remember what you said to me the first day you saw me?' I asked.

He shrugged. 'I suppose I said to you what I always say to people who look lost. I probably told you that salvation was only a few blocks away.'

I shook my head. I felt oddly disappointed. He didn't remember at all.

'You told me there was a barbecue. You offered me lunch. I asked what the catch was, and you said, I had to be quiet when you said grace.'

He leaned back just a little. I had surprised him. 'I did?'

I nodded.

'And you came?'

'I hadn't had a good meal all month,' I said.

He laughed. His eyes twinkled, and he looked at me with warmth.

'They even had me believing it,' he said as if we were old friends who understood each other.

I was appalled by his familiarity. 'Believing what?'

'Those lies. Those hateful lies told by men who couldn't accept what their lives had become. I never did anything, except do my best to exemplify God's love.'

My breath caught. He had been here at least ten years, and he still thought himself innocent. He thought himself the victim.

I hadn't expected that. I hadn't expected this man before me, an older version of the younger one, eyes still bright with intelligence.

I had convinced myself I would find one of two men here: a monster who knew what hell he had brought into the world, or a broken man who begged for forgiveness.

I had found neither. I had found an older version of Father Joe, and I realised with a chill that had he been at some parish with families and children and teenage boys, he would still be trying to show them what he so horribly called God's love.

I almost stood and left, but I made myself stay. I had sat across from murderers, people still covered in blood, people who never took responsibility for the lives they had taken, and none of them had upset me as deeply as this man did, right now.

I guess that boy was still inside me, the one who needed the order and discipline of the Church. I guess that boy wanted to know – needed to believe – that this remedy worked, that exile turned men like Father Joe into someone else, someone who asked for and finally received the forgiveness promised in the Scriptures.

He didn't even know he needed forgiveness. He believed he was more sinned against than sinning.

'You're not here to take me back, are you?' he asked, and this time, I recognised the bitterness in his voice. It was deep and practised, a well-worn groove in a life gone wrong.

'No,' I said, and noted with a touch of surprise, I could no longer call him Father Joe.

'So why are you here? To get some kind of personal satisfaction by accusing me of hurting you? You have to see me face to face, is that it?'

My breath caught. Had he hurt me? For one brief moment, I worried that I had repressed old memories.

But I knew I hadn't. I hadn't been one of Father Joe's boys. I had watched from the outside. Father Donnelly had actually seen me one afternoon, staring longingly at the troop who flocked behind Father Joe, and had said, *You think you want to be part of that. But nothing is as it seems, my son. And the fact that you're here, now, while those boys are walking away shows me just how much God loves you.*

I swallowed hard. If God had loved me, had he hated the other boys? I couldn't believe that.

I was taught that such things didn't follow one after the other, but I recognised now what emotion had fuelled my quest. Not just curiosity, but guilt. Guilt that I had somehow – through luck or the love of God – dodged something awful.

Father Joe was watching me, his expression guarded.

He didn't remember. He didn't remember if he had touched me or not. I would have wagered in that moment – and I would wager now – that he didn't know the names of most of the boys he hurt.

He reached across the emptiness between us and grabbed my arm. I resisted the urge to pull away.

'I rescued you once,' he said. 'I took you away from an awful life. You owe me.'

I stared at his hand. The hand I didn't want on me now, the hand those boys hadn't wanted on them then.

'You want me to rescue you,' I said.

'That's why you're here, isn't it? To get answers? And sometimes getting answers requires action. Such as simply returning a favour long past.'

A feeling of calm descended over me.

'I can do that,' I said.

He smiled that old Father Joe smile. I had forgotten what

charisma he had and what great charm. Anything felt possible in the wake of that smile.

Or it had. Now that smile looked odd on such an angry and battered face.

'Thank you,' he said, pulling his hand away as he started to stand up.

'Sit down,' I said.

The tone I used wasn't a boy's. It was a voice I hadn't used in years, not since interview rooms in the Chicago PD. I didn't yell or speak any louder than I had before, but this voice of mine, learned over long difficult years, made the most hardened criminal sit down.

Father Joe sat down.

He watched me like they used to in those Chicago interrogation rooms, uncertain what I would do next.

'When I was a boy,' I said, 'my father was drinking his way into the gutter. I tried to get him to stop, and finally I told you about him.'

Father Joe was watching me, obviously confused about why I was bringing this up now.

'You told me that God gave everyone the freedom to choose his own life, and I had to respect that choice, even if it was a bad one.'

Father Joe leaned back just a little, his mouth open slightly, as if he were going to argue.

'You said I just had to be there when the other person realised how bad his choice had been, maybe to catch him, or maybe to help him recover.'

I leaned forward. 'But you left something out. You left out the most important part.'

He turned his head, but his gaze remained on me. I could feel how desperately he wanted to look away, and how he was too frightened to.

'I learned,' I said, 'that there are people who like their bad choices so much that it doesn't matter how many opportunities you give them. It doesn't matter how many hands get extended to them, how many times someone offers to rescue them. They don't want to be rescued.'

'I do want rescue,' he said tightly.

'No, you don't,' I said. 'Because you don't even see what's wrong with this moment.'

'That I asked a boy I rescued to return the favour and he won't?' His voice vibrated with fury.

'That you sit in the most beautiful church I have ever seen, in the presence of a God that you vowed to serve every day of your life, and you beg *me* for rescue. Me, a former cop, with no powers at all.'

His face flushed.

'I can't rescue you, Father,' I said. 'You don't want to be rescued. You don't think you did anything wrong.'

He watched me, his eyes glittering with rage.

I stood.

'You were right, all those years ago,' I said. 'God gave us free will so that we could choose the right path. And part of choosing that path is recognising that most people won't.'

'You came here to tell me that?' he asked.

'No,' I said quietly. 'I think I had come here to see what a monster looked like. And instead, I found that you look no different at all.'

*

I left the room, and climbed the stairs.

The sun had moved, muting the light through the stained glass. The sanctuary looked like half a dozen sanctuaries I'd been in, that moment of reverence gone.

I did then what I hadn't done when we hovered in the back: I walked up front, knelt, and bowed my head.

Not to pray for Father Joe. Others could do that.

Not even to ask for forgiveness for all I had done in my life.

But to give thanks for that moment of clarity.

I wanted order so badly that I somehow believed the Church's very existence would provide it. Even as I aged, I hoped that something magical in these places would take a man and make him something he wasn't.

A man's redemption didn't come from the outside.

It came from the inside.

And I had already found it, even back then, even as a boy. I had wanted to change. I had wanted to make my life better, and I had known – somehow – that *I* had to do it. No one else could.

Perhaps that was why Father Joe never touched me. I hadn't been lost or desperate. I had just been hungry and grieving. Father Donnelly, with his baseball, Father Bill with his jokes, they had been enough for me.

And the world they all opened for me had enough rules to give me guidance, and enough freedom to let me walk away if I needed to.

I wasn't sure God could forgive men like Father Joe. I never believed in prison conversions. They were too easy. And people who had destroyed lives like Father Joe had didn't deserve easy.

I stood, my knees cracking with age and effort.

This place was aptly named. It was Hell Island. Hell's waiting room. Even here, though, there was a chance for salvation. I stood inside that chance right now, with the light from the stained glass fading around me.

I doubted any of these men would take that salvation offered them.

Which made the island's nickname apt as well.

The Island of Lost Priests.

This island wasn't even a detour on the road to eternal damnation.

It was the end of the road.

The last stop, before true punishment could begin.

Ω

There is much work still to be done on uncovering the secrets of the Island of Lost Priests – not least, ascertaining just where it is, 'one of many unoccupied islands found in the world's oceans'. The writer of this account indicated that the Church owned other hidden islands as well; perhaps the island he visited was just one of several performing the same job, or perhaps other islands have other purposes.

In the mid-1970s, when he wrote this account, the Church was only just beginning to admit to abuse by its priests, but the extent of it had still not been revealed; the writer admits that he 'had to sign all kinds of confidentiality stuff'. Only since Pope John Paul launched the Commission of Enquiry into Abuse in the Church, with police and social services working closely together with Church officials, has it not only been honest about the issue, but shown its determination to root it out and deal with it.

1978

This account of events in the necropolis far below St Peter's Basilica, on the night of 6–7 August 1978, must be one of the very last documents to be placed in the Vatican Vaults before the election of Pope John Paul.

It reveals the existence of a covert intelligence network within the Catholic Church – but that is the least of its revelations.

Apocryphon

Stephen Marley

'I have lived my life according to a simple maxim: what can exist does exist.'

Monsignor Felici's parting words haunted Father Jerome as he descended the spiral stairway to the Vatican necropolis beneath St Peter's. As he passed below the foundations of the fourth-century Constantine basilica, Jerome was still puzzling over the significance of the monsignor's remark, delivered barely ten minutes ago in the Italian dignitary's office in the Apostolic Palace.

As Sister Yi Zhenmei was fond of observing, Monsignor Felici 'majored in Cryptic'. Appropriate enough for a cleric who exerted considerable influence in the Crypt, as the Catholic Church's covert intelligence network was known to its close-mouthed insiders, who were themselves designated as 'ghosts'. As a novice ghost to the Crypt, summoned from his first parish in North Yorkshire barely six months after arriving fresh-faced at its presbytery door, Father Jerome was still trying to find his way in the protean power structure of the Vatican secret service.

So it was all the more inexplicable that Felici had chosen him to keep vigil in the Chamber of the Vates. And wasn't Monsignor Ortega the assigned watcher for tonight's vigil? Although, with the necessary 'sanitising' of records and 'disappearing' of sensitive files necessitated by the prospect of a new Pope, that particular monsignor may well have been called away to take charge of 'Cleansing'. True enough, Felici had assured him that Sister Yi Zhenmei would try to get to the Chamber before him, but there was no guarantee. She might be an hour – two hours – late. In the meantime, he would be alone. The only reason he could fathom for the responsibility falling on him, after barely three weeks in the Crypt, was that everyone else was too busy rushing hither and thither since the death of His Holiness less than two hours before Jerome was summoned to Felici's office. By now, almost midnight, the Camerlengo would have taken the Fisherman's Ring from the Pope's finger and ceremonially destroyed its signet. The Catholic Church was bereft of a leader. This was the time of the *sede vacante*, the interregnum of the Empty Chair.

Jerome shook his head. Life as a parish priest was much simpler. He was out of his depth in Rome.

And descending into the depths. The air became denser, drier, warmer, as he trod the final steps down into the necropolis, six storeys below St Peter's marble floor. When his feet touched level ground and he stared down the narrow street of the dead, he experienced a sudden sense of . . . what? – apprehension? – dread?

What can exist does exist.

He brushed off the presentiment, berating himself for foolishness. He was as bad as those visitors on the ninety-minute guided *Scavi* tour, suffering panic attacks the moment they entered the first passageway, squeezed by claustrophobia as the walls of ancient brickwork closed in. No such misgiving had troubled him on his two previous visits, tagging along behind the tourists. He should know better. He *did* know better.

The necropolis was no Stygian underworld, bedevilled by wraiths. It was once, simply, a network of miniature streets, open to the sky and lined with replica houses for the dead, on the south-west flank of Vatican Hill stretching down to the banks of the Tiber. When the Emperor Constantine ordered the construction of the original St Peter's in 326, the city of the dead was buried under tons of soil and masonry fragments that provided the foundations of the mighty basilica. Not until 1940 was it rediscovered. The story of the necropolis was archaeology, not demonology.

He followed the southernmost of the two excavated main streets, each orientated in an east–west direction and providing a double-spine to the complex uncovered in the 1940s archaeological digs. Even back in those early days, some one thousand burial sites were identified. After October 1950, many more thousands were uncovered in successive popes' plans to explore the necropolis almost to the banks of the Tiber. A gargantuan enterprise, and a secret one. Perhaps only the Vatican could have maintained the necessary secrecy for such a mammoth project, knowledge of its existence restricted to the Pope, five cardinals, the *Scavi* guides and some members of the Crypt. And why the secrecy? Four days ago, before Felici first informed him of the hidden regions of the necropolis and the new-found Chamber of the Vates, he wouldn't have asked that question because he was as ignorant of the secret excavations as the rest of the world. Now that he knew of their existence, and the reason for keeping them concealed, he wished he'd remained ignorant.

But Jerome had little time to brood, even while breathing in ancient dust and surrounded by the stern brickwork façades enclosing mausoleums with elaborate tombs and faded frescoes, each casting a sombre spell, a spell no less potent in the humbler tombs with their utilitarian loculi. In the breathless air of the necropolis, rich and poor were as one, a democracy of the dead.

There was also, he reflected wryly, a tacit ecumenism between Pagan and Christian. Even in death, they had grown old together, differences forgotten. In truth, many mausoleums were in their origin Pagan Christian, Christian Pagan. In one tomb, Christ was portrayed as Helios in his chariot of the sun. In another, he was Sol Invictus, the Unconquered Sun, the god of Constantine. Theologies converged.

He turned into a narrow corridor that led south-west to a tomb draped in tarpaulin worksheets. It was one of three entrances to the restricted necropolis. Regular followers of the *Scavi* tour might have noticed that three tombs, close together, had one of them 'under refurbishment' at any given time. The open entrance was always 'under refurbishment'. The opening of each portal was alternated randomly every three or four months; as one was opened, the former entrance was sealed. A single tomb, permanently 'under refurbishment', would have roused suspicion.

Quickly consulting his map, he entered a nondescript vault, brushing aside the tarpaulin. He approached a faded mural depicting the upper body of the double-headed god, Janus, then took out an Introibo, which was designed to resemble a black cigarette case. He opened the Introibo and jabbed out a sixteen-digit sequence of numbers on the button display. Crypt code entered, he held up the device to Janus's right eye and pressed the activation button inside the case.

Signal transmitted, the wall slid to the right, disclosing an open doorway. After a moment's hesitation he walked through. Seconds later, he heard the wall slide shut behind him.

From here on, the necropolis became a fully-fledged labyrinth. He constantly checked his map, carefully navigating a way through the maze. Even with the map it was quite possible to get lost in the dimly lit, twisting tunnels, so he was reassured by the feel of the handheld transceiver strapped to his belt.

He was further reassured when he entered a cramped court-yard that he identified, from its layout, as the Court of Uriel. From here, according to Monsignor Felici, it was less than five minutes to his destination, the Chamber of the Vates, named after the soothsayers of Vatican Hill, decades before the birth of Christ, but rediscovered only five days ago.

For reasons best known to the Holy Father, the Chamber of the Vates was declared forbidden to anyone outside the covert Crypt, whether the outsider was a humble priest or exalted cardinal. You had to be a ghost to enter this chamber.

*

'So this is the famous crypt – a suitable location for a ghost.'

Sister Yi Zhenmei lofted an imperious eyebrow at the trite remark from Father Dieter. 'Yeah, yeah,' she sighed ostentatiously, 'that joke gets funnier each time I hear it. Crypt as in Catholic secret operations. Ghost as in Catholic secret agent. I get it. I keep getting it. Hilarious.'

Sister Yi planted fists on hips and tapped her foot, the sound echoing faintly in the spacious rectangle of the underground chamber.

The German priest raised submissive palms. 'Sorry, Sister Yi. Really sorry. You can stop aiming that eyebrow at me.'

'And this isn't a crypt *anyway*. The Chamber of the Vates was a temple. This is the last time I take you down here, breaking all the rules. You're not an assigned watcher. You're not even a ghost. If another watcher turns up it will be me who'll get it in the neck from Felici. I'll probably have to say a hundred rosaries.'

Dieter's brow furrowed. 'Hey, all this theatrical fury, it *is* an act . . .' His tone became more tentative. 'Isn't it?'

She angled her chin with a haughty air, then burst into laughter. 'Of course it is, you idiot.' Catching his piqued expression, she shrugged. 'All right, all right, I overplayed it. *Mea culpa.* Truth is, I'm dying for a cigarette. I couldn't sneak a smoke all day, what with Pope Paul passing from the world.'

'A cigarette-smoking nun,' he snorted. 'I don't know how you get away with it.'

'Because I'm young and beautiful and a cool secret agent.'

'And a favourite of Monsignor Felici,' he added.

'That too.' She turned on her heel and strode towards a limestone wall whose expanse was covered in a vast mural, an extravaganza of the divine and diabolic so intricately intertwined that it appeared that the one was forever turning into the other. No clear images could be discerned. Everything was suggestion: protofaces, rudimentary horns or haloes, embryonic limbs, constantly disconcerting. Since her initial sighting of the first-century mural, five days ago, she didn't care to study it for too long.

Reaching a relatively unadorned patch on the wall she stretched out her arm and pointed at a circular carving some five feet in span, its base two feet from the ground. '*Voila!* Look upon it and weep. But not too long in case another watcher turns up.'

He leaned forward and viewed the carving. It was the face of a bearded god, mouth agape. Moments later, he stepped back. 'It's a copy of the Bocca della Verità. The Mouth of Truth. Pretty exact copy, from what I remember. You put your hand in its mouth and, if you're a liar, it bites it off. This is what you brought me here for, a Roman Holiday?'

'Well, this is no movie and I'm no Audrey Hepburn and you're definitely no Gregory Peck.' She angled her head. 'Put your hand in the mouth.'

He studied her expression. 'Is this a joke?'

'No joke. Look – I'm wearing my serious face. Go ahead and stick your hand in.'

'I think I'll just go.'

'Try it. You're the one who pleaded to see the great mystery in the secret chamber. Come on, it'll take only a second.'

'Okay, okay, just to keep you happy.' He expelled a sharp breath and thrust his hand into the mouth.

And missed. His fingertips pressed on the stony lips. With a self-conscious attempt at laughter, he darted a look at Sister Yi. 'Well, that was pretty clumsy.'

Slowly, she shook her head. 'No, it wasn't.'

'It certainly was,' he said, aiming his fingers at the mouth. Only to miss again.

He tried again. And again.

And again.

He lowered his arm. 'What the hell?'

She folded her arms, tucking her hands inside the wide sleeves of her black habit. 'It's the same for everyone. I can't touch it. Nobody can touch it. It doesn't seem to exist. Look inside that mouth and you'll see nothing but blackness. We tried ultrasono-graphic readings but they showed nothing. Absolute vacuum. That's why the facial image was carved around it, in the first century, a ring around a mystery.'

He stepped back from the wall. 'First century? How was its age established so soon after finding it?'

'We already knew its age before we found it. The exact year, in fact. The first year of the reign of the emperor Claudius. AD 41. By the way, it's not a copy, it's the original. The Bocca della Verità is the copy, fashioned soon after and installed in the Temple of Hercules.'

'You knew its age *before* you found it? How, exactly?'

She indicated one of four tunnels that radiated from the cham-ber. 'You'll have to leave in a couple of minutes but I'll be stuck in here all night. I fancy a stroll though the tunnels. Let's walk as I talk.' She moved away. 'You probably won't believe what I have to tell you.'

He kept pace with her long strides. 'Whatever you have to say, it can't be any more astounding than that – that thing back there.'

She stayed silent for a few moments as she strode down the tunnel. Then, barely above a murmur: 'You have no idea what's back there.'

*

'My God!'

Jerome pulled to an abrupt halt a second after entering the chamber. The sight of the vast mural on the right-hand wall froze him to the spot. What *was* that? And what inspired lunatic painted it, a first-century soothsayer? His vision was compelled to trace a convoluted path up, down, across and even *into* the interweaving cavalcade of saint and sinner, angel and demon. And, with a sudden shift of perspective, he saw sinner saints and angel demons, interchangeable. Then he recalled what Felici had told him of this mural: it operated in a similar manner to a Rorschach test. You saw what you wanted to see in it. Equally, you saw what you didn't want to see.

He forced his gaze from the perplexing sight and studied the remainder of the Chamber of the Vates. In severe contrast to the painted expanse, the other walls were coated in plain, unadorned plaster. And the vault contained nothing but two canvas chairs. It looked as if Sister Yi Zhenmei was going to arrive late.

Well, if he was a watcher for tonight (and please God let Sister Yi join him soon) he was turning one of those chairs to face away from the demented spectacle. But first . . .

Keeping his eyes lowered, he approached the giant mural. His steps slowed as he reached the Mouth, as Felici had described it. Not Mouth of Truth, but simply, the Mouth, and the main reason for the hasty creation of a watcher class. The monsignor had calmly described the negative properties of the gaping aperture as if it were no more than an interesting novelty. Jerome had listened with blank-faced incredulity.

Now that he stood before it, he was less incredulous. He had, like so many others, placed his hand in the Bocca della Verità in Santa Maria in Cosmedin, and this image, its prototype, looked no different. But it *felt* different. He bent down and peered into the mouth. It must be imagination, but he felt that through the yawning aperture he saw the emptiness between the stars.

He straightened up and studied the face. Like the face in Santa Maria in Cosmedin it evoked, for him, a simple, one-word description – mindless.

As for what Felici had claimed about the nature of what lay inside that mouth . . .

'It's not possible,' he muttered, directing his shaky hand to the vast face. 'It can't exist.' He pushed a tentative finger at the mouth, and gasped as it landed on the surrounding stone. He tried again. Same result.

There followed a minute's experimentation, including throwing coins at the mouth, each of which was diverted from the target.

Finally he relented. It was impossible, but it was real. He smiled the thinnest of smiles as he grasped why Felici had sent him here: to undermine his empirical world view, confront the sceptic with the supernatural. He had always had faith in the divine spark in the human spirit, but not in miracles, and now he faced a dark miracle.

He closed his eyes, lips moving in silent prayer.

Father, you give us grace through sacramental signs,
Which tell us of the wonders of your unseen power.

Then he heard a voice, faint, distant, oddly familiar.

'*My God . . .*' it sighed.

His eyes sprang open. It was surely an auditory illusion, but the voice had seemed to come from the mouth. If not an illusion, then what? Quirky acoustics?

The voice sounded again, nearer, more distinct:

'*Deliver us from evil.*'

He stepped back, the tempo of his pulse accelerating. 'I know that voice.'

It was his own.

And then came something that had no voice, or face, or shape.

*

'It all started,' said Sister Yi, 'at Nag Hammadi.' She slowed her pace in the curved, tomb-lined corridor and glanced at Dieter. 'I presume you're familiar with the Nag Hammadi discovery?'

He grimaced. 'I have a sketchy idea. Truth to tell . . . very sketchy. It's a long time since my student days at the Gregorian.'

She shook her head in reproach. 'And you a Jesuit . . . Oh well, here goes: in December of 1945 a group of farmers led by Muhammad Ali Samman unearthed a sealed jar at Nag Hammadi in Upper Egypt. Hidden inside the jar were leather-bound papyrus codices containing no fewer than fifty-two Gnostic texts dating from the fourth century. The Arabs who discovered the jar kept its contents quiet, as Muhammad and his brothers became involved in a blood feud. Their father had been killed, and they avenged his death by hacking to pieces his alleged killer, Ahmed Ismail, and devouring his heart between them. As you can imagine, they had good reason to lie low from the Egyptian police until they could dispose of the literary treasure on the black market. Muhammad later showed the Gnostic texts to a local Coptic priest who, over the following years, helped secrete them to Cairo where they were revealed to a fascinated world.'

Dieter nodded. 'Yes, it's all coming back to me, although I didn't know about the blood feud.'

'Uh-huh. Another fact you won't know is that Pius XII personally oversaw the formation of an archaeological team – all Crypt members – in February 1949. Their mission was secret, *hyper*secret. Pius had personally located a codex in the Secret Archives that indicated a literary trove underneath the ruins of St Pachomius monastery, within walking distance of the 1945 Nag Hammadi discovery. Long story short, after five months the Crypt team unearthed similar Gnostic texts to the earlier find – with one addition, an exquisitely preserved papyrus scroll inside an ebony cylinder. The author had dated the scroll as the second year of the reign of the emperor Claudius. He also put his name to the document: Simon of Gitta.'

'Simon of Gitta? Isn't that—'

'Simon Magus, who followed Christ in Galilee – at a distance, and who was a thorn in St Peter's side after Christ's crucifixion. Yes, Simon Magus, the heresiarch himself. Quite a find. But the authorship is dwarfed by the content of the work, the Apocryphon of Simon Magus.' She halted at the juncture of two tunnels and took a deep breath. 'Prepare to hear the greatest story ever untold. It transpires that Simon had spent many years studying in the Library of Alexandria, which we learn from him was *not* accidentally burned by Julius Caesar, merely a few harbourside book depositories. The Library – in fact a combination of a library of half a million books, a university and several temples – was a source of wisdom from the time of Ptolemy, companion of Alexander the Great. It was also an inspiration for the future. Centuries before Simon's era, Eratosthenes calculated the circumference of the earth and Aristarchus proposed a heliocentric model of the solar system as well as providing a close approximation of the size of the moon. However, Simon's prime interest lay in theories of a multiverse. An infinity of universes in which everything that can happen, does happen.'

Dieter's tilted head and pursed lips were the soul of scepticism. 'Surely not. Wasn't the many worlds theory first posited in the 1950s?'

'A little out in your chronology there. The multiverse concept was familiar to such ancient scholars as Parmenides, Democritus, Epicurus and Lucretius. Cicero, in his *Academica*, discussing the topic of innumerable worlds, puts it this way: "Just as we are at this moment close to Bauli and are looking towards Puteoli, so there are countless persons in exactly similar spots with our names, our honours, our achievements, our minds, our shapes, our ages, discussing the very same subject."'

Dieter raised his hands in surrender. 'I stand corrected. So, the *Apocryphon of Simon Magus* contains, what, proof of numerous worlds?'

'Not theoretical proof. But an indication of where to find such proof . . . in the Temple of the Vates, which gave Vatican Hill its very name. The menace that the temple presented was sufficient cause to keep further exploration of the necropolis secret, from 1950 to the present. The year before he composed the apocryphon, Simon Magus hired a stonemason to carve a face around an – absence – on a wall of that temple. The face was intended as a warning.'

'Ah! It was carved around a pre-existing mouth . . .'

She nodded. 'A mouth in which, according to Simon, you can hear voices.'

'Echoes, you mean?'

'Not echoes.' She glanced at her watch. 'And there's something else. At the end of the apocryphon there's a warning: "Take care lest you invite the Creator into his creation."'

He chuckled. 'Too big for us?'

'That's the least of it.' She tapped her watch. 'You've overstayed your welcome. Twenty minutes, remember? That was the agreement. Now make your own way back. I have watcher duties to resume. Oh, and take one of the tunnels that go around the Chamber of the Vates. If another watcher sees you in there I'll have a lot of explaining to do.'

He frowned as he extracted a folded paper from his jacket pocket. 'Are you sure this map won't get me lost in this maze?'

'Oh, you'll be fine. Go on, vamoose.'

'See you for coffee tomorrow?'

She shrugged. 'If you're paying.'

She watched him trudge down a side-tunnel, then leaned against a wall and expelled a gradual breath. Bringing Dieter into the necropolis had been a bad idea. Why did she give in and indulge his curiosity? She really should have grown out of kicking against the rules by now.

She straightened up and headed back down the passage. A couple of minutes and she'd be where she ought to be, keeping watch on the Mouth. As she threaded her way though the labyrinth, her thoughts returned to the teasing half-hints she had given Dieter. She had, she admitted to herself, been a bit of a minx. But then, what was she supposed to do, blab everything she knew for an unauthorised visitor's entertainment?

The Creator, for example: she had allowed her friend to assume that Simon was referring to Jehovah or the Trinity. He wasn't. In Simon's apocryphon, the Creator was given a name: Ialdabaoth. The name was Hebrew. And translated into English: son of chaos.

'I've a feeling it's going to be one of those nights.'

*

Jerome sat on the stone floor of the chamber in a far corner from the stony mouth, his shoulders slumped, his gaze averted from both mouth and mural. He shouldn't have lost his nerve. What kind of priest was he, panicking at the sound of his own voice? No matter how bizarre the circumstances, he should have held his ground.

'But it wasn't just the voice,' he murmured.

There had been something else, something the human mind wasn't meant to contain. It had enveloped . . . smothered . . . the voice he'd heard. It could be called the soul of nightmare. But that didn't begin to describe it. It could never be described.

He leaned back and rested his head against the wall, gradually clearing his thoughts. It took a while, but eventually he was sufficiently composed to formulate a plan. First option, retrace his steps through the necropolis and report his experience to Felici. Second option, stay and see his mission through to the end, in which case he'd need Crypt support. Despite the upheaval following the Pope's death there was a chance that a Crypt agent was working somewhere in this underworld. And, with luck, Sister Yi might be on her way through the maze right now.

He detached the transceiver from his belt and pressed the com button. 'Father Jerome here, requesting assistance. Location, necropolis. Please respond.'

He almost laughed in relief as a cheery voice answered moments later.

'Hi! Sister Yi here, Double-O-VII, Licensed to Excommunicate.'

'Sister Yi! Thank God! You're in the necropolis . . .'

'For my sins. You're that Crypt newbie, right?'

He found himself nodding. As they had met several times it was deflating to be dismissed as a Crypt newbie, but apparently he was small potatoes in the world she worked in. 'Yes, but I was assigned as a watcher, and, well, I think I'm in this over my head.'

'I was assigned as a watcher too. Felici wouldn't drop you into this without an experienced partner. So, what's the catastrophe?'

*

Sister Yi slowly circled the Chamber of the Vates as she listened to Jerome's somewhat breathless account.

'Uh-huh, uh-huh.' She frowned in concentration. 'And you're sure this voice sounded like your own?'

'I think so. I believe so.' To her ears, Jerome's voice on the transceiver had a curious, distorted tone, making it difficult to catch every word.

'Uh-huh. And that "presence" you mentioned, the one that followed the voice, how would you describe it?'

A brief silence. 'It was a nameless horror.'

'Right. Right. Um, do you think you could improve on "nameless horror"? It's a bit, you know, H. P. Lovecraft. No, scrub that – Lovecraft would do better . . . No, I'm kidding. Seriously, Felici shouldn't have assigned you. And no I don't blame you for running away. Good move. Go straight back and report to Felici in the Apostolic Palace. Tell him I sent you.'

'I'm going to see this through to the end.'

'No, you're not. Get out of here, reach safe ground, pronto.'

'I was taught to face my fear. A while ago I failed. I won't fail a second time.'

She groaned inwardly. Why were novices so damn gung ho? 'You don't get it, do you? I'm not asking, I'm giving you an order. Get out of here! No more discussion.'

She terminated the connection and ceased pacing. If Jerome hadn't the sense to leave the necropolis, he would almost certainly return to the Chamber of the Vates. She would deal with him then. On entering the chamber a few minutes ago she'd glimpsed his fleeing figure an instant before he disappeared into the farther tunnel. Now the source of his panic was revealed, she earnestly wished that he'd kept on running.

She stepped over to one of the canvas chairs, angled it to face the Mouth directly, and sat down. Whatever Jerome had sensed in the chamber, she caught no hint of it. Either it had gone or she wasn't attuned to its presence.

But if the entity (non-entity?) was what she suspected, she was confronted with an onerous task. She drew out her notepad and flipped up some observations she'd written in the five days since the chamber was breached. Within seconds she added a new line:

Who is the Creator?

She scanned the notes, seeking inspiration. Sifting the evidence, weighing probabilities, she started to scribble more comments, occasionally peering up at the visage in stone.

A couple of minutes later she leaned back and studied her additions:

6 August 1978

Circa **6.30 p.m., the Pope laid low by suspected pulmonary edema in Castel Gandolfo. Was opening of the Temple of the Vates the final straw to his failing heart? He is reported to have mumbled 'Where there's a hell, there's a heaven.' He died at 9.41 p.m. The interregnum begins.**

Did he who made the Lamb make thee?

Creator . . . Ialdabaoth? Also known as Saklas, idiot god, and Samael, blind god.

Mentioned H. P. Lovecraft to Jerome. Unconscious association? Lovecraft's Azathoth the idiot creator at the centre of chaos. Ialdabaoth, god of chaos. Maybe the Puritan Atheist of Rhode Island was an authentic mystic after all.

She winced. 'That was a bit harsh. Sorry, H. P.'

What can exist does exist. In a multiverse, innumerable heavens, numberless hells.

'I believe in God, and I believe in gods.'

Simon Magus writes that the door opens <u>from both sides</u> with a burst of lightning (release of energy on contact?) and that the door is found where the walls of the world have worn thin. Further . . . it opens with a touch.

She placed the notebook on the adjoining chair, the rudiments of a plan forming in her mind. It was a truly awful plan, so simple it was borderline moronic, but the best she could come up with. There was no authority she could seek. She was the authority.

'And with that thought, God help us all.'

*

Once again, Jerome reached out to press the transceiver's com button. Once again, he withdrew his hand. The nun, albeit an offbeat nun, had made herself clear as ice. As she was second only to Felici, himself the de facto head of the Crypt, her orders should be followed without question.

But he couldn't do it. For all he knew, Sister Yi was in danger, somewhere in the necropolis. He had thought she would have come here, to the Chamber of the Vates. It seemed the logical destination. But, sitting on the ground in this empty vault, not the faintest echo of approaching feet resonated from its walls. The chamber was quiet.

Finally he rose to his feet. He had waited long enough. Since he ran from what he felt was an emerging presence, sprinting clean across the chamber to the far wall, he had cowered on the ground. At least he'd resisted the temptation to flee the vault. He hadn't held his ground in front of the Mouth, but he hadn't fled the scene. Although that wasn't saying much.

Well, he would try to make up for his cowardice. Taking a deep breath, he walked across the chamber, past the canvas chairs, and halted in front of the stone face with its lip-ringed aperture of – nothing. This time he'd face out his fear.

He lifted the transceiver and pressed for contact. 'Sister Yi, we must talk.'

*

Standing in front of the Mouth, she closed her eyes as she prepared to summon whatever lay beyond it.

And nearly jumped out of her skin at the loud buzz of the transceiver. Cursing, she lifted the transceiver to her mouth.

'Sister Yi, we must talk.' The priest's voice was as distorted as in the first call, and this time there was a peculiar echo, as if in stereo.

'No we don't. Do as you're told, get clear of here.'

'Wherever you are, Sister, I want to help you.'

'Well you can't. Go away.'

A pause. 'Very well. But if you need me, I'm only a call away. I just want you to know, I'll be fulfilling my mission as a watcher. I'll keep vigil all night.'

Lines puzzled her forehead. 'What are you talking about? Where are you?'

'I'm in the Chamber of the Vates.'

She involuntarily looked over her shoulder at the chamber, realised the futility of the action, then stared at the transceiver as though the device had gone insane.

'You're *where*?'

'In the Chamber of the Vates,' he repeated in a tone that certainly sounded quite sane.

'*Jerome*, I saw you run out of the chamber.'

'But I didn't! I ran across the room to the far wall. I've been here ever since. But how could you—'

'Count that as the most unsuccessful lie of your life. Guess how I know it's a lie? Because *I'm* in the Chamber of the Vates!'

'You can't be!'

'Well, if you're not lying, then one of us is nuts, and it's not me. *Dominus vobiscum* and *adios!*'

She returned the transceiver to its belt loop and expelled a sharp breath. 'What a liar.'

'I'm telling the truth.' The voice was small and remote, yet more distinct than before. No distortion.

Startled, she darted a look at the transceiver.

'Why won't she believe I'm telling the truth?'

The transceiver was mute.

Her gaze shifted to the Mouth. That's where Jerome's voice was coming from. Now she recalled the echo on the radio: it was Jerome-beyond-the-wall double-tracking the priest on the radio.

The implications were staggering. It would take weeks to absorb them. She had seconds. She made the best of them.

Just as we are at this moment close to Bauli and are looking towards Puteoli, so there are countless persons in exactly similar spots ...

Backing away from the mouth, she lifted the transceiver. She definitely wasn't inclined to talk to a wall.

'Jerome, I'm back. Now I'm going to ask you some very silly questions. All you have to do is answer. No laughing, no querying, just answer. Got that?'

'Okay.' The tone was guarded.

'Fine,' she said. 'Are you standing directly in front of the Mouth?'

'Right in front of it.'

'That fits. So far, so good. Now, was there a major event in Castel Gandolfo today?'

'Of course. The death of His Holiness.'

'Right. And what time did Pope Paul die?'

'Pope Paul?' he echoed.

'Pope Paul VI, successor of John XXIII.'

'What's wrong with you? Celestine VI is the Pope.'

A stealthy cold seeped down her spine. She tried her best to ignore it. 'Let's be scrupulously exact here. Are you saying that Celestine VI is the direct successor to John XXIII, and that he died tonight?'

'Well, *yes*. Pope Celestine succeeded John XXIII. And Celestine died over five hours ago.'

In your world, Jerome, not in mine.

'And was Celestine the former Cardinal Montini?' she asked.

'*Yes*. You know he was!'

She nodded. Same man, different papal title.

'One last question, of paramount importance. You know me – right? I mean, I've never actually spoken to you before but—'

'Of course you have! Many times!'

'Well, yes and no. From where I'm standing, I haven't. But from where you're standing . . . what did I say to you? Do you know my plans for the chamber?'

'You've made no secret of them in the Crypt. The plans are to contact some timeless power. Bring God into the world.'

She shut her eyes for a moment. *You have a fool for an alter ego, Sister Yi. Although, with a toss of the coin, I might have made the same mistake.*

'Thanks for telling me,' she said. 'Oh, and I apologise for accusing you of fleeing the chamber. That wasn't you. It was another you. He has probably arrived at the Apostolic Palace by now.'

'Are you feeling all right?' There was genuine concern in his tone.

'Actually, I'm not, but that's irrelevant.' She drew a deep breath. 'Listen closely – we live in different universes, and I'm not speaking metaphorically.'

'What!'

'That's the easy part. It gets a lot worse. Hold on to your hat. From the presence you described, or rather didn't describe, I think I might know its identity. According to Simon Magus, Ialdabaoth is the creator of your universe – and mine. A mindless creator that knows not what he creates.'

'I believe in God! I'm a priest, after all. Don't you believe, *Sister*?'

'Indeed I do. I believe in God, and gods, but I don't require God to be my creator. I'm more than happy with God as my Redeemer. According to the Gnostics, there's a crack in our dark universe. The crack lets in the light – and not only the light.'

'The old Gnostic heresy . . .' A lengthy silence. 'If you can prove we're in different worlds, I might consider what you say. How can we be talking via radio? Nothing can pass between universes.'

'Sound and electromagnetic waves seem able to do that, for a start,' she said. 'That's evident, at least to me. Or I should say, they pass through where the walls of the world are worn thin.'

'That's no proof.'

'Okay, what if I talk to you through the Mouth, would that convince you?'

'There could be a hidden transmitter,' he responded. 'You'll have to do better than that.'

She sighed. 'I knew it would come to this. Okay, you must know about the strange properties of the Mouth. It can't be touched. What do you think will happen if we touch it simultaneously?'

'Nothing?'

'My guess is you're wrong. I've had the advantage of reading a certain apocryphon and certain phrases are lodged in my mind. Phrases like "the door is found where the walls of the world are worn thin . . .", "the door opens from both sides" . . . perhaps only from both sides *simultaneously* . . . "opens with a touch – and lightning".'

'No offence, but that sounds like babbling.'

A smile spread her lips. 'As always, "no offence" is a prefix to offence. But point taken. Let's just say there's a witless creator, a demiurge, *between* universes. And it's creeping – no, squeezing

– into our worlds, expanding into space itself like some sort of – what shall I call it? – negative energy . . . dark energy . . .'

'Does it matter what you call it?'

'Not sure. I think I may have been on to something there. However, to the task in hand . . . how do we get light – lightning – into our worlds, a weapon against Ialdabaoth? Where there's a hell, there's a heaven. We invite the light, perhaps, by reaching through the door.'

'You mean through the Mouth? But it can't be touched because—'

'Because it isn't really there,' she broke in. 'But if two people on each side of the door touch as much as a fingertip simultaneously, who knows?'

She stretched out her arm, index finger pointed at the nothingness between the stone lips. 'My fingertip is two inches from the Mouth. Place yours in the same position.'

*

Jerome reluctantly did as requested. For all his sceptical words to Sister Yi, he still quailed at the memory of the nightmare presence that had emanated from the wall. His main impulse was to run again. He glanced up at the mural. That presence – was it the source of the celestial-infernal madhouse painted in ancient times?

He tried to take in what Sister Yi was telling him, but it was so confusing: *there are many cracks in the universe, and not all of them let in light . . . the door opens with a touch . . . the door opens with lightning . . .*

He gave up, and concentrated on moving his fingertip nearer to the Mouth, now less than an inch away.

'Almost there,' he said. 'How close are you?'

'Within an inch. When I say "now", push forward. Oh – and Jerome – what do you have faith in?'

'The divine in the human spirit.' He hesitated a moment. 'And you?'

'The unknown. If there are innumerable hells then there are innumerable heavens.' A brief silence. 'Before we touch, you think of your faith and I'll think of mine. Don't allow anything else to enter your mind – or something else might come.'

'Ialdabaoth?' He heard the tremble in his voice. 'But isn't that . . . thing . . . coming anyway?'

'Sure, but let's not hasten its arrival. Ready?'

He shut his eyes, and summoned an image of a child he had known once, a girl in a terminal cancer ward who had set about giving away her toys to other children in the few weeks left to her. Her smile as she handed over the toys was, for him, proof of the divine.

He sucked in a deep breath. 'Ready.'

'Now!'

He pushed his finger forward.

*

She pushed her finger forward.

And the world vanished.

There was nothing. Nothing that could be seen, or heard.

Vacuum.

Plenum.

Everything and nothing were co-existent.

Then . . . a point of contact, infinitely small.

A touch.

A quantum event that happened and didn't happen.

A cosmos of lightning.

*

A burst of light flung Monsignor Felici back in his chair, which tilted and crashed backward, depositing him on the carpet. He sprawled there, heart thudding, vision swimming.

Thunder from under the earth. Down from where he'd sent Sister Yi to serve as sentinel.

Something was breaking into the world.

'*Libera nos a malo*,' he gasped. 'Oh God, Sister Yi . . . what have you done?'

*

Lightning blasted Sister Yi across the floor of the chamber.

Prostrate on the stone, she struggled to lift her head. A hazy vision of the vault. Then even that hazy vision faded.

Then nothing.

Time may have passed.

Her eyes flickered open. Her other senses awoke. And sensed something unholy in the air.

They had failed. Before losing consciousness she had sensed rather than seen the lightning. Now she knew that light was more than simply the lightning. This was not lightning from heaven, but the blast of infernal energy. Hell was coming from between universes.

She pulled up the transceiver as she swayed to her feet. 'Jerome! Jerome! We summoned Ialdabaoth! We have to try again – *now!*'

After an excruciating wait, his dazed tone issued from the radio. 'It was me. At the last moment I forgot – my faith – just saw the cancer . . .'

'One last try!' She staggered to the Mouth. 'Tell me when you're ready.'

Mercifully, the wait was short. 'Say when, Sister.'

A terrible Nothing bulged out of the wall. The mural burst into a celebration of bedlam.

'Now!'

＊

As he reached towards the Mouth, Jerome fixed his thoughts on the girl with her toys in the hospital ward. On the previous attempt, at the last instant, the girl's smile had been swallowed in the image of her wasted body, riddled with cancer.

And with the thought of cancer, that terrible presence returned.

He mustn't fail a second time. He must remember the smile.

His hand stretched into . . .

Nothing and nowhere. Everywhere.

An impossible coincidence of the subatomic and the cosmic.

In this nothing and everything, he sought the human spirit.

And reaching out to the human, the human reached back.

Two ghosts made contact, a phantom touch.

Revelatory lightning.

Thunder of the soul.

The mighty bells of heaven.

*

Monsignor Felici sat up on the floor, sprung from despair to exaltation.

Ialdabaoth, Saklas, Samael . . . whatever name was ascribed to that unhallowed presence, it was, for now, cast back into the nothing between the worlds.

'You did it, Sister Yi!' He subsided into the relief of laughter. 'Thank God, you did it.'

*

'We did it.'

Sister Yi stepped back from the Mouth and lowered her arm.

'Yes,' Jerome answered from another world. 'We did it.'

Sister Yi knelt down, lowered her head, and smiled.

*

Slowly, two ghosts scaled the spiral staircase out of the necropolis to the slate grey predawn of Vatican City.

The two never spoke, or exchanged glances. They existed, after all, in different universes.

But Sister Yi and Jerome had the same thought.

Lightning had struck the same spot twice. The second time was the cure. Where there was a hell, there was a heaven.

Ialdabaoth had not conquered.

And if heaven had not conquered either, at least now the battle was evenly matched.

Ω

In a note attached to this account, Sister Yi explains that she and Father Jerome spent some hours talking in the Chamber of the Vates before, in each of their worlds, their replacements as watchers arrived and they were able to leave.

Her account of that night includes her reconstruction from what Jerome told her of his own thoughts and feelings as he had worked his way down to the chamber on his own. They agreed that he should write a similar account including what she told him. We cannot know whether his account remains in the Vatican Vaults in his world or whether it too has been brought to light.

Nor can we know whether later that August Cardinal Albino Luciani succeeded to St Peter's Chair in Jerome's world, as he did in ours, and if so, what name he took as Pope. We can only hope that the second lightning strike heralded a new age of openness in his Vatican, as in ours.

The Writers

KristaLyn Amber

KristaLyn Amber was born and raised in Pennsylvania and became addicted to travelling early in life. She has travelled to more than twenty countries for both mission and leisure and gains a lot of inspiration for her stories this way. She graduated from Susquehanna University with a degree in English Literature and has published five books including her most recent, *Pure Fyre*. KristaLyn now lives in Virginia, working for the Walt Disney Company and continuing to write. Her website is www.kristalyn.biz.

Sarah Ash

Sarah Ash trained as a musician – and music just keeps on finding its way into her stories. She's also fascinated by the possibilities of alternate histories – and when researching Allegri's *Miserere*, she came upon so many different versions and apocryphal accounts that it was difficult to tell where history blended into myth and vice versa. Her fantasy series *The Tears of Artamon* is set in an alternate late eighteenth century, but her new novel *The Flood Dragon's Sacrifice* grew out of her love of Japanese mythology (and, of course, manga and anime!). Her website is www.sarah-ash.com.

Cherith Baldry

Cherith Baldry was born in Lancaster, UK, and studied at Manchester University and St Anne's College, Oxford. She worked as a teacher for a number of years, including a spell at the

University of Sierra Leone. She is now a full-time writer for adults, young adults and children, and is currently working as part of the team writing the *Warriors and Seekers* series under the name of Erin Hunter. She is widowed with two grown-up sons and a granddaughter, and lives in Surrey as housekeeper for two cats. Her interests are medieval literature, especially Arthurian legend, early music and travel.

David V. Barrett

Tales from the Vatican Vaults is David V. Barrett's second SF/fantasy anthology; his first was *Digital Dreams* (NEL 1990). In the years in between he has written more than twenty non-fiction books, mainly on new religious movements and esoteric societies, and has contributed to numerous encyclopaedias. He has had over a dozen short stories published. He is a regular contributor to *Fortean Times* magazine, and co-founded the London Fortean Society.

Alex Bell

Alex Bell wrote her debut novel whilst studying Law at university. Since then she has had both adult and young adult books published, along with articles about fairtrade gold and ethical fashion. In her spare time she enjoys volunteering for St John Ambulance and catering to the whims of her neurotic Siamese cat.

J.-M. Brugée

J.-M. Brugée has been fascinated with troubadours and their music since hearing Ensemble Perceval performing in the château at Chinon, in the Loire Valley in France, some twenty years ago. The first draft of 'Songs of Love' was written in Chinon to the accompaniment of their music.

Patrice Chaplin

Patrice Chaplin has published over thirty books and her work is widely translated. *City Of Secrets* was the first of her metaphysical series followed by *The Portal* and in 2015 *The Stone Cradle*. She has worked in drama for the BBC and her stage play *Sessions* was performed in Paris in spring 2015. She lives in London and is the director of a charity using creativity against addiction.

Storm Constantine

Storm Constantine has written twenty-eight books, both fiction and non-fiction, and well over fifty short stories. Her novels span several genres, from literary fantasy to science fiction to dark fantasy. She is most well known for her Wraeththu trilogy. Storm is founder of the independent publishing house, Immanion Press, created in order to get classic titles from established writers back in print and innovative new authors an audience. She's currently working on several ideas for new books, as well as short stories. She lives in the Midlands of England with her husband, Jim, and five cats.

Lionel & Patricia Fanthorpe

Lionel and Patricia were born in Norfolk and married there in 1957. They have two daughters and two grandchildren. Lionel has worked over the years as a journalist, Anglican priest, teacher and author of over 250 books, many of which he and Patricia have written together. He also lectures and broadcasts on radio and TV. He and Patricia have researched Fortean-type unsolved mysteries all over the world and have written numerous books and articles about their findings. He was the presenter of the *Fortean TV* series on Channel 4. Lionel and Patricia were also among the pioneers investigating the Rennes-le-Château mystery in 1975. They now live in Cardiff, Wales.

Jaine Fenn

Although best known for the *Hidden Empire* series of far future SF novels published by Gollancz, Jaine Fenn also has an interest in conspiracies, alternative history and Fortean phenomena generally. She has a particular fascination with pre-Columbian American history, going back to one of her first published short stories in 2002. Despite her interests she subscribes to the cock-up, rather than the conspiracy, theory of history.

Mary Gentle

Born: once. Got it right the first time.

Interests: sword-fighting, Airsoft rifles (preferably with someone else at the business end of either). Animal communication (pet rats, pet pigs).

Hobby: being a mature student (BA English and Politics; MA, seventeenth-century history; MA, War Studies).

Books: favourites among her own are *Ancient Light* (there *is* no sequel), *Rats & Gargoyles* (Hermetic fantasy; gives new meaning to 'obscure'), *Grunts!* (orc marines give new meaning to 'bad taste'), *Ash* (weird-shit fifteenth-century behemoth). And, naturally, the next one.

Lives: Hertfordshire, with her partner and several pigs. He is the one with the hat.

John Grant

John Grant is the author of some 70 books and the recipient of two Hugo Awards, a World Fantasy Award and various others. His stories have appeared in *Interzone, Postscripts, The Third Alternative, Black Static, Nautilus, Nature* and other magazines, as well as in numerous anthologies. For some years he ran the famous fantasy–artbook imprint Paper Tiger. Among his nonfiction books are *The Encyclopedia of Fantasy* (with John Clute) and the series begun with *Discarded Science* and including most recently *Denying Science*. His *A Comprehensive Encyclopedia of Film Noir* was published in autumn 2013 and his YA non-fiction book *Debunk It!* in spring 2015, while an adult non-fiction book provisionally titled *Spooky Science* is due for fall 2015; his second story collection, *Tell No Lies*, appeared in late 2014. He writes about usually obscure movies at Noirish: http://noirencyclopedia. wordpress.com.

Terry Grimwood

Writer, editor, publisher, playwright, college lecturer, open-mic harp blower and blues growler, oh and electrician, Terry Grimwood has three novels under his belt (*Bloody War, Axe* and *The Places Between*), numerous short stories in numerous magazines and anthologies (many of them collected in *The Exaggerated*

Man) and has contributed to, and co-written, a number of electrical and engineering text books for Pearson Educational press. He runs theEXAGGERATEDpress (http://exaggeratedpress.weebly.com) and edits *Wordland* magazine (http://wordlandhome.weebly.com). Terry is married to his muse, the translatlantic poet Jessica Lawrence.

Dave Hutchinson

Dave Hutchinson was born in Sheffield. After reading American Studies at the University of Nottingham, he became a journalist. He's the author of five collections of short stories and the novels *The Villages* and *Europe In Autumn*, and his novella 'The Push' was shortlisted for the 2010 BSFA award for short fiction. He has also edited two anthologies and co-edited a third. His short story 'The Incredible Exploding Man' featured in the first *Solaris Rising* anthology, and appeared in *Year's Best Science Fiction*. He lives in north London with his wife and several cats.

Kleo Kay

Kleo's interests lie in mystery and magic, oracles and divination, religions and belief systems from long ago. She is currently working on a series of books about the Gods and Goddesses of Egypt, Greece and Rome, and also enjoys writing short stories with an esoteric and mysterious edge. Kleo runs themed workshops on several of these topics in London, England. www.godsandgoddessesforyou.co.uk.

Garry Kilworth

Garry Kilworth has been a full-time novelist and short story writer for thirty-five years and has published over eighty books. His great loves are speculative and imaginative fiction in the genres of science fiction and fantasy, but he also indulges in historical fiction. His latest work is a collection of strange tales, including three Anglo-Saxon fantasy stories, under the generic title *The Fabulous Beast* published by Infinity Plus Books. He has just completed a science fiction novel *The Sometimes Spurious Travels through Time and Space of James Ovit*, which currently resides with his literary agent, John Jarrold.

Paul Kincaid

Paul Kincaid is the author of several works of criticism, including *What It Is We Do When We Read Science Fiction* and, most recently, *Call And Response*. He has received the Thomas Clareson Award from the SFRA and the Best Non-Fiction Award from the BSFA. He keeps meaning to write more fiction, but this is still a rare event.

Stephen Marley

Stephen Marley, author of eight novels, was born in Derby, England. He was expelled from one school and left another with no qualifications but somehow made it to university where he gained an MSc in the sociology of science and almost finished a PhD in ancient Chinese science. He left academia to take up writing full time and lives by a Derbyshire river a shot-put throw from Augustus Pugin's first church and a javelin throw from the world's oldest factory. His likes include *Buffy the Vampire Slayer* and boxer dogs and he describes himself as a Leonard Cohen Catholic.

Damian P. O'Connor

Damian P. O'Connor, sometime soldier, academic and teacher, has two dozen academic books, articles and reviews on historical and African themes to his name. Having travelled widely in Africa, he has been awarded a medal from the Chief of the Zulus as well as being recognised in the Brenthurst Foundation Nelson Mandela Prize Essay competition. Now back from being stuck as far up the Yang-Tse river as it seemed feasible to go, he is based in the relative sanity of Essex. He is also a member of the T Party Writers Group.

K. J. Parker

After brief and inglorious careers in photocopiers, a leading auction house and the legal profession, K. J. Parker took to writing full time and has to date produced three trilogies, five standalone novels, five novellas (two of which won the World Fantasy Award) and a gaggle of short stories. When not writing, Parker works on a tiny smallholding in the West of England and makes things out of wood and metal.

K. J. Parker isn't K. J. Parker's real name; but even if you knew K. J. Parker's real name, it wouldn't mean anything to you.

Marion Pitman

Marion Pitman is a Londoner exiled to Reading, and has no car, no television, no cats and no money. She sells second-hand books online since her shop burned down, and has three unpublished novels. She has had short fiction and poetry published in a number of magazines and anthologies, most recently in Alchemy Press *Urban Mythic 2* and Fringeworks *Potatoes*; and poetry in *Sein und Werden* and *Unspoken Water*. Her hobbies include watching cricket, listening to folk music, and theological argument.

Stephanie Potter

Stephanie Potter has been telling stories all her life, mostly through her work as a chartered school librarian. She has recommended the work of many other authors, so has decided to add her voice to the multitude with her first published story. She is married, lives in Cornwall and enjoys gardening.

Rosanne Rabinowitz

Rosanne started writing when she helped produce 'zines in the 1990s, contributing articles and reviews. Then she began to make stuff up. Her fiction has since found its way to places like *Postscripts*, *Midnight Street* and *Black Static*, and anthologies such as *Rustblind and Silverbright* (with Mat Joiner), *Never Again: Weird Fiction Against Racism and Fascism* and *Extended Play: the Elastic Book of Music*. Her novella *Helen's Story* (PS Publishing) was shortlisted for the 2013 Shirley Jackson Awards. Rosanne lives in South London; unsurprisingly she has a story called 'Lambeth North' in the anthology *Horror Without Victims*. Her website is at rosannerabinowitz.wordpress.com.

Kristine Kathryn Rusch

USA Today bestseller and Hugo-award winner Kristine Kathryn Rusch writes in all genres under various names, including Kris Nelscott for mystery. Her short fiction has been nominated for every award in SF and mystery, and has been featured in twenty

...best collections as well as a Best of the twentieth century. She is the former Hugo-award winning editor of the *Magazine of Fantasy & Science Fiction*, and currently edits the acclaimed anthology series *Fiction River*. In the first six months of 2015 WMG Publishing published the remaining six books in her *Anniversary Day* saga. She's relieved to turn her attention to something else.

E. Saxey

E. Saxey is a queer Londoner with a longstanding interest in religious orders. Their short fiction has appeared in *Holdfast*, *Spacewitch Moonshots*, *Daily Science Fiction*, *Aghast*, *Apex Magazine*, and in the anthologies *The Lowest Heaven* and *The Rite of Spring* (both by Jurassic London).

Douglas Thompson

Douglas Thompson's short stories have appeared in a wide range of magazines and anthologies. His first book, *Ultrameta*, was published by Eibonvale Press in August 2009, nominated for the Edge Hill Prize, and shortlisted for the BFS Best Newcomer Award, and since then he has published seven subsequent novels, *Sylvow* (Eibonvale, 2010), *Apoidea* (The Exaggerated Press, 2011), *Mechagnosis* (Dog Horn, 2012), *Entanglement* (Elsewhen Press, 2012), *The Rhymer* (Elsewhen Press, 2014), *Volwys* (Dog Horn, 2014), and *The Brahan Seer* (Acair Publishing, 2014). He is a director of The Scottish Writers' Centre. http://douglasthompson.wordpress.com.

Jean Marie Ward

Jean Marie Ward writes fiction, non-fiction and everything in between, including art books, novels (2008 Indie Book double-finalist *With Nine You Get Vanyr*), and short stories such as the 2011 WSFA Small Press Award finalist 'Lord Bai's Discovery' (from the anthology *Dragon's Lure*) and 'Personal Demons' in the award-winning anthology *Hellebore and Rue*. She edited the web magazine *Crescent Blues* for eight years and now writes for other online venues, including *Buzzy Mag*. Her website is JeanMarieWard.com.

Geraldine Warner

Geraldine Warner is a London-based musician, whose career has ranged from performance work to choral conducting and university lecturing. She has just completed an MA in Creative Writing at West Dean College with Lesley Thomson and Elly Griffiths. 'The Missing Journal of Captain James Cook' is her first published story.